Gods of Nabban

ALSO BY K. V. JOHANSEN

Blackdog

The Leopard

The Lady

Gods of Nabban

K. V. JOHANSEN

an imprint of **Prometheus Books**
Amherst, NY

Published 2016 by Pyr®, an imprint of Prometheus Books

Cover design by Liz Scinta
Cover illustration by Raymond Swanland
Cover design © Prometheus Books

Inquiries should be addressed to
Pyr
59 John Glenn Drive
Amherst, New York 14228
VOICE: 716–691–0133
FAX: 716–691–0137
WWW.PYRSF.com

20 19 18 17 16   5 4 3 2 1

Library of Congress Cataloging-in-Publication Data

Names: Johansen, K. V. (Krista V.), 1968- author.
Title: Gods of Nabban / K. V. Johansen.
Description: Amherst, NY : Pyr, an imprint of Prometheus Books, 2016.
Identifiers: LCCN 2016012441 (print) | LCCN 2016019561 (ebook) |
    ISBN 9781633882034 (softcover : acid-free paper) |
    ISBN 9781633882041 (ebook)
Subjects: LCSH: Gods—Fiction. | Demonology—Fiction. | BISAC: FICTION /
    Fantasy / Epic. | GSAFD: Fantasy fiction. | Occult fiction.
Classification: LCC PR9199.3.J555 G63 2016 (print) | LCC PR9199.3.J555 (ebook) |
    DDC 813/.54—dc23
LC record available at https://lccn.loc.gov/2016012441

Printed in the United States of America

For Tristanne and Marina

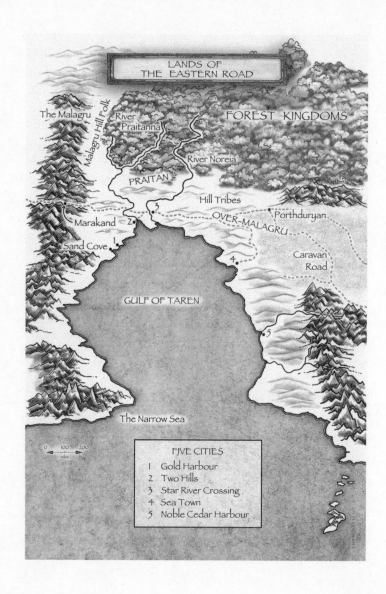

LANDS OF
THE EASTERN ROAD

The Malagru

Malagru Hill Folk

River
Praitanna

River Noreia

FOREST KINGDOMS

PRAITAN

Hill Tribes

Marakand   2

3

Porthduryan

OVER-MALAGRU

Sand Cove   1

4

Caravan
Road

5

GULF OF TAREN

The Narrow Sea

0   100   200
miles

FIVE CITIES

1 Gold Harbour
2 Two Hills
3 Star River Crossing
4 Sea Town
5 Noble Cedar Harbour

On the nature of the demons, gods, and devils, from the common introduction to the cycle of histories of the devils' wars told and sung by the Northron skalds:

The demons—*Though the demons may wander all the secret places of the world, their hearts are bound each to their own place, and though they once served and once defied the Old Great Gods and are no friends to humanfolk, they are no enemies either, and want only to be left in peace.*

The devils—*In the days of the first kings in the North there were seven devils escaped from the cold hells where the Old Great Gods had sealed them after the war in the heavens, and their names were Honeytongued Ogada, Jasberek Fireborn, Vartu Kingsbane, Tu'usha the Restless, Jochiz Stonebreaker, Dotemon the Dreamshaper, and Twice-Betrayed Ghatai. And there were seven wizards, who desired to know yet more, and see yet more, and to live forever. The seven devils, having no place, had no body, but were like smoke, or like a flame. They hungered to be of the stuff of the world, like the gods and the goddesses and the demons at will, and as men and women are whether they will or no, and having a body, to find a place. So they made a bargain with the seven wizards, that they would join their souls to the wizards' souls, and share the wizards' bodies, sharing knowledge, and unending life, and power.*

The gods and goddesses of the high places and the waters—*As all should know, the gods and the goddesses of the earth live in their own places, the high places and the waters, and are bound each to their own place, and aid those who worship them, and protect their own.*

The Old Great Gods—*They watch and judge and cherish the souls of humanfolk after death and take no part in the affairs of the living world, save once only, when the pleas and prayers of the folk and the gods and goddesses of the earth themselves brought them into the world, to defeat and bind the seven devils . . . but afterwards the Old Great Gods withdrew again to their own place, to await the souls of humanfolk in the heavens beyond the stars.*

DRAMATIS PERSONAE

[Freeborn Nabbani are listed by their personal, rather than clan, name.]

Aoda (Daro Aoda)—A priestess of Father Nabban in Dernang.

Ahjvar—Former assassin of the Five Cities cursed to remain undying in the world; now a companion to his onetime groom and shield-bearer Ghu; also called the Leopard. A long lifetime ago, prince and king's champion (or *rihswera*) of the Duina Catairna in Praitan. See also Catairlau.

An-Chaq (I)—A wizard-talented daughter of Emperor Yao of Nabban who fled west; mother of Ivah.

An-Chaq (II)—Wizard, artist, stone-carver.

An-Chi—Yeh-Lin's daughter, a wizard who sided with her brother Min-Jan against their mother.

Anlau—See Rat.

Anri—Captain of the Wind in the Reeds, the imperial order of spies and assassins, under Emperor Otono.

Ario (Zhung Ario)—a banner-lord of Zhung Musan's army who defects to Ghu.

Attalissa—Goddess of the lake and town of Lissavakail in the mountains called the Pillars of the Sky, west of Marakand beyond the Four Deserts.

Awan (Shouja Awan)—A priest drawn to Ghu's service, who had helped him years before when he was a runaway.

Baril—Yuro's second-in-command over the horses and stables of the White River Dragon, a slave of Daro Korat's.

Barrast—An ox, possibly a demon aurochs, of Grasslander legend; a constellation.

Baya (Dwei Baya)—A banner-lady, niece of Dwei Ontari.

Big Yen—General servant and compound watchman at the Flowering Orange playhouse in the Golden City.

The Blackdog—Formerly the guardian dog-spirit of Attalissa, now bonded to its last host, the Westgrasslander caravaneer Holla-Sayan, as a double-souled shapeshifter.

Bolan (Lai Bolan)—High lord of Argya, rebel against Buri-Nai, self-styled prince.

Buri-Nai—Princess, later empress, of Nabban and eldest child of Emperor Yao; full sister of Emperor Otono, half-sister of Dan and of An-Chaq.

Buryan—Praitannec caravaneer (from the Duina Noreia); member of Kharduin's gang; cousin of Seoyin.

Catairanach—Goddess of the Duina Catairna in Praitan, who cursed Catairlau to live as an undying host for the soul of Hyllau.

Catairlau—A prince, wizard, and king's champion of the Duina Catairna roughly ninety-some years before this time; counted among the kings of the *duina* by the bards. See Ahjvar.

Chago—A slave horseman of Daro Korat's; a contemporary of Ghu's.

Chichi—An imperial slave; drummer for Buri-Nai's boat.

Dan—Youngest son of the late emperor Yao; Traditionalist and rebel; sometimes uses his mother's clan-name Dwei rather than the imperial Min-Jan.

Debira—Serakallashi caravaneer of Kharduin's gang.

Deyandara—A Praitannec princess and singer; former student of Yeh-Lin's. Ghu calls her "the little bard"; Ahjvar looks on her as a granddaughter.

Diman—An assassin of the Wind in the Reeds assigned to Princess Buri-Nai's household; later captain of the company.

Dotemon—One of the seven devils, bonded with the Nabbani wizard, empress, and usurper Yeh-Lin.

Dolan (Dwei Dolan)—An old peasant woman met by Ahjvar and Ghu in a deserted village in southern Alwu Province.

Duri—Slave house-master at the castle of the White River Dragon.

Etic—A legendary Grasslander hero; a constellation.

Evening Cloud—See Niaul.

Father Nabban—God of the high places of all Nabban, who came into being when all the gods of the land became one to defeat Yeh-Lin Dotemon during the devils' wars.

Faullen—A Praitannec warrior of Deyandara's household.

Gahur (Hani Gahur)—A lord of the Hani Clan; General Zhung Musan's second-in-command.

Galicha—Goddess of a spring in Denanbak, the deity of the chieftain Ganzu's folk.

Ganzu—Chieftain of a tribe in Denanbak.

The Gentle Sister—One of the three great rivers of Nabban; formerly also a goddess.

Ghatai—One of the seven devils, bonded with the Grasslander chieftain and wizard Tamghiz.

Ghu—Stray who followed an assassin home one day from the streets of Gold Harbour and wouldn't leave. Horseman, fugitive slave—saviour, so far as Ahjvar is concerned, and the dying gods of Nabban might agree.

Gomul—Slave of the stables at the White River Dragon, who rescued the infant Ghu from the river.

Gorthuerniaul—Praitannec translation of the name Evening Cloud. See Niaul.

Gurhan—The hill-god of Marakand.

Guthrun—Northron camel-leech, caravaneer of Kharduin's gang.

Hadidu—Nour's foster-brother and widowed brother-in-law; priest of Gurhan in Marakand.

The hag—See Hyllau.

Haliya—An eastern desert woman in Kharduin's gang.

Hana (Zhung Hana)—First Minister under Emperor Otono.

Holla-Sayan—Westgrasslander caravan-mercenary. See the Blackdog.

Huong (Zhung Huong)—Brother of Ti-So'aro; imperial officer; governor of Dernang under Ghu.

Hyllau—The ghost which possessed Ahjvar for much of his life.

Ilbialla—A lost well-goddess of Marakand.

Irtennin—A half-demon Grasslander hero of legend; a constellation. His tribe was said to have settled the Western Grass.

Ivah—Grasslander wizard, caravaneer, scholar, scribe; daughter of An-Chaq (I) and of the devil Tamghiz Ghatai.

Jang—A slave in the castle gardens at the White River Dragon; becomes one of Yeh-Lin's pages and takes the Daro clan-name.

Jasberek—The most mysterious of the seven devils; bonded with the wanderer Anganurth.

Jian—One of the co-ruling sacerdotal queens of Darru and Lathi, who are also called the Wild Girls.

Jilin (Lai Jilin)—Author of a classic treatise on the dramatic arts.

Jiot—One of the two dogs who followed Ghu from Marakand; tan and black.

Jochiz—One of the seven devils; bonded with Sien-Shava, a wizard from the islands in the ocean south of Nabban.

Jui—Ghu's other dog; white and grey.

Jula—Orphaned child adopted by Prince Dan.

Kaeo—Slave-actor and singer of the company of the Flowering Orange; of Dwei Clan before his impoverished and desperate mother sold him. An agent of the rebel Prince Dan, and possibly a prophet.

Kangju (Nang Kangju)—An imperial wizard of Plum Badge rank; he is a dreamer of true dreams.

Ketkuiz—A shaman of Denanbak, belonging to the folk of the goddess Galicha.

Ketsim—A Grasslander warlord who followed Ivah's father Tamghat until the latter met his end; then a mercenary in the service of the Lady of Marakand in the conquest of the Duina Catairna.

Kharduin—A caravan-master, exile of a tribe of the eastern deserts; lover and business-partner of Nour; friend of Ivah.

Kiaswa (Swajui Kiaswa)—An elderly priestess of the Mother. The Swajui clan-name is taken from the shrine of the springs of the Mother's rising.

Korat (Daro Korat)—Kho'anzi, or high lord and border lord, of Choa

Province and head of the Daro Clan; a man of Traditionalist leanings; Ghu's former owner.

Koulang—Bithan-born son of Wolan; a caravaneer of Kharduin's gang.

Kufu—A slave in the castle gardens of the White River Dragon; becomes one of Yeh-Lin's pages, taking the clan-name Daro.

The Lady of Marakand—Late goddess of the city of Marakand.

Lau—Name under which Rat serves in Princess Buri-Nai's household.

The Leopard—The byname by which Ahjvar was most recently known when he was an assassin of the Five Cities. He has used it on previous occasions as well.

Liamin—Slave and personal attendant of Lord Daro Korat, trained as a physician's assistant.

Lin (Nang Lin)—name sometimes used by Yeh-Lin; quite possibly her original name, as the courtly "Yeh-Lin" is rather grander than the status to which she claims she was born.

The Little Sister—One of the three great rivers of Nabban; also the long-gone goddess of that river, who became a part of Mother Nabban.

Maka—An imperial soldier of Buri-Nai's household troop.

Marnoch—King of the Duina Catairna; betrothed to Deyandara.

Meli—A weaver; a former slave of the Kho'anzi of Choa Province; a rebel and bandit.

Mia—A slave and actress of the company of the Flowering Orange in the Golden City.

Miara—Ahjvar's lover, a widowed wizard murdered in Praitan long ago.

Mikki—A bear—sometimes. A Northron half-demon. Also a carpenter.

Min-Jan—Emperor of Nabban at the time of the devils' wars; son of Yeh-Lin. His descendants use Min-Jan as their clan-name.

Moth—Northron skald, storyteller, warrior, singer, devil . . . The name preferred by Ulfhild Vartu, q.v.

Mother Nabban—The one goddess of Nabban, who came into being from the merging of all the goddesses of all the waters of Nabban to defeat Yeh-Lin Dotemon during the devils' wars.

Mulgo Miar—Pine Lord, highest ranked of the imperial corps of wizards, under Buri-Nai; defected to Prince Dan.

Musan (Zhung Musan)—General serving Buri-Nai; victor in retaking Choa Province.

Nai (Daro Nai)—A soldier of Lord Daro Korat's household.

Nasutani—A young Grasslander woman in Kharduin's caravan-gang.

Nawa—Eldest of the co-ruling sacerdotal queens of Darru and Lathi, who are also called the Wild Girls.

Niaul—Dark bay Denanbaki stallion given to Ahjvar by Ghu, who did not quite steal him from Lord Daro Korat. Short for Gorthuerniaul, q.v.

Nour—A Marakander wizard and caravaneer, lover and business-partner of Kharduin, whom he keeps on the straight and narrow, mostly. Close friend of Ivah.

Ogada—One of the seven devils, bonded with the Northron wizard Heuslar. Rumoured slain in the north a generation or two previously.

Ontari (Dwei Ontari)—A Dwei Clan lord, Prince Dan's right-hand man.

Oro (Gar Oro)—A scout of Dwei Ontari's forces.

Oryo—Captain of the imperial bodyguard of giants.

Osion (Daro Osion)—A woman of Dernang who joined Lord Sia's rebels.

Otono—Emperor of Nabban; brother of Buri-Nai, An-Chaq, and Dan.

Raku (Daro Raku)—A Daro Clan lord, cousin of and military commander for Lord Daro Korat.

Rat—A young woman of many talents; a Dar-Lathan or, as she would say, of Darru—or of Lathi. She may choose not to be specific.

Rozen—A Praitannec warrior of Deyandara's household.

Rust—A camel belonging to Ghu, or at least stolen by Ghu, which comes to the same thing.

Salar—An eastern desert caravan-mistress.

Sand—Another camel, also belonging to Ghu.

Sanguhar—An emperor of Nabban.

Sen—A slave of the stables at the White River Dragon.

Seoyin—A colony-Nabbani man from Two Hills; caravaneer and cook in Kharduin's gang and cousin of Buryan.

Shaiveh—Grasslander *noekar*, or vassal, of Tamghat's; Ivah's late bodyguard and lover.

Shui—Young daughter and heir of the Denanbaki chieftain Ganzu, poisoned by Nabbani assassins.

Sia (Daro Sia)—Daro Korat's son; an adherent of the Traditionalist philosophy, rebel against the empress and an ally of Prince Dan. Not, however, someone remembered fondly by Ghu.

Sien-Mor—A wizard from the islands south of Nabban; became the devil Tu'usha; sister of Sien-Shava.

Sien-Shava—A wizard from the islands south of Nabban; went to the north and became the devil Jochiz; brother of Sien-Mor.

Silla (Yeon Silla)—A poet beloved of an empress.

Sisu (Gar Sisu)—A young imperial wizard of Palm Badge rank.

Snow—A white stallion born on Father Nabban's mountain. Belongs, so far as Ghu and the horse are concerned, to Ghu, whatever Daro Korat, the lord of Choa and legal owner of the horse, may have to say about it.

Sohi—A Denanbaki woman, wife of the chieftain Ganzu and mother of Shui.

Storm/Styrma—A Northron bone-horse, or necromantic creation made from the soul-memory and skull of a long-dead horse, of Moth's. Currently misplaced . . .

Sujin—A slave of Daro Korat's stables who joined Sia's rebellion.

Sula (Lai Sula)—An imperial general under Buri-Nai.

Tai'aurenlo—A god of "the burning hills" in Lathi, father of the three Wild Girls who lead the tribes.

Tamghat—Name used by the Grasslander warlord and devil Tamghiz Ghatai at the time of his conquest of the mountain lands of the goddess Attalissa; Ivah's father. His followers took the tribal name Tamghati from him.

Tamareva—A woman of the southern islands living in Nabban; a dealer in mother-of-pearl and an agent of Prince Dan's.

Ti—A slave from the castle kitchens of the White River Dragon; taken by Yeh-Lin to be her page, she gives him her clan-name, Nang.

Ti-So'aro (Zhung Ti-So'aro)—A Zhung banner-lady; officer in Zhung Musan's imperial army who defects to Ghu.

Toba—An elderly shaman of Dar-Lathi, counsellor of the queens.

Toi (Lai Toi)—A deserter from the imperial army.

Tu'usha—One of the seven devils, bonded with the Islander wizard Sien-Mor.

Ulfhild—A Northron warrior and wizard, sister of one of the first Kings in the North; King's Sword of Ulvsness; bonded with the devil Vartu. See Moth.

Urumchiat—A Grasslander shaman and hero of legend; a constellation is named after him.

Vardar—One of Kharduin's caravaneers; of the Malagru hillfolk.

Vartu—One of the seven devils, bonded with the Northron wizard Ulfhild. See Moth.

Vixen—Deyandara's dog.

Wey (Shouja Wey)—Owner of the acting company of the Flowering Orange, and of Kaeo.

The Wild Girls—Sacerdotal co-ruling queens of the tribes of the jungles and highlands of Darru and Lathi; human-born daughters of the god Tai'aurenlo.

The Wild Sister—The greatest of the rivers of Nabban, and the goddess of that river, absorbed into Mother Nabban.

Willow (Daro Willow)—Illegitimate daughter of Daro Korat's youngest daughter.

Wisan (Lai Wisan)—A wizard of the Plum Badge rank; the diviner who testifies at Kaeo's trial.

Wolan (Daro Wolan)—A Nabbani man in Kharduin's gang, originally from Choa Province.

Yao—Late emperor of Nabban, called "Bloody Yao." Father of Otono, Buri-Nai, An-Chaq, and Dan.

Yeh-Lin—A wizard of Nabban; formerly an emperor's wife, usurper, empress, exile, and conqueror. Bonded with the devil Dotemon.

Yuro—Daro Korat's slave-born master of horses and later castellan; the man largely responsible for what upbringing Ghu had before he fled.

Zial and Wujian—Legendary lovers in a quite-probably tragic Nabbani epic.

PART ONE

CHAPTER I

Something stalked him through his dreams. She was hungry, reaching . . . *Hyllau, reaching for him. The Lady of Marakand, but her face was burnt black, charred and flaking away like Hyllau's and she closed her mouth over his, pressing down on him, tongue forcing . . . He caught her by the throat, to choke and throttle, to end this one slavery, at least—*

There was more strength than one might think in Ghu's compact frame. He jerked Ahjvar's arms open, away from his neck, and pinned him to the ground like a wrestler. Ahjvar woke as his head thumped the earth and the ground hit him hard in the back.

Bunched muscles turned to water, as if he had run to the point of exhaustion. Ghu's fingers bit into his wrists, forcing Ahjvar's arms down as he leaned over him, a knee heavy on his chest. The blind dark of a cloudy night wrapped them; their fire was nearly smothered in its ashes.

"Awake?"

He couldn't answer yet. Breath wheezed and sobbed in his throat.

Ghu released his grip, cautiously, and Ahjvar rolled away, arm over his face, shaking, teeth clenched on the plea. He could not ask to be set free; he had promised, so he would not, not yet. But he had to swallow the words, choking on them. *Let me go. Let me die now. I can't do this.*

Ghu put an arm over him, pulled close and held him tightly, till his shuddering eased to mere shivering against a cold that was not the autumn air.

"Hush." The command was hardly more than a stir of air against him. "Listen. I was going to wake you before long anyway. They've caught up. We're watched."

There was nothing to hear but his own harsh gasping, still too fast, too shallow, too loud.

"Shh, shh. It's all right, Ahj." A hand on his chest, breath in his hair. Encircled, safe. The Lady was dead. Hyllau's very soul was destroyed. He caught at Ghu's hand, gripped it, but didn't push him away. Lay still that moment longer, being safe and trying to settle his breathing, to be awake and sane and of some use.

He remembered. They had been stalked through the hills all that day, since early in the morning. Six riders on horseback, never closing in, never letting themselves, they thought, be seen. Ghu had kept the dogs, white and grey Jui and dun Jiot, in close, though they had been alert and bristling, wanting to investigate. Most likely the six were after the camels and, if they had seen it, Ahjvar's sword and the rings in his ears; they couldn't think Ahjvar and Ghu had any other wealth, just two more masterless wanderers come east from the defeat of Marakand's mercenaries at the Orsamoss. They might be ragged and growing gaunt with short commons, but to such men they would still be worth robbing. There was the gold and sea-ivory of the sword's hilt and the camels were still in good condition, better fed than their masters. Ghu cared for them well and had stolen only the best to start with, not but what the Praitannec kings had owed him more than the price of two camels for their victory.

When no attack came by dusk, Ahjvar and Ghu had made their camp with a careful eye to the ground. Trying to outrace the dogged pursuit, when they had no safe fastness to run to, seemed futile, as did making any great effort to lose them in the hills. Besides . . . they had been fairly certain who the six were. If the brigands lost Ahjvar and Ghu, they would only go looking for other prey, less able to deal with them.

At Ghu's insistence, Ahjvar had slept the first half of the night; he had insisted in turn that Ghu wake him, let him take the second watch.

Ghu had done so, and Old Great Gods forgive him, Ahjvar had slept. He did not even remember lying down.

He might as well be an invalid for all the use he was. His body healed. Wounds did, far more quickly than another man's might. He had only clean scars to mark his road from Sand Cove to Marakand and the Lady's well, to the battle at the Orsamoss and the burning tower at Dinaz Catairna. His mind, heart, soul, whatever, was another matter. A cripple. Even waking, there were long gaps in his days, as though his mind slept, or curled away small somewhere, leaving the body to manage the camel and the business of not falling. He would wake to awareness, though his eyes had never closed, and the light would be changed, the sun travelled several hours on its way, the land about them new.

Ghu should have known better than to trust him.

In some moods, he was strongly tempted to threaten to knock Ghu around the ears for treating him as a struggling child, letting him run, there to pick him up when he found he couldn't. Even for a grumble that would not be meant or taken seriously, he wasn't going to complain of the nursemaiding, though; it was Ghu who risked hurt, lying near to seize him back when the nightmares turned too foul. They might be only memories, festering unhealed wounds of the mind that he deserved to carry, not madness, no possessing ghost lurking in them, but even so . . . fast as Ghu was, the fading bruise on his cheek was Ahjvar's doing, two nights old. It was the murdered shepherd who had woken the dreams again, when he'd been a week without them. He turned over, face-to-face, muttered on a sigh, "Sorry." No atonement, and none for sleeping when he should have watched.

Bar himself from dreaming? He had attempted it, briefly, a few weeks back. The nightmares had leaked foul and vicious into his waking mind, or his half-waking; the periods where he lost time and place and self turned to horrors, and that . . . that was worse. To be mad in the daylight world . . . He had burnt the woven knot of herbs he had made against the nights, but the spell had been already failing, too weak to hold against the strength of the dreaming.

His sins; the dreams were his just punishment and atonement to

bear for them, maybe, whether on the Old Great Gods' road, or Ghu's.
He could not set them aside.

"Watched? Where are they?"

Neither dog was by them. He rose on an elbow to look. There. Pale,
slinking wolf shape: Jui, just barely visible in the thinning night. The
dog came up, keeping low, lay at Ghu's feet, watching the deeper darkness along the willow-lined bend of the coulee, just where a pool of
water still lasted. That was where Ahjvar would have been. The rest of
the slowly rising land was open of any cover but the night, grazed earlier
in the summer, though no herds were near now.

"Four in the trees. Two up on the high ground, lying flat. They've
been there a while." Ghu sounded apologetic. "You needed to sleep."

That someone had been keeping watch after all made him feel no
less shamed for his failure.

"You get downstream, keep out of it." Old habit, to make sure the
boy was safe out of any killing when he went about his work in the Five
Cities. But Ghu was not that boy.

"And leave you alone? No, Ahj." After a moment, Ghu added, "We
knew they were going to come on us sometime, once they started following. It may as well be now. These *are* the same who murdered the
shepherd."

Ahjvar had been a king's champion once, and a king's wizard, too, a
long lifetime ago. The king's wizards might divine truth from lie, when
charges were brought for royal judgement, but those thus condemned
might still appeal for the justice of the sword, a trial by combat within
the circle of nine witnesses, which was generally only to have a more
honourable death than the slow hanging that was the fate of wilful mur-
derers and certain other most heinous criminals, the king's champion
being the best sword of the tribe. He did wonder if Ghu had gone so
far as to make the two of them bait, if he had on his own decreed a trial
by deed, to give the justice the little chieftains of this land might fear
to exact from the lordless mercenaries when they travelled in gangs. He
could not be certain any more what Ghu might and might not do, but
the man would do it quiet and clear-eyed and whole. His simpleton

groom—hah. He would trust Ghu's instinct for guilt or innocence over any wizard's divination, including his own, and Ghu's judgement, too, and set his sword to serve what Ghu appointed.

Two days past, they'd come upon a shepherd slain with her dog, her hut burnt and her ghost confused and lost on the hillside, what was left of her flock still keeping close, sensing her there. Six, she had told them. Foreigners, four men and two women, and they'd killed her the previous day for the bit of barley meal and cheese in her summer hut and a couple of sheep they could have driven off unchallenged. She had had more sense than to face them; she'd been hiding in the thorn thicket, she and her dog in silence, but they searched and found her and dragged her out . . .

Ahjvar and Ghu had buried the shepherd and the dog together, setting them free to take the road to the Old Great Gods, getting well away before her kin could come seeking her, to make mistakes about which wild and lawless wanderers might have done such a thing. The two of them could have been the warlord Ketsim's followers, Praitannecman and colony-Nabbani together, Ahjvar dressed in battlefield gleanings and Ghu, barefoot, having worn through the soles of his boots, in a too-tight caravaneer's coat scorched and shredded to rags.

The road ran over a thousand miles through the hills beyond the eastern boundaries of the Praitannec kingdoms before it climbed to the dry uplands that became the eastern deserts, near enough now that sometimes the sun rose in the yellow haze of some distant, dust-bearing wind. These hills they travelled, though, were not so unlike Praitan, but wilder, emptier. There was dry scrub forest, the trees low and tangled, where reclusive demons, spirits of the land, watched warily as they passed: a blue-eyed stag, an owl, a white wolf without a pack. When they ventured into the shade of such woodlands, the camels paced crunching along paths drifted with past years' curled leaves, brown and leathery, smelling of resin. When there was a demon, it would trail them, unspeaking, attracted to Ghu, uncertain about Ahjvar.

For the most part, Ahjvar and Ghu had kept to the open lands, the rolling hills where lower scrub and autumn-yellowing grasses were grazed by wild goats and antelope and the sheep, asses, and camels of the semi-nomadic hillfolk. They were Praitannec kin, pale of hair and eye, skin an oak-tanned brown; Ahjvar could have passed for native here, but for his tongue. They spoke the same language, or near enough, but with a guttural desert-harsh intonation, not the singing lilt of the seven kingdoms farther west. They had no kings, only chieftains ruling tribes of a few families, which drifted seasonally up and down their hills between high summer camps and the stone and sod huts of their winter villages, nearly abandoned in this season, in the sheltered valleys. The goddesses of the shallow, stony rivers, like the gods of the hills, were quiet folk. If either had priest or priestess it would be only some gentle holy person living apart, half a shaman, or a wise elder who had settled to be companion of their god in their old age. Such gods did not always denounce Ahjvar as cursed or an abomination in their land, and sometimes the holy ones would offer them a meal and shelter for the night, drawn, like the demons, to Ghu. Sometimes they asked for the tale of the western upheavals and an accounting of why their lands, usually disturbed only by bands of young folk who took to caravan-raiding or an outbreak of reiving between neighbouring chains of hills, were so beset now with wandering bands of lordless foreign folk, desperate and rapacious brigands. Ghu would tell them of Marakand's war on Praitan and the victory of the kings of Praitan. Ahjvar left the talking to him.

Some of the mercenaries and Catairnan traitors, Praitannec warriors who had betrayed their queen, might be looking for honest work, hoping to find hire on the road or in Porthduryan, the town at the desert edge. Not many. The three cities on the coast south of Praitan would have been the better destination for such. Any who had come so far east as this were brigands now, even if they had not started out so.

And what was there to tell the folk of the land that Ghu and Ahjvar were any different? Only the god-touched holy ones saw otherwise. The brigands certainly did not.

Not long to wait now; enough light to see the shadow-shape of the dun dog Jiot, settling by the hobbled camels, who were likewise wakeful but chewing their cuds, unperturbed.

Ahjvar reached over Ghu, feeling for his sword. He wouldn't sleep with it within reach, nor a knife. He didn't trust himself. His hand found the hilt, ivory and gilded bronze, the pommel a snarling leopard's head. Northron work, very old. Lost heirloom of an ill-fated house. He slid it clear of the scabbard, laid it by his hip while he groped again and pulled his boots on, lay on his back. Ghu rolled over, chin on his arm, his forage-knife under his hand, that broad-bladed, angled tool that could cut a man's throat as easily as an armful of fodder. Ahjvar still heard nothing, but he was not sure Ghu did either, or if in some way he might perceive what the dogs did.

The trees along the coulee had solidified out of the thinning night. He could see them now, leaves hanging still, heavy against the windless dark blue. Mist crept off the pool, fingers of white snaking about the lower trunks. A shout. The trees birthed running shapes, a single figure pulling ahead. Ghu rose to one knee, ignoring them, watching up the hill. Ahjvar leapt the embers of the fire and went the other way. The woman in the lead was Northron tall, with an axe. Without a shield, he didn't much want to deal with that axe face-to-face. He dodged at the last, struck low as she tried to follow him, cutting across the backs of her knees, and continued around to drive the circling weight of his long Northron sword up and into the following man's belly, steel grating between the bronze plaques stitched to the man's jerkin, bearing him down. A second woman came at his unguarded side. He abandoned his sword and the dead weight on it, hooked her feet out from under her, seized the hilt and shoved the dying man clear of his blade with his foot, and had the sword free again as the woman flung herself up and closed in on him, grim-faced. He might have asked her why it took six of them to kill one unarmed girl. He might have offered quarter and told her to run, if for no other reason than to show himself he did not have to kill her but by his own choice, yet there was Ghu, with no better weapon than a peasant's knife. So that was his choice. They were convicted and dead anyway. His father would have hanged them.

She was a Grasslander with a horseman's sabre and the small buckler they used, and so was the last man of the four who rushed at him from the side, blade sweeping, braids flying. He had to turn between the two of them. Could have used a shield, yes, or a stick, or just about anything, really, to block that. It was a harried few moments, till he took the woman's head half off. The blade had dulled its edge, scraping armour and bone, and he paid in blood for that delay in jerking his sword free, felt the man's sabre skim and bite his warding arm, but it saved his face, and the man's savage grin gaped as he ran him through. No armour. He pushed him down and cut his throat, a mercy he likely did not notice, and killed the crippled axe-woman on the ground as she tried to drag herself away, before looking around for Ghu.

Both dogs were barking now, loud and angry, and Ahjvar, all unwilling, could hear the wailing of the confused and angry ghosts. No other human cries, though, now that the last woman was silent. A camel, finally, decided something was amiss and bellowed.

There. Ghu rose from where he had crouched, wiping the blade of his forage-knife clean on a handful of grass. *Someday I may have to learn to kill*, he had once said, and, *Not this day.* It seemed so long ago. A lifetime's journey. Even before that, they had argued over whether Ghu would learn to use a sword, once it began to seem inevitable that the boy was his, a stray cat that could not be driven off. Ghu had persisted in his refusal, but he surely had not tracked Ahjvar across half Praitan and hauled him from the Lady's hell in the midst of battle without shedding blood.

To mourn that sacrificed innocence seemed ungrateful of the gift.

No. What Ghu had set aside to claim Ahjvar from the curses that held him was not a child's innocence, but his freedom. A doom chosen before he would otherwise have done so, or one he might still have rejected altogether. He could have abandoned Ahjvar to the mercy and the death the devil Dotemon might have given him, and kept on his westward wanderings. But he had not, and so he was bound to the east, and Ahjvar would not abandon him. Not this day. That was all he could promise, yet. Each day anew—not this day.

Sometime, too, the starveling boy had become a man, slight, but with a muscular grace and power in movement that ought to be turning the girls' heads in some king's hall, not . . . Anyway, he should have a better weapon than that damned peasant's knife.

"We should look for their horses," Ghu called matter-of-factly. The torn ruin of the coat he had been wearing since Marakand was sprayed with blood. Not, Ahjvar trusted, his own, in that quantity, or he would not be standing. Ghu shrugged the filthy rags from his shoulders as Ahjvar crossed to him, frowned at the hand, still gripping his sword, that Ahj pressed to his left arm.

"Bad?"

"No," Ahjvar said firmly. It was only seeping.

Ghu made some exasperated noise. Ahjvar ignored him and warily took his hand away, but no great spreading of blood followed, so he had spoken truth. Shallow. He wasn't the only one with a dulled blade.

There were no ghosts hovering over the still humps of the dead Ghu had left. A man with his throat cut, neatly, if you could say that, and precisely. The other had been stabbed, a wide mouth of a wound ripping up through leather, between horn plates. They had carried Grasslander sabres and a spear.

"You shouldn't be getting in close like that. Great Gods, Ghu—"

"Once I am in that close, there's not much they can do." Ghu considered the smallest man and hauled off his boots, caravaneer's leather-soled felt.

"You can't take on a swordsman with a knife!"

Ghu's eyes flicked up at him, brows raised, but he didn't deign to answer. And the boots appeared to fit. He considered the taller of the two, who likewise seemed mostly dressed for the caravan road. Not Ahjvar's height, but large feet.

"No," Ahjvar protested.

"We're heading for the desert, Ahj. And winter is coming."

Ahjvar's footwear was a horseman's heeled leather, no warmth, and ill-fitting anyway. The last remnant of the Red Mask's gear, uniform of the servants of the Lady of Marakand. He should be glad to be rid of it.

"Robbing the dead. Fine. Take a sword, too, then. You need—"

"Ahj, you think you can make me a good swordsman before we come to Nabban?"

He had no idea what Ghu was capable of. "Maybe. Probably. Competent." Ghu would not be merely competent, whatever he set his hand to, but not likely they would have the energy, travelling hard, to spare for such things when they made their evening's camp. Ahjvar doubted he would, anyway. He wanted, right now, nothing but to lie down and lose himself in nothingness. A dream-free nothingness. "Probably not."

"Then don't bother."

"And what if you can't dance in and cut throats?" He crouched to clean in the grass his sword and the hand sticky with his own blood.

"I hide behind you." Ghu's smile down at him was that of the inno-cent of Sand Cove. "Put those boots on."

Ahjvar took an undamaged shield from one of the Grasslanders for good measure, one of Ghu's. He had stopped caring how he was hurt years ago, but it was Ghu going to pay, now, if he got himself laid out half dead in the midst of a fight. Half dead, or—whatever. He didn't feel up to peeling one of the better-equipped out of their armour and Ghu didn't suggest it.

No sign Ghu had flung even the token handful of earth over the brigands he had slain, yet by the time Ahjvar trailed him down towards the coulee, trying not to cringe at feeling the shape of a dead man's feet, the ghosts were silent and gone from the others too. A word from Ghu might be blessing enough. He supposed even they deserved it. Less blood on their hands than on his, whatever they had done, and yet theirs would be a long road to the Old Great Gods. It was unlikely the shep-herd had been their only innocent victim.

He gave in to having his arm bandaged before they broke camp and set out to follow the dogs, who found the horses downstream, though regretfully they turned the beasts loose to be claimed by whoever might find them. Trying to trade them wasn't going to be worth the risk of being mistaken for part of some brigand gang themselves. They took what spare clothing from the saddlebags seemed a reasonable fit, and what gear would be of use, which was much of it. The greatest prize was a bulky Grasslander-style sheepskin coat, rolled tight and carried against the winter. Too small across the shoulders for Ahjvar, it was a loose fit on Ghu. They would be glad of it before they came to Nabban, he supposed. Even such things as a whetstone, a flint and firesteel, the woman's axe—all might get them further on their road. A case of needles, which he dissuaded Ghu from trying out on his arm; it was really not all that bad. Blankets, food, a couple of purses of Marakander coin, a sack of barley, which the camels were going to need if they were to do more than meander, grazing as they went . . . Ahjvar left the looting to Ghu and went to sit by the stream, methodically working over his sword's edge with the stone. It had seen little use, all things considered, in the last ninety years or so. Just as well, no doubt, from its maker's point of view, or the blade's steel edge would have been taken back to its pith; his weapons in the Five Cities had generally been less honourable ones, knives and poison and the garrotter's cord.

His arm throbbed and still bled sullenly, his head ached, and he would have lain down to sleep again if it were not for fear of the nightmares or some local chieftain's handful of spearmen coming upon Ghu at his methodical robbery. Satisfied with the blade's restoration at last, Ahjvar leant his head on the bole of a willow and found he had shut his eyes anyway.

Nabban. Ghu was drawn east now as the geese were pulled north in spring. The empire was a land of what, in any other place, would be many gods protecting many folks. There were only two gods in all Nabban now—Mother Nabban of the rivers, Father Nabban of the heights—and they called Ghu home . . . but what followed on that?

"You'll like this."

He had slept. The sun was hot, even through the willow leaves, climbing towards noon. Ghu dropped something at his side. A stirrup crossbow cased in oiled leather, and a quiver, six bolts left. Good Gold Harbour work. He recognized the maker by the patterning of ships on the stock.

"We could go back down to the Five Cities," Ahjvar said.

He had lost track of time, the passing weeks and the phases of the moon; they had wandered far from the road, their course more winding than a slow river of the plains, and some days he had not been fit to travel at all. Days. Weeks, maybe. He couldn't say. He wasn't sure where they were, except well east of the kingdoms of Praitan, nearly to Porthduryan, where the eastern desert road began. There was a second land route to Nabban, a way that ran south of the deserts, north of the eastern forests, but it climbed high into mountains before dropping to the free city of Bitha. Not a road for winter. The third route was by sea from the former colony cities, a dangerous voyage, very long; the coast was savage and the sea beset by storms, and yet it would leave behind the assumption that they were more of the warlord Ketsim's brigands; Ghu, at least, would be in a known world on board ship. He had worked his way west from Nabban by sea. From here, the nearest port of the Five Cities would be Sea Town, far away south somewhere. Noble Cedar Harbour was seven hundred miles down the coast from there. It had been a long time since the Leopard had hunted in either. A lifetime, for other men.

"I could easily earn enough to pay our passage by sea."

Ghu's face went still, utterly without expression, black eyes dark as night, as ageless. "No."

Ahjvar hadn't felt much but weariness and fear since the battle at Orsamoss, but that woke some spark of anger. Difficult enough, what Ghu set out to do, but he made it worse dragging Ahjvar with him, and the desert . . . "You want to try to cross a desert you know only from caravaneer's tales, in winter, with what we can steal from bandits hardly better off than we are?"

"You don't kill for me, Ahjvar. Not like that."

He looked away. Ghu crouched down by him, took his arm, turned it to look at the deep purple bruises blooming on Ahjvar's wrist. Brushed a thumb over one, as if to undo it. Or the rope scars beneath, and the mottled burns, livid, not yet fading to silver. "Besides, we still have your bracelets, remember?"

He did not. So many things lost, but the memories he would leave by the wayside he could not shed. But yes, hazily, he remembered. Thick gold rings with leopard's-head terminals, heirlooms, like the sword, of his house. Useful now and then over the years when he had needed to swagger as a noble of Praitan in some disguise about his work. Not robbed for the temple after all; they had been taken and restored; he had been sent out wearing them, her captain, her—don't think of her. Bracelets. His. Gold. Wealth to outfit them for several journeys, but difficult to sell for anything near their worth. Difficult, in this land, to find anyone who could afford to buy, or who would want such killable wealth under their roof, in a land so brigand-plagued. In the cities, though . . .

"We could buy passage fit for most respectable merchants, once we came to a place to sell that gold, ragged as we are," said Ghu. "But Ahj . . . you want to be shut up in the close quarters of a ship? For months, if the season's bad? Dreaming?"

"No." He kept his eyes on the water. He dreamed of water, flowing into him, burning in the lungs like fire, the deep still water of the Lady's well. He'd gone into the sea once, long ago, when he had still hoped there might be a way to die and take his curses with him.

"Come away," Ghu said quietly. "They had still the haunch of a sheep. We might as well have the good of it, once we put enough miles between ourselves and this place to risk a fire. There's bread to eat till then. And you do need stitches in that cut if it's to heal clean."

Ahjvar nodded, trying to summon the will to move.

"It was the coffee I meant you might like, actually. Not the crossbow."

"Coffee?" He looked around at that.

Ghu laughed, shook a rattling cotton bag. "Nothing to grind it with, but there's bound to be stones wherever we camp. Now—come." As if he were one of the dogs.

The dying gods dream of salvation, a gambler's doomed hope. Do they see him? He thinks not. Their own dreams drown them: they dream of their child, cast to the winds—all their last and fading thought. Their hopes of him leak, and the prophets spill words of storm and a land made new.

It will be so, but not by the heir of the gods.

A gift to the emperor's daughter, an ambassador from far, far in the west, sent to great Yao of Nabban, famed even in distant Tiypur, with tribute of sea-silk and cameo-work in onyx and agate, and drugs and dyestuffs and poisons. A rough, barbarian thing, the gift, a trinket that drew her eye, hers out of all those who looked on it, displayed in the mother-of-pearl-inlaid chest with the greater jewels destined for the imperial treasury. He had made it so, like a caravan-mercenary's amulet, to prevent it being desired, and so lost to some imperial wife or favoured lord who would be no use to him. It would draw the one he sought: the lever, the stepping stone, the pebble of his avalanche. He had not been certain who it might be, but there was faint wizardry lingering in all Min-Jan's descendants, their foremother's legacy, and he had been certain the seed he sent would find some fertile ground in which to sink its roots.

A door, to be opened.

And so it has proved.

CHAPTER II

Mia leapt onto the stage flourishing a scarlet-painted wooden sword, the comet's tail of her horse-hair wig swirling after her. The basswood mask, eyes edged in red to show the character's devil-bonded nature, was also meant to show feminine perfection, a smooth, small-mouthed oval, subtly carved and tinted. Kaeo sprang before her with a shout and they fought back and forth, omitting none of the nine significant forms, each held a moment for the appreciation of the audience, who, here in the Golden City, the imperial capital, knew precisely what they should be seeing and would be loud in disapproval if there were any flaw in the performance. His own mask was a masculine mirror of the Yeh-Lin one Mia wore, manly perfection, the eyes outlined in gold, the faint colouring likewise mixed with gold dust. The pair of masks was the most valuable of all the troupe's possessions save the theatre itself, carved by a master over a century before, heirlooms, and the master of the company kept them under lock and key in his own home, entrusting them to his slave-actors only just before each performance. Not the way to get to know a mask, to learn to live it. Kaeo would have hung his on the wall and meditated before it while learning his part if he had been able to treat it in the usual way.

The Min-Jan robes were the real thing, cast-off brocades passed down through some upper servant of the palace, even if the armour was nothing but lacquered paper-pulp. Would any sane warrior have worn armour over a full court robe? Kaeo thought not. His mind was wandering and he sweated, though it was autumn and, even in the lands below the lower mouths of the Wild Sister, the days were cooling in a welcome manner, for all that the season brought storms to smash the shore and destroy the harvest.

And to drive impoverished free peasants to the money-lenders, and to debt, and the selling of their children.

Almost time. Mia rolled to Kaeo's feet, arms flung wide. She was still the most athletic of the women, still boyishly slim; she was twice his age and complained of painful joints in the winter damp, though not where Master Wey could hear.

"My son," she cried, and sang the long verse about sparing the breast he had suckled, parting the neck of her robe, though not enough to reveal her still-high and lovely, well Kaeo knew it, bosom. It was an old play, much honoured, but what imperial woman these days would suckle her own child? The audience took it to show Yeh-Lin's coarseness, her peasant origins, rather than as a touching plea for filial mercy.

Some vulgarian called out, "Show us what you've got!" A figure moved, down by the raised causeway that crossed the courtyard from the encircling veranda to the stage. Master Wey did not stand for that sort of thing. The Flowering Orange company was one of the oldest and grandest of the many theatre troupes of the city. The heckler would be shown the gate, most ungently. Or possibly the canal, if he put up a fight and annoyed Big Yen, who would even now be forcing a way through the crowd, a stirring as though a pig marched through grass, unseen. But there was a second stirring, people moving from the gate, crossing the packed yard, and the audience pushing to move back. Those who had paid for a place and a seat on the veranda or upper galleries leaned to look down, distracted.

Magistrate's guard of the Osmanthus Moon district. Nothing to do with him. Could not be. Sweat trickled down chest and back, slicked Kaeo's face. The air felt heavy, smothering, as if a typhoon were pushing up along the coast, but there had been no warning of it from the office of the Pine Lord of Wizards, no criers in the public squares. Kaeo blinked sweat from his eyes. Not a typhoon. He was abruptly light-headed, chilled and weak in the knees. Afraid. Dear Father Nabban, Mother Nabban, let him get through this. They pursued some thief who had taken refuge among the crowd, that was all.

Mother Nabban and Father Nabban, the two gods of great Nabban, drifted onto the stage with little mincing steps, robed in white and black respectively. Their masks, white-haired, serene, were not as old as the Min-Jan and Yeh-Lin set, but were nonetheless done in the ancient style in which the faces of the gods were delineated strictly in white and black. They seemed to swim and pulse and turn to mist.

Yeh-Lin—Mia—clasped his ankles. "My son, my son," she moaned, which was not the line; she had spoken the line, his cue, and he had been silent, staring away at the misty gods, whose outstretched hands—no, they did not reach for him; they stood correctly remote and serene, hands tucked inside the sleeves of their robes.

Kaeo dragged his attention back to her. "Foul mother!" he cried. "Murderess of the folk! Destroyer of the gods!"

Which was not historically accurate. When Emperor Min-Jan defeated his usurping mother in battle on the Solan Plain, she was an ageing wizard, not a beautiful, immortal devil. It was later that she returned as Dotemon the Dreamshaper, to seize the Peony Throne and make war on the manifold gods of Nabban. Kaeo knew he read too much poetry, too much history. His mind overflowed with irrelevancies, distracted him—good to be distracted, there might be a wizard and who knew what a wizard of the imperial corps might pluck from a fearful man's thoughts—the play, the play, he must think of nothing but the play. Concentrate. Breathe. It was too late to run . . . Line?

He drew a breath, standing with the tip of the lacquered wooden sword on Mia's bared throat, and began to sing. Min-Jan had shown mercy, of course. He was no matricide. He had exiled his mother, who had ruled as regent since his infancy, bade her be gone from Nabban and never return. A great and misguided mercy, the historians would say, and the one folly of his reign. She had returned a devil.

He could not remember the words, but they poured through him. He could have sung Min-Jan in his sleep.

The audience stirred, the silence gone sharp and deep. The drums whispered with his pulse. The flute rose and coiled around him, but it faltered, uncertain. Yeh-Lin—Mia, it was Mia, pinched his ankle, her hand hidden by his robes. Inside the mask, her eyes were wide and her lips moved.

The leading pair of guards vaulted onto the stage and, at the back of the courtyard, a woman shrieked. As if that were a signal, the silence shattered. Shouting, cursing, wailing of children, as the nearer crowd surged and seethed and tried all at once to flee out the narrow gates, while those further back shoved and elbowed and tried to force closer to see.

Kaeo's knees gave way and he sank down on the boards of the stage.

A wind blew through the courtyard, and the canopy that protected the stage cracked like a sail. Very dramatic, he thought, in some mad, distant part of his mind. Master Wey would approve. Something smashed. The tall ceramic pots of the orange trees flanking the gate had fallen. Trees old as the masks. As beautiful. As pointless.

He was a dead man. His words were gone. He was alone, trembling, on a stage in the eyes of the city, and the play was ruined and he was a dead man. Mia scrambled to her feet and backed away, gulping sobs, as the guards laid hands on him, shouting for Shouja Wey, demanding, was this the slave Kaeo, was this Kaeo the actor?

Kaeo was drowning, and a cold wind roared in his ears. He could not move. Kick, bite, curse—the boy he had been in another life might have done so, Dwei Kaeo might have hoped to fight and squirm away and run, but Kaeo of the Flowering Orange had learnt years ago that the only hope, ever, was to cower small inside himself and wait for it to end. Whatever it might be.

Stupid. His only end was death. But still he could not fight.

They dragged him from the stage and stripped him of mask and robes. Shouja Wey raged up and down, demanding to know for what cause they came to ruin the performance, did they not know that the second secretary of the office of the Pine Lord of Wizards was a patron of their company?

Treason, the captain over the guards said, a spy of the rebel and heretic Dan. Wey, generally a most unviolent master, went silent and then kicked Kaeo in the ribs and turned his back.

Kaeo understood and did not blame him. Mia wept and wailed, and half of the company wept and wailed with her. Fear as much as grief.

They bundled him, shivering in his loincloth, out the gate. He walked stumbling and as if blind, the very paving stones of the narrow street between buildings and canal seeming to rise and fall like waves, the bridges betraying him, rising in unexpected humps, tumbling downwards. Boats on the canals. He ought to heave himself free and throw himself in to drown, but they had roped him between them.

Shouja Wey and Mia were taken as well, and in the public rooms of the magistrate's mansion on the broad South Branch Canal they were all beaten, slaves and master alike, while the magistrate demanded of him things Kaeo told himself he was too stupid to answer or even understand, told himself he did not understand, because he was so very far away and the wind, the roaring water, so loud in his ears. He heard Mia's sobbing, like the crying of the children, the lost ones, lost Kaeo whose mother had sold him and his sister to feed his younger brothers, to put one more season's seed into the grudging earth.

Kaeo told them in the end, of course he did. He cringed and whined and grovelled and gave them the Islander woman who dealt in mother-of-pearl for the makers of jewellery—because they must already have her, or she was traitor. She was the only one who knew his name.

She was dead. They let that slip, somewhere along the way. Her heart failed under the questioning. She had not been young. Dead, but not soon enough for Kaeo, to whom she had passed small packages, scrolls of poetry, classics wrapped in oiled silk and some secret messages, for those who could read them, pricked in the paper.

Who did he give them to? He did not know. Men, women. Wey was a kindly master and did not object to his actors and musicians earning some little extra, when an admirer wanted to hire a performer for an evening of poetry recital or music or . . . other things. He took only the half-share the law allowed him, too. A slave might save for their own freedom so. Who did he meet? Kaeo might be hired for an evening of wine-drinking and poetry in some upper room, and find there was no party, no gathering of friends at all, only, perhaps, a private little dinner, one or two people, and he might be invited to join them, and he might be asked to sing or recite, because there had to be a reason for his absence and his meeting, did there not, and if you had Kaeo for the evening, of course you would want him to sing or recite. Was there anything else? Once, he did admit, he had spent the whole of the night. No, he did not know the names of that woman, either. No, she hadn't paid him, not for that; she was a guard to the old man he had been meeting with and they had taken a liking to one another, he and she. Had he ever taken payment for such—sniff—services . . . ? Of course he had received gifts, but not that night. What was her name? He didn't know; he hadn't asked; she hadn't said. A foreigner, Five Cities, a mercenary. Someone called him a common whore, then, and they were distracted, making him suffer for that. But they remembered their purpose after a while. Was her master a colony man too? No, he didn't think so. He had no accent. How did he know them? There might be a phrase given, a line of a song, the old folk-ballad of the Brother Swans, and he would hand over what he carried. Never the same person twice, and they were always strangers to the city, he thought; he did not know their faces. The names they gave were only clan-names, Master Lai, Mistress Zhung, which was not the proper form, and often the clan and the accent or face were from opposite ends of the empire. There was even a man of Dar-Lathi once, who carried himself with the arrogance of a prince, and a woman with the ivory-cream skin of the north coastal province of Argya, who smelt so of spices she might have been a merchant, but her hands were calloused and her body hard with muscle. . . . He noticed these things; he kept them to himself as long as he could, and he had no true names, and they were gone, all long gone. The grey-haired man with the missing two fingers and the accent of Shihpan Province in the west he kept and swallowed. He had been only last week. He might not yet have left the Golden City for—for—Kaeo did not know, he did not know, how could he know? He only took the parcels and passed them on, he knew nothing of how they were marked; he never read them.

Was it Prince Dan he served? The Wild Girls, the so-called queens of the rebel tribes of the jungles and highlands of Dar-Lathi? He did not know, he did not know, he only did what he was asked. . . .

Prince Dan. The traitor, the rebel, the Traditionalist who defied the manifest will of Mother and Father Nabban and the blessed emperor with his lies of a return to a golden age that never was. . . .

Eventually, Kaeo gave them even the eight-fingered man. He would surely have fled by now. He surely would flee; to arrest Kaeo so publicly was folly; all the city would talk of it. The governor of the city might have meant a warning to any rebel sympathisers: see, this celebrated actor, this singer beloved of so many—a traitor and a traitor's death, even for him. But it would be another warning as well. It must be. Kaeo did not want to carry the Shihpan man's death.

His pulse was loud in his ears. Drums. The flute rose, coiling about him again, as in the dance of the battle. Yeh-Lin's mask. . . . A great pressure of words, a flood drowning his heart. *"Are you deaf that you can't hear?"*

He screamed at them, spewing words like the vomit of too much wine. He could not contain the agony, the grief, the helpless wrath. *"The children torn from their parents' arms, the old hungry by the canals, the young dying alone far from home. We cannot comfort them, we cannot reach them, we cannot stand. This weight. They weep in the night. We cry out. Don't you hear? The broken hearts. Children torn from their gods.*

"A storm comes, a dawn. From the desert comes the scouring wind and in its wrack and wake the land is reborn. The heir of Nabban brings the death of the gods and the birth of the gods and the rising of the folk. The years of the Peony Throne are ended."

Kaeo thrashed and twisted and screamed and drowned, and it was not his pain but theirs that flooded him, that tore his heart and poured from his throat.

"Justice—mercy—the weeping folk set free." A wind. A mountain wind, cold with ice, roaring through the sea-damp room. They did not feel it.

They did not hear or see. They shouted and they tried to pin him against the wall.

"—before he breaks his neck—"

"—get him down, sit on him—"

"—look out!"

"Possessed."

"The word of the gods—"

"You'll be for the Isle yourself. A false prophecy of the dead gods."

"Blind! Blind and deaf! Don't you see them? Don't you hear them? Storm. Wrath. The Peony Throne is broken."

They beat him again, into red darkness and silence.

Later, at the end of it all, there was a dry-voiced man, a wizard of the imperial corps, who, amid the smell of hot iron and smoke, read a sheep's blade-bone cracked by the poker's heat and said Kaeo uttered truth when he denied knowing the true names of any he met, the truth when he named himself a servant of the traitor Dan, seduced by his vision of a land without slaves, truth when he swore his master, Shouja Wey, and the slave Mia, his known lover, were blameless and ignorant of his treason.

The questioner-wizard saved Master Wey and Mia, at least, named them innocent of all complicity in his treason, though Mia's hand had been broken by then and she would never again make the smooth, elegant gestures of the seven-flowers dance or grip the painted sword; he had seen her on the floor, half-naked, seen the boot, heard the shriek. Could the wizard not have performed his divination at the start, and cleared them then, condemned Kaeo then, without all this pain?

But there must still be testimony given, for the record. The clerk of the magistrate's court kept smacking her lips, pointing her brush.

Shouja Wey, his voice shaking, as if he were on the verge of tears: "Kaeo has been in my company for fourteen years now. I bought him as a boy, a singer, from the House of Canaries; they look out for likely prospects for me, talented youths. Oh yes, he was one of the best. To hear him recite 'The Parting of Zial and Wujian' would make a stone weep. Drunk? No, not before a performance, never. No, he has never shown any signs of taking opium, never spoken any improper sentiment against the blessed emperor, the Exalted, not in my hearing. I've never knowingly allowed my people to make improper associations. Well, yes, they do have followers. I don't let them go with those I think might be harmful to them. Respectable people, I thought them. Merchants, ship-owners. How could I have known? The enemies of the Exalted are subtle. Yes, he can read, I did tell you that. A little, only a little. It is necessary, in my business, that they learn at least the—that they learn the syllabics. Acting is not a mere matter of recitation. As Lady Lai Jilin wrote in her treatise on the five true arts of the theatre, an actor must make himself the mask and the soul behind the mask. He must make the words his own. If they learn only from hearing another's reading, they will never do more than parrot another's reading . . ." Master Wey's voice, which had woken for a moment into a lecturing passion, grew fainter again. "I don't think reading the texts of the twelve classics could have led him into such wickedness. They uphold the virtues and praise the imperial family most highly. Half of them are about Glorious Min-Jan. I can't account for it. I was greatly deceived in him. He never showed any sign of rebelliousness; he always seemed to accept the will of the gods and the place they had decreed for him most meekly. A most accomplished liar, born to deceive and betray."

The wizard's voice again, dry, dispassionate. "He is in full possession of his wits. He entered into this treason and heresy of his own will, out of hatred for the Exalted and the gods and the master his fate and the will of the gods had appointed him. And as for the second matter—as for his heresy." A hesitation. "He has spoken a false prophecy. He has made himself a vessel for the lies of the enemies of Nabban. His words were no true voice of Mother or Father Nabban, whom we know are weak and fading and do not speak. Their will is manifest in the will of the Exalted. To claim otherwise, to usurp the Exalted's right to speak for the gods, is heresy. For that alone he could be condemned."

Kaeo's eyes found focus. Floor of bare wood. Booted feet. Slippered feet on the worn brocade of a footstool, hem of an orange robe. Magistrate.

"I have taken the oracles. I testify, this is so. The slave Kaeo of the

Flowering Orange is a traitor and heretic, a knowing servant of the renegade Dan, an enemy of our emperor, the Exalted Otono, and of the gods
of Nabban, a vessel of lies, damned by the gods themselves for falsely
claiming to speak with their voice."

Magistrate's court. He looked higher, to a grey beard, a face smooth
with fat, eyes tiny and lost in the folds of it, a silk tasselled hat. The
wizard, in a blue court robe with his badge of rank glittering gold on his
chest, stood beside the magistrate.

The butt of a halberd struck between Kaeo's shoulders and he flattened himself, eyes, teeth, hands all clenched on the pain that burned
white, blinding, deafening him.

The dry voice, when he could hear again, said, as if bored, "He is
only another of the tools of the renegade prince, and a rebel himself,
a heretic who defies the will of Mother and Father Nabban, a traitor
in the household of his master the theatre-owner Shouja Wey, and a
whore who has given himself to strangers for money. He is corrupted
and unclean. He is damned. You may do your duty to the Exalted with
a clear conscience."

"The slave Kaeo, an actor of the Flowering Orange company," said
the magistrate, slowly, so that his clerk missed no word. "He is a man in
full possession of his wits, not a foolish child led astray. The testimony
of his master proves it, for all Wey of the Shouja Clan wants to believe
otherwise, being a merciful man. By his own testimony under the question, confirmed by witness of the arts of the Plum Badge Diviner Lai
Wisan, servant at the feet of the Exalted, this said Kaeo is a spy of the
traitor and heretic Dan. He has spoken heresy and treason in the hearing
of servants of this court. He has pretended to prophesy, which is heresy
and blasphemy. He was named a fellow-conspirator by the spy Tamareva
of the Islands. He has confessed to meeting with agents of the rebel Dan
and passing on to them documents obtained from Tamareva, injurious to
the rule of the Exalted Otono and the peace of the land. For doing so he
is found to be a malicious enemy of order and peace. For the treason he
has committed, the slave Kaeo's life is forfeit. For this treason, he will be
delivered to the imperial guard for a traitor's death on the Isle of Crows.

And for his blasphemy, once he is dead, his body will be given to the sea, without prayer or blessing. Kaeo, formerly of the Flowering Orange company, do you understand?"

A magistrate's guard kicked him where he knelt, face to the floor. A hero might have defied them. A prophet of the gods, dedicated to restoring justice and the right of every man and woman of the land to stand before them, might denounce the court and emperor and all. In the end, he was only a slave, and the words he had, the poetry of the plays, belonged to others.

"Have him flogged," said the magistrate. "Demonstrate to the Exalted and the gods our contempt for his blasphemy."

Footsteps departed, shuffling slippers, slapping sandals, boots. The guards kicked him to rise and he could not; his joints were water, and he trembled and could not push himself from the floor. They dragged him.

Not to the hands of waiting imperial guards. Not yet.

"They'll come for you in the morning," one jeered. "You're bound for the crows. A nice day out for the palace."

They hauled him to a bare stone room, where the tide's damp lay in the corners and watermarks made white lines of salt on the wall. A high niche held a statue of the Exalted to look down over him—blankly serene, no emperor and all emperors, and no reference to the gods at all. They turned Kaeo face to the wall, wrists tied to iron rings, and took a cutting whip to his back. Why? Because he was so vile a thing, so loathsome. Because they were filled with hatred, fat with it, and must spew its poison somewhere. In the end, the world turned dark about him and he slid away and left it behind.

CHAPTER III

Ahjvar, Ghu thought, had nearly forgotten the dead shepherd and the mercenaries-turned-brigand they had lured to a judgement at the blade's edge, though he wore a dead man's boots and his sheepskin coat was bought with plundered coin in Porthduryan. They had come, at a guess, over six hundred miles since then on the desert road—a rutted track marked by dung, the occasional bones of camels, and cairns over the graves of men and women dead on the way—crossing sandy yellow hills and a waterless plain of broken black slate, back into a land of tightly folded ridges, all gravel and sand and thorny, winter-dead things.

A dead man, too.

He should have ridden by. For all the harshness of the land, the long days on short commons, and the scouring dust on the cold, dry wind that cracked lips and fingers and sucked the moisture from your very throat, Ahj had been well, as if the clean desert horizons gave him space to begin to find a way back. He had been over a month without the worst nightmares; it was like watching him return to life, to see him take an interest in the world again, in ordinary things: the herds of antelope in the sand hills, the shower of falling stars they watched half one night in the black land, which Ahj said came every year in this season, though in Sand Cove the winters had been rainy and it was the ever-changing

44

sea they had watched when they sat out by summer nights, while before
. . . before there had been no one to tell Ghu such things. He had never
known Ahj at such peace. A fragile, new-born peace, needing space and
calm and silence in which to sink enduring roots.

But then there was the dead man. He should have gone on, except
that the last well had been brackish, and their water was low, and the
dogs, with one accord, turned onto the well-used trail that plunged into
a deep valley before he had quite sorted out that his unease and the smell
of something dead, along with water, was their awareness, not his own.
Even then, he might have called them back, but Ahjvar had leapt down
to lead his camel on the precipitous path, and so Ghu followed.

Vultures climbed from behind a wall of interlaced thorn brush.
Their wings brushed the air with a noise like pines in the wind.

"He's several days dead," Ghu said, while Jui and Jiot sniffed, lips
curling in distaste.

No need for a dog's nose to smell that. Rotten-sweet in the sun;
what ragged flesh remained to the bones had been shielded by clothing.
And seared flesh, like old cooking. Overhead, the vultures circled,
waiting for the human presence to be gone. The man looked to have
been a hermit: a body in a robe of undyed wool, barefoot. He lay half in
the ashes of his own firepit, sleeve burnt away, hand and arm, what was
left of them—cooked.

The ghost of the man was there, a faint presence. Aware, but not
pressing. Not present enough to take form that Ahjvar could see, or Ahj
was ignoring it, Ghu was not certain. Ghosts had visible form for Ahj,
as they did not for him, but Ahjvar had turned away, gone to the wall to
look over at the camels.

Smell of burnt flesh.

He should have ridden by. But they were here now. Ghu ducked
into the low doorway of the domed drystone hut, pushing the sheepskin
curtain aside.

"Ghu?" Ahjvar muttered something about fools and half-wits,
which sounded more like Ahj and reassured him, before crawling after.

The hut held nothing but a pile of dingy sheepskins for bedding, a few baskets and leather sacks hung from pegs driven between the stones, and some hand-shaped pots and bowls.

"Don't take the food," Ahjvar said. "We're not so far gone this time that we need to steal a dead man's stores, are we? Leave it for the truly desperate."

Ghu was not so sure of that. They lost time by hunting everything from antelope to speckled sandgrouse, so as to leave more of the dried peas purchased in Porthduryan for the camels, and he was not certain how far yet they had to go and whether they truly gained anything by such diversions. He had asked about the road, but estimates of the stages of the journey varied wildly. There was still a dividing of ways before them, a choice between longer and easier, or shorter and more dangerous. Winter deepened over them. The real killing cold was yet to come, but even now, though the sun stood at noon, the shallow scrape of the well outside the thorn fence here had been iced too thickly for the camels to break. They would water after and then be on their way, though the recently broken ice was going to be another sign to the unseen caravan that followed them that there were travellers ahead. He knew it was behind by the dust when the sun slanted down into the west, and every time they turned aside to hunt, it gained on them.

"Maybe," he said, about the food. There wasn't much. A small sack of peas, another of millet, a brick of tea, partially carved away, shrivelled garlic. A very meagre existence the hermit had lived. Various dark and dusty herbs, carefully sorted into bowls and little bags, did not smell like anything for cooking. "Ahjvar?"

Ahj came crouching over; he couldn't stand upright. Even Ghu had to duck. Ahj rubbed leathery, dry black things that might have been some sort of mushroom, sniffed his fingers and shrugged, but held up a fistful of wizened, once-fleshy roots, scraping a little of the scabby dark skin away with a thumbnail to show fibrous yellow flesh. "This one I know. We call it tranceroot. Poison yourself with that, all too easily."

"Wizards use it?" Maybe that was what had killed the man. Fallen dead and into his own fire.

"*I* don't," Ahjvar said pointedly, and returned it to its place. "It comes from the desert, though. One of the shaman's nine holy herbs, I think. The apothecaries call it dreamer's yellowroot in Nabbani."

He hadn't heard of it by either name. It probably meant, though, that this was a holy man of the tribes whose territories lay hereabouts. But not a priest with frequent visitors.

"We should go." Ahjvar had a tight, weary look about the eyes again. It wasn't the death; it was the burning. Ghu led the way back outside, leaving even the brick of tea. They had plenty of that, at least. Now, if there had been coffee . . . hah, the Leopard of Gold Harbour wouldn't be above looting coffee, no.

"Yes," he said, but when Ahjvar headed for the gap in the thorns he turned aside to crouch by the corpse, taking up a handful of ashy dust.

"A wandering god?" The ghost's voice—thought, perhaps, more than voice—was soft, bemused. "So far from your land. A river. Are you? A man and a river? Are you come here seeking answers?"

"No."

"They do come."

"Who?"

"The folk."

Ahjvar stopped and turned back to him, knelt down, a careful hand on his shoulder. "Ghu . . ."

"Do you see him?" he asked.

"The ghost? Old man. Yes. A little. Thin old man."

"Wandering god. And a web of bone and fire. Why do you hold this man here, when he should be gone to his road?" Not accusing, just mildly curious.

"Don't." Ahjvar backed away. "Ghu, let him go. Come away."

"A wandering god. You should hurry home. They'll take your land from you."

"Who will?"

"A fallen star." The thought drifted, attention sharpened. "A lie. A hungry fire. The road . . . it calls, and I cannot answer. Let me go?"

"Would you have us bury you? Do you have kin near, someone we should take word of your death?"

"Oh, let the birds feed. They are the desert. I am the desert. Let me go back to the desert, bone to dust. It was always kinder than kin. They would have taken me back to snuffle and dribble in their tents, scolded and babied in the smoke and the squabbling. Better it came this way, quiet and quick and kind. I only fell, a little pain in the heart and I fell, and . . . and then I was free. Why do they make death so difficult? They will find the bones, when they come again, and bones are all we are, bones and dust and the fire of the stars . . . You ride to war, young wandering god. Is it worth it? Why do the gods demand the blood of their folk to feed their land?"

"Why say so? It's the folk who make war, not the gods."

"Not you. Not your land. Not the one who hunts you."

"Who?"

"A lie. False god, false truth, false hope for a dying land. A waking devil. Is she? Not she, hunting, but you are the quarry none the less. A false true god, yes, hunting. Take care, young river, take care lest you fall and fail and fade and leave an emptiness and an empty folk that will welcome what crouches quiet, waiting, in the west and reaching fingers even into . . ."

"*Ghu!*" Sharp fear in Ahjvar's voice.

The presence of the ghost drew in on itself, shivered small and weak and afraid. "You should not linger on the way, child of river, child of mountain."

Ghu held up a hand to Ahjvar, who stooped to take up a handful of sand and would have cast the ghost away with it.

"Do you say I do?" he asked. Ahjvar swore and turned his back.

"I say nothing. I only dream. I would drink the tea and dream true visions for you, wandering child, but . . . I am gone. Am I gone?"

"You're dreaming still."

"I do dream. I always did. They are heavy, dreams. Too great a weight to bear, sometimes. They said I should not have killed him, because he was my brother, but what choice did he give me? But the dreams are heavy. Must I bear them to the road?"

"The road takes all."

"So the gods say."

"So the gods know. Go, find your way."

Ghu scattered the ash and sand, sat back on his heels, dusting his hands and watching Ahjvar, standing now in the gap in the thorn fence, looking away. Something had frightened him, and nothing waking ever did. Some echo of nightmare.

Old man. Seer. Hermit. Murderer?

Gone to his road now, anyhow. And wanted his body left to feed the birds. Well, it was a rite among some folk, or so he had heard, and why not? Ghu straightened the disordered limbs at least, scrubbed his hands in the sand, though dead flesh was a scent hard to lose.

"He wished his body left for the birds to clean," he told Ahjvar, who only gave a jerky nod. "He died of his age, is all, his heart failed and he fell over where he sat. Nobody meant to burn him. It's all right. Go break the ice so we can water?"

Another nod. The camels were nosing at the ice, the dogs waiting patiently by. Ahjvar used the axe to cut a hole, filled their depleted waterskins before the animals drank. Ghu cast a look around the horizon of this long hollow in the grey-gravelled waves. Nothing to show that anyone had been or gone in the past days, but the wind might erase all tracks. It felt like the whole of the world for a moment, empty, desolate, lifeless.

"Wait," he said, and went back for the peas and millet. Ahjvar leaned on his camel's shoulder and shook his head at the sky.

"I have no idea," Ghu said, "how far we have yet to go." He made the sacks fast to the baggage frame behind the saddle, about his camel's second hump.

By noon, when they would usually halt to rest the camels for an hour or two, they had come to a fork in the road; the dividing of the ways of which he had been warned, so many weeks ago. North or south? He knew which pulled him.

"Which?" Ahjvar asked.

Ghu considered the horizon and their choices, trying to discount the pull in his blood, trying to think of Ahjvar, and the camels, and the husbanding of their strength. Both roads led, in the end, to the border town of Dernang. South, they had told him in Porthduryan, had better wells, a safer road, but was a longer way by several stages, maybe a week, maybe more. They had also told him he was a fool to think of setting out on the desert road without the protection of a caravan. One lamed camel, one mistaken path, and they would die, especially at this time of year. Only a few caravan-masters would have risked the journey even then, and in a few weeks more, they said, it would be too late altogether to set out. But what choice had he had? The caravan-masters of Porthduryan had eyed Ahj askance, a tall Praitannecman with a mane of yellow hair and an untidy beard, blue eyes fever-bright in a face gaunt and grey-tinged, shadowed like old bruising. He startled at sudden movements and flinched from anyone who passed close enough to touch, hand on his sword. They said they were not hiring guards, nor grooms, no, nor cooks. Not, at least, if they had to take on Ahjvar as well as Ghu. He had not told Ahj of that part of it. Nor of the caravan-mistress, a fox-tattooed woman of the eastern deserts, who had made him another offer. He might have taken her up on it; she had been good-humoured and not overly pressing, handsome, too, dark and lean and clean. Not an unappealing offer, by any means. He'd done worse, endured worse, willing and otherwise, but she hadn't wanted Ahjvar along either.

"That one's mad," she had said, with a jerk of her head back towards the tea-house doorway. Her braids, all wound with silver rings, had danced and tinkled. "Watched you prowling about town with him trailing like your shadow. Wondered about you, but him, I've seen those eyes before. Boy I used to know went off as a mercenary to fight in Nabban's wars in the south. Came home, married the girl who'd been waiting for him, cousin of mine. Don't know what had happened to him in the wars, but he was broken like that. Smothered her, one night, and cut his wrists. That friend of yours is the same. Dangerous mad, the sort that's quiet till someday he kills for no reason and maybe takes someone else with him. You don't want to be the one standing next to him when that time comes."

"He's not mad," Ghu had said. "He's getting better." Which was perhaps not quite the contradiction he had meant it to be. And he had collected Ahjvar, waiting propped against the wall outside because he would not go into a crowded room, and they had gone back to the hill of the god and the shepherd-priest who let them shelter in his shed in return for Ghu's help doctoring the lame asses and coughing sheep of the hillfolk. Neither god nor priest spoke ill of Ahjvar; they had left him space and quietude. It was Porthduryan had set Ahjvar sidling and tense as a misused yearling, but he hadn't trusted Ghu to be safe there without him. He would do better by the time they came to Nabban. Ahjvar healed. He must.

Ghu rather thought it might be the silver-ringed eastern desert caravan-mistress whose caravan trod so close on their heels. She had been preparing to leave about the time he decided Ahj would be better off if they went on their own, and that he himself could not wait in Porthduryan all winter. Travelling as they did, they should have pulled well ahead of any caravan that followed, but with so much wandering aside, they lost what they gained in travelling light and at a faster pace than the heavily laden baggage train could maintain.

Time. He should not feel time gathered and began to outrace him, flowing like the tide. But it did. Ghu knew it. Powers moved of which he understood nothing, except that Nabban lay beneath their uncaring feet.

They left the camels, already fed from their nosebags, browsing some twiggy brush that Ghu trusted wasn't poisonous, to climb the nearest height. The northerly branch of the trail continued more easterly, heading down into a sinking, stony land, ridged and tightly folded. To the southeast there were higher hills, yellow-dun with old grasses between the drifts of sand, and the right-hand road angled into these, rising, falling, curving. It was clearer, the same well-trodden, well-dunged track that they had followed all this way. The northerly route was more difficult for the eye to follow. Southerly, too, lay the lands of the eastern desert tribes, pastoral, nomadic folk from whom so many of the eastern road caravaneers came. Their gods were many and small; they drifted between them on their yearly cycle of grazing, so that the folk of one tribe, one family even, might be born to different gods, depending on the seasons of their births.

"South?" Ahjvar suggested.

Common sense said it was safer to stick to the better-travelled road. The caravan-masters knew what they were about. Yet, there was that caravan behind. It would likely swing south of the badlands. Most did. The flowing tide tugged at him . . . *You should not linger on the way.*

"The northerly road is straighter," Ghu said.

"And worse terrain," Ahjvar countered. "Stone."

It was lying up a day with a lame camel, a blister turned to a deep sore in the sandy one's pad, that had first let the never-seen caravan creep up on them. He had remembered caravaneers' talk in the market of Dernang, of patching a camel's pad. Eventually, they had improvised a boot for her instead. It seemed simpler than trying to truss her, just the two of them, and stitch a patch to the pad itself, and the boot had lasted long enough for the foot to heal, though he'd done something to speed it and to keep any other sores from going so bad or deep.

"I know," Ghu said. "But I think nonetheless . . . the left-hand way. We'll try the badlands."

Ahjvar didn't debate the point further, only nodded. They headed back down to the camels, mounted, and set out again. Yes. The northerly road pulled at him, drawing him.

"Maybe we'll be able to buy grain from the tribes in Denanbak, if we go among them," he said, mostly to drive that fish-on-a-line feeling from his mind. "We'll come to settled lands sooner this way. We'd run short of feed for the camels and food for ourselves both before we came to Dernang or even to the winter camps of lower Denanbak, if we took the southern route here."

"Does that matter? We have no money left. Do we?"

"A few coins," Ghu said guardedly. He had no idea if any trader of Denanbak would even take the three diviner's coins he carried, they were so old. Maybe they'd have some value for the weight of the blackened bronze. There were Ahjvar's bracelets, though. A lord of the west, decently outfitted as such, could sell his barbarian gold if he chose, though they would melt down the lovely work, no doubt, and never see the beauty in it. Truth was, he would like to see Ahjvar wear them again, well and whole and bright in the sun on a good horse. . . . "The gold—it's the same problem, bring trouble after us, I think, selling or trading it in that land. Better to wait for Nabban and the cities. But I have a book I can sell. A thing like that won't draw half a chieftain's hall out after us the next night in hope of more as the bracelets would, but they would take it, thinking to sell it on to some caravan wizard."

"You have a book? Ghu, you can't read."

"It's not my book."

"You can always be counted on to have something that doesn't belong to you. Purses. Horses. Camels. Now books. I thought gods were more upright and moral. Let me see."

"It doesn't matter, Ahj. It was a friend's, but she's dead in Marakand, I think."

"Let me see. You'll have no idea what it should be worth, will you?"

Ghu, with reluctance, twisted around to root through the bag closest behind his saddle. What he passed to Ahjvar was a fat leather scroll-case, worn, but well cared for. Ahjvar slid the scroll out and unrolled the first pasted paper page of it, to study close, fine Nabbani writing. Ghu craned to see. There was also an illustration of a lord and lady, sun and crescent moon raying their respective heads, and an ornate seal stamped in red, a flower surrounded by characters, which overlaid the elegant calligraphy of the title. Another few turns and Ghu could see bold black lines making little blocks of tracks down each page, surrounded by much dense writing.

"The hexagrams for coin-throwing," Ahjvar said. "The book's called *The Balance of the Sun and the Moon*. Nabbani divination."

Yes, Ahjvar could probably read it. He said he had learnt to read the court characters long ago, when to pass the years he had studied for a lawyer in Star River Crossing. Why, he didn't seem too clear on himself. Maybe because the Leopard, or whatever he had called himself in those days, had needed some cloak of respectability.

He also said, small wonder they had turned to a syllabic script in Yeh-Lin's day, and generally from there he moved on to the subject of Ghu learning to read. Not this time, no. Ahjvar said only, "Your friend was a wizard."

"Yes."

"The Red Masks."

"She was taken by Red Masks, she and another man I met, another wizard. If they were made Red Mask by the time I freed you, then they were already dead, Ahj. You didn't kill them." He added, because Ahjvar kept looking at him, "I couldn't go after them. I had to follow you."

In silence, Ahjvar rolled the book up and returned it to its case, handed it back.

"It's old," he said. "It's valuable, yes, but not uncommon. Something every Nabbani wizard would have a copy of, but this is a fine one, beautiful calligraphy, worth a decent price for that alone. And it's stolen. It has the seal of the imperial palace library stamped on its first sheet."

Ghu shrugged. "Better to sell it before we come to the Golden City, then."

If they did. He had not thought about where they would go in Nabban, but . . . there must be destination. A time and an ending. A place. A chill touch on his spine. He had kept Dernang and the castle of the lord of Choa ever in his mind, never looking beyond. But that was the half-wit boy again. He could not wander blind and trust to the winds of chance. Not now.

CHAPTER IV

The sound of the wheeling gulls was loud overhead, and the crows clamoured . . .

The man whined like a miserable dog. They were tearing his dirty loincloth from him, leaving not a rag for his modesty, shaving his head.

That a human being should come to this. His bruised and bloody face, his raw back, turned her stomach. It was wrong. Whatever the treason, the heresy, he had committed, it was wrong. He could have been a monster, a cannibal, a tormentor of children, and yet such a death as this would have been wrong. Of course the empire would execute those who worked against it, the spies, the rebels, which this man had been; one expected that; one knew it one's doom when one took on such a task, but a headsman's axe made a sufficient end. He had been taken by prophecy in his agonies, they said. When the gods of the land moved a man to speak and their words were met with this . . .

The man's entire body was blackened and swollen in broken lumps; blood seeped down his legs; his hands were crusted black with it. Why the magistrates bothered with torture, when they had every right to send at once for an imperially-licensed diviner . . . but that was not how things were done in the Nabban Bloody Yao had made.

Kill him and have done with. It had been this Emperor Otono's father who instituted the death of disembowelling. His brother had rebelled against him, and Yao had made certain his death taught his lords and generals a lesson of loyalty, and perhaps his own children too, though it did not seem they had learnt it well. There was one prince dead by suicide while still a youth and a daughter who had fled, pursued by assassins for the defiance of fleeing. Rumour was, whispered most warily, that she, wizard-talented and permitted only the most minor of studies, in accordance with Min-Jan's law forbidding imperial daughters and sisters to wield any power, had secretly achieved the rank of Bamboo Badge, the highest tier under the Pine Lord. Or perhaps rumour exaggerated and lost Princess An-Chaq had been only Plum or Palm. No matter. No second Yeh-Lin, Min-Jan her son had declared. Imperial women were also forbidden holding any minor office, or undertaking any scholarship even of a non-wizardly bent, or having lovers, male or female. Might as well smother them at birth, in Rat's opinion.

Most recently Dan, the youngest prince, had risen in rebellion, fleeing the palace for his maternal Dwei-Clan cousins in Shihpan Province in the northwest the night after his father's death. Yao had died of an apoplexy this past spring, falling dead from the Peony Throne in the act of condemning to death his Minister of Festivals in a rage. A punishment of the gods, striking him down? The Minister had been executed by Emperor Otono as his first act in his father's memory, followed by the proscribing of Prince Dan as traitor and heretic. Dan was inspired by such very prophecies as this man had spoken, the fool's dream of the golden age the Traditionalists celebrated, a time when lords were answerable for how they used their folk, the emperor a mere priest of a land of petty princes and shrines, and slaves were debtors with a term to serve, no more. Or unknown.

Interestingly, Dan had not been condemned for the murder of his father. Too evidently an act of the gods.

Rat was not so certain. She had not been in the palace, then, but what she had seen since . . .

They were condemning the victim as a false prophet now, too, as if they could kill him two and three times, pile crime upon crime. Had he cursed them in the name of his gods, of Father and Mother, whose poor wandering dreams he had tasted, as they tortured him? She hoped so. She remembered the actor, the voice that seemed as though it spoke to you and you alone, giving living breath to the old, old poetry of the plays.

The land wanted to change, yet Mother and Father vouchsafed no clear visions at all to their servants in these times, unless the vague words of prophets—drunk, mad, imbecile, as though such fragmented and open minds caught the edges of another's uneasy dreams—were truly holy. Some few might truly be moved to speak by a god's hand falling upon them, Rat supposed.

She could hardly deny that the gods might reach out and touch their folk, after all.

Emperor Otono stirred unhappily on his little folding chair, the only one who might sit here. She might hope conscience made him uncomfortable, that he might suddenly declare an end to this, order someone to behead the man and have done with, but Otono, from what she observed, was a man who would cling to what had been done, because it had been done. Weak. Uncertain. Cursed by the gods, it was whispered in the palace. Three wives, as permitted an emperor under Min-Jan's law, but childless. An epidemic of croup had swept through the palace around the time of Yao's death, and many children had died, slave, free, and imperial. All six of the emperor's sons and daughters.

Poison or wizardry rather than disease, Rat would have said, but the imperial physicians and the wizards of the corps said otherwise. Rat considered that they were blind fools, but it was not her place to say so, being a slave in the household of the elder princess, Buri-Nai, Otono's full sister.

A slave, and yet she wore court robes of silk and had jewelled combs—the jewels were only glass, but nonetheless—fixed in her cropped hair. The nobles were like a garden of scented flowers, bright, sweet, whispering—whispering robes of silk, so thin, so fine, almost iridescent, so heavy in their multilayered wonder. Whispering voices hidden behind painted fans, as if they viewed an entertainment and must discuss it as it happened. Compare it to previous such entertainments. The emperor's robes were the grandest, the most translucent, held the most colours:

a garden of a dozen red flowers in shades ranging from palest rose to deepest carmine, each just short enough to expose the embroidered hem of the one below, with an over-robe of cloth of gold. His broad sash was a red so dark it was nearly black. His cylindrical cap was cloth of gold as well, and an array of golden, ruby-headed pins fastened the bun at the nape of his neck. She saw the glint of them as he turned his head to murmur some word to the captain of the Wind in the Reeds, the imperial assassins and spies, who stood at his side. He wore gloves, not to sully imperial hands with any touch of the mundane world, and his slippers were embroidered in golden thread on crimson.

This was how you dressed to watch a man be torn apart to die?

The princess was an echo of the emperor in the same imperial colours; Rat, who was called Lau in the palace, was the woman who held her parasol.

Captain Anri of the Wind in the Reeds did not watch the prisoner, but the courtiers. There were others, who looked like slaves of the court and carried no obvious weapons, but whose eyes watched all about. One of the princess's ladies was such. Diman.

The wizards of the imperial corps wore many-layered court gowns too, but their outer one was a deep, clear blue. They worked by rote and book and dared nothing that had not been well-tested and attested and set down.

No priests. The priests of the Father and Mother were not in favour at court these days. The last attendants at the shrine of the Father in the palace gardens had quietly withdrawn to some hermitage after Yao's death. Otono's anger had at least been confined to destroying the shrine and ending all imperial gifts to the thousand others throughout the land.

Rat touched the amulet she wore about her neck, against her skin. A hidden trinket, a river-stone with a hole worn through it, strung on a leather thong. Comfort. Promise. Not of a god, as the barbarians of other lands might wear amulets of their gods when they went travelling far from the land of their birth and their folk. Promise of the memory of a god.

The prisoner whimpered, wailed, wordless. The sound trailed away into sobbing, then dissolved into screams as the executioner's assistants laid hands on his raw flesh again. They bound him to the brass rings set into the stone table that was the only man-made structure other than the wharves on this islet, which lay just beyond the sandbanks and break-water walls of the lagoon.

To be disembowelled alive, gutted like a fish and unpacked, spread out for the gulls and ravens . . . that was what was meant by a traitor's death. He screamed and screamed in his animal terror, not yet touched with the knife.

The emperor's bodyguard, the full troop of eight giants, none under seven feet tall, stood ranged behind Otono, a half-circle about him. For a moment, as if in the corner of her eye, half-seen, and yet not seen at all, there was light, gathering nowhere and everywhere, as if it might pour through from somewhere, make—someone, the prisoner, the executioner, the emperor, someone or anyone—a blazing beacon of flesh, a fire shaped in human form.

There was no time to gather any defence against it, to know what it might be, breaking into the world, where it might unloose itself. All in a heartbeat.

There was a great shout that bypassed the ears.

A sound like thunder, and the rock beneath her feet lurched. Branched lightning struck, searing the eye. Not from the blue sky; it arced over the table, snapped between rocks. The earth heaved. Waves leapt, flinging spray into the air from the far side of the isle. The executioner lay dead, a charred sprawl, smoking. The table was shattered and fallen. She could see the bare and bloody foot, that only, of the condemned man, a lightning-broken shackle beside his ankle. The rest of him was hidden behind the shattered table from which he had been spilt. The emperor lay flat on the ground among his guards and his wizards and his ladies. All that, Rat saw in a single flash as she fell side-ways, deafened, blinded, but sound returned in voices screaming. To lie stunned, to gather her wits, to try to comprehend . . . no time. Move. Act. She crawled to where she could look again.

They were stirring all about her, the fallen flowers of the court, the bright silks, the guards in gilded scale and silk-swathed helmets. They clambered like clumsy, uncertain kittens on all fours, mewling. The emperor's parasol-bearer sat up on her knees and wailed, pawing at the emperor, who flopped all limp and slack as she hauled him into her arms. Foolish woman. She should be giving thanks to the Old Great Gods she was spared.

The emperor was certainly dead. That fine silk was scorched black over his heart. One of the giants dragged the parasol-woman away, shouting. So much shouting.

"The gods!" A wizard stumbled to her feet, hands clapped to her ears, her coiled braids shedding their pins and tumbling down. "The gods, the gods have struck down the Exalted!"

Well, someone certainly had.

"The emperor is dead!"

"Wizards of Prince Dan!" someone else cried.

Old Great Gods, were they fools? This was no wizardry. But the old Pine Lord did not deny the possibility. He was among those who failed to stir.

"The wrath of the Old Great Gods!" Princess Buri-Nai staggered to her feet. "It is the wrath of the Old Great Gods!" She jerked her arm away from the giant who presumed to seize her. "Diman, come. We must save him."

"Who, princess?" The assassin had shed the outer layers of her court robes. Beneath she wore leather armour, snug leggings. No sword, but a long knife in each hand, putting herself between her princess and the glowering giant who would have been a hero and carried her to safety.

"The prophet! The prophet of the gods."

"Princess, he's fried," Diman said bluntly. Rat had an unholy urge to snicker at that coarseness. Shock.

"Exalted," Buri-Nai said.

Rat felt as though her heart stopped, as if the world held its breath, though none but she and Diman had heard.

Diman gaped. Her face was painted for court, powdered pale, eyes outlined in blue, mouth made small and red. It hid the pock-marks that scarred her. Now her gaping made her a theatre mask, an expression of shock or horror.

Not a plot between the two of them, then. The Wind in the Reeds were better actors than that.

The Pine Lord, maybe? But he had died in the attack. Some other wizardry—but Rat knew the taste of wizardry in the air and this lightning had not been—

—had not been any work of the gods, either. No.

"The gods have struck down the emperor for the death of their prophet!" someone cried. "We are all damned, we are all damned!"

Very likely.

Diman's mouth snapped shut. "Exalted Buri-Nai," she said, and pushed past Rat, who was fumbling with stupidly shaking hands to retrieve her parasol, as a good attendant should. But she followed close, courting a blow from a princess always too quick with the sharp edge of her bamboo-bladed fan, to see for herself what horror lay beyond the broken table.

The prisoner was not dead. His eyes stared at the sky, dark, dilated, and his body shook with little panting breaths.

"Prophet of the gods," Buri-Nai said, stooping to him. She pulled off a glove, laid a hand on him, his skin against her forbidden imperial skin. Rat was not certain what she was seeing. Concern? Prurient curiosity? Theatre? He was cold and sweating and gritty with ash blowing from somewhere. "Prophet of the gods, do you hear me?"

Theatre. Others had followed—two wizards of Bamboo rank, Captain Oryo of the giants, the First Minister, the Master of the Treasury, the Lady Governess of the Wives.

"Prophet of the gods, do you hear? Do you see me, know me? I am Buri-Nai, daughter of Yao and heir to this land now. I am the chosen, the fulfilment of your prophecy. The line of the sons of Min-Jan is ended, as you foretold. I am the Daughter of the Old Great Gods, and you have been deceived by the lies of the devils, to think Nabban's salvation lies elsewhere. Do you know me?"

The man blinked. His lips moved, swollen and bleeding. Shaped a word, maybe. His eyes drifted closed.

"Bring him," Buri-Nai ordered, looking over her shoulder. Captain Oryo frowned.

"You heard the Exalted," Diman said. "You've witnessed the judge-ment of the gods, captain. Bring the prophet, as the empress commands."

Empress.

The space of a breath, two.

Buri-Nai straightened up. "Captain Diman—"

It was the *captain* decided Oryo. A glance back at the dead, at Anri the captain of assassins sprawled unmoving by his master.

"Exalted Buri-Nai." Oryo bowed, stooped to gather up the limp and senseless prophet. Shouted names, orders, and they were engulfed in the giants. They formed around the princess—empress, if she survived the day to come. Rat was only an adjunct, like the parasol itself.

Some of the court had already fled, their boats seeking the gap in the breakwater, oarsmen driving them into the lagoon, frantic with terror, frantic to be the first to carry the news.

Dan, far in the north and his rebellion going badly, was emperor now, by Min-Jan's law, but by the time news of his brother's death and an empty throne reached him, Buri-Nai would have the reins of empire firmly in her hands, if she were not dead. Her sudden seizure of power was not so mad as it might seem—if it was sudden at all, which Rat might doubt. Dan's Traditionalists called for an end to slavery, a diminishment of the powers of the great lords and of the very emperor. The lords, save those inclined to the gods, and certainly the court, would rather not see him take the Peony Throne. But a woman, a defiance of Min-Jan's law—and "Daughter of the Old Great Gods?" An unheralded revolution in religion . . .

There would be chaos. Anarchy. There would be . . .

The nebulous opportunity that had been foreseen, that had brought her here.

No time to delay, for any of them. Rat followed meekly as Diman helped the *empress* into her own boat—they were taking the emperor's body in his.

Buri-Nai's boat left the choppy waters of the open sea to follow the emperor's back across the green waters of the lagoon. Her boatmen bent their backs to their oars in silence, broken only by the creak of rowlocks and the tap of Chichi, the drumming girl who kept their time. The Old

Great Gods had never entered into the affairs of the living world, save only the once, when the seven devils warred over the world. Was even the rot of Nabban enough to call them back? Rat doubted. And did not the oldest stories of the wars say that the devils, in their final act of rage and hatred, had sealed the road of the heavens against the passage, not of human souls, but of the Gods?

Prophets, minor and—so even the priests of the shrines said— mostly deluded, wandered the land, imprisoned, flogged, even executed by magistrates in almost every town. There was a commonality in some of their claims, the priests would admit, in secret, to those they thought—sometimes mistakenly—could be trusted. The destruction and salvation of the empire, the rebirth of the gods . . . More rare was mention, often from the most mad, of a messenger of the Old Great Gods in the west, but those who raved of that never spoke of Nabban and Nabban's fate. Even the priests of the shrines did not speak of any return of the Old Great Gods into the world.

Daughter of the Gods.

Was the self-proclaimed empress mad? Could even the ruin of Nabban be enough, to bring back the Old Great Gods? Or—what other powers might stir, in this time of chaos?

They skirted around the city—the city of a hundred islands, the floating city, the Golden City of Yeh-Lin—rather than cutting through where their wide-spread oars would be a hazard in the maze of canals, then crossed more open water, fought the current at the lower mouth of the Gentle Sister, the tide running against them, and headed upriver for the stone wharf and water-stairs of the red-pillared gatehouse reserved for the imperial family alone. Buri-Nai's boat hung back to allow the dead emperor and those who guarded him—two of the giants, his slaves, a few courtiers who had found themselves with no other transport—to make his landing undisturbed. The rest of the flotilla would be putting in at the lower wharves by the river mouth, jostling, quarrelling over slights, in haste to spread their news.

Reserved for the imperial family, but the boat of First Minister Zhung Hana pushed past them to follow the emperor.

Buri-Nai's own boatmen, grim-mouthed but silent, shot in to the wharf hard on Lord Hana's stern. There would be angry words in the boatmen's stilt-village, undoubtedly. Buri-Nai permitted herself be handed out, climbing the stone steps, scrubbed twice a day to keep them from being slimed with algae and weed, on Diman's arm, her hand again protected by its silken glove. Rat followed, unaided, ignored, and silently cursed the delicate slippers that made her footing so insecure. The boat arrowed away, making for the dyke-enclosed pound upriver, where the vessels of the imperial court were kept.

Oryo gave hasty orders. The emperor was rolled in the silk canopy that had shaded his seat in the boat. A shroud. His household slaves linked arms to carry him on their shoulders under the direction of one of the giants. They waited for Buri-Nai to precede them.

The heir's right. The—call her empress-presumptive?—bowed gravely to her brother's body and took the place she meant to claim. The giants fell in about her, rather than the corpse. A message no watcher could ignore. One carried the senseless prophet as though he were a child.

Slaves and peasants rising in revolt in answer to Dan's Traditionalist preaching in the north and west. In the south, rebellions in Dar-Lathi, where the tribes of the hills and lowland jungles had risen with Bloody Yao's death in the spring. Only a week ago news had come of the massacre of the governor and all in his palace. There were horrified whispers of the feast that had followed. It was said that the garrison of Ogu, the fortified town that was the centre of Nabbani rule in what had once been Lathi, had been overrun and scattered, that the gods of the hills and the goddesses of the little waters had put on their aspects of war and joined with the queens.

The Wild Girls. They were sisters, human daughters of the god of the barren mountain that brooded over the green highlands. Not monarchs as the term was understood in Nabban, not priestesses, either, but revered as having aspects of both by all the chieftains of all the tribes.

The head of the governor, preserved in a chest of salt, had been left on the very seat of the Peony Throne. Even the wizards could not tell how it had come there.

Another sign of the wrath of the gods, perhaps. But which gods?

Rat followed at Buri-Nai's heels with her parasol.

The imperial palace could have been a walled town in its own right, set on the only high ground for miles, on what had once been an island in the marsh and the fortress of the pirate-lords who had held this lawless coast. The deepest channel of the Gentle Sister curled round its southern side; the high wall, studded with guard-towers, had been expanded to include all the hill. There was no fortress within now, only the main palace itself and any number of auxiliary buildings. One could walk for miles within the landscaped grounds, around and around as the paths circled and twined in on themselves, and never look on precisely the same view twice. Buri-Nai kept to the straight, brick-paved road.

Just within the Emperor's Door, which only the imperial family and those attending them might use, Lord Zhung Hana stood.

He had gone so far as to bare his ceremonial sword.

"You are overcome with your grief, princess," he said. "Your forget that the emperor must precede you. Captain Oryo will escort you and your women to a suitable retreat for your mourning. Perhaps the House of the Pines."

A traditional lodging for elderly imperial widows, away in the northwest corner, out of sight of the main palace.

Oryo waited to see what she would do. Well, in his place, Rat considered, she might do the same. She did not step away from the princess, but she considered it.

"I am empress by the will of the Old Great Gods. You will kneel."

Lord Hana laughed.

Did he think he could seize the Peony Throne himself? He might dream so. The Zhung were powerful and counted Kho'anzis—high lords—of four provinces among their great nobles.

Other courtiers crowded behind him. Witnesses, Rat thought, and began to feel an edge of fear.

Oryo expected Buri-Nai to order him to remove Zhung Hana, and Zhung Hana expected that Oryo would refuse to obey her. Diman was the one to watch, and Diman only waited. She did not hide the long knife in her hand. A nod, and Lord Hana would be dead.

Buri-Nai stepped forward past her assassin. Rat did not feel this was a moment for the parasol-bearer to follow. She stayed where she was and considered the swiftest route to cover.

"Do you deny entry to the empress?"

Zhung Hana was a fool. He—slowly, not striking, making it clear he was not striking—brought his sword's point to touch Buri-Nai, just below the breast. Only her upraised hand stopped Diman.

"Captain Oryo," Lord Hana said, "escort the princess to the House of Pines and detain her there. She is deranged in her grief."

"The gods are dying." Buri-Nai spoke clearly, pitched her voice to carry to those beyond. "Their prophets say it, as do the priests of the shrines. We see it in the rebellion of slaves and peasants against the order of the land, in the treason of brother against brother, in the failure of our soldiers to stand against the headhunters and cannibals of Dar-Lathi. But the Old Great Gods have chosen Nabban for the greatest of blessings. The Old Great Gods send a saviour, their chosen, their Daughter. They name me empress of Nabban. Min-Jan's law is overthrown, as the prophets foretold. Kneel. I am your empress. I am your goddess."

Zhung Hana's lip curled. Buri-Nai folded her hands over her heart. A gesture of prayer. Raised her eyes to the sky, clear and blue.

Rat felt again the light that was not a light gathering. She was already backing away as Buri-Nai clapped hands either side of his blade.

There was a flash of white light, as if lightning, a very small bolt of lightning, had run the length of the sword.

The First Minister fell backwards, his heels on the threshold of the door. His arms were outflung, his mouth and eyes open, strangely dark.

For a long moment, they all stood as if cast in bronze. Then the courtiers beyond the corpse were falling to make obeisance as though someone had slashed the cords of their knees.

"The counsellors of the Blessed Otono will come before me in the hall of the Peony Throne," Buri-Nai said. "And they will offer their fealty to the empress and the Daughter of the Gods. Oryo, have my prophet taken to some secure place—for his own safety—and a physician brought to tend him."

She hitched up the trailing hem of her inner robes and stepped delicately around Zhung Hana. He smelt of smoked meat, and fouler things.
Rat, knowing her place, stooped to catch up the princess's trailing imperial hair. He had puddled the floor like a puppy as he fell.

She would go over the wall tonight and take her canoe from its
hiding place in the marsh grass. It would be a long message she must
dictate to the hermit in the Mother's shrine on the river island, two
miles up.

The Wild Girls must know of this.

*The deaths of the prophets first became necessary in her brother's day, when with
her father's death they began to speak. It was not her father's death that set
their visions stirring. The rising, west of the desert, of the winds of change. The
moment when the heir of the gods put out his hand and began to gather in the
power that would be his. The gods knew it, and the land, and the vulnerable
minds of the land, were steeped in their dreaming hope.*

*She will keep this one close, let his words be her warning. Through his
visions, she will see what the messenger of the Old Great Gods cannot or will not
show her, her enemy's approach.*

*She does not need this broken prophet, he says. "My daughter, trust to the
wisdom of those who have chosen you."*

"In your wisdom you chose me. So trust in your choice. I do as I see necessary."

*Wilful. He would punish her, but . . . what does it matter? Let her have
her toys. But he whispers of the drugs that will open the gates of that dreamer's
mind to vision, not only open them but tear them wide. There will be a satisfaction in watching her struggle to make sense of the broken flood that spills from
the wretched man.*

CHAPTER V

The sounds of the komuz were distant, a faint wandering song in the night. The king's bard was playing her great harp in the king's hall, but her apprentice the princess had promised a new song and was sitting in the doorway of her bower trying it out one more time.

An awkward turn of phrase, that. Yeh-Lin heard Deyandara falter, realizing it herself. Another run at that verse, a word changed. The song was not something that would be picked up by the bards, not yet, and yet there was something there. The girl had the bones, now, the burning heart. Mastery would follow. A small song, this. It sounded as though it ought to be a piece of a larger whole, a longer tale of which this was only a moment, like a scene caught in faint colour and hasty lines. Riders by night, passing ghostly under the moon and fading away towards distant horizons. A vision woven of words, a glimpse of something viewed from afar, something never to be known in its entirety. She had hold of something, that child.

Yeh-Lin thought she might put a name to the riders. The child would no doubt deny it.

Child. Her pupil, once, but now? Deyandara was a young woman, the new king's betrothed and a bard in the making. She had spear-carriers of her own and the king's besides to keep her safe, and the wizards of the king's hall. She carried no ancestral curse; she had no particular enemies any longer; the child—woman—needed no guardian wizard, nor yet a tutor, now that she had chosen to belong to the bards.

Yeh-Lin angled the inscribed silver mirror to catch the moon. Something had been nagging on the edges of her dreams, prickling when she drifted on the edge of sleep, for some time now. She had found herself unusually reluctant to pursue it. That fact . . . began to interest her.

Clouds, swirling, captured in silver beneath a cloudless sky. The spiralling path of text was in no script of human lands or tongue of human voice. She followed it, fell into cloud and moon, hung still and seeing.

A man lay on a pallet-bed. He was young, Nabbani, she thought, from his straight black hair, but he was so bruised and bloodied and bandaged, blood seeping through his bandages, too, that it was hard to guess at the bones underlying his swollen features or even the shade of his skin. He laboured to breathe, but he breathed. A woman entered, knelt. Her many-layered robes spread in a great pool of colour about her. Her hair was loose, a river of black over the silk, long enough to fall to her heels when she stood. The room was panelled in dark, carved wood, lit by golden lamps in the shapes of flowers, no two the same. Far grander than the bed, which was a makeshift thing. Not this man's own place, she deduced. Ornate shutters closed the window; impossible to see if were day or night. Yeh-Lin could see only the one corner of the room; she might have seized the vision, entered into it more fully, but . . . better to be soft, to be quiet, no will but the watching, until she knew what she saw.

Nabban, of course. A woman of the imperial family . . . that cherished hair.

She pulled off silk gloves, laid her hands on the man, on his chest and forehead, careful to set skin on skin, not wrappings, even though that meant touching swollen and crusted blackness, which every human instinct should say to leave be. The man twitched feebly, as if, had he strength and waking wits, he would be flinching, struggling, crying out against such handling of what must be agonizing pain. Perhaps he was drugged.

The woman bent low over him. Praying, maybe. She took her hand from his forehead, drew a pendant of some sort out of the breast of her robes, laid it on his forehead. Her hand went over it, with more prayers. Yeh-Lin had only the faintest glimpse. Something pale.

There was a third presence in the room, an attenuated thread.

The man grew still. His breathing eased, deepened.

Yeh-Lin touched the surface of the woman's mind to taste what she found there—

Was slammed away as though by a lion's paw.

The last glimpse she had was of the woman's eyes as her head snapped around. Fury, and an energy she could feel through the spurt of—*fear*, damn it, that she felt—like a blast of wind from an opened door. Red and gold and silver pursued her, a shivering wash of cold fire, of light that cracked and ripped as if through the sky of the frozen north, before she flung herself away, palm clapped over her mirror. Her heart pounded.

Well. So.

The night was silent, except for Deyandara strumming the komuz, gathering her thoughts, perhaps, for then her voice was raised again, that verse, a new turn of phrase.

Once her heart slowed—it had only been a momentary alarm, *not* fear—Yeh-Lin tucked her mirror away and walked across the crunching frosted grass, breath a cloud, to the stone-built bower. A stocky man leaning against the wall a little distance away nodded to her; the woman sitting with her spear at her feet and her hands tucked into her sleeves looked up and tilted her head towards the hall. Faullen and Rozen, chief of the princess's spears. *Get her and us out of the cold, my lady, please . . .* Yeh-Lin smiled. The black herding bitch, Vixen, bounced up to greet her. It never failed to warm Yeh-Lin's heart, that affection. Animals knew what she was, an alien note in the song of the world, but the little dog had come to trust where her mistress did. Deyandara played a rippling arpeggio and three ringing final chords and smiled shyly, flipping a coppery braid back over her shoulder. "That's it, I think."

"Yes. I liked it. Shall we go to the hall before your fingers freeze on the strings?"

"Before we give the old man an attack of rheumatism," said Rozen, climbing to her feet. "Devils take this frost. I was meant for warmer lands."

"Old?" demanded Faullen. "Old enough to know that if I plant my bony behind on the frozen ground I'll give myself piles, as you and my lady are so set on doing." He gave Deyandara a hand and hauled her to her feet.

"In the kingdoms of the north, they'd call this a fine springlike day, Rozen," Yeh-Lin said. She did like the folk of Praitan. Here was the rightful queen of the land who had stood aside for one better suited to lead it, and a scout and groom and a wandering foreign wizard—princess and her banner-lords, as her own folk would name them—and they all strolled companionably together and joked and grumbled, and gave respect and trust where it was earned. Sometimes she wished it could feel like home to her. Sometimes she wished she could stay.

She would not spoil the girl's evening. Deyandara sang often as a bard's apprentice, but it was no small thing, to offer a new song. Nor would Yeh-Lin betray friendship and oaths by vanishing in the night. She had sworn service; she would seek leave. It would be given. They had gone east, those wanderers Deyandara saw in her mind's eye beneath the moon. One should be dead and gone to his road by now, though the girl, she thought, had not understood that was his doom and she would not tell her so. The empire drew the other, but there was something coiled waiting in its heart. Yeh-Lin did not think he ought to face it alone. Deyandara would not think so, either. She trusted the child for that.

CHAPTER VI

T he northerly road might be the straighter route, for the crow, or vulture, but once it descended into the barren lowland, it began to twist through narrow ways that set Ahjvar on edge, taking the crossbow from its bag and slinging it at his knee, as if he expected ambush. Difficult to be certain of the road; the wind seemed to have scoured most tracks away or buried them under shifting drifts. Their path wound through strange pillars of stone, striped russet and grey and yellow, smoothed and rounded as if by years of rushing water, and oddly sculpted, so that, wherever the way broadened out, it seemed they rode through a forest of giant toadstools. In other places, boulders balanced precariously atop more boulders that seemed mere pebbles, or dark cave mouths glowered down from cliffs curved and rounded as a sleeping woman's flank. The wind whistled and sighed and gusted oddly, but at least there was no smell of smoke, no sign of human habitation.

No gods, either, though Ghu would have expected one amid all this stone. There was something, though.

"A goddess, I think," he said aloud. "But she's faded long ago. The stones remember her."

Ahjvar looked around the heights above. "You mean we're at the bottom of a lake? Or is it a dead river like the ravine of Marakand? How long ago?"

Ghu shook his head. The world had its own life that rose and faded regardless of humanfolk. "More what we would call a demon, maybe," he said. "Maybe they're not so different after all. Long ago. Very long. She was a spirit of the living earth, nothing more. Before humanfolk ever walked. No shape, no voice, no memory. Dead and gone, or changed out of all understanding."

They rode in silence a little longer, the camels striding on soft pads, no bells on their harness to proclaim their passage to the world. A hawk cried out of sight. The dogs appeared and disappeared, weaving their own way, hunting for the same small, fluffy-tailed rats the hawk would be after. "What happens," Ahjvar asked suddenly, "when a god dies?"

"Life fades to life. After that, I don't know."

"The gods of Nabban—the tales I heard growing up said Nabban's gods were lost in a devil's war and became Mother Nabban and Father Nabban. Lost, died. Were eaten by two of their own to become greater, strong as devils themselves."

"Not eaten. You should ask Yeh-Lin. She was there."

"I'm hoping we don't see her again. Anyway, do you think she'd tell me the truth? Don't you know? Ghu, when we come to Nabban . . ."

"I don't know," he said, a bit desperately. "The gods and goddesses of Nabban, the old gods, they became two. No, they put themselves into two, dissolved and merged, the two greatest of the northerly lands of Nabban, the god of one mountain, the goddess of one river, to stand against the devil. To be greater, to be all the land. It was a willing sacrifice."

"And now?"

"The gods of the earth and the goddesses of the water shouldn't be so. They were only one mountain, one river, and now they hold all the land and all the folk of the land, north and south and west and the coast, and it's too great a weight, one they're not fitted to carry. They're *tired*."

"What happens, when we come to Nabban? What happens to you?" Ahjvar turned his camel across to cut Ghu off.

"I don't know."

"Ghu, I need to know. You're becoming Nabban, you said. You said, come with you, not to be your champion or your captain or your assassin. Why say so? Are you going to *need* any of those? What are we heading into?"

He had also said, *not my lover*. Ahjvar didn't mention that one.

"I don't know, Ahj. I don't know. Yet. But the land is sick. I knew it, then, when I didn't understand. I know it now. The gods are dying and the land dies with them. Rots, like a man with a poisoned wound."

"And you are the god of Nabban."

"Maybe . . . better to say, the heir of the gods of Nabban."

"To carry what the gods who defeated Yeh-Lin Dotemon cannot bear? You're a man. One man, and mortal, and . . . Great Gods, Ghu, you—you can't even read."

He burst out laughing, gathered up his rein and nudged the camel alongside. "Not a necessity for godhead, Ahj. Even in Nabban." He grinned back over his shoulder as he took the lead again. Ahjvar was not laughing. "Be my clerk, then. Come to read for me."

Ahjvar scowled, flicked his crop to set his camel pacing after Ghu's. "Ghu, there are priests, there's an emperor, there's a whole great empire and its folk that pay so little heed to their gods they sell their own children in the marketplace. I know what you are, or that you are *something*—Nabban, if you say so, because—because I'm still here in the world. Because what but a god greater than the gods of Praitan could have—"

"Not a god. Not yet. A mortal man. As you said. Mostly." Sometimes. Somewhat. He had not been, not in that night.

"—could have taken me from my goddess and freed me of the hag? But how do you make the empire know you are even the heir of its gods? What are we *doing*?"

"Going to Nabban. All else follows. You're right, though. There is something I need to know, something I can't see. Would you make a divination for me, tonight?"

Ghu glanced back. After a moment Ahjvar shrugged. "If you ask, I'll try. But it's been a long time, and you know what they say about Praitannec wizards."

Ghu shook his head.

"It takes three wizards of Praitan, soaked to the skin, to tell you it's raining."

"In you I have faith, if it rains hard enough."

So weak, the wizardry in her, but the narrow channel is enough. He can set his hand to hers. He can teach her to write what must be written. A seal of their dedication, he says. A promise of their faith.

A barbarian art. She brings a mistress of the art from the city, a free woman, but free, slave, what does it matter? She is empress of Nabban and Daughter of the Old Great Gods; she takes what she desires and the woman will never go home to the islands again.

Her own blood in the ink. Sacred, he tells her. A rite of dedication, the blood of the Chosen Daughter of the Old Great Gods.

A Northron wizardry, he does not say. They went to the kingdoms of the north in search of new magics, he and his sister, his lover, who betrayed him at the end. Buri-Nai will never do so; she cannot. She has no claim on his heart. The sickle does not betray, when it is put down at the end of the day's reaping.

She insists on binding the prophet. It does not matter. Her dedicated, her faithful . . . strong souls, fierce, single-minded. But he will have dreamers, too, and from them he will weave a web to bind the others as they are, in the fullness of time, gathered in.

A harvest.

CHAPTER VII

A sword. She dreamed it. The blade was black, polished glass. Ice. Obsidian, frozen fire. The silvered hilt held words, a voice, a will laid in its words and she could not read them. Yeh-Lin strained to see, to tilt it into the starlight, but the light flowed like water and could not be held on the silver, and the flowing thorny lines filled in niello shifted and twisted and vanished under plain rough leather that was braided to wrap the grip. Hoarfrost grew into flowers, feathers, a delicate fringe edging the blade, but then it was not she who held the sword and the blade was levelled at her throat. No fringe of rime; it kindled the air to a burning edge of fire, blue and white and cold, and a wind rushed past her, into the blade, which was not stone but a rip in the night, a hungry wound to swallow her.

She could not see the hand that wielded it.

Yeh-Lin opened her eyes. She sat at a roadside fire, sharing tea with a family of travelling players heading down towards Sea Town for a clan wedding, a caravan of three wagons. The dream had been but the thing of a moment, a breath and gone. She shivered, and a boy called her "grandmother" and refilled the earthenware cup, offered her a second blanket. She smiled brightly, assured him it was but a passing chill, a breeze down the neck. She wrapped her headscarf more tightly.

Old woman travelling alone. They were kind. She would leave them as soon as she could without causing alarm; a mistake to have fallen in with them and their slow-travelling oxen, but it was exhausting to ride the winds for long, and she had chosen to vary that with walking, as a vigorous old warrior might. Good to keep an ear to the roads, to the voice of the lands she travelled through. Perhaps a poor decision, to have adopted the face of her latter years when first meeting this gregarious clan, since they would not countenance the thought of an ageing woman travelling alone in these barren hills, a warrior armed and able to defend herself or not, but their ways would part soon when she took the road to Porthduryan and the desert edge. Invent old friends who expected her there, assure them she *was* expected, that she would be alone in this brigand-plagued land no more than a day and a night. Strange, though, how often she did choose to wear that image of herself. Strange that she felt herself more free. It was not that old woman who had learnt the lessons that set her on this road; that had come later. Perhaps she simply did not want the bother of fending off young men.

Or the emotional complications of failing to do so, as the case might be.

Not on this particular road, at any rate.

Yeh-Lin shut her eyes and sipped the tea, trying to shut out the sound of singing, of laughter, of the baby fussing until a teat quietened it. The vision, though, did not return.

CHAPTER VIII

*S*now *on the mountain. Cold wind, biting. Cold water, the river's depths. Dark, dark. Kaeo is drowning deep in the dark.*

The wind smells of snow, dry, cold, burning his nose, his throat, sucking the heat from him; lips crack, bleed in the cold. Rank barnyard stench. Animals. Something groans, some beast. He cannot see it; he sees only the stars, the distant stars falling. They leave streaks of light like the colours inside the shell of a mussel. Faint crunch, rocking. A canoe crossing the great pool of the market by deserted night, the stars over him, under him. Stars over him, cold and sharp and close in the blackness, white expanse and the wind wails like a trapped ghost. There are ghosts trapped in Yeh-Lin's sunken palace in the Golden City, damned to guard it forever.

Sharp pain. She has struck him in the face. She does, when Kaeo does not see what she wishes, when the words leave his tongue and pour from him meaningless, or when she believes they do. She is a fool, a fool; the empress is a fool to believe herself a goddess and the chosen daughter of the Old Great Gods. She is a fool who wishes to see and punishes him when he does not see what she desires.

But he does see, he does, he does. What dreams the gods dream come only fractured, broken to smallest fragments. Shattered and tossed in the ferment the tea makes of his poisoned mind.

The desert. Snow in the desert. Stone like a madman's dream. Corals in the desert. A beetle, he, dragging a slow way through a forest of lichen frozen to stone, old logs rotting in the lord's forest preserve to grow mushrooms, delicacies for his table and they'll be beaten at the very least if they are taken here, poaching, and his sister clings close as something shoots by but it is only a woodpecker, big as a crow, black, white, flash of red. His mother beats them; the lord might take them and brand them his slaves for their crime, but she cooks the mushrooms. It is the next spring she sells them. Stone formed like lichen, like mushrooms for the lord's table, towering high against the stars. He is the madman. He is the dream. Stone. Storm.

The desert, the empress says, seizing that. He comes from the desert. The badlands. Fool, ranting of mushrooms. Who is he? The false heir of the gods, who is he, how do I know him? The messenger of my Gods cannot see him. Tell me, tell me, how can he die?

The heir of the gods, the child of Nabban. The false god is here, false, lie, dupe of—

She strikes him, or maybe it is the fist of the captain of giants. He did not know he had risen to his feet, but he must have because he falls, he feels himself falling, a long time falling, like a star, and like a star he bursts in shards and fire.

A star, a broken shell, crushed, all meat prised out, empty, dead. She prays to raise a storm, and storm rises in the night. The heir of the gods of Nabban will not die of a storm, he says, not like the wives of the Exalted Otono, sent into exile on the island province of Vansaka and sunk in an autumn storm, which is why the Kho'anzi of Lower Lat Province, father of the second wife, made a treaty with the Wild Girls of the tribes and withdrew his army from the border, letting the hordes who had slaughtered the governor of Dar-Lathi and burnt the fortress-town of Ogu pour out, across Lower Lat and into Taiji, a flood rolling inexorable now towards the lands of the Imperial Demesne. The high lord suspects sabotage; he does not suspect the storm itself. Buri-Nai's fan clatters a threat. She does not want to hear his opinions. The queens of the tribes are cannibals, barbarian headhunters of no account; the reverence the chieftains hold them in founded on the lie that they are the daughters of the paramount god of the highlands, the perverse marriage ritual enacted in every generation ended by Bloody Yao's civilizing conquest. The Old Great Gods will never let them come within sight of the Golden City.

His tongue is thick and swollen again, and he chokes on blood and bile. The tea is yellow as bile, and he has given up resisting when they bring it to him. When the empress wants the prophet of the Daughter of the Gods to dream for her, they will pour it into him regardless, and he will choke and gag and dream the same in the end.

Prophet of the Daughter of the Old Great Gods. Prophet of the empress. Prophet of the gods she says are dead and gone but their dreams flow through him when drinks the tea, and she has killed five wizards, diviners who dreamed, since she brought him to the palace, trying to see if their dreams would show her the enemy she wants to see.

She strikes him. The guards throw him to the floor. It has happened, will happen. It is happening again. She cannot see. She is the mask and the mask wears her, the mask hides unseen and she strikes him, the guards throw him to the floor. He dreams, but he is only an actor, a singer of songs, his words have never been his own. He vomits at her feet, but that is the poison they steep for him, yellow as bile, bitter in the throat, in his nose, foul on the tongue, churning his stomach so he cannot eat. She is only a ghost, he says, a forgotten ghost, nameless.

The heir of the gods comes from the desert and the north and the snow and his shield is fire and ash and bone. The heir of the gods comes like a king and the sky is the banner over him and his horse is white as snow. He is the wind that blows off the mountains; he will sweep you all away.

CHAPTER IX

Her breath made clouds in the cold air, drawn into the smoke of the fire, rising with it to the stars. Ivah blew on her hands, fingers going numb and shrivelled, scooped up the three Gold Harbour silver gulls she kept for divination, and plunged her hands back into her sheepskin mittens. The coins were not telling her anything useful anyhow. She did far better when it wasn't her own meanings she sought. Too conscious, too much an observer of herself.

In the Palace of the Moon, the sleeping goddess turns her face away. Death, abandonment, rejection, said *The Balance of the Sun and the Moon*. She didn't need to look up the hexagram. She hardly ever did, these days, having transcribed herself a new copy and bound it into a practical codex in the great library of Marakand, to replace the scroll she had inherited from her mother, lost when the Red Masks took her. The copying seemed to have fixed it in the mind better than all her childhood study, spurred on by An-Chaq's fan rapping knuckles or ear at Ivah's far-too-frequent faltering. The book was in the deep square pocket of her sheepskin coat, folded in soft antelope leather, but she didn't bother to dig it out, even to read the half page of further commentary.

She had begun to distrust the Nabbani manual of divination, with its strict division, like the questioning of the sheep's blade-bone, of all readings into sun and moon, positive and negative, male and female. It had

never sat comfortably in her mind, and Nour said his tutor, a woman of
Gold Harbour he had spent a year with when he was a young man, had
told him that the wizards of the Emperor Min-Jan had burnt all the old
books of commentaries and written others at his imperial order, in the
days when the old gods of Nabban were recently dead or dissolved into the
great new deities of the Mother and the Father. Min-Jan had been noto-
rious both for his distrust of the female, a reaction against his usurping,
devil-bonded mother, and for his tyranny, which came close to equalling
or surpassing the Empress Yeh-Lin's own. The coin-diviners in the tradition of the Five Cities argued different interpretations of the hexagrams,
but all their commentaries and alternates to *The Balance of the Sun and
the Moon* were recreations from memory, or old books so muddled with
later copying, intrusions, and outright inventions that Ivah found Nour's
explanations worse than what she started with. But then, Nour admitted
he was no scholar, and of no great note as a diviner, either.

Dreams. Perhaps what she ought instead to try was a divination in
the Grasslander manner, with the coloured pebbles, red, black, yellow,
thrown onto the painted calfskin that charted the constellations and
their stories. That might have a greater truth for dreams, being more
dreamlike itself. She had been working, since they left Porthduryan, on
making herself such a sky chart, finding herself more and more drawn to
her father's technique, though she had no intention of taking to some of
his other methods, the Grasslander shaman's trance-inducing smoke and
the like. Besides, she had the feeling it might be best to come to Nabban
as a Grasslander, despite her more-Nabbani-than-not looks.

Her chart wasn't completed yet, though. There was little time to
spare for such work when they made their evening camp.

Dreams. What she wanted, truly, was not a divination, but just
to tell someone. It had been Nasutani and Haliya who had the watch
before her and Wolan. Woken into the cold in the low tent she shared
with those two, the dream heavy and frightening—and why it had been
frightening she could not yet understand—she had almost caught at
Nasu's sleeve to ask her to come out to the fire, to talk. But self-preser-
vation had reined her tongue. "I had a dream about a man—" was going

to have to struggle through a thicket of good-humoured teasing before it got to any common sense. And what could Nasutani tell her? A good friend, a most cheerful and indomitable heart, a fellow Grasslander who spoke the same native tongue and had the same song of the grass and sky in her blood, almost like the kinship of sharing a god, which they did not—but Nasutani was not a wizard or a shaman or one who wasted much time on deep thought.

Footsteps crunched on gravel, and Wolan, a greying, slightly-built man originally from Choa Province in Nabban, though he had gone to the free city of Bitha after his marriage and to the road with his son after his wife's death, came down the slope to the fire, squatting to warm his hands.

"Bit of dust to the south," he said. "Nothing much. Bit of high haze, too, in the north. Might be snow coming in a day or two."

"I'll take a look." She was still learning the signs of the eastern deserts, the meanings of the colours of the horizon, the shapes of the clouds. Ivah picked up her spear and climbed to her feet to take a turn wandering the camp.

An odd sort of family, a caravan-gang. The caravan-master, Kharduin, was from some tribe of the deserts south of here—territory they would not be crossing. Nobody seemed to know details, but Nasutani hinted, with the air of one confessing forbidden secrets, of outlawry and a raider past. His partner Nour was from Marakand; Wolan and his son Koulang from Nabban or Bitha, depending on how you counted them; hawk-tattooed Haliya from the deserts, a different tribe from Kharduin, though; and Nasutani and Ivah from the Great Grass. Then there was Guthrun the camel-leech, a pale-skinned Northron; Seoyin, who was colony-Nabbani from Two Hills and his cousin Buryan, a Praitannecman from the Duina Noreia; Vardar, a man of the Malagru hillfolk; and Debira, a horse-tattooed woman of Serakallash—though one already gone to the eastern road in the days of that town's conquest by the warlord Tamghat, for which Tamghat's daughter was greatly relieved. Folk of so many lands and gods, drawn from across half the world. They were happy to enfold her into their family: Nour's friend, Nour's saviour, the great wizard and hero of Marakand.

Abandonment. Rejection.

Not they of her. Truth in the coins. She of them. This wasn't a life that could hold her. Oh, she could be a caravan-guard and she could do her work well; she knew camels, she was trained to sabre and spear and bow from her youth, and she was moreover a wizard such as few gang-masters could dream of hiring. With her along, Kharduin and Nour could have offered their protection to merchants carrying the most precious lures for brigands, northern amber, ambergris, the rarest dyestuffs and medicines of Tiypur . . . but the pair of them rarely took merchants in convoy, doing most of their trading on their own behalf or for their Nabbani-side patron, the high lord of Choa himself. Kharduin didn't need a great wizard, only a moderately competent one to set wards about the camp against hostile wizardry of raiding tribes or to warn of dangers unseen, storms that came suddenly without that warning haze on the horizon. And every one of them, even Seoyin the cook, was a competent camel-driver and a fighter at need. They didn't *need* her, and she needed something more. She felt . . . dulled, a blade rusting, already, and this was only one journey. What would a lifetime do to her? Out here there were no thoughts but the camels, the weather, the animal wariness of movement on the horizon, and the spark of hunter's eagerness that went with it.

They had fought a skirmish, with what Kharduin dismissed as a rabble of outcasts adrift, and driven them off with no injury or loss, only a few days into the desert crossing. It seemed almost a season ago now. More recently, they had found a dead hermit at his shrine, a regular stopping-place before the badlands, and had buried him with a prayer to the god of his distant folk. She divined for the safest road to take, the southern or the northern, at the forks where a caravan had to choose whether to venture the stone valleys of the badlands; her divination warned of a blizzard striking there, meaning they took the southern route, which would bring them into Denanbak at its westernmost edge. It was nothing Nour could not have done, and hardly a challenge. More truth to be faced: the reason she had not completed her star map was not the difficulty of working with ink and tanned hide in the cold; it was a creeping mental laziness, the body worked to exhaustion in the cold days but the mind growing soft with lack of exercise.

There was nothing for a scholar-wizard in Nabban, though, but to be taken into the imperial corps of wizards in the emperor's service.

Her father's daughter, her mother's daughter, would be no servant of any lord. That was not the arrogance of high birth, but simply that she had claimed her own soul from her father's overmastery; she had sworn she would make her own choices, think her own thoughts, find her own beliefs. She would not surrender that.

That need only mean Nabban was not her destination, as she had once thought it might be. She could stay with the gang, return westwards in the summer. Maybe go back to become a scholar of the library in Marakand after all. Maybe to the Five Cities, where there were also houses of scholarship, and patrons for wizards.

She could tell herself that, but Nabban had the weight in her thoughts of a mountain on her horizon from which she could not look away.

The dream had had much the same feeling.

Ivah checked the hobbled camels, studied the haze against the stars of the horizons to north and south, noting how they differed, the long fingers of cloud in the north, the subtlety of the blurring of the southern edge of the sky, which she might not have noticed at all had Wolan not made it something she should look for. She circled the camp, the several tents. What she wanted was to talk to Nour, but she was hardly going to go crawling in to drag him from Kharduin's side to babble of dreams. But if ever she had truly loved another person, and sometimes she wondered, it was he—though not in any way that wanted to take anything from Kharduin—and she wanted, achingly, to try to put this dream to words, to have someone hear her, before it all faded with the morning's light and the routine bustle of the day and left her lost, wondering if she even remembered truly what she had felt.

Friendship had its roots in their imprisonment beneath the temple of the Lady; there was a debt on either side for survival and a bond born of horrors no one else could understand. It need not have become anything more, but over the months in Marakand and on the road, it had.

Her brother of the soul. She was not a child, though, to go clamouring for a comforting word because of a dream. If daylight burned it away, perhaps that was for the best. Ivah turned her back on the clustered tents and studied the rising constellation. It was named for the shaman Urumchiat, who had danced the winter down in the years of ice. Tomorrow she would work on her sky chart.

Footsteps crunching, sliding gravel and frosted grass. She turned. Not Wolan, too tall. Nour, climbing to the ridge with a quilt wrapped over his shoulders.

"You don't have a watch tonight," she pointed out.

He shrugged. "Woke up thinking I heard you call me."

"Oh."

They both considered the horizon.

"Did you?"

"No."

He yawned. "Too early to get up. Must have dreamed it. I'm going back, then, before Khar rolls himself and all the quilts into a cocoon?" He made it a question. Ivah had come to think Nour had a stronger natural talent than he knew, stunted by long suppression in Marakand in the years when to be known a wizard meant worse than death in the Lady's well, and by lack of proper teaching.

"Nour, I did—I was wishing you'd wake up."

"What, you some sort of wizard or something?"

"Sorry." Her father had walked unseen in her dreams when he sent her out to hunt the goddess Attalissa on the road. She did not want to think she could do such a thing and not even be aware of it.

"No, you're not." He leaned to bump her with his shoulder, not sparing a hand outside the blanket. "You need me? I'm here. Twins. Blood-bound."

She snorted. "Of course. My mother forgot to mention it."

He yawned again. "Funny. So did mine. Why did you want me?"

"I was just thinking—I had a strange dream. I wanted to tell someone." She shrugged. "I wanted to fix it in my own mind, I suppose. I don't know."

"How strange?"

"Shaman-strange." But that might not mean much to a city-bred Marakander. "It doesn't sound like much. I dreamed . . . in the dream I wasn't really there, you understand. I was just seeing. There was a man, very far away. A rider on a white horse. Desert-bred, I think."

"Tell me about the man, not the horse, Grasslander."

"You say that like it's an insult, shopkeeper."

"Man or woman, are you certain? You said far away. Anyone you knew?"

"No. A man, though. I couldn't see . . . I knew. I just know. A man." She shut her eyes, trying to see again. "Dark haired," she decided. "I'd have noticed if he wasn't, probably. Black hair." Not wearing a carava- neer's many long braids, either, or she might have thought it was Nour or the Blackdog; at distance either's hair was dark enough to be taken for black, and she hadn't seen the face, to see tattoos or the shape of his cheeks, the shade of his skin. Black-haired man on a white horse, and dressed—"He was all in black. Not a caravaneer's coat. I don't know, just, black. He was that far away. He wasn't looking at me. He was looking away." And was that the abandonment, rejection, of the coins? It hadn't felt so, though she had wanted him to look around. "I couldn't see where he was. It was just . . . there was nothing but the man, and the horse. When I try to see it, that's all there is, no grass, no road, no sand, no snow. As if everything is dark and the only sunlight is there, on him. And the sky. The sky over him was bright as noon, as blue, and it turned all to banners, blue banners, blowing from the sky like great sheets of silk around him, and that was all. I woke up. The thing was—"

Nour didn't laugh, though in the light of the setting moon and the grey edge of the coming dawn she thought he was smiling, a little.

"—the thing was, I knew it was a true dream. I knew it dreaming, and I knew it when I woke. A shaman's dream, we'd say."

He shook his head. "Remember I'm a half-trained wizard at best and not in a tradition of shamans, either. Does that mean he was a real person, somewhere, sometime, or is it only the meaning of it, whatever that is, that's true?"

"Oh. It could be either, in a true dream. He might be only a symbol of something, a man out of a story of the stars or the past, or someone in the world now. It felt—it was both. He is real. I'd know him, I think, even though I never saw his face. I'd recognize the weight of him in the world. But what I felt, that's what was—" She shook her head.

"Frightening?"

"Yes. I—I belong to him. Old Great Gods, Nasutani would never let me hear the end of it if I said that. I don't mean it the way she'd take it. I don't mean like, like falling in love." Not that she had any experience in that, really. She had never fallen love with Shaiveh; her *noekar* bodyguard had simply taken her over when she was a very young woman. Ivah could think now, with guilt for Shai's death faced and accepted, that Shaiveh had been attracted not so much by her person as by power at second-hand, attracted by the knowledge that she possessed something of her lord's daughter. "It felt like what it must be, to come to a place and realize it's your home, even if you've never seen it before. Knowing it."

"Or if you've lost it, and come back to it after years away," said Nour.

"*Yes.* I need to—to find him. I—" She remembered something Nour had said about his brother-in-law Hadidu, the last priest of a murdered goddess. "Nour, you know what you said about Hadidu when the god Gurhan called him, when he was so devastated and lost, and he just got up and—went? That. If the man had turned his head to see me, if he had called my name, I'd have gone and knelt and said, what do you need of me? I'd have gone right into the dream, if he had called me then."

"Good thing you didn't. You'd be an awful burden to lug around if your soul went wandering."

"I would not. I'm the smallest one of you. You could roll me in a quilt behind the back hump and your camel would never notice the extra weight."

"You think you dreamed a god?"

"I didn't," she said slowly, considering. "But now you say it . . . yes. Yes. I saw a god. That's why I wanted to talk to you, now, before the day, before I forgot how it felt and it turned into just a dream of a man on a horse. A god. I've met gods—" Attalissa, in whom she had never seen any holiness and who no doubt hated Ivah, with good cause. The gang knew she had been in Tamghat's service, if not exactly all that she had done, but it didn't matter anymore, and Nour, at least, knew all of it, even the truth of her father, confessed walking on Gurhan's wooded hill in the night. "I spent a lot of time with your god Gurhan, last summer. He felt like that, but he didn't make me feel like that, if you know what I mean. I've sat and talked with him, long hours . . ." Drunk tea with him, told him her crimes, given into his trust to keep for their rightful owners strange things that had come into her possession: a Northron axe and a carpenter's chisels and an ancient horse's skull, smears of runes painted in old blood between its eye-sockets. "I could understand and feel Gurhan's godhead. I felt—as though all my burdens were eased, when I was with him. But I didn't want to give myself away to Gurhan. He wasn't—my soul's home."

"Some people—most people, maybe, never feel that for their god at all," Nour said gently.

"Oh."

"The ones who do, we generally call priests."

"Nour!"

But he was serious, and he put an arm and the quilt with it around her, pulled her against his side. She leaned there, head against his shoulder.

"I was born godless," Ivah said. "My parents were travelling in some territory between folks, between tribes and gods on the Great Grass. Not even a little wild god without a folk."

"You have a god, and he's calling you home."

"Not to the Grass."

"Do you know that?"

"Nabban," she said. A mountain on her horizon.

"There are only two gods in Nabban, the Mother and the Father. The priesthood of the Mother are born to their service, the way the servants of Gurhan and Ilbialla used to be in Marakand. The priests and priestesses of the Father are those who feel themselves called. They're mostly scholars, I think, what little scholarship isn't the preserve of the imperial wizards. But neither order is held in very great esteem by the court or the rulers of the land, and their shrines are very poor and unregarded, for the most part."

There had been nothing fatherly, nothing of the quiet scholar, about that man on the horse.

"A warrior," she said. "Sky-blue banners. I don't think he was Father Nabban."

More footsteps, heavy. She shrugged free of the arm and turned, as Nour was saying, suddenly unhappy, "Something that wants you to think it a god and isn't, Ivah . . ."

Kharduin. He didn't say anything, just tramped up to stand beside them, a burly shadow.

"Storm coming?" he asked after a while.

"Ivah is . . ." Nour shrugged, not going to betray her confidences. "Needed to talk, is all."

"Dreaming strange dreams," Ivah said. "I wanted a wizard's thoughts. Nothing to do with the gang at all, though, no danger. Just, dreams of things that might be, far from here. But Wolan says there's a sandstorm coming in the south, and snow north."

"Should die down before we meet it," Kharduin said, after a glance to the southern horizon. "Nearly dawn. No point trying to go back to sleep in a cold bed. Someone walked off with the quilts."

"One quilt."

"Tea." Kharduin growled that like a bear.

"Yeah. Good idea. You go do that, Khar. Ivah—"

"I heard. But I don't think—I don't think what you're thinking could feel like that, Nour. I—" *My father was a devil and I never knew.* "I just don't think so."

But she was chilled, and her dream-certainty that she must find this man, this mountain that drew her, that claimed her, was shaken.

Dawn was just pushing at the east, a grey twilight, a yellow edge. Tea and porridge, to warm the belly and the heart. Ivah followed Nour and Kharduin back to the fire.

A woman burns, fierce and bright and how has he not seen her before, Min-Jan's blood, Yeh-Lin's—obnoxious, mocking old woman, but Dotemon was always so and found her true mate in the aging empress. The bright, fierce woman dreams . . . dreams and her dreams touch the edges of the prophet's dreams and he finds her there, dreaming of her god.

"He is a lie, and weak, and will perish," he warns. "You are stronger than he will ever be. Daughter of emperors, daughter of . . ." He sees it in her mind, her shame, her love, her regret for lost love, her anger for betrayal. Evil, she thinks her father, the warlord, the conqueror, the tyrant of the lake. She regrets her child's proper love and yet loves him still. "Daughter of devils. Will you be empress? They have grown weak here, and they look only inward, all this empire festers and seethes in its own poisons. A wind from the north, the west . . . a daughter of the Grass, to make all new again under a new god."

In her dreaming mind she weaves fences of cord against him, cord rolled of grass of the steppes. She says, "I know you." She turns her back on him, and fixes her mind on the white horse that rides in her dreams, and the blue banners flying.

She thinks she has driven him out. She thinks the barriers she raises against him, grass and sky, are enough. She thinks she has learnt not to listen to the doubt and the fear, having grown up within them, the voices that are never silenced, that say she is never enough, never good enough, can never be right, no matter what act, what choice, what deed she offers. She thinks that angry stone core that has always stood within her, mute and stubborn and raw as the ice-dropped boulders they take for altars in this land, will resist him.

Women, in his experience, always do mistake obstinacy for strength.

They do learn differently in the end. His sister did, long and long ago.

This one will be an empress to fear, when she is his. But Buri-Nai will suffice to hold a place for her for now. When he has what he has come here to have, when what he has foreseen he may have, the foundation, the keystone, the great soul wound into the soul of this living world, then he will snare and take his new empress, his worthy queen, to serve him in the east.

He hesitates. Now the grass surrounds him, green and trackless, shifting, moving like water. She is gone, she and the black horse of childhood she rides in her dreams, but he holds still the threads he has wound into her, the roots. He has not lost his way. There. But she is a sly one. He did not expect that she could have done that, slipped from sight, not while he yet wanted her to remain.

He withdraws and leaves her to her dreams. She will not remember. Her god will not see.

She will be there, when he wants her. She is the daughter of Tamghiz, the daughter in many generations of Yeh-Lin. Ambition, power . . . he knows the shape of such desires.

CHAPTER X

B y evening, the sky was streaked with grey cloud in long ridges, and the wind was bitter, tearing the white smoke of their breath away. The camels' muzzles were bearded with frost.

They had no proper tent, but a cobbled-together shelter of poles and felted blankets, the edges of which they weighted down with rocks. Here, though, there were caves, like wormholes in the cliff sides. It seemed more practical to make a heap of every blanket they owned at the back of one such cave, out of the cutting wind. The one Ahjvar chose was about twenty feet above the valley floor, up a slope rounded like edges of the channels through the mudflats along the lagoon of the Golden City. The camels they left in the lee of a turn of the rock, unhobbled. They would not stray far. Camels wanted the safety of their herd, which included Ghu and Ahjvar, now, and they had had their ration of peas and browsed on what few wiry plants grew about the base of the rocks. Ghu checked their feet and legs and the points their harness might gall, scratched their cheeks and ears, praised them for their day's work, and lingered to warm cold hands in their fleeces, grown winter-long. A moment of peace for all of them. Good beasts, quiet and patient. Sand and Rust, he called them, for their colours, which Ahjvar, who never named his horses, said was unimaginative, but then said, so were the camels, though maybe that was a virtue. Ghu left them chewing their cuds in drowsy contentment and climbed higher up the cliff to cut a few armfuls of the sparse weeds that grew in the cracks of this place for extra bedding in the cave. The camels could breakfast on it.

Ahjvar had a fire just inside the cave mouth when he came down. There wasn't much fuel; dung gathered from the passing of earlier caravans, a few sticks gleaned along the way. Enough to boil up some tea and take the edge off the chill wind. Fuel would be a problem soon, since the shifting sand in these ravines had buried most traces of the caravans. He shaved tea into the smaller kettle, scraped lumps of the morning's cold pease porridge out of the larger of their two bronze pots onto a wooden platter, rationed out water into that kettle to start more dried peas and some strips of smoke-dried mutton simmering for the morrow's meals. He let the dogs drink, too. No watering-place till the third day into the badlands, at least in summer, by what he had heard. They didn't want to delay here, but if he went out at first light with his sling, he might bring down a sandgrouse or two. The dogs watched the platter of cold porridge hungrily, though they had dug out a nest of desert rats nearly rabbit-sized and dispatched the lot of them that morning. He should have called them off long enough to add one to their own pot.

"Tomorrow we hunt," he told them, doling out a dollop to each dog.

"Won't be much in these stones," Ahjvar said, which meant, much that he could stalk and that the heavy war-bolt of the crossbow wouldn't tear through, to shatter itself on a rock. Days since they'd seen an antelope or wild sheep.

"There was that hawk, and I heard an owl as I was coming down the cliff. There's something about for those, at least." Ghu sliced an onion, their last, over the mound of thick porridge. "Here, eat, before Jui gets his nose into the plate."

They shared the food between them, eating lumps of congealed pease porridge and onions with their fingers, washing it down with the smoky tea, which warmed them. Afterwards, while Ghu stirred up the peas, which would soak through the night once they let the fire die and be faster to finish cooking in the morning (if it all didn't freeze solid instead), Ahjvar fetched a handful of the weeds cut for bedding and sorted through them, frowning.

"I was never much of a soothsayer," he confessed.

No, he would not have been, Ghu thought, sitting back, arms around his knees. Ahjvar's edge was the sword's, hard and certain, not the poet's dreaming borderland where the tides of fate and chance might brush the world, like waves on a shingled shore, rushing up, flowing back, leaving streaks of foam and drifts of flotsam. Ahj walled himself too strongly against the darkness between breath and breath, though when pushed, when he let go and fell—he didn't walk, in that place. He soared. Maybe it was always so, for the truest depths of poetry, of wizardry, that there must be walls not easily breached, because you could not live day to day in such a fire.

"What do you need?"

"Trees," Ahjvar said. "Twigs of trees, mostly, and a few lesser plants. This is hay."

"Someone, somewhere, must divine with hay."

"It's not even good hay." Ahjvar held a stalk of something in the fire until it flared and was gone, leaving a spicy scent. "The thing about Praitannec divination is that it's a very formal ritual, a performance. Three wizards. One plays a drum." He smiled at some memory, a rare and beautiful sight. It took the years from him. "Usually me, because I am—was—notoriously unlikely to achieve anything resembling a trance, which is expected of the speaker. But a divination in the hall—I was my father's champion, his bodyguard—the wizardry was wasted in me. What use would I be lost half in a dream? I should have been two sons. My first duty was always the sword."

"First love?"

"That, too." He considered. "I was possibly young and stupid. Or lazy. Probably lazy."

Ghu doubted one became the foremost swordsman of a *duina* of Praitan while still a very young man through laziness. Long, long sweating, aching hours with something to prove, he rather suspected. And a song the little bard had once managed to sing all through, when Ahj was not listening to interrupt, called the doomed prince Catairlau one of the great wizards of all Praitan in those days, too. The golden hope and ruin of the Duina Catairna. The goddess Catairanach, wilful-blind though she had been, had had the sense to seal Ahjvar's wizardry away when she made him the vessel to preserve her mad daughter's soul, lest she loose an even worse monster on the world than she had.

"So pretend. You did before. You said it's all symbolism, anyway."

"I was inspired. Or mad. Or desperate." Ahjvar fed another withered stalk to the fire. This one smelt bitter. It had been growing too dark for Ghu to be certain what he cut. Nothing poisonous to camels, he hoped. "What do you want to ask, anyway?"

Ahjvar was watching the fire, not him.

Ahjvar was not making the idle conversation it might have seemed. The next stalk was tossed aside onto the gritty floor of the cave. His gaze never left the fire.

"Something in the west . . ." Ghu said slowly. "The hermit said so. Something in Nabban as well? We may have to do with the watcher in the west, but not . . . not yet, I think. Not for a long time yet." His own soul was drifting, dreaming. Shadow, and fire in its heart. He shook his head. "No. There is waiting in Nabban something we do have to face. Something has woken. Powers. One. Two. I don't know. Or maybe I only see them, feel them, now, as though . . . the hermit stirred something, reminded me, an echo—and now I'm listening for it. A storm. A wave that gathers force unseen. Your question was the true one. What do we ride to in Nabban?"

"That's two. There should be three. There are always three." Ahjvar's eyes were more than half-closed now, but he still spoke as if they argued the merits of some plan over the tea. His long fingers sorted stalks, burning some, tossing some aside, and the smoke wrapped them. It was pungent, heavy, and slowed the thoughts. If there was pattern in what Ahjvar laid aside, Ghu didn't see it yet.

Two questions. He hadn't meant to make the west one, but apparently he had after all.

"A third . . ." *What do I do?* But he knew that answer, or the beginning of that answer, and so it did not need asking. The third came unsought, words spoken unconsidered, rising out of the thickening smoke and the true question that troubled his heart, the one that mattered. "If I go back, what follows for Nabban?"

Ahjvar nodded and burnt the last of his handful of straws. He held up a hand when Ghu would have spoken, raked ash back from the edge of the fire with a knife, and gathered that ash into his hand, flinging it over the cave floor where he had been tossing the plant stalks. Jiot sneezed and sat up. Ahjvar, too, sat up on his knees now.

"We don't write books in Praitan," he said, his voice low. "We never wrote much at all, till Nabban's colonists took the coast and built their cities. But the wizards and the bards had their own writing, long before. Not for books, not for letters between the kings. For words of power, for memorial stones, for secrets too precious to be left to breath and memory alone. The characters were named for the sacred trees and the herbs of wizardry and divination. They could carry the sounds of the tongue, but they didn't need to."

The straws had fallen in a random scatter, one by one, withered leaves and seedheads touching, overlying, crossing. The ash bound and also separated them. The eye could make patterns. A stick-horse such as a child might draw in the dust. Almost a circle, like the moon a little eaten away. Ahjvar's finger traced other shapes, though, strokes like the scratching of hens in the dirt.

"Here, together. Yew, which is death, most often, but it can mean deceit, illusion, even treachery, the attributes of the devils. Or simple fear. Darkness. And with it pine, which is the sign of the Old Great Gods, the formless fire of the soul, the hope that survives even death. That, crossing it—" His finger traced other lines. "—that is the berried holly, which is battle. The sword. Which may be an edge. Or a boundary, a borderland. A decision. You can see why this is not useful." His voice rose.

"Shh, yes. It is."

"I don't know how to read this for you." Ahjvar hugged his arms close, shivering, distressed. He feared dreams, feared losing himself, and this drew too close to that loss of control; Ghu should not have asked it of him, not yet.

"I do. Almost. I see it. A little. Enough," he said, soothing, as he might have spoken to a frightened horse. It was not enough. A shape he could not quite grasp. Ahjvar drew a breath.

"The third, here . . ." The ash made a swirl, cutting off a complex arc of straws, no more meaningful than any other to Ghu's eye. "Here— elder, which is rebirth, renewal. Willow, which is water. Movement. Change. This, elm, which is peace. Except, the forms can be read either way. There is no left and right with it between us so, and this form, this circle, from here—" His hand touched, halfway between the two of them. "—from here they all make flowering ash, which is grief and sorrow, and prickly ash, which is undoing, and reversal, and the negating of all that comes under its influence. Balanced. And between them, the berried holly again."

"The sword's edge. Balance."

"Yes."

"You said the third. Are the two readings in the second group two questions?"

Ahjvar's hand passed over the ashes, touched a twisting bit of dry vetch, moved on. "No," he said. "There's nothing else. That—" He spread his fingers, covering the first muddle of signs he had found. "—is your first and your second, the same answer to both, the questions inter- twined. Here, in the second gathering—one question but two answers. The sword's edge, you said. Balance. You see it more clearly than I do." He swept them all into a heap, back towards the dying fire, and looked Ghu in the face at last. "What in the west? The—She feared the west. It was why she wanted to make Marakand her own. A fortress, and an empire behind it."

She. "The Lady?"

A jerky nod. Better they had not spoken of the Lady so close to time for sleeping.

"She is dead, Ahj. And the west—I don't know. I don't think it's something we need to fear, not yet, not for many long years. We go east." *A devil. You are the quarry. A fallen star and a lie.* Devil and Old Great Gods and war, grief and sorrow perhaps undone. All balanced. On choice, of course. On himself.

Ahjvar only rubbed his face, leaving ashy streaks, and asked wearily. "Did that make any sense to you?"

"Yes." Maybe. He didn't know, except yes, to know he rode not to peace, but to the turmoil of a land dying with its gods. And a devil . . . There was more there than Ahjvar understood. More there than Ghu did himself. "Thank you."

Ahjvar still shivered. "We're going to need that fire all night."

Ghu climbed down to check on the camels once more before sleeping. They seemed undisturbed, nosing at him for more scratching. It would take more than this cold to bother them.

He and Ahjvar rolled themselves into the blankets under their sheepskin coats, with the dogs curled up against them, one to either side. Ghu didn't sleep, much, but lay listening to the wind. Owls, maybe. Ghosts. The ghost of a sea. The night was starless with thickening cloud, very black beyond the low glow of the fire, which he crawled out to feed whenever it threatened to die away. Ahjvar twitched and muttered. Snow, hard, small stinging flakes, whipped past the mouth of the cave and swirled in to sizzle on the flames. Ahjvar whimpered like a dreaming dog and struck out at his ghosts. Ghu caught his arm before he could hit Jui, tucked it against his own chest.

"Hush. Sleep." The nightmare faded; Ahj didn't struggle further, didn't wake, though his breathing still came too fast and his hand clenched painfully on Ghu's like that of a drowning man.

Could he refuse to go on? Turn his back, chase the sun west again, as he had once set out to do with the god's and goddess's good grace and blessing, to see the greater world, to learn, to find new ways?

Nabban pulled him, stone and water, almost a physical pain, hooks set in his heart. He could not turn away now.

Change and rebirth, or destruction, and he balanced between. The wrong choice, the wrong moment . . . the wrong man. He might yet be that. His gods had shaped him, set him on the road, and he had started in innocence, in service, wholehearted, but did he set his will over theirs? He was no god; he had borrowed against his inheritance, one could say, to free Ahjvar. No. He could not claim that had been his end, because Ahjvar was not free. Ghu had taken on, that night, a borrowed godhead, only to steal the web of a curse worked by a desperate and unbalanced goddess in hatred and love, and could he do so in any greater virtue or any less sin than she, whatever his intention? Ahjvar was a perversion of nature, a knot of powers that twisted the world to keep itself in life. Ghu had sworn he would release him, if he asked, when he asked, and—Ahjvar had no wish in himself to live. He only endured because he saw no more peace in death than in this unnatural life, only a long and terrible road to the Old Great Gods beneath the burden of the evil worked with his hands. Did Ghu prolong the curse of the goddess Catairanach to give Ahjvar time to heal, so that death would not seem mere release to continued torment, or to keep him by his own side, tied to him, for his own selfish desires?

Both?

He had killed, not even in defending himself or defending others, but in battle in a cause that was not his or Nabban's, only because a man stood between himself and Ahjvar. Who, yes, was killing others, who would have slain the kings of Praitan if Ghu had not been able to free him from the Lady. . . . Justified, then? Who was there to judge, but the gods? And the little bard would have died.

What else? He had set himself in judgement and lured the guilty to death, and waited without compunction to kill them. They might yet have found their way to some atonement. He gave Ahj that chance but took it from those brigands in the eastern Over-Malagru. But they chose to attack a sick man in the night.

He had done worse, far worse. He had destroyed a human soul. Evil as Hyllau had been, no god of the earth could have that right.

He must come to his gods and lay that before their feet with all the rest. If they judged him unworthy, corrupted, too weak . . . that was his doom and his failure. It might also be Nabban's. They poured their wish and will into him—their blessing, their child, their heir. The gods might yet make another child between them, choose another discarded infant and begin again, but another child would be another lifetime lost as Nabban died about them and they died with it.

There were godless lands in the west.

He waited, unsleeping, for the morning, as the wind rose to a howl and lashed the rocks with snow. Still Ahjvar gripped him, an anchor against whatever storm he battled in his sleep.

It is groping into a fog, shaping, at great remove, a dream, a will to action, out of repressed anger and half-formed thought. She is a mind born keen and hungry but left to stagnate, to fester.

Obstinate. She hears, and yet she does not listen. "Let him come. Draw him to you," he says. "My daughter, you do not need to fear." But she is the Daughter of the Old Great Gods. He has said so. She will not allow this challenge, these prophets who should speak of her, and her alone. She, she only, is salvation. He has said so. The land and the folk will know it.

So let her send her assassins. If they succeed, the heir of the gods is not what he should be, and he is no loss.

Yeh-Lin held the inscribed mirror flat across both palms, a little darkened moon. It clouded with her breath, caught the light of her campfire, flickered with flowing shadows. Or a pattern of frost, growing, flowing. There had been a black sword, edged in ice. She breathed on the mirror again, banishing ice, willing to look beyond, but there was only night sky, stars. Frost. No. *Snow, white beneath bright sun, and young saplings, stark and dark and dead, not winter-bare but blasted of branches, and the wreckage of a cabin and outbuildings, built of upright logs in the Northron style: only the burnt ruin of them, almost buried in the snow.*

A bear, a giant of the forest, tawny gold, not brown. She had never hunted one so large in the days when such sports had amused her. A bear, and not denned in winter sleep?

It stood in the clearing of the dead saplings, with dark forest, spruce and white birch, ringing it, heavy with snow, unmarred by the fire that had swept the yard about the cabin, and it seemed to observe, with more than animal interest, the ruin of the cabin. Trod forward, ploughing through snow halfway up its flanks, and went in between the stumps of the doorpost, though there was little wall left to make a barrier and the drifts climbed over. It circled through, as if seeking something. Looked up. Snarled, at the sky, at the empty forest—at her?

Eyes found hers, like a blow, and she lost the vision, felt as though she staggered, a heavy paw slamming past to dash the mirror from her hands.

No, she held it still, clutched in her left-hand fingers, but the arm she had flung up to ward off the blow was numb and then tingling.

"What," Yeh-Lin asked, "in the cold hells, was that?" The stars, cold and high over the hills of the desert borderlands, gave her no answer.

CHAPTER XI

"So what news?" Kharduin called, as soon as Wolan and Guthrun were within earshot. Ahead of them, low mountains clawed the horizon, and the road climbed to the pass and the Nabbani border. Nearer, though, was the smoky smudge of an encampment almost the size of a town, straggling across the road.

"What we've been hearing since we left the desert," Guthrun said in disgust. "War. The emperor was assassinated, the imperial family's at war with itself, the clans are taking sides. Dernang's been attacked and captured twice since the autumn."

"That," Wolan said, with a jerk of his head back towards the camp, "is a mess of caravan-folk who were wintering in Dernang and were able to run for it before their camels could be confiscated, *and* deserters from at least two armies, *and* slaves who've taken the chance to bolt, begging and stealing and selling whatever they've got to sell, which is mostly themselves, for a mouthful of food." His face was grim. "There's a handful of gang-bosses and merchants calling themselves camp guild-masters. You want to go into that?"

"No," said Nour firmly, with a look at Kharduin.

"No." Kharduin scratched his beard. "Me and a bunch of merchants calling themselves guild-masters? There'd be blood on the snow before the week was out. Any word of Daro Korat?"

"Besieged in the castle. He's at war with his son, the one who declared for Prince Dan, but an imperial army crossed from Numiya while the river was still low. The general's retaken most of Choa Province from the young lord. He's retreating to Dernang, they're saying—the young lord, that is, not the empress's general."

"Empress?"

"Buri-Nai, I suppose. The old emperor's sisters are both dead long ago and so's his younger daughter."

Ivah flushed hot and cold.

"So was it old Yao or Otono who was assassinated?"

"Otono, like the Denanbaki told us. Someone got Yao last spring, or maybe he just died. That's when the younger prince launched his rebellion. If it was him killed Otono in the autumn, he doesn't seem to have been able to take much advantage of it."

"But their law says a woman can't rule. Her claim's being contested?"

"There's rebellion every which way, so far as I can make out."

"This isn't going to settle quickly. Damnation. And we owe the Kho'anzi money from last year, if Nour's accounts are right." Kharduin grinned, not happily. "Or not. Poor old soul. Best he cut his own throat, I suspect. Old Great Gods, now what? Dernang's going to be a battleground, if it isn't already. Nour?"

Nour brought his camel up alongside. "We need to resupply."

"Can sort that out with some of the Denanbaki winter camps. They'll trade for Tiypurian reds."

"We can go a while longer if we get good feed, but the camels will need pasturage and rest to fatten up before we turn west for the long haul. We can't just turn for home, even if we could find someone to deal with quickly here. Bitha . . ."

"The hill-road?" Kharduin considered. "It'll be blocked with snow yet."

"That or turn north, try to make a deal for pasturage with some of the tribes, see if things quiet down."

"They'd know what advantage they had and rob us blind."

"Bitha, then, Khar. Before this mob lose their hope that Dernang'll settle and all get the same idea."

Kharduin sighed. "Yeah. Might be thawing, or at least passable, by the time we get there."

"What's the hill road?" Ivah asked.

"Four hundred miles back west along the edge of the mountains and then a horrible track that skirts between the mountains and the great hills, down to Bitha," said Nour. "A brigand's road."

Kharduin chuckled.

"We can still make a profit there, even if a small one," Nour calculated. "Head to Noble Cedar Harbour on the southern road."

"Guthrun?" Kharduin pointed at the Northron camel-leech. "Can they make it?"

She shrugged. "We might lose the old dark brown cow, maybe one or two others. The road will be bad, but, yes, we can make it."

"Better than Choa Province." Kharduin nodded. "Bitha, then. Nour?"

Nour nodded. "Bitha." He turned his camel to head back to the caravan, which they had left waiting, wary for any threat from the unexpected encampment, a half mile to the north.

Ivah swallowed. "Kharduin, Nour . . ."

"No," Nour said. "Not on your own."

"I have to."

"No!"

"Have to what?" Guthrun asked, as the five of them rode back, Wolan as rearguard casting a frequent eye behind.

"Go to Nabban."

"Why?"

She hesitated, not sure what to say to convince them, but Guthrun formed her own conclusion.

"Family in that mess? You never did say what your clan was. It's mostly Daro and Zhung fighting in Choa, from what we heard in the camp, Daros loyal to their lord the Kho'anzi and Zhung officers and banner-lords come with the imperial general."

"No, neither of those."

"Later," Kharduin said firmly, for which she was thankful.

Later was more argument, the three of them lagging behind the caravan, and another caravan, one they'd been leapfrogging since they turned south of the badlands, veering to intercept them for the latest news. Mistress Salar, a fox-tattooed desert woman not, fortunately, holding any particular enmity against Kharduin. They retreated to the west, made camp, planned to journey to Bitha together, pool their resources for the winter hill-road crossing.

Ivah's personal quest—and of course by then all the gang and the strangers as well knew she was determined to go to Nabban, was hashed out by them all, advice and warnings in equal measure. At least it was not anything mad as a god they believed she sought, but her mother's kinsfolk.

There were embraces and tears and people slipping small gifts into her pockets, people giving advice serious and joking, good and bad. A shy and fleeting kiss from Nasutani, who had turned down an invitation for anything more months ago. Growling from Kharduin, advice on what caravan-masters to trust, should she decide to head west again; where—since it did not look like their wanderings would bring the gang to Nabban for a few years—to leave messages in Bitha or Porthduryan or Noble Cedar Harbour in hope he would get at least one; reminders, again and again, that in Marakand she had a home for the asking, she had only to find her way there, half a world away. . . .

Only Nour rode back with her the next day, taking a route through the lower hills to come within sight of the border crossing again, bypassing the camp of refugees, which seemed, seen at a distance and from a height, to have doubled in size overnight.

"You still think you saw a god?"

Ivah did. "I don't know," she said.

"There are five devils still free in the world."

"Four," she said, and added, to his look, "There's a Northron skald's story that Ogada was killed long ago. I believe it. And Sien-Mor—Tu'usha—we know is dead, and," she swallowed, "Tamghiz Ghatai." *Father.* "That leaves four. And Ulfhild Vartu—I know her. She doesn't frighten me."

Nour stared.

"Well, she does, but not in that way. She wouldn't—she wouldn't be claiming a false godhead and trying to use me. She's—not a friend." Family, by some odd reasoning. Mother of the only siblings Ivah had ever had, dead though they were generations before she was ever born. Ulfhild, strangely, seemed to look on her that way. Stepdaughter? "If she wanted me for something she'd just—tell me. She'd wear her own face. But she isn't interested in conquest, in having people serve her and follow her, not anymore." That, she was sure of. "Jochiz and Jasberek—I don't know anything about them. But the Northrons call Dotemon the Dreamshaper, and Nabban was her land, so she's most likely, and—but Old Great Gods, Nour, I can't believe a lie could—could feel so true."

"Just remember Marakand worshipped the Lady."

"I know," she said, low-voiced. "And my father's folk saw him as a great wizard and a warlord. But they feared him and loved him as a man. He didn't deceive them with a pretended godhead, for all he aspired to make himself a god."

"Be careful."

"Why would Dotemon call me with visions of a false god? How would she even know I exist? She never pretended to be anything she was not, in all the stories of her. If she wanted Nabban, I think she would come and conquer it as Yeh-Lin the Beautiful again, and not work plots in the shadows, hiding behind masks. And yet, *Dreamshaper*. When I think, I doubt, but when I remember the dream—I don't. I'm going to find a priest of Father Nabban, first of all things. A true priest, who understands gods and faith, which I don't. I'm not a fool. I am—wary. But Nour, I've been thinking, too—how do you judge the truth and the worth of a man or a woman?"

He shrugged. "Experience of them?"

"Yes. By their deeds. It has to be as true of gods as it is of human-folk, doesn't it? *You* never worshipped the Lady, even when you thought her a true goddess. You knew she was evil, whatever she was. There have been true gods no more worth following than—" Maybe not worse than the Lady. "—than my father. If I find this god, or this thing that I feel is a god, and it, he, is—is—not worth reverence, it doesn't matter if he's truly a god or not. I won't give myself away again to serve someone who does evil in the world."

But Nabban was an empire of tyranny, and evil, by all accounts, was rooted deep in its rule. Her grandfather, her uncle . . . If she had taken, after her father's defeat, his place, asserted herself as warlord over the broken and fleeing remnant of his followers who had gone as mercenaries to the lands Over-Malagru in Marakand's service—she would still not have commanded the swords and riders a conqueror would need to take Nabban, to seize it and drag it to some new faith . . .

She shivered at the thought. She had never wanted a warlord's place. Why consider it now?

They rode in silence for a long time.

"I ever tell you how I met Kharduin?" Nour asked abruptly.

"No."

"When I first went to the road, my first job, in fact. I'd hired on with a caravan-mistress out of Two Hills, someone who took the Bitha road. And that was a bad road in those days; there was war between the southern tribes, wells going dry, all sorts of things unsettling the folk. The sort of thing that leads to brigandage and raiders, wild folk and desperate folk and those who just enjoy the chaos and take what they can from it. We were attacked by a band of raiders one evening about dusk, before we'd made camp. About three times our numbers. They cut out half the train, I think. My camel was killed, and I was wounded and left behind in the confusion and the dark."

He stopped, as if that were all.

"And?"

"Well, Khar."

"Came back for you?"

"No. But he did find me, rounding up his own strays."

"One of the raiders? I thought Nasutani was just telling tales when she told me he'd been a bandit when he was young."

"She was. She doesn't know more than the gossip that's around the caravanserais, and it's all old rumour and half of that lies. They don't know anything for certain, except Haliya, who knows full well who he is and who his kinsfolk are—old enemies of hers. And Wolan, who dealt with him in Bitha before he came to the road himself, after his wife died. Kharduin wasn't just one of the raiders. Their damned captain."

"Oh."

"But . . . he was Khar. And it was like that, you know." He shrugged. "For both of us."

"Ah." Ivah didn't, not really. But *like falling in love* she had said, only half knowing what she meant, and perhaps sudden love was like seeing her god, in a more human and earthy way. As little to be resisted.

"And that was that. But after a year or so, I couldn't, well, live with myself any longer. That life. My sister and Hadidu, they'd be thinking I was dead, and I started thinking, better I was, than to have them know how I was living, a desert brigand. I've a few deaths to my account I'll carry to the road to the heavens, ones that weren't any justified fight. Not that we ever set out to do murder, not against the caravans, anyway, but it happened, and Kharduin was deep in the tribal feuding, too, and carrying on this war of revenge against his sister. . . . We weren't like those young fools we ran off this crossing, just trying to grab and run. The caravans feared us."

"Oh."

"So I said I was leaving him, and why, and after all the shouting and the throwing things I took his best two camels and I went. To Bitha, and he didn't come after me. I was half afraid he would, half afraid he wouldn't, and half expecting just to be shot down as I rode some hot noon. His temper's mellowed some since those days."

"That's three halves."

"I know. I lead a full life, right? But nothing. And then from Bitha across two provinces as a merchant's guard to Dernang, and found hire there and home by the northern road, to be sure I didn't get within his reach again. Or . . . put myself where I could change my mind, maybe."

"Oh," she said again.

"So a year after that, he shows up in Marakand, master of his own caravan, and he says, 'Fine, you win. Come with me.'"

"Ah."

He shrugged again. "I'm not sure what my point was."

"Don't be like you and get swept out of all sense for some first over-whelming vision?"

"Maybe." He grinned. "Though he was a pretty overwhelming first vision, even if I hadn't been bleeding on the sand with a few broken ribs for good measure, and the jackals singing not so far off, and anyone willing to tie up my leg rather than cut my throat looking like my dearest friend at that point. No, actually, I was thinking, you're a great wizard, a—a weapon if you let yourself be that. And you have this link with the devils through your father, and this, I don't know, hollow-ness—you wouldn't say so often that you're godless if it didn't matter to you, if you didn't feel it a lack, an emptiness you want to fill."

"Do I?"

"It's there. I notice. If someone wanted to lure you—they've found the right bait, haven't they? Not the seduction of love or wealth or power, but a god calling you, father and mother and beloved all in one. You think you've done things you have to atone for now. So've I. But like Hadidu told me at the time, when I trailed all broken-hearted and angry and hollow back to Marakand, you do it through the life you live. Do right with what's before you, yes, but don't go making yourself a—a damned offering to something you can't really see, blinded by guilt and looking for some, some wholeness that you should be finding in yourself, not in a god."

"Says the priest's brother."

"Well, he's the priest, not me."

"He'd give me different advice?"

"The first part would be the same. Not the last. Hadidu would end by telling you to go find your god," Nour said glumly, but then added, "I'm sure he'd say, be damned sure your god's a true one."

"I'm not, I think. Blinded, I mean." She considered Nour, going home again and again to Marakand, where they had killed wizards, and a lifetime spent at the heart of the loyalist conspiracy, Hadidu and he and Kharduin smuggling wizard-talented children out of the city and away to safety. *Go on and remember and choose differently*, the devil Ulfhild Vartu had told her.

"You don't need to go to Nabban," Nour said.

"I do, Nour."

"Well, then. Nothing more to be said. Just remember you've got a home with us, and resources you can call on. You're not meant for the road—your heart's not in it. If you wanted to set up and live a scholar's life or as a respectable wizard in Marakand or Two Hills or someplace, you just need to ask. We'll be taking a big loss on this trip, but that's not to say we haven't got something laid by. And if you're wondering, Kharduin said, tell the woman that."

"Ah. I'll remember."

They rode on in silence.

Where the road began its snaking climb up the pass, they embraced, and kissed, and he left her.

CHAPTER XII

When they bring Kaeo to the empress, he is her prophet, the prophet of the Daughter of the Gods. They walk him through the palace from a high room under the eaves in a robe of white silk, two of the giants escorting him and a slave to open doors, whenever the empress is moved by the desire for prophecy. The wizards fear her. There is madness in the yellowroot and it poisons them for a vision of her enemy, the false heir of the gods, the deceit of the devils who is sent to bring Nabban to war and anarchy, as if it were not already there, and while she hunts for dreams of the prophets' heir of the gods in the north, her generals mutiny and retreat, serve the provincial lords their cousins, and slaves and peasants seize manors and butcher the banner-lords who hold them. She executes other prophets who say only what Kaeo has said. She executes the priests who shelter them, and burns the shrines, and builds her own temples in the towns. Priests and priestesses are ordered to proclaim the holiness of the Daughter of the Gods. Some do. Some flee into the wilderness. Some die martyrs. And while she wars on the priests of the gods, the two armies that have flowed out of Dar-Lathi to cross the Little Sister into Lower Lat and into Taiji plunder and burn. The folk flee, or they join their Lathan kin and the wild jungle-folk of Darru.

He dreams this. He says it. He says, the empress of the folk must defend the folk. She strikes him. He is scarred from the edge of her fan.

She has sent Captain Diman from her, sent her north into the winter with a handful of her assassins to murder her enemy before ever he comes against her, and Kaeo dreams and speaks his dreams and says, there is death in the dead land, where the dead god sleeps. He laughs and laughs and laughs, because she is a fool, and if she kills him, still the heir of the gods will come.

She sends assassins to kill the Wild Girls, but they do not survive to come to the army of Dar-Lathi. The queens, too, have their guardians.

"You do not see, you do not see," he cries.

She orders diviners of the imperial corps of wizards brought to her, and the tea poisons some, but some survive and dream as Kaeo dreams. Unjust. He is no wizard.

She likes their dreams no better. They see too little. He is the prophet, while they are merely diviners. The gods speak through him, while they only strive to see echoes of what pours through him, and they die for their failure. The youngest of the giants, most often made her executioner, has haunted eyes. One night he walks off the roof of the moon-viewing tower.

Kaeo wishes he could die, but he endures and keeps enduring.

The heir of the gods is coming. He tells her so, and laughs.

All the palace gossips how the prophet falls in the grip of his visions, how he injures himself in his violent seizures; the price of prophecy.

There are nightmares in the aftermath of her questioning, always nightmares, and the room they keep him in—where none come but the giants and a slave-attendant he knows for a trusted spy of the Wind in the Reeds, because he has felt the knives the young woman wears beneath her court gowns when once he fell against her half-fainting, though he has not yet figured out how to abstract one unseen—whirls about him as though he has drunk far too much.

The tattoo over his heart burns. It is black as fresh ink on the brush and he thinks the caged words that he cannot read writhe like the legs of a knot of insects, scorpions interwoven. He thinks it a chain, binding him, the iron collar of a runaway dragged back to be branded on the face. He cannot see, the gods do not know, to what he had been bound.

Death, death, death. He screams the word after them as they leave him.

The hangover, when the delirium leaves him, will be worse. He has discovered, though, that if he can manage to vomit, it will not be so bad as it can be. Perhaps this is why the wizards so often die; they have not learned this secret.

He wishes he could give up and simply die, but there is something in him that is angry, too angry, the ghost of the man who carried messages in coded books for Prince Dan and his rebels, the man whose deep-buried anger remembers that he is Dwei Kaeo and a free man before the gods, a child of Nabban, a soul that cannot be owned.

He is Dwei Kaeo. He always has been. The gods know it.

And in the nightmares, sometimes, he can find a place of quiet. In the distance he will see a rider, a white horse, and banners, blue like the sky, black like the night.

He wakes from those dreams broken and sobbing, bruises burning, scabs cracked and bleeding again, and all the scars of his torture aching and pulling. He weeps because he is alone and his god is gone into dreams and he does not know when the empress will send for him again, to torment and poison him and open the way again for that briefest of glimpses of his god.

He hungers for the oily bitterness of the tea.

CHAPTER XIII

It seemed to Ghu that for Ahjvar, the days rapidly faded again into a haze of dreaming, a confusion of wind and snow, cold and stone. The divination had woken some sleeping fear, torn some half-scabbed scar of the soul, Ghu thought. He should never have asked it of him. Maybe what Ahjvar had foreseen walked too closely with what had been, or he had read it so and sent the underlayer of his mind down that path again. Maybe, Ahj said himself, on one of his good days—when he was speaking, when the words were not too great a weight to deliver and he was capable of seeing and reacting to the world around him—it was only that the tide of his madness turned to flood again, its ebbtime over.

"You aren't mad," Ghu said, which only stopped him speaking again. He was as bad as when they had first set out for the east, or worse. Even Ghu found he began to have doubts Ahjvar could find his way back. When, after half a month more of blurring cold and wind and hunger, the land rose in a day to softer hills and there was turf beneath the thin skin of snow, Ahjvar did not at first seem to understand the desert passage was over. He did not react to the flock of brown and white ground-pigeons that went up in a great wing-clapping cloud from feeding among the grass-seeds—Ahj, who, like the leopard of his sword's hilt, wild and wary predator, had twitched to every movement and possibility of threat.

Ghu had his sling out and felled five of them in as many breaths.

Denanbak was the name of this country, a land of small gods and summer-nomad herders who pastured their herds on the hills, while related tribes tilled the green, better-watered valleys to the east. A folk he knew, not Nabbani, but kin, maybe, coarser-boned and lighter-skinned than Praitan-folk or most Nabbani, and free. Their own gods still lived and they owned no emperor, rarely even cast up a paramount warlord to unite them. Traders, familiar neighbours, enemies old in history, who sold their fleeces, horses, and camels, as well as mutton on the hoof, in the market of Dernang. Almost home. He felt it not with any gladness; Nabban was a weight pulling him down, his return an icy slope he could not climb again. They turned to the southeast. The camels' humps were going slack, the dogs ribby, and Ahj, Ahj was grey, sunken-eyed. His hands shook, and he stumbled like an old man at uneven ground. They should have gone seeking the winter settlements of the Denanbaki to buy provisions, but "Do we need to?" he had asked, low-voiced. "Just keep going. Go where you need to be. No people. I don't want people." A mistake, maybe, to listen to Ahjvar then, to let his unreasoning fears grow, but Ghu suggested it again a few days later and was sworn at, which meant nothing, but there was fear in his eyes. . . .

Meat. There were the ground-feeding pigeons, hare and pheasants on the hills, and a gazelle would feed them for several days, sparing more peas and barley for the camels. He took the crossbow himself to bring down a gazelle, since when they crossed the trail of the herd Ahjvar was having one of his bad days and better left wrapped up by the fire, staring unseeing at nothing, with Jiot to watch him. The good meat revived him, for a little, and put flesh on the dogs' bones.

Here, the desert gnawed the edge of the land, and the wind blew bitter and biting out of the northwest, a constant whistle in the ears, stinging with desert dust and sometimes a fine, hard snow. In the kinder seasons, the chieftains of the land would no doubt watch the road more closely, to claim tolls of the caravan-masters and also to prevent their poaching the chieftain's game. He had never met a lord yet of any folk who did not think the deer of the hills his own. They wandered far from the braided ruts of the caravan road, taking a twisting way that kept them remote from the winter villages, whose sod-built houses were dug half into the hillsides, so that from a distance it seemed the earth was smoking.

A caravan passed them, keeping to the road, the one that had dogged their heels through the desert. He thought of trying to persuade Ahjvar of the wisdom of overtaking it, joining it for the last leg. It would be a way to get themselves past the border legitimate and accounted for, set down on paper as caravaneers of a gang. But he did not think any caravan-master was likely to be more pleased by Ahjvar now than they had been in Porthduryan, so he let them go. It would likely have meant an argument with Ahj, anyway. The border was going to be a problem. Wanderers did not just wander in without giving some good account of themselves. There were other ways, smugglers' ways, high and dangerous ways . . . they would have to abandon the camels. Well, it could be done, when the time came. He would find a way. Every ridge and fold and tree of the god's mountain seemed to be held in his mind, when he sat silent and listened for it.

In less than a fortnight's travelling, in which Ghu knew they were spotted twice, once by children driving cattle along a snowy ridge and once by a hunting party, they came, on the road itself rather than shadowing it, to where a great hogsback hill rose against the southern sky. The caravan road curled around it to the east, crossing an avenue of broken pillars. Ruined walls and snow-filled hollows spread out about the skirts of the hill and halfway up its terraced slopes, where the snow drifted against hard angles of stone. The crest of the hill was bare of any sign of human working, save for the stump of what must have been a tower, a broken ring of great stone blocks, with bushes growing from the joins and thick-girthed poplars inside.

"Letin," Ghu said. It must be. There could not be so many ruined cities on the road, and that meant they were very near the border, two days, maybe, or three, at their current pace. But he had known as much by the way the land lifted and by the low mountains, which made a ragged wall to the south.

Ahjvar made an effort and looked around, flinched when he looked at Ghu, who had a split lip from last night's dreaming. It ached in the cold, and the scab broke and bled when he spoke, and how did he make that better for Ahjvar?

"What's Letin?"

Words. Words were good.

"Godless Letin, they call it, in a song we still sing in the north of Nabban. It was a great city where the queen of all Denanbak was wed to the god, but the devil Dotemon duelled and slew him, sword to sword, in fire and thunder and the breaking of the sky. The tower of his worship fell. He was the paramount god of Denanbak and the queen the overlord of all the chieftains and all the tribes, so Nabban took Denanbak and made it a province of the empire. There was a hero united all the tribes again and drove Nabban out during the rule of Yeh-Lin's grandson, a descendant of the last queen, maybe, but we don't sing songs about that." He chuckled. "Probably the Denanbaki do."

No folk dwelt there now. It had the emptiness of utter desertion. When they followed the pillared avenue towards what might once have been the city's heart, they found that good water still welled up from a broken fountain, oozing over its own mound of ice to fill a stone-curbed pool. It flowed away down a channel overhung with bush-willow and red dogwood and dead reeds, bridged with occasional slabs of stone, all that was left of some culvert through the city.

"Camp here," Ghu decided, though it was little past noon and usually they would only stop to rest the camels a while, before going on into the dusk. "It should be safe enough. Let the camels forage. You can rest. I'll hunt."

Ahjvar didn't argue. Ghu didn't expect he would; too much effort. They offloaded the camels, working in silence, one to each side. Ghu let them wander free of hobble or picket and they headed for the bushes along the broken culvert. Don't fall in and break a leg, he wished them, but it was mostly eroded to a slope-banked stream now, nature taking back the course it had followed before ever a city grew at the god's feet.

That was the emptiness he felt; not that the people were gone, but the god.

He cleared snow, sent Ahjvar with the axe to cut branches, and built a lean-to in one of the hollows, in the corner of two walls below the wind.

"Make a fire," he said. "Make tea. Sleep. Stay warm. I'll be back by dusk, and I'll leave Jiot to keep watch."

Ahjvar just watched him, kneeling on the floor of brush he had made in the shelter. As if the words made no sense, as if Ghu suddenly spoke Denanbaki or some tongue of Pirakul, sound without meaning.

"Ahj . . ." He dropped down by him, helpless, hurting so badly.

Ahjvar touched the swollen corner of Ghu's mouth. That hurt, too.

"It's all right," Ghu said.

"It isn't."

"I was tired. I wasn't fast enough to wake."

"Old Great Gods . . ." Ahjvar bowed his head to Ghu's shoulder, shaking. "I am damned. I can't . . . I can't . . ."

"Hush." Ghu held him, tight against his shivering, rocking him. "You'll find a way out. You will. We will. Remember the desert, before the badlands? You were better in the desert. You will be better again. You will come through this."

"What if I don't?" That was a whisper, a breath.

Ghu didn't need to answer. He pressed his face to Ahjvar's hair and thought, not yet, not now, and let him go when Ahj sat back on his heels, eyes shut, hands fisted on his knees.

"Do you want me to stay?"

"No." Ahjvar opened his eyes, swiped a palm over his face. "Go," he said hoarsely. "Go. Don't get yourself taken for poaching. I'm in no state to talk you out of some angry chieftain's stronghold peaceably."

"Yes, Ahj. Ahj . . ."

"What?"

He caught up Ahjvar's hands. A tremor in the right. In the cold, scars were blanched dead white against the brown. He raised the hands and kissed them, and left Ahj kneeling there. A sharp whistle brought Jui to his side. Ghu headed down the watercourse, gathering pebbles as he went. Jiot remained without a word needed, lying alert in the sun.

Ghu was gone, and the silence heavy. Wind over the stones. A distant raven. A flock of grey juncos flitted and twittered into the brush and weeds rooted along the edge of the fountain, taking flight again when Jiot, lying atop the wall, turned his head to watch them.

Cold. Ahjvar got to his feet, stiff as if every year he had lived lay on his body. Fire, Ghu had said, but he didn't think fire would warm him. One word, three maybe. *Let me die.* All he need say to end this, to end everything. He could still feel the touch of Ghu's lips against his hands, still a smear of blood on the right. He pressed that angrily to his own mouth, going out into the sunlight, taking his shield from the baggage, climbing up to a broad plateau and into the harsh wind. Jiot followed, chose another stone. The dun dog turned his head into the wind, sniffing, alert, but after a moment settled and lay down again. The camels browsed unconcerned among the bushes away below, eating with determination. Ghu and the white and grey dog were already lost to sight in some fold of the land.

Ahjvar stripped to his shirt, laying his coats, sheepskin and camel-woollen, on a bare patch of wall. Jiot, being a dog of good sense, immediately moved over to lie on them.

He drew his sword and, slowly at first, set himself to work through all the practice-patterns of his long-dead boyhood sword-masters, as he had so rarely since leaving Sand Cove. It hadn't seemed to matter, when the sword was no longer his first weapon and he had thought he was riding to a final death. Again, and yet again, until he had trampled a great circle in the snow, like a courting grouse's dancing ground, and was soaking in sweat, folly in this land and season, aching in muscles that had not been so driven since they took to this road. It was something to do. He thought it might shut his mind away, but it did not. No stillness here, no peace.

Better he were dead. Better dead than dangerous as a mad dog. Better dead than casting divinations that warned so vaguely of doom and forces they had already survived more by chance than any power of their own—if he could be said to have survived, useless as he was.

Yew and pine. Death and the Old Great Gods. The devils and hope. Betrayal, the berried holly of battle, peace and peace unmade.

Did he tell Ghu anything he did not already know, or only confirm it? Confirm something Ghu wanted denied. His simpleton boy was fore-sighted. He had known that much years ago.

Ghu should be seeking a shaman of this land if he wanted a true div-ination for the shape of his return to Nabban, not the wreckage Ahjvar had become. He was no wizard to put trust in. He never had been. If anything, it was the king's champion that the heir of Nabban would need, and not a damned sick and broken madman and self-doubting wizard who cried out at dreams that had no power over him—*no power over him*, burn that into his heart—and struck out witless at his bedmate.

Friend.

Whatever.

Ghu was peace, yes. A stillness he could hide in. Useless, to be a child and hide, loathing himself, to let someone else ward him against the world and the screaming in his own mind.

He could try, at the least, to be a king's swordsman again. And maybe exhaust himself to the point the body would sleep, deeper than dreaming could reach.

Ghu brought down a pair of cock pheasants so intent on their rivalry he could almost have walked up to take them by hand as they danced and strutted with the first stirrings of spring in their blood, but he kept going after that, the birds hanging at his shoulder, for all it felt an effort to put one foot ahead of the other. Jui flushed a hare. He added that to his catch. Two men and two dogs to feed, and he wanted to make good time the coming day. Something was making him edgy, the dead city, maybe, or . . . he couldn't say what. He wanted to be out of this naked land. He wanted mountains, trees, white water over stones. This land was too quiet, and he began to feel he moved across it a bright and alien thing, out of place, a glitter of forces that did not belong. Kingfisher-bright against the snow, to senses that could see. Something watched. In his own land he might be a quieter thing. You didn't see the kingfisher in the woods for all its brilliant blue.

The wind gusted wildly about him, snow rising in a sudden flurry, a whirlwind. Jui set up a great outraged barking, leaping as if a taunting crow circled him.

She plunged from the sky in a swirl of colour, peacock-blue and green, red and brown. High boots and red leather leggings, short gown of quilted silk brocade, a confusion of bright flowers wrapped tight with a broad embroidered sash. Incongruous Praitannec plaid blanket worn over her shoulder, Praitannec plaid scarf about her neck, and her sword on her back. The scarlet tassel of its hilt tangled with her black hair loose and long, streaming like a banner in the wind that still gusted around her. Her face was all elegance—high cheekbones, deep brown eyes, warm complexion. A little taller than he. Perfection of beauty. He loved beauty, could see it in even those, man or woman, the world called plain, but she left him cold.

"Dotemon." He did not reach for his knife.

"Nabban." The devil, the usurping empress of Nabban, the conqueror of Denanbak and Dar-Lathi, north and south, bowed with full and formal mockery. "Yeh-Lin, please."

"What are you doing here?"

"Looking for you."

"I thought you took oath to Deyandara. Broken so soon?"

Yeh-Lin shrugged, and waved a languid hand. The captive wind settled and died away. Jui had retreated behind Ghu's legs, where he grumbled softly.

"She doesn't need a tutor any longer. She's betrothed to the king and gone to the bards. I told her I wanted to go to you and she released me. Here I am."

"We don't want you."

"We? Catairlau is with you still?"

"His name is Ahjvar."

"He should have died. I thought you were going to take him from his goddess and let him go. It was for that I put his mad goddess to sleep in the earth." A red ember woke in her eyes. "You did not leave him walking this world with that hungry thing still in him."

"Hyllau I destroyed. Ahjvar is free."

"He can't be free. He is—"

"I know what he is. *He* knows what he is. He comes with me by his own will and I will let him go when *he* wills it. And you will not touch him, Dotemon, or Nabban will see you into a grave there will be no escaping."

Wind raised snow about them, snapped at her hair.

"This is not Nabban," the devil said, and did not step away, but he saw it—almost she had.

"Ask him what he wants, if you doubt me."

The fire he had seen faded. She did take a step back, to bow again, no mockery this time. "I do not think you would lie to me, Nabban, or to him. Young fools, the pair of you. Is he even sane?"

"He's—better. Sometimes."

"Poor fools. Take care not to damn him before the Old Great Gods. They're jealous of what they've marked as their own."

"The dead, you mean? He isn't. He may have died, but he lives and breathes and bleeds and keeps his soul. As do you."

"*I* am not under discussion." She shrugged. "Even I have no idea what to call him, truly." Her lips curled up. "But 'dead king' does annoy him so."

"Well, don't annoy him. I won't stop him hitting *you*. What do you want?"

"Your company."

"We don't want yours."

"No? You might need it. What exactly do you plan to do in Nabban? They are at war, you know. Civil war, the surviving children of Emperor Yao, who died a year ago, fighting for the Peony Throne. Uprisings of slaves. Lord and generals seizing what they think they can hold, and revolt of the tribes in the highlands and jungles of Dar-Lathi. I've seen it in the mirror. I can show you."

"No."

"Will you retreat to the wilderness of the gods and fade to sleep? Nabban will break and die around you."

"No."

"What, then?"

Ghu shook his head. "I don't know. Yet. I will know, when I see."

She studied him. "You do know. You do see—"

"I don't know what I will do," he snapped. "I only know what needs to be done."

"And that is?"

"None of your concern."

"It is," she said. "I sowed the seeds of it, did I not? This rot that you must mend?"

She spoke the truth in that.

"You do need me. What do you know of war? You may fight well in a corner and your dead king was a captain, yes, but the armies of the Praitannec tribes are rabble and their idea of a war is a hundred riders on a cattle raid."

"Not entirely true."

"Not entirely untrue. They're a folk who esteem geldings as warhorses!"

"For raiding, yes. They find them quieter when they're stealing their neighbours' mares. So?"

"They didn't defeat Marakand by any tactical skill or strategy of their own; it was the loss of the Red Masks and the Lady's fall let the kings claim the day. It was you and your dead man gave them their victory. Catairlau—"

"—Ahjvar—"

"—has no more idea what to do with a real army than you have."

"I'm sure he's read a book on it."

"A book! You—" Her brows lowered and she snorted. "Not a matter for joking, Nabban. I swear—"

"Don't. You make oaths too lightly."

"Deyandara sent me to you. Truly, she did. The damned Old Great Gods be my witness—"

"Don't. Don't swear."

"By the tree that held me and released me, whom I do respect, I will not cross the border without your leave. I put myself at your service, Nabban." She went down on her knees in the snow, like a Praitannec spearwoman exchanging vows with her lord, offered her hands. "If you won't take my oath, how do I prove that? How do I give you some word you will believe?"

"No words. By your deeds, Dotemon. Day by day."

And that, how could he lay that before his dying gods? That he brought Yeh-Lin Dotemon, whom they had sacrificed themselves to vanquish, back to Nabban?

But it felt . . . necessary.

"I want," she said softly, "to come home."

She was a devil, and one whom the songs said had ever worked subtly on men's minds. Yeh-Lin the Beautiful, Dotemon Dreamshaper. He wanted simply to like her—he did like her, he enjoyed her company, which worried him. No enchantment there, surely, though danger none the less. It was with a more obvious form of seduction that the songs usually concerned themselves, though he did not think she needed either wizardry or devilry for that. The face she wore was her own, no glamour.

And it was for Ahjvar's own sake she had been outraged, to find him still walking the world. That—he could forgive her much that he should not, for that care for Ahj.

"Get up," he said, and offered his hand. "You can come with us. For now."

Her grip felt real and human, warm, with a swordswoman's hardness. But underneath, underneath flesh and bone, within it, she was fire and frozen light.

He wondered what she felt in him beneath the stiff and wind-chilled flesh and pulled his hand from hers, pocketing his sling, putting on his mittens.

"I'm hunting," he said. "Make yourself useful and carry the game."

"Ah," she said. "Yes. I should have said at the start. There were a handful of riders to the northeast, heading for the ruins of Letin. They don't look like a hunting party. They have no dogs. There is a wizard of minor power with them."

"You should have—"

"You distracted me, talking of your dead king."

"Who is alone in the ruins of Letin."

"Well, if all you did was take over the goddess's curse intact, they can't kill him, can they?"

At Ghu's look, Dotemon bowed again.

"I am," she said, "possibly, too fond of the sound of my own voice."

"Yes. Possibly, if you're going to live in this world and do it no more harm, you should cease looking on it as all a game laid out for your amusement."

Ghu turned back on his tracks and left the devil to follow.

Jiot sat up, sniffing the wind. Ahjvar was drawn out of his half-dreaming concentration to watch him. The dog settled once more but then lifted his head again, casting back and forth, nose high. Turned around to watch the other direction. Ahjvar, alert now, moved with him. Nothing stirred against the white and dun landscape. There must be something faint in the air, but not upwind, he thought. No unaccounted-for tracks marred the snow. Ghu, the dogs, the camels wandering along the watercourse . . . The camels browsed undisturbed; nothing prowled along the stream that they could sense, but the land was rippled and folded, more than he had realized. To come down from the north and around the rising ground of the ruined city unseen would be possible. Careful stalking might have gotten near and left no betraying tracks, using the lines of bushes rooted in drifts along the stone ridges and ditches, their own footprints, even. The hollows, the walls that still stood a course or two high—there was far too much cover, in fact, for a skilful hunter to use, and the shadows were stretching long and blue with the dying afternoon.

Now that he stood still, even for a few moments, the wind froze his shirt to hard folds and ridges against his skin. He might have frozen his hands. Surely should have. They ached, instead, merely red with cold. He forced his fingers to flex, considering. A moment's dizziness, white spots in his eyes, ears ringing, a moment's deep weariness. He shook it off. He wanted the crossbow, but, as he judged the lay of things, if he were stalking an inattentive sleepwalker out exercising on the hillside, and if he had worked around from the northeast in so doing, he would be down in that very hollow, or behind the further slumped ridge of stone.

It was possible, of course, that Jiot had only scented uncertainly some distant fox.

He left his coats lying and started purposefully down the slope towards the camp, not keeping to cover himself. If anyone were going to shoot him, they could already have done so. Watching, uncertain whether to approach, maybe. He didn't break his loping stride when in the corner of his eye a patch of dirty white heaved over a broken wall to the north and raced towards him, but vaulted the ridge down into the hollow of the camp, striking the person who rose up there with his shield. She reeled back and fell, caught herself on one hand and was on her feet again, a hooked forage-knife slashing. It could have laid bare his ribs, but he turned out of her reach and struck her hand with the flat of his blade, knocking her arm wide, sending the knife spinning away. She had a bow at her back and a quiver on her belt, could have shot him any time.

"We're no enemies of the lords of this land," he said in the Nabbani of the road, and stepped back, giving her room. A breathing space, there, as the second—second and third—topped the wall. Time enough for her to call a truce, a word—time for all to hesitate and change the moment. The urge to kill them, to make a clean silent space with no one near to hurt him, was loud, but he did not have to listen, he did not; it was madness and the nightmares and not himself. He knew it, and so he made himself say it again, "Wait—"

She flung herself after her knife and a man leapt down from the wall, swinging as he came. Ahjvar pivoted away and back, slashed up across his belly as he landed, took the other's faltering blow on his shield and cut the cords of the woman's neck and reeled, ears ringing and spots again, bile rising in his throat.

Wizardry, to break and hold him. Wizard, the fourth enemy, hidden in the shelter. The last warrior came after him wielding a two-handed sword, swift and sure for all the snow and blood-slick ground, which ran and shifted like water in Ahjvar's vision, unbalancing him, never quite where his feet thought they were. He gritted his teeth on the burning in his throat and went down on one knee as the world whirled around him, but the man's sword was a fixed and steady thing in his vision, and his splintering shield was there to take it as he rocked up again, Northron steel driving through his attacker's guts and up, back ribs shattering, grating. The man fell, spewing blood as Ahjvar yanked his sword loose, choking and swiftly dead. The wizard knelt keening over her clasped hands, a chant rising and falling, what had been a whisper lost in the wind risen only now to audible song. She flung a scatter of pebbles at Ahjvar's feet and bowed her head, hands open and empty. The fever-dizziness vanished with the dropping of the pebbles. No. Not his enemy. Maybe. Ahjvar put the bloody point of his sword to the woman's throat and raised her chin.

She swallowed and licked dry lips, placing her hands carefully on her knees, sitting back on her heels. She was young, little older than Ghu, and tattooed with a mask of black braids about her brown eyes. Ahjvar did not remember seeing tattooing on any Denanbaki carava-neers. A sign of her calling, maybe. She wore feathers worked into the end of her long braid. He only now had time to think that the other three had been Nabbani, alien to this land.

"Jiot!" he called, and risked a glance around, but the shaman did not take even that slight chance and stayed as she was. The dog stood on the wall, hackles raised, but tail wagging gently.

"Much help you were. Any more?" Easier to talk to the dog than the woman.

Jiot sat.

"What kind of an answer is that? Out," he told the shaman, switching languages again and making his point with the sword. He didn't want to be down in this blind hollow, even if he trusted the dog to know this was the lot, which he did not.

The shaman crawled out of the shelter and stood in silence. She was dressed in a quilted grey coat and sheepskin boots, with a sheepskin over her shoulders, the legs tied about her neck, and a white headscarf over her hat. The dead all wore white headscarves and sheepskin coats with the fleece turned outermost.

So, they had come—from where?—prepared to stalk Ahjvar and Ghu, or someone, over the snow. That did not suggest a curious hunting party or a chieftain's men out to claim a passage-toll, even leaving aside that the three dead were no natives of this place.

"Go on, up."

He took the crossbow and hooked the quiver to his belt before he followed.

"Who were they?" he demanded, as the shaman, keeping a wary distance from Jiot, climbed the wall.

The Denanbaki glanced down at the nearest. "Nabbani," she said briefly, and spat on the body. "Assassins."

"Not friends of yours?" He prodded and pointed to steer the woman up what might once have been a street of the city, picking up his coats on the way. "Up. Right up to the top of the hill." The words came more easily with each one he managed. Speak like she was a dog, an honest creature in the world, which she might, after all, be. "I want to see who else is crawling around here wearing a dead sheep."

"No one is here. Only the dead. We don't come here," the woman said. "It is cursed."

"Today, you did. And it isn't cursed. I'm cursed," he said, and suddenly laughed, as if he were on the bare edge of too much wine. "I cursed a whole folk, once. So trust me, I can tell. This hill is quite empty of curses and gods and anything at all, except maybe more of your friends."

"Nabbani," she said again. "Not my friends. There are no more, only you and I, alive. The hill is cursed, even its stones. The hill remembers the god who died and the devil who killed him." But the shaman nevertheless trudged upward without demur, moving as Ahjvar directed, using her hands on the bare turf of the steep banks of the terraces.

"I kill people who work spells on me," he said.

The shaman nodded, resigned, and did not point out that she was the only one still alive. Ahjvar found this irritating, but he still felt drunk with the aftermath of the fight, the fire in the blood dancing in the void of exhaustion, and perhaps he was not thinking clearly.

Up on the height, the wind sounded like rushing water in the crown of trees about the ruined tower. He pointed at the ground and she sat meekly with her back against a stone, hands withdrawn into her sleeves and folded on her knees. He knelt to clean his sword and shrug on his coats again. Shivering. So was she, but not with cold.

Lots of weeds growing here, dead stalks about the base of the stones and the narrow trees. He didn't see exactly what he wanted, but, if he let his mind drift, didn't watch his hands, it didn't matter. Old grass would do. She watched as he knotted brittle stalks.

"You weren't with those Nabbani of your own will, were you?"

The shaman hesitated. "You speak for a god?"

"I'm not speaking for anyone."

The woman frowned, nodded at the grasses in his working hands. "Shaman. Wizard. God-touched."

"Maybe."

"You are an enemy of Nabban?"

"No."

"The Nabbani said you were. Not you, but the one you serve. They said."

"The Nabbani didn't know me. Obviously. Or him. No, first, who are you? What were the Nabbani to you, if not your friends? You were working with them."

"They have poisoned my brother's daughter."

"I don't understand."

"They said they would cure her if we gave them aid. But I think it was a lie. We had to hope it was not a lie, of course we had to hope, but we thought they lied, my brother and I, and now they are dead and you will kill me, so I will not even be able to search them. She will die, too."

"I'm not going to kill you."

"Those who come to Letin hunting this enemy of Nabban will die. I saw it."

"Seeing does not set the pattern. Deeds do. We're not enemies of Nabban. And you're not hunting me, are you?"

She shook her head.

"Not my enemy, not my friend's enemy?"

"No."

"Good. No reason to kill you, then. Stay here."

He cast the knotted grasses to the wind and watched how they broke apart, falling, the scatter of them on the snow. They told of emptiness, not concealment. And, because he no longer trusted himself, he spanned and loaded the bow, left the shaman sitting and walked the circuit of the tower. No tracks crossed the snow to shelter in the brush there, no patches of bare grass were so placed as to let someone reach it without leaving a sign, and nothing stirred anywhere up the road to the north or on the empty hills. They had followed in his and Ghu's own camel-tracks, of course, to reach the ruins.

The shaman sat resigned where he had left her. No place to run, no safety she could reach from a man with a crossbow in the time his circuit had taken him, but she should have tried. Either she trusted his word, or she believed her own foreseeing and counted herself already dead. Or possibly, with Jiot lying close by and watching her, she had not dared to move.

"They poisoned your niece. Why?" He stood with his back against a poplar trunk, watching the east along the watercourse where Ghu had gone.

"They came to us because we are close to the road, close to the border, too. They said they were servants of the empress in Nabban."

"Empress?"

"The emperor is dead. The empress wars against her younger brother. These said only, they were servants. It's said the new empress claims the title of Daughter of the Old Great Gods, that a prophet has said she is chosen by the Mother and Father to take their place. They speak of her so in Dernang. We hear. These said, an enemy came, an enemy of Nabban, a false prophet who would bring war and the destruction of the empire."

"From what I've heard, the Nabbani are doing that quite well on their own."

"They said we were to give them aid in finding and killing him. They needed a wizard, because their own had stayed behind in Nabban to serve the lord of the empress's army there. The lord of Dernang wars with the empress in the name of the Mother and Father, I think." She looked up at him. "Thus they came to our winter settlement, to demand the service of shamans from the chieftain Ganzu, who is my brother. There is only the one, myself. I went to the spring of our goddess and sang the prayers and danced for her, and slept there and dreamed. I saw that those who sought to hunt this enemy of Nabban would die, but our goddess told me, aid Nabban and you may yet live, but be certain it is the truth of Nabban you aid. I rode back to the settlement and they had poisoned my brother's daughter, Shui his heir. They thought to enforce our obedience to their will, as if we were slaves of their own. They demanded I track their enemy with the gifts of my goddess. I told my brother what I had seen, that those who went would die, and I asked him to send me. He would have killed them then and buried them at his daughter's feet, knowing they lied when they said they could undo what they had done, but I thought I might yet find if they did have some means to save her, and I went back to the spring and begged our goddess Galicha of the spring to do all she could, to preserve the girl's life a little longer. Her hand is on Shui, but she cannot drive the poison from the child's blood. Shui's feet are on the road to the Old Great Gods already, our goddess says. And yet I had to have hope. That, she said as well, our goddess did. I should have hope in our enemy. I thought she meant Nabban. Nabban has always been our enemy.

"Then I threw the stones and saw that the one they sought would be at Letin, so we rode here, and watched from a distance as the one walked away to the east. We came here first, thinking the servant hunted and the master waited, but we found only you. The Nabbani decided to wait while you made your prayers with the sword, thinking to take you unawares as you came back wearied to your camp to make a fire against your master's return. They would question you before they killed you, they said, and learn more of your lord and what power had sent him against their new god. They did not tell me these things. They did not think I had the true Imperial tongue, but we sell horses and fleeces in Dernang, and I speak for my brother with the lord of Choa, so I heard and understood them, and I said nothing. I hoped they would speak of my niece, but they did not."

Ahjvar rubbed his forehead. Headache. Prayers with the sword?

Maybe. What power in Nabban was there to foresee a threat in Ghu and seek his death? Not the god and goddess who called him back. Surely not. The empress the heir of the gods? He did not like the sound of that.

That was not what mattered, there and then. "I know poisons. Some. Tell me."

He knew the symptoms: vomiting, purging of the bowels, deathly chill alternating with fever, and the bloody pinpricks that wept on skin and coloured the tears and saliva, seizures and an agony of the joints that left brave men weeping and begging for death. They called it *tears of repentance* in the Five Cities, which was only the usual Nabbani poetic circumlocution. It was some blended distillation that cost a fortune, a foul thing that took its time and left its victim lingering all too long. A poison for hatred and revenge, not expediency. They had pricked her with a forked needle, the shaman said. A small dose, then. But a child. And even a small dose was deadly, only . . . slower. He had used it a time or two, when some clan-father insisted and could not be argued out of a cruel vengeance. Pointless. Such slow deaths had done little to feed the hag and keep her quiescent, which had been Ahjvar's reason for selling himself in the cities in the first place. The girl might linger a day or two yet in the hands of her goddess, but there was no antidote he had ever heard of. To work wizardry against poison was no more effective than to battle it by a physician's skills—both required understanding of what the poison did, and that the damage be not more than what the body could overcome.

The assassins had come prepared to compel by such tactics, or prepared, Old Great Gods damn them and make their road a long one, to use such a poison on their ultimate victim.

He thought of the arrows in the quiver at the dead archer's belt and sweat chilled him.

"Come," he said abruptly. "There's no antidote, but we'll see what else they're carrying. What's your name?"

"Ketkuiz."

"Ketkuiz. I'm Ahjvar. We'll go back down. Let me search them. You build a fire."

Two distant figures, dark and abrupt against the white hills, had risen out of a fold in the land, proof of how easy stalking was, for all the barren ground. He stopped Ketkuiz with a hand on her shoulder, but he and she were against the trees, dull-coloured, hidden.

"Your people or more Nabbani?"

"Ours, no, not on foot. There were only the three Nabbani. Your master?"

That was where he had expected to see Ghu, yes, but not with another person. Yet something moved white on white, four-legged. Jui, and he breathed again. It was Ghu after all, moving at a steady jog-trot. The one who followed was taller, more slender, long hair loose in the wind and a flash of red at the shoulder, all bird-bright colours against the snow . . . Surely . . . no.

"Cold hells." Now he was cold, yes. "Ketkuiz, these assassins, when they said they were sent against an enemy of Nabban, did they say *he* or *she?*"

"A man," she said. And, losing some of her dull resignation. "Why?"

He shook his head. "Maybe Letin's past returns to haunt it after all." But he left that remark in untranslated Praitannec. "Come. A fire."

He waved an arm, stepping away from the concealing trees. Ghu saw him on the instant, waved back.

All right, then. Both of them all right, for all they each had a shadowing stranger.

Ahjvar burnt the arrows clean in the fire Ketkuiz kindled, setting the iron points into the hottest heart of the flames. He did not like the glossy dark gleam on them, no. He fed the bamboo quiver to the fire as well, and searched the bodies, inert and awkward weights to move and fouling to the hands. Each wore an enamelled badge on a chain about the neck, some device identifying their service, intricate as a coin or a seal, interwoven geometric shapes, flowers, maybe, on one side, and two characters just as intricate and intertwined on the other. Court script, but so ornately stylized he couldn't make it out. Each had a tattoo, as well, deep black and new-looking over the heart, a round-cornered rectangle like the border of a slave's brand. He found the first by accident, getting at the chain of the badge, which that man wore inside his inmost shirt, then pulled open the shirts of the other two and found them marked the same. The script within he could not read, either, but did not even recognize it or what language it might be. Flowing, yet jagged and barbed with thorns. Wrenched further at clothing and found that all three had a slave's brand on the back of the shoulder. Min-Jan, the imperial clan. Slave-assassins of the emperor? He did not know how to interpret what any of that meant.

Every damned blade they had carried he laid on the fire, burning clean any poison that might taint them. Good knives, a fine sword, but they could lie here and rust. In a satchel under the last swordsman's coat Ketkuiz found an array of small jars, stoppered, some sealed in wax and some with their seals cracked, and a roll of soft leather containing several two-tined bronze needles, a blowpipe, darts.

"Don't touch," he snapped, though the shaman had used a dead man's scarf wrapped about her hand to open the bag. "Let me."

The jars were labelled in court Nabbani. All poisons, every one. Most he knew, by name or by sight. Seeds, resins, dust, oil.

"Out!" he roared when Jiot came nosing in. "Ketkuiz, more wood, a hotter fire. Gods, I hate this, I hate it."

"Is there—" she began to ask.

"No, no antidotes to poison here, not even for these—" He pointed to the jar of small red beans. "—and there is a leaf that taken soon after will cure their victim, often. But there is no antidote to *tears of repentance* at all, unless maybe you vomited it up the moment after it was taken, though I doubt even that—and certainly not when it was given in the blood. I'm sorry. But we need to burn all this, so there is no accident. *Out*, dog." He certainly wasn't going to carry those foul little jars; he was through with such deaths.

The ghosts of the slain Nabbani were very still, unnaturally so, not a flicker in the corner of the eye, not a pressure of presence on the mind. He was used to that. The dead saw the wrongness of him, as the living did not. He worked the stoppers out of the jars using one of the assassins' knives and upended each into the flames, dropping in the emptied jars and corks.

"Take the dog and get upwind," he advised, and thought to look to see where the camels had gone. They were far enough away to be safe from the smoke, which turned first heavy and yellowish, then greasy black. Only when every jar and every edge had been given to the fire did he try to reach out to the ghosts, thinking he might persuade them to speak of their master, this empress of Nabban who foresaw and feared Ghu so.

Nothing remained of the assassins but cooling flesh. He had felt nothing, handling them, but now that he searched—still nothing. Empty, not shocked and quiet, confused and lost as a new infant, which was not uncommon in a murdered soul. Empty, as if . . . but the hag was dead.

"Did you free the souls?" he demanded angrily of Ketkuiz, who had gone to sit on the wall, Jiot at her side.

"No. I don't see ghosts. Are they already gone to the road to the Old Great Gods? I would have left them unblessed with the ghosts of Letin."

Earth, fire, deep water, even salt in the corpse's mouth might set a soul free to the road. Or a god's blessing, which death by Ahjvar's sword certainly was not. Baffling, and contrary to nature.

"There are no ghosts in Letin," he growled. "Not even these ones that should be here."

Except of course the devil Yeh-Lin herself, striding up at Ghu's side. She had, since he saw her from the hilltop, taken on her old woman's guise again, her lovely face lined, waist a little thickened, her hair iron-grey and swinging short about her shoulders. Even the splash of brilliant colour she had made against the snow was muted, brocades faded to something more in keeping with her Praitannec plaids. Only the scarlet tassel of her hilt was still bright as blood and flame.

"Dead king," she murmured in Praitannec, as Ghu, silent, stepped up on the wall to look down on Ahjvar's butchery. Ketkuiz watched him, eyes gone wide. Ghu did strike some women that way.

"You're still here—Ahjvar." The devil made the name sound like a child's pretence she condescended to share. "Are you sure that's a good idea?"

"I'm not sure you're a good idea. I thought you swore service to Deyandara. What are you doing here?"

"Your granddaughter, or whatever you call her, is content and well and in no need of a tutor, as I have already told Nabban. She sends me after you, with instructions to be useful. So. Here I am. Being useful, as you can see." She offered the dead winter-white hare and brace of pheasants she carried as proof. "What have you done to make Nabbani enemies? You haven't even crossed the border."

"I was wondering if you might know that."

"They're nothing to do with me."

"They were sent, the shaman says, by the empress of Nabban, to destroy the enemy of Nabban. He, this enemy, not she, although now I wonder if perhaps whatever oracle sent them made a mistake."

Yeh-Lin raised her eyebrows. "Interesting."

"Can you read this?" Delicately, he worked the chain and badge off over the dead woman's head, tossed it up to Yeh-Lin. She snatched it from the air and held it in the light.

"Oh, you are in trouble, and you haven't even crossed the border yet. That device is meant to be peonies—the badge of the imperial family." She turned it. "And this says, in a very obscure form, *wind in the reeds*. Or *reeds in the wind*. You could read it either way. Spies. Assassins. The emperor's own. The Company of the Wind in the Reeds, they were when I formed them to be my eyes and ears in the land. Interesting." She slipped it inside her gown.

"What about that?" He rolled over one of the men, exposed the tattoo. Her nose wrinkled fastidiously, but she hopped down, forgetting to seem to have a care for old knees, and came to squat beside him. Touched carefully with a forefinger.

"Huh."

"What does it say?"

"Interesting."

"It's not Nabbani."

"No." She shrugged. "It is—a calligraphy you would not know."

"I know I don't know it. That's why I'm asking you."

"It's a phrase. *The gate and the bridge.* That's all. It means nothing to me. Poetry, maybe. It sounds like something your granddaughter could make a song of."

Ahjvar turned away in annoyance.

Ketkuiz still watched Ghu up on the wall, not the devil. Finally she looked to the old woman, back to Ghu, to Ahjvar, and licked dry lips. No powers here for a great empress to fear, he could see her thinking. No blessings here to save her niece. "Your master," she said to Ahjvar, softly, as if that might stop the others hearing. "Is he a priest?"

"No!"

"He looks no priest. No wizard, either. But they feared him, and I do see there is the hand of a god on him. My lord—" She slid off the wall herself and bowed to Ghu, deeply, in the Nabbani fashion, hands together. "Forgive our aiding your enemies. We were forced. Your swordsman Ahjvar has freed us but please, if you will, lord, come to my brother's hall. If my niece still lives, perhaps—perhaps she might yet be saved, by your will."

Ghu looked down at her, but Ahjvar didn't think he saw. Fallen into that old deep darkness, maybe, the world losing him. Perhaps he did hear his gods. Or ran, to hide.

"Your master?" Yeh-Lin murmured. "My, my. I can't help but notice neither of you has rushed to correct her. And here I thought he was your horseboy."

"Shield-bearer," Ahjvar said. "So? Now I follow him. Ghu?"

"What sent them to the road?" Ghu asked, returning to himself, coming down to crouch by the dead.

"I don't know. They were just gone. I don't know when."

Yeh-Lin spread her hand on the man's chest, frowned, now. "Interesting. They aren't gone to the road, Nabban. Can't you tell? There would be a . . . a scent of it, an echo, the call of the stars. . . ."

Ghu shook his head.

"Something has taken them."

"No," Ahjvar said flatly. He felt nauseous, cold and yet sweating again.

The devil shot him a sharp look. "Not destroyed," she said. "Not necromancy, either, not exactly. Just . . . taken."

"By what?" Ghu asked.

"I can't say. I don't know."

"What do you think?"

"I think—nothing," she said. "What does the shaman know?"

"Nothing," Ahjvar said. "She wouldn't have given them any blessing even if the ghosts had begged."

Ketkuiz had waited out the Praitannec discussion in a tense silence, but when they all stood up from the body, she bowed yet again. "My lord—"

"Wait," Ghu said. "I don't know what you want of us. Ahjvar?" He might be asking for an explanation, but he meant, *Will you try? Can you try?* Try to bear being among people.

'Yes," he said, before the tide of his fear could start to rise and swamp him again. "We should go. We don't want to cook here where I've been burning poisons, and we owe Ketkuiz all the help we can give. Poison. They forced the folk of this land to aid them against us by poisoning a child. There's no cure I know, but she wasn't dead yet when the shaman set out with the assassins. Lin?" He in his turn made the shortened name a question.

"Ah," said Yeh-Lin, eyes narrowing. "No promises. Tell me."

He did, as briefly as he could. Weariness, now that he had stopped moving, seemed to crawl his veins. Cold beyond hope of warmth, and words a labour. He would not let it pull him under, not yet. Not his doing, this child's death, but nonetheless . . . he felt the sin of it. It came because they were here, in this land.

"Maybe," Yeh-Lin said briefly. And to the shaman, "I don't think our lord—" and no whiff of irony touched the words, "—can help you, but I know something of medicine and of healing wizardry. I can promise nothing, you must know that, except perhaps to ease her suffering until the end. But I will try what I can do. If," she said, with what still seemed utter sincerity, "my lord Ghu says I may try."

The look Ghu gave her was unreadable.

"Yes," he told Ketkuiz. "We'll help if we can. But we know nothing of these assassins. We're only travellers. We're only going home." As the shaman bowed to him again, he gave Ahjvar's shoulder a reassuring touch before climbing back to the top of the wall and whistling. Only Ahjvar failed to look impressed when the camels appeared shortly thereafter, looking down and snuffing inquiry.

They walked, the laden camels following, no need to lead them. Ahjvar fell back to Ghu's side. They had no language between them that the devil did not speak, but a glance was enough. Ghu shrugged.

"For now," he said.

Yeh-Lin, walking beside the shaman, looked over her shoulder and smiled.

CHAPTER XIV

The winter camp of the shaman's tribe was a village of houses half dug into a south-facing hillside. Riding the horses Ketkuiz and the assassins had left in a gully a mile from the ruins, they wound their way up to the wooden gate between walls of turf and thorn; sheep, roan cattle, tall horses, a few camels—some corralled, some free in the valley below where they could dig for grass—raised their heads to watch them pass. Dusk filled the sunken lane with darkness. Armed warriors met them at the gate, three men and a woman eyeing them with suspicion, two spears crossed to bar the way.

Ketkuiz called out and launched into long and hurried speech in her own language. Ghu listened, head cocked to one side.

"You speak Denanbaki?" Ahjvar asked.

"No." But then he added, "Not yet."

The spears were raised, one man setting off uphill at a run, the woman going to take the camels' heads.

"She will see your animals tended and your gear bestowed in a guesthouse," Ketkuiz said. "Come to my brother."

Houses and outbuildings were clustered with no defined yards except here and there a pen of hurdles sheltering a calf or ewes with the first of the new lambs, but the chieftain's long hall was set within its own low bank of turf, more symbolic than practical as a fence. As with the smaller huts, even the portion of the hall downslope was dug into the earth, while at the rear the roof rose nearly from the ground. They dismounted there and a girl—a sister, maybe, for she looked very like a younger copy of the shaman—flew at Ketkuiz and hugged her, before inclining her head solemnly to the strangers and driving the horses off towards one of the outbuildings.

"This way." Ketkuiz led them into the hall, but it was empty. A clay stove, cold and dark, ringed by an earthen bench, held the centre, with cushions and rugs laid out in arcs around it. Not a dwelling but a meeting-place of the chief men and women of the settlement, Ahjvar judged. A heap of hunting dogs, sleeping on the rug-covered dais at one end, stirred and stared in silence, offering no challenge to Jui and Jiot. Ketkuiz hesitated there.

"No," she said, half to herself. "He will not come. He will not leave her now." So they followed Ketkuiz through and out a door on the other side, to a house not distinguished from any other, except by its location within the hall's yard and the presence of the man who had carried the news from the gate now standing at the door.

A few anxious words were exchanged. Ahjvar could imagine. Of course strangers must be brought before the chief to learn his will, and courtesy also demanded he greet his sister's guests, if that was what they were, but to intrude strangers on the child's deathbed. . . .

A second man came to the doorway, wearing feathers in his braid and a many-stranded necklace of pierced coins over his chest. He didn't embrace the shaman before strangers, but his look of relief was telling, and as she spoke, giving their names and possibly much more, his eyes measured them. He inclined his head to Ahjvar, but his attention was mostly for Yeh-Lin as Ketkuiz spoke on.

"Ganzu my brother offers his thanks for the deaths of the poisoners, Ahjvar," Ketkuiz said. "He says, if you are enemies of this ruler who sends assassins to poison children, then you are welcome as our guests, though there will be no fire in the hall until the seven days of the funeral prayers are over—no, she is not dead, but it must be soon." Her voice cracked. "My lord Ghu—"

"No lord," Ghu said quietly. "No physician, no healer. This isn't my land. It's Lin you must let see her."

More urgent Denanbaki, to which Ghu added a few careful words. Neither Ketkuiz or Ganzu the chieftain seemed surprised by that. Nor had Ketkuiz questioned Yeh-Lin's appearance, though by her own witness she knew only two had made camp in Letin and that Ghu had left to go hunting alone.

Dreamshaper.

"Come," the chieftain said, in rough caravan-Nabbani. "See. You cannot help. No help her. But you see. You carry my vengeance to Nabban."

"I want to know more about what exactly you plan to do in Nabban," said Yeh-Lin, as they all ducked in the low doorway. "Two of you, both half dead on your feet, and an empire that is already trying to kill you?"

Small though it was, woven rugs hanging from the beams partitioned the house. These were mostly tied back, bedding rolled up for the day, leaving two bed-platforms covered in cushions for seats, with a loom against the wall between them, but a third corner was screened from view. The small clay stove was roaring, the room stiflingly hot.

Ahjvar could hear the laboured breathing from the doorway and the sudden muffled drumming, like distant hooves, of a body jerking in convulsions.

"I can't," he said, not knowing he had spoken, till Ghu said, "Stay," and left him, pushing back the hangings of the secluded corner and going down to his knees at the bedside.

"Ah, damn," he heard Yeh-Lin say, following Ghu, and for all she spoke Praitannec, her tone could be no comfort to the family. "This is ugly." The room smelt of urine and bile and sweat, stronger than the smoke, and he had to look. Several women knelt by the bed, two elderly, one younger. Ketkuiz knelt too, arms around the largely-pregnant younger, and they clung together before the shaman sat back and, voice unsteady, began to sing. A prayer, no magic in it. A raw plea, but he thought the goddess of the spring had already done all she could to delay the inevitable a little longer for a hope they all knew was futile, that the assassins had not lied and carried some cure. The girl was tiny, four maybe, or five, and she briefly made a shrill whining as her body arched and began to jerk again. Then the chieftain, who had stood for a moment holding the hangings, crouched down by the pregnant woman's side, pulling her head to his chest, and the striped rugs fell back to hide the spasming heap again.

Ahjvar set his shoulders to the doorpost and found Ganzu's guardsman his reflection. The man gave him a nod. Waited, which was all such hands as his could do, in such a time. There was nothing wizardry or gods could do but still her and, in mercy, send her on her way.

He heard a murmur from Ghu. "Hush. Sleep." A slowing of the gasping breath, maybe. At least a stillness.

"Give me your hand," Yeh-Lin ordered, still speaking Praitannec.

"I'm no god," Ghu said. "Only, Nabban that might be, and this is not Nabban."

"Nevertheless you are shelter and shade like a rock-rooted pine, a weight even in this place. Don't you know? The shaman saw, for all she does not know what she sees. Give me your hand. I want some anchor of this earth."

Ahjvar closed his eyes, but he could not help seeing another room, another deathbed, where he had waited because he was being paid to wait, in the days when he was still new to trading in death. The senior-most clan-father of the Sea Town Daisua, who had sent assassins to kill all the family of his own ambitious nephew, even the young children. The man had tried to hire Ahjvar for that and been turned down; he had been on retainer to the Sea Town Aka Clan then, and the nephew had, in defiance of his uncle, taken a high-ranking Aka wife. They had been warned, the nephew and his family. They had been guarded, not well enough. Ahjvar had refused the bodyguarding. As well put a mad dog to keep your sheep safe, though he'd given some other excuse to the Aka clan-mother who thought she had him on a leash in those days. But he had done what the Aka lady asked of him, after the family's death. The wife had been her daughter, stepdaughter, he didn't remember now. Remembered he had bought the poison himself; she wanted rumour, she wanted it known the Leopard would come for the clan-father of the

Daisua and what it was he should be fearing. That fat little apothecary in the crooked street just up from the harbour. He couldn't remember the name. It ran uphill with a dog-leg turn and the shop had had yellow shutters. The mind held on to such odd and trivial things. That was eighty years ago. Before he had gone to Star River Crossing for the first time. The reason he had gone to Star River Crossing . . . he had met Miara, in the years he lived wild in the hills upriver and worked in that city . . . don't think about the Star River Crossing years. He'd gone all the way down to Noble Cedar Harbour after, under yet another name, though he always came back to the Leopard, whatever else he called himself. That fat little apothecary, what had she said . . .?

"Ye—" He caught himself and turned it to a cough. "Lin!" He crossed the room in a few strides and pushed through the hangings, his fellow guard warily at his heels. "There's said to be an urchin in the deep waters off Tiypur, the colour of garnets, with venom in its spines. It causes deadly seizures if handled, if one gets caught up in a fisherman's nets. If that's true, that venom may be a component of this poison. At least, someone told me so, once."

"Yes?" She sat kneeling with her right hand spread on the child's bare chest, her other hand holding Ghu. The child Shui was still now, corpse-still. Her face was skull-like, skin sunken, all a child's proper fleshiness gone. Face and chest smeared with a thousand pinpricks of weeping red. Did she even breathe? Yes. Yeh-Lin looked up at him, and there was something cold, an emptiness, to her eyes, and an ember of light that should not have reflected there. "An urchin. So. A thing of water, not earth, or so your wizardry would say. One could try to work against that, to find a balance, but that is not the true pattern of things and I think you would fail. Besides, there is so much damage, nerves, muscle . . . the heart is a muscle, dead king, did you know? And the mind lives in the brain, which is the greatest web of the nerves of man. It is only the beginning, to call back her soul when she stands with her face to the road and her feet on its threshold, and that we have done, her goddess aiding."

"You," said Ghu.

"We. But she will nevertheless die. I must restore what has been burnt and scarred and utterly destroyed and that is no work of this earth. There was more than this poison of the sea in what she was given."

"I said so."

"You did, Ahjvar, yes. I'm talking to myself. The bleeding looks like arjibe-seed oil, which is not necessarily fatal, wouldn't you say? Not in small doses, at least. Whatever caused the purging is long gone out of her. So. But this is beyond human skill, even for the greatest of the wizard-surgeons and healers, and they are all long dead."

The devil began to murmur to herself in something other than Praitannec. It might have been a prayer, but he didn't believe so. The air grew cold, Ahjvar thought, and Ghu suddenly hissed, as if in pain.

"Felt that, did you?" Yeh-Lin asked, as if from very far away. "I don't know that you can really call yourself human any longer, heir of Nabban. Think on that, and speak for me to the goddess of this folk if need be. She watches us in the shadows. She may have seen. Or maybe not. She is a small thing, and we are such a confusion of powers, we three, all hidden and tangled in your holiness."

"Not," said Ghu through gritted teeth, "yet—a god." Ahjvar put a hand on his shoulder. He was shivering.

"We three," said Yeh-Lin, in clear Nabbani, "are servants of the gods of Nabban. Small lady of the spring of Galicha, what was done was done by no will of the true gods of Nabban, but by their enemies, and in the name of the gods, we will do what we can to make amends to this child of your land."

He could not see what the devil did. No wizardry, for all her talk of elements, but he thought for a moment that there were threads of light woven through her flesh, and they extended and sank into the girl, growing like root tendrils, and it was Ghu who caught at him, then, before he could make any move towards her, and said, "Leave her, Ahj. It's all right."

Nothing changed, but a heaviness in the room seemed to lighten. The presence of the goddess of the spring, carried in the shaman's prayers? Yeh-Lin finally released her hold on Ghu, who sighed and brought Ahjvar's hand to his face. The man was cold, chilled as if he had been standing out in the bitter wind, and he shivered, leaning on Ahjvar's leg. Lin folded the child's hands over her chest and drew the blankets up to her chin, brushed the sweat-soaked hair back from the little girl's forehead, and bent to kiss her cheek.

She had been a mother and grandmother, Yeh-Lin, before she gave herself to the devil.

Ketkuiz ended her chant and regarded them anxiously.

"Let her sleep," Yeh-Lin said. "When she wakes, give her broth. No milk, no bread, no meat, only broth, and in a day or two, when she can swallow it, a little gruel, very, very thin, thin enough to drink. Think that her throat, her stomach, all her inward parts are burned as if a fire has been in her, and judge her care by that."

"She will live?"

"She has a good chance of living. Tell her parents that. A good chance, if she takes no other illness in her weakness. There is no certainty. I—we, with the gods of Nabban, who are kind and merciful, have done what can be done. We were given a great blessing, to be able to do so much. But it may not be enough. They must have hope and take great care of her, and seek the blessing of your goddess Galicha, whose hand must ever be on the child."

Ketkuiz spoke to the anxious parents. The chieftain wept, and went to his knees to pat Ghu's feet, and Ahjvar's, and last of all Yeh-Lin's, bowing to touch his forehead to them. His wife simply embraced her, mother to mother, maybe, and Yeh-Lin, an odd look on her face, awkwardly, and then firmly, put her arms about the woman and let her cry on her breast.

"She will always be frail, if she lives," Yeh-Lin said, over the mother's head. "Ketkuiz, make sure they understand this, please. Shui will be frail. Her heart will be weak. It took a great injury. The fever and seizures have done her mind no damage, though—if I could not have saved her there, I would not have damned her to the life of an idiot," she added in Praitannec, and then in Nabbani again, "She will not be a warrior. She must not do any great and heavy labour. She must not—when she is

older, you must make her understand, she must not bear children. She
will not have the strength."

"She my heir," Ganzu said, following more Imperial Nabbani than
he spoke. "She to take my sword."

"If she is still to be your heir, then her brother or sister must fight
for her," Yeh-Lin said. "Better, maybe, to name another heir, and let your
daughter be trained to some quiet craft."

The mother put a hand to her belly, then went to the bed and lay
down by her daughter, curled around her, protective, stroking her hair.

Probably that was not the way of this folk, to have a chieftain who
could not fight. Petty wars among the tribes, raids into or defence
against the desert, every few generations some unifying warlord arising
and an attack on northern Nabban, that would be the pattern of their
life. Well, they would find their way.

More Denanbaki talk, and then Ganzu said, "Sohi my wife watches
with the child. The aunts with her. We eat with our guests. We praise
the gods, ours and yours. We drink!"

Word had spread through all the settlement. Folk were crowding to
the hall, waiting for news. Ganzu cried out to them, arms spread, and
some scattered away, voices loud. Dogs barked. They brought burning
brands into the hall and lit the stone lamps, which burnt mutton-fat
and gave as much smoke as light, and a fire was made in the stove,
bronze braziers brought too, to add their share of light and smoke and
warmth. The travellers were swept in a crowd to cushions on the dais
with Ganzu and the chief folk of his household, the place of honour,
displacing the hounds. Food began to appear almost at once, first cold
flatbread, leftovers of the day, and bowls of new milk, and soft cheese.
A feast was not made in a moment. Bread, cheese, and milk made good
enough a feast for Ahjvar. Bone flutes and Nabbani fiddles swirled into
music, and Ganzu the chieftain stood to speak, gestured the three of
them up in order to embrace them before the hall, kissing both cheeks.
Ahjvar saw it coming and succeeded in not flinching at strange arms
seizing him, but his heart ran too fast and his mouth went dry. Ketkuiz

joined in the embracing and kissing, but added, with a glint of mischief, a kiss on the lips for both Ghu and Ahjvar. He swallowed and rubbed sweating palms on his cushions, sitting again, and saw that his hands were shaking; he wrapped both around the bowl of sweet milk to hold them still. It wasn't even he who held her eye; that was Ghu, not hiding now in wordlessness, not in Ahjvar's shadow, but the centre of them, talking Denanbaki in which Ahjvar caught Nabbani names, *Choa*, the province of the northwest, *kho'anzi*—the title for a lord of a border province, *Dernang*, the town of the northwest pass. *Emperor*. No, *empress*. Yeh-Lin listened, nodding sometimes, frowning, as if she too began to absorb the tribal language. It was oddly isolating, as if amid the noise he alone sat in deafness. Distancing. Safe? No. But he had Ghu on one side and Yeh-Lin on the other and up here on the chieftain's dais no one crowded close against him, except Yeh-Lin, leaning across to speak to Ghu and Ketkuiz on his other side. The shaman's eyes, intent on Ghu, were bright within her tattooed mask.

He shifted back, a little behind them, where Yeh-Lin did not have to touch him when she leaned to catch a word.

Game stews began to appear, Ghu's pheasants and the hare some contribution there, maybe, and collops of mutton hastily seared on skewers. Jugs of buttermilk that fizzed but seemed no stronger than weak beer were passed around, and then more bread, hot, with rice and both sour pickled fruits and others in syrup, some that he knew from the markets of the Five Cities, some he did not. Finally the serving-folk of the hall came with jugs of something that even in the dim lamplight showed a clear yellow-green as it was poured into the drinking-bowls. The taste was strange, not the golden barley-spirit of the lands Over-Malagru. A complexity of herbs. Sweetness. An underlying bitter edge. But definitely the oily, burning kick of distilled spirits unwatered.

"Oh, very nice, very fine," Yeh-Lin murmured over it. "But not, I'm afraid, meant to be served in bowls that thirsty hunters might take their kefir from."

Some, most notably the spear-carriers of the chieftain, did not drink, or took only a token mouthful, even in this night of celebration, so Ahjvar trusted he could safely do likewise without giving offence, standing in the same relationship to Ghu. Yeh-Lin did not seem object to having her bowl filled, overgenerous serving or not.

People wandered in, stayed a little, wandered out, the faces changing. All the settlement passed through, he thought, even children darting in for sweets, being chased off back to their beds by their parents. A slim girl in a grass-green coat drifted in like mist, her face marked like that of the shaman, but the pattern was waving grass. Galicha, the goddess of this region. Few saw, and sometimes she was no more than smoke and shadow and streaks of light. She paused a moment, inscrutable, to look down on them. Blue eyes, in this brown-eyed land, deep and dark as the twilit sky, and she looked at Ahjvar as if it gave her some pain to do so, as if he were the false and ugly note in the song. Fine with him. He wanted no truck with gods. But when she turned her gaze to Yeh-Lin the goddess wavered and was for a moment a reflection in water, cloud-shadow on the grass, no more. Yeh-Lin bowed where she sat and Ghu, saying nothing, reached over to put a hand on her. Claiming her. The goddess, a slight human woman again, backed a step away. Now she carried a bronze spear. She had not, before.

Letin is not forgotten, Galicha said. Ahjvar understood her, though the words were not Nabbani, nor even spoken aloud.

"We'll be gone in the morning," said Ghu. "All three of us. We mean no harm to your folk or your land. Dotemon is . . . other than she was, she claims. She has so far proven herself so. And she did save the little daughter of your folk. Grant her willing passage through your land, for that."

And what could a small goddess of the earth do against a devil, but hide and hope for it soon to leave? Galicha of the spring inclined her head and turned to Ketkuiz, who bowed deeply. The goddess rested a hand on her head in blessing. She was gone altogether the next moment, smoke and shadow taking her place.

"Well," said Ghu, on a long sigh, and since Ahjvar had no more than touched his green whatever it was, drained it for him. "One of us," he said, "needs to be not falling over, when we leave this place."

Fair enough. Ahjvar found the words he ought to say, the light jesting of such an evening, but that finding took thought and effort. "Me, is it?"

"You're too heavy for me to carry." But Ghu's gaze was sober. "Ahjvar . . ."

"I'm all right," he said. It was a lie, but he would make it truth, or he would sit up and not sleep. The Great Gods knew, if anyone deserved a night when he did not have to put someone else before himself, it was surely Ghu.

Ketkuiz leaned in and asked a question, waved a hand, circling and inviting, taking in the hall. Ghu answered; she asked something further. Ghu was doing most of the talking now, Ketkuiz and Ganzu and the whole of the hall fallen largely silent to listen. Strangers in the hall. Of course they must offer a story. *Marakand*, he heard. *Praitan*. *Deyandara*. There would have been caravans pass through in the autumn with pieces, at least, of that tale, and more would come in the summer. *Marnoch, Ketsim the Grasslander*. Ghu gestured, sweeping armies here and there, a glint of enjoyment in his eyes. Not the full true tale, but a bard's telling, Ahjvar could trust that. He still did not want to hear, even without understanding.

Ketkuiz sat very close to Ghu's side now, hip touching hip, and sometimes it seemed he spoke to her, smiling, eye meeting eye, before offering the tale up to all the hall again. Yeh-Lin, a wry smile on her lips, told some little part. Unlike Ghu, she might lie outright and enjoy it. Ghu's bowl was filled again, and Yeh-Lin's.

Too many people, too much noise, and Ahjvar's head ached. It didn't need strong drink to make him feel on the verge of falling over.

He touched Ghu's shoulder in a moment when Yeh-Lin was talking, spoke in his ear. "Too much smoke in here. Headache. I'm going out to walk in the fresh air. You stay. Enjoy yourself. I'll be fine."

"Ahjvar . . ."

"I think I chased some nightmares away for a little, having someone to fight. It's fine. I'm going to walk and look at the stars. You take care of charming the women. Or whatever."

Ghu had Ketkuiz's hand in his, but he leaned his forehead against Ahjvar's temple. Said nothing. He never did.

After a long moment, Ahjvar pushed him off, two fingers on his chest. Ghu was, if not drunk, getting there. "She's not married or betrothed or anything, is she?"

"Ketkuiz? Not that she's mentioned."

"Well, find out before you do anything that's going to involve me in any more fighting today, all right?"

"I'll ask."

Ahjvar rose and bowed to Ganzu the chieftain before picking a winding way out of the hall into the clean, cold night. The dogs followed him, stretching and yawning.

"Camels?" he suggested, so they went to find Sand and Rust, who were tethered in the lee of a hut wall, the remnants of a heap of dry fodder before them. They woke enough to regard him warily, no doubt dreading, in whatever passed for a camel's imagination, another journey so soon. He wandered farther. No one followed him.

Down to the gate, closed now. A young woman kept watch there and spoke with him, a few halting words to the effect that it was good the Nabbani assassins were dead and the little girl would live if the Old Great Gods willed it, and Ahjvar wandered off again. He stood for a while leaning on a rough fence, watching a pair of foal-rounded mares standing head to tail. Tall, clean-legged, long-backed animals; the style Ghu favoured. Not, he thought, what he himself wanted for close work over hills, battle or cattle-driving. Though for a long race over the open . . . they were not here to buy horses, nor yet to steal them.

Well after midnight, by the stars. He should reclaim his companions before he did have to carry them both to bed, though it would be tempting to leave Yeh-Lin, at least, to sleep it off wherever she fell.

It was not like Ghu to talk so much in company. He usually faded away when there were many eyes to see. Hard to do that when assassins had proclaimed you the great enemy of the empire. Any seer who feared a traveller in Denanbak should be dreaming of Dotemon, not Ghu. What could his simpleton boy do in Nabban? What would he?

Not like Ghu to drink much, either. Ahjvar knew that weary urge to let everything go, just for a few hours. Abandon care. It never worked, but while it lasted . . .

Ahjvar stumbled now with weariness and the dark, feet uncertain on uneven, unfamiliar ground, rutted, crossed with shallow ditches, pockmarked with hooves, made hummocky with frozen droppings. The brief calm that had come with watching the horses faded, left his thoughts fretting in circles, spiralling down into darkness again. Find Ghu. Sleep. Travel. Another day. That was all his concern. Ghu's quest, this. He only followed, and once he saw Ghu safely to wherever it was he needed to be, he could—could let it all go. For good. Stop. At last. And face the road of death, and he was damned. It would be a long one. He would rather his soul was lost into the living pulse of the earth. Better to be an animal and pass on so than to endure his own memory, until at last the long road made him fit for the presence of the Old Great Gods, if ever it could. Rather be destroyed, ended. Out, like a flame, clean and gone. No god would contemplate such an abominable thing, the death of the soul, but Ghu had destroyed Hyllau. He could wish for the same end himself, but Ghu—he did not think Ghu would give him that. It was too great a wrong to the nature of the world.

The feast was fading away. Some of the lamps and braziers had gone out, the fire in the stove had burned low, and most of the revellers were away to their beds. Ganzu the chief was gone. So was Ketkuiz. So was Ghu. Yeh-Lin, unfortunately, was still there.

"Ah, there you are," Yeh-Lin said. "I have had," and she smiled at a threesome of old women clustered by her, drinking tea, who smiled back and politely waited out the foreign speech, "quite enough of discussing the virtues of my nonexistent grandchildren back in Praitan in my little Denanbaki. I'm your young god's dear old auntie from Two Hills, by the way, if anyone asks."

Ahjvar dragged himself to speech again. "Are they likely to?"

"Probably. They have prised every detail of my two, or maybe it was three, late husbands, my six sons and daughters, and their assorted offspring out of me. I doubt I'll remember any of it by morning."

"It very nearly is morning. Where's Ghu?"

"Ah," said Yeh-Lin. "He and the pretty shaman disappeared not long after you took yourself off. She had him by the hand, but I didn't notice that he was putting up a struggle."

"Good. Where are we sleeping? Here?" Serving-folk were gathering dishes, shaking crumbs from cushions and stacking them on the dais, pinching out the lamps. A few of the women, one man, eyed him with interest. A bit of elbowing back and forth and giggling. He ignored them. Pointedly.

"There is a guest-house made ready, apparently. I was waiting to see if you would reappear, while being outdrunk by old grandmothers."

"That's tea."

"Yes, and I am awash in it." She offered a hand and without thinking he took it to help her up. "Give me your arm, like a good boy, till we're outside, and I'll totter off to find some discreet corner."

"Y—Lin."

"I'm probably your beloved old auntie from Two Hills, too. Old aunties are supposed to be vulgar and embarrassing. It's what we do. My dears, it's been a pleasure." She patted Ahjvar's arm and said something that left the old women grinning and chuckling.

Ahjvar freed himself from her clutch as soon as they were out the door. He might as well be drunk; arms and legs weighed twice what they should. If any assassins lurked, the devil could deal with them. He was through with this day.

"Oh look, that must be the privy."

He walked off and left her, which would have been more effective if he had known where he was going. Any cow-shed out of the wind would do. But Yeh-Lin caught up again while he stood irresolute, and recaptured his arm. "This way. Down in the eastern corner of the hall enclosure, they said. Our belongings were taken there."

"*Our* belongings."

"I trust you can spare an old woman an extra blanket."

It was, of course, the same hut where he had found the camels.

Even Yeh-Lin had to duck under the lintel, stepping down into the pit-house. The floor was cobbled, with a clay stove set in the middle on a raised hearth and a smoke-hole over it. The bed was a platform covering half the floor, with their harness and bundles set neatly by. Even the crossbow, the one thing he might have worried about if he had remembered to worry about such things, was there in its bag, with its quiver beside it. No need to dig out their own gritty blankets: sheepskins and thick quilts were stacked ready.

He left the devil to make the fire, which took her no time at all, and made up two beds on the platform—against opposite walls. Yeh-Lin burrowed into one and turned her back on him. For once, he kept his weapons close by, not sure he would sleep, anyway. The place felt too much like a barrow, suffocating. Even the roof was turf, and too low for a tall man's comfort except under the peak.

Don't think that. Just, sleep, properly warm for the first time in months. No nightmares; he'd told Ghu so. The dogs jumped up to join him and took over most of the sheepskins when he only sat, his back against the wall.

"Yeh-Lin?"

A stirring in the heap of quilts she had made, and she emerged into the spill of light from the stove's mouth rubbing her eyes like a sleepy child. "Yes?"

"Nightmares," he said, watching the deepest shadows of the roof. The light dimmed and she was only a shape, a voice. He still should have been startled to find himself speaking, but . . . she was unexpectedly easy to be with. She knew him, and he did not have pretend he was sane, or whole, or anything but what he was.

"Nightmares. I'm not surprised."

"I've hurt Ghu, thinking they have me, thinking I can escape if I can kill them—I can't find my way back. I know I'm free of them all: Catairanach, Hyllau, the Lady, I *know* it, but in my dreams, they're there, and I am so afraid." Low-voiced, he said, "They call you the Dreamshaper."

"A Northron bit of poetry and almost entirely without meaning. That I ever fashioned dreams to draw unwilling men to my bed is a *lie*."

That drew his gaze down to her, but her eyes burned in the darkness, a flicker of fire behind them. Ahjvar flinched back, hand going to a knife, sick with a cold sweat.

Yeh-Lin frowned. "What?"

He shook his head, swallowed a panic that had nothing to do with her, could surely have little to do with the Lady of Marakand either. The sick fear was older than that; it had its birth in his own hands and a limp beloved body—but it was worse than it ever had been, bad as the dreams—there was water in his lungs and blood in his mouth and her tongue and her breath forcing into him.

He did not remember that. Did not. Would not.

Yeh-Lin kept still and watched him. Only when he drew a long, deep breath and wrapped his arms around his knees at last did she say, "Better." Or maybe it was a question.

The dogs, who had sprung alert, pressed close, Jiot's nose on his shoulder, Jui's on his feet. Warmth.

"Are you so desperate you would turn to me for help?"

"I hit him again," he said, speaking to the shadows, not her eyes. "You saw his mouth. I did that, last night. I've tried to ward myself against the nightmares, but nothing I do is strong enough. They run too deep. I would kill myself rather than hurt him, but—it's him I have to ask to let me die."

"Which would hurt him. You are a fine pair of fools. And you trust me?"

"Who else is there who knows what I am? No, I do not."

"Just as well. I can't say I entirely trust myself, but regardless of that, I do not think your dreams are a place you want me. I think I would do more harm than good. What did you see just now that set you shying like a whipped colt?"

He did not answer, but she did. "I am Dotemon. I am one of the seven. The Lady who enslaved you was my kin and my kind. I do not think you would see the difference between us, naked of the body of this earth."

"I want to know if a strong wizard could pluck the memories out of me like weeds. Like cutting off a rotting limb. It would be better than this. I don't think a human wizard could. *I* couldn't. But *you?*"

"Not—so easily as weeds," Yeh-Lin said. "It would not be so easy as amputating a limb, no, and you know how very easy that is, and what the consequences can be. I think—I think you would lose a great deal else, too, Ahjvar. A great deal of yourself. And your young god would not let me wound you so. He would not let me try. Trust him for that. No," she said. "Look at me."

He did, meeting the fire in her eyes again. He did not flinch this time, but he was cold and his pulse was loud in his ears.

"I will not. You've surely had enough of gods and wizards and worse tearing at your soul. These dreams are wounds like any other. They will heal."

"I can't believe that any more. For a while in the desert I thought I had mastered them, but it took nothing at all to bring them back. *Nothing.* A shadow, a foretelling—of you, I think, Great Gods, was that all? You? Ghu lies awake to keep the dreams off and it's wearing him to exhaustion. He won't say so, but I do see it and what's the use of it? Even then I don't sleep well. I can feel them: dreams taking shape, even when I'm awake and by daylight. Maybe I've lived too long, maybe I am mad and he needs to let me go. When I do sleep—some night he won't be fast enough to stop me, some night I'll forget to put a knife out of reach and he won't be fast enough or strong enough—I don't want to kill another—another friend."

"You're sleeping with him?"

"Yes. No! He sleeps by me. Not the same thing."

She snorted. "No. No, of course it isn't. Ahjvar . . . What my wisdom, such as it is, tells me is, you dream. You know you dream. You know the dreams have no power over you—no, listen, they have no power over you, those who have possessed and tormented you and abused you, they are memories and shadows; they are gone. The one you knew as the Lady is dead; I have seen that in *my* dreams, and the sword that slew her, though I don't see whose hand—not your concern. She is dead and the devil she was is gone from this earth with no returning. The goddess Catairanach I put into the ground myself. The monster that possessed you so long is destroyed and you are free of her, there is no taint of her left in you. The dreams of all three are like a sickness, expelling poison. You know this in your head, but you need to learn it in bone and blood and heart. You need to understand it in your dreams, so that they are no longer real."

"I *know* that."

"You know, but you aren't paying attention to what it means. Listen to me. Knowing is not enough. You need to learn to feel it in your bones. Maybe he needs to leave you to dream, to find your own way out."

Ahjvar said nothing. She saw it in his face despite the darkness, he knew she did, felt it in his soul, the scream. *What if I do not wake?* That was his nightmare, and Ghu knew it. What if the thing Hyllau had made of him had become his truth? "And if—" he managed.

"Then he will break the goddess's curse he took himself to hold you in the world, and let you go," she said. "Do you think he is so weak he would not, or so cruel he would bind you here undying if you became even a shadow of that monstrous thing in your own self?"

"No."

"Trust him. Go to sleep." She added, "We elders need our rest."

He made himself ask, "You or me?"

"However you count it, I'm older than you by a few centuries."

"But for how many of those were you sealed in your grave?"

"Hah. Boy, don't mock my hard-won old age. You never lived long enough the first time for your joints to start creaking. I win either way. Go to sleep, dead king."

He woke to a gust of cold air and Ghu sitting on the edge of the bed-platform.

"Morning?" Ahjvar asked hazily.

"Not yet." Ghu pulled off his boots, crawled under the quilts, shoving dogs aside. "Ketkuiz went to take a turn sitting with the child. Ah, Ahj, I didn't realize I was so tired. And I'd forgotten what it was to be warm." He lay up against Ahjvar, nuzzling into his hair.

"Don't do that," Ahjvar said, acutely conscious of Yeh-Lin not much more than an arm's reach away, undoubtedly awake and probably snickering. "You're drunk. Still."

"Yes. Yes, I think I am. Somewhat. She threw the stones to tell my fortune."

"Hah. Are you going to claim that was what you were doing all this time?"

"Well, no. Mostly not." Ghu laughed softly. "But do you know, I am to die in Nabban and find what I have most sought?"

"In that order?"

"Maybe. Maybe not. Ketkuiz said the stones fell both ways."

"Was she drunk too?"

"Oh, yes. Moderately so."

"Then don't take it too seriously."

"Nothing I didn't know. It could read far more ways than she sees. Ahj, I am human, aren't I?"

"Yes." Blue-lipped with cold, battered, starving, huddled on his garden wall on the cliff. Yes.

"Good. Do you want to turn back?"

"What? No. I go where you go. Ghu . . ." whose face was in his hair again and breath warm on his ear. *"Don't."*

"Sorry." Ghu rolled over, and, so far as Ahjvar could tell, fell at once into a deep sleep. There was a faintly strangled sound from the other corner.

After a time, "That man," Yeh-Lin observed out of the darkness, "is in love with you."

"I know."

"That must be rather . . . frustrating, for him, pretty shamans notwithstanding. I'd be happy to trade beds with you."

"No."

"Or with him."

"No."

"That last was a serious offer, just so you know. Dreams and all. Though you smell like rancid *rykersyld*, the pair of you. When did you last bathe?"

"Hot water, you mean? Soap? Sand Cove."

"I said when, not where."

"Sand Cove. Last summer. Though I think Ghu made it to a bathhouse in Marakand. What's a—no, I don't care, I don't want to know. Yeh-Lin?"

"Yes?"

"He is drunk. If I dream, don't let me hurt him."

"I am within reach, and faster than you, sword of the Duina Catairna. Stronger, too. You will not hurt him." She did snicker, then. "And also a very light sleeper. They do say that thirteen-herb white-spirit is very . . . invigorating. Do try not to disturb your elders, eh?"

Ahjvar didn't dignify that with an answer. And he did sleep again. He dreamed of searching for something in the fat little apothecary's shop in Sea Town, hurling jars to the floor in the fury of his search, and not able to find whatever it was, though it held, he thought, some matter of life and death. But that was only a dream such as anyone might have. He woke on his own, heart racing, feeling he had lost something. Ghu was still there, stretched alongside him. That was all right, then. Ahjvar went back to sleep with a hand on Ghu's chest.

There was no justice in the world. Ghu ought to have had a foul hangover, but it was his cheerful whistling as the kettle came to a boil and he made the tea that woke Ahjvar and Yeh-Lin.

It was not advisable to enter Nabban by the road. The pass was fortified and guarded, and they had no idea who might be watching for them. There had been a camp, also, a market, almost a town, along the road not too far from the border. Caravans fugitive from the fighting, and the remnant of some broken rebel force had been there, but more soldiers— the Denanbaki didn't know whose—had come through the pass and Nabbani had fought Nabbani there not so many days before. Some had fled east with the caravaneers, out of Ganzu's lands; many Nabbani captives had been taken back into Nabban. Others might still roam; his patrols watched for such outlaws, though if they left his people alone, he let them be, Ketkuiz had told Ghu. Better they were free to creep south and make trouble for Nabban or harass the imperial soldiers guarding the road down from the Denanbaki pass. Just who those imperial soldiers served, or even who held Choa now, Ganzu did not know.

"Isn't the whole of the frontier watched?" Ahjvar wanted to know, blowing on his tea.

"Yes," said Ghu, "but usually for raiding parties and caravans trying to avoid paying taxes, not a few folk on foot. Now, who can say? But with only three of us, we may be able to cross."

"Afoot?"

"I think, yes. Ketkuiz has said Ganzu will lend us horses and a guide to the border."

"Good."

Ghu shrugged. "They're grateful, but they want us gone. 'Before the eye of your enemy falls on us again,' she said. The goddess spoke in her dreams."

"Ah. Useful if Galicha thought to mention who this enemy is. I suppose she doesn't see."

"What we need to ask," said Yeh-Lin, "is, why fear the heir of the gods? And, since little love though I have for the Old Great Gods, I do not believe they have taken a sudden passionate interest in the rule of Nabban, what power other than a servant of the gods would know of him?"

Neither Ahjvar nor Ghu offered an answer.

Their leave-taking was long with Denanbaki courtesies in the hall, another incomprehensible speech that no one translated for Ahjvar, more embracing and kissing—all very proper and formal, this time. They drank the green liquor again, in one silver cup shared by all. Ghu gave the camels Sand and Rust to be Shui's, the foundation of a herd of her own, he said, because she had lost her birthright by the act of his enemies, and added that both were in calf, which Ahjvar had not known. Ghu and Ketkuiz must have planned it in the night, because there seemed some ritual involved for which Ghu had come prepared, a handing over of a lock of long wool cut from each beast, which Ketkuiz accepted on her niece's behalf.

The shaman followed them back to watch their packing, afterwards. There was little to leave behind except the camels' gear; they had carried so little anyway. Food and skins of kefir were given them, and she came with them so far as the gate, where their two guides waited with the horses.

A less formal leave-taking, then, and Ahjvar did get kissed on the mouth, which this time he was expecting and braced for. She and Ghu took their time, twined in one another. Ahjvar looked away.

Horses, at last, and a clear sky, snow sparking bright beneath the sun. They would not pass by Letin again, angling west away from the road instead and rising into the low green and grey mountains of the border there. Two days, their escort said, then they could go on alone afoot and had only to climb the knees of the westerly mountains, keeping out of sight of the watchtowers, find a path up the cold north-facing cliff of some particular hanging valley or scale the turf and stone wall that barred slightly more passable sections of the wilderness border to horses, cross the spine of the range, and they could come down into the deep and forested Nabbani valleys west of the town of Dernang.

"And then?" Ahjvar asked.

"We'll see," said Ghu. "I suppose, I go to the mountain."

CHAPTER XV

The Golden City could stand a siege forever, if the fleet stayed true. The empress had said something about the fleet sailing from Kozing, but there were few ships of war in the lagoon that Kaeo could see. Merchant ships carrying supplies for city and palace, yes; merchant ships carrying folk away. He had a good view of the distant city from the narrow window in this room up under the eaves of the main palace. Cowards, the empress named those who were inclined to desert the city, and ships were searched, and any residents trying to flee were stripped of rank and sent as labourers for the army of the Imperial Demesne, which was meant to hold the border with Taiji Province but had been falling back towards the city these several days, by all reports. The tribal armies of the Wild Girls were coming. Soldiers and slaves of the imperial estates were erecting fortifications along the line of bare hills on the western horizon, the Beacon Hills, they were called. He knew this, though he had not seen it, not even in a vision. She had given Captain Oryo that order when Kaeo had spoken of the palace burning.

"The palace will burn," he had said. "A beacon brighter than the hills. It will drown, it will be forgotten, a pasture for wild cattle, a story for peasant firesides. Once there was a castle on the island, and a wicked empress who thought herself a goddess—" And he had laughed, unable to stop. He was not sure which half-healed scar he had to remember that by. There were so many. He could not remember, now, if what he spoke had been the delirium of prophecy or drug-addled defiance. He rarely heard the dreams of the gods any longer. They had faded and failed, were gone from him, but still she pressed.

Death in the dead city, he had said once. Months ago, he thought, but time dragged and rushed and confused him and sometimes the visions of prophecy came back as dreams in the night. He knew it was the end of winter, with spring warm in the air, nothing more. You send your spies to their deaths, he had said. That had been even earlier, hadn't it? Captain Diman no longer followed at her back. Diman was sent to her death. He laughed when he told her that Diman would die; the empress had been fond of Diman, as close to a friend as an imperial princess could ever have, maybe, and he liked to see her hurt. But he was sorry, because Diman was a slave made to be what she was, and all through the winter, till she was ordered north herself, she had never beaten him or hit him for doing as the empress asked and speaking the truth the gods gave him. He had thought sometimes Diman looked as though she might, if only he knew how to ask, to persuade her, let him have a knife.

To use on himself or on the empress? He had thought the empress would kill him, the time he had screamed and screamed, the Peony Throne is broken, the devils are loosed in our land and the Peony Throne is broken.

It was not, of course. But it would be. He had seen it struck and split by lightning. He spoke of a sign, Buri-Nai said, of her new dynasty. That was what it was. Not the wrath of the gods.

But he knew the city. The whispers of the canals would know the wrath of the gods when they heard of it, when it came.

A knife. He still did not know how to get one from the slave-woman who had charge of his care and who was no true servant but a spy and assassin of the Wind in the Reeds. He played at being even weaker and frailer than he was when she came to his room. There was always a guard outside to be called for—probably the guard did not rank highly enough to know her for more than what she seemed, a girl even younger than himself, thin and quick in her movements, but he had felt her muscles firm as wood as he sagged to his knees in her grip, she trying to wrestle the soiled silks from him. Any hero of a play would by now have seduced her, taken the best of her weapons, and with her at his side—either to be wedded or to die tragically in the final scene, slain the guard at the door and fought his way out to some waiting ship of his allies.

Kaeo's face had been a pleasing one, once. People had always professed themselves delighted to discover that there was beauty behind the masks of the stage, beauty to match the voice and the grace in movement. He did not think he had much beauty any longer. He limped; he moved stiff as an old man, for all he tried every day they left him alone to work through all the seventy-two forms that were the syllabary, as it were, of dance. His face pulled and bled; there were always new cuts from the fan as the old scabs healed. His nose had been broken at some point; he did not remember how that had come to happen. Some of his seizures he had in truth; not all were lies to cover the blows of the empress's temper.

Perhaps pity could seduce the girl. Her name was Lau. He had no pride left.

She was Wind in the Reeds. Pity would get nowhere.

He leaned on the window frame and watched the sky, the sea, the city veiled in fog as the tide rolled in, cold water over the sun-warmed mudflats. The setting sun threw shadows out over the lagoon. The first geese came on their way to seek the north, and the empress's fowlers went out into the marshes and onto the creeks with nets.

There was rebellion in Choa and Alwu and Shihpan, led by Prince Dan, or in his name. The wind from the north. The empress said her enemy came from the caravan road. She had ordered an army into Choa, to take the province and hold the town, to split Dan's alliance of rebel lords and slaves turned wild brigands. Rebellion in Vanai and Taihu and Upper Lat as well, and in Argya in the far northeast, but not in any unity with Dan or his god. Too many high lords were taking advantage of the imperial disarray to seize their own territory, making princedoms in all but name—though Lai Bolan of Argya did style himself prince, and the empress had prayed to the Old Great Gods who protected her to make his Denanbaki wife barren. There was no philosophy, no dream behind it when such lords claimed autonomy. Mostly, they put down revolts of the folk and the slaves as brutally as ever imperial troops could. Kaeo heard these things. The chamber-slave Lau chattered, as if the empress's prophet might be hungry for the gossip and news in his holy isolation.

There was some excitement in the palace. He could hear nothing in this high room, but earlier there had been parties of labourers clad only in loincloth and smock swarming like ants about the paths between the artfully-sited buildings and disappearing down towards the eastern water-gate and the wharves that faced the city. Troops of soldiers followed the same route, and once a party of wizards in their blue robes, surrounding a handcart.

Muffled thunder. Water burst upward like a fountain, visible above the height of the curtain wall. Again, and this time the fountain was red mud. Shouting carried on the wind, excited. There were other thumps, low, shaking the air, the floor he stood on.

He wondered if the warriors of Dar-Lathi would kill him when the palace finally fell. It would fall. He had seen it burning.

Kaeo stood rigid at the click of the lock on the door, heart speeding up, mouth going dry. His hands shook. His eagerness disgusted him. Excitement. Fear. He made himself turn slowly.

It was Lau; it always was. The empress did not want very many to know the secrets of her prophet.

No covered cup in Lau's hands, though. He had already had his evening meal, plain rice and a little fish with greens, which he had not finished. No appetite. He thought again about the heroes of tales. He was not so very tall; she a little shorter, and slender. Even thin and poisoned-sick as he was, he might outweigh her. Maybe not. Wind in the Reeds, remember that. And there was the guard outside the door. A precaution against assassins who might be sent by Prince Dan or the Wild Girls to slay the empress's prophet, of course.

"Get dressed," Lau ordered. "Quick."

Kaeo who had been the darling of the Flowering Orange might

have smiled and pointed out that he was already dressed and that maybe he was in fact wearing a little too much, at least if it was seduction and getting his hands on her knives he had in mind. Kaeo who was the broken prophet of the empress only stared at her blankly. He wore cotton trousers and smock and there was a heavy quilted gown on the bed, cover for the night, which remembered they still stood in the shadow of winter's rains, but the order usually accompanied the white silk that made him respectable for his passage through the palace. "Dressed," she repeated and pointed at the gown, which was plain brown wool and cotton and patched, a cast-off from some lesser servant or guardsman. He pulled it on. No sash. Too obvious an invitation to strangling himself, perhaps. Another reason there was always a guardsman on the door.

"No sandals," she said, frowning.

"No." He was barefoot. He had been since they took him to the prison. No one had minded before. Holy hermits often were.

"You'll have to do. Come. Stay close to me."

"Why?"

"The Wild Girls have taken the Beacon Hills. The empress is breaking the dykes to flood the marshes. The imperial companies are fighting Dar-Lathans at the western gate and the boatmen's village is burning."

"The palace will burn," he said. "It will drown."

"I hope not. You should see the library. You read, don't you? A sin to burn it. They ought to evacuate it, but the empress is sending only folk she finds useless mouths off to the city. No wizards, but lots of courtiers and officials. Even so, I noticed a bit of furtive scurrying down there. I think some are taking the chance to make themselves scarce, and taking their pet books with them. I'd have a go at pinching a few myself if—" She shrugged, gave him a strange smile. "I hope you appreciate the sacrifice, Dwei Kaeo. There are some histories I'd really like to get my hands on."

He frowned. He did not remember that his clan-name had ever escaped him in her hearing. She winked, opened the door, and stepped out. There was a broad-bladed dagger in her hand and she punched it deep into the guard, right through his leather, between the bronze plates of his coat. His mouth opened and closed like that of a feeding fish, and the blood was nearly black in the lantern-light as she stepped away from the falling man. He was still trying to breathe, but he made no cry and the gasping stopped as she wrestled him over face-up to unfasten the buckle of his belt and take his short sword. She hauled Kaeo's gown off one shoulder, slung the refastened belt over him as a baldric, the sword under his arm.

"You know how to use it?"

"Yes. No. Not a real one!"

"Pretend it's wood. Just thrust harder. You want to do more than tickle their ribs." She snickered. "You could make a dirty joke if you like."

He didn't like. He was watching a man die and wondering what he felt and if he felt anything. She cleaned her knife carefully on the man's trousers and stowed it away inside her own quilted gown.

"I'm sorry, not that you'd be in my place," she said, and squatted down to push something into the dead man's mouth. "Salt," she said. "Better to send him to his road than leave him for a wizard to question, eh? Come on."

"Wind in the Reeds. I knew you were Wind in the Reeds, but—you're Prince Dan's," he gasped, wits returning. He had to run to catch up, trying to get his left arm back into the wide sleeve, the sword swinging wildly.

"Old Great Gods, no!" A strange gesture sent light flaring wildly down a dark stairwell. "It's clear, come on."

"But—"

She grinned back over her shoulder. She had a sharp, pointed little face and her short hair, free of the jewelled combs she wore when attending the empress, stood up every which way.

"You're a wizard? One of the ones who fled to Dan in the north?"

She yelped with laughter, as if she were drunk.

"Try again. Third time lucky, boy." She waited at the bottom of the stairs, caught his hand, tugged him around into a dark corner. Kissed him, to his astonishment.

"For luck," she said, and stooped to drag out a big basketry chest. "And because it's been a long time since anyone laid a friendly touch on you, hasn't it? Here, you take the back end and try to keep up close to it, keep your gown from falling open. Don't want anyone seeing that sword. Keep your head down, too."

Play a slave and hide his face, she meant. He could do that. She took the front handle and they set off. The chest was not light, not to his weakened arms, anyway. But she must have put it there herself. He was feeble as an invalid, that was his problem. Head down, fall into step with her so that it did not sway wildly. More stairs, corridors where herds of people ran back and forth shouting. Two of the giants passed, running, shouting over heads something about the empress's boat being taken down the river to safety. Stairs, passageways, lamplit receiving halls where crowds gathered making a noise like geese. The basket grew heavier and heavier and Lau had to brace herself against it going down the stairs, to stop him losing his grip on it altogether.

Outdoors. He didn't know where they were, which direction they faced, but there was fire on a nearby mound, within the curtain wall. Some villa or tower burning. Away to his left, shouting, screaming, a hideous din, metallic thunder. The gate that faced the inlet of the boatmen's village. Fire lit the sky there, too.

Lau dropped her end of the chest, and it twisted before he could let go, spilling out silks. That was all that weight, a few gowns. He was ashamed. Also terrified. She dragged him sideways into a bush sweet with leathery, evergreen leaves. A party of men rushed by towards the burning tower. The sounds of fighting faded and the night was filled with more men, tight-packed herds of them, with officers shouting. The remnant of the forces that had held the Beacon Hills? Pursued to the very gates of the palace. At least these had made it inside. It sounded as though the Dar-Lathan pursuit had been driven off, or maybe only given up, retreating. Carrying with them the heads of officers to strip clean for trophies. Bodies for their victory-feast. But perhaps that came later, when they took the empress. There was nothing in the old plays about the Dar-Lathans eating their enemies; he remembered Shouja Wey adding lines about it. Kaeo had wished Master Wey had not done that; it took out a beautiful, hard-edged line about the hero's brother's death.

Fires painted a constellation in scarlet across the line of the Beacon Hills. The Dar-Lathans.

The soldiers had passed into the night, around to the south. He followed like an obedient child when Lau led him by the hand along narrow paths in the dark.

"Down." Hand on his head, pressing him. He ducked, crawled after her, into a sort of den beneath vines growing on a framework completely obscured by the mound they made. Wisteria, naked, but dense in its grey tangle. Just enough faint light from the distant fire and the rising moon, a few days past the full, to see that. He squatted on the ground trying to steady his breath.

"You are a wizard," he protested.

"More a sort of priestess, I think you'd say."

"A sort of priestess."

"Of the Little Sister."

"Of the Mother? There aren't any priestesses of the Little Sister."

"Not," she said, "on your side of the river."

She caught him, a hand over his mouth against his yelp, but gentle, her other arm around his shoulders.

"Consider," she said. "It's not as though your empress has shown any great affection for you, prophet of the god of Nabban. And we're not cannibals; really, we're not. That's a Nabbani lie Bloody Yao started to justify the last war. We're not so different from you, really, except we never lost our gods." She appeared to consider, holding him in the dark. "Heads, I'll grant you. But I'm sure nobody has any use for your skull. I certainly don't." She kissed him again, his cheek this time.

"Will you stop doing that?"

"Sorry. You looked like you needed it."

"It's too dark for you to see what I need." The words sounded odd in his own ears, as though his mouth remembered friends and how to trade light words, but his mind did not recognize what he did.

"I can see in the dark better than you. How about, I wanted to? Take it as a mother's kiss."

"I'd rather not take it at all." Again, something he might have said a year ago, not now. As if she had woken something he'd thought dead.

"There's a lie in your voice, prophet of Nabban. Even a smile. There." She squeezed his shoulders. "I've made you laugh. Good. They haven't damaged you all that much, not where it matters. That's what I wanted to know. Caught your breath? That's the way. We can't lurk here all night. That fire won't keep them distracted forever."

"You started it?"

"A beacon to be seen from the Beacon Hills. I did. It's just a moon-viewing tower, nobody in there. Are you sitting on a sword, by the way?"

"I hope not." There was something beneath him. Cloth. Heavy, when he lifted it. A jacket reinforced with horn plates. The sword and its baldric were beneath.

"My name's Anlau, but you can call me Rat," she said, changing her gown for the jacket. "Everyone does."

"Why?"

"Oh, you know. Pointy nose, good at getting in everywhere . . . Stay close."

Kaeo followed, keeping close as he could without actually grabbing hold of her hem. It was a long way in the dark, wherever they were going, with much twisting and winding through the groves and up the hill that the grounds of the palace covered. The fury at the gates had subsided; the tower still burned.

Fog was rising above the walls. Cold water, mud and reed-beds still holding warmth from the day's sun. The scent of the sea was strong. Buffalo bellowed.

"Tide's coming in," Lau—Anlau—Rat, said. "Drowning the marsh. It'll be all pools and bogs and sucking mud at low tide, and those ditches turning to channels. We don't have many boats, and there's not much forest around. She's made herself a safe island, for now. Devils take her." Poked him. "Which maybe they will, if you're right."

"What did I say?"

"Hmm, what haven't you said? There's a devil loose in the land. Maybe more than one. Maybe the empress is one, though you haven't said that."

"It's not a damned play. Don't sound so cheerful!"

172 Gods of Nabban

"You want me to actually let go and throw off the mask? I'll be hiding under a bush howling in terror and saying not me, not me, not here, not now. What good does that do anyone?"

"Can I join you?"

"Don't think two of us howling under a bush will help, either." She caught at his hand.

"Do you really think the empress is one of the seven?"

"No. But she might be allied with one. I don't know. It seemed like wizardry murdered old Yao, not poison, which was what caught my interest, and then realizing how very suspicious it was Otono's children all dying. But it wasn't wizardry, that's the thing. It really was more like some god's or demon's power set loose. We—I—did a bit of scouting around the palace. It's not too difficult, really. You thought I was Nabbani."

"You look Nabbani."

"Pah. It's your gods and your language make you *of* a folk, not your looks. We're the same folk in the blood, folk of what's Nabban now, and Darru and Lathi, only those of us from south of the Little Sister are better looking. And that doesn't make us Nabbani belonging to Nabban, no matter what Yeh-Lin thought. It's the tongue that's the trick of passing, not the looks, so long as I don't pretend to be some flat-faced, pale-skinned lout of a herdsman from Argya or Alwu. Anyway— my goddess is—"

"There's no goddess in the river. The Little Sister gave herself up to become Mother Nabban."

"My goddess," she said, "is dead and gone, yes, but sometimes I used to dream her dreams, lost in the Mother as they were, and the gods and the goddesses of Darru and Lathi speak to me. I travel a lot, to see them. Sometimes I think I've been doing nothing but roaming all this land from Upper Lat to the coast of Darru since I was a baby. My sisters and brothers who serve our gods and I all gathered—we were dreaming echoes of—we weren't sure what. And my sisters—the Wild Sisters— were eager for war, the omens said it was time . . . I ended up back in the palace, taking the place of a messenger-girl."

"What happened to her?"

"Ran away to be a soldier."

He remembered, though, how easily she had stabbed that guard.

"Really, she did, and was very glad of the chance. Her name really was Lau, too. After the last queen of Lathi, like me. She was Lathan, or her mother was, and brought up on old stories until they took her from the fields at one of the imperial manors for palace service. Easy enough to start sliding myself into things, and people thinking, there's something a bit different about that girl, maybe, and forgetting the thought as they have it."

"Wizardry."

"It's not exactly wizardry, in my case. But call it that if you like. So I put myself, very quietly, into Buri-Nai's household to see what she was."

"What she was up to?"

"That too. And then she killed Otono and snatched you. Just as well. There wasn't anything I could have done for you without revealing myself to—well, probably the wizards, and definitely the empress."

She was still holding his hand, almost towing him along. Hard to catch his breath, climbing along the hillside.

"Where are we going?"

"Far, far away . . . not really. Downhill soon."

That was good to know. His head ached. "Water?" he suggested.

"There's water. Not far. Springs and wells all over the hill—very romantic for trysting in the night."

"Not trysting," he gasped. She was Wind in the Reeds, or whatever the Dar-Lathans had that was the same. Spy, assassin, wizard—lunatic who wanted to flirt on the edge of a battlefield. It was just her light-hearted manner, a way of encouraging him to talk, to give her all he knew, which she knew already, or maybe just a way to keep him moving and not realizing how much he hurt, scars, wounds, headache, craving for the free-floating release of the yellowroot. It was not anything she really meant, but it warmed his heart somehow regardless. "The empress. She's not a goddess."

"I can tell that. What do your gods tell you about her?"

"That she's a lie. She's not some saviour chosen by the Old Great Gods. The heir of the gods is in the north. I've seen him."

"Really?"

"I—think so. I don't know. It was strange."

"Dreams can be that. What about the empress?"

"They don't know. I mean, I don't know." Kaeo considered. "The gods fear her."

"I thought she might be Yeh-Lin returned, taking the princess's place as I took young Lau's, but she seems too—confused."

Buri-Nai had not struck him as confused. A ruler ill-suited to a time of war, but she had hardly been given the education for that, he supposed.

"Yeh-Lin would have pushed us back over the Little Sister long ago, not sat in her palace worrying about prophecies of a solitary enemy. Buri-Nai sends her generals scurrying about worshipping her as a goddess, but she lacks any clear strategy or a rein to hold them in. And making enemies of all the priests, decreeing the shrines unhallowed? Ordering them killed if they don't offer their allegiance to her cult instead? The folk hate her as well as fear her now, as they never hated even Bloody Yao, for all the misery he brought them. That was stupid, and Yeh-Lin was never said to be stupid. Here. I told you there was a well."

The well was surrounded by ferns, overshadowed by pale-barked fan-leaf trees, naked now. Some convenience for the gardeners. Kaeo sank down gratefully on damp paving stones, let Rat draw water in a wooden pail. So cold it almost burned in his throat, which was raw and sore anyway.

He did not want yellowroot. He did not want to dream. The headaches would fade in time.

"Why did you save me?" It did not sound as though they needed a dreamer.

"Honestly?"

"Yes."

"A whim. You're no use to us. We don't need your prophecies and anyway I've heard all you've had to say so far and it isn't much use. Nothing we couldn't have found out on our own with a more reverent use of a shaman's proper rite of dreaming. But I was there when she saved you—a little diversion after assassinating her brother—and I helped the physician keep you from taking the road, which you were about ready to do—not that she noticed my help, but you can thank me. I guess I've gotten fond of you, young Kaeo."

"I'm older than you."

"And you look it. You need fattening up. Also I used to go to plays at the Flowering Orange, when I was in the city, before I turned myself into a palace slave. You're going to sing for me, someday, my boy, when you've recovered."

"Am I?"

"Oh yes."

She confused him and warmed his heart. "I might." More water.

"And largely," she said, her voice serious, "it was because you were where I could get at you, and I figured you wouldn't slow me down all that much, and the risk wasn't too great. And it defied her, taking you. Just so you know, I'd have stolen her dog if the same considerations held good, and if she had one."

"If the dog could sing, you mean?"

"Well, obviously. Ready to go on?"

Kaeo could have slept right there on the stones, damp and all, but he pushed himself wearily to his feet and fell in behind Rat as she led off across close-shorn grass and down a snaking sanded path. They had been walking hours, or so it felt, though the stars said not quite so long as all that. His legs felt each as though they were his own weight again and his bare feet, gone soft with only trudging the palace corridors or dancing in his prison, were bruised and tender and probably bleeding. The empress was going to discover his escape before they were out of the palace grounds, if they didn't find some way out soon. Perhaps she would have too many other important things to deal with this night. He had been getting the feeling her interest in him had waned. One day soon Buri-Nai would have given Oryo the order to kill him in one of his fits, and it would have been over. Better to be out walking beneath the moon with a whimsical not-a-cannibal spy. Take what little kindness life offered. Perhaps Rat would kiss him again.

The moon climbed until it was nearly overhead. Rat had fallen into silence, and Kaeo had dropped behind, stumbling along wondering if they would circle through the gardens forever or only until the dawn, when ahead, someone snapped out a challenge.

'Stand, in the name of the empress."

"Ah, cold hells."

"I said—"

"Keep back." She was gone in a rush, and someone yelled. Up to him to save himself, abandoned as the empress's dog would have been. Kaeo set his back against a tree and, feeling a fool, tugged the sword free. Heavier than painted wood, of course it was. But it felt unsettlingly familiar anyway. Shorter than the false court swords he had fought with playing Min-Jan and other heroes of legend. A soldier's sword. Thrust, don't slash, he heard Master Wey's voice telling one of the others, some comedy piece involving merchant's guards. No armour, no old-fashioned shield. Maybe he wouldn't be seen. Metal rang loudly and someone gasped and grunted. Someone else shouted, "There's another!" and he was seen, a wrong shape in the moonlight, not a tree, and they came out of the darkness. Two of them.

At least they didn't just walk up and kill him. They moved a little apart to come one from each side, as if he might know what he was doing. Foot had touched something. Fallen branch or root. Root was no use, but he dropped and seized it in his left hand. It was a dead branch as he had hoped and their rush at his movement found him on one knee on the ground, so he swung the branch sideways with all his strength across the knees of one man and then lunged up stabbing at the other, who leapt back and seemed to expect Kaeo to follow, but he backed up against the tree again. Stabbed with the broken branch at the other man's face as he closed in. It was a long branch. The man swatted it aside with his sword, and while he was doing that Kaeo yelled—because a good yell always pleased the audience in a fight, if there were no lines to say—and stabbed and the sword bit something and grated and the man yelled and stumbled. He jerked his blade clear and slashed around at the other man, forgetting the bit about thrusting—and what did Shouja Wey know, he was a theatre master not a swordsman. He hit something hard and yielding in one and felt the shock of it up his arm, dodged the thrust he knew was coming—back to the tree once more, dodged and fended off strike after strike and struck blows himself that twice found a mark, but his arm was shaking and so were his knees and his breath panted like a runner's. The man he'd first wounded was standing off and watching, hurt or confident in his friend, and suddenly he pitched forward and Rat was there behind him.

"Leave him," she snarled, and put herself in the way. Kaeo slid down to the ground, fighting for breath, and now the man he had been fighting was fighting for his life and knew it. The blades flashed, catching light, and then the soldier was staggering back and falling and thrashing a little. Rat whirled around, watching for movement all about. There was none save the light, a moving light, and he tried to gasp a warning but she dropped down by him, took his face in her hands.

"All right?"

He nodded, unable to speak.

"Sorry they got past. There were four of them. I didn't think the patrols would come around so far with all the excitement at the gates and my nice little fire on the tower and all. And you took on two at once. Not bad for an actor."

She did kiss him again. He took his fair part in it, this time, and was sorry when she sat back on her heels away from him. "Better get my kissing in while I can." Her face twisted, a smile fighting to lay itself over something else, and she wiped at blood on his face. "Thought I'd got you killed before I even got you away." He was fumbling for his sword and as his mouth opened on a warning, breath for it at last, she bounced to her feet again and spun around, loosing a torrent of words that sounded Nabbani and were not.

Allies. Ah. Dar-Lathan tribal warriors, with painted faces and not a torch but some sort of wizard-made light caged in a sphere of woven bamboo. It faded slowly away to the faintest of fox-light again once the man who bore it dangling from a long staff had recognized Rat.

There was a grove of pines near the wall, the landmark Rat's escort had used to find their meeting-place. They went back over the wall using ropes and grappling irons—more shame for him, because his grip failed him and they had to haul him like a sack. Down a steep bank. The flat grasslands of the marsh seemed to squirm and undulate in the moonlight. Water where there was water only during the bad typhoons, but not come over the dykes in storm and fury, water running up channels usually blocked against salt inflow by tide-gates, water flowing in breaches in the dykes, reclaiming the saltings that the Exalted Min-Jan had barred to them when he dyked the marsh for his hunting preserve and turned the old pirate-fortress island into his palace. Tall reed-grass stood in water, broken seedheads and leaf-tips of the previous summer lying on the surface. A herd of buffalo stood on an isolated stretch of dyke, statues against the sky, waiting for the tide to drop. Easy for small parties to come and go, but not unseen, not by daylight. For any force to come against the walls now on ground soft and getting softer, clay dissolving into mudflats, would be next to impossible.

A man whose face was all painted in dark slashes and swirls murmured something to Rat.

"We have canoes pinched from the imperial boat-pound, good. Can you swim, Kaeo?"

"Will I need to? Yes." He doubted he could swim far, the shape he was in.

"Let's hope not, but it's good to know."

They had three canoes, one an outrigger meant for the sea. Shadowy shapes about him, more than had been inside the palace. The lantern was dark and they all, even Rat, kept silent, running the canoes out into the strange sea of winter-grey grass. The water was not deep, but there would be hidden ditches and creeks and currents in them. No one offered him a paddle. He was a prisoner, he supposed, but no one took his sword from him.

His sword. As if he had become a warrior by holding his ground even so short a time.

They paddled along the lines of drowned drainage ditches, where bordering bushes and wind-slanted trees would hide them. The moon was treacherously bright. It must be past midnight. Every other Dar-Lathan seemed to be an archer, and they knelt each with an arrow in hand, ready for the string, but no alarm was cried from the palace walls and nothing else stirred on the marshland. A frantic rabbit thrashed past. Three foxes sat together on a piece of flotsam, a heavy plank that had once bridged some ditch. Kaeo watched them watching the canoes, imagined them thinking, if only we had a paddle. He was delirious. Perhaps they smelt the rabbit. But the water was lower than it had been. The tide was ebbing. The shallow lagoon created by the dykes might not drain completely, but creatures would pick a way through puddles and pools and muck to move inland out of the softening ground.

Why worry about the foxes and rabbits? There were men and women dead in the boatmen's burning village and at the gates, and there would be more, hundreds more. But he hoped the foxes would come safely ashore. And the rabbit.

They took the canoes up a brook that had become a creek of the sea. It was guarded by a Dar-Lathan outpost that he never saw; there was only a brief exchange of low-voiced words, and they passed on by, though the party with the outrigger put into the bank and did not follow on up the narrowing water. When it became a ditch, they abandoned the canoes—or maybe left them guarded. At any rate, their numbers kept falling away, until in the end there were only five, including he and Rat, who came to where sentries guarded the crossing of a new-dug defensive trench on the rising ground. Kaeo was staggering with weariness by then; he sank down on his haunches the moment they stopped moving, but it was only a moment's rest. Rat hauled him up. Winding their way into a camp. Huts of brush, tents. The fires were mostly banked with sods, but a whiff of cooking smells started him retching. A dog barked and was hushed. There were few people to be seen. Asleep. Just guards here and there. From the height of the hill, the sullen dying fire of the burning moon-tower still made its signal in the gardens, and there was torchlight about the palace walls. Windows showed lamplit yellow where palace folk still planned, or panicked, or where wizards worked, preparing who-knew-what defences or attacks. He had never walked on grass, he realized, in all his time in the Golden City. He had not felt simple earth under his feet until Rat dragged him out into the gardens.

Priestess of a goddess centuries gone. What authority did she carry here? He wasn't any use to the Dar-Lathans; she said so herself. A whim. They didn't take slaves. Or prisoners, from what he had heard. Maybe someone would want a singer.

They paused outside an enclosure that was a not a hut but a circle, a brush wall enclosing firelight. Echo of one of the storied roundhouses, he realized, and there were, there really were, skulls, ivory-white, jawless, hung like fruit in bunches from two tall posts that marked an entryway. The high lord of Taiji? Commanders of the army of Dar-Lathi, lords of the city of Ogu? Surely they would not want his; he was only an actor.

Here, at last, came a challenge, and they had lost all their escort but the one man with the lantern. A man and a woman armed with spears barred a gap in the thorny fence. The wizard brought up his light to a golden brightness with a pass of his hand, swinging it to shine on Kaeo's face. Rat spoke, quick and urgent words. He heard his own name, the full Dwei Kaeo, and Buri-Nai's. The spearman made a gesture at Kaeo. His gown was flapping like a bat's wings, exposing his sword. Kaeo meekly began to drag the belt off over his head, but Rat's hand seized his arm.

"No you don't, my boy. You've earned it."

Argument, brief. The man shrugged, stepped back. The woman likewise gave way, looking amused. Rat gave both of them a cheerful wave as she towed Kaeo through.

A woman in armour paced back and forth before a fire. Other people sat about under a thatched roof on posts, or stretched out sleeping, but most of them were already stirring, disturbed by the argument at the gate. The pacing woman paused long enough to prod another with her toe, and that one leapt up as if kicked, then launched herself at them, shouting something. Kaeo had an impulse to leap in front of Rat and an even stronger one to hide behind her, and ended up only twitching, as the older woman grabbed Rat and shook her, laughing. The other strolled up in time to fling her arms about both as they embraced, all talking at once.

"All right, all right." Rat disentangled herself. "Here. This is Dwei Kaeo. He's a singer and actor and was a spy for Prince Dan until one of his fellows betrayed him under torture. He's also a prophet of the heir of the gods of the land, or was taken by the gods to be so, when the magistrates tortured him to the very threshold of the road, and the empress has been drugging him back there at regular intervals ever since with dreamer's yellowroot, though he's no wizard. He may be useful, if we want to talk to either Dan or whatever or whoever it is who's coming into the land to take the place of the gods. Kaeo—"

He was already bowing to the armoured women. They looked very close in age, their mid-twenties, maybe, older than Rat, but they shared her pointed face and keen eyes. Their armour was lacquered jade-green, mottled like the stone, and both wore jade pendants in their ears, jade rings braided into their hair. The elder was plucking at Rat's cropped head, scowling.

"It'll grow," she said, distracted. "It's only hair. Kaeo, these are my sisters, Nawa and Jian."

Father Nabban, she meant real sisters, not fellow priests or fellow commanders. Raised in the furthest wilderness of the highlands and the coastal swamps, hunted by the corps of wizards, hidden by the gods and goddesses of their many tribes. The Wild Girls. Daughters of the grim god Tai'aurenlo of the burning hills and a human mother. The queens. He hadn't heard that there were three of them.

A queen of the south thought him worth kissing? A halfling god did?

"Give him to the priests, then," Nawa? Jian? said, dismissing him, and followed that with more in whatever the language of Dar-Lathi was called. People were gathering at the fire—some council meeting. The wizard took Kaeo's arm.

"Dwei Kaeo, come." So he spoke Nabbani after all. Rat must have seen his frantic look around for her.

"Go on with Toba. He's more a shaman than a wizard, to put it in your terms. It's possible you are too. Anyhow, he probably knows what to do with someone half dead of overdosing on yellowroot. We're talking boring sisterly things—"

One of the queens laughed, not pleasantly, in his opinion. Said something about Buri-Nai.

"Well, if you wanted her head, Nawa, you should have told me sooner. Though odds are she'd have sent mine back to you. Nicely charred. So." Rat left her sisters to run after him, take him by the shoulders. "You'll be fine. I told you, nobody wants your skull. You're safe. We're friends." She wiped at something on his face. Mud, he hoped, and nothing worse. "Get some sleep."

Kaeo found a smile from somewhere, though in truth he was so tired he had no energy left for worry over what they meant to do with him in the morning, if only they would let him sleep now. "You think your sisters would have let you keep the empress's dog?"

"Only if it could sing."

No whimsical kissing here, just a brief tightening of her grip on him before she turned away, back to her sisters and their council and the fire.

Water, plain rice, a quiet corner. Toba seemed a civilized man of quiet good sense, not a headhunting cannibal shaman. The last thing Kaeo saw as sleep pulled him under its darkness was the wizard sitting nearby, his lantern-pole stabbed into the earth, its light glowing dimly over a pattern of small white bones that he gathered up, breathed on, and threw again. Maybe not civilized. They were human finger-bones, he was certain.

Toba looked over at Kaeo. Nodded. Gathered, breathed, threw again.

CHAPTER XVI

*T*he fleet begins to arrive with the dusk, ships dark on the lagoon. A strong wind has blown from the east all day, as they came along the southern coast of Nan-Ya. He promised the empress it would be so, once she summoned the admiral. She is the Daughter of the Old Great Gods and the empress of all Nabban. The Gods bless her and by their grace the winds will serve. But now they grow wilder, swinging, shifting. They swing to a southerly, bringing cloud and rain, and the summer warmth of the ocean, unseasonably early. Not the following wind she will no doubt wish for, but it will serve.

I am weak in your world, he reminds her. The heavens are very far from me.

"The palace will burn," her prophet told her, and she believes his words, all his words, even the ones that were spite.

The fleet could have carried soldiers from Kozing, could have landed them, driven the Wild Girls back, but—why bother? The south does not interest him. Why should she struggle to hold it? It is in the north that the heir of the gods is moving, shifting the currents of the land.

The palace will burn. She does not intend to be there.

All the first half of the night, there has been much stir. Torchlight and lanterns moving, and noise, too, human voices like the distant babble of waves, rising and falling and never ceasing.

Wait, he says, when Buri-Nai would go, the last of all with her company about her. Look back, he tells her.

Buri-Nai obeys, impatiently.

What? she asks, shaping the word with lips and tongue, no breath. The Daughter of the Gods must not mutter and whisper to herself, but sometimes she treats him as a tutor, a counsellor—an irritant who forgets she is empress and divine, by his own testimony. He intends to teach her otherwise, eventually. Not yet. The messenger of the Old Great Gods must be patient, kindly even when stern.

Her urgency to be gone is not fear, which rather surprises him, but Buri-Nai has a serene and utter confidence in her sanctity and her invulnerability. Merely, she is finished with this place. Through. The Wild Girls can sack it, for all she cares.

That suits him.

He asks, Should the throne of your ancestors be left to those who will pick through the wreckage here?

He feels her pleasure as she considers that wreckage, the ruin to come of the palace so long her cage.

"The years of the Peony Throne are ended," *she says aloud, quoting her prophet, who vanished in the first abortive attack on the palace walls. Stolen, he presumes, by Dar-Lathan assassins who thought him of some value. Their mistake. They seem recently to have killed him, perhaps in some jungle rite of their wizardry. A soul stolen from the braid he weaves, the foundation he lays. Aside from that, the man is no loss, though she was angry. He did not bother to search when the man was first taken, though she turned humble, asking him to. Obstinate, clinging to the idea that secrets of the gods might be revealed, if only she pressed him hard enough. Or an ageing woman besotted with a once-attractive face. He was annoyed, though, to lose that soul as he had, opened as it was to vision and dream, stronger than the man who had borne it.*

Yes, he says patiently. The Peony Throne will be cast down. They say so, in the markets throughout the provinces.

"A prophecy for me or against me?" *She laughs, her hand on her amulet.* "Or does the Daughter of the Old Great Gods cast down the Min-Jan throne along with the laws of Min-Jan? I shall."

The air grows tense with the breath of storm. He takes her, courses through her. She draws a breath that is almost a gasp; there is pain in the white light that burns an instant through her veins. Lightning tears the air.

The throne is split from carved canopy to seat, fallen into two halves, and the edges, and the delicate patterning of the floor, inlaid in many woods, smoulder.

"No cannibal tribeswoman is going to defile the throne of my father," she says. "And what need have I of it? The years of the Min-Jan are ended. These are the years of the Daughter of the Gods."

She turns on her heel and strides from the long throne-room, walking like a warrior, not with the soft steps of a courtier. He has taught her that. Carry yourself as what you mean to be.

The dark of the moon. Beacon Hill is spattered red with the fires of the tribal horde. By the time the dawn comes, Buri-Nai and all the folk of the palace, those she has not sent to the city to have them out of her court, are aboard and the ships are nosing out the gap in the breakwater, seeking the open sea.

By the time the dawn comes, the palace is a beacon, burning, to be seen far offshore.

Let the Wild Girls have the ruin and gloat in their triumph, for the short time they can. The heir of the gods is in the north, and he must come into the empress's reach.

Far out to sea, the winds shift. The waters stir uncertainly.

The heir of the gods is coming home . . . Kaeo thrashed himself out of smothering blankets, awake, heart thudding. Echo of a dream.

Toba woke. The old wizard had been physicking him with assorted unpleasant brews to stop the headaches, the vomiting and the shaking, that had kept hitting in waves over the first days of his freedom. He was better, now, but one of the less-foul teas, which Toba still insisted he drink, still gave him dreams. Vague and troublesome ones, mostly, elusive on waking. This . . .

"The queens," he said. "The empress is gone. The god . . ."

He was hardly coherent.

Come dawn, they stood on the crest of the highest of the Beacon Hills, looking down. The queens in armour, jade in their hair, their ears, about their throats, heavy collars of it. Faces painted for battle that, apparently, would not come. Rat looked older, a stranger, almost, masked in green and brown swirls like light through leaves and birds in flight, till she winked at him.

They had been already awake. Only he, drugged on his pallet in Toba's little hut, had slept through the uproar of the sentries, the messengers going to and from the Council House of the queens, the preparation for the attack that had not come, as the palace went up in flames.

The ambassador of the Kho'anzi of Lower Lat was with them, speaking of his lord's most certain trust in their promises . . . He thought it some great wizardry of their own.

"You dreamed," Nawa, the eldest of the sisters, said.

"The heir of the gods. The one the prophets speak of. The empress has gone—some threat against him, I don't know. Some—" Sometimes he dreamed her outlined in fire, sometimes the last emperor, falling, the lightning drawing him against the sky. "Some *thing* is with the empress, and it means death to the god, it does. We need to go to him."

"We have the Golden City," Nawa countered, and he should feel afraid, that he argued with a queen. He did not. "The empress has realized she can't retake Taiji, now that Lower Lat has turned against her. She couldn't even take the Imperial Demesne back."

"We don't have the city," Jian said. "We have no ships. Unless you want to paddle over in stolen canoes to burn it, and what would be the point of that? Send to their lords or their rich grandmothers or whoever will surface to rule now that the court is gone, and talk them over to us."

"The god," Kaeo said. "We—you should send someone to speak for you to him. When he comes. If he does. If we can find him."

"Listen to him," said Rat. And her sisters had a brief conversation in Lathan.

"No," said Nawa. "The empress has gone to make war on him. You would only be putting yourself in her way, and she knows you now."

"Who looks at a slave?"

"A slave who stole her prophet. And it might not be the empress who recognizes you. You said yourself, some other power was there in the palace."

"But we need the god," Rat said simply. "What do we have? Provinces we can't hold, once Nabban settles its quarrels within itself.

A border hard to defend, because we can keep no standing army. We need—to talk."

"So wait, to see what happens in the north."

"Yes," Jian agreed.

Rat shook her head, but she made no further argument. The queens ruled so. Argued themselves into some consensus—not always a majority. But Rat was letting this go, for now.

At least until her sisters left them.

"We will go, Kaeo," she said. "I—am sure of it. A few days, a week or two . . . we need to go. We will." Smiled at him. "Sorry. Prophecy's your game. Ignore me. Sometimes I get feelings, that's all. I'm sure I'll grow out of it."

"We'll go," he said, more certain than she. "But just the two of us?"

"We'll be enough. Faster that way. Less arguing. Best leave Jian and Nawa here, and Toba's too old. He'll throw the bones of his grandmother for us before we go."

His grandmother. Left to him on her death, as the wizard said he had left his own bones to his newest grandson, who already showed signs of the wizard-gift.

A strange people. Kaeo did not like to think of someone handling his fleshless bones after he was dead. But it was the way of the mountain folk south of the Little Sister.

Bones clean and wrapped in a straw-woven rug, a cave high on a mountain, the place of a god. It is very peaceful there, and the sky is very blue, like banners. The forests below are green and dark and hide secrets of the highland folk and the jungle folk, and the river guards their border, and the folk go freely over and back.

"We remember his name," a white-haired old woman says. "He was mine."

As fragments of dreams went, there were worse.

"We don't need the bones," Kaeo said. "We go north. I'm not his—the new god's. I never asked to be made a prophet. I never prayed, or thought that much on the gods at all. I honoured the Father and Mother, but . . . it was Prince Dan and what he promised that I served. The gods weren't my concern, ever. They still aren't. I only want—a life of my own. But I can find him."

As surely as knowing he faced the sun, Kaeo thought. He did not entirely like that feeling. As if a part of him had been taken, enslaved, however accidentally, by the dying gods, as he was dying on the Isle of Crows.

PART TWO

CHAPTER XVII

"Papers," the young soldier said, and Ivah, bowing, dug in the pocket of her caravaneer's coat for the short section of bamboo that held the rolled paper. One only needed a pass if one was travelling between towns, but here in Dernang imperial officials had gone house to house making a census of inhabitants, each vouched for by the others, and any deemed suspicious investigated further. Suspected runaway slaves had been stripped to check for brands.

General Zhung Musan still searched the town for agents and sympathizers of Prince Dan's and held executions every morning, before he allowed the market to open. The road to the south was a stinking riot of crows, the heads of Lord Sia's banner-lords and officers and all who remained with him to the end as they were driven back into Dernang. The old lord had refused to open the gates of the castle to them. The young lord had refused, so they said in the town, refused to ask him to, so that the old lord could not be accused of aiding his son's rebellion. Dead now, or as good as, prisoner in his own castle and doomed to a traitor's death on the Isle of Crows with the empress presiding.

Ivah the Grasslander, formerly a caravaneer, now servant of the priestess Daro Aoda of the shrine of Father Nabban in Dernang in Choa.

The soldier, a boy still high-voiced, frowned over the brief few characters and the red stamped seal, lips pursed. Illiterate. They were all conscripts, Aoda had told her, poor tenant-farmers' sons summoned to the emperor's service and eating no better now than they had been before they were impounded for this duty that might, after a few years, release them, maybe far from home, to become beggars and vagrants and bandits on the road. Sons only. Conscripted girls were too likely to end up pregnant.

Ivah kept her face impassive, bored. She had seen this particular soldier around, watching her as she did Mother Aoda's marketing, seen him watching the shrine of Father Nabban. Looking for an excuse to harass them in the name of the empress, the new goddess of the land, she assumed; twice they had been searched for fugitives from the rebel army. The most recent time, the soldiers had taken the last of Aoda's yams and barley, along with the copper bells that had chimed in the wind on the holy pine tree. There was nothing left to loot, unless they plundered her library. Now the soldier held the paper turned sideways. Ivah resisted the urge to correct it for him. A caravaneer who read court Nabbani would be suspicious.

"Good," the soldier said, looking up at Ivah, his stare intense. "You work for the priestess."

"Yes," she said, carefully using the form of the word that indicated submissive respect. It did not often enter her vocabulary. And she must be very, very careful with her pronouns. Remember how Wolan and Koulang mocked her use of regal forms. It wasn't teasing she'd bring down on herself here, letting her mother's speech slip through.

"The priestess," the soldier said, frowning down as he slowly rolled the paper again and slipped it into its bamboo envelope, "has had too much to drink."

"Oh?" Ivah said, wary. Food was in short supply in the town, at least for all but the occupying imperial army of the empress, but Mother Aoda had a large jar of white-spirit from somewhere. For three nights now she had sat under her holy tree, with the jar and a cup beside her. She never drank; she simply sat cross-legged, lips moving in silent prayer, rocking with the cycle of her words, and breaking off only to snarl at any who approached to leave her to her meditations.

"She's at the building site of the new temple."

"Oh." Ivah kept her eyes from turning that way, across the length of the market.

"She's speaking against the goddess of Nabban."

"Ah." Devils damn.

The soldier held her eyes a moment, licked his lips, offered her back her pass. His hand shook. Ivah returned it automatically to her pocket. "I don't know what you can do," he said. "It's too late, far too late. But there are children at your shrine. They shouldn't be there."

Her stomach clenched, sick. Ivah gave the boy a curt nod of understanding, in thanks that could not be spoken, and was waved off. The soldier turned on his heel and continued down the street, the clusters of people venturing out to the market making way for him, eyes averted. He stopped an old man, demanded his residence and business, barely listened to the answer, and moved on.

Ivah didn't turn her stroll through the market into a run, though she quickened her pace. There was a stir over in the northwest, where three big merchant houses had been demolished by deliberate fires and the rubble already carted away. The outer wall of the new temple was rising there, a clamour of masons and labourers, slave and conscripts of the town, starting with the dawn. They would demand Aoda serve there, when it was done, and if she refused . . .

Almost running. Don't. Stand and gawk like all the rest. A figure in a faded gown, easy to see up on the bamboo scaffolding. Speaking, her voice a thin thread of words. She glanced down, turned and scrambled, gained greater height, heaving herself to the top of the unfinished wall.

Soldiers were clambering after the old woman. She stood straight, raised her voice again.

"The heir of the gods of Nabban will come among you, and he will throw down the temples of the empress, the false daughter of the Gods, and break the land, and remake the land, and the days of the sons of Min-Jan will be ended!" Aoda shouted. "I am a priestess of Father Nabban. I have seen."

She spread her arms as though she blessed them . . . jumped. Her gown billowed up obscenely to expose scrawny legs, sagging drawers. The crowd cried out, almost as one, and then began to shove and shout, some to push closer, others to take themselves away. Screams and shrieks. *Help her! Don't touch her!* A bellow. *Don't kill her—take her alive! The general will have your head if you . . . !* Old Great Gods, was Aoda not dead? Something squealed shrill, high, unending, like a rabbit in a snare. Abruptly, it ceased.

Ivah had already been backing away. So much for worries about how to make the gruel go further. Now she began to run, one among many, until she was hidden in the shadows of the porch of the shrine, built against the town wall at the southeast corner of the market square.

The fool. What had Aoda been thinking? She might as well have set fire to the shrine and torn down its walls herself.

Someone within heard her pounding, a distinctive rhythm of two and three, and the door, always barred these days, jerked open.

"What's happening?" the old man there asked. Elderly potter, left behind by his family, his hands too crooked and stiff to handle the clay any longer.

"Aoda," she said.

The potter peered past her at the crowd in the upper end of the market. "She went out. I couldn't stop her. She said the gods had given her the words she must speak. Mistress Ivah, what has she done?"

"She's dead," she said. "She spoke heresy and treason and jumped off the wall of the new temple, and when that didn't kill her the soldiers did. You've got maybe long enough to grab your blanket and get out before they get here. I'm sorry. We all need to scatter."

For a moment the shrine seemed very still and peaceful, a haven, a hiding place inviolable. There were weeds rooted between the cracked roof tiles, new green sprouting there in the first spring sun, and moss bright in the damp about the well. A bird sang in the pine.

The bird could fly.

Ivah could not save them all. She headed for the stairs to the gallery and second floor of the hollow square of the shrine. "Go!" she called as she started up. "Aoda is dead. Soldiers are coming. Run!"

Others were joining the potter in the courtyard. When she looked back again, she could see the woman with her two grandchildren, the three slave-boys from the livery stable that had burned when the wizards and fire-masters of General Zhung Musan broke down the town's southern gate in dust and thunder and destroyed half the street in the following inferno, and the man with the terrible, barely healed wounds to his head, who could not seem to speak or see despite his intact tongue and eyes. What chance did any of them have? The man was too clearly an officer, maybe even a banner-lord, with his well-fed height and his sword-calloused hands. Imperial or rebel, who could say? What did it matter, Aoda had asked, when a soul came to the gods? There were others, too, all pinched and frightened and staring eyes.

"Go!" Ivah yelled in sudden panic for them all. "Now! Don't wait!"

The littlest child began to wail.

The grandmother grabbed the witless banner-ranked and shoved the little one into his arms. "Look after her," she said, and grabbed the boy, a few years older, by the hand. "Come, come quick, we'll fetch our basket."

The old potter hobbled in haste, leaning on his stick, for the little room he had claimed as his own. A cape or blanket was a precious thing in this town, in this time. The probable-lord had stridden off, not staying for any possessions, the little girl's cries muffled against his shoulder, feeling his way out of the gate of the shrine with his bamboo pole, leaving it open behind him. The grandmother—the boys from the stables had run for Aoda's chambers, as if perhaps she had any better blankets than the rest of them, or some secret stash of food. Another old man ran to grab the bottle of white-spirit that sat by the holy tree. Still sealed, Ivah noticed. Oh, Aoda.

Folly to delay for anything. But she ran for the long upper room Aoda had called the library, though half its cupboards were bare, scrolls long crumbled beyond repair or claimed, if they had any uniqueness in content or ornament, by the corps of wizards. She slept there, her heavy sheepskin overcoat, her bow-case, her scribe's portable desk, all tucked down in the far corner. Old habit: her heavy quilt was rolled and tied.

She snatched the nearest scroll-case, a book she had been studying for hints of the gods in the days before they gave themselves up to become the Father and Mother. It would only be looted by the soldiers or torn for lighting cookfires. A translation of a very ancient account of a Pirakuli wizard's journey through Nabban a hundred years before Yeh-Lin's time. It recounted stories of the many kings and queens and the emperor, wonder-tales of the myriad gods, but it also contained many strange characters she had never seen or heard, the sound of which she could not even guess. Into her pack, with her change of linen and the painted calfskin star-chart. She grabbed brushes and ink-cakes from her desk, the inkstone, the little knife, her last few scraps of paper, stowed them in her quiver. The desk must be abandoned, and she had carried it all the way from Marakand, thinking she might take up a scribe's position again here. The winter coat likewise, a treasure for someone, if they didn't burn the place first. Pack, bow, quiver, her sabre hidden under her striped camel-hair coat, bedroll last of all because it was still too cold for sleeping out without cover.

They were on the stairs. Thumping of bare feet and sandals.

She stood where she was, spat on her wrist and drew characters there, felt not so much the words as the whole intent of them flowing into the shape, drawing close about her. Took a breath. Walked, quiet in her felt boots, to the door, stepping aside as half a dozen soldiers poured in.

They did not notice her.

She wove through more of them, went along the gallery to the ladder-like stairs to the attic. An officer was shouting in the courtyard. Someone screamed. She did not look down. They swarmed down there like a pack of wolves about a staggering fawn, and what could she do? She did look, one hasty glance too many. The old grandmother, the boy. It was swiftly over.

They should have run. Why didn't they run?

They had done no more than she had, lingered to gather what little they had left. Old Great Gods keep them safe on their road.

Shuttered window. Bats stirred, clinging to the beams.

She hauled the shutters opened on oiled hinges. She and Aoda had planned this when it seemed likely the town would fall, a route out, at least for the fit and able, of which there were hardly any sheltering in the shrine, of course.

Only she, really, and the boys from the livery stable.

She looked out, and down. Quite far down, to the alleyway between the shrine and a joiner's workshop. The roof of the workshop was lower, and not too steep. No one below. She had made the jump to show Aoda it could be done, but not with all her belongings on her back. And if she threw them, they would simply roll off. Nothing for it, unless she meant to abandon all but the clothes on her back and her sword.

Burdened as she was, she fit, barely, into the window frame, if she crouched like a frog.

Jumped like one, arms and legs splayed, landing flat as she could on the tiles to keep her weight low.

More screaming, someone hauled out of hiding down below. Sudden silence. General Zhung Musan had led an attack on the mountain shrine of the Mother and the family of priests there in person, just over a week ago. They had been sheltering spies of Prince Dan, it was said, or maybe the prince himself, though that could not have been true, or he or parts of him at least would have been brought back to the town for triumphant display. There had nonetheless been a great slaughter. A shrine was no place of safety. The so-called Daughter of the Gods did not tolerate priests who denied her godhead for long. This would have come to the shrine here anyway, today, tomorrow, in a week.

They should have sent these homeless folk to the street and gone themselves before this. Foolish hope, not us, not here, not today . . .

Carefully, Ivah began to crawl, up to the ridgepole, over and down, angling towards where there was a lower shed for ageing wood. She slipped, slid ten feet, horribly close to the eaves. Lost her hold on the spell of concealment. Travelled sideways sweating until she could drop to the shed roof and lie there to catch her breath and reform the spell. It did not render her invisible, really, but it made the eye slide away, think her only shadows, leaf-shimmer, a broken form of light and dark. An intent searcher might still discover her.

None of those here. All busy ransacking the shrine. She heard axes on wood. Destroying it, rather. Felling the sacred tree.

She dropped to the ground and walked down the laneway, out to the street.

Best find some place to lie up for a little, where she could clear her mind, throw the coins, or the stones, and find her way again. Dernang had seemed the place to be, but she had found nothing here of gods on white horses, no god in the old tales whose colours were black and sky-blue. She should head south—to the cities? To rebel-held Shihpan? The road to Bitha ran west from Shihpan.

The ruin of the livery stable by the south gate offered a fragment of roof and a cavelike back room still intact. The soldiers had cleared out squatters; that was where the stableboys had come from. She could shield it from any chance inspection, if only an imperial wizard did not come by to notice the working.

It would do for a night or two, at any rate. Perhaps the coins would guide her to a road. Nothing else seemed to be helping to make a choice.

If she stole a horse, she might reach Bitha before Kharduin's gang ever did.

CHAPTER XVIII

No clear line defined the border here for human eyes. Away to the left and below them, a turf wall cut off a valley like a snow-filled bowl, barring what might otherwise have been a trail away to the north and Denanbak, but it did not stand on the true border, the boundary between stone and stone. Nearer, on the clifftop, a square grey watchtower stood. Not on the border that Ghu could feel. Not, any longer, a guarded border, either. Not today. The dogs sniffed the wind.

"It's deserted," Ghu said, and Yeh-Lin nodded agreement.

They had come from higher up a steep and unstable slope down a shoulder of mountain, keeping well in among the juniper to work around the tower. No need for such caution. Wind whipped fine, stinging snow over what tracks they left; Yeh-Lin's doing.

At their feet, now, the ground dropped away in two directions, towards the tower, and to the south, in a long, broken fall of stone and occasional pines, thickening with the descent until they hid the land, though still they fell away into the green depths. Snow, here, and wind-bared grey rock. The rising air already smelt warmer. Living. Home?

Here. At his feet. The line of the land, the lip of the slope. It followed in a curve, around, angling to the northeast. Here. He could just barely see the mountain, the Father, away to the east. A small and regular peak behind others, white against the blue; greater than them all, in truth.

Ghu caught Ahjvar's arm when he would have started down. "Wait."

The land pulled at him. Stone and water. He could fall forward into it. Drown. Again.

Not yet.

Without a word, Ahjvar went wearily down to one knee, sitting back on his heel. The dogs sat, likewise waiting.

Yeh-Lin, too, waited, turning to look up again at the deserted watchtower.

He could still turn back. Now. This moment, no other. And then what?

Chase the sun to its setting. Sand, forest, sea.

Ahjvar would die. But he had come this far only to see Ghu to Nabban. He still had no desire to live for his own sake, for life itself. On or back, his choosing or Ghu's, Ahjvar would die when the knotted curse was released, when Ghu no longer held what the goddess Catairanach had made, what he had stolen from her in his borrowed godhead. For Ghu to pull himself from the hands of his gods was to let Ahjvar go, but that came, and probably soon, regardless of what doom he chose for himself. He had promised. Sworn himself to it.

To be free, to go where he would, do what he would, alone and seeking . . . nothing.

He could smell the land: stone, root, leaf, water. Hear it. Hear them, Mother Nabban, Father Nabban, in their silence, waiting. Their hope. Their apprehension.

Dotemon. They recognized her, and they remembered.

He could hear the land. The folk of the land. If he listened . . .

He never in his life had been free. Sand Cove. A timeless time. That had been his. That only.

Ahjvar's head was against his hip, sliding into sleep again. He gripped tangled hair and Ahj looked up at him, shadowed eyes the colour of the sky, awake after all, and sombre, seeing what he did not say. "We could go back," Ahjvar said.

"I could, Ahj. You—"

"I don't weigh in the balance. Go, if you will."

"No." Ghu tried to speak lightly, but he felt his smile twist. "It's not for your sake, Ahj. Don't think that." He drew a deep breath. "I know where I need to be."

"So, then." Ahjvar caught Ghu's arm to pull himself upright again. "All downhill from here, at least."

No choice, really. Far too late for that. Ghu nodded and started to pick his way down, taking a slantwise path. Loose stones rattled away from his feet, for all his care. The land whispered, a slow weight growing against the ears, a light touch like the brushing coil of a cat around the ankles. A wave, rising over him.

"Son of Nabban." He caught himself on the nearest stable thing, which was Ahjvar, and looked back. Yeh-Lin still stood above them, a twist of smoky darkness against the sky, edged in light, veins of fire glowing within. He blinked that vision away. Only a woman dressed in the fashion of another age.

She waved a hand along the line of the border. So, she felt it too. No surprise. "This. I . . . would rather not, unasked. I would return in your service, or not at all. I swore so."

"To whom?" Ahjvar demanded.

"To myself, when I left Praitan to follow your young god. You're not the only who doesn't trust himself without a polestar."

"When did I say that?"

"You never did. Will you tell me it is not your truth nonetheless, dead king? Nabban, I swear—"

"*Don't*," Ghu said.

"But I do. I did not kill the goddess who wrapped my grave in her roots above the buried river, beyond the green mountains of the priests, in the dry south across the sea. No other one of the seven came to battle her and call me back. The chains of the Old Great Gods were weakened, yes, and I could have put forth my strength and broken them, and I did not. She let me go, Nabban. She told me, 'You have work to do in service to this world before the end. Redeem yourself. Go.' She said that, my tree, my old river-goddess, and she set me free. But still she holds a part of me, that I may not—be the danger I was. I am—leashed. I do not fight my leash. She is right to constrain me. Do you see it?"

There was a tremor in Dotemon's voice that Ghu did not know if he could swear was truth. That she was restrained—he did not know either. He did not know how she might appear, that fire in her, in her full strength. She was a devil. The tales said there was no truth in them.

The wordless gods, aware through him, grew small and hard with apprehension, the way some sea-thing might draw in on itself. But they did not wake into any anger, any denial, even in their fear. Their judgement lay surrendered, in this moment, to him.

Why? How could they trust to his judgement? He was too small and young and human for this.

He could not look to Ahjvar for guidance. Ahj, as the devil claimed of herself, only waited. Only followed, with no strength but to carry himself, if that.

He did like her, wanted to like her or the person she seemed to be, but she had charmed armies to their destruction and set the pattern for Nabban to become what it was.

So might he. In what cause?

"Where will you go, if I send you away?" he asked.

"I don't know, Nabban. To find the others, I suppose. To find my death, maybe. There is a sword of ice waiting for us all." The last was a whisper.

He tried to listen to the land. It feared. In her, there was fear, too, that he would send her away. That she would be alone. Was that why she followed, simple loneliness? Fear of her fellows. It was not his, to save her from her fears. But in her, too, there was a yearning, a reaching for peace, for place, to know the green hills and the wild and the slow-snaking rivers again.

Ghu found words. Tasted them. Reluctant. Uncertain.

"Come, then. You've given your oath. I take it. And I hold you to it, Dotemon. Serve Nabban. Serve me."

Yeh-Lin drew her sword, then, one swift movement, and closed both her hands over the blade. He saw the blood fall, *felt* it, hot drops on the boundary of Nabban soaking his earth, his skin. Could taste it in his mouth, warm and salt.

"Yours," she said. Only that, and she went to her knees, forehead to the stones, sword laid before her.

"Idiot," he said. "Stand up and come on."

But there had been no mockery in her prostration.

Yeh-Lin came down to them slowly, stood breathing deeply, looking down into the valley. The thin red lines across her palms were already scabbing.

"Hah." She looked up then, meeting his eyes. Grinned. "Home, Nabban. Do you feel it? We're *home.*"

"Yes."

"Well, come, then." She laughed aloud and dodged past, clapping him on the arm as she went. Abandoning all caution, she plunged a zigzag course like a hare down the slope, ploughing through snow, slithering on stone, catching herself on the isolated grey trunks to change course, exuberant as a girl. The dogs surged after her, Jui yapping like a pup, skittering and skidding.

Ghu watched her disappear into the first thick stand of pines, a bright flash of colour before she was lost amid the crooked boles. A flock of birds took flight, scolding, wheeling against the sky. He laughed and caught at Ahjvar again.

"Come on. It's spring down there."

They followed breakneck in the devil's wake.

After the first stand of woods they all lost their reckless abandon. The light began to fail, the sun plunging towards the unending mountains that stretched west, and there were long and sudden drops, deep gulleys filled with ice, the meltwater chiming through it, woken by sun and soon to sleep again.

Darkness wrapped them by the time they reached the thick forest of the valley bottom, and scents of pines and moss. It was as though they had walked out the dying of the old year and into the new, the big flower-buds swelling on the understorey rhododendrons, a chorus of frogs singing in the branches overhead.

Ahjvar dropped his pack and slid to sit himself against a tree, eyes closed, as if too tired to stand. But he spoke. He had not, much of the day past. "Yeh-Lin the Beautiful. Loose in Nabban."

"Like you, dead king, I am but another of Nabban's hounds." Yeh-Lin bowed to them both. "Though handsomer than the four-legged ones and better-tempered than you."

"Do you want to be buried again?" Ghu asked lightly. "Plenty of trees here to put you under."

"One of his hounds, until he sends me away," she amended.

"And what cause would you give him to do that, old woman?" Ahjvar demanded, opening his eyes again.

"I don't know. But he will, someday. I see it." Her eyes were shadowed. "I—Old Great Gods, I do not care. Not for any betrayal of mine, I swear it, again. And we are here, now." She chuckled. "And there is a civilized town only another day's march distant, and in the foreigners' ward there are bathhouses that will admit even the likes of you, barbarian that you are, and if you two will avail yourselves of them, I will finally be rid of the stink of rancid *rykersyld*. Or filthy, unwashed male, which is almost the same thing."

"No money," Ghu said. "And we're not going into the town."

"Then the first brook we come to, you are going to wash. Both of you."

"No soap," Ghu said.

"I," Yeh-Lin said, "have soap."

"Do you?"

"Yes, Nabban, I do. But what you need is a razor, because those few otter's whiskers that seem to be all you can grow are not going to charm the girls."

"Ketkuiz didn't complain."

"Ketkuiz probably thought a man who smelt like camels was at least a change from men who smell like horses. And do I look to you as if I have ever in my life been in need of a razor?"

"I don't know. Old women. Bristly chins."

"The first brook we come to, heir of Nabban, I am going to push you in and hold your head under."

"I can't drown, you know. And it's barely spring."

"Cold baths are good for you," Yeh-Lin said. "At least if soap is involved. And you'll wash what of your clothing can be washed. Damned Great Gods, listen to me! I am not here to be mother to either of you."

"Dotemon the Dreamshaper lures us to our doom," Ahjvar muttered. "We survive the badlands in winter and she kills us with a spring ague."

"A long-laid plan," said Yeh-Lin. "I shall then rob you of your— your—you have absolutely nothing I would think worth the stealing. And bury you under a tree, I suppose. Both of you in one grave. A touching ballad."

"A cautionary tale," Ahjvar countered, eyes shut again. Last night he had nearly flung himself and Ghu both into the fire in his dreaming.

"Children, you really do reek. Why aren't we going into town? I was looking forward to a hot meal and a soft bed, even one with fleas, in addition to the bathhouse."

"We have no papers, no caravan-master to say we're his folk," Ghu said. "They'd have turned us back at the border for that alone. Ahjvar looks like trouble—you do, Ahj. No magistrate's guard is going to let you walk the streets without question. And I'm a runaway. There are people in this part of the world who might even know me, for all I've grown up since then."

"Slave, Nabban?"

"Yes," he said shortly.

"I said Ghu was a slave's name, when first we met. I only meant to be rude. I didn't know. I'm sorry."

"Why a slave's name?" Ahjvar asked. He caught at Ghu's arm, heaved himself up again as the night settled around them, mountains claiming the sun.

"Because it's a joke," Ghu said. "It's Lathan, from the south. Listen, I hear water. There's a brook near. We'll camp by it."

"Why is it a joke?" Ahjvar persisted.

"It's a name you'd give a dog," said Yeh-Lin.

"Or a horse," Ghu said. "It doesn't matter. It's my name. I didn't see any smoke, coming down from the mountain. No villages, no soldiers. We should be safe to make a fire. I'll cook. Find wood, you two."

Her eyes were open, blue-grey, empty. Lips blue, mouth bruised, and the marks of his thumbs on her throat. Brown hair, a few white threads shining in the candlelight, snarled his hands.
  No. No. No.

Two of them, dead where they had scrambled in confusion from their sleep. Old man, old woman, blood pooling together on the rush-strewn floor. The door hung broken.

King, champion, sword. Hot hands on him, digging in, burning. A body lying over him.
  Open your eyes, dead man.
  Blistered skin, crumbling to the touch. Slimed with stagnant water.
  Knife in his hand, the small, fine blade.
  There was a fire behind her eyes.
  Pain, a sharp blow. Hand opened.
  "Ahjvar. *Ahj!*"
  Eyes opened too, on night, on firelight. Ghu, who had struck his hand against a twisted root to break his grip on the knife. Ghu, who snapped, "Get that," at the devil. Ghu kneeling over him, pinning him down. Yeh-Lin far too close beside him, on one knee, plaid over her shoulders as she had slept, sweeping up his small last knife in her hand.
  He gasped for air, throat raw. Not smoke. Not water. He had forgotten how to breathe. Ghu hauled him up, dragged him close. He pressed closer yet, shaking.
  "Great Gods damn, we need to search him before we lie down to sleep," Yeh-Lin said, and rubbed a tear below her breast, a dark smear in the amber firelight. "It's all very well saying the dogs will keep watch, but they don't seem to have been watching *him*."
  Safe. Ghu had him. Yeh-Lin flicked the bloodstain with angry fingertips and the darkness was gone, the brocade whole.

"Not faster than me after all," he muttered into Ghu's shoulder, but the words came broken, stuttering.

"I was *asleep.*" Outrage in her voice. Yeh-Lin drove the knife point down into the moss at his side. And then, more gently, "Tu'usha—the Lady—is dead. That is truth. You know it. I saw it in the mirror. I told you before—I can show you, if you will. If that would help."

"No."

"She has no hold on you; she will not touch you again. She is gone from this world; the black sword took her. I am not she. And I'm not hurt. You couldn't do me lasting harm if you tried, Ahjvar, so sleep, both of you. I'll sit up. No more dreams tonight." He flinched from her hand, but she did not touch him, only sketched something in the air. "Possession atop possession. I suppose the wonder is you're as sane as you are."

"Don't—"

"Too late. And it's only small wizardry. It won't hold you if you fight it. So don't fight it. Let it be. Sleep."

"Don't."

"*Sleep.*"

The weariness was too heavy and the panic that wanted to break free was muffled, stilled against warmth, a song half-whispered.

"Not a horse." Mumbled protest. Ghu sang to horses. But he gave up the struggle, did not want to wake, after all, to remember he had forgotten the knife at his wrist. Ghu had him still, lay down with him on their coats. Ahjvar curled against him, head on his chest, held to Ghu as if the night might yet tear him away. Yeh-Lin piled blankets over them and retreated to the fire. He shut his eyes, not to see the flames reflected in hers.

Sleep, she said, or maybe it was memory. *Know you dream. Learn to fight the dreams, not your friends.*

The sun was high when Ahjvar awoke, standing almost at noon. The fire was down to embers and no one was near but the dogs. He crawled out of the nest of blankets and coats chilled and stiff. Spring, maybe, but winter's cold had rolled down off the mountain in the night. Splashing, out of sight. Under the densest pines the ground was clear, soft-carpeted with bronze needles, but where the canopy was thinner, leather-leafed bushes were snarled and woven into impenetrable thickets. He wound around several such and found Ghu downstream, crouched on stone, wringing out a sodden bundle of greyed linen in water already climbing its banks.

Shirtless, roughly-shaved—and that was his little knife tossed into the moss—wet-haired, and goose-bumped. "You missed breakfast, Ahj, what there was of it," Ghu said over his shoulder. "Soap, there, on that rock. Wash off one layer of grime at least and make the devil happy."

"We can't go on avoiding settled areas much longer, can we?" Ahjvar asked. "Soldiers? City guard, that sort of thing?"

Better lost in the wilderness forever?

"Checkpoints on the road, on gates, yes. Probably more than usual, with the fighting the Denanbaki warned of. We'll need to dodge all that. We don't have papers."

"At some point there'll be people."

He did not want people. It had been a relief, like a weight taken away, when the Denanbaki left them.

"Yes, Ahj."

"Let me look at that brand."

Ghu rose and mutely turned his back. The slave-mark was old and silvery white against the skin of his left shoulder.

Ahjvar traced the outline, a round-cornered rectangle long as his thumb, three fingers wide. Not too distorted. Born into slavery, but at least they hadn't set the iron to the little child's flesh. This had been done when he was nearly full-grown, or it would not be still as legible as it was on the man. He had never given it much thought. The old burn was puckered and hard beneath his fingertips. *Daro Clan*, it said within, in ornate and searing calligraphy even the blind could read.

"How do they cancel it for a freedman?"

"A second brand set near it. And papers, too. There's always papers. Everyone in the empire needs papers, if they travel even so far as the next town."

"Another brand. Great Gods be merciful." Ahjvar flattened his hand, hiding the scar. Dripping black hair brushed his fingers. Ghu usually hacked it off before it grew long enough to reach his shoulders. "Papers I can forge, if I have the wording and the pattern of the seal. Well, and ink and paper and brushes too, but—"

"Yes. Ahjvar, don't do that unless you mean it. It's, it's very hard not to notice. I try, but—gods, don't do that. Please."

He had, unthinking, drawn his hand down, thumb tracing the spine.

Ghu turned against his hand, solemn, watching him. His eyes were not dark brown but black, truly black, night and deep water. Not men, nor gods, Ahjvar had said, what seemed very long ago. It had always been women who drew him, women he had tangled, in the long dark years, with his memory of that waking, of Miara dead, so that he never forgot, ever, what he had become, and desire died stillborn. Mad. Unclean. A horror in the world. He had grown to be sickened by almost any human touch at all, however casual, knowing what he was, what his hands had done, but Ghu had never—he had never feared Ghu near him, his mere presence a refuge and a stillness that he had craved before he ever recognized that deep enfolding calm as what kept him from trying too hard to drive the boy away.

This, though . . .

Ghu was . . . Ghu. Only Ghu. Water-chilled skin warming to skin. The chiming of the brook over stones sounded very loud.

He still tried to kill the ghosts of his past in the night. His mouth was dry. The knife had bitten flesh. An edge fit to shave with. It could have been Ghu.

"Children," Yeh-Lin sang out, from the camp farther upstream. "Someone come gut these fish for me. I did not come back to Nabban to be your cook, but if I must, I expect help."

"Can you cook?" Ahjvar called over his shoulder. He retreated a step, dropping his hand in something like relief.

"Can I cook? Champion of the Duina Catairna, I grew up in a one-room hut in a village of Solan, on the southern banks of the Wild Sister where she grows tame and broad among the canals. I was a virtuous maiden planning to marry the son of a woman whose hut was across the village paddies from ours, until a banner-lord's son murdered him thinking thus to make me his mistress. Which is when I ran away to what they call now the Old Capital, to seek my fortune, as they say. Can I cook? If there is anything to cook, I can cook it. I can also butcher a pig, heckle hemp, spin, weave, milk a buffalo, drive an ox, and handle a boat. You'd be surprised. But that doesn't mean I enjoy it or that you get out of gutting fish."

Ghu caught Ahjvar, hand on the back of his neck. "Later," he said on a breath, and left him.

"Do you darn?" he heard Ghu asking Yeh-Lin with easy interest in his voice. "Because we have quite a bit of mending that no one ever seems to get around to doing."

"Not unless you have your pet assassin put a knife to my throat do I do any kind of sewing."

"Could arrange that."

"Do you want another war with me, Nabban?"

"Not this morning. You caught fish. Did you find my fish-hooks? I thought them lost."

"I learnt to tickle trout in the kingdoms of the north. These are not trout, but I caught them just the same. And look—cresses. Greens! And eggs! I found a duck's nest, and do not look at me like that; it was not a full clutch and she wasn't setting yet. I took only three, which is one each, if you don't insist the dogs have their share, and left her with a blessing that nothing else would disturb her nest. The world returns to life. Don't stand there dripping and shivering at me. Hang that shirt by the fire—at least it will smell of fresher smoke then—and wrap up in a blanket or something. Dead king, you with the knives, come and earn your keep!"

Ahjvar ignored her, stripped and waded into the deep pool below the rocks instead. Ice cold and numbing, and when he did trudge barefoot back to the fire, his knife reclaimed, and the few bits of ragged clothing he thought he could spare for the afternoon washed, after a fashion, and dripping in one hand, the fish were sizzling on skewers and the eggs just boiled in the tea. Taking the time to wash, even in ice-water, had its merits.

"Unmerciful Great Gods," Yeh-Lin said, eyeing his chest as she passed him tea in a cracked earthenware cup. "Has everyone you ever met in the past century tried to take a slice out of you?"

"Yes," he growled, and pulled his coat on shirtless to hide the scars, for all that probably undid the good of ever having washed. It reeked of camels.

"Perhaps they weren't entirely to blame." She rubbed a fist over her ribcage. "So, here we are. Home, I suppose. Now what?"

"I . . . go to find my gods," Ghu said.

And what then? What point asking? If the gods claimed Ghu and took him from the world, there was little Ahjvar could do.

Die, he supposed. At last.

Ghu said he did not know this forest, these valleys, and yet, when they set out again, he led them with the assurance of familiarity. Unknown birds whistled and carolled overhead and flashed away, half-seen flecks of colour. Small deer no bigger than a goat broke cover and darted across their path, crashing through brush and vanishing. A leopard, dapples fading into dappled light, stood and stared with burning yellow eyes. The dogs froze, flattened themselves to the ground. Ahjvar reached slowly for the crossbow, but Ghu, in the lead, held back a hand, not looking around.

"Go on," he said softly, and the leopard blinked and paced on her way, not a rustle of leaves to betray her as she vanished from sight.

"Reminds me of someone . . ." Yeh-Lin remarked.

By evening, they were smelling smoke and seeing signs of human activity, stumps of felled trees—saplings, mostly—and trampled patches along the brook where the tightly coiled new fern fronds had been gathered. The ground was marshy here, flooding as the brook rose, carrying meltwater from the mountain snows. They spread out away from the watercourse, the dogs slinking and silent, not a sound from Ghu or Yeh-Lin either. Ahjvar paused to span and load the crossbow, worked his way ahead of the others again. No sign of any outlying sentries. A rooster crowed. If it was a village, there should be fields.

No fields, but, abruptly, a lean-to of poles built against the trunk of a pine, roofed with bark thoughtlessly stripped to kill that same sheltering pine. Ahjvar knelt slowly, shielded by a tall stand of some thick, winter-yellowed grasses. More huts were scattered about, no order to them, built against trees or freestanding, with just one communal fire in the centre. An old woman in a ragged gown sat on her haunches, turning the stone of a quern and tugging at a naked little child, leashed with a rope about the middle, whenever he tried to crawl away. Another woman milked a goat. Lean swine rooted around the shelters, churning the ground to muck with their tusks. Women worked at the fire, chopping fish into chunks for a steaming pot. Children, more women young and old, a handful of old men, were away on the other side of the encampment, grubbing up roots and trying to turn the soil around newfelled trees with spades and hoes. The smallest ones worked in the rough furrows, dragging baskets, planting and tramping down some brown tubers. Hardly any adult men, and they all looked half-starved; all wore little more than knee-length gowns and maybe a headscarf or a shawl. The naked child began to wail and was cuffed to a snivelling silence.

The ones in the field straightened up, watching, with a sort of sullen blankness, three newcomers, two women and a man. Better clothed— loose trousers, sandals, jackets, though all of brown or undyed cloth. One woman had a spear over her shoulder, the other a short, single-edged sword slung from a scarf knotted into a baldric of sorts, the man an axe.

"Nothin' for the pot tonight," the man called as they crossed the field, paying no heed to what had just been planted, and the older of the two women laughed and mimed a thrust at a child with her spear when the boy wasn't fast enough to get out of her way. What game had they hoped to take, trampling and kicking along as they did and with only a single spear between them? The younger woman yelled in what sounded indignation, spotting the swine, and began shouting at the nearest children to get them out of her hut, though one only was poking its head in a doorway. She ran at them herself, beating with the flat of her blade, kicking snouts with her heel, and the creatures scattered, squealing and grunting. Her comrades flung themselves down by the fire, made no move to help the women preparing the food.

Gods, but Ghu could move like a cat when he wished. A touch on Ahjvar's shoulder, a shadow in the corner of his eye. He had heard nothing. No sign of Yeh-Lin or the dogs at all.

"Fugitives from the fighting?" Ahjvar guessed, hardly more than a whisper.

"Likely. I know her." Ghu raised his chin at the young woman, now picking her way, grumbling, around the stumps and muddy patches towards the stream. She was pregnant, enough to show but not yet heavy and slow.

"Send one of the kids for water," the other hunting woman shouted, but the young one retorted, "Snares," and kept on her way, scowling.

"Friend?"

"No."

"Who is she?" Deserter, adrift from the fighting, would be his guess.

"Meli. One of the girls from my lord's estate. A household slave's daughter. They were training her for a silk-weaver."

"Not your lord."

"No, Ahj."

"Good. Remember that. Don't say it." A conversation they had had years ago, he was certain.

"No, Ahj."

"Will she know anything useful?"

"How she came here may be good to know."

"Yes, then?"

"Yes," Ghu said, "if you think we can get away without a hunt raised for us, after, and without harming her."

Ahjvar retreated into the trees, eased off the bow and returned the bolt to the quiver. Ghu trailed him, around through the forest, down towards the water again, moving quickly, but his quarry turned their way, leaving the muddy ford where the animals watered and following a path along the bank upstream. Ahjvar shed his pack and slipped through brush still winter-bare, into a stand of some gnarled, broad-leafed evergreens, and rose to pull the woman down, hand over mouth, arms pinned to her sides, when she bent to glower at an empty sinew snare. He dragged her, kicking and twisting, back to clearer ground. Ghu plucked her chopping blade away and shoved it through his own belt. Still too close to the camp. Ahjvar gagged her with her dirty scarf, heaved her over his shoulder and set off upstream, until he found a place they could cross, keeping dry on stones. Ghu, with both packs, followed. She didn't weigh all that much more than a child and hung limp, as if resigned to her fate. He wouldn't make the mistake of thinking she was.

With distance and the sound of the water roaring down a narrow, rocky defile to cloak any shouting, he set her at the foot of a tree and pulled the cloth from her mouth, a knife in his hand for a wordless warning.

Ghu stood looking down on them both and asked, "Who are they?"

The woman cowered back against the tree, licked her lips.

"What's left of Taza village, aren't they?" she muttered. "A Zhung man, aren't you? You should know."

"But I don't. And I'm no one's man. What happened to Taza?"

"Burnt, wasn't it?"

"Where are all the men?"

"Soldiers took them, didn't they? You lot. General Zhung Musan's soldiers. Labourers for the town, they said, but they won't come home. They never come home."

"What's Taza?" Ahjvar asked, speaking Praitannec.

"A Daro manor," Ghu answered, "south of Dernang."

"They're slaves?"

"Taza? No, serfs."

"Same thing."

"No," said Ghu. "More like Grasslander bondfolk. They're not owned outright—they can't be sold. They're folk of the clan and have a name."

"The land's not their own."

"The land is the gods'," Ghu said. "Neither do your folk own the land they hold under their lords."

"They can leave it. The lords can't wilfully take it from them. They can choose to pass their tenure of it to another. They can choose their heirs. They're free. These aren't."

"No."

"These people are starving."

"Yes. My—Daro Korat was not so hard a lord. A philosopher, Ahj. He did not starve them. But their lives aren't their own, you're right. No rights, except not to be sold, no rights but to their own souls. Not even to live, if they offend their lord. And many lords do starve them, taking all, time and labour and all that the land will give." Ghu turned back to the woman. "Who are the other two with you, Meli?"

"How d'you know my name? I've seen you before. You're one of the assassins they sent in to spy on Lord Sia, looking for the prince." But she frowned in doubt.

"No. Who are the other two?"

"Osion and Toi. I don't know about her. She's a pig. She's from the town. Freewoman, I think, at least she claims the Daro name. Lai Toi's a soldier. A deserter. But he's a pig too, and what I'd pay to see his head along the road with the rest—" Her voice took on a whine. "If I help you take him, will you let me go, my master?"

"Not your master. Tell me about Lord Sia and the prince."

"I don't know anything. They said the prince was in Alwu and came over to Sia, but what does it matter? They're all dead, you killed them all— there's only us left and it's not my fault, Toi made me come with him, him and Osion, into the forest to starve, but we found these witless dirt-grubbers and it's better than being taken as a rebel. Show them a blade and they roll over like a dog. Look, it's Toi you want, isn't it? He's the deserter—he's the real soldier—I'm just a woman. You can let me go, or take me with you, you don't have to give me to your lord. I can—" She licked her lips again, plucked at the neck of her jacket, glanced up at Ahjvar and cringed, tried to smile, straightening her back, thrusting out her breasts.

"Lord Daro Sia, Meli?"

"I only went with him because everybody did. I was afraid. I never spoke against the empress. I never did."

Ghu dropped down to his heels, face-to-face with her. "You don't remember me, do you?"

She frowned, squinted, rubbed her nose.

"We're not imperial assassins. We're not the empress's men. It was a long time ago."

"Mother be damned, you're one of Horsemaster Yuro's boys. From the stables. The simpleton. Ghu. You've grown."

"Boys do."

"You talk more than you used to."

Ghu shrugged. "Lord Sia, Meli. You said rebels. He fought his father, the empress, who? What prince? What's been happening here?"

"What's it to you? Everyone thought you were dead, fallen in the river at last. You never ran away on your own, not you—caravaneers stole you, did they? I can guess what for. You always did have pretty eyes." A glance up at Ahjvar again. "That doesn't look so bad, better than Toi. You his, horseboy? Does he like women, too?"

"He's mine," Ghu said serenely. "And no, he does not. Not at all." The corner of his mouth lifted, meeting Ahjvar's eyes. Ahjvar kept a king's guard's impassive face. "Tell me about Daro Sia and the prince, Meli."

"Stupid horseboy." Contempt soured her voice. "You always were slow. Who cares about Sia? He's dead and he never was anything to you so don't pretend you care. Toi'll kill the both of you. He's a real soldier. And I can't be bullied by some half-witted—" She flung herself forward and clawed at him, but Ghu was simply not there, rising and stepping aside. Ahjvar jerked her back, struck her face.

"Do that again and I will take your hand off," he told her, pushing her against the tree, her arm hauled up over her head. He scored a line over the skin of her wrist. "Right—there." She whimpered as the blood beaded in the knife's wake.

"No, Ahj," Ghu said gently. Just that.

Old Great Gods have mercy, what was he doing? The rage that boiled in him—it was her contempt for Ghu far more than the futile and childish attack that had ignited his temper. He had barely checked himself from putting the knife in her back.

"Sit down, Meli."

She sat, shivering, her wrist to her mouth.

"Tell us about Lord Sia and the prince."

"There's a war. There's been war ever since the old emperor died. War in the south forever, but you know that." That was meant to be a sneer, but Ahjvar couldn't see why. "Last spring they took all the boys from the villages for the army, not just the usual conscription levy. And Prince Dan tried to make himself a king down in Shihpan. So there was fighting everywhere. And I don't know, some of the provinces were for Prince Dan and some for the emperor, and the headhunters from Dar-Lathi were going to come and kill us all, they said. They said the rebel prince freed the slaves if they'd fight for him. And then the emperor got killed—not the old one that died but the new one. The gods killed him, struck him down for murdering the prophet that said the princess was the daughter of the Old Great Gods and brought the prophet back to life, too. And nobody knew who was emperor any more, but the princess said she was the empress and a goddess too, and she sent for our master to come take oath to her. The Kho'anzi didn't go. He was sick. A fever in his joints." She glanced up at Ahjvar, cringed. "He didn't want to go. Everyone knew that. Everyone knows the Kho'anzi is a Traditionalist at heart and thinks the gods will come back someday and overturn Min-Jan's laws, make everyone free, which is what Prince Dan was doing, and the empress says the gods are dead and she's the only goddess of the land, so he wouldn't go to her, would he? There's a prophecy going around the markets that the heir of the gods will break the emperors and make the land new. Mad old woman's talk, and the magistrates arrest them, of course, and flog them for madness, which doesn't make sense, if the empress is a goddess, because that's what she's done, isn't it? Broke the emperors. But Lord Sia thought it was true and it didn't mean the empress. He said he would be the sword of the gods in Choa. He thought Prince Dan might be the heir of the gods. So Lord Sia wanted to raise Choa and declare for Prince Dan, and Lord Korat said he was waiting and praying for a sign from the gods, that's what he said. They argued about it, him and Sia. Yelling. I had a friend served in Lord Sia's apartments. He heard. The Kho'anzi and Lord Sia fought about what the gods wanted."

Then a rush, bitter. "And the old man wouldn't. Our lord could say the gods meant all folk to be free someday, like in the long ago before Yeh-Lin, but he wouldn't see anything changed now. He had to keep everything as it was, because the gods set him over us all and he had to keep us safe, all Choa Province safe, as if he ever could, and he said Prince Dan wasn't the one the gods wanted us to wait for, and he was going to lose his war, and it wasn't the empress either. So Lord Sia called all the folk of the castle one night without his father knowing, and said, who would fight for him and not be a slave, a lot of Traditionalist rubbish about how everyone was born free in the eyes of the gods. And we all went with him, well, a lot of us. Some. All of us who were children with him, and others, too. All fools together. We took Dernang, and the village serfs rose because he said he'd give them the lands they worked for their own and they believed him, and half the soldiers of the province and some of the young Daro lords and ladies too, from the other families of the clan, even banner-lords, and we said we'd have Prince Dan as emperor. We fought the Kho'anzi's officers and the soldiers that wouldn't come in with us, but the old lord wouldn't fight. Locked himself up in the castle and prayed, I expect," she said in disgust. "So we had the town and we took the courier-stations, and some banner-ranked from Shihpan took the border-posts in the south—Shihpan's all for Prince Dan—and General Lord Zhung Musan came up with an army through Numiya and there was fighting. Numiya was for the emperor in the summer, so now it's for the empress. Zhung Musan's the empress's man. There was a lot of fighting. We were all penned up in Dernang in the end and the old lord closed up the castle—"

"Where was Prince Dan? In Dernang?"

"Stupid, how would I know? Dan was in Alwu. There was some big battle over there and he killed some Tua general, a lady from Numiya, I forget her name. We got a lot of soldiers from that, men of the general's that escaped, and rebels, slaves and serfs from Numiya, useless rabble, mostly, Toi says." She sniffed. "He should know; he was one of them, an imperial, before he decided he was through with fighting for anyone. They say the prince came into Choa with a picked band to help Sia but I don't believe it. Why would he? And sometimes they said he was in Shihpan and sometimes they said he was still over in Alwu, so they didn't really know, did they? And if he did he was too late. Or he got killed before he ever got to Dernang. I heard that. Whatever. So imperial wizards blew open the gates. They had fire-powder. Smoke everywhere. Toi and Osion and I got away with a couple of others. They're dead. I thought we were going to die too, but we found this lot and they feed us. We protect them, Toi says. We hunt for them, see? The whole town's full of soldiers and there's all tents in the horsemarket, and they patrol all the roads in the daylight, but soldiers don't like the night and they don't come into the forest. Scared of demons."

"Most of the demons of Nabban died in Yeh-Lin's day. What happened to Lord Sia?"

"Killed in the fighting, killed himself, I don't know. He's dead, anyway. I saw his head along the road. But that was lucky for him. They'd have sent him to the Golden City, otherwise, I guess." She hunched herself up. "Stupid fool. I believed him, didn't I? I—we all did. Sia talked and it was like he was a priest of the shrines, like he'd come from sitting at Father Nabban's feet to set all right. He killed us all. The gods don't care. Maybe the ones that say they're dead are right."

"No," Ghu said.

"The castle held out for a while, but they took it not long ago. The old lord surrendered to them at last, himself to die for Lord Sia's crimes and his family allowed to renounce their name and go to live quiet in exile in Bitha or the colonies or somewhere. He went out to the general and let him put chains on him, and had his banner-lords march out with him and lay down their swords. That's what they say. General Musan lied, though. He sacked the castle, once he had the lord and his banner-lords. Don't know who survived that—I snuck as far as Waterfield market a few days ago and saw one of the girls from the kitchen-gardens there, with a man she called her husband. She said both the ladies, our lord's daughters—their husbands died with Sia—both the ladies and

Sia's wife barricaded the keep and killed themselves rather than be taken by General Musan's men, and poisoned their children, and it's only then the house-master opened the door of the keep itself. The general had said they could have all the women once he had the old lord in his hands—"

"Even in this gods-forsaking land that's against every—" Ahjvar began.

"Who cares about that? But they already had our master then without an arrow wasted, old fool, and he's back in the keep in his chains, they say. They'll be sending him to the empress in Lord Sia's place." Her eyes shifted between Ghu and Ahjvar. "You understand, horseboy? Everyone's dead. The empress's armies'll come up the rivers once the floods ebb and that'll be the end of Prince Dan's rebels in Shihpan and wherever, if he's dead or if he isn't. Don't know why you'd come back, anyway. Go away with your caravan man."

"Things I need to do," Ghu said. "You think the Kho'anzi is still prisoner, or have they sent him to the empress already?"

She shrugged. "How should I know? Nothing to me, anyway. Except I think it's Sia's baby, not Toi's. I went with him one night. We all did, us girls from the manor. He said we were all men and women alike, all the same before the gods. Doesn't matter. Nobody's going to make it lord of Daro Clan once the old lord dies. Toi'll probably drown it. Babies cry too much and we might have to run away, he says, if the emperor's soldiers do come into the forest."

Nasty little wretch. This land was sick. Poisoned with itself.

"Would the Northron take me, too, with his caravan? I always liked you, Ghu. I did. I wasn't one of the ones that threw things. I didn't hit you. I didn't call names, not worse than anyone else. And you can't blame me if I did. You were only a dirty brat in the stables and acting like you couldn't understand plain speech half the time, such a stupid little staring thing. But I did like you. You remember that."

"No."

"Yes, you do. I could lose the baby; it wouldn't be a bother to your master, tell him. Osion gave me something, I just haven't . . . not yet. It's so far along. She said I might bleed too much. But I will. I'll show you which huts are ours. You can kill Toi and Osion too. It'll be easy when they're asleep."

"No," Ahjvar said, and, "Not his master. You don't listen, do you?" while Ghu was saying, "He's not Northron."

Ghu settled down on his heels again, looking up at Ahjvar. No words. Troubled.

"No," Ahjvar said in Praitannec. "She's stupid and treacherous. Too dangerous to trust her."

"Pity her, though."

"I don't."

"Well, try. But no, there's nothing to trust in her, as she is now, and too much danger in doing so. She'll sell us wherever she sees a passing advantage."

He was going to have to kill her. Ghu would ask him, as quietly as he said, pity her. And he himself would care no more than he would wringing a hen's neck for supper. There was something wrong with him.

She watched Ghu, trying again to smile. "I did like you. I thought you had pretty eyes. I had to come when all the house-children went looking for you. They'd have thought I was demon-touched too if I didn't. But it was just in fun. Nobody meant anything. You know that. You know what children are like. You can't blame me for that now. We were just playing."

"Oh, yes." Ghu sighed. "Meli, there's no truth or trust in you. You know this. I'm not putting my friends in your hands. You're not coming with us, but you shouldn't go back to the camp."

Her face twisted to a sneer. "Like you can stop me going where I want."

Too stupid to live, Ahjvar thought.

"We could stop you, but we won't. Don't go back to the camp. The village folk are going to realize that what makes you masters over them is habit, nothing more. They're going to realize they have far more weapons than the three of you do. You can't say that you're all the same before the gods, and then make yourselves lords over a village of slaves through fear of an axe. If he keeps on as he is, Toi will die in the night, and soon, as you said, but not at our hands. Go to Waterfield or go west, take the road to Bitha. You're a silk-weaver; you have work you can do."

"And end up some man's whore again? That's all the likes of you and me ever will be, horseboy, if we're not in some safe place with a master to hold his hand over us, and I can go whoring here, get taken and be burnt on the face for a runaway here too, just as easy as trying to get to Bitha. All foreigners there anyway. Better than what'll come to you, coming back speaking words the Northron puts in your mouth."

Ahjvar felt the devil before he saw her, behind him, coming around the tree. A prickling on the back of his neck, like a wind risen up.

"Put her to sleep for a while," Ghu said. "Give us time to get away."

"Leave her for the leopard," Ahjvar muttered and caught the woman by the hair to prevent her, when she would have looked around.

"I can do better than sleep." Yeh-Lin pushed Ahjvar aside, kneeling down to take Meli's head between her hands. The woman stiffened and then sagged, not in sleep, but relaxing to the verge of it. Yeh-Lin leaned close. "Dreams," she murmured. "Hush, be still. You were checking the snares. You wandered from the stream. You were lost. Do you see it? Do you remember? You were afraid. A noise. An animal. You didn't see it, but you heard it snarl. You smelt it. You ran. A branch scratched you. Your wrist hurts. There were thorns. You're out of breath now. You've sat down to catch your breath. You're not quite sure where you are, all alone in the forest."

Meli put her wrist to her mouth, chest heaving. Her head turned and Yeh-Lin let her move, looking this way, that. She didn't seem to see Ghu, still standing before her.

Yeh-Lin looked up at him, touched the woman again. "It's getting dark now. Night's almost on us. You hate this hiding in the forest, don't you, Meli? You're going to leave it. You're going to run away from them, tomorrow, when they go hunting, yes, you'll stay behind and then you'll leave them, because you hate the trees and the wild animals, the cold and the wet, you hate it all. You're going to go away, far from here. But now you're going to try to find your way back. You remember now, you crossed the stream, you're all turned around. Your legs are all wet from wading. You need to cross the stream again and get back to your camp before all the light goes."

Ahjvar could feel it himself, a haze of memory, running, cold wet skin, trees and shadows and fear not to be admitted aloud to the others—fear was the core of it, her fear of him shifted aside to the forest, to threats unseen, and her anger, her contempt for Ghu slid over to lodge with thoughts of her comrades, the emotions still there, but turned away, leaving nothing but shadows where he and Ghu had been. Ahjvar shook his head and stepped out of Meli's line of sight as she surged up and floundered off, heading, in a dodging, uncertain way, for the brook. Ghu dropped her blade at the foot of the tree.

"Tidy," Yeh-Lin said, and rubbed her hands in the moss as if to clean them. "Well, now, it is getting dark, but I don't think we want to camp here, do we?"

"No. The highway." Ghu slung Ahjvar's pack to him. "We go towards the town, for now."

They came out of the forest into a landscape of more tended woods, open and barrenly rocky between coppiced stands of charcoal works and the high lord's timber lands, and then the land dropped away from the plateau in a crumbling escarpment, down into terraced fields and orchards standing leafless, limbless. Ahjvar had thought at first it was only spring pruning, trees pollarded for some farmer's purpose he didn't know, until the wind brought the lingering scent of old burning that even rain could not dispel. Skeletons of hacked and fire-ravaged fruit-trees, acre after acre. Wanton destruction. Malice. The moon, just waning from its third quarter, was rising, and the stone-paved highway gleamed like pale water. The roadside clay was churned to muck by the passage of feet and hooves, bridges thrown down and replaced with rough work of newly felled timbers. The winter-flattened weeds of the ditches were trampled and torn to a morass. Beyond the road, easterly and south, the land was flat, flooded fields reflecting moonlight. A stretch of the river lay in that distance, marked by a line of trees rising from the water, a darkness against the gleam and the stars. Walking up the road they passed one village of a couple of dozen close-huddled huts on the edge of the river's broad interval just above the flooding, sleeping and lightless, another that was nothing but scattered stone and burnt posts, and on a small hill like an island east of it, the raw remains of a wooden stockade and the buildings it had enclosed, a fortified manor house, some vassal of the Daro lord. Taza, Ghu said, where the runaway serfs in the forest had come from. There had been graves, as well, hasty and too shallow, not single graves but pits and trenches of them, wet earth clumped and hummocked, and the furtive scurryings of scavenging rats that the dogs took off chasing, until Ghu called them back.

The smell of rotting flesh. Creatures larger than rats had been unearthing the dead. More than once they came on a disarticulated long bone dragged away and gnawed not quite clean enough. The empress's general may have taken Dernang, but there had been hard fighting before he ever came to its walls.

Deep night when they saw the walls of Dernang looming before them, with the mountains dark beyond to the north. With those walls a blackness like the mountains against the night sky, the faint tang of death grew heavy and foul. Not ruined trees, these rising poles that flanked the highway on either side. Stakes. Heads.

"We need to get off the road," Ahjvar pointed out, but he didn't much like the open fields either. "You said we weren't going into the town. What are we doing here?"

"Looking," Ghu said, his voice faint.

"Why?" Yeh-Lin demanded.

He didn't answer.

They were all inhuman in the night, set just high enough to look down on even a rider. Shapes only, and stench, mostly from the scatter of leavings dropped by crows about the skulls, rotting and half bared. Ghu found one worth looking at. Featureless, not just because of the night. Hair lifted and stirred in a rising wind.

"You know him?" He didn't see how anyone could.

"Her," Ghu said distantly. "Sujin. From the stables. Why Meli and not her, to survive? But I thought she'd be here, if Lord Sia was." It was that soft, distant, soul-wandering voice that always chilled Ahjvar.

"A friend?"

Ghu only shrugged.

"There are torches burning at the gate," Yeh-Lin observed. "Presumably there are guards. Shall we perhaps not stand here talking?"

"I need to see Lord Sia."

"Why?"

"To know he's here."

"Does it matter?" Yeh-Lin asked.

"To know what Meli said is truth—yes, it matters," Ghu said wearily. "We need them."

"Who?" Ahjvar demanded, as Ghu, both dogs sticking close and subdued, tails low, walked on.

"Choa. We need Choa Province. We need this rebel prince, maybe, if he's still alive and free, if he will serve the gods. We need the Daros."

With Daro Clan burned into his shoulder, as one might notch a sheep's ear?

"*No*," Ahjvar said.

"If Sia is dead, we need the Kho'anzi."

"I'll kill him for you. Both of them, if the young one isn't dead already."

"No, Ahj."

"We were going to the mountain to find your gods."

"This, first."

"What," Yeh-Lin asked, "do we need Choa Province *for?* It's hardly a good base, and poor besides. Barely grows enough grain to feed itself."

Better to ask, who is *we?* was Ahjvar's thought. Ghu had found another head worth standing before.

This one . . . the soul was gone, though they may not have intended that. He had heard of chaining a ghost into the world as some ancient punishment long ago, in Nabban or Pirakul, he didn't remember which. A necromancer's blasphemy made perverted justice. He hadn't thought it was literal, but this was a higher post with a crossbar below the smashed skull—even in the night the misshaping of some great blow was plain—and body parts wrapped in chains swinging from it. Yeh-Lin gagged and wrapped her scarf over her face.

"This one, they hated," she observed. "Prince Dan? Lord Daro Sia?"

"Could be anyone," Ahjvar muttered, but he didn't believe it.

"Sia," Ghu said. He knelt down with a hand splayed against the mud of the roadside, head bowed. Not grief. Thinking. Or listening.

Abruptly, Ghu surged to his feet again. "The castle, Ahj. Come."

"*Why?*"

"Need to talk to someone," Ghu said.

"It's held by the general who did this. You can't—"

"Now, while we still have the dark."

A mist was rising from the chill ditches, tendrils of fog snaking over the terraces, wrapping their legs, clasping like white arms across the road.

"We are three—" But Ghu, the dogs at his heels, was already lost in the dark fields and the rising blindness of the fog.

"Well," said Yeh-Lin.

Ahjvar's hands were fisted. Nothing to hit.

"If we don't follow, will he turn back?" Yeh-Lin asked.

He spun on her, didn't raise his hand, but she froze where she was. "Do I put faith in him, or not?"

"The boy is hardly infallible."

Ahjvar turned away again and leapt the ditch, catching up with Ghu in a few long strides.

The fog rose to engulf them like an incoming tide.

CHAPTER XIX

The storm had been brewing for three days; first a heavy, wet wind from the south, then growing stronger, setting in from the east, summer-hot, and the high clouds streaked in a way that made men and women of the coastal tribes uneasy.

The folk of the Golden City, too, had a hard time keeping their minds to what they did. They were not comfortable in the new-built Council House anyway, though most of them hid it well. These were not courtiers, but great merchants and masters of merchant fleets, which meant they knew to bend with the wind, and if that meant they must walk past the polished skulls of the lords of their land and sit on woven grass mats on the earth to drink tea with women they thought cannibals, they would.

It was that or face the fact that though the Wild Girls had no fleet, they did have the coast. The Golden City might bring its rice from Nan-Ya, but a city could not live on rice alone, and the Imperial Demesne, smallest of the provinces of the empire, had been its market-garden.

And with Taiji under the rule of the queens and the Kho'anzi of Lower Lat having sworn oaths as their vassal and taken the title of prince under them . . . the city must feel very much besieged, ships or no ships.

Further . . . there were ships in the small ports of Taiji. There were crews who were as much Lathan and Darrian as Nabbani.

All in all, better to avert one's eyes from the skulls and drink the Wild Girls' tea.

Kaeo sat at Rat's left hand. He felt a stranger to himself, wearing a coat stitched with plates of hardened leather, sword at his shoulder, jade bead pendant at his throat. Some honour, that meant. Rat's gift, setting him apart from the ambassador from the Kho'anzi of Lower Lat and his retinue. Making it clear, to them and to her sisters, that he was not to be counted among the Nabbani, whatever language he spoke or did not speak. His face was not painted as those of the Dar-Lathans were, but he was marked in a fashion neither Nabbani nor Lathan, as though he were some barbarian come with the caravans from the west. At least the representatives of the Golden City couldn't see it. Toba and Rat had done it in the first days he had been among them, pricking out what would be a tiger in red and black. It crouched snarling and spread defiant, defensive claws on his left breast. The sign the empress's woman had put there was completely obscured, worked into it and remade, lost in stripes and bunched tiger-muscle and fang.

"Better," Rat had said. "Safer. There's some power I don't understand in that mark and we've changed it. Did you know a tiger was the physical form of the Little Sister most often, when she went among the Lathan-folk, at least?"

A tigress, then. That rather pleased him, despite not feeling it was quite a part of him. But neither had the empress's mark been.

Maybe when it healed. His chest was scabbed and itching. He knew how to shut mere physical discomfort from his mind, at least. This was only another mask, another part to perform.

Jian herself dragged him up every morning to practise with the sword. The part was fast becoming his reality.

The Wild Sisters—specifically Nawa—argued now that there must be a council of the city representing all its districts and guilds and classes of folk, to speak for it to the queens, since it had no sensible division into families and roundhouses. The self-appointed lords of the city said that a freeport acknowledged no lords and that they made a treaty, not an offer of submission.

Jian said, the queens intended to offer the city to Prince Dan in return for acknowledgement of their borders and they could damn well do as they liked till he sorted them out, but she said it in smiling Lathan and it was only Rat whispering translation in Kaeo's ear that told him what was said.

"The slaves will be free," she said, breath tickling. "Whatever's decided today, in the end, your prince and your god will have the city." But then she frowned, and looked at him, sitting back.

"No," she said aloud. "Kaeo—I don't see it, I don't see the city free—come outside."

Sharp speech from Nawa. Jian set her hand to her sword.

"What does the elder queen say?" asked a stout, white-haired woman, an importer of Gold Harbour wines. They had no translator but Rat. They had brought one, but he had been left outside, and the ambassador of the new prince of Lower Lat was not admitting his fluency to the folk of the city, though he had not looked best pleased at Jian's asides.

Kaeo rose obediently. He bowed politely to the other two queens, the ambassador, the representatives of the city, and walked around the outside of the circle. Rat caught his arm at the door, dragged him into a jogging trot. Toba came long-legged after them, demanding to know what was happening.

He was beginning to catch the Lathan words, to hear the echoes in them of their kinship with Nabbani.

"Storm," said Rat.

"We're well above even the spring tide line," Kaeo said. "It's too early in the season for a typhoon."

"Is it? But the Daughter of the Old Great Gods has left the city to us, for all she burned her palace. Do you think she's the sort to let others hold her cast-offs? I said it was a trap."

A trap, the abandoned and burning palace. They had looted what was left from the free-standing towers and villas, after the ruins of the main building began to cool. Much left. Much taken. If it was a gesture of defiance, it had only served to hearten them. Jian had been all for shifting their camp to the palace island. Symbolic.

Trap, Rat had said, though Toba and the other wizards of their following found no evidence of any spells set against them. When Rat spoke so, the other two ceased whatever protest they were making. Priestess, of a sort.

Outside the camp and along the crest of the Beacon Hills, to where view of the lagoon and the sea beyond was unobscured by the palace island. Voices behind. Kaeo glanced back. The whole of the gathering in the Council House was following, led by Nawa and Jian, the city merchants looking more apprehensive than ever. High view of the lagoon, here, the city beyond, and the breakwater. Waves smashed against it, black and white and high. Waves dashed themselves against the city, too, over breakwaters there. He could see some boats leaving the mouths of the canals, heading over the lagoon towards the barren shore or the second lagoon created by the dykes of the marsh, or for the Gentle Sister's mouth.

"That," said the wine-merchant, her not-quite-court-accent dropping from her, "has come up a lot since the morning." She sounded now what she probably was, a ship-captain climbed to higher rank through marriage.

Nearly noon, but the day was dark, the sky to the southeast almost black. A greyness on the water, out to sea.

"Rat . . ." Kaeo said.

Sweating. He wasn't used to wearing armour made of anything but paper. The air was hot and heavy as late summer. He glanced at the city folk, but it didn't matter what they thought now, or who they thought him. There was at least one woman there he did know . . . rather better than he would want Rat to know about. A dealer in exotic weaves and spices from Pirakul, mostly, and a connoisseur of poetry of the unfashionable heroic mode, which he rather liked himself. She was carefully not catching his eye.

Listeners far too close. He whispered. "The palace will burn, I said, and it did. The palace will drown. I said that, too. Didn't I say it?" He could not remember.

"You said a lot when they drugged you," she said, head close to his.

"Yes." And some of it had been his own anger finding a way out to spite the empress, if he could not hurt her. But it was loud in his ears. "The palace will drown."

"Trap," Nawa said. "My sister Anlau saw it and said so, when Buri-Nai fled. It was a trap. Dwei Kaeo, blessed by your gods, has said it. The palace will drown, and your Daughter of the Old Great Gods intended that we drown with it, lured to shift our camp to the palace hill, as if we needed to demonstrate our hold of the coast by squatting on her leavings."

"We need to evacuate the city," the wine-merchant said. "And the harbour—my ships—three in port and it's already too late to get them out to sea and run out of its path."

"Can the city stand such a storm?" Jian asked. She was looking at Kaeo, as if his opinion mattered more than what the great folk might say.

"It did last time," Kaeo said. "That was when the typhoon came on the day of the Harvest Festival, the year they celebrated Yao's fortieth year of rule. It stood, but—the canals were choked with bodies, after, like—like weed washed in." An image that he thought he had put from his mind.

More boats on the water. Some in the city were deciding to risk cannibal tribesmen rather than face the certainty of the storm.

"The Golden City has faced storms every year since its founding," another merchant-lord said. "There's no reason to panic like children who've never heard—"

Lighting flared along the horizon, a fire high in the clouds. No sound of the thunder reached them. The sky was black and purple-grey as bruising, and down among the bushes on the lower hillside the birds were singing songs of dusk.

"I," said the wine-merchant, "am bringing my people to the mainland. Honoured queens, I beg we adjourn this council until another time."

Rat had been standing with her eyes shut, face tilted to the sky. Now she looked around at them all.

"Go," she said. "Don't bring only your own people. Tell them on the canals and in the markets, in every quarter and on every island, this will be no storm like any that has struck the city before. This is the work of the one you've called the Daughter of the Old Great Gods. This is a weapon, aimed at us by the evil of your empress, without regard for what other lives it destroys. She's safe away. Did she give you any warning to follow? She did not. We do, Dwei Kaeo the prophet of your true god does. Bring the folk to the hills inland, so swiftly as you can. All your folk," she added, with a glance at Kaeo. "The canal-side traders, the shopkeepers, the boatmen, the slaves, the beggars. All folk of all rank, if ever you hope to face your god or your road to the Gods with a clean heart. So many of the folk as you can. You have ships. Fill them, run them ashore on the mudflats if you must. The prophet of the god of Nabban, your god, the heir of the Mother and Father, has warned of it, and we did not understand. The palace will drown. The city will drown. There is nothing we can do now but save what we can and spite our enemy so. Go!"

"Yes," Nawa said, and began issuing orders to her own people.

Kaeo stayed where he was, as Rat did, when even Toba went back to the camp. They were tearing down the shelters, when he looked. Better to endure the rain and the wind than to lose tents and the reed-bundle huts and have no roof to put up again when all was over.

"What are you watching for?" he asked, after a while. The boats of the merchants had fought their way across the lagoon to the city, and it was truly a fight, the oarsmen straining against the wind and waves. Boats were leaving the city. One canoe went down into the trough of a wave and never came up. They had left it too late, and so many vessels were meant only for the canals.

"She's going to kill her own folk to strike at us," Rat said.

"She's mad. She thinks she's become a goddess."

"But she isn't mad. She truly believes it, because she's been told it, and had it proven to her, the way all her path is cleared by miracle—the powers she commands, or thinks she commands."

"Who's told her?" Kaeo asked.

"Something next to her heart." Rat looked at him, her smile a little crooked. "She rather liked you, I think. You should have tried compliments instead of cursing her. You might have got to find out what she wears there. I never did, for all I was slave of her chamber."

He rubbed at the tattoo. Rat squatted down on her heels. "Stay with me here? I don't know what I can do. I'm only the priestess of the memory of a goddess, and a faint hope of . . . growing into something more. But what I can do, I need to."

He nodded. Stood like a guard over her, because he did not know what else to do. Toba came back to them, to wordlessly offer the little bag of his grandmother's finger-bones. Rat nodded and laid them out in a semicircle before them, as if she set a wall. Toba clapped a hand to Kaeo's shoulder that seemed to be some approval and went back to the other queens.

Ships, flying wild before the wind, only the least of sails set. They really did careen themselves in the mudflats beyond the dykes, and there were people struggling to drag canoes and small boats to take the folk over the marshes. Dar-Lathans were down there with the outriggers they had taken from conquered villages, and riverboats. Smaller boats still came from the city, too. He watched another swamped, the folk disappearing, the waves too great to be conquered by even the strongest swimmer. Another. Rat stood. There was a grey wall over the ocean now. A dark and straggling line of folk winding up the lower hills northward of their camp. So many carried bundles, dragged possessions—what space in those ships was given up to hasty grasping after things that the gods would not judge in the balance against even a slave's life as having the weight of a feather?

Up the rising hump of the hill, the banners of the camp were snapping and streaming inland. Thatch was tearing off the Council House.

"I was going to say, we should leave in a day or so," Rat said, conversational. "We can't delay any longer, or we'll never come to your god before the empress does. She can move swiftly by water, at least, and we'll be walking. Horses would draw too much attention, more than I could shift away."

"I can't ride, anyhow."

"You'd learn. You wouldn't enjoy it."

They were shouting into the wind. Leaning into it. The first drops of rain struck, hot and fat and hard as hail, and in the space of a few breaths they were drenched, blinded. Thunder rolled above them, and the sky over the lagoon was lit a strange pinkish white, like lightning high in the clouds at night. The city vanished in the rain as if eaten by mist, and then even the palace hill, so heavy the storm. They crouched together, holding to each other as if the wind might blow either away, alone. Impossible to see much farther than the reach of his hand. The water drowned his eyes, stinging, poured down his neck, down his spine, into his boots. Rat groped for the bones, sitting up on her knees. Touched each in turn, singing something. A prayer, he thought. He heard a few words he almost understood. *Sister* and *tiger* and *safe*.

The wind knocked her backwards.

He caught her arm and pulled her down beside him, both of them lying on their bellies, the rain pounding them into the earth.

"Pray," she said, or he thought she did. There was a light on the bones before her, as if moonlight lay in them, escaping slowly. She drew breath and sang again.

He did pray, uncertainly. Wondering, did he betray his gods, if with Rat he prayed to some memory of the Little Sister's tiger-goddess. It was a tiger that filled his mind, a tigress, red-gold and fierce, and the itching of his chest was soothed by the soaking he was getting. Warm, though, the tattoo. As if he took a fever in it, but it was not a bad feeling. He put a fingertip, hesitantly, on one of the bones. Rat had taken one up in her hand, sang whatever her words were, a pattern of twenty lines or so, he thought, with it cradled almost to her mouth.

"We ask the memory of our foremothers and forefathers to strength us," she broke off to shout at him. "They're gone to the Old Great Gods but there's memory of them in their bones, memory going back to the days of the goddess, and memory of all our own living gods and goddesses."

The finger-bone was smooth and warm and the light felt almost like a human touch. He matched his voice to Rat's and sang, not a prayer, but a deeper undercurrent to hers, making a wordless music. An offering. To what god, he could not have said. Mostly it was the warmth of the tigress tattoo and of Rat lying against his side, warm even with their armoured coats between them, that shaped his music, not the thought of the dying Father or Mother, or their promised heir. He could hardly hear Rat, to follow and wrap around her voice. The wind screamed, roared. Thunder crashed, and waves, and things snapped and cracked and boomed. Trees, buildings, the end of what was left of the palace and of the palace gardens. The end of the ships run onto the mud. How many had come ashore, of all those in the city? Best not to think of it. Shut it from his mind, let the music carry him in Rat's footsteps, whatever it was she did.

She fell silent, eventually, and he did, throat raw, rain in the mouth a blessing to be swallowed. Their hands were clasped together over the bone and the rain drummed hard. The wind would seem briefly to weaken, and then roar again with renewed strength. Dark shapes moved, new leaves, birds, who knew what hurled inland. When finally it did begin to die, Kaeo could not trust he did not imagine it. The darkness did not lift. The air was colder, though. He dared to lift his head. Softer rain, and icy. He could see—not much. Night had come on them. Rat whispered something, and spread light above an opened hand, but when she unclasped the other from his, the bone they had held together was only a little white dust. She touched it to her lips, then to his, then wiped it away. Tried to take up the rest of the bones and found them gone, a little white graininess in the mud.

She shivered. "Toba's grandmother," she said. "Did you feel her memory with us?"

He shook his head. "I don't understand these things." The warmth of the tigress tattoo was gone, though. So was the lingering soreness, and the itch of it. "Why say you're not a wizard?"

"Powers lent me," she said wearily. Her teeth chattered. The pale light smearing her other hand faded and died. "That's all. I don't think it was enough. This is Nabban, not the shores of the Little Sister, and your god is not even—a god, yet."

She picked herself up. The wind was blowing from the north, where a few stars showed.

They went to find what was left of the camp.

The palisade still stood, and the Council House, mostly roofless, but filled with elderly Nabbani, small children, babies. Little else. Fires were already being built—a good thought, whoever had ensured some fuel was kept dry. People everywhere, and all down the sheltered side of the Beacon Hills, where the wind had been a little less.

No food, no tea. Fire was enough. Someone made a place for them closest to the warmth and they sat shoulder to shoulder. Rat fell asleep against him, which was—awkward, when Jian came searching for the youngest queen, to find him with his arm about her. She said nothing, though, except, "Nawa says, come and see."

Dawn. He shook Rat awake and they went out into the open again.

The marshes were flooded deep, and the waves still rolled high, spitting over the dykes. The palace hill looked as though it had been struck by a thousand hammers, trees splintered, smashed, buildings that been spared the fire gone as if they had never been, or lying in shattered heaps.

"Plenty to burn," Jian said. "Plenty to build with, too."

"Look further," Nawa told them.

He did. Found he was holding Rat's hand.

"Yes," said Jian, to something in his face.

The Golden City was—gone.

Waves churned rough and white. Sandbars, ancient pilings of massive logs, stone-paved plazas, and canal-side streets, there. Buildings—a few. Broken things, sagging, leaning. A scum of flotsam heaved with the waves, made rafts that drifted on the surface of the lagoon. Mia. Shouja Wey. The Flowering Orange, the masks, the scrolls of the plays.

Yeh-Lin's ghost-haunted and long-deserted palace loomed over all, roofless now, but still standing.

He had not thought wind and wave could do so much.

"We were spared," Nawa said. "The full force of the wind was weakened as it came over the hill, a little. Our walls and fences still stand, and they were better shelter than none. The Little Sister is with us."

A wall of finger-bones, a memory holding out its hands, to guard them. A tiger, crouched defiant, snarling into the wind.

He looked at Rat.

"No," she said. "It was only the last memory of Toba's grandmother. The last strength in her bones. We have nothing to set against the power the empress holds, whatever it is and however she came by it. We need alliance with the god of Nabban. We'll go to him, Kaeo and I. Kaeo is his prophet. I—go only as the youngest of the queens, I think. Find us food, if there is any. We'll leave today."

Neither Nawa nor Jian made any protest this time.

CHAPTER XX

The Daro castle, called the White River Dragon for an old, old tale of its founding, sat to the northeast of the town, separated from it by a broad moat. The spring flooding often reached so far, lapping at the town's eastern flank, mingling with the waters of the moat, but Dernang was on a low mound and the castle itself on a higher, safely above the waters in most years. The castle's main gate faced the town, with a bridge between, but its second gate looked east and flung out a raised roadway towards the river. Ghu did not want to keep too close under the city walls, so he led them out into the fields, heading cross-country to circle to the river road, across wet fields that sank into ankle-deep water. The ditches became drowningly treacherous, marked only by lines of cattail and reed. Ghu and Ahjvar went barefoot; there was water even over the road, and boots meant for the winter desert were no use for wading. The cold numbed Ghu's feet. These were the waters of the Wild Sister, Mother Nabban's own river, whose three main sources converged two and three hundred miles south of here, carrying the waters of the mountains that bordered Choa and Alwu over shallow, stony beds. Spring melt, always, and sometimes the autumn rains in the mountains, swelled her waters to push over the land, a shallow lake drowning thin clay and the beds of ancient stone beneath. He felt her in the water, felt him in the stone, the Mother, the Father, like a slow,

slow breathing, a tide in his blood, rising. The river's tree-lined banks were only a weight in his mind, lost now in the night. The bridges over the small streams that fed her rose humped and forlorn, like the hulls of overturned boats, from the lake she was becoming, and then even they faded, as the fog thickened and they moved blind in darkness that felt muffling, no reflection of moonlight on water to guide them. The drowned lanes he followed through the fields were only memory to his feet. In the fog, he could fade to nothing himself, to memory, instinct, with only the shuffling splash of Ahjvar and Yeh-Lin, the more rapid spatter of the dogs, to anchor him.

Something brushed over him like a trailing cobweb, an insect on the skin. Something drawn by the fog, wondering at it. An awareness, searching.

He held himself very still, very small, as he had when the eyes of the Lady passed over him in Marakand. There was nothing. Only fog, cold air and day-warmed water, damp fields breathing. Fog was common to the season, fog was blinding, muffling, a blanket in the dark.

The touch faded, distant as a dream and he slid down again into his own place, the night and the fog. Found the pattern . . . became a part of it.

The Mother stirred uneasily, like a sleeper disturbed, but she did not reach to touch him as the gods had when he crossed the border. Already, she was less than she had been, even then.

No matter, in this moment. What might be, what must be—what could, what should be if only he could move the world about him as he needed—hovered. No words. Pattern, yes, a juggler's wild spinning of pieces, a weaver's threads flung all in the air but he could seize and move and bind and shape if only he kept all moving to his hand.

No words. Easier to have no words, to let them go. Ahjvar grew angry when he forgot to speak, when he let the words go because they were too thin and yet too complicated and cumbersome a thing to hold in mind. No words in the fog, in the night, only the flying threads, the pieces of a shattered shape all tumbling through the air, falling, and *this* one, *now*, to save, others to lock into it, others it would draw, and hold in strength, to build . . .

Ahj was angry now. Not for silence. For this place, for the old lord, for Meli. Ghu was not sorry it was so. It warmed him, oddly, and awed him. There had been no one to be angry for him, for them all, when he was a child.

He climbed the bank to the raised road and broke into a jogging trot. The way beneath him was his, and the night, and the fog. When the castle loomed, an artificial island the size of a Praitannec village, it was as though it was a mere slow thickening of the fog. Stone walls and whitewashed towers, low spreading roofs upon roofs, only a faint solidity. The moat was lost in the still floodwaters, but the shallow fishback arch of the bridge showed where its depths lay. The eastern gatehouse rose dark over them, wings of the roof held out like a swooping bat.

Too cold for swimming. He waited for the other two to come up beside him.

"Take my pack. I'm going around to the postern. There's a boat there. Keep well back and follow along on the shore. Don't splash. Don't fall in."

"I could open those for you," Yeh-Lin whispered against him.

"No." It must not be her doing, not Dotemon's, to be the first assertion of—of what he would claim. He knew that, felt it in the marrow, and the riverwater that for this moment seemed to flow in his veins.

But he did not want to pass over this threshold. He did not want to be again within these massive walls. He had not wanted to bring Ahjvar to this place. Deep in his chest there was a slow-smouldering anger that had never died, all his life. He had taken it in with his mother's blood, been nourished on it within her womb. The lord, the castle, all Nabban . . . he did not know which it was for. Pity, mercy . . . they were what he needed. He had found them for Meli. The Kho'anzi Daro Korat had been a fair master, on the rare occasions when he had had to do with such as Ghu—small things, the least of things, within the great compass of his lordship. He had had far worse treatment from fellow slaves and from folk in other lands who would call slavery a sin against their gods. But something burned. He did not want Ahjvar, who would have killed that spiteful, stupid, pitiable fool Meli for striking him, to know of it, to unleash on the folk of this place the rage that burned undying in Ghu himself. Nor to be by him here, where he had been owned and despised and beaten and of no worth. It sickened him to stand here.

Ghu took a breath, and crossed the bridge before there could be any further debate, most of all with himself. Torches burned there to show up any approach but the fog swallowed them, muffled their light. He passed under the blackness of the outflung eaves of the gatehouse; wings, but not for his sheltering. The outermost gate was a grille of age-dark cypress, bronze-studded. He set a hand to it. The river's breath wrapped him. He could bring it down, the gate, the whole weighty stone strength of this tower. In this moment . . . he turned away, to move a little longer in quietness, like the river's rising in this broad vale.

The angle of the high scarp where the moat rose to meet the curtain wall was steep, faced in smooth stone. Just around the next bend to the north there was a postern gate and no bridge, only a boat, usually, moored to a ring in the wall. There were carp stocked in the moat once the floods subsided, harvested for the family's dinner. Slaves of the outer services, stables and gardens, weaving-sheds and workshops, potters, carpenters, smiths, masons, tile-setters and all, had poached them when they could. He remembered that, now. Much he had put from his mind and pretended it was forever. Steeper than he remembered, this scarp, almost vertical, a great cliff, but he had been smaller last time he clambered along it. He splayed himself flat, toes and fingers seeking the joins in the stone. If he slipped, it would be a splash too great to be dismissed as a leaping fish or disturbed duck. If he slipped, better to have swum after all. He remembered the water, deep but swampy, stinking—it would be fresher now in the floods, if colder. He'd been thrown in more times than he wanted to remember.

Too much he did not want to remember. But he remembered everything, everything since the river. His mother drowned him . . .

Foot slithered. He clung by fingers alone a moment, till toes found a hold. Crawled up and went on. Finally, the first of the many rounded corners, but the only one he needed to pass. There, the jutting darkness of the postern gate, a stone porch, and the punt where it had always been, as if he had never gone. It dipped and bobbed as he used it to scramble around to the little landing-stage, still an inch above the waters. No torches here to gild the fog, which had thickened as he worked along the scarp, until he could see neither the far side of the moat nor the moving shadows of Ahjvar and Yeh-Lin. He leaned against the door and closed his eyes, fingers spread on the wood. Let himself go again, into cold, into night, into biting frost and the death of the year, when even mountain oaks might crack and stone split, hillsides sheer away . . .

Iron bolts, top and bottom, secured the door. Wood cracked. Stone split, a snap like breaking ice. Loud, but there was no other sound within. Ghu leaned, gently. The door moved.

Not, Ahjvar would say, subtle. But it was done.

He left it to cast off the punt, sculling over the stern. The oar creaked on its pin. Too loud. Ahjvar caught the blunt prow and steadied it as Yeh-Lin and the dogs leapt in, followed them, pushing off from the drowned and stony shore, leaning up to his elbows in the water.

Ghu sensed, rather than saw, Yeh-Lin's movement to speak and touched her hand to silence her. Once inside, he picked up the bolts, fallen with splintered wood and flaked stone, staples and nails and all. They were still white with frost, but warmed to his hand. He closed the door behind them, cutting off the fog that reached to follow, and fitted the broken ironwork back in place. Even by day the passage was dark. It would fool the eye until someone tried to draw the bolt. Time enough.

The passage was narrower, lower, than he remembered. A sharp bend, a grille suspended above, meant to be dropped to trap an enemy, and gaps in the ceiling through which to finish the work. Mostly, in the peaceful years he had known, it had been a passageway to the punt and the fish for the kitchen staff. There were two men in the chamber above, asleep. He wondered if they were meant to be, and wished them to stay so. Through the thickness of the wall to a covered passage and out into a cobbled yard. The fog pooled there, wrapped him as if in welcome, followed him.

The castle was a maze of interconnected baileys, buildings, towers, lanes, and narrow passages on many levels. The main keep was a serene and lofty island floating amid gardens at the centre of it all, stronghold without, palace within. Neither slave nor free servant of the outer castle crossed those gardens on the green moss of the lawns or the white-gravelled paths unsummoned. Ghu was not sure he would even know the way, but the keep wasn't his aim—not yet. He threaded a path between walls, through gates, across cobbled yards and hard-packed earth, along narrow alleys, up and down steep, shallow steps and around broken-backed turns, making for the stables near the western gate, but taking a shortcut he would not have dared as a boy, along the bamboo-laid pathway from the house-slaves' quarters. Burnt ruin of a weaving-shed. Burnt ruin of the soldiers' kitchens. The potters' building with its doors smashed in. Gates into yards wrenched off their hinges. Truly a village, this, but one made to be a maze as well. Dawn could not be far distant. Past the household troop's barracks, its doors hacked open, a reed screen hung to keep out drafts. No one kept a watch there, though many slept within. The stable complex, beyond an intact granary, was familiar. Strong scent of horse. He crossed the square of it to the western stable block, with its grand entry porch and low square tower over it. Sacked, Meli had claimed, but the damage could have been far worse. The general would have wanted the castle whole and fit to live in. A watchdog stirred and came to him, nosing at his hand. Not one he knew—he had been gone almost a dog's lifetime—but it did not growl even at Jui and Jiot.

Here, he risked a whisper, a few words, sending Ahjvar and Yeh-Lin to wait, with the dogs, in a corner behind a stack of straw. Ahjvar stood a moment, but then followed Yeh-Lin in silence.

Through the door. Not a homecoming, no. He had a strong impression of the ruined broch on the cliff with the unending sound of the sea below, smoky, salt air, the shaft of light where their attempt at a turf roof had fallen in. A deep and painful yearning to be back there, not here, not in this place again, whelmed up in him, choking, but horses stirred, and horses were welcoming. He quietened them, not even a word, urged the boys asleep in the far corner room with the lord's most expensive harness to sink deeper in their dreams, and took the stairs to the tower room.

The door opened silently when he lifted the latch. Much as he remembered, smell of horses and oiled leather. He found his way to the side of the bed, a pallet on the floor, without tripping on anything. The room seemed smaller than he remembered, only a few paces to cross. He crouched just out of reach. The shutters of the windows were closed against the night. It was some sense other than vision that assured him this was Horsemaster Yuro. Fortunate he was here, and not over the river with the foaling mares. In a nest of blankets in the far corner, like a dog's bed, a child curled sleeping. Ill, Ghu thought. Usually the ill of the stables were handed over to Baril, who oversaw the eastern stable wing and the girls and womenfolk of the horses, especially if they were female, as this child was. Baril was the one who made the salves and the potions for drenching. Fever on the child. Her dreams were formless, fearful, dark things, hard to grasp.

"Master Yuro?"

The man stirred.

"Master Yuro! Wake up."

He woke with a groan and a snort and a mumbled, "What is it? Ghu . . .?"

Eight, nine years it must be at the least since he had gone off down the river—time was a bit vague before he came to Gold Harbour, and he had been a boy then. The man couldn't know his voice.

"Ghu," he confirmed. "Master Yuro—"

"What?" More alert now. "Is that—? No . . . Who?"

"It's Ghu." The room was cold, no embers in the brazier, nothing at which to light a candle. He rose and opened the shutters. From here the fog was a sea of white, hugging the ground, but the sky was clear and there was enough light to make out shapes; the moon would not set until after sunrise. Yuro folded a gown around himself. "Oh, Sen. What is it?"

"No, it's Ghu, Master Yuro," he said patiently, and stood still while the man trod close and peered into his face.

"Ghu? No." Hesitantly, "I was dreaming of Ghu. Come back drowned out of the river looking for that damned white colt."

"Yes." Words fled him, but Yuro thought he still dreamed. He must speak. "Not dreaming, Master Yuro. The gods' truth, I'm Ghu. I've been in the west."

"Ghu. Ghu! You damnable *fool*, what did you want to come back for?"

Ghu turned aside from the swinging arm and hooked the man's feet out from under him, reflex more than anything, as the failed slap had been. Yuro lurched up and flung a punch, not now the mere back-handed cuff that had driven so many words home when he thought a boy wasn't listening. Ghu knocked him flat on his back, standing off warily as the man gasped for breath. The dog down with the horses barked once at the thump, which would likely wake someone, but if nothing else followed they wouldn't bother crawling out of warm blankets . . . No one called out, not even Ahjvar.

Yuro sat up, didn't move to come after him again, so Ghu offered his hand and Yuro did take it to help himself up. Ghu gripped his wrist and jerked him close. "Don't hit me. Ever. I have a friend down below will kill you for it." His own anger surprised him. Yuro had never had too heavy a hand, compared to some.

The horsemaster stood frozen, till Ghu let him go. He moved away, rubbing his wrist. "You're not Ghu. The boy's long dead."

"I am. Truly."

Master Yuro groped on a shelf, seeking flint and steel, from the sound. Eventually he struck a spark into a dish of tinder and lit a tallow candle at it. The yellow light showed his hair grey-streaked, which it had not been, his broad weathered face more lined than formerly. He brought the candle too close to Ghu's face, peering at him, only half a head taller now.

"You look like him. Maybe. Grown up."

"It's been a long time. If you didn't think it was me, why hit me?"

"I thought I was dreaming."

He could hear Ahjvar's acidic comment on that. Even in their dreams, people hit him.

"You shouldn't have come here. They'll burn your face for you." A glance at the heap in the corner. "At best. They've killed her, I think."

"Who is she?"

"Doesn't matter. Let her sleep. Maybe she won't wake ever. What in the cold hells did you come back for, if you actually survived to get away? I figured you were in a ditch with your throat cut years ago."

"I needed to come back."

"I used to dream you were drowned. I don't know why. It was the snow nearly took you."

"But I was drowned."

"That. No, you weren't. You were alive and wailing when Gomul fished you out."

"I know, I remember. But I was drowned, regardless."

"You don't remember; you were a newborn babe."

"I do." Smell of mud and water and crushed green reeds. Cold water that wasn't cold, that carried him . . . The boy whose hands felt so hot they burned, though it was only that he was cold as the water himself, when they plucked him up, thumping his back, and words . . . no meaning in the words then. It was a long time before words had meaning. The world had been such a vast and overwhelming thing . . .

That Dar-Lathan girl, the one they had to keep in chains . . .

They spread them around the imperial manors, after the last battle of the war. Never too many. Gave them to the lords. They didn't make good slaves, the warriors of Dar-Lathi. A lot of them died, one way and another.

She got the baby on the long march north . . .

Wouldn't give suck to the infant . . . They kept her chained to stop her killing it. To stop her running.

The lord didn't know they'd chained her. He wouldn't have stood for that. Old Duri's orders . . .

Worked the staple out of the wall and walked into the river in her chains, with the baby . . .

It was Gomul who named him, and the stable-folk used to hold him to suckle among a litter of puppies until the scandalized and furious house-master Duri found out about it and, since the Kho'anzi forbade that he be thrown back to the river, which Duri at first ordered, made one of the under-cooks his wet-nurse. Gomul was dead of a bad fall by the time Ghu was sent back to the stables, four years old, maybe, or five, not old enough to be any use among the horses but judged too slow of mind for the kitchens, and mute besides.

He remembered the smell of the kitchens. Disorder wild like a storm. Incomprehensible noise. Heat and shouting and the kitchen-master who struck out with an iron ladle at any failing or slowness. The stables were better.

He took the candle from an unresisting hand, stuck it back in the horn-paned lantern on the shelf. "Sit down, Master Yuro." But it was the polite honorific of the road he gave him, not the Imperial word for one's owner or a higher ranking servant of the house. Slightest of differences in sound, a world of meaning. Yuro raised his eyebrows at it, hand folded across a probably-sore midriff. Ahj didn't always hear that difference when he snarled about it.

"Where do they have Lord Daro Korat? I need to find him."

"Old Great Gods have mercy, do you not know what's been happening here?"

"Don't shout. Yes, I do. I need to get the Kho'anzi away. I need his name, to take this province."

"*Need?*" Yuro, who had not sat, took a step back. "The province? Do you know what you're saying?" A frown. "You never used to put enough words together to make sense."

"I've had to learn. My friend growls at me when I don't."

"You're not the boy. You look like him, maybe. If he went north. All sorts of wild things in the Denanbaki hills and the desert. Demons. Spirits of the wind and the sand. The stories the caravaneers tell . . . You're not him. Something's putting words in your mouth. His mouth."

"I went south, Yuro, and east. To the cities and the sea. And west, after, to the Five Cities and beyond. Now I'm back. Do you want Daro Korat to die?"

"No! Never such a death as they mean for him."

"You didn't join Sia."

"Lord Sia was a fool and damned all his family. Once he had the Kho'anzi, the general said he was going to kill even the children. Don't know if he meant it, but the ladies poisoned them to spare them. Their own children."

"Who's the girl?" Ghu tilted his head towards the heap of blankets.

"Lady Daro Willow." Yuro's lips thinned. He had not meant to answer.

"The baby?" The Kho'anzi's third and last daughter's baby. A scandal, that had been. She had been refusing a betrothal to a young lord of Musa Clan in Taihu, an alliance the old emperor had strongly hinted would be to his liking, when her pregnancy became obvious. The father had never been named that Ghu knew of, but it ruined her marriage prospects. She had always wanted an officer's commission in the couriers anyway, not to be lady of a household. She gave that up, as well, to raise her baby herself and not leave it entirely to slaves and her brother's wife. Or maybe she had had other reasons for not wanting to leave the castle . . . riding down along the river, and a man who thought himself out of sight in the willows at the stony spit where the coltsfoot bloomed so thickly in spring. *Take my dogs for a good run, Ghu*, she said. *Take both horses. I'm going to sit and watch the water.* . . . Lord Sia's confidential secretary, he had been, secreted in the willows, some minor banner-lady's younger child, landless, rankless. No fit match for a high lord's daughter. Ghu had always understood the baby's name, if nobody else did.

"So you know who the child was. Doesn't mean anything. You could know what's in Ghu's mind, maybe, what he remembers. Whatever you are."

"Two of the Kho'anzi's family left to him. And he himself."

"One."

"I am Ghu, Yuro. And if I did not talk much, I listened. Are you going to let your father be sent to die in the Golden City, or will you help him?"

Yuro sat, then, as if the wind had been knocked out of him a second time.

"Where did you hear that? Old Great Gods, not even—no one—"

"It's in your heart," he said gently. "Every time you stood before him. And in his."

Yuro said nothing, so Ghu bowed and turned away. It would have to be the river, then. The punt would not hold so many, once they had Lord Korat, but he could swim the moat, and they could raid the village on the mound southward for a proper boat—would the Kho'anzi in hiding be enough to rouse the province, with an imperial army in Dernang? He needed—he knew what he needed and could not see any way to it, but through the devil.

To start so . . .

He paused by the girl. "What did they do to her?"

"She ran from her aunts—her mother's dead. I mean, two years dead. Died in childbirth with a second baby and no father known for that one, either. Though—Sia's secretary had died of winter fever not long before and I saw the life going out of her with that, if no one else did." He added, "She always liked the horses."

Yuro had had affection for her, then, the sister who did not know him her brother. Ghu had liked her too. It spoke well of both of them.

"But Willow, she hid, when the family—did what they did. House-master Duri couldn't roll over fast enough for the Zhung general. He told him who the girl was, when they found her halfway down the fish-pond overflow drain. General Musan said a bastard Daro brat wasn't much of threat if she was put in her proper place and ordered her branded for Zhung Clan and set in the castle records as a captive of war. As if she were a foreigner! They sent her to the kitchens, and I don't think that lot were any too kindly. Scared for their own skins if they were, maybe. So the child took the punt across the moat, three nights ago now—the flood hadn't come up so high yet. She stole a horse from a courier station—no one knows how she managed that—but they caught up with her, of course. Don't know where she thought she was going. So Musan marked her as a runaway."

"Someone meant her to die," Ghu said.

"General Musan. With his own hand on the iron. I took the girl out of the kitchens to see what I could do, for her mother's sake, but I'll have to send her back in the morning. If she's still breathing. Musan is—" He shook his head. "To execute rebels is one thing but—"

"Bring the light."

Yuro hesitated, just long enough to make it clear he was not jumping to the order. But he brought the lantern and held it up. The child lay on her side. Her skin was slick with sweat and a flushed, unhealthy colour; her hair had been shorn to a knuckle's length all over her head.

The wound on her face was a crusted burn, purple, black, red, oozing. The iron left in place too long, searing too deeply. The eye above it was swollen and her breath heavy and wheezing. Ghu knelt and pulled back the thin gown. The brand on her shoulder had nearly healed, deep and livid though it was, only seeping a little, and crusted, smeared like her face with some rank-smelling salve Ghu doubted was doing any good. He put his hand over the festering new burn on the girl's face. She was dreaming now of the moat, of cold, lightless water, struggling to reach it, to drown herself, while hands like claws clutched her back.

"You're stronger than that," he whispered, because it was true, but despair and surrender were heavy on the child, as killing a force as the fever that ate her. "Be stronger, Willow." The little hand found and gripped his suddenly. Eyes flickered, not quite opening.

"Tell me again," Yuro said abruptly. "Tell me again, why you're here. Why you've come back, why you talk so. To take the province. Are you mad?"

"No. Yuro, do you truly think a newborn baby should survive, in the river? How long was my mother dead when Gomul found me? How long had I been in the water?" Almost a whisper. "Yuro, I am here; I belong to the gods, who send me to you, to Nabban, and if you love the gods, believe me. I need Daro Korat."

"You need. You tell me what you are, before the gods." The horsemaster's voice shook. "What thing you are and what you did to young Ghu."

The fever was cooling. Ghu put a palm over the burn on the girl's back.

"Why come back?" Yuro demanded. "Whatever you are, and I don't believe you, why? What's the old lord to the gods? I know what's planned for him; I know how the emperor killed his enemies and the empress's rule is no different. Worse. She executed all her brother's counsellors before his body had even cooled, that's what they're saying. If it's true. Had them summoned to her and murdered by Wind in the Reeds there before her, to show what would happen to those who didn't accept her. I don't want the old man to die a traitor's death for defying that kind of tyranny. He was always—he wasn't like Sia, after anything with breasts.

Whatever my mother was to him, it was something that mattered, and to both of them. He was always kind to me as he could be, while his mother lived and ruled the Daro, and kind to my mother who was mistress of the stables before me, and after—she died in the same year as the old lady so it was too late, wasn't it? But the little lady—he let Willow have the Daro name and set her in the family descent acknowledged in her lordship and that was for—for what he hadn't done for me, as much as for his daughter's child, I knew it. But Lord Korat will die. So many have, and the gods have done nothing. If they exist at all. Why? Why say you need him?"

"I told you. I need his name—"

"The Daro name is worth nothing now but death. Look at Willow."

"I need the Kho'anzi. I need the army of Choa, the banner-lords of the Daro Clan."

"There is no Daro Clan in Choa. The name is forbidden. They're to be Zhung, all Zhung, even the banner-lords, those few who'll keep their rank. Or their heads. There is only General Zhung Musan's army; he's been appointed Kho'anzi of Choa now. All the companies of the town and the border posts are his. Prince Dan's army—I don't know if it ever existed, or it was just a wish of Lord Sia's. There were certainly companies from over in Alwu roaming like brigands here, mostly harassing the imperial forces, but they've scattered. There's rumour that there's still a rebel army over in Alwu, but we haven't seen them here. Here, the garrison of the castle, our lord's own banner-lords and his soldiery—they were disarmed when Lord Daro surrendered himself to the general. They laid down their weapons trusting in General Musan's word and honour, and they're imprisoned now and to be sent in chains to the Old Capital with the Kho'anzi, to die with him. The younger sons, the warrior daughters of every Daro family, the household armsfolk. There is no Daro army. They're all prisoners here."

"The Kho'anzi was a good lord and the soldiers of the clan and lords of the province and their banner-lords will find their heart again for him," Ghu said. "But they won't follow Daro Korat's horseboy."

"Why should they?" But it sounded a plea.

Ghu sighed, sitting back on his heels. "Yuro—I am all I ever was, and I become all that the gods, who claimed me before Gomul ever fished me from the river, mean me to be. Believe, or don't."

"The empress—her people say the gods are dead. They pray to her as a goddess, Chosen Daughter of the Old Great Gods. They're tearing down the shrines of the woods and waters, building temples and altars to the empress. They kill the old priests, now, if they don't turn from the Father and Mother to serve the new cult-centres in the towns. The family of the Swajui shrine are dead. You think the gods have sent you to fight *that*?"

"Yes. They have. The gods aren't dead yet, but they are dying, Yuro. They have been dying a long time. But they have not set any child of Min-Jan's line to take their place."

"That's not a prophecy to bring the folk to follow you, boy, or to bring them to the Kho'anzi's banner either. Anyway, there's not a mad fool who claims to hear the whispers of the gods who doesn't die for it in short order."

"There is more honour in fighting to renew this land than in making yourself a slave, surrendering choice and leaving the struggle to others. I don't claim to be a prophet, but it is the true heir of Nabban who will shape the fate of this land now, not the children of Min-Jan. Not the empress."

Yuro snorted. "Not the Min-Jan. That's what the prophets say. Old Great Gods—yourself, you mean?"

Ghu looked up. "Yes."

Something touched him again, brushed over him, hesitated, lost in fog, and passed on.

Yuro was silent, lips working as if he chewed his thoughts.

"You're mad," he said at last. "But you'll take Lady Willow away? You've been in foreign lands. You've been out in the world. You'll take her over the border to Denanbak?"

He could not answer that. It felt wrong. Where? *Swajui, the shrine of the Mother's rising.* No. *He* must go to Swajui, to the holy spring, and up the mountain to the Father, but Daro Korat—the Kho'anzi was where he needed to be. Here.

Prince Dan. If the man was not dead, he must find him, too.

He was mad. They were three, against a castle.

But they were already inside the walls.

"How do you think you can get her out? Demon magic?"

"I'm not a demon." But he had a devil leashed by her word. For now. If he thought it right to use her.

He did not. But she was the only weapon he had to hand.

Yuro shrugged. The little girl, beneath Ghu's hand, mumbled and curled up smaller, like a dog getting comfortable. Her grip on Ghu slackened. "How?" Yuro persisted.

How, indeed. "We'll manage."

"Who's we?"

"Friends."

"Caravan-folk?" Eyeing Ghu's sheepskin coat.

"Not exactly." Ghu sighed. "It's you I wanted, Yuro. Your help. Your sense. Your care for your father. But if you will not, at least stay quiet here. Bar your door and keep the child safe. I don't think we'll get Daro Korat away without bloodshed."

"I'll meet you on the road," Yuro said. "With horses and the girl. We can run for Denanbak."

"There are two wizards." Yeh-Lin's voice, the door ajar. "There were wards and guards on this castle, and you walked through them without a stir, my lord, I don't know how, but the attention of something has been drawn by this fog, and now one at least of the wizards is waking and knows things run amiss. We're out of time."

"*My lord?*" Yuro repeated.

Time. The moment, flying. Not away. *Here.* Now.

"Daro soldiers," Ghu said. "Prisoners. Where?"

"What? Cellars of the western tower," Yuro said. "If they're not drowned. It's flooding down there."

"Get them out. Arm them. Where's Daro Korat?"

"At the top of the great keep in the sunset room. Don't be a fool. You can't—"

"Ahj!" He was out the door and halfway down the stairs, with Ahjvar coming out of the darkness there to fall in at his side.

"What?"

"The Kho'anzi," he said. "We need to take this place. Now. Tonight. We need to hold it. Come."

The gods in him gathered strength, and the thing that watched the fog, the tendril of awareness that had touched him, wary, wondering, was dispersed. For a time. It did not see him clearly, not yet. But one of the imperial wizards stirred ink in a silver shell, and breathed on it. *Eyes met his, widening, lit by candle's flame.*

"No," Ghu said aloud, and brushed the man away.

"What?" Ahjvar asked.

"Wizards. Watching."

Ahj shed their packs in the mulberry orchard, cut a thin branch from a tree they passed and stripped the bark from it as they went. "Wait," he said, and as Ghu paused, impatient and yearning to run, Ahjvar split the wand, leaning back against the wall, and scored lines on it, muttering, "Walnut, mountain ash, grape . . ." none of which would be growing in this enclosure. There was some shape of will there, made between his hand and the knife and the green wood. That which was hidden and the reversal of sight. *The wizard, away in the keep, cried out and dropped his silver shell, blinded and clutching his eyes. A woman demanded of him that he speak, say where the danger lay, and he cried, "We are cursed by the gods, lady. Forgive me, Father forgive me." Another . . . another wizard, somewhere in the keep, walked into a wall, rubbed her eyes, and began to run.*

"Damn. I've lost one," Ahjvar said. "Where's—" But no point asking, Yeh-Lin was not with them. He snapped the stick in his hand, dry and brittle now as if a year dead, and dropped it, loaded the crossbow. "Go on?"

"Yes. Run." A bell jangled alarm somewhere high above.

They ran where they could, crossing gardens, went warily in the narrow passages between buildings and on the shallow steps. The place was designed to lose and trap. The Zhung soldiers had been quartered here only a few weeks. More likely they would trap themselves in dead ends than he would. And from the cries, they were mostly being sent to the gate and the outermost yard, after the stables. The air smelt suddenly of smoke.

"She wouldn't fire the stables," Ahjvar said, and gave him a shove when he broke stride, almost turning back.

No. She would not. Trust. The smoke was doing what she meant, drawing enemies away from the keep. He ducked into a narrow gap between buildings, damp walls, mossy stones underfoot, eaves nearly touching. Steep climb, three sharp-angled turns. Broader passage, a gate, closed. He jumped to catch the top and swung over it, dropping down into a family garden. Ahjvar followed one-handed, holding the crossbow. Soft lawn, clouds of magnolia opened like white stars, and dark mountains of juniper. The ornamental fishpond, a stone statue of a leaping fish. Beyond, there was a low retaining wall and then a raised platform of crunching white gravel to cross, before the towering keep itself.

Torches burned at the entry porch. Lanterns lit the perimeter of the keep's platform. Light glinted up high. No windows in the stone-built ground storey.

They were two, and this was madness. Fog, which had trailed them through the passages, across the garden, thickened over the pond, climbed to blur the lights.

There was a darkness against the plastered walls high above. Shapes. Not shuttered windows. Elongated . . .

Death.

They cried out to him, wordless, beseeching. Ghosts, trapped souls. Bodies. Four. Old man. Young man. Young woman. Girl-child.

Hanged from the upper windows of the keep, swinging over the eaves of the next storey down.

He swayed and would have fallen as their fear and pain and loss poured through him, but Ahj seized him as he crumpled, and he caught himself on the top of the retaining wall.

"Who?" A whisper. Ahjvar could see ghosts, and must see these.

Ghu shook his head, could not speak.

The old man—the old man he knew, the old man had turned on his heel once, in the horsefair, eyes wide, and bowed to him, stable-grimed slave that he was, leading a pair of yearlings Lord Sia had purchased for racing, and hurried away . . .

He knew all of them, even the child, who could not have been born when he fled. He knew them. They knew him.

The family of the Swajui shrine.

The shrine, burning. Soldiers. The shrine, burning. The general, a face of terror, a moustache, a helmet with a crest like antlers. Soldiers, and more soldiers.

The gods were dead, they cried. The empress's will would have no gods set before herself, no prophets crying of the wind from the desert, the wind from the northern mountain, the fall of the house of Min-Jan and the Peony Throne cast down.

Soldiers hunted them through the forest. Soldiers dragged them away and beat them and kicked them, and the shrine burned and the house and they hacked at the holy tree.

They were kept with the former Kho'anzi, to die with him for hiding his rebels, which they had not done, but two days past the priestess who kept the shrine of Father Nabban in the town had preached against the new goddess in the market of Dernang. The empress as goddess was a lie, she cried. The time of the Min-Jan emperors was ended. She was cut down by soldiers in the town, and then in his rage, because that was not punishment enough, the general hanged the family of priests of the Mother, the child last of all, grinning, laughing, as he put the rope around her neck. Hanged them from the window of the upper room, while the lame old lord in his chains tore his wrists raw to come at him.

They fled to him, the ghosts, nothing to see, memory and soul, scent and light—they flung themselves into him, and the river was waking in him to set them free, to give that blessing and break those bonds, to end the pain and let them go.

The corpses hung empty and he was on his knees, leaning his forehead on the cold and fog-damp stone, fingers clawed against it.

He could break the stone, in this moment, this place. Shatter it, pull down every tower. He had but to call to Dotemon and turn her loose to do what she would. He hanged our *priests*, whose family vows forbade them weapons. His thought. Theirs, Mother and Father. Zhung Musan hanged a *child*. He made the child watch, till the end, the last of them, as they were thrown out the window. There were no words.

He shivered as with deep cold. Ahjvar laid down the crossbow and crouched by him, hands on his shoulders.

"Zhung Musan," Ghu said. Words. There, he had found words. But too few. Found more. Enough, if they could ever be so. "Priests. The family. Because a priestess in the town spoke against the new lying empress, the false goddess. The child. It was not a swift death, hers, Ahj, she was so light. Ahj, they are all our folk, all Nabban, but I will not, we offer no quarter to Zhung Musan."

There was a weight of oppression lying on the gods, crushing them. Smothering. But their rage went deep as their sorrow, and he was their outlet. It flooded blood and bone.

"Yes," Ahjvar said, and caught up the crossbow to follow when he went over the edge and strode to the door, and the torches flared like bonfires and the fog roiled and spread like wings about them.

CHAPTER XXI

Rising ramp and shallow steps making two right-angled turns to the second-storey entrance hall. Soldiers in short, banded cuirasses, on their helmets a badge Ghu knew for the imperial peony, came out from the cover of the porch to bar the way, but they stood in a cloud of fear and they saw . . . he did not know what. The world was little more solid than the fog, and Ahj, to his sight, had gone like a ghost to something that vision could not quite truly grasp: hearthfire, the warmth of the sun and the shadows of the forest, and the harsh web of the curse that bound him in the world, spun steel and adamant, tied into Ghu himself.

"Stand aside," he said, and to his ears his voice sounded little more than a whisper. The soldiers scattered back as if some great wave of mountain snow bore down on them, and the dogs poured by, wolf, snake, dragon, smoke. They milled about, waiting. Ahjvar put his shoulder to the door and flung it wide.

Beyond the axe-scarred entry-hall more guards, who fled like the first, and they found the stairs that climbed inside the outer wall. No time to stop and wonder what he did, would do. The river's flood, the snowslip moving . . . He brought the dogs back to follow at his heels, to not run their fool heads into trouble. Two women on the landing, hard to see, one in bright-lacquered armour, one with the taste of wizardry in her, the one who had walked into a wall before she shed Ahjvar's spell of blindness. Power gathered to her and she cried, "The depths of the river swallow all!" flinging out her arms, but the rushing darkness of her magic fled into the river's depths in him with no harm, though the line of poetry was meant to choke and blind and drown them. In the spell's loss, she gasped and fell fainting. Ahjvar took his hand from the trigger of the bow and pointed it ceilingward again when the banner-lady laid down her sword and went to her knees, and they pushed past, but the wizard recovered, crying out, "The curse of the Old Great Gods!" Ghu felt the air burn as she swept at him with some weapon that trailed fire. Ahjvar rounded on her to kick and she went off the stairs over the single rail of the banister. She died when she hit the floor, the burning flail smouldering in the air, then dying with her.

Her soul, stunned and afraid and overwhelmed . . . a momentary coldness, a pull as inexorable as that of the road to the Old Great Gods and she slipped away. Gone, and not to the road. Taken.

Wrong.

Another landing, and footsteps. The warrior lady they had passed came racing up the stairs after them with two common soldiers sent on before her, angry, fearful, shouting incoherent threats. "Devil" was in their words, taken from her. Ahj shot the foremost and the bolt passed through the soldier's chest and the left arm of the lady behind to thunk into the wall. The soldier pitched back dying into the lady but she yelled, staggered sideways, and shoved the body rolling down the stairs. Ahjvar flung the crossbow aside to draw his sword, gone cold and still in the flaming heart of him. "Go," he said, so Ghu went on. He heard them fall behind him, felt their dying, near enough he could reach in pity to free them and let them answer the pull to their road. The coldness that had taken the wizard did not claim them. He felt rather than heard Ahj following him, even if it was no more than the touch of reins of cobweb binding them, broken soul to mountain's heart, as he swung around the turn of the stairs.

More banner-lords, the least of the nobles of the land, assembling, half-dressed, half-armed, shedding attendants and servants, when the stairs ended and he must cross through a lamplit hall with a dais and the scattered cushions of a court. One went to his knees, forehead to the floor, and whispered, "My lord," in a voice like a dreamer, and some of them drew back, but they were many, and between him and the screened passage to the further stairs.

Ahjvar was there again, sword blooded, shield notched. "Behind me, remember? Get back."

"We're come for Lord Daro Korat," Ghu told the warriors, ignoring him. "Best you stand aside, for love of the gods of Nabban."

One lord laughed, but most were afraid.

"Zhung Musan," he added. "Where is he?"

"The general went up to the Kho'anzi," a woman answered, and moved away from the far passage. Not the answer she should have made, being a Zhung banner-lady wearing the imperial badge.

He gave her the slightest of acknowledging bows and walked forward, and the dogs went again before him. Ahjvar followed, and was not happy with that. There was fear in that audience-chamber, and confusion, and they were not sure what they saw, but some of the young attendants had bows. He felt very far away from it all, very heavy, as though the world, the very stone and flesh of it, was nothing but shadows and light on the water, and he alone a thing of weight and matter.

"In the name of the Old Great Gods," another woman cried out, and a man, "Daro traitor!" and with one move drew his sword and half severed the neck of the lady who had answered Ghu. That, after the ghosts of the priests—he was braced to endure, a rock in the stream, did not let himself falter, not drown in her flooding emotions, but stepped aside as Ahjvar went past him, and the dogs swept ahead, singing in their throats. He had his knife in his own hand for the first who came against him, and the Zhung lord who had knelt rose and went for those who would block the upper stairs.

Then they were through, he with Ahjvar close ahead, with a following, and there was blood on his knife, his hand.

Their own folk. His. The gods mourned.

But some followed him. He could not wonder at that, in this place and time. Only take what they offered to whatever of their gods they perceived in him and use it worthily.

"Up," he said and they went up together.

Shouting above, something about rebels and a prince, gates breached.

A woman's voice rose shrilly. "They can't have crossed without word coming. It isn't Prince Dan, it can't be. The beacons—"

From a window, a glimpse of distant fire, away towards the western gate. A man's voice: "But the empress's orders—"

"Her orders were to bring Choa back to her, and if that means killing the Daro traitor now to keep him from the rebels—" A crashing, as of furniture overturned.

The upper landing, glazed porcelain lamps like waterlilies, a choice of two doors, both double-leaved, both ornately painted in intricate figures. They hit the door of what would be the west-facing room together. Not barred; the latch shattered. Ahjvar swung in front of him and a knife had left his hand as a soldier with a crossbow turned to face them. That one pitched into the floor, hilt standing out from his eye, and the bolt hit the ceiling. Two more came on in a rush. Ghu left them to Ahjvar and went around, to where the old man had been half dragged from his couch, a table overturned. A woman he thought vaguely familiar sprawled weeping and cursing all in a tangle with him, her arms twisted awkwardly. There was a rope about Daro Korat's neck. She had thrust her hands into the noose and struggled still to free him.

Ghu slashed the rope first of all and the woman, never leaving off her sobbing or her invocation of all seven devils against the general, tugged frantically and got the noose free as the two tumbled the rest of the way onto the floor. The argument—he thought it had been that—of the Zhung commanders broke up, the woman and the younger man, great lady and lord by their gilded helms and fine armour, turning to Ahjvar. Soldiers and a pair of banner-lords scattered in confusion from those who had followed Ghu. Shouting, each group accusing the other of treachery, demanding surrender to the will of their gods. The soldiers attacked and the two banner-ranked went for Ahjvar.

No place for Ghu in that fight. The general, with a roar like a thwarted animal, drew his sword—Ghu leapt over Daro Korat and the woman who shielded the old man with her body as the man came at him, leaving the dogs to defend the lord of the Daro and the woman from any Zhung soldier who might sidle around behind. He faced what the little priestess-child had seen. Snarling face, antlered helm—a lust to instil fear, to see submission, to know his enemies broken and debased before him—baffled simpleton's rage that he should be opposed, his power not acknowledged . . .

I see you. You think they will have you god of this land? No priest, no holy man, not even full-blooded Nabbani—

Were the words even spoken? No, and that was not the general's thought, either, though his strangely simple mind made an open road for it. Ghu ducked the sweeping blade, felt himself battered by the grinning hunger of the man wielding it. A joy in anticipated death. Monstrous, and the rage of the god and goddess was a deep, hot, and black-hearted thing, kindled for one child, in one moment. It thought nothing of the folk and the land and all the great injustice and the great suffering, but stood for it. And burnt all his own away.

Those who found their pleasure in the torment of others went to the Old Great Gods unblessed, unforgiven. No pity for such from the gods of their birth, no pity for what they would find, on their long, long road.

Good armour, no opening for the forage-knife to hook and bite. He retreated, a line away from the old lord, and the general followed, still grinning and yet spitting foulest insults, till the wall was at Ghu's back. He was not where the general struck, and the sword caught in the panelling. Rolling off the floor, he slashed the tendons at the back of the knee, was up and out of the way as the general staggered down, still raging and obscene.

The few of the general's soldiers still living had fallen back to the furthest corner and knelt, weapons cast down. Ahjvar. Ghu stepped out of his way, and Ahj had no compunction at all about finishing Zhung Musan unseen from behind, the Northron blade thrust up under the brim of his helmet, kicking him aside as he crumpled like he was so much rubbish.

Lord Korat was praying; he had struggled free of the old woman's frantic hands and stood supporting himself on her shoulder. She was— who? A house-slave, a woman of the family chambers. Physician's assistant. Liamin. Her name came to Ghu, but he did not think he had ever known it. It was an old rote prayer the Kho'anzi chanted, but all his soul was in it.

"Hear us, lord of the mountains and the hills, hear us, lady of the rivers and the lakes, let the heights be our comfort, let the waters be our consolation, hold us and guard us, defend us and bless us for the road in the hour of our dying . . ."

Other voices joined in. There was a white light in the room, a pearliness to the currents of flowing fog, as though they waded in the ghost of a river that had drowned the moon.

But the gods fell away, leaving Ghu empty, a hollow ruin in the wind and the night, so he could not see or think. There was grey dawn seeping in, and the fog withdrawing. There was Ahjvar, hazed in light, darkness and starlight, snowlight and river of Ghu's own will wrapping the flame of a human soul that was all scarlet and gold, holding him together. There was Ahj to drag him close, speaking into his hair Praitannec words he could not hear, not understand through the emptiness that was in him. His silence was frightening Ahj. Feeling as though he groped and gathered some scattered basket of yarn, Ghu pulled tangled strands of himself together. So weak and dizzy and strangely light, but that was the passage of the gods through him. So cold. He was shuddering with it.

"All right," he said, because Ahjvar was trying to get the coat off him. "All right, all right. It's not my blood. I'm scratched, no more."

Ahj was a reassuringly solid bulk to lean his head on nonetheless.

"That," Ahjvar was saying, "is why you don't fight swordsmen with a damned knife. He nearly had you."

"No," he said vaguely. "I knew you would be there."

"I was on the other side of the room!"

"Yes."

The chamber was a roiling confusion of the living and the dead, souls in confusion, souls drawn to him as if he were sun to warm them, for all his chill shivering. One soul was all fury and terror still. He tried to brush them from him but they clung like cobwebs till he whispered blessings, sent them to their road. Zhung Musan last of all.

"Go," he said. Only that, to cast him free, unforgiven, as the gods had declared. He would not leave him here to haunt this place. But—in that moment, he had already gone.

Or been taken.

Wrong.

At least the general was dead. He felt warmer then, or maybe that was Ahjvar's coat slung over his shoulders atop his own, but the warmth made little difference; he still could not sort out sense in the room. Voices, movement, colour, stench. Slid down to his knees, shut his eyes against it all, dropped away to where there was nothing but the whisper of water, and Ahj like a stone in the current to shield him. There, he could be still. Gather himself together again in quiet.

"Ghu. Ghu, damn you, don't. Don't sleep."

He wasn't, but he had to open his eyes to prove it. He had drifted only a few moments, he thought.

"All right," he said yet again, and pulled himself up, using Ahjvar as a prop. "I'm all right, truly." But Ahjvar did not look as though he believed him. "So many dead," he said. "So heavy."

The dogs, anxious ears flattened, crowded close.

Ahjvar waved off the woman Liamin, who approached clutching a basket of surgeon's tools—yes, with Ahjvar's coat about him Ghu looked like he ought to be on the floor and bleeding his last. She did not protest but bobbed a bow before going—fleeing—to where other folk clustered, near the door, about a man who groaned and writhed.

His shoulder ached. He must have struck the wall harder than he thought. Or the floor.

"I thought he had you," Ahjvar was saying. "He was frothing mad, and I thought—what were you *thinking?*"

"The gods," he said wearily. "They were angry. But I can't carry them for long like that."

"*Damn* all gods," Ahjvar said, and meant it. He leant slumped, back to the wall, head bowed, speaking to his feet. "You should have gone west. You should have let me bloody well go and been free."

"Didn't come back for your sake."

"Didn't you? I don't believe you when you say you don't lie." Ahjvar's voice was rough with his anger and he looked up, glaring. Not shouting, no, but the quiet, careful words were worse. "You should have let me go, back at the Orsamoss, left me to go back to bone and ash. You should have run till you were free. Are they just going to take you so, whenever they have a mind? Is that what you've come back to?"

Possession. All Ahjvar's nightmares.

"No. Ahjvar, *no*." He took Ahjvar by the shoulders, the better to meet that—deep, deep rage, that fear. To stop him turning away, to stop the rage finding some other outlet, nightmare or the next and nearest soldier to look a threat . . . Blue eyes burned, and how to make him understand, to quell that fear, which was for Ghu's own sake, that rage for him, and who had ever feared or been roused to anger for Ghu's sake in all his life, but Ahj—"No. No. Not that. If I am their eyes and their voice, it is—they are so weak, Ahj. They have so little left in this world. They borrow from me, maybe, as I from them, I don't know, but—no, not that. What they take I give of my own will."

"And these prophets they take and use, these prophets who die for them—"

"That is not their will. That is—their dreams and their nightmares, spilling into the souls of this land. Not their will. We will end it. We will end it soon."

He felt Ahjvar stiffen at *we*.

"The gods and I," he said, which probably did not help, though it separated him from them, a little. "I am whole," he said. Words were too weak a thing to say what he meant. "I am myself. Always. Trust."

Silence, and a long sigh. He did not think Ahjvar conceded anything, but the man let it go for the time, and some of the tension went out of his shoulders. "Good," Ghu said, and that brought the shadow of a smile. It had been what Ahjvar called his talking to horses and idiots voice, though he hadn't meant to sound so. "Are you hurt?" he thought to ask.

"Not so it matters." Ahjvar flexed his shoulders and finally looked around. A deep breath. "Now what? Did your gods think of that? They'll burn us out."

"Not if we hold the whole of the castle."

He moved away from the wall, only a step or two, and shrugged the ruin of Ahjvar's coat away. The movement drew a tassel-helmeted banner-lord's attention and the man bowed, and then they watched, seeing him again, all that upper chamber, and there was awe in their eyes. Not for him, please the gods, who had been there. It was surely Ahjvar who was the bright-burning alien thing in the room. But they did not see Ahjvar as Ghu did. Ahj was only a filthy foreign caravaneer stained with blood not his own. It was Ghu they saw. Only him. He had brought the gods to them. The dying man was gone, Liamin's attention turned to the wounded she could help. Zhung man, confused, filled with sorrow in the presence of his gods. "Go," he whispered wearily, as that ghost flew to him. "Safe journey, be free."

Figure in the open door and Ahjvar put himself before Ghu again. It was an armoured banner-lady, her face smeared with soot, her helmet under her arm. No imperial badge on her helmet. None on any here, save for the dead. She dropped to her knees and, in the widening of her eyes, Ghu saw his godhead reflected. He was—too present, in this place. No hiding. Filthy, bloody caravaneer though he might seem to be.

"Holy one? Holy one, Lady Nang Lin sends me to say, we hold the gatehouse and the stable block, and the empress's company of the barracks has surrendered. What will you have her do with them, she says? And men of my banner have the entry-hall of the castle and hold all the stairs for you, Zhung though they are. The Daro soldiers are freed from the cellars and armed. Lady Lin has set them to take back the castle ward by ward, gathering the Daro folk to them as they go. I am Lady Zhung Ti-So'aro and I swear myself and the soldiers of my following to the holy one and Lord Daro Korat under the true gods. And Lady Nang Lin says, is the Kho'anzi Daro Korat in good health, or will you have her act as your seneschal this day, to set all in order until you can make better provision?"

He caught himself before he asked, "Who?" Nang was a common Solan Province name. Maybe it was even Yeh-Lin's own true clan. And she asked most circumspectly who commanded here, while taking charge herself. Doing only what he would have had to order done himself, if he had thought of it. To hold this room was not to hold the keep; to hold the keep was not to hold the castle.

Or Choa Province.

"The empress's soldiers not of your own households, not trusted by you personally—disarm them," he said. "Confine them. The Kho'anzi will take their oaths and yours, too. Later."

It already was morning. He might know it, if a soldier meant his swearing, when he gave his hands to the Daro lord. He could weed out those already unfaithful in their hearts, set them to guarded tasks of rebuilding, maybe, whatever it was Yeh-Lin had burnt, or Zhung Musan before her, and the postern gate was broken open. . . . He should be there to see what she did, but he did not think he could walk down all those stairs now, and there was still the Kho'anzi to face. Lord Daro Korat, his master, who had papers to say Ghu was his chattel, seated now on the couch, his swollen foot propped on a cushion, white hair all cascading down in disorder, frowning at him, not in disapproval so much as puzzlement.

"They'll swear to the holy one of the gods, their captains say," Lady Ti-So'aro told him, "if it's your will to show mercy, holy one. Lady Nang Lin sent that word too. They saw, we all saw, the great light that came upon the tower, as if the moon became a river and poured into it. It's on you still, holy one."

What?

Moon on fog. Maybe. Moon on fog and a yearning for some wrongness to be set right and done with. He did not think the Zhung warriors and imperial soldiery had been happy in their general. Though he would not put it past Yeh-Lin to have made some false wonder, to awe them. He would argue that with her later.

Faint pearly shadow lingered yet, in the corner of his eye when he moved.

"Later," he said. "We will do all that must be done later. Tell Lady Nang Lin to do what I would have her do—" safe as he could make that command, "to hold the castle for the Kho'anzi and the gods, till he is recovered. Thank her. Thank you, Ti-So'aro."

"My lord." She bowed, on her knees.

"And stand up," he added, in unreasonable irritation.

She rose to bow again, before she left him.

Thus he stole the castle from his master, and did anyone notice? Not the Kho'anzi. There was another came in, before he could cross to the old man. Horsemaster Yuro, looking awkward, head ducked a little like a dog expecting reprimand, cudgel in one hand and the other clasping that of the girl Willow. Willow, on her feet, was still in the grubby scant gown of the lowest scullion, bruised above the black scabbing of her cheek, but her skin was dry and her eyes clear. She did not let go to run to her grandfather, but jerked at Yuro's hand and brought him forward, when the stablemaster would have gone to his knees, the lord's eye falling on him.

"Grandfather." Willow bowed, most properly, but Lord Korat rocked to his feet and embraced her.

"Willow, my girl, Willow." Whispering, as if a cry might blow the child away, show her to be nothing but a ghost. When Yuro would have stepped away to kneel, Daro Korat caught the horsemaster's arm and pulled him close as well. "My boy," he said. Yuro looked stricken.

Well. So. Ghu took a breath and crossed to them, with Ahjvar at his shoulder and the dogs to either side.

And the old man, clutching at Yuro to keep himself from falling, knelt. To him.

"*Don't.*" No honorific came to his tongue, not with Ahjvar beside him, a knot of anger against not only gods but this feeble old man, but he caught at the Kho'anzi's arm and steadied him to his feet again. A knob-jointed hand seized his sleeve, clutched him, staring close.

"Holy one. I dreamed of you. In all the nights, in the darkness, since the priests died, I have dreamed you were coming. . . ."

"That's only three nights, Lord Korat," Liamin murmured, edging close behind, reaching for him, not touching, but wanting to take him, to make him sit again. "You remember?"

The Kho'anzi frowned. "Yes, yes. Of course. But holy one, I know you . . . ?"

"It's Ghu, my lord," Master Yuro said. "One of my boys. The one who brought the white colt down from the sacred mountain after that spring storm? We'd thought the boy drowned, some years ago." A sideways glance at Ghu. "He claims—"

The old lord never took his gaze from Ghu's face, but his frown melted to a smile. "Ah! I knew that I knew you, holy one. And you were here among my folk?" He hobbled a step back and Liamin was there to take his elbow. He bowed, most formally. "Tell me what you will of me, and if I can, it will be done. How would the gods have me serve?"

Dernang. Choa. Castle, town, province. A road. South. The rebel prince, somewhere, and the wreckage of his army, his lords and his clerks and all. . . .

A questing coldness reached again for him, threads like cobweb, drifting on the wind, to cling.

Ghu brushed them away. They drifted back. A breath. A long exhalation, steadying himself. He was nothing, only the water and the mist off the river, nothing to see, nothing to touch, nothing to hold. An emptiness. But the lord watched him, wanting words.

"Make this place safe," he said. "We start from here." Remembered. "Make yourself known to your own folk again; the prisoners are freed. There's a Zhung banner-lady, Ti-So'aro. She'll swear herself and her retainers to you, she says. Fold her into your own folk; there was truth in her heart. She's with—with my—" What was Yeh-Lin? And where? "My captain, Nang Lin. She's taking the castle with the Daro soldiers Yuro freed." Or has taken? "There's a Zhung banner-lord. I don't know his name." His eye found the man, leaning wounded on one of his retainers. A nod. The man bowed low. The name came to him. "Zhung Ario. Others who serve the true gods." Another thought. "No revenge on the Zhung and the empress's soldiers. My lord, swear them to you if they will and if not, guard them. We can't begin with the killing of those who've surrendered to us, with the murder of prisoners. We will not."

Begin what? The Kho'anzi did not ask. Did he know himself? He was no longer certain. But there was an imperial army in the town still, and it would hold the roads and the border posts. He must learn the truth behind Meli's vague and confused understanding; he must understand the shape of things. . . .

"We will do no murder," Daro Korat said. His voice was firm now, however flushed his cheeks with fever. "Holy one . . ."

Ghu needed out of this room. He understood of a sudden how Ahj must feel, in a small closed space with people all around him crowding close, a weight of eyes and attention, crushing—and that reaching awareness found him again. It sought the presence of the river. He was only a man, and weary and battered. Only a man among the many here.

He was not.

The room seemed very unsteady around him. A ship, swaying deck. The walls were smoke. Or moving water. Ahjvar steadied him.

"Liamin." The Kho'anzi transferred his grip to a startled Yuro's arm. "Find my own chamber-servants, if they're still among the living, or any of the household you trust. Have them tend the holy one."

"I can't sleep inside here, under this roof," Ahjvar said abruptly, almost a whisper, desperate. "Ghu, they are too many, they keep moving. I can't watch them all and I can hear—something's burning."

He touched Ahjvar's hand for reassurance that he had heard the Praitannec murmur. "No, it is not, not inside here. There was a fire down towards the gates, but Y—but Lin will have dealt with it." And was probably the one to have started it. Fire to frighten out those who held out against her. . . . Although the Kho'anzi was right; he craved rest and drink and food, and he was hardly the only one in such desperate need. He forced his dizziness away. No time. Ahjvar's hands shook; his speech had been slow and slurring. He looked ready to fold to the floor.

"Some quiet chamber where the holy one will not be troubled. I don't know . . ." The old man looked around the room, his expression baffled. "We can't stay in here. None of us can stay in here." The old man was too weak to sustain any authority for long, overwhelmed and undone. Someone needed to take thought for all that needed doing.

"Yes," Ghu said. "You need to find some better place to rest, Lord Korat, and someone you can trust to order things in your name. Your house-master is traitor to you and may be dead."

Already was dead. Murder done, hard on the heels of rumour that the Daros rose again. Willow clung to her grandfather's side and Ghu was not feeling very forgiving. Other needs were more pressing. He gathered his thoughts again.

"Lord Korat, you're ill. You can't take thought for everything. Appoint your son your castellan."

"My son," Daro Korat said, softly, slowly, as if turning the words over, bringing them out into light and air.

"He can run these great stables, so he can run this castle. They're not so different. Advise him yourself, and he'll learn what he needs. I'll want Lady Nang Lin elsewhere."

"Yuro," the Kho'anzi said. Closed his eyes a moment, ran a hand over his lips. "Yes."

"My lord!" Yuro protested. "You can't—"

"Do it, Yuro," Ghu said flatly. "Because there are others less fit will be quick to put themselves in that place." And the old man's in no shape to resist them, he did not need to say, not to Yuro.

The stable-master gave him a long, considering look. Bowed to his father. "My lord."

Daro Korat reached for him, took his arm to pull himself upright again.

"Witness," he called, and—they were already the focus of all attention, but the silence deepened. "Witness all of you. This is my natural son, Daro Yuro, and so it will be set down in the records of the clan. I acknowledge and claim him, before you and the gods and the holy one of the gods."

And so Yuro was freed. So simply. Words. Ink would make it lasting truth, ink, and the iron, and sick smell of seared skin.

Not in his Nabban that would be, no. Set it witnessed in the records of the Daros, for the law, for the clan, that Daro Korat acknowledged his son, yes. But the other, *no*. Here it ended. There would be no burning to prove the slave was freed.

No slave and free.

"He will hold the keys—someone find the keys; Zhung Musan's man will have had them. I appoint Lord Yuro castellan of the White River Dragon, to order all as he sees fit and needful in my name. Further, I name him guardian to my granddaughter and heir Daro Willow should the Old Great Gods call me before Lady Willow's majority, the gods and the Old Great Gods and the holy one of the gods being witness."

Trust, indeed, to name one bastard of his blood guardian of the other.

The child had seniority in the records of the clan, acknowledged from her birth, but—wise to confirm her his heir? That depended on Yuro.

The Kho'anzi let himself down again. Liamin frowned at Ghu.

"You look to the Kho'anzi," he told her and Yuro both. "We'll take care of ourselves. Castellan, send to Lady Nang Lin if there's anything . . ." He waved a vague hand. "Ahj. Come." Praitannec. "I want to find the devil." And pass by the kitchens outside on the way to the north tower where he felt she now was, filch themselves a dish of cold barley or millet porridge and weak beer, of which there would be plenty, always, unless things were very much changed. He did not think any were going to deny him, or even his dogs. Not for godhead. For Ahjvar at his back.

"He's right, though," Ahjvar said. "You should sleep."

"Not yet." Keep moving now, or be washed over and drowned. "If you held the town, Ahj, and suspected the castle had been taken from within by the Daro Clan again—would you sit and wait?"

"No. We don't even hold the castle yet."

"Yeh-Lin will, soon enough." She would have thrown down the bridges, surely, which it seemed Daro Korat never had done, either against his son, who had probably never pressed a siege, or against Zhung Musan. "But we'll be besieged here so soon as whoever has command over the moat in Dernang realizes something is wrong."

"Yes."

"So. I need to talk to Yeh-Lin. Then we sleep, a little. Food first."

"Not hungry."

"You will *eat*."

At one turn of the stairs, Ahjvar walked into the corner of a wall, as if vision failed him, though the light grew with the morning. Nacrous mist still trailed in the corner of Ghu's eye, in the shadows. Illusion of his weariness, trickery of Yeh-Lin's—he did not believe that. Last breath of the goddess? Folk of the castle, slave and free, huddled whispering behind doors, with furtive scuttlings, always out of sight behind or before them, as rumour ran on slippered feet. Runners passed them, boys and girls wide-eyed with wonder and fear relieved. Soldiers, a lord, a lady with them, held vital points—stairways, the central halls. Daro soldiers, ragged and soiled with imprisonment. Zhung sitting weaponless, under guard, commoners and banner-ranked and their esquires together in the great hall. Many had cast off their helmet-badges, but prudent to disarm them anyway. The floor was bloodstained, but the bodies had already been carried away.

"Holy one . . ."

A whisper in the air, a susurration of voices, a thought.

"Holy one—?" Movement out of the shadows of a square pillar, and Ahjvar slammed past him. Ghu flung himself sideways, shoulder into Ahjvar's swordarm. Supplicant, groping—blind, he realized now, having registered only the empty hands as Ahjvar had reacted. The man fell, colliding with them. Ahjvar froze where he was, arm pinned against the pillar, breathing hard.

No soldier. The man wore the simplest of court robes, three layers and fine blue leaf-printed cotton outermost, dishevelled, sashless and all unfastened. Some amulet or badge swinging on a bright chain. His cap had fallen from his balding head and the thin bun of greying hair at the nape of his neck was straggling loose. Wounded. The white tunic of his underclothing was bloodstained over the left breast, but Ahjvar had not touched him.

Ghu wasn't sure he dared remove his weight from Ahjvar to take the groping hand of the fallen man.

Fallen wizard. Plum Badge rank, second of the five. Above a mere diviner, but no powerful worker, more likely to be a scholar. That was knowledge he did not think he had possessed even a few days ago. The hand found his foot, gripped, and the man bowed his head over Ghu's boot. "Holy one," he whispered again. "Forgive me, forgive me, I didn't know."

Ahjvar dragged a breath almost as near a sob as the crouching wizard's and jerked away from them both.

"Outside," he said in Praitannec. "Ghu—"

"I know. It's all right, Ahj, just—just put up your sword and wait. You, Nang Kangju—" the name was there in his mind—"Stand up."

"I didn't know it was you, I didn't know you were come. I knew it must be a lie, when they said the gods were dead and the empress had become the goddess of the land, but I was afraid to speak. Even when they killed the priests, I was afraid to speak, and I knew I shamed the gods, but I did not speak. I did not know, forgive me . . ."

Ghu stooped and pulled him up. What to say? This Kangju was hardly the only one to be silenced by fear. In all the empire, the thousands . . . He shook his head, wordless. The man stared, pupils dilated black, spilling tears, and clutched Ghu's hands. Not blind, but blinded. The wizardry still clung about him, isolating him from—something else. Ahjvar's doing. Scent of sap, torn bark. He pulled the man's inner tunic back from his chest, scored and bleeding, slashed and slashed again, not deep but savage. The cloth itself was not cut.

"Who did this to you?" he asked gently. "Nang Kangju . . ."

"I couldn't come to you with her mark on me," the wizard said simply.

"Whose mark?"

"The goddess's. The sign of our service to the empress."

"All of the empress's servants are marked?"

"No, holy one. Only the chosen."

"The wizards?"

"No, holy one. Only a few of us. We aren't to speak of it. We don't know who, but—people talk. Or one sees. I don't know why I was among them. Perhaps because I was always a true dreamer, I don't know. I only know we are summoned, a few. And she has us marked by her own tattooist. It was a great honour." His face twisted, tears spilling. "Forgive me, lord."

Black, amidst the sticky red. Tattoo. Ghu covered it again. Better it did scar, maybe. Break the pattern, whatever it was. Whatever it did.

A dreamer, not a scholar after all. Souls drawn away, lost to the Old Great Gods. Would the wizard Ahjvar had thrown from the stairs have such a tattoo? Would Zhung Musan? He must have Yeh-Lin look before the bodies were buried. But Kangju's sightless eyes were a more immediate matter.

"Ahjvar, can you—did you mean to blind him?"

Ahjvar stood back to him now, watching the room, sword still in hand. They were the focus of all eyes, but from a safe distance.

"What?" Weary confusion, not looking around. "I don't know. What did I do?"

Ghu did not think it would be lasting. It was only a spell worked in haste, to stop him seeing . . . mirror, there had been a mirror or some reflecting surface, Kangju had watched as they crossed the mulberry orchard. He was only dazed, dazzled, not so much blind as unseeing, to prevent him being the eyes of another . . .

Eyes of another, bound in blood and ink. But for a soul to be snatched away—

Later.

The shape of Ahjvar's spell—neat and precise, it was, for all its haste, which maybe should not have surprised him—was indescribable, not to be grasped by eyes or hands, but a shape none the less. Ghu simply unmade it, released the channelled power, borrowed of the earth's life, to flow as it would again; the wizardry did not resist him.

The wizard blinked, more tears spilling, and tried again to kneel.

"Go to the Kho'anzi, to Lord Daro Korat," Ghu said, and looked around, beckoned a young Daro soldier. That name, too, he could find, if he sought it, as if the Mother held them all, every breathing soul of the land, and her passage through him had left them here. And what else? "Take him to the Kho'anzi, Daro Nai. Tell your lord, here is an imperial wizard who wants to swear renewed service to the gods."

The soldier bowed and took the wizard's arm, not ungently, when Ghu handed him off. He gave Ahjvar a wide berth, though.

Ahj did not look well, grey and sweating, when he turned back from watching the soldier away.

"Ahj?"

He seemed to have to grope for words, swallowing, frowning. "Burning," he said at last.

Ghu's heart clenched. "No, Ahjvar, it's not." *You're not?* Now he was afraid, as he had not been even with Zhung Musan's blade swinging for his throat.

"Smoke."

"That's outside, remember?" He took Ahjvar's arm, wanted to pry that sword from his hand but did not suppose Ahjvar was going to let it go. "Yeh-Lin will take care of it, whatever it is. Maybe only the kitchens. We're going that way. Come. Walk."

"I know it's not real. I can see—I can see you. You're all white light. I can—but there's fire. That—who was he?"

"Wizard, Ahj. You didn't hurt him. He meant no harm. I sent him to the Kho'anzi."

"Wizard. I—he was—a thing, in the fire." Barely audible. "He was her. Burning. Black and still moving. Don't let me go. Don't let me *near* anyone. I can hear the fire, Great Gods, Ghu, help me. I'm so tired now and I can't trust what I see—"

"Look at me. Look at *me*, not the wall." Ahjvar's eyes were wide, blind as the wizard's had been, and staring over Ghu's shoulder. "See me. You're—dreaming. Awake and dreaming. Come."

"Too many people." But the eyes found him, did see.

"Good. Yes. We'll go outside. Come."

He gripped hard, didn't let Ahjvar break away from him. He spoke Praitannec, not allowing silence in which shadows could grow. Warning him of every encounter, as if he did guide a blind man through a perilous landscape.

Across the gravelled terrace again, bright now in new sunlight, down steps into another walled yard, where the buildings of the kitchens and kitchen-stores were. Ahjvar shrugged himself free from Ghu's grasp, dragged the back of a hand across his face.

"I can't stay here," he said.

"I know."

Stir and bustle and shouting, all the usual life within. People must eat, whoever ruled the keep, but here was a quiet corner behind the woodshed, shadowed and mossy and overlooked. Ghu led Ahjvar into it.

"Too many people." Ahjvar shook his head as if to clear it. "Even silent, there's too much noise, something like noise, I can't—"

"It's all right, Ahj. It's all right."

Eyes shut, Ahjvar sank down to his heels. He shivered, coatless, wet with others' blood. His own, too.

Ahjvar couldn't go on this way. Not among people. Ghu could not always hope to stop him when he saw some horror that wasn't there and struck to kill enemies a year gone from the world. He squatted down on his heels as well and tilted his face to the sun.

There truly was a tang of smoke, harsh in the air. That could not help. None clouded the sky, though.

"Ghu . . ." Ahjvar's hand groped and found his. Cold, as if there were no life left in him.

No peace. No healing in this world. He began to fear that was so, and he could not hold Ahjvar here in torment, he would not.

Not yet, not here, not like this. Not in blood and fear and weary defeat, with the unburied dead all around him. Let him at least die in some tranquil place, let there be beauty about him, not walls, not—

"You can't have a madman at heel and call yourself the gods' chosen heir. I'll hurt someone."

No answer to that. He rubbed the hand he gripped, trying to warm it.

"I can still hear fire," Ahjvar said, very low.

"No. You can't."

"I *know*. I'm just telling you."

"Ahjvar . . ."

"I can see you. I know you're true. I'm not so sure of anything else now. Why? I've gone longer than this without sleep, and merciful Great Gods, that was an honest fight if ever there was one, no murder."

Maybe. It was not the greatest weight that made a camel's knees buckle, but the last. The last wave that drowned a man. And there was fire here, and death, many deaths, the pressure of too many unshriven ghosts, and wizardry. Ahjvar was lost, drowning, and every buffeting wave one closer to too many. No sleep, either.

Ahjvar flinched, a convulsive clenching of his fingers and a hard grip he did not relax, as if Ghu's hand were the only certainty, an anchor in a raging sea. The movement that startled him had only been a sparrow dropping down to the woodshed eaves, lifting away again in alarm as great as Ahjvar's.

Anchor. With his free hand, Ghu dug into his coat's deep pocket, found his purse, worked its neck open. Shells, picked up along the shore below the cliff. No. Pretty, but they were dead things. He was not sure why it should matter, but it did. Acorns, a few long, smooth acorns, capless, from the cork-oak grove behind the village. Curiosities gathered and carried because they caught the eye or were smooth to the touch. Memories of Sand Cove, of a place that was anchor for something that mattered, a time that had made him, as another person might carry some token of their god's holy place when they went wandering, to remind them. Unlike the shells, the acorns held life.

"Hand." Ahjvar didn't react, so Ghu uncurled the one he held, pressed three acorns into the palm, folded the fingers over them. "There."

"What?"

"Hold those. Acorns, from Sand Cove."

"Why?"

"They're real. So you'll know. The acorns are real. Remember that. I picked them up—I think it was the day before the grape festival, that last autumn. You were just back; you'd gone to Gold Harbour without me."

"That was a bad one."

"Don't. It's the oaks you should remember. You don't dream of acorns."

Ahjvar turned them in his hand. Bemused? Distracted, anyhow. Distracted was good. And, "No," he did agree. "I don't."

"So hold on to them, and know the fire you hear isn't real. All right?"

Ahjvar eyed him. Ghu waited on *half-wit boy*, hoped for it, really, but Ahj only carefully, deliberately, transferred them to his left fist instead, to leave his swordhand free. He rolled them in his fingers as a man might some amulet of his god or a hermit's meditation-beads. Then back to leaning on the wall, eyes shut again.

"I don't know why it's worse under a roof," he said at last.

"Nowhere to run?"

"Huh. Nowhere for them to run, maybe. You think, thinking that in the back of my mind makes it worse?"

"Maybe."

"Head aches," he said, and sighed. "No coffee in this whole damned land, is there?"

"Coffeehouses in the Golden City and Kozing Port. Lots of trade, lots of merchants and sailors from south over the sea. It's not coffee you need. Breakfast. Stay here. It's safe, no one will come near."

Ghu raided the kitchens and met with no protest, only wide-eyed service, saw the dogs fed, sent dishes up to be taken in to the Kho'anzi and all with him, since Liamin had not yet sent for food herself. Eat first, deal with corpses after, would have been his concern. Back to Ahjvar, who was turning an acorn through his fingers, staring at the ground. Ghu wrapped his own coat over him and made him eat the better half of the dish of rice and eggs and vegetables he had carried off. The beer was that meant for the slaves of the outer offices, not the folk of the household, and no better than he remembered, but Ahj had a little better colour afterwards, though he then fell asleep where he sat.

Ghu took Ahjvar's sword, laid at his feet, and threw it aside out of reach, with himself between. He didn't dare leave him to go in search of Yeh-Lin.

A blackbird was singing, but all else in this corner seemed quiet. An island, smelling of river and green and growing things. Despite himself Ghu sank away, uncoiling into the river that lived now within him, wrapping all the land in its waters.

Few words were left to the Mother. Ghu had only ever had few of his own, before he found Ahjvar and learnt in his silences to speak and not to fear.

He feared for Ahj, but Mother Nabban spared no thought for him or for the sin that was Ghu's in taking over the curse that had bound murdered Catairlau into the world. Too late, too spent, too weak for judgement. Nothing left but the deep yearning to gather and hold all the land and ease its pain. Nothing left, so worn away was she with the too-great weight she had borne too long, since the days when all the goddesses had drawn into her and become one, to oppose the devil Dotemon and bind her in her grave.

Ghu's greater sin was not his dead man, his living ghost, but that he brought Yeh-Lin Dotemon back into Nabban, and deluded himself he could use her.

All laid on the Mother's lap. Offering.

Taken, and returned, gift for gift, for the Wild Sister within the Mother had dared what could not be dared, had been the heart and the passion and the will of her in the days when they fought the devil, and the Wild Sister's will would dare yet. The Wild Sister within the Mother saw a darkness and a fire within the land, and what was there to set against it, but a darkness and a fire sworn to serve? So he might dare, her will, their will—his will was to dare to think Dotemon honest. For this time, in this place. He saw no other way.

The river was all rivers, all waters, the lakes about him, quiet with lilies white and blue, secret, tree-lined, stirring with swan and duck and crane, fringed with villages rising on stilts, boats swift and darting, cutting the surface, dragging their nets. The cold secret forest wells where deer and bear, monkey and great cat came to drink. Streams swift and stony and ringing loud, calm and earthen between green and growing fields, subjugated in canals, in pounds and paddies, alive and flowing, always flowing, from the mountains to the sea.

She, he, was pregnant with them, rebirth awaiting, in all their names, in all their waters.

But not yet. Not this lifetime. New strength must grow, the land must take back its heart.

She, Mother Nabban, drowned herself in him. Nothing left but the deep heart of her, of him, in him. A spring, the small upwelling, to seep and spread and overflow, to flood him, drown him, dissolve him, make him river. It hurt, as drowning, as birth, ever did.

Then there was only the river.

The mountain, distant, waited.

"Nabban?"

He woke slow and groggy. "Nabban!" The whisper was repeated, breath tickling his ear. Yeh-Lin, crouched beside him. Ahjvar was slumped over against him, heavy head on his shoulder, the sore one, and it ached. He slid himself free and lowered the man to the ground, shoving a sleeve of the coat under his head. Ahjvar stirred, but only to clench his fingers into the turf. It was worrying that he had not woken before Ghu did at Yeh-Lin's approach.

She seemed to think so too. "Is he wounded?"

Ghu moved a few yards away and she followed. "No. Not to speak of."

"Is he all right?"

"No."

She sighed. "Ah, Nabban, what will you do with him?"

He shrugged. Not her concern. "The castle?" Sunset painting stripes of copper and fire on the white walls. The gods forgive, he had slept the day away. He felt half-drowned in sleep yet. He had dreamed . . .

"I have the north tower, and that was the last holding out for Zhung Musan. I went in myself after their captain, since he would not come out. He will not trouble you further. A patrol led by an imperial officer came against the western gate demanding entry from the town, much surprised to find it shut against them. I suggested Ti-So'aro inform him there was an outbreak of the bloody pox. They came in greater numbers and with a banner-lord, demanding speech with Zhung Musan. She said he was ill. They have retreated from the bridge back into the town and closed the gate at the town's end, and there is a company at the eastern gate as well. Not openly threatening yet, but . . . now what? They are not such fools as to believe that tale for long, when there is no outbreak in the town. We have, maybe, the night, before they assault the gates, I would guess. If we had any allies at all I would order the bridges destroyed, but as it is, if we do not break out of here and take the town, somehow, we are finished. For now, any I thought we could not trust are confined. I have walked the walls to ward them against the spying of wizards and—and anything else which might seek to know what we do here. Will you come? Whatever else we do, the Kho'anzi must take the oaths of the soldiers and the Zhung lords willing to renounce the emperor, which is most of them, and they are in such a fervour of faith . . . they must swear to you, before it ebbs. They have to swear to something, after all."

Ghu hesitated. "They can make their oaths to the gods of Nabban. You don't need me. You'll know who lies."

"You must—"

"No. No 'must.'" Grimly. "Let them lay their hands on the bier of the daughter of the priests to make their oaths to the Father and Mother. I won't be there."

Ahjvar muttered in his sleep.

"Nabban, you—"

"They think they've seen the will of their gods. Good. They have. They don't need to see a slave of the stables. I need to go to my gods. You, Yuro, Liamin, Ti-So'aro, Ario, the wizard Nang Kangju, the Kho'anzi's faithful lords and captains—you can do what must be done here. Look at Kangju's chest, a tattoo he's tried to cut. Find out what it is. Look for tattoos on the soulless dead. Zhung Musan. The other wizard. Look on the living. They were marked by the empress herself, for this goddess that she claims she has become."

"Ah? As on the assassins of the Wind in the Reeds in Denanbak? Very well. So. What of Dernang? Do we take it?"

"Yes," Ghu said. Did it need saying? "Of course. What else can we do? But I'm going to the mountain. You do what you can, when you can."

"You're leaving? Just you and your madman?"

"And the dogs."

"Oh, and the dogs. We have enemies at our gates, Nabban."

"I go the way I came."

"Just slipping out in the night? They will kill you on the roads."

"No."

"The town is garrisoned with half the army Zhung Musan brought north."

"I know. Make them ours."

"How?"

"You are Yeh-Lin. What would you do?"

"You want them as allies?" she hissed. "I would destroy the gates of their town and pull down the houses of their commanders, and set a fire upon the tents of the camp in the horsefair."

"Did I say, Dotemon?"

"Ah." She blinked at him. Smiled. "So you do trust me, heir of Nabban?"

"Was that a test of *my* intentions?"

She shrugged, still smiling. "Ti-So'aro and I have spoken—a young woman of energy and enthusiasm, that. Rash, perhaps. She reminds me of myself as a girl, a little. The Kho'anzi, too, has made suggestions. He has rested and woken with more of his wits about him. Ti-So'aro has kin among those of the lesser nobility of Zhung Clan who serve with this army, and though the lords have their household troops, most of the common soldiers are conscripts. They hardly know who or what they serve, and few are truly happy at being told their gods are dead and that they must worship a new god of the empress's court. It will be easy enough to get into the camp, which is outside the town walls, and Ti-So'aro thinks getting within the town will not prove too difficult, either. Her elder brother commands at the southern gate. A ruin and a makeshift barricade is all it is, still. They put their rebuilding efforts to some temple rather than their walls. So she and hers will go, once darkness falls, and tell that the true heir of the gods is come to bring justice to the land. She says, some will listen. Thus I till the ground and sow my seeds. After that . . . I do what I can."

"Don't unleash devilry upon my land. Don't kill my folk needlessly."

My land. My folk. He had meant, that of the gods. Had he not?

He felt too small and overwhelmed, apt to flee away into the child again, where it was safe, where Ahjvar could stand between him and the world. The last of the fury of the Mother and Father had gone from him, all certainty fled except in this one thing. He must go up the mountain to the god, as he had meant to. Ghu sighed and pulled himself together, all his scattered thoughts, all the waters . . .

"If you would come, so that the folk might see you—"

"No, Yeh-Lin. I am not the lord of this folk. I will not be general of this army, nor the Kho'anzi's seneschal. You are my captain and Daro Korat must make himself lord of this province again, under the gods. Do what your wisdom says needs doing. Tell him I said so. Do it without devilry and without murder and don't let yourselves be caged in this castle, or we'll have lost before we begin. Send over the river to these stray companies of Prince Dan's that are rumoured, send all the way to

Alwu if you must, to try to find the rebels there, and down to Shihpan, see if you can win his folk as allies. Tell all the officers and lords of the town they must choose to either obey a lie, or defy the empress and serve the will of the gods and the heir of the gods. And let me *be*."

"And what is the heir of the gods of Nabban going to be doing, then? Wandering on the mountain?"

"Yes."

"Madness. But three of us took a castle, so . . . I will give you Dernang, if you will."

"Yes."

"But I think they will need to see something they can believe in, even Ti-So'aro's kin. They will need more than a rumour and a tale."

"Make do with that for now. I'll come back. I will. If I do not—do what you must." Better Yeh-Lin than . . . what?

"And will both of you be coming back?"

He said nothing.

"Ah, Nabban. Better he had gone to the Old Great Gods when I put his goddess into the ground."

"No." Ahjvar had been better in the desert. That was worth this pain now. To have known him so. Worth it even for Ahj, to have been, for a little while, free again? Or was it sin and selfish greed that tried to believe so?

Yeh-Lin eyed him and let that go. "So what am I to tell the Kho'anzi? What do I tell the banner-ranked and the soldiers and the slaves who have seen you and been stricken with hope of their gods, who have offered their lives now, for hope of the gods?"

"That they must pray the Father sends me back," he snapped. "I don't know, I don't know. I go where I must; I didn't plan to come *here* yet."

"And yet you have, and they have put all their lives in your hands. They will die, all of them, and terribly, if this castle comes again under those who serve the empress. Do you know how they execute traitors in this land now?"

"I know!" He heard his voice crack, almost a shout.

Ahjvar surged to his feet and put himself between them, not as a friend between quarrelling friends but silent and fluid as a cat, focused on that one dangerous thing, which was Yeh-Lin. Not truly awake and not even recognizing her, Ghu thought. Sword in his hand. Yeh-Lin's eyes narrowed. She stepped back, very carefully, bowed, hands together, as Ghu put his hands over Ahjvar's on the sword.

"I am afraid for you, my lord," Yeh-Lin said. "Are you sure you know what you are doing? Don't let what you feel for this place drive you to—something ill considered."

She saw too clearly.

"I never know what I'm doing," he said. "Just what I must do. Ahj, it's all right."

"If you will go, must it be now? The oath-taking and the prayers—they are gathering already on the great terrace."

"Yes." Or there would be more questions, and more, and more people standing between him and his leaving, more needs between him and the mountain.

"As you are?"

"Food," he said. "Tea." *Horses.* No, not with enemies sitting before the gates.

"Your *gewdeyn*—" Yeh-Lin used the Praitannec word for a spear-carrier, an armed follower who went at a lord's shoulder and should be friend and counsellor as much as armed retainer. Better than the Nabbani word for a bodyguard, who might be free, but was more often a slave. "Your *gewdeyn* still looks a ragged madman. What happened to his coat?"

"What do you think?" Ahjvar growled. "Probably with my bow." He frowned. "Where are we going?"

"To the mountain."

"Crossbow," said Yeh-Lin. "Do you want one?"

"I don't know. Yes."

Ghu did not contradict him.

She let go a long breath. "I have set a guard on the postern door, since it had neither lock nor latch and I have not had time to find the smith. I will take you over the moat myself. At least folly won't extend to leaving that punt on the other side. And you, dead king, should wash.

There is blood in your beard. I've told them the holy one's man is a king of Praitan who left his land to serve the heir of the gods of Nabban. Even if you cannot find any respect for yourself, for your young god's honour in the eyes of his folk, make some effort to look—less mad. Give me a little time, then meet me there." She turned on her heel and stalked off.

"Angry," Ahjvar said. "What was that about?"

"We're going up the mountain to the place of the gods, you and I. She wants me here."

"Need to take the town."

"Others can do that. Come."

The folk they met on their way bowed and murmured a greeting and went on with whatever they were about. Ghu shed no light, looked only a small and ragged and weary vagrant, but perhaps that was not what the eyes of the newly faith-filled saw. Ahjvar, who had rubbed dried blood off his face on his shirt-sleeve and found a cut beneath it, did not understand such awe, and mistrusted it. Dotemon Dreamshaper. But Ghu seemed to find it . . . his due, and yet accepted it in all humility. Ghu would not let the devil spin lies for him. He would know if she did. Surely.

Ahjvar had never heard Ghu raise his voice in anger before. Never known him angry, he thought, till they came to this place. The anger in that raised voice, he had not dreamed.

Jui and Jiot slunk close at Ghu's heels.

Yuro the stable-master—castellan, now, and bastard son of the high lord, was he? He waited in the dark tunnel to the postern gate and the landing stage. No guards.

"Leaving?" he asked, standing arms folded in the open door. The twilight beyond made him a faceless silhouette. Fog was smoking off the water again. The flood had risen, lapping over the landing stage.

"The mountain and Swajui," Ghu said.

The stable-master waited, and Ghu stood between them. Ahjvar would have to push Ghu aside to heave Yuro out of the way.

"I will come back, the gods willing. They—I need to be there. I only came here first for Daro Korat."

"You're like a child throwing a pebble. No idea where the waves are going to wash up."

"No."

"You will come back. You swear, you will come back, and not leave us to die here betrayed by our gods."

"The gods willing, yes."

"And if they're not?"

"Then—look to Lady Lin. There is something lairing in the empire's heart. The Old Great Gods do not send messengers seeking the worship of living folk and the empress is no goddess. Whatever can stand against that lie, must. But I will come back."

Ahjvar thought the man frowned, maybe. Certainly he shifted his weight, turned to look over his shoulder, out to the moat, and back.

"Prophecy, boy?"

No answer.

Yuro snorted. "Long walk up the mountain and you should come back swift as you can. I sent mares up to the thorn-flower pasture early. Chago's in charge there. If you get so far without getting yourself killed, tell him I said, give you the horses you want."

"Mares in foal, Yuro?"

"Maybe a few others. They sent Sia's warhorse back, before the town fell. Before Sia died, he sent him back. Knew he wasn't going to be riding out of there. Proving to his folk he wasn't going to flee at the last, maybe. I didn't figure the white needed to be sent off as a prize for the empress, so I made sure he wasn't here when Zhung Musan took the place. Tell Chago, give you whatever horses you want, even that one. Knock him down if he argues."

Ghu laughed, a strange, bright sound in that place.

"Yes," he said. "Good."

And Yuro stood aside out of their way.

Ghu turned back, though, in the doorway. "He always was mine, you know," he said.

"Holy one." The man bowed. "I'll look to see you riding back."

Yeh-Lin sat in the stern of the punt, bundles at her feet, which were their own packs, left in the orchard. Full quiver, heavy stirrup bow, not the one Ahjvar had carried.

"Food," she said softly, prodding one pack with a toe. "Tea, a bow, and dead king, put this on." She twitched the folded Praitannec blanket from her own shoulder, flung it in a swirl of blue and greens over his back. "Here." A pin to hold it, a simple thing, but heavy, twisted red gold like a tongue of flame. And then her scarf as well, green and grey and russet wound about his throat. "From Deyandara. There's not a man in this castle with your height to borrow a coat from. It will be cold before morning. Cold to call the fog out of the river. Frost in the hills."

She sculled them across the moat ably enough. He could believe her some peasant woman, except for the sword at her shoulder. Impossible to see where the moat ended and the flooded fields began, and the fog was already thickening so that the castle loomed a strange and topless mountain, but she turned the punt and Ghu steadied it with a hand under the water, braced against unseen ground, and with boots tied to their packs and trousers rolled they disembarked. Even the dogs slunk, contriving not to splash. A distant horse whinnied.

In this fog, a sortie from the gates might be chanced, but what then? Yeh-Lin's business. Ahjvar hoped they would not return to find all Choa under her hand, and Dotemon Dreamshaper halfway to making herself empress again. Though she had never hanged children.

"Nabban . . ."

Ghu, already gazing away to the north as if he saw through fog and twilight to the mountain's height, turned back.

Yeh-Lin held out a hand and he gave her his. She raised and kissed it. "My lord. Go safely to your gods. Come back safely to your folk. And you, dead king . . ."

He kept out of reach.

She only shook her head, pushed the boat away.

CHAPTER XXII

The White River Dragon and Dernang were joined like two bubbles on the surface of a river, clinging but separate, with castle wall and broad moat and town wall between the castle's west and the town's northeastern gate. Or like a double-yolked egg, Yeh-Lin thought, and grinned at the homely image. Eggs boiled in the tea. So long since she'd handled an oar . . . strange, the memories a few simple actions brought back. What would that girl have made of young Nabban and his soul-wounded shadow? What of this woman who wore her face and her name? Suspicion and calculation in equal parts for the latter, she suspected. No sense of humour, that girl. She rather preferred the old woman.

And her young god wanted Dernang. No fool, whatever fools might think. Dernang, and the army encamped in the horsefair, and all Choa, three strides to take to a place they could stand in strength . . . for a little. It had taken only the three of them to seize the castle. Well, three, and the gods' own hands laid on their young heir. And they left her to him? Perhaps they also had developed a sense of humour, which was to say, perspective. Some might think there were worse things to have loose in your land than a tame devil. She laughed, looking down from this balcony under the highest gable of the many-gabled keep.

Grey light, the harbinger of dawn, and the moon a broken coin, high, hazy behind thin and drizzling cloud. From here she could see into the town, almost a bird's view. Still sleeping, the bell to end the night's curfew not yet rung, but the army's camp in the old horsefair was astir and there was a busy back-and-forth down several of the larger streets. Officers and officials of Zhung Musan's following had taken over a street of grand merchants' houses and guildhalls for their headquarters, Ti-So'aro said, before the castle fell; many had been left there when the general shifted his headquarters to the keep, to ensure the town still felt his boot on its neck. The market square by the northern gate was empty yet, save for bodies on the gallows—nice to thing to hang over your vendors of vegetables—and a flock of crows busy at them. Fresher meat than the foul display they had passed beneath on the road in the night. The squat gatehouse of the north and the ruin of the south, the gate there roughly barricaded to a single cart's-width with rubble, and the small tower that watched the gate of the castle's bridge, all flew the imperial banners, deep purple-red and gold, with the Zhung characters black on white in a centre roundel to show which clan here represented the imperial will. The imperial banners—Zhung, not Daro—still hung from this keep as well, and from their gatehouses. She did not suppose that Zhung Musan's deputy believed the story of an outbreak of disease, despite the banners' proclamation of continued Zhung supremacy, but his failure to take any decisive action in the night was encouraging.

If his hesitation continued, though . . . she had not the forces to storm the town, whatever the Kho'anzi and his officers hoped, nor yet to besiege it, and she did not think that to come upon this lieutenant to the general, this Lord Hani Gahur, with lightning and storm, to blast down his walls and scatter his army in terror and death, was quite what her young god had in mind, when he said, "Do what I would have you do." Ill-advised to destroy the town's defences, which he might yet have need of. And these were Nabban's folk, all of them; she rather thought he was going to need them, too, living souls and his.

What did peasant conscripts know of emperors, of gods in this land where few had ever seen or spoken with their gods? They saw only their sergeants and officers and the banners carried ahead of them, knew only what they were told, repeated it without understanding. Uneducated, unthinking beyond the day to day—whatever they might have been had they had other lives and other education, they were sheep now. They would bunch and mill and hesitate, and go, when they went, in a rush and as a flock. She need only drive them where she would have them go; it was those over them that she must win, or destroy and replace.

Down there beyond the moat the rumour was spreading, if Ti-So'aro and Nang Kangju and the rest who had been ferried over the moat in the punt, two by two, to slip away to the camp at the north gate or the town's hopefully welcoming and vulnerable southern entrance had found the willing ears they expected. *The heir of the gods* . . . a whisper and a hope. Seeds, so that when—what followed—followed, there would already be rooted among the under-officers, the banner-ranked and their personal troops, and among small islands of the conscripts, too, the shoots of new faith, a will to a new Nabban, ephemeral though such shallowly planted notions might be, to grow and spread until by sheer mass they proved too firmly fixed for eradication. Or at least, the whispers might be a spur to turn suspicion of the empress, whose general had murdered priests, to mutiny.

A company of Lord Hani Gahur's horse waited on the road below the castle to prevent any outbreak from the main gates, but the waters still rose, lapping over the road now, beginning to meet at its crown; they could make no camp and would be driven back before long.

In the town, some move, surely against the castle, was mustering, order emerging from the scurrying consultation, a company—embassy? —assembling.

"Children!"

They were sleeping in a huddle under a blanket filched from a chamber within, but they came alert at her word, yawning and rubbing their eyes. A few hours' rest, while she had composed spells against the morning's need, gathering formal wizardry about her once more. They had slept deep in exhaustion, poor things, oblivious to the characters that glowed in the air as if traced by fireflies, written in mind, breathed out with a word, sent to settle and fade to secrecy where she would have them lodge.

Yeh-Lin had, in the end, rested herself, sitting precarious on the parapet, cross-legged, hands open on her knees, eyes fixed unseeing on the cloud-troubled stars. If she dreamed, back in Nabban with all in chaos and wanting only a strong hand . . . well, that was a matter for the night, and it was past, and the day lay before her. She had sworn.

They blinked at her and offered wary bows: her pages, newly named so, and still wondering and uncertain in their elevation. In their freedom. She must remember their names and not keep thinking of them as the little one and the girl and the other boy.

The previous evening, Yeh-Lin had realized that she needed and would go on needing loyal message-runners, willing fetch-and-carriers. She had conscripted three young slaves from garden and kitchen work as she passed through the castle, liking the look of them. Watchful intelligence behind those warily downcast eyes, all three. They ran at her heels and were dispatched about the castle with messages as she met with the Kho'anzi, with his captains and banner-lords, with the castellan, with all she must persuade and order and chivvy into obedience and action. They had been most helpful in rooting through the storerooms, too, for what, even she had not been certain. "Something to make a banner of . . ."

It had been the battered littlest one who found the sky-blue silk, several bolts of it, and had said, with un-slavelike confidence, "This, mistress! This is what you want."

It had been so, most certainly.

There was a name for such service, even in Nabban, that was not slavery. Begin as her young god meant to go on?

They had helped her lug the several heavy bolts of silk to this balcony beneath the highest gable facing the town, and they had rested and eaten cold dumplings and tea together, the four of them.

She had dropped words into the dark of the night, startling their yawning into an apprehensive, disbelieving silence. "Children. I have decided that you three are to be my pages, if you will. Do you under-stand that? Only if you will. And if so, you must call me 'my lady' or 'Captain Nang Lin,' not 'my mistress.'"

Pages came of high and free birth. They had not quite dared to understand.

"The heir of the gods of Nabban will have no slaves in his land." So—it was said, and the castle must know it. How he thought this could be done and the land brought to peace and a place found for all, she did not know. There had always been debt-slaves in the law, with some limits on their terms and their service, even when she was a child. And then . . . there had been captives from Dar-Lathi, and from what were now the western provinces from Choa down to Asagama, once those were conquered, their kings and queens becoming Kho'anzis and high lords of their clans, but many of the lesser nobility had been taken captive and never freed. Hands had been required to work the land when the army called up the sons and daughters of the free peasantry to become soldiers for the invasion of Pirakul and the war there, where Jasberek Fireborn united the temples of the many gods against her. . . . And so it had grown, and sunk deep roots, and now it was the support and the frame of all the land.

Her god must surely understand that it was easier to break than to make. They must take thought for that future, not, as it seemed Prince Dan had done, wake rebellion with no consideration how the folk of the land, slave or serf or free, would then feed themselves.

Slave himself, and devoted servant, grown to manhood in his mad assassin's shadow trying only to keep him from the dark, had Nabban yet learnt to look more than a move or two ahead, when he set a force in play?

The game of long calculation held also the risk of paralysis. Dotemon had learnt that.

Sometimes, was it not better to unleash the storm and hope to ride it? Yeh-Lin had taught her so.

For now, they must all—all this castle's folk swept, whether they adored or doubted, to follow Nabban—feed on hope.

"If anyone presumes to order you back to your old places, you say you are the pages of the captain of the heir of the gods and they must come to me. And if you come to find you do not want to be in my service, we will find some other work you are suited to do, yes? But in these next days, I will need some quick-witted and willing servants. I would have those servants be you."

"Yes, mistress." The round-faced boy—Kufu, that was the name, and he was the grandson of the garden-mistress, no doubt an aristocrat among the hierarchy of at least the outdoor slaves—had seemed doubtful, mistrusting but not disagreeing. He had licked nervous lips. "Yes . . . Captain Lin." But the eyes of the skinny lad from the kitchens, Ti, the little one with the bruised face, had been wide with an adoration he could not have known she saw. The tall, bushy-haired girl, Jang, another belonging to the gardens, had given a brisk nod, and a "Yes, my lady."

Pages. So they must learn to read and write and have some training in arms and . . . had she so very much enjoyed playing tutor? Or did she yearn to be a mother and grandmother again? Perhaps she could do better this time around.

"Children, Lord Gahur is coming. I said he would. The silk—you remember what to do?"

"Yes, my lady." That was Jang. Confident in the morning.

She sent them to relieve themselves in whatever chamber-pot they could find in the abandoned room of Lord Daro's imprisonment. Of such things must the god's captain—and a good grannie—take thought.

"Then wait. It may be a long wait. Kufu, you'll go to the kitchens and fetch back something to eat. Don't let them keep you. Don't send Ti near the kitchens. I do not have time to argue with cooks to get him back." And she would have a word with Castellan Yuro about how the kitchen-master treated his underlings, so soon as she had a moment to spare. "It may be a long wait, but you must keep watch faithfully and not let anyone drive you out or order you away."

A round of bows, nicely judged to the appropriate degree, but little Ti was frowning at her.

"Yes, Ti?"

He shook his head, suddenly afraid, staring at his bare feet, shoulders hunched.

Yeh-Lin dropped to her knees, a finger tilting his chin up. Eye to eye, she said, "Never be afraid to ask me a question, Ti. *Nang* Ti." A full and formal name, freedman, free man. Her name, but it ought to have been Daro, as they were of the Daros. Too late. "What is it?"

"You changed your colour." Whispered.

She laughed and sat back on her heels. "Good. I did. And did Daro Kufu and Daro Jang think it would not be polite to mention it, or did they not notice?"

"But you're a wizard, my lady," said Jang, unquashed.

"Ah, but what Ti wants to know, really, is *why* I changed the colour—am I right?"

The boy still hardly dared nod. She ruffled his hair.

Changed her colours. Black-lacquered armour. Yesterday it had been deep-blue and rose, old colours from before the time of Min-Jan, which only an historian would know. The armour, her brocades, were all formed of memory, but as real as the roof beneath her, as the body she wore. What, stripped of the workings of power, had she actually clothed herself in? Some simple shirt and trousers of Praitan, she suspected. She did not remember. She shaped them to what she would. The blanket and scarf she had given Ahjvar were real enough; she had them from Deyandara when they parted.

"I changed the colour in the night, yes. Black is my god's colour, your new god's colour, the heir of Nabban. Black for the night sky, and blue," she added, as his frown returned, puzzling over a god of night, maybe, or thinking of the bolts of silk, "for the day. As you knew was right, when you helped me in the storeroom." And she touched the trailing silk ribbons of the helmet she had set on the parapet, drew them through her fingers and let them see the azure spread, like morn breaking upon the world. But she left the scarlet of her sword's tassel. Hers. Always. Real as her bones.

She vaulted back up to stand on the railing, forgetting till too late her grey hair. Ah well.

"Hah! They come from the town now, to demand word with their general. Perhaps I should go to greet them. Keep your watch, my faithful pages. You won't mistake my signal."

"No, my lady."

"No, Captain Lin."

"It will be like in a song," little Ti said abruptly, as she leapt down again and strode for the door.

Yeh-Lin paused, one foot over the threshold, to look back. "Yes," she said. She had better find some instructor in the pipa or another minstrel's instrument for that one, it occurred to her, and some books of the old poetry. That was the seed that struggled to sprout in his heart. "Do it right, and it will be a song. And it may be that someday you will make it."

"You can't mean to let them in," Lord Daro Raku, the Kho'anzi's cousin and commander, protested. He leaned heavily on his sergeant rather than the pike he had taken as a prop. The last of the Daro prisoners to be released, he had been thought dead; mere chance found him in the deepest cellar, alone, with the water rising past his waist. Raw and festering wounds from his shackles girdled both ankles, though Yeh-Lin had claimed to have a minor talent in physician's wizardry and driven out the rot that would have killed him. The sergeant glowered at Yeh-Lin, as if holding her responsible for her commander's refusal to withdraw safely to his bed.

Lord Yuro chewed his lip, straightened up when he caught Yeh-Lin's eye on him. "She does mean it," the new castellan said, which was vulgar, to talk about her so before her face, no title.

The sergeant switched her frown to him, but he was only as blunt and forthright as the peasant girl from Solan had been when first she sat smiling in the tea-house by the gate of Solan, hunting, as the orchid-spider hunted, by waiting under the guise of a passive flower for some lordling who might give her a chance at a wizard's education. No corps of imperial wizards to take her in, in *those* days.

"But what does she mean to do after?" Yuro asked. "Captain Lin?"

He was unnerved, greatly, though he hid it well. That he should take counsel with captains and lords, and be heard.

Yeh-Lin smiled sunnily. "We shall see," she said. "That depends, of course, entirely on Lord Hani Gahur. Mount."

Because their enemies were coming mounted, and it would not do to be looked down upon, or overridden. The blue-eyed piebald stallion a woman held for her was showy and restless. Yuro's choice. A test, a message, or an acknowledgement of confidence, she wasn't certain. No time to persuade it of her benevolence. It knew her for an alien thing and twitched its skin as if swarmed by flies, rolled its eyes. She took the lightest of holds on its mind, as if she seized a lock of mane in her fist. Twisted, to tighten her grip.

"Shh, shh. Behave," she told the rolling eye, and settled it, not in any manner either Yuro or Nabban would approve, as she allowed the stable-hand to hold the stirrup for her mounting.

Despite the thick walls, they could hear the hooves on the bridge already. Bold. Stupid? Genuinely deceived by the banners and the report of illness? Surely not that stupid. *She* would not have trusted that the timbers were not sawn through. A sudden thunder of drums demanded entrance. She fastened her helmet, but left the mask raised.

A soldier signalled from over the gatehouse. Twenty. Was that really all? Yeh-Lin half-shut her eyes, counted what she felt, the small warmths of their souls, and the beasts they rode. Twenty-two riders, and many more afoot back behind the gate of the town on the other side of the moat. Three wizards out there somewhere, one of modest talent, something more than a common Camellia Badge diviner, the sort who could be Plum or Palm depending on how hard they strove, two surely among the greater of Palm Badge Rank, if not a Bamboo lord or lady. No, only one, somewhere; the others she had thought she had felt were gone. Both. A mistake? Unlikely. Odd. No time to pursue that vanished tickling presence.

"Open the gate," she said.

No hesitation in obedience. Hesitation beyond, though, the bridge-narrow front of imperial officers clearly having expected some shouted negotiation from the gatehouse and an ultimate refusal.

The imperial commander faced pikes and crossbows, two dense wings of them, and a complete stranger in anonymous black armour flanked by lords blazoned with the Daro roundel.

They could, of course, still charge the gate, and they might very probably win through in the end, but it would be those in the van who died in the first piercing hail. She did not give them time to nerve themselves to it.

"Lieutenant-Commander Lord Hani Gahur? I am Nang Yeh-Lin, the captain-general of the Holy One of Nabban. With Lord Daro Korat the Kho'anzi of Choa, I hold the White River Dragon for my lord, the heir of the gods of Nabban. You will surrender Dernang and command of its army to me, in the name of the heir of the gods."

Lord Gahur, his helmet slung at his saddle-bow, was a young man, soft-faced. Fat would come with age if he were not careful, but for the moment he had only a still-boyish roundness, and his arrogance was a boy's, too. His brief moment of startlement turned to a smile.

"Yeh-Lin? Your mother chose you an ill-omened name." An appraising look, a curl of the lip. Was his youth and high rank a sign of competence, or was he some kin of the general's? Or promoted for an apparent lack of ambition, perhaps, but there was a cunning in his study of her, a calculation. Miscalculation. The look assessed and dismissed her. "I'm surprised the traitor Daro Korat would trust a colony mercenary." His bow in the saddle was entirely mocking. "Ah, Daro Raku, a pleasure to find you in good health."

"You will dismount and lay down your arms, and order your banners struck. Dernang is claimed for the heir of Nabban."

"Don't be a fool, woman. Where is General Zhung Musan? Release him, and I may let you flee over the border."

A lie on his tongue.

"Quite dead. He attacked the gods' chosen. You haven't had the pleasure of meeting the—" Not *gewdeyn*, no. *Rihswera*. That was the word she wanted, and very much on her mind now, because—this young lordling was too arrogant to be bluffed into caution, into negotiation and the putting aside of his advantages. Ahjvar was not here, but there was more than one sword would serve Nabban. "—the *rihswera*, which is to say, the champion, of the young god. I assure you, there are some would rather face me than him. And that is saying more than you know."

"Would this be the man and his—creature, who fled the castle last evening?"

Lord Raku's horse jibbed at some twitch of the bridle-hand. Yuro did better, impassive, but Hani Gahur smiled, seeing his words find their mark.

"Oh, yes, my wizard was watching your walls. Did you think not? We expected spies, but the Daro puppet seems to have had second thoughts about his role in your wretched last gasp of rebellion. He's run for the hills."

Creature? Wizard enough to see something amiss in Ahjvar—definitely Bamboo Badge, and that was dangerous. But even a Bamboo lord was not necessarily more wizard than Ahjvar could deal with, she told herself. Wizard, Hani Gahur said, not wizards. He had been careful about that. Too careful? *My* wizard . . . How easily and arrogantly he put himself in General Musan's place.

"Wizard or wizards, Lord Gahur? Did you send your best strength after the holy one on his pilgrimage and keep only your diviner here? I hope you took a proper farewell; he or she is marked for death. The heir of the gods has gone to speak with his gods, and when he returns, it will be to take all Choa in his hand. Will you give me your sword now, and spare yourself?"

Hani Gahur was disinterested rather than baffled, impatient, turning to speak to the man beside him.

She shrugged. "No? And I asked most courteously, too." She raised her sword, wished for a moment she did have a god to pray to. Lord Gahur's gaze snapped back to her, eyes widening, lips beginning to part. *Do not let the crossbows mistake the gesture, horseboy, as you love me, as I and they are yours.* "The new goddess is a lie and the empress is a traitor to the gods, an usurper of the land, no daughter of any gods small or Great. The throne of Min-Jan will be cast down."

Behind her the castle was a range of swooping eaves, white and dark, against the dawn and the sun just showing a burning edge, a shaft of light piercing through the clouds and the gaps of the buildings to strike on her uplifted blade. She breathed a word. It was wizardry, a great wizardry such as she doubted even the Pine Lord or Lady, whoever they might be in this time, could work single-handed, but it gave no offence to the gods. She did not promise them, or Nabban, that she would always work so.

Yeh-Lin did not need to look behind to see the sudden glint on gilded thunder-charms rearing on the peaks. It was before her eyes like a reflection on water, and in the staring eyes of Hani Gahur and those about him, two-score uplifted mirrors. The banners of the Min-Jan flared like polished copper catching the sun.

And they burned.

Scarlet, yellow, white flame—roaring, announcing itself as if all the keep were afire. Folk cried out, staring, even Yuro and Raku turning in the saddle, the horses laying back their ears, nostrils flaring. The imperial banners shrivelled to black, floated away in ashy flakes like dry leaves dropped on a bonfire. Too brief a fury, maybe. Had enough seen in all the yards of the castle, in the town, the camp . . . throughout the land, as every banner of the Min-Jan in all the empire turned to ash? Neither soot nor smoke would be staining the plastered walls of the White River Dragon; no charring would mar its beams. She would not swear it was so at the imperial palace in the Golden City.

A small miracle of the new god. She did hope the empress, wherever she might be, had word of it and took due note of the omen.

Or challenge.

And now—almost she held her breath. Now Yeh-Lin did risk a glance back, and up, but the children were true to their time. A push was all it would take—yes. The three bolts of heavy silk unrolled, spilling down the white wall, rippling like water, floating out on the wind like the dragon the Wild Sister had once been. Against the lime-washed plaster and the curdling grey of the clouds that closed again over the sun they blazoned the promise of clear skies.

"I will have Dernang for my god," she said. "Lord Hani Gahur, our forces are more evenly matched than you know—" A lie, but she did not think the wizard back somewhere among the footsoldiers was capable of sifting *her* truth. "—and we are all folk of Nabban and folk of Nabban's god. Dernang has seen enough of blood. Will you fight me, champion against champion in the manner of Praitan, for command of this place and this army?"

His mouth, open to gawp like a child for all he must recognize wizardry, snapped shut. "Are you insane, old woman?"

"If you would rather not face me, you may of course appoint another champion to stand for the empress and her false god."

"In the manner of *what?*"

"A tradition of the king's justice of Praitan, particularly apt, here, where we two can agree on no god's judgement."

"You want to fight me? Old woman—"

"Not so old as all that," she snapped, with careful indignation. "Some might say, there is an imbalance here yes, of long experience set against a young man so clearly promoted above his competence for—what, family connections, a pretty face?" Though not one to her taste, especially when he flushed the colour of old brick. All flesh and no bones. "All I have heard of you assures me—" *you are arrogant and a fool* "—that you are an honourable man who would keep his oath once given and would abide by the judgement of fate and the sword, and would demand the oaths of the lords and officers under you to do likewise, or I would not have offered this challenge. If you fear—"

"Fear has nothing to do with it. Why would I fight for what I have only to take? And why would I trust some wizard from the colonies, which you clearly are?"

"What you have only to take?" She glanced aside at the crossbows. "I hear that your army is on the edge of mutiny, Lord Gahur."

"Then you have heard lies."

"Word of the return of the heir of the gods passes among your soldiery. The overthrow of the tyranny of the line of Min-Jan is proclaimed. Neither the conscripts nor the banner-lords and -ladies have any faith in this lie of the empress as goddess. She has murdered her brother and her father. Priests are slain throughout the land by her word." Young Ti-So'aro had provided much rumour that would be of service this day. "Buri-Nai and the emperors before her have shown no care for the folk of this land, and the folk of the land are turning against her. A sensible man would lay down his sword and surrender command of the town to its rightful lord under the gods, but if you will not, then at least settle this with honour."

His lip curled.

"Or I will have you shot down, here, now, and proclaim *that* the will of the gods, and if you say, we have not the numbers to withstand you, I say, are you so devoted to the usurper that your ghost will find consolation in that? Count the crossbows, Lord Hani Gahur. All with you alone their target. Your company may ride over us, but your armour could be dragon-scale wrought by the true Yeh-Lin herself and still you personally would not survive it. Don't!" she snapped, as he raised a hand to lower the mask of his helmet, and he froze.

"Good," she said, as he dropped his hand again and sat back. She pushed at him, just that little, not to bend his will but to nudge it. Would her god approve? No. But it bought lives. Not excuse enough? She restrained herself. A nudge, no more. He was all nerves and fear, not of her but of the eyes of his own officers. That need to be admired and an arrogant temper made a seething soup.

"It's you who should be appointing another champion for this fight," Gahur said. "*Grandmother*. But since you've made the challenge I'll take it, and let Dernang be the prize."

"And should fate give you the victory, the Kho'anzi Daro Korat and all his folk, and all your folk who have given their oath to the holy one of the gods, will suffer no reprisal from you, but be allowed to depart over the border to Denanbak." She must make such a condition; he would expect it. "We fight not only for Dernang, but for command of your army, and the oaths of your officers to turn their backs on the empress and her false god and serve the true heir of the gods."

"Very well. But I can't command their oaths to the gods."

Yeh-Lin gave a brief bow to the truth of that, which she had not expected him to acknowledge even to present a face worthy of respect to his officers. It was plain as mud in water he meant to honour nothing of this agreement once she was dead.

"You will have to make do with their oath to surrender to your command," Hani Gahur continued, "on condition that they be allowed free passage to the Old Capital and return to the empress's service." His turn to make conditions for the look of the thing, his lip curling in a sneer. But he was confident. Wary, a little, suspecting some trickery, but confident in himself against a woman old enough to be—surely not his grandmother? Yes.

She ought to have left more black in her hair.

They rode together to meet face-to-face under the shadow of the gatehouse, each with two witnesses to hear their bargain made again and formally, invoking the Old Great Gods. He ordered up the young Palm Badge wizard who had hung back among the ranks, to ensure no wizardly trickery. Yeh-Lin took Yuro and Lord Raku from the small company which had followed her. Her own wizard was busy with Lady Ti-So'aro, sowing mutiny throughout the town, and she feared no treachery any wizard of Hani Gahur's could arrange, even were there another, hidden from her. But no, when she reached out briefly searching again . . . nothing. She shrugged off the nagging feeling that there should be.

The negotiations were tedious and exasperating, and she would concede to none of Lord Gahur's fishing for greater delay. She would not have him sending the most faithful of his officers off to find the truth of rumours of mutiny; she wanted haste to keep his anger and contempt, his humouring of the rebel folly and their misplaced faith in their pretender divine heir, on the boil. Have this over and done with, and send Daro Korat's head rather than his person to Buri-Nai, that was Hani Gahur's thought. And the head of this arrogant mercenary captain, too. She pressed, encouraging that set of his mind. Glory, when the empress received the salt-packed boxes. His success, blazing over Zhung Musan's failure.

Here, now, not noon, not tomorrow's dawn, by which time the rational sense of Daro Raku would have overruled the fool old woman. Here in the market square of the town, and Hani Gahur agreed, yes, laughing behind his teeth at her folly, her willingness to bring her little band into town, but she would not have him within the castle gates where he—or more practical officers among his following—might yet overturn all.

A play. A game for children. But he demanded further solemn oaths from her, by the Old Great Gods, that she would use no wizardry. She gave her most pious word.

Nine witnesses. He argued, for form's sake, that there could be no fairness in that, no even balance. Nine, she said. It was the tradition of Praitan. The circle was made of nine, who should be bards and wizards of the tribes, but of course Nabban had no equivalent of the bards of Praitan. The scholars, those who were not clerks of the imperial court, were all poor scrabbling things, holy folk of Father Nabban, and the priestess of the town was, they told her, a crow-picked corpse.

Three from the castle—Yuro and Raku and a commoner, a middle-aged Zhung archer of Ti-So'aro's following whom Yeh-Lin chose for her grim face. Three from Hani Gahur's corps of officers, including his young wizard. Three picked from the streets of the town, witness for the judgement of fate—Yeh-Lin pointed at random to a man in a cara-vaneer's coat, his head wrapped in a loose turban. He was Nabbani, but he wore his hair long, hanging in the many braids of the road. The man gave her a slow look, as if he considered protest, but then bowed and stepped forward. He moved like a warrior, fluid as a cat, and his face did not have the pinched look of this town's hard winter. Mercenary? Spy? She would think the worse of Prince Dan's competence if he did not have folk in this town. The caravaneer would bear investigation, later. Hani Gahur pointed to another caravaneer. Random chance or did he think strangers were required? This one was a woman, maybe a Marakander, with the amber eyes of the Grass, though her features were more north-provinces Nabbani, delicate and rounded, and she was very pale for a Grasslander. Well, make sure the next was for Dernang, then. Yeh-Lin pointed to an old man, beckoned him forward. So. Done.

Nine witnesses to make the circle, under the Old Great Gods. Neither she nor Hani Gahur believed anything but skill of the blade would determine this meeting, but they made yet again, and publicly, their most pious oaths, and declared again the stakes, command of castle and town and army, for all to hear.

Raku was seething; only the Kho'anzi's order that Captain Lin was to be obeyed as if she spoke with Daro Korat's own voice had kept him denouncing her and seizing mastery of the situation himself. Even so, he had given final orders behind her back. The castle gate was closed again, his sergeant left behind to prepare for what he believed was inevitable assault, after the deaths of all dragged by Yeh-Lin's folly into the town.

"They'll slaughter us, even if you can defeat Gahur," he hissed in her ear now. "For the gods' sake, for my lord and all the castle, let me take this fight. For your god's sake, if you believe that's what the horseboy is, don't throw away what we've already won. We can stand a siege, wait for Prince Dan—"

"Shh, shh. I begin to think Prince Dan and his various ever-defeated armies nothing but foxfire. Trust me, my lord. Yuro does."

The castellan, close by and looking worried despite her claim of his trust, pursed his lips but said nothing.

"A slave-born bastard—"

"Hardly fit words to give your lord's son." Yeh-Lin didn't need to pretend to coldness. Daro Yuro stood close enough to have heard that, and she was deciding she rather liked the man. Pity she hadn't shown up looking twenty years younger.

"No, I mean—my apologies, my lord Yuro—" That sounded stiff, but honest. "—I don't doubt his—his honour, but what experience does he have to judge?"

"You think he rose to stable-master blindfold and stopping his ears with wax? A wiser man in judging men and women than a lord who sees only the bowing masks of servility. He trusts me—do you not, my lord castellan? And your lord the Kho'anzi does, and my young god does, and your word if not your faith is given there. Now go to your place, like a good boy."

"He's almost twice your weight, woman, and less than half your age!"

"Oh, please. He is neither. Well, perhaps the latter, I will grant you, but I intend neither to wrestle nor seduce him. *Trust* me." She winked. "After all, I was ruling this empire when your great-great-greats were in their swaddling clothes, was I not?"

Raku blew out his breath in a groan. "And what was the purpose of that? Childish! It didn't have a chance of intimidating him. It only lowered you to a fool in his eyes and gained you his contempt. He thinks you're a joke, a symptom of our lord's desperation and delusion."

"It did indeed." She shook her head. "Poor fool."

Yuro gave her a long look as he stepped away to his place, and, in his narrowed eyes, a little uncertainty. Raku turned on his heel and stalked to the station she had appointed him, between the male caravaneer and the Palm Rank wizard. Brave man. He thought he would not live out the morning. Or perhaps foolish, when it was only honour and his lord's command that held him here against all his better judgement.

Same thing in the end, the girl she had been might once have said. Dotemon . . . would now disagree.

"I serve the young god of Nabban," she said, bowing to the imperial commander. "With my blade and my life, I will prove the truth of my words. He is heir of the dying gods, and this land and its folk are his, and your empress is a tyrant and a usurper and a false goddess, a deceit and an outright lie."

He had been warned. She had given him her name. He ought to have doubted his own impulse to take this challenge and silence the mocking old woman. He need not have given in to it, embraced it, even, in anger at the insult of her existence, in the mingled fear and relief he felt at Zhung Musan's death, in his desire to come to the notice of the empress. And he stood in the circle of witness before the Old Great Gods with deceit in his heart, faithless in his word. If she fell, Yuro and Raku and the handful of officers and their escort of crossbows would be butchered, and the castle taken, and Lord Daro Korat slain. He intended it.

A ritual of execution with a throw of the dice, a nod to reckless fate. Had Catairlau enjoyed this moment, in the days when he stood as his father's *rihswera*, the king's champion of the Duina Catairna? Savoured the heat that smouldered in the heart under the cold and observing eye?

Lord Hani Gahur bowed. She did. Visors lowered.

They met with formality, the careful sparring of training. Hani Gahur—nearly all the lords—favoured broad, single-edged blades, heavier than the sabres of the Great Grass style that were the preferred sword of the caravan road. Shorter than her double-edged antique of the old empire. She doubted his edge could match hers, though she would as soon lay her limbs under a meat cleaver as let him test it on her.

No one could say he had not been warned.

Ivah had more than half a mind to pull concealment around her and slip away, the moment they all began moving away from the bridge, up to the wider space of the market square, but she had to admit a fascination, too, in the outcome of this challenge. She recognized the form of the duel from her Praitannec gang-mate Buryan's stories. It was a judgement of the gods, or an execution. But the woman was no warrior of Praitan. No one of her age who had lived by the sword would show so little sign of it. Leanly muscular, as a dancer was. Beautiful, before she hid herself with the helmet's ornate mask. If she had been younger, Ivah thought she might have fallen in love with such a face, or at least been moved to contemplate it, and its no doubt complete disinterest in her, gloomily over a cup of wine if there was one to be had in Dernang. High cheekbones, long, slender hands, long-lashed eyes warm, dark brown. She had been unscarred. Unmarked by care, by sun, by wind; she might have spent a lifetime keeping carefully withindoors and cosseting her face with orangewater and milk baths. Her sword was not in the style of any other weapon Ivah had yet seen in Nabban, and yet the brocade-covered scabbard was without doubt Nabbani work. She had seen such long, straight blades, with the silk ribbons of the tassel flying from the hilt, in the illustrations of old Nabbani scrolls in the library of Marakand when she had been making her new copy of *The Balance of the Sun and the Moon.*

Yeh-Lin. The woman dropped the name either to rattle Hani Gahur's nerves, or to have him think her a senile braggart. A game.

Old woman playing games, with a province at stake . . .

A grandmother dances at the funeral, the coins had told her that morning, which was one of the more cryptic hexagrams. Ivah was still not certain what she ought to make of that, as advice, and had decided ruefully that a hasty throw to determine the tenor of the day bordered on uneducated superstition and she ought not to do it.

She told herself so, every time she did.

Perhaps she ought not to have ventured out.

Yeh-Lin, after all, was her grandmother—rather a few generations removed.

Which made that brief moment of even hypothetical attraction—well, never mind.

The centre of the market was cleared. "You," the captain-general said, pointing at Ivah. "Stand there. You are a witness for the Old Great Gods. And you . . ." She arrayed them all, while Lord Hani stretched and went through self-conscious exercises, nearly preening for the crowd. Ivah eyed sidelong the blank-faced rebel lord with a mace who was placed to one side of her and the nervous-looking young imperial wizard in her indigo-blue robe on the other. Neither took any interest in her. Her fellow caravaneer was not someone she had seen around town, or on the road. He looked very well-fed; he had not been in Dernang long. A handsome man a little younger than the captain seemed, fifty, perhaps, grey but still in his full strength.

Caravaneer. Huh. She had walked beside him. His coat did not reek of camels, and he too, watched everything, studying them all. His face showed nothing.

He would not have come from the winter desert or Denanbak in those horseman's boots.

No more formality, no prayers. The captain saluted, touching her blade to her forehead.

"Are you quite ready, my lord?" She lunged at him, a mere warning.

At first they were careful, as if each knew what the other meant to do and only went through an exercise. They circled like two dogs sniffing, finding their place, a rhythm. A fight to the death. The tassel of the captain's sword was red, but the ribbons of her helmet were blue, blue as the silk that unfurled from the top of the castle keep as the banners burned.

Blue as the sky, breaking to ribbons and banners around her god.

A grandmother dances at the funeral. Ivah was cold as if hit with a gust of wind off the winter desert. Hard to swallow. Here. She was blind. She had come where she ought to be. And in that dizzying moment she saw the woman truly, black hair long, not cut short, flying out from beneath her helmet, her armour, a style so different from what the other lords wore, not black but bright rose and deep blue, gleaming like a beetle in the sun. She knew the grin, the teeth bared, half concentration, half pure pleasure, even if she could not see it, and for a moment there was an echo dancing with her, the faintest hint of a trailing aurora, shimmering pearl-colours. Blinked and it was gone.

Devils shaping dreams. A part of her wanted to cry out for her god, as if he faded, vanished, revealed as the devil's lie.

She still could not doubt her vision. No. But he was not here.

Hani Gahur was no poser; she would not want to face him herself. They moved like dancers in silk. The devil did dance, a willow in the wind, a wind in the bamboo, a swallow in the air. Her ribbons, blue and scarlet, traced patterns in the air like the passage of dragons.

Now they were much closer to this side of the circle than they had been. The devil leapt the lord's heavy blade as it swept low and sent him backwards, off balance the briefest of moments, with an elbow in the chest as she whirled past him, drawing him back towards the centre. Ivah heard the grunt of his breath then, and the devil kicked his blade aside as he came at her. Her stroke hissed over his armour. They became as leaves in a gale, the flash and the flicker and swirl of them. A long dagger bloomed in Yeh-Lin's left hand. No wizardry; she had drawn it from her belt in the time it took to blink. Perhaps it was a technique of the old court sword. Scrape and thump as Hani Gahur's sword struck and the devil went down to the dirty paving stones. Someone cried out, but Ivah had seen it coming; Yeh-Lin had already been moving that way. The blow had done nothing; it was the lord who staggered back grace-less and was suddenly loud in his gasping for breath. Yeh-Lin's long dagger was wet, two fingers' breadth of it stained and all of one edge. No hesitation, no merciful pause to ask if Hani Gahur would yield as she rolled gracefully up to follow him. Her blade struck past his once and again and then she thrust with a grunt, the first sound she had made.

With her dagger-hand she struck the lord's forearm aside and he was on his knees, her sword slick and dark withdrawing.

Lord Gahur was not yet dead, but his sword had fallen from his grip and he swayed, kneeling, sunken back on his heels. Yeh-Lin slashed and cut the strings of his helmet and knocked it off with the dagger again, before she dropped the shorter blade and took a two-handed grip on her sword to sweep, in a single stroke, his head away.

The body tipped and spurted and flooded and folded to the ground. The head fell with a horrible soft thud. It stared, mouth open, and eyes. Ivah shut her own eyes, swallowed hard. *Her mother's head flying, taken in one clean blow, and her long hair trailing out, a beautiful banner as it flew . . .*

The devil caught up her dagger and shoved it filthy through her belt. She spun in the centre of the circle to catch them all with her eye, a whirl of black and scarlet and blue, and she cried out, "Witness! It is done! By the will of the Old Great Gods! I claim command of Dernang and Choa and the imperial army in Choa for the heir of the gods of Nabban."

Now there was a thought. Challenge the empress to name a champion—Old Great Gods, she did not *want* the empire. It was her god she sought.

There were cries from the crowd. *The heir of the gods! The holy one of the gods is coming! The holy one of the gods!* And, *Find the priest-killers! Death to the usurper! Death to the sons of Min-Jan! The fall of the Peony Throne!*

The market square was crowded, and it was soldiers packed the space behind the unwary townsfolk, trapped now where they had thought to learn the news and skulk away, and the soldiers were crying out too, *The true gods and their holy one! Death to the empress! The heir of the gods!*

Bodies began to push and surge; Ivah could not see beyond the shove and shift of them, but there was shouting, words becoming lost, and a man roaring and then screaming. She thought the soldiers were killing an officer, there away beyond the shoving shrieking townsfolk, and suddenly some group broke through, running, and others surged into the circle. Yeh-Lin shouted, "Daro and the true gods! To horse!" and leapt to the magpie-brilliant piebald she had ridden into the square.

But Ivah had distinctly heard her say, in the bastard Nabbani of the road, "Ah, *damn!* A bloody riot. He's going to *kill* me!" as she passed. Ivah almost burst out laughing. That, that was not a weaver of dreams and schemes and a master of puppets. That was some warlord's *noekar* who had overstepped her authority and had her lord to face.

Her god came to Dernang. Not here now, but he came. And she would know him when he came.

The devil on her circling piebald caught her eye. Ivah didn't care. She grinned, bowed, hands together, and slipped away through the crowd that ran and milled like confused cattle.

She found a safe sanctuary on the roof of a porch, hid herself. Judge gods by their deeds. And their servants as well.

The scaffolding of the temple of the Daughter of the Gods was burning, and so was something beyond the half-built wall. In the market, by the town keep, she could see soldiers on their knees, officers too. There were other soldiers standing over them, gesturing, shouting, but not nearly the blood and mess and horror she had expected must follow, though it was bad enough. Bodies lay about the square, soldiers and bright-armoured lords and townsfolk. Trampled or slaughtered in the first fury. Now came a hurrying back and forth towards the north gate, and to the silk-merchants' street where lay the grand houses expropriated for officers' lodgings before the castle fell. But the fire of the scaffolding had spread to the next courtyard house, and there was smoke from other streets, too, and shouts and cries. She did not suppose all the soldiers rushing off were doing so to put out fires.

Orders shouted. Parties of other soldiers went after them, more orderly. Officers grim. These ones wore blue ribbons on their helmets or scraps of blue cloth about their arms.

"Go home!" the townsfolk were being ordered. "Go to your houses, clear the streets, the god has gone to the mountain, he comes but not today, go home, keep the peace; the Kho'anzi Daro Korat of Choa will send criers to tell you what follows. For now, go home."

Good advice. Ivah dropped down and made her stealthy way back to her new base, an inn where, for Kharduin's name, she had been given a corner and one meagre meal a day in return for scouring pots and sweeping the yard. Better than her den in the ruined stable, though she had never before in her entire life wielded a broom.

Kaeo and Rat marched swifter than any army ever could, begged passage on the riverboats in trade for a song, and went cross-country by winding paths only the peasants knew, but which Rat could always find. There were whispers, as if the thought rose from the grass, the wind. The empress lied. She was denied by the Mother and the Father. The heir of the gods would come to the north. One morning in a small town whose name he never knew, somewhere in Choian Province, the imperial banner that hung faded and tatty at the magistrate's gate burst suddenly into flame and was burnt to ash. Folk went to see it, Rat and Kaeo among them. That story followed them, met them everywhere. Banners had burned throughout the land. A sign.

It was forbidden to speak of it. The magistrates flogged those who repeated it. The folk gathered in the half-built temples dedicated to the empress as the Daughter of the Gods to pray for her protection against their enemies in north and south, and yet still that whisper followed and met them. *The heir of the gods comes to the north and the weeping land will be set free.* Word born from the wind, from the rustling leaves of the willows . . . from the dreams of the fled and hidden priests, more likely, yet Kaeo did not hear it in his own.

Everywhere, they found shrines deserted, priestless, burnt. They sheltered in such ruins, and Rat shed her levity to pray, briefly, in the shadow of a great grey boulder that was the only altar such shrines ever had, while whatever millet or lentils and rice they had bought with Rat's coins simmered on a small and careful fire with fish she had caught and the wild greens he foraged for. Kaeo would make his own prayers, such as they were, to add to hers. He offered a waiting silence, at any rate, kneeling, holding to stillness. But waking, he could not touch the gods.

They were dying. Dead? Why should he feel that they should be there as more than a thought in his mind, a hope, a wish? They never had been, in all his life. It was they who had reached blind and desperate out of the deep darkness and found him. But when Rat prayed, he tried to make his own stillness an echo to hers, a shared reverence, at least, for the place where the gods should be.

One such night-in-day, while he knelt with closed eyes, waiting in a silence that had no answer, her hand touched the back of his neck. Rested there. He looked up, expecting a grin, a joke, a poke in the ribs and a comment on men who fell asleep at their prayers. Her lips smiled, ever so slightly, but her eyes were—her eyes were wide and solemn.

"Kaeo," she said. Only that, and he reached for her where she knelt beside him, as her arms came around him, and her mouth all uncertain, most un-Rat-like uncertain, found his.

No uncertainty on his part, only a startled wonder. She was all sharp bones and hard muscles until Kaeo found the curve of hips that clothing hid and the small breasts, soft and warm, to fill a hand. Clothes shed all anyhow, laughing, and under her shawl and shirt, along with a simple amulet of a flat and naturally-holed river-stone, she wore a heavy collar, many strands of variegated jade, that would betray them entirely if they were ever searched. It was the green of forests, a dream, he thought, of hidden pools, of a goddess's eyes, and the colours shifted and moved like leaf-shadow against her brown skin. She was gentle when her hands travelled his autumn's scars, fiery fierce when she pulled him over atop her, wrapped him in arms and legs. At some point they remembered to move their supper off the fire. It would keep.

They were late rising that evening. The sun was set and the young moon following it, before hand in hand they took to the road again.

CHAPTER XXIII

For Ahjvar, the journey to the god's mountain passed like a dream, like memory of fever. Night. Fog. Cold water. The road rising from the flooded lands, angling to the northeast. Not the highway to the pass to Denanbak. Lanes and trackways Ghu seemed to know blind. Crouched silent, waiting, as some patrol rode by, betrayed by their hooves and desultory voices, by their torches sullen red in the fog. Meat-filled dumplings and cold tea from a flask in the lee of an empty herder's hut. They were among hills, climbing out of the fog and into a slow dawn, a sunken track through a grove of drily-whispering bamboo, then trees about them, a rocky, boulder-strewn ground. Lee of a boulder, warm in the sun. Dragged by Ghu out of dreams so foul he could only crouch, gasping and retching, for what seemed an age but probably was not. Arms hard around him, breath against his hair. His name, over and over, until he turned his face against Ghu's shoulder and sobbed like a child, while the dogs nosed at him in concern.

Ahjvar didn't speak, even once he could. The only words he could find in that place would ask for his death.

They climbed another mile in silence. Maybe it was two. Hay meadows, and thorn-hedged pastures, winter-brown and with snow still drifted in the northern shadows. Ghu led; Ahjvar followed. Ghu looked back often, waited when he lagged, feet heavy. More grey pastures, horses tiny and distant in a steep valley, a stream tumbling down shelving stone ledges between slender smooth-barked trees, some white flower like a carpet of snow between their interlaced roots.

"I'm going for horses," Ghu said. Watched his face. They had drunk. The water was cold, with the taste of stone in it. They sat on a stony step, spray misting over them. "All right here for a little?"

Ghu looked drawn and grey, older than his years now. No god but a man pushed to the fraying edge.

Ahjvar went to kneel by the water again, drank again, bathed his face. The little brook had risen up over the flat stones of the ledges. In the deeper channel, small fish hung, wriggling to hold position, gathering strength to leap, to climb to the next stair.

"Go," he said hoarsely. "I'll wait."

Ghu still hesitated.

"Go on."

Ghu nodded, touched his shoulder as he sat down, back against the stone, sword across his lap, and left him, keeping under the shadow of the trees. Both dogs stayed, this time.

Ahjvar found the acorns shoved into his purse, sat hunched forward, worrying one through his fingers. He drifted, fighting sleep. No thoughts. Only the shape of the nut, the sound of the water, birds. Jui scratched and shook himself and curled on the stone to sleep. Jiot came to lie with his muzzle on Ahjvar's boot. Small white clouds, scudding like a flock of sheep before the wind. Change in the weather. Rain on its way. Maybe not this night. He must have touched the edge of sleep again, or dreams came into his waking. Wizardry seeking to fix a hold on him, to catch at his sleeve. . . . He walked about and broke the stalks of last year's dead weeds, stripped a few twigs. Some kind of beech, but he had given up keeping to the strict patterns of the spellcasting of Praitan. Let the weeds and twigs be what he told them they were. Laid out three patterns, one within the other, of three points each, the innermost three paces a side. Heather for dreams, hazel to purify, cypress for sleep and healing. Then mountain ash at all three points, for protection. Outermost three all prickly ash, to break and scatter and turn the illusion of wizardry that he dreamed against itself. To keep it from him, in his waking. He didn't sit down again but shed Yeh-Lin's blanket and began to work through the old exercises, making something new of them. Weaving a pattern through the wizardry. To keep his mind from wandering into dreams, to feel sun and sweat and blood coursing in his veins, to know he lived, he alone, the hag gone from him and the deeds of his hands his own.

The sun was dropping into the west when the dogs stirred and the wind brought the scent of horses and oiled leather.

Horses at an easy canter. Ghu. A great black-legged white Denanbaki stallion, moving like flowing water, bright as the moon, and following it, no leading rein, a dusky bay. They jumped the stream lower down, came up through the trees at a long-swinging walk.

Ghu on a swift horse was an eagle on the wind. He should always be so, not worn and bruised and shadowed.

Ghu looked down on him, faintly smiling. "My white colt. Isn't he grown fine?"

A king of horses, this was. Ahjvar remembered some night—Sand Cove, it was, and a storm, and the waves lashing and raging at the cliff, and the wind howling like the ghosts of wolves. The two of them sitting against the wall, out of the downpour, warming themselves with spiced wine—their roof repairs of the ruined broch never did last well and sodden turf followed by the weather had come down on the hearth, for neither the first nor the last time. Ghu had spoken of a wind that shrieked with the voices of dragons, and snow driving hard as whips on the mountain of the god, a difficult foaling, a mare strayed high above the trees and the snow burying them, boy and mare and foal together. But it was the god's mountain, he had said, as if that mattered. And he had brought them down, sometimes carrying the foal, who must have weighed as much as he did then, after the blizzard, and . . . that was all the story. It had been maybe the most words Ahjvar had ever heard from him, at that point. He had been shivering in that autumn storm with cold or remembered cold. Ahjvar hadn't supposed the value of the slave nearly lost to death on the mountain's forbidden height had been counted anything to compare to that of the mare he had been sent to find, and he had not gotten up and moved away when Ghu huddled over to press against his side.

That foal, here and real, tying time together.

Standing still, his shirt soaked through with sweat—the light wind cut with an edge of snow. Ahjvar shivered. "Yes." Beautiful, yes, hard and sudden as an arrow to the chest. Horse and rider. He turned away. "For a race on the flat. For hill-work—"

"They were born to hills, Ahj. You're thinking of western desert-breds. But if we do go cattle-raiding, I'll let you choose."

He snorted, heading to the stream, to drink and wash at least his face once more. Water like ice. He felt chilled to the bone. "They let you take them, or are your Castellan Yuro's men coming after us to get them back?"

"I knocked Chago down," Ghu said seriously, as Ahjvar returned, swinging the blanket over a shoulder, pinning it with the devil's gold. "Nothing to do with the horses. Old. Settled. Chago says, the bay they bought from Denanbak two years ago and his name is Evening Cloud, a stablemate to the white and trained to battle. Oh, and he—Chago, I mean—gave me food and a gourd of millet beer. I expect it's very bad. What they make up here at the high pastures always is. Eat, sleep, or ride through the twilight?"

"Ride. What's the white named?" Ahjvar asked. He didn't really care, but Ghu did.

"Sia gave him another name. I've always called him Snow."

A name a child might give a puppy. Ghu had given all their horses such simple and obvious names, the ones Ahjvar owned, the ones they had stolen, once, twice, when he had gone to Two Hills on business of the Tenju clan-father. Born in a blizzard. Snow. What else? Ahjvar startled himself, laughing.

They rode past the twilight, eating soggy buns and passing the sour beer back and forth between them. The dogs went crashing off in pursuit of some small beast, came back bloody-muzzled and pleased with themselves. When they lost the last light and stopped in the shelter of a fern-hung outcropping of rock, making no fire, Ahjvar found he could not bring himself to lie down. Dreams prowled the edges of his mind. He felt them there, gnawing, waiting.

"You sleep," he said. "I'll watch."

Measure of Ghu's exhaustion that he didn't debate it, just lay down rolled in his filthy sheepskin coat, the dogs curled nearby. Ahjvar paced a little, checked the horses, turned loose without hobble or picket. The stallions were quiet, not disturbed by the oddity of their night. Ahjvar set his back against the rock, tilted his head to watch the stars turning slowly through the leafless branches overhead. Frogs sang in a loud chorus, echoing and answering, all around. Up in the trees, maybe. Distant water rang over stone. Always water, it seemed, in these mountain foothills. The birth of the Mother of Nabban. Eyes closed. No good. He paced a circuit of their camp again, ended up squatting on his heels by Ghu. Touched the back of his hand. He didn't stir. Ahjvar spread Yeh-Lin's blanket over him. Cold to keep himself wakeful. Maybe. He drew his sword, drove it into the earth a pace from Ghu's head, and walked off, climbing several low shelves of stone, choosing a way that seemed thick with the boles of trees, and—he found by blundering into it—a thicket of that bush with the hanging, leathery leaves. Good to have all that between them. He found a way around and still wouldn't lie down, but sat leaning on a tree, watching the sky again. If he slept, he would probably fall over. If he didn't wake himself tipping, and if he dreamed, he would probably make enough noise to wake Ghu, either shouting or—Old Great Gods prevent that he walked in his sleep, don't even think it, don't let thought of the hag rise—if he did walk he would be sleepwalking, only sleepwalking, as men did, not hunting open-eyed and ghost-ridden, and walking blind in his sleep he would crash and trip and fall or tangle himself in the brush, and Ghu would wake. . . .

Best he could do. But he would fight to stay awake, waiting for moonrise, and then for the following dawn. Name the constellations as they cleared that gap between the branches, count the hours thus. Tally them in the leaf-mould, each he could name, to have that focus to his watching. Thin ribbons of cloud trailed over the stars. Eddying like smoke. Drifting.

Fingers still clenched on her throat, though she had stopped fighting, stopped moving long before. Words, broken, the mind could not hold even the echo of them, the woven patterns of the twigs on the beaten earth floor where they had knelt broken and torn by her thrashing, the three beeswax candles set likewise on the floor knocked over. One had set a pattern of thorn to smouldering. Stench of burning hair, strong, and roasting flesh, but Miara was not burning, that was another time, another woman. Miara was dead, Miara dying, gasping and choking beneath him, the spell they had designed and she had worked, his wizardry having been sealed beyond his reach or the hag's, broken as its patterns, as the cords of her throat, and he was on his knees, gasping to breathe, torn fingers splayed where they had clawed against the stony ground.

He had shouted. Hadn't woken Ghu. That, at least. Let him sleep. His throat was raw with some cry, with rising bile, and he gagged on the stink of burning. No fire. Not real. No death. He sweated and shivered and simply lay down where he was.

He could still feel her under his hands, feel her weight, always, every day. Lifting her, how cold she had become, by the time he had dug her grave on the hilltop by the hawthorn, and her ghost was gone, gone, the hag left no ghosts. . . . He began retching again, pushed himself to hands and knees and crawled back to the tree. Narrow-bladed knife in his hand. The edge sliced flesh of his arm with hardly any pressure. In the past he had tried a knife under his own ribs, more than once; the curse wouldn't let him go so easily and he didn't mean to try it now, but the blade was cold and real, the blood hot, welling up, trickling down into his palm. The pain only a dull ache among others, not enough. He felt himself falling, pulled, hands on him—

No. Sank the knife in the earth, drew his knees up, and sat huddled.

Couldn't go on this way. Couldn't.

Leave Ghu alone at the mercy of his gods, with only the devil his friend.

"You know you dream. You need to learn it in bone and blood and heart. You need to understand it in your dreams, so that they are no longer real when you dream them."

Yeh-Lin sat down by him. Ahjvar lifted his head. She stretched out her legs, crossing her ankles. Hadn't heard her approach. The dogs hadn't barked any warning. She'd changed her appearance once more, a woman in her prime again, long hair black as Ghu's, but smooth and sleek as silk in the moonlight.

He'd been waiting for moonrise. Only a silver sickle, now. Scant light, but she seemed to gather it to herself. His forearm throbbed where he had cut it.

"I *know* that."

"You know. So you say. You don't seem to understand what it means. Listen to me. Knowing is not enough. You need to learn to feel it in your bones. Maybe he needs to leave you to dream, to find your own way out."

Had they not had this conversation before? Maybe he had dreamed that.

"What good did that do?" By the churning of the mould, it had been no swift waking. He had fought—nothing. Scrabbling like a man in a fit. Because there had been no one within reach. Time enough to hurt someone, oh yes. Time enough to kill. It had gone on until his own choking pulled him back.

"At least you did wake."

He had feared he might not, that some echo of the hag's nighttime killing might take him over forever, if Ghu were not there to pull him back. So yes, he could be thankful that at least he had woken.

"Dead king, do you want to die?"

"Are you offering to kill me?" His voice rasped, raw and weary. Kill him. The devil likely could, at that. The Lady hadn't managed it, for all she had slain a goddess. Hadn't understood what she dealt with, that was all. Dotemon, however, knew.

She chuckled. "Your young god has made threats of what he will do to me, should I do so. I have no wish to make him act on them. No, I am not offering to unmake you. I am merely asking what you want. And you are not answering, dead king."

"Will you stop calling me that? My father was king. My brother—my son was king. I was a few hours between them."

"But all the songs will have it the day of the three kings. Two is so . . . un-Praitannec. Unsatisfying as poetry. I notice you are still not answering."

"I thought you were going to take Dernang." He should have been angrier that she trailed after them and did not busy herself with whatever it was Ghu had set her to do, but he was too exhausted for anger now. He should have been afraid.

"Dernang is mine. I do as I am bidden. I think you will find my method to have been—amusing. You do know you are followed?"

"Yes."

"Good. Be wary. The wizard is Bamboo rank. See how I watch over your former shield-bearer? And over you. Are you not fortunate? Your young god takes my empire, which I could reach out my hand and reclaim, and I serve him most faithfully as he does so. So—is it that you will not leave him, or is it that you fear the road?"

No, he did not fear the road to the Old Great Gods. Only he was so mortally weary, and the way was so long, and his burden so great. . . . To be lost on the way in his torment. To fail, and fall, and lie forever in nightmare, dead and trapped and unending . . . a hell he inhabited already. That, he feared.

Hyllau's oblivion had been mercy, whatever Ghu thought.

Yeh-Lin was a warm pressure against his side, too close and yet—a comfort. When had she become a friend? "Still no answer? Tell me, what do you want of him?"

"Nothing. Death." No. Nothingness. To end. For pain to end. For Ahjvar who had been the Leopard, who had been so many other names, and in the beginning of all Catairlau, for Catairlau to end, simply end.

"He was angry once when I called you that. Your name is Ahjvar, he said." She answered thought, not speech.

"Catairlau is long dead."

"So are you. Or you should be."

He remembered burning. Remembered seeing his own hands, black crust and white bone. Seeing with eyes that should have been shrivelled and blind.

"Fire is warmth and life, too. Light in the darkness."

You drew me like a fire, Ghu had said, after the battle at the Orsamoss. Ghu was not fire. He was deep, clean, quiet water; he was the peace in the darkness of the night; he was warm silence. *I wanted to be some light in your darkness.*

And he had left Ghu sleeping alone, without fire or warmth or watch. Alone, maybe, always. Doomed to godhead.

"This is a dream."

"You think so? Do you have so much imagination, to dream me? Imagine you can change your dreams, then. Kiss me."

He turned his head to stare. "Why?" That put his face far too close to hers, almost nose to nose as she watched him with a wry smile, but pride wouldn't let him flinch away then. She knew it, too.

"To prove you can."

"What does that mean?"

Yeh-Lin looked away. "What honour do you do your lover's memory, letting the faintest hint of desire make you ill, making her a horror you carry with you, a corpse lying between you and any passion you might find? What of her life, her love, her courage—what she dared, to fight with her human wizardry against the god-bound ghost that rode you? What of her joy in you?"

"I shouldn't ever have let myself be near her."

"No. That, you should not have done. But you did, and there was a good time, before the end. Do you even remember her, Miara, in herself? Or is all that is left of her what you have made of her, a horror to yourself? Is that justice to her memory?"

"No." Very quietly.

"So. So kiss me. Great Gods above, I am Yeh-Lin the Beautiful and I should not have to beg. I am not used to begging."

"Beg away," he growled.

"Or is it that you prefer your women older?" She glanced at him sidelong, grey streaks running back from her temples, the laugh-lines crinkling about her eyes and mouth.

There should not be light to notice such things. He shrugged and shifted sideways a handspan or so, couldn't summon the energy to move further.

"Ahjvar." So quietly. Yeh-Lin knelt up facing him, put a hand on his chest. He clenched his jaw, trapped and not going to give her the satisfaction of seeing him jerk away like a dog from a blow. "Do think on what you want, what you need from him. You are a weight on him, a burden of his own choosing, yes, but all Nabban falls on him and he needs either his champion at his back to help him bear it, or to be free of ghosts. Your ghosts. You."

Racing pulse, drumming in his ears. He could hurl her away. He had moved so that the knife pressed against his hip, and he was hardly unarmed, besides. He held himself still.

"Tell your own ghosts they are dreams. They are dead and gone. They are a sickness of your own mind. Tell Miara, she is dead and gone to the Old Great Gods—"

But the hag had fed—

"Don't! She is free and gone, beyond pain, beyond reach of hurt, beyond any saving or damnation and whatever came to her soul, all that is of her in *this* world is what you carry. Do you want that memory to be the manner of her death, or her life and her valiant heart? Start there. Tell me."

"Tell you what?" His voice croaked.

"Tell me she lived. She loved. She was beautiful."

He swallowed. Took her hand, carefully, off his chest. But her fingers folded around his, very lightly, and he made himself not pull away, as Yeh-Lin sat back on her heels, facing him. Let himself hold her hand. "Tell me."

"She wasn't, really."

"Tell me who she was."

"She—she served in the queen's hall, when she was younger. Not the first of the royal wizards, but not the least. But when her husband died and her sons were grown Miara went to the hills. She belonged on the hills. She liked the silences, and the wind. She tamed hawks and flew them. She didn't take them from their nests, she coaxed them from the sky, wild birds, and they hunted for her. . . ."

He could see her. Plain, broad-faced, blue-grey eyes. A woman with her brown hair greying and in a long and wind-ravelled plait. Grinning at him, triumphant, having got a red-tail to settle on his arm a moment, for all the corrupted taint of him. Laughing at his pleasure in her joy, in this place on the hills where for a little the cities and the work he found there to keep the hag quiescent and fed could be forgotten, almost.

Only ever *almost*.

"Remember her truly, now. If you are dreaming now, think: you dream her truly." Yeh-Lin touched his face. Wet. Tears, or dew. Sitting out in the cold night, grappling ghosts. "Look at me. I am not the Lady. I am not Tu'usha. One woman is not another. One devil is not another. One love is not another. If I am only your dream, I can do you no harm, and if I am not, I will not, I say it. Do you need to be afraid?"

There was a fire within her. It was not his nightmare, his memory of burning, of Hyllau burning; it was the devil's soul, a flicker in her eyes. The Lady had burned so.

"I am not the Lady, Ahjvar, and you are stronger than she ever was. For all of her, and Hyllau, and your viciously foolish goddess, you are unbroken yet."

He leaned abruptly forward and did kiss her, with his heart racing too fast and not from any arousal of desire. She put her hands, not about him—he stiffened and almost pulled away when she moved—but only on his shoulders. What she made that kiss was neither chaste nor brief, but her lips and tongue were sweet and careful. When finally she pulled away from him, smiling, he was most definitely . . . not without any arousal of desire.

"There," she said. "Now I have something worth dreaming of, to keep me warm tonight, if Nabban's tasks allow me any time for sleep. You—I could wish it so for you as well, but I doubt it. This is the best you'll allow yourself."

"Now you'll say you are a dream after all?" Amused in spite of himself. Annoyed, too, as if he were the butt of a joke and could not quite see how.

"I claim nothing. Certainly not you. But dead king, you should not kiss someone so if you don't mean it."

"*I* shouldn't!"

She laughed at him again.

"Tell your ghosts they are dreams and you are done with them. Teach yourself to wake; learn to make some truth in your dreams. Find your way out of the fire, or go to find your road. Choose. Choose soon, for young Nabban's sake." She tugged him to her by the collar of his ragged shirt and kissed him again, on the cheek this time, sisterly. Pressed her face to his a moment, hair sliding soft and scented, oddly, of gorse and thyme like the hills of southern Praitan, clean and homely, before she stood up, a mist he had not seen arise eddying about her. He turned his head to watch her going, but she was not there.

The thin moon was climbing through the trees, trailing scarves of cloud. He could still feel the devil's mouth on his, warm and soft and insistent, and his eyes had that hot, swollen feeling. A man might shed tears in his dreams. A change, to dream of kissing the damned devil, to dream a kiss that was not a horror. It still heated him. But what put those words in her mouth? A bard, a wizard grown old enough to be wise might say she spoke the thoughts that he, waking, could not shape; that he counselled himself.

Ahjvar did not trust that he had come to any wisdom yet, but of a sudden sleep was heavy on him, and did not seem worth fearing. He curled up where he was and dreamed again of wizardry brushing at the edges of his mind, though it was the cold that woke him. Chilled to the bone and shivering in a grey and drizzling morning, though he was under both the blanket and Ghu's coat. Ghu himself was sitting where Yeh-Lin—where he had dreamed Yeh-Lin had sat, with Ahjvar's sword beside him, turning that discarded knife in his hands.

He dropped it point down by Ahjvar's face when he saw him stirring, and got to his feet, sweeping up his coat. "Idiot. What good will taking a cold do?" He sounded—angry.

Ghu walked off without waiting for Ahjvar to gather himself up. Dry brown blood crackled and flaked away as he flexed his hand. Ah. Ahjvar rubbed away what traces he could, too late. The cut on his forearm was scabbed black and healing. Nothing to do about the stained

sleeve. Wash it when he could, but that shirt would really be better off
decently buried. The fresh stain on the arm was the least of it. He caught
up back where they had first camped, found the horses lipping up a last
trace of spilled grain. The man at the foaling pasture had sent them off
with more than bad beer, obviously.

"Eat," Ghu said. "Don't feed the dogs. They've been hunting zokors.
They'll do."

Whatever those were. He took a stale bun and the flask of water Ghu
passed him, ate in silence, watching while Ghu bridled and saddled the
horses, moving about them with quiet efficiency. Still Ahjvar's groom,
halfway to godhead or not.

"Ghu? This holy place of your god—much farther?"

Ghu turned from cinching the bay's girth, stood scratching the
horse's cheek. "Late afternoon, maybe, if we don't push it. Before
evening, anyway. Up above the trees."

"Do you need me?"

"Ahjvar—"

"I'd rather—just wait. Here. Somewhere. Quiet. Alone."

A long, long silence, then. The bay turned his head against the motionless hand. "Swajui," Ghu said at last. "Nobody goes up to the Father's
sanctuary on the mountain, unless they're called. Not even the priests. I
would have taken you regardless. But Swajui is the Mother's place here on
the mountain. The name's for the shrine and sanctuary both."

"There's a difference?"

"A shrine—people go there. They went for the healing waters and
the counsel and prayers of the priests, but the sanctuaries are the holy
places of the gods, places for the gods alone. I don't know what you'll
find at the shrine of Swajui. It—hurts. Even to think of it, it hurts. I
don't think you should go there. There are none living left. I think it
was burnt. But that wasn't the Mother's sanctuary. If you go higher, go
up to the pines where the cold springs rise, that's the true holy place,
the Wild Sister's own. The priests went there. Folk did, sometimes.
Called, or seeking her in solitude. I don't think Zhung Musan's soldiers went so far. The shrine was enough for them. Visible and known.

There's nothing to show the holiness of the sanctuary, to folk that don't know it or can't recognize it. If you can't recognize it, you can't find it, I suppose." Another long look. "You'll know. Wait for me there."

"Your goddess won't want me there. Gods don't."

"She's gone, Ahj. She—died, I suppose. As we took the castle."

"Ah, *Ghu.*"

"Go to the sanctuary of Swajui. Go up to the pines. I'll find you there. A day, a few days, I don't know. Wait for me."

They rode slowly, as if, for all Ghu's urgency to flee the castle—and it had felt like flight, Ahjvar thought now—he was reluctant at the last. The drizzle gave way to a damp wind, but the clouds did not thin. Despite the grey day, the birds were loud with spring song. Once a swarm of sandy-furred monkeys went leaping, almost flying, away overhead through the upper branches of the barren trees, exciting the dogs, but Ghu called them back before they could launch themselves into the forest. Ahjvar dropped behind, watching the trail they had ridden, but the grey woods covered all the winding, climbing, plunging track.

Prickling unease. Neither Ghu, nor the dogs nor horses, seemed to feel it. He wondered, though, if he would really dream vague and subtle spells pressing against him. He never had before. Subtlety was not a notable feature in his nightmares.

Ghu reined in after perhaps three wandering miles; they had been riding along a ridge like some hunched spine of stone, but ahead it entered a narrow place, overhung with stone and trees. Another track branched away, plunging down to the west.

"Here," he said quietly, pointing to the left. "That goes to the shrine of Swajui. The main road to the shrine comes up from Dernang; we came east of that, through the greater hills. From the shrine, there's a path that climbs north. Steep and twisting. Nothing to mark it from any other forest trail, but it follows a stream. You'll know it, I think. Ahjvar . . ."

"Better you face your god without dragging me along."

"Don't—" But whatever Ghu meant to say he thought better of. Held out an open hand, letting the words go. Urged Snow on into the narrow defile. Halted, though, before the first turn that would have taken him out of sight, looked back. "Talk to the horse," he called. "Use his name."

"I don't speak Denanbaki."

"Try Nabbani, Praitannec—Evening Cloud doesn't care." A flashing grin, a nod like a salute, and he was gone. The dogs lingered, watching Ahjvar.

"No," he said. "I don't need nursemaiding. Scram. Go with Ghu."

Jui gave one sharp bark. Protest or agreement? But they both left him, breaking into a flying lope to overtake the vanished horse. The bay raised his head and whinnied after them.

Ahjvar turned him aside to take the descending western trail.

Not far, though. He hadn't survived decades as a Five Cities assassin on immortality alone, and to ignore the little nagging prickles of unease was—never wise. Even when they were nothing more than a bad dream or a grey day. Sometimes they weren't.

The horse sidled around restlessly when Ahjvar dismounted, not happy at being separated from the others. Ahjvar tugged at the bridle, addressed one dark eye. "Stand, damn it." No idea what commands or signs a Nabbani-trained warhorse knew. "Evening Cloud. What sort of name is that for a horse? Sounds like someone should write lovesick poetry to you." He tried the Praitannec. "Gorthuerniaul . . ." Shook his head. Too long. "You. Niaul. Stand, or I will tie you to a tree."

The head turned to study him, but the sidling stopped. "Better." He unslung the bow in its leather wrappings, hung the quiver over his shoulder, and led the horse off the trail. They were out of sight from the fork and someone would have to come beyond the first bend to see that his tracks turned aside.

It wasn't the landscape for a mounted fight. He shoved the plaid blanket and the scarf with its flashes of kingfisher blue into a saddlebag, fished out a headscarf that might have been russet originally but had faded in the past year to a mottled dun, and wrapped it as if against desert snow and sand, covering pale hair and beard. He left the horse with another terse, "Niaul, stand," heading up a steep shoulder, stone beneath the moss and groping tree-roots, worked his way down from that height, back to where he could see the trail down the mountain and the path to Swajui branching off. A good vantage-point and a long, clear stretch of the trail. This western slope of the ridge dropped away abruptly, almost a low cliff. Little cover, with the trees and bushes so bare. The thin soil supported only sparse undergrowth, but rid of the plaid and with hair covered he was dull and drab as a nesting bird. A winter-broken bough would make a scribble of twigs before and alongside him; there were a few stalks of some seedy weed, but mostly it was stillness that would hide him.

He spanned the bow, slotted in a bolt, put quiver and sword where he could quickly lay hand on either, and settled himself to wait. He might have had only a couple hours of sleep in the past gods alone knew how long, but no heaviness tried to close his eyes now.

Might have been dreaming. It had been a night of strange dreams, surely enough. Devils damn all devils. But for the same vague, subtle pressure of a spell to come twice, when he had never dreamed anything of the like before . . . No. He didn't have such dreams.

No wizardry raised his hackles now. Nothing. Birdsong. The shrill barking cry of some animal he didn't recognize, far in the distance to the east. Blackflies settling to bite, a first crop of spring annoyance. He hadn't noticed them, riding with Ghu. If the horse was too badly tormented, he was going to wander off.

Was it quieter, down the trail?

A bright blue bird flew up crying alarm, raising a flock of little black twittering ones.

Hooves.

Could, of course, be some hunter, even a pilgrim seeking the gods. Not very damned likely. Not even a fluffy seedhead fouled his line of vision down to the bend. So.

They came around the corner, two riders abreast. Good sturdy horses. Lacquered scale armour, helmets with ribbons. Not Zhung, the characters on the breast of their deep rose surcoats. Min-Jan. Imperial officers, not banner-lords or the spear-carriers of banner-lords. Imperial officers' livery, at any rate, and the enamelled badge on their helmets the same. How many behind them?

He let them come on, farther than he had intended, waiting for their followers, but none appeared, and the two were deep in some low-voiced discussion, the horses walking. Argument, he thought, from the way the thick-bodied older man gestured.

Still no followers. Very, very slowly, he shifted position a little, lining up the bow to cover the area where the trail forked. Much closer than he wanted, really; there would be no time to prepare a second shot. He wanted to hear what they said, know what they were. Not a troop riding to the destruction of Father Nabban's holy site, as he had for a moment thought, seeing the livery. The regular army did not conscript women for the common soldiery. He wasn't sure about the officers.

They reined in and the woman, thinner, younger, her face flecked with pale pock-marks and her hair cut short, leaned to study the tracks, not dismounting.

"They've split up."

The older man pulled off his gloves, tucked them into his belt, and licked a finger. Not testing the wind but writing on his wrist in saliva. Wizard. Ahjvar felt the subtle pressure again, a will imposing itself on the world. The man pressed his wrist to his lips, eyes shut. Not officers, just the uniform as a mask.

"The holy man went up the mountain," the wizard said.

"Don't call him that. It sounds like treason. Or heresy. Something."

The wizard ignored that. "The guardian, whatever he is, left him and turned west."

"Seems unlikely."

"That's the path to Swajui, captain. It's a holy place. Why not?"

"Why not? Would he leave the holy man? If they've split up, it's because they know they're followed and he's doubling back behind us."

"I've made sure they don't." Smug bastard. Mistaken.

"You say. They killed three of our best in Denanbak. Hope you appreciate I didn't send you with them." The woman considered, eyed the wizard sidelong and tilted her chin up the trail. "That one is the one who matters." She hesitated. Artfully. Did the wizard feel a prickle of warning on his spine? He should. She was about to make him a stalking goat, if he had the wit to see it. "What do you foresee if we do split up here?"

"Nothing," the wizard spat. "I see nothing. I have seen nothing. They've been hidden from me since yesterday. Only glimpses, hints . . ."

"Are we even following the right men? If you've led me a wild goose chase . . ."

"*I* don't make that kind of mistake, captain."

"Fine, fine, they've split up. You head to Swajui and I'll—"

No question which of these two was most dangerous to himself. An assassin of the Wind in the Reeds. One shot. Ahjvar took aim on the woman's eye. At this range, he could have hit her with a thrown pebble.

And just as he would have squeezed the trigger, the wizard spurred his horse forward, coming between him and the assassin. "I'm not going after that guardian alone, whatever he is, and I'm not going to be bait in any trap for him for you. He'll be no threat once the holy man is dead."

Likely true enough. Bones and ash. Ahjvar shot the wizard instead, since the man now blocked the assassin. The iron head of the quarrel shattered his cheekbone, tore through his brain. Ahjvar was on his feet, sword in hand and slithering trunk to trunk down the steep slope, leaping the last drop even as the wizard fell, caught in his stirrups, spooking his horse, which bucked and shed the corpse. The other spurred forward, sword sweeping around. Ahjvar dropped under the blade and slashed open the beast's belly as he rose. Ghu would not like that, and he was sorry for the need. The assassin vaulted clear of the screaming, kicking shambles and landed on her feet.

Shield lost in the keep. The woman was armoured, but a head and a half shorter than Ahjvar, her blade likewise shorter than the Northron sword, single-edged like a Grasslands sabre but broader, heavy. Ahjvar drove in hard, forcing her back, but she circled away, moving uphill. Fast, damnably fast, and balanced and confident. Professional, in fact. And she'd probably both slept and fed better for many days. On the other hand, Ahjvar wasn't worried about dying.

He counted on that too damned much and he knew it. Tried not to. He could be laid out on death's threshold for days, recovering from what should have been fatal. Time enough for the assassin to catch up with Ghu and kill them both with that one death. Time to stop being a death-wooing fool, but he'd said that before. Should have told the devil to find him a shield. Heavy dagger to guard his side. He didn't follow in close again, shifting slowly around, inviting—he was too damnably tired to let this be dragged out, and the other probably intended that, Ahjvar's haggard face betraying his weakness.

Had her, the assassin moving in where Ahjvar wanted her. Sweeping kick as if to hook the woman's legs out from beneath her, contemptuously avoided along with the sword's swing she shouldn't have been so focussed on. Dropped his shoulder, dagger punching swiftly below the skirt of scales, slashing upward. Ahjvar let the dagger go and shifted to a two-handed grip on his sword, weight and height his advantage now as the wounded woman staggered back, blood darkening her bright trousers. Maybe he'd gotten lucky and hit the great vessel of her thigh. Ahjvar didn't wait to find out, struck the woman's left wrist and likely broke it, though the glove was armoured and he didn't take the hand off. The slender knife the Nabbani had snatched for went flying. Poisons in Denanbak. Didn't want any edge to touch him. Battered the woman down with both hands on the sword again, breaking more bones, stamped on her swordhand as she tried weakly to rise, and thrust still two-handed beneath her jaw.

Death, and no lingering ghost. A moment's shock and fear and rage and she was gone. Ahjvar went back, scooping up his dagger, shaky, to finish the poor blessed horse. A beast-soul returned to the earth it belonged to; that, at least, was as it should be.

He had no desire to strip either victim of armour to look for the tattoo he was almost certain he would find, at least on the woman. Leave that mystery for Yeh-Lin. He did fish in the neck of her armour to pull out the ornate badge on its chain, just to confirm. Wind in the Reeds, though neither stealthy nor secret here, riding out as an officer of the army in all confidence. And the wizard—raging ghost.

He considered questioning him. Ghosts didn't lie. Couldn't be compelled, either. To draw anything useful from a reluctant and resisting ghost took patience and calm he currently lacked. This one was inchoate and might take days to draw himself together. Ahjvar gave him earth and checked for his badge. Not Wind in the Reeds, no, but a wizard of the imperial corps, Bamboo Badge Rank, the second highest, was it not? Conscripted from Zhung Musan's service before the castle fell by the assassin . . . or had she been set to serve with him in response to some alarm the wizard had taken, some foretelling of Ghu's coming? He should have asked Yeh-Lin for news of the town, but he forgot—that was only a dream.

Habit of the past year meant he considered for a moment what might be salvaged, but no, he didn't even want to check the saddlebags for food. And no point pulling the bodies off the road, since he couldn't hide the dead horse. Leave them for a warning. He cleaned his blades and scrubbed blood from his hands in dirt and old leaves before climbing back up the ridge of stone to hunt for quiver and crossbow, retraced his steps to check on the horse. Horses. The wizard's was out among the trees nearby, reins tangled in one of those evergreen bushes. He gave the bay a pat and praise for standing and went, circling carefully, talking soothing nonsense as he would have so long ago, before he'd stopped caring for anything, and was able to come up to the stray without panicking it, though the bay—Niaul—trailed after him, trampling through brush like an ox. He dumped the other horse's saddle, freed it of its bridle, and it bolted away. He caught Niaul, took him further down the trail to Swajui, and left him to stand again. He'd be a fool to trust there were only the two.

But drifting a mile back down the trail, concealed in the forest, watching, only found him the straying horse again, peacefully grazing the first shoots of new grass on a sunny edge, though he waited until well into the afternoon. Cast his own spell, too, weaving it of the old patterns and the sword's edge. Nothing followed, nothing stirred, either on the track or in the forest. He picked his way back up to his own horse, not wandered too far, and took the path to Swajui.

CHAPTER XXIV

The mountain of the god rose grey, banners of mist trailing west, fading into cloud. The air bit harsh and clean; breath began to smoke like the high winds. No trees, now, only low juniper spilling from cracks in the rocks and snow deep in the shadows, while the first brief flowers, pale yellow, vivid blue, splashed colour over the south and the eastern slopes.

There was a path, if you knew to find it. Holy folk, drawn to the god, might find it. A foal-heavy mare might, driven from the shelter of the lower forest by bear or wolf or leopard. A boy might, seeking that mare, with the warmth of the god burning like a hearthfire to draw him on, and the wind rising. Geese crying high overhead. It had been spring then, too, till the storm fell on him.

The standing stones were cold and dark, when he came to them. It was only that shadow fell on them, but they seemed a warning. Two on the ridge, and two more distant over it, only the tops visible, and the last yet out of sight where the shallow stream crossed the valley that was more a ravine.

There were ravens. They rose from the carcass of a dead musk deer, wandered up out of the forest to die in the winter. It was gone nearly to clean bones now, as a boy and a horse might have been. The ravens circled, croaking. One dropped to his wrist. Snow laid his ears back, shook his mane and stamped. The raven studied Ghu, obsidian eye—one side, the other. Beak like the point of a spear. Cried hoarsely and flew. Ghu rode on between the stones, reined in again, looking down. The valley was cast all in shadow and ice fringed the narrow meltwater stream. There were trees down there, pines that grew more as creeping bushes than great towers, bare, red-barked willow no higher than his head. And stones. Mostly stones. Clumps of wiry grass not yet greening held a little thin soil in place. No flowers yet at all among the stones, and snow at the head of the ravine and in all the shadowed places, feeding the stream, the great peak rising white over them. He dismounted and went afoot, leading Snow down the steep way that was barely a memory of a path, angling towards the second pair of standing stones, then made a sharp turn to the south and crossed the ravine-valley to the brook and the stepping stones. There he dismounted and unsaddled Snow, removed his bridle. Cleaned the horse's feet and groomed him as if at the end of an ordinary day and his stall waiting, while the shadows thickened colder and darker over them, and in the west the sky turned sullen orange. Grain—mostly with Ahjvar. He poured out a little of what there was, murmuring to the horse of the danger of the unseen cliff, where the brook fell away in a great plume that turned to mist before it ever reached a lower valley, and left him, crossing the stepping stones of the brook and up between the third pair of stones.

Another cliff towered beyond, fissured and broken, spilling scree and snow.

The seventh standing stone, alone, twice the height of the others, a roughly squared pillar, or a broken slab embedded where it had plummeted from above . . . who, now, remembered?

Ghu climbed the rising ground and stood before it. The wind hissed in the creeping pines below. Darkness thickened, the sun behind the clouds falling away into the west, over mountains, deserts. Sun on the hills of Praitan, maybe. Sunlight still sparking on the waves of the Gulf of Taren, the tiled roofs of Gold Harbour. The stones of the ruin on the headland they had called home warm in the sun, and the garden wall, and the garden he had dug and tended gone to weeds and wild things, but the gulls still floating on the wind and crying, and the sea still running away into the sky.

He sat down with his back against the stone, legs crossed, leaned his head back, looking into the west. The light was gone, starless, moonless, black cloud low and thick. The horse Snow was no more to be seen than the snow-heavy heights.

"I'm here," he said.

Another night, not quite yet a year gone by since then. Summer air, and the damp smell of the mist still, and the swamp called the Orsamoss. Smoke clinging to clothes and hair, the reek of the burning tower. A bank overgrown with junipers sheltered them, spice-scented. Ahjvar had dragged himself that far, could do no more, and had lain down like an exhausted child with his head in Ghu's lap. He wanted to die. His goddess was silenced and put to undreaming sleep in the earth, but his curse still bound him to her and held him in the world, and the hungry ghost of Hyllau still possessed him, waiting to rise and hunt. He could die, at last. Ghu had promised it. He would not wake again with innocent blood on his hands. And the hag had taken him then, hungry to hunt, and Ghu had taken on himself the grace of the gods who would claim him and broken the binding curse, dragged her struggling from Ahjvar's soul, and when the savage will of hate that was all she had left of humanity would have burnt the man, again, he destroyed her. A human soul, not released to the road to the Old Great Gods but made nothing, ash and nothing, a piece of the universe unmade.

He had taken the other part of the curse of Ahjvar's goddess then, put himself in the goddess's place to anchor it. By doing so, he made himself a necromancer, some might judge. Wizards, priests . . . gods. An enslaver of the dead. And he had asked, come with me to Nabban. Because he was afraid, and lonely, and afraid to be alone. Selfish.

And Ahjvar had said he would try, and had held him for his own comfort when the nights were bad.

If he were no god, he could not hold this curse, and Ahjvar would be dead, as he should be, and go to his road.

If he were no god, he could return to the west.

If he were no god . . . what changed, for Nabban?

The land died soulless, unknown, unloved.

And Ahj died regardless. He could not hold him here.

He could. He would not.

The Mother had not denied Ahjvar, but she had had so little will, so little left of her being. The Father could still take that decision from him. Cast Ahjvar to his road, without a word, a farewell. *Do not let him burn again, do not let there be pain and fear, just let him go.* He prayed that, if his heart was prayer, beyond words.

He gives himself to you. The Father's thought, deep, resonating, stone and marrow. *How do we deny that?*

They had sent him to follow the sun, to find what he needed to become in a world they could not know, and Ahjvar had been what he had needed to find, the sun he had found to follow. Or the rock he had needed in that time, to brace his back against, to be able to find his stillness, to see. A man, who made the silences in which he found how to speak.

He gives himself to you, and not from fear of death. He gives himself to you—to you, through you to us, to the mountain and the river, in service of our children. How should we deny that?

He accepted that. It was forgiveness. It was his, the deed and what must follow. Father Nabban did not take Ahjvar from him.

He would let him go. That awaited, at Swajui. But there would be time for leave-taking, and so Ahjvar could go free and clean and at peace, without pain, between breath and breath, and lie among the roots of the pines with the wind and the sky over him.

You have come back, the Father said, *with a devil at your side. You have brought Yeh-Lin Dotemon back to this land.*

To say she would have come anyhow was a child's argument.

"Yes," he said aloud. "I don't know; I'm afraid of what I've done, allowing her. I don't know I've done right. But I see her, I . . . need her. Will need her. There is something among us that should not be. It was in the Golden City. It . . ." Eyes shut. Darkness to hold him. He shook his head. "It's a fish, too swift for snatching."

You would set fire against fire? All may burn.

"Maybe. But maybe not. I would trust her, a little. We are Nabban. All Nabban. For a little—" And was it he or he and he-the-Mother who had been the Wild Sister, and a dragon in the dawn of the world, who spoke those words, held that thought? "—while we are that, while the gods and goddess are growing within us unborn, we may match her. She is not what she was."

We made you. You are what we are.

You are what we are not.

Angry.

Alive.

Newborn in the world. Do what lies before you.

Find your own road. Ours has failed us.

Find your own road.

Or make it.

They reached to enfold him. Father, Mother, Sisters, Brothers, dragons, tigers, peaks unknown and waters unnamed, forgotten, rebirths awaiting. Snow, stone, deep brown water.

My mother, my father, he told them, voiceless, and let himself fall.

CHAPTER XXV

The track plunged down a long hillside, then followed a valley upwards again, crossing and recrossing a brook. It ran swift and noisy in its rocky channel, bright with green mosses on its banks, new ferns uncoiling. One of the many sources of the Wild Sister. The path left it, though, where it poured in a plume like a white horse's tail down a sudden broken cliffside rising to the north. Now there was smoke on the wind, not fresh but damp old burning. Ahjvar rolled an acorn through his fingers and told the horse, "The soldiers will have fired the buildings." Give the words voice. Maybe he would hear them himself. He rode alert for any movement in the barred light and shadow of the trees, largely maples of some sort, by the cushioning leaf-litter that muffled the slow beat of Niaul's hooves. Pale early flowers spread in carpets beneath. All very peaceful. If he had seen his shrine burnt and his family hauled captive off to their deaths, he would be greeting the next intruders with an arrow on the string from ambush, though he thought the priests of Mother and Father Nabban took vows not to kill and even ate no meat.

Under the circumstances, he thought they might be tempted to forswear such vows. At least he could not be mistaken for an imperial soldier.

But Ghu had said there would be no one here. No survivors.

A raven flapped heavily overhead, followed by a second. A third. Heading away to roost.

Late-slanting sun breaking through the clouds at last to shine in his eyes, and a gateway, of sorts, marking where the path entered the precinct of the bamboo-fenced shrine. Two trunks, pines, scaly and grey, rose like pillars to either side of a narrow gap in a high palisade. There had been a simple gate hung between the trees, but it had been torn down—gate and destruction alike symbolic, because it was little more than a screen of split and woven bamboo and its latch a loop of cord, no defensible barrier, nothing that would keep even a determined sheep in or out. The track passed between boles of the trees, over a web of roots like the bone and tendon of two elderly hands interlaced, and descended by three stone steps. The way was just broad enough to admit a rider. The steps were shallow, leading down to the lowest level of an enclosure of three terraces, much larger than he had expected, five acres, maybe, with stone paved yards and paths and the roofless, blackened ruins of a dozen sizeable wooden buildings. A broader road climbed up from the south; its wide-spaced gate-pillars had likewise been great pines, but they were scorched and scarred by fire. There were pools between the buildings, some with wooden pillars extending out into them as though they had been half roofed over. The water steamed in the cooling evening air. Charred wood and rubbish floated in the pools now. And rags. The horse blew and snorted and shifted his weight. Ahjvar wrapped his scarf over his face again, for what good that would do. Layering camel over corpse. The overflow of the pools ran in stone-lined drains to gather to a single channel, dropping over ledges, passing under flat bridges formed each of a single slab of stone. Iris blades and some yellow mounding flower and mats of sky blue forget-me-not thrust up from gravelled beds to border the flowing water. Greenery grew back over trampled patches, nearly hiding them. The stream ran out at what must be the main gate to the south; he heard it chiming down another fall, natural, that one, or so he expected. Not the waters he and horse had played leapfrog with.

A single bare tree, not an evergreen, reared up and spread broad branches over the central—bathhouse? Shrine? Priests' house? The holy shrine itself, he guessed, too small to be more than a henhouse, really. A black stone boulder sat squat amidst the wreckage there. He would have called it an altar, but that it was unworked.

More ravens sat in the branches, watching him.

He could picture the place crowded with folk come to ease rheumatic joints and wheezing lungs. Not his idea of holiness, something that had more in common with a city bathhouse.

No pilgrims seeking ease and healing now. The great central tree had been girdled, its bark stripped with axes in a broad band all the way around. In that, he saw General Zhung Musan's hand. And the will of what power, that hid behind Zhung Musan and the empress he served?

Something that harvested the souls of its servants. Or devoured them.

He was nearly sick, and not from knowing what he was going to find in this place.

He had given up looking ahead . . . long since. Left Ghu to carry that, too.

Go up the pines, go to the sanctuary, Ghu had said. Had not wanted Ahjvar here, where there was burning and death and horror.

Ghosts, still tied to unburied bodies. Those who had sunk beneath the Mother's waters were gone—water of the earth was one of the blessings to free a soul—but there were others here, still bound to the world. Ahjvar rode slowly out into the open, not reaching for a weapon. The horse moved alert and tense, his weariness fallen from him, but he did not fight or refuse Ahjvar, though nostrils flared and ears were back. The smell of death. Old death. The massacre was not recent. The priests hanged at the keep had been prisoner some time. The ravens launched themselves away with a susurration of feathers as he rode up to the middle terrace and around behind the ruin. Niaul's ears went back.

Young woman, Ahjvar thought. Long hair, brown robe half torn off, the pale shift beneath shredded, ribs opened out, spread to the sky. A disjointed foot lay some distance away. Nose, cheeks, eyes gone, body long past bloating, turned soft and greasy, falling in on itself. But she made the effort to stand visible before him, hair braided with rings of white shell, memory of those crushed about her body, hands tucked into her sleeves—ghost holding to the dignity her unswift death had ripped away. It was not the foxes and ravens, nor even the flies and crawling maggots, had defiled her body.

"Please . . ."

She was faint and uncertain, and afraid, even dead and beyond further harm. Ahjvar dismounted, though that put him closer to the stink and he had to fight the gagging urge of his throat. It seemed discourteous to loom from the stallion's height.

Others were aware, but were only light, warmth in the corner of the eye, not to be seen by staring. One drifted nearer, a growing presence. Old woman.

"He comes from the gods. From the god who will be. The child dead and born of the river, born of the snow."

They considered him, two women of light and shadow and smoke, like enough to be one alone viewed in youth and age. Grandmother, granddaughter?

"Is he coming?" the elder asked. "In the Mother's dreams, I saw him. But she left us."

"Yes," Ahjvar said.

Both ghosts regarded him, quiet, calm now, the fear he had seen in the younger gone. "She is born into him?" the younger asked. "And he has sent you?"

"Yes." Agreeing with the last, at least.

Some spark of the young woman she had been before horrors took her still endured. Her eyebrows went up, and the corners of her mouth. "*You* are the priest of the god who will be? My grandmother's mother—" And she bowed to the older ghost—who showed herself now a woman little older than the other, in the way of ghosts, since few were elderly in their own hearts. "—foresaw that one would come, but I would not have taken you for a priest."

Well, Ghu had not mentioned *that* one, that night after they left the gathering of the kings at the Orsamoss. Ahjvar didn't debate the term, but grinned suddenly beneath his scarf. "Neither did Zhung Musan."

This time teeth flashed fierce in her smile.

"But what are you?" the grandmother asked. "A living man?" She sounded doubtful. "You—look very strange, although to see beyond the flesh of the living at all is . . . very strange. I wonder if the gods see us so? Light and fire and shadow. But you are—"

"Does it matter what I am, grandmother?"

"No. You are the god's. That's enough. You'll do what must be done here."

"Did any survive?" That seemed to him the most urgent question. The dead were going nowhere.

"My son—"

"My sister and her husband. Our little cousin."

"They escaped to the forest. I don't think they escaped for long."

"No," he said. That was the tally of the hanged priests of the keep. "No. They were taken. I think they were prisoners some time, but they were killed a few days ago. We came too late." There was no apology he could make for that. "They're blessed and gone to the road."

"The Mother in the god-who-will-be came to them. I know. I dreamed. I did not think that dead, I could dream. Young man—" The old one looked younger than he did, now. "—you will want a spade. But—" And an old woman's weariness slowed her voice. "—I don't know what has been left. It burned. All burning, all the night . . ."

He stooped to gather earth, but the young priestess put a hand over his. Her touch was like warm water, barely felt. "No. Give us to our graves. You can't dig them in a night. We'll wait with you, priest of the god."

"If you will."

The younger lost form, became nothing but an impression of misty light in the corner of the eye. The elder trailed him as he led Niaul across the terrace. He breathed through his teeth, through his scarf, and the horse pulled ahead. He headed for the western side of the enclosure, where there was another narrow, pine-sentried gate; the evening wind came from the west and he wanted to get upwind before he was sick. The burnt buildings here seemed to have been smaller, less formally placed. Scattered, blackened timbers gone to charcoal ridged like scab. A few oddments of metal. Sickle, there at his feet. Tools.

No spades, as she had said; they'd have been wooden, with a metal cutting edge. Maybe some of these rusted strips among the ashes.

"You'll want water. The springs within the shrine are better for bathing than drinking, and . . . and they cut the throat of my other son over the well, and threw him in after he bled dry. He is gone to the Old Great Gods in the blessing of water, but the . . . the well will not be fit for use. There is another spring dug to a well by the gardens. Come. Let's see if it is unpolluted."

A ghost could not travel far from its anchoring body, but the old priestess walked ahead of him, a shadowy woman's figure, long hair loose down her back, and then fading to a streak of silvery mist, but still very much there. A handful of hens scattered from her as if she walked in the flesh.

"Hah," she said. "They missed a few. I suppose the foxes are taking them."

Ahjvar said nothing, concentrating on breathing clean air, still swallowing the body's urge to retch itself clean of the corruption it only inhaled. The western path led to a steep hillside cut and walled into terraces facing the southwest, muddy, puddled with water, trampled with boots. Ranks of grey cabbage-stalks not yet cleared, tangled dead vines of pea or bean. The spring there came out among rocks, its natural well expanded to a broad, deep pool, with stone steps descending and a stone-lined channel carrying it to many branches, some blocked with wooden boards, to water the gardens at need. Nothing in the water that he could see. The soldiers would have wanted fresh water themselves. Would they have poisoned the well as they left? There had been hate here, not just enmity. The general had been one of those sick souls who took pleasure in power over others, and in death, besides.

The horse pulled again, wanting water.

"Wait."

There were tracks in the earth by the stones. Fox. Prints almost like small hands. Pheasant. All made since the night's rain. No small beast-corpses in the bursting ferns. Besides, though Zhung Musan had not destroyed the shrine immediately on taking Dernang, this massacre was still a week or two old. Poison ought to have been flushed away.

He thought only after Niaul had plunged his muzzle in, that to clear the water of potential poison was a spell simple enough. Slow and stupid.

"The water is clean and blessed," the ghost said. She had been drifting like mist along the channel, down to the terraces, but now returned. "I think you'll have the easiest time of it if you make our grave here. It's a stony land, and this is the best you'll find. The cairns of my parents and my other sons are high on the opposite side of this valley. You would find it too far to carry all of us. I don't suppose there is any dishonour in laying our bones in clean earth, even if it is last year's onion bed."

"I suppose not," he agreed, bemused. He had never met a ghost so—so solidly of earth and self. Usually they yearned to be gone, pulled to the Old Great Gods.

"And the sun is setting. Another night makes little difference. What the ravens and foxes and rats will do, they do. You should make a camp. Perhaps here? I don't think the wind will change."

"No." He tried to sound less brusque. "No, grandmother."

The corner-of-the-eye presence was close, at his shoulder. "I don't think I'm old enough to be your grandmother. And I would have lived a hundred years, if I had lived until midsummer, though I'm no wizard. My name is Swajui Kiaswa, elder brother."

"Ahjvar," he said. "I—" He did not want to discuss why he would not camp near death and old burning, nor where there were any strangers to witness the night, dead souls or living. "I'm going up to the sanctuary of the Mother. I'll return in the morning."

"Is the air bad even here? I can't smell. Isn't that strange? I can only imagine. I'm sorry." The light began to drift back towards the fenced compound of the shrine. "Come with the dawn, then, Ahjvar."

Nothing to be seen, but he felt the gathered force of them still, a gentle pressure of—not life. Souls in pain, trapped. Even she. Yet Kiaswa dressed herself in the cares of the family matriarch she had been in life, and thus staved off her pain and fear and the forlorn anguish of a soul held back from the road. They chose to, both of the priestesses, all of these holy folk, no ghost asking to be set to the road this night. Why? To defy their enemy his triumph. They were murdered and deliberately left as ghosts, for the torment of their souls, but they would take their leave of their gods and go to the Old Great Gods of the far heavens with due care at the hands of one they chose to believe a priest, a successor to themselves.

He was no priest but a murderer many times over. Ghu should have come himself, but his god had pulled him as fiercely as the road called these, Ahjvar suspected.

At least he could dig graves. The ghosts could make their own prayers.

An owl dropped from a tree, soaring over the nearer terrace. The last of the sun cut redly through the broken clouds and the lacing branches. Dusk was thickening as he found, easily enough, a path climbing up behind the shrine, wandering aimless between the trees but always upward. Narrow, but not overgrown, at least for one afoot. He walked, leading the horse, and always found the way under his feet, even once the light faded to blackness. It would be dawn before the last of the waning moon rose. At some point water began to sing alongside, maybe even the same stream he had crossed and recrossed riding from the east, and then the feel of the ground underfoot changed from leaf-mould and occasional beds of stone to springy layers of fallen needles. The air was bright and clean and living with the scent of pines.

Cold mountain air, though. He should not be a fool and sit up chilled through the night, but he was exhausted, and if he lay close enough to a fire for its heat to be any comfort, he risked throwing himself into it.

The thick trees opened out into spaciousness. It was more the sound of the air about him than any certainty of shadowy trunks. The feel of a compressed path beneath his feet faded away, as though it had come where it meant to be. The singing note of the water grew louder, then quieted. Whispering of pines more lofty. Water and wind in the needles, branches moving. A bird singing like liquid silver, strange and beautiful and nothing he had heard in the Nabbani forest below the mountains. In the far distance another echoed it, or challenged, or merely sang an answer.

Ahjvar was abruptly so weary he could not bear the thought of standing any longer, but he unsaddled the horse by touch, found a sack that felt like feed and shook out a small measure of grain of some sort for him, made sure the soft, questing muzzle found it, and left Niaul to it. He still had the stench of rot in his throat, in his hair, his clothes, or maybe it was only in his mind.

Water called him. The ground was all fallen needles ribbed with roots. Softer ground under foot, and stones too. Scent of bruised green. He knelt down to feel for the water. Cold as winter's breath, running fast and shallow. Cupped his hands and drank, and drank, and then bathed his face. Got out of the way as he heard the horse walk up by him, splash and begin to suck. He found a tree, a vast trunk, and lay down between the spreading roots, wrapped in his plaid blanket. Cold. No idea where he had left the saddle and gear. There was one of their old blankets rolled and tied behind the saddle and he couldn't be bothered to seek it. Hollow belly and no stomach for food. Just . . . sleep. Stars like chips of ice between the clearing clouds. He missed the warmth of a body beside him. Admit that. Hoped the horse wouldn't stray too far or fall over any cliffs in the night. Should have tied him, not trusted to Ghu's horse-magic, god-magic, sweet fool's innocence. . . .

Slept. And drowned in nightmares, was drowned, choking beneath the waters of the well, hit his head on the root he lay by, skinned the back of his hand on the rough bark of the trunk, slept and woke with a cry lying alongside a corpse and woke choking on smoke, white bones, woke . . . Did not set the knife's blade to his skin, though he had it in his hand. Rocked and told himself he was awake, he only imagined the smoke and it was old smoke, old horrors, not his horrors but the poor blessed ghosts he was called to serve here and the morning was coming, the morning would come. . . . Counted out acorns, three, turned them through his hand and tried to count the trees of the cork grove, so carefully peeled and tended by the villagers of Sand Cove. Say he stood at the turn of the road, or sat on the stone wall *there*, and looked from the south, how many? First the old great grandfather tree, lightning scarred, the outrider. Then . . . He drew it in his mind as an artist might, this tree, the next, an intrusive dark holly there. The next . . . did he remember? That one had a crooked branch . . .

When he realized the first grey was upon him he staggered stiffly up, whistled for the horse, which came as obediently as a beast would for Ghu, and found a little more barley. Discovered pick and comb and brush, so cleaned Niaul's feet, worked till the gleaming dark hide was free from mud and sweat and dried blood. A long time since he'd had to tend his own horse. There was cracked barley, too, meant for men to boil to a porridge rather than for horses to eat, and he seemed to have both the larger and the smaller kettle among his gear, bad luck for Ghu, but he thought he would rather face the dead, or their remains, with his stomach empty.

Brick of caravan-tea.

Not even tea.

But he did not feel so—empty—of the soul, as such a night should have left him. There was a quiet here, a deep, calm quiet, even knowing the goddess of the place dead. Dawn spilled golden through the pines, and birds all around sang, though not the silver outpouring of the early night. The axe taken from the Northron brigand so long ago and the roll of the old blanket over his shoulder, the horse following, he headed down to the ghosts.

Ahjvar half expected some hovering overseer, Kiaswa herself, to be vocal at his ear with instruction; the ghosts were only a presence like the birdsong, though—there, but belonging to the background. He stirred through the debris of the outbuilding until he found what he thought he had noticed without giving it much heed the evening before, the head of an iron mattock, undamaged, rust-flaking but sound, though its shaft was burnt away. He took it and his axe and went in search of a good strong sapling, the ghost of Kiaswa with him as faint presence, while Niaul grazed along the ditches and greening banks of the terraces. There were buds showing swollen on the trees, and a mist of pale green over the lower forest, viewed from the terrace heights. How long till the waters receded and armies could move again?

It was rough work—Ahjvar was no carpenter—but the mattock's head showed no inclination to fly off its new haft when he swung. Good. He left the horse still grazing and, after consideration, left shirt and plaid as well, wrapping the old headscarf over his face again as he climbed to the western gateway. The wind was out of the southeast, today, and smelt again of rain. And the damp air held more scent.

Smoke might be preferable.

The waiting dead. He had walked a battlefield once, long ago. Cattle-raiding, Yeh-Lin might jeer, but it had been claim to rights over a section of the caravan road they contested, that war between his father's folk and the Duina Broasora. He was just eighteen and newly named his father's champion, the woman who had held that place before him having stood aside, saying she had yet a few years for childbearing and meant to make the most of them with a bard of the Duina Lellandi she had met. Sword-mistress . . . he had not forgotten her name . . . Ailsa. Not the master who had trained him, that was her father. His mind wandering, not to think of what he breathed. Battlefield. And a princess of the Duina Broasora dead, a young woman he knew well. They had been friends in another summer. Maybe might have been something more, especially after such a season of blood, and peace sought with autumn, before the harvest, but she was dead. If that prince had married that princess . . . who could say. But as there, so here: on that field the dead had waited, to be known and named and claimed.

Only he, here, to walk among them, though their names were Kiaswa's and her granddaughter's to speak. He took the old man from the well first of all, with a sapling cut and trimmed, a low pair of angled branches left a foot long or so, to make a grappling hook. His body was gone soft and strange, but the cold water had kept it from decaying so badly as some of the others. He was still . . . in one piece. Ahjvar laid him by the gate, limbs straight, white hair parted from his face.

One.

He hauled them from the pools, next. Those were . . . bad. Disjointed. Sunken beneath the surface again, torn clothing swaying like weeds. Bones, flesh slowly poached off of them. The water steamed not from cold air alone, but because it flowed bath-warm from its springs. Clothing held them together. Some had been put in naked. He had to cut another sapling, leave more branches, not exactly a rake but . . . fit for raking. He gathered them onto the blanket, not his plaid but the old one, camel-rancid and desert-gritted, and dragged them to lie by the old man.

The old woman and the young were a pressure against his back, a presence. Naming names. Kin born to the service of the Wild Sister, the Mother of all Nabban. Marriage kin from hills to the east who had chosen the service of the goddess, the tending of the pilgrims. Children.

Twelve. At least the souls of those who had been given to the water had taken the road, their feet safe on their way, blessed and set free.

He considered the defiled well. The springs that made the bathing-pools would flush them clean and purify them, in time, but the well that had been given the old priest's lifeblood. . . .

"What will you?" the younger priestess asked, as he walked a circuit of it, laying gathered twigs from the dykes of the terraces, carefully pat-terned. "You're wizard as well as priest?"

"I can't leave this here and open. If someone comes—if anyone came, and drew water—"

"No," she sombrely, and "No," Kiaswa said, drawing slowly to her body's form. "But it could wait."

"No." It gave him the horrors, that dark water, reflecting the bright sky and concealing a man's worth of blood. How long till that was clean again? Never, sunk deep in the goddess's earth or not.

He walked his pattern, sword in hand, cutting lines through the symbols he had set. The square wooden coping of the well, which had sur-vived all the burning, crumbled inwards, and the earth beneath it, stones sliding. Then there was only a sunken hollow and the earth all disturbed.

"So."

Back to gathering bodies. Those who waited. The granddaughter, whom he had rolled in the blanket and carried, trying to wrap her opened ribs back together, not forgetting the foot. Some lying where they had fallen at the public southern gate.

Seventeen.

Two boys close under the wall, dragged up from the terraces, where they had been turning the ground for peas, the granddaughter said.

Brutally used, ribs cracked open, like herself under the tree. Brothers. Silent ghosts, but even they . . . "No," Kiaswa said, when he asked. "They wish to wait with us. We will wait to take the road till we are in our grave, all of us left here. We will not leave you to this alone." And the boys pressed close to her, to Ahjvar, and still did not speak, but he felt their fierce will, their agreement.

Nineteen.

Kiaswa herself. She lay at the north, hidden away under a bush sticky with pregnant buds, and a baby lying where they had dropped it, torn from her arms. Frail, shrunken little woman, white hair gone thin and fine as silk floss, limbs all sprawled and her skull beaten in.

"Don't see me so," she said. Illogically. "Don't look."

"My baby," the young priestess said, and light gathered in light, but the ghost could not hold the ghost, not here, and the infant was a little thing without words, wanting its mother, unable to join with her. On the road—a baby was drawn pure and direct to the Gods, it was said. A baby had no sins to face and know. A baby . . . should have had a life with its mother, Gods or no Gods to hold it now. He wrapped it into her robe when he took it to the gate with its great-great-grandmother, and nearly fell, so dizzy, when he stood again from setting them down. Ears buzzing like wasps, light and high with fasting.

Twenty-one.

Late afternoon already. How had the day passed and so little done? Not hot, though sweat ran in runnels down his chest and back. He was cold.

"You should rest. You should eat," Kiaswa said.

"Could you, grandmother?"

"Go away. We shouldn't have asked this. It's enough. I was wrong. Bless us and go, give us the quick blessing of earth and leave us under the sky, let the crows and ravens do their work."

"No."

He trudged away to the gardens with the mattock. No ghost followed, then. Kiaswa drifted near, later, as sunset stretched the shadows into twilight.

"Ahjvar."

He looked up. Nearly, he thought, deep enough, broad enough. One bed to hold them all. Stones, grubbed up from below the level of their tillage, ringed the pit.

"Go. Come in the morning, but go, now. It's dark. You'll take your own toe off," she added tartly.

He leaned on the mattock, hardly understanding her.

"Elder brother, promise me something."

He nodded, vaguely.

"Cook something. Eat. Drink tea."

He considered her, sorting words.

"You promised." She flicked a finger at him. "Say yes."

He didn't answer.

"Ahjvar!"

"Yes. Grandmother."

She made a sound halfway between laughter and a sigh, and faded away towards the shrine. He left the mattock where it was, climbed out of the pit, and wandered in search of his way again. He remembered to take his shirt and the plaid blanket only because they hung on a bushy willow where had cut his first sapling.

Niaul saw he was going and followed after him.

Not so dark, this evening, the last light still lingering. He could see what he had not noticed even in the morning, that there were three springs in that wide sloping open space beneath the ancient pines, one high, two lower, all twining together to one as they plunged down a set of shallow rapids. Was there any sanctity to that little brook from which the Wild Sister arose—would there be any taboos as to its use? He stripped regardless and slid into the largest pool below those rapids, stayed till the cold cut to his bones and teeth chattered, washed his linens and dried himself on the same blanket he meant to sleep in.

But he made no fire, and brewed no tea.

Know in your dreams you are dreaming.

New moon: blackest of nights, but cloudless. Starlight was cold. Frost in the air. He drowned in exhaustion, lay deep in graves, in a grave, with Miara. Groped after others the hag had destroyed, bodies buried, the ones in the quiet hills, if he found them again, or abandoned in the nighttime streets. That old couple, the man who had tried to be kind . . . graves he had dug with his bare hands. It was Miara he fished rotten and disintegrating from the Lady's well in the cavern beneath Marakand, and Miara who kissed him, mouth hot with his blood, and pulled him in to drown, devoured, smothered, chained.

Something he needed to find. Lost somewhere. Memory. Shape. Warm body next to him. Burning beneath him, grappling him close and his burning hands clutched her, his thumbs pressed—*no.* Feel of an acorn clenched against his palm. Real. Acorns were real. He was awake, and choking on smoke. He still held the acorn. He had gone to sleep holding it.

No smoke, of course not. Dawn lightening the east.

He drank and washed and fed Niaul the last of the coarse grain, saddled the horse with no intention to ride, but lacking any other better harness, the ornate breast-strap would do to pull against. Odds were the stallion had never been set to such work in his life. He thought it about two winding miles from the shrine up to the cold springs, but it seemed to take more than an hour to walk down, this time, and twice he found himself standing, holding himself up with a hand against some tree trunk, without knowing he had paused. Dreams pressed at him, ate time. He heard Miara screaming his name, which shocked him awake, still walking. A lie. He had not used this name in that time. A little, dog-sized brown creature—deer? goat? overgrown cloven-hoofed rabbit?—stood staring in the path. Fanged. Niaul stretched out his neck, snuffing, and it bounded into the air and vanished.

He had not dreamed that. A tiny fanged deer. Maybe. He could ask Kiaswa if there were such things. He had forgotten it, though, by the time he rounded the next sharp bend in the descending track. Stared stupidly at stepping stones where the path crossed the brook—he did not remember crossing the brook this way. Did not remember that the path had crossed any brook at all, before. Suddenly could not work out the pattern of the stones, how he should step from one to the next. As though he had never seen such a thing, could not think how to get his foot to a stone, or what followed. As though he must think of each muscle, to move it, to set a foot in place without thought was—he did not understand how to *walk*.

Niaul paced impatiently forward, and Ahjvar, who had been leaning against him with a hand hooked through the breast-strap, having forgotten to bridle the beast, stumbled alongside him. There, he had not forgotten how to walk after all and the stones did not matter. Boots were wet. No matter.

The path forked. It had not forked before. Had it? Small sweet yellow flowers on a leafless bush. Niaul stood to tear several mouthfuls, looked round at him, still chewing, led off again, right-hand fork. Steep plunge down, up again. Ferns. Moss. Weeds with rosettes of leaf just greening beneath last year's rattling seed-stalks. Open ground. The terraced garden plots. Not lost after all. He let the horse go and sank down to his heels, eyes shut. The paths through this forest shifted and changed. He would believe that, not that he hallucinated the ordinary.

Twenty-one. It was not broad enough yet, nor deep enough to hold them safe. There would be bear in such a forest, larger scavengers. He stripped off his shirt and sword and went down into the grave to widen and deepen it. The sun grew hot. He cut new ferns and the yellow flowers that Niaul wanted to eat, laid them over mud that was winter-sodden and puddling, and when that was not enough, gathered old leaves too, the earthy scent of autumn. He was coated dark with clay, a thick second skin, boots heavy. The ghost followed him, seeming worried, but if she spoke he could not hear. He cut poles for the frame of a travois, made a sling of the old blanket across it, and whistled dry-mouthed for the horse. No good. He stumbled to the pool to drink and tried again, and when Niaul came, led him up to the narrow western gateway of the shrine, frightening off three ravens and a handful of squabbling crows. The smell was something he could shut out, now. It belonged to some place other than this staggering dream. Foxes or something had been among them, scattering . . . parts, in the night. He gathered them again. Niaul was unhappy with being harnessed to the travois, tied with torn strips of the brown scarf, but he stood even to have rotten flesh loaded behind him, and was praised in mumbled Praitannec whispers. Ahjvar took them two at a time, first the bodies of those whose souls were gone, carried each down into the grave, no rough tumbling. It mattered. He forgot why it mattered but this he must do, with care and reverence. This service, to these innocents he had not killed.

Niaul proved patient and biddable, obeying spoken commands like a good herd-dog. Ghu's lingering horse-magic, surely. They tramped a mucky trail, many trips, and when they were done Ahjvar brought a load of ferns, which were unrolling with the growing warmth of the day, to cover them, and more twigs of yellow flowers, before he cut the horse free of his knots and the travois.

"Pray," he told the old priestess, who had taken form again. "I can't."

"But you do, elder brother. With your every breath."

The younger touched his hand again. Warm now, almost as the living. Shy. Smiled. The small bright soul of her child was twined with her own. They all came in forms of life, those that remained, old, young, the two boys, and touched him, which he should not have felt, hands brushing his, clasping fingers. Solemn eyes. Then they were gone to light again. Kiaswa lingered last of all, reaching her hands to his shoulders. "Duck."

He bowed his head obediently and she stretched up to kiss his brow. Her lips were dry and warm and he was surely dreaming wakeful, to think he felt them. "Find healing. Be free. Be blessed. You have surely blessed us."

"Go to your road with the blessing of the god," he told them hoarsely. Praitannec words, he realized after, but he did not suppose they minded. They had let go their will to remain; they were pulled, urgent to answer, no longer concerned with him, with what they left behind. He spread the first handfuls of earth by hand.

Free. Gone. He felt it then, the pull, like standing on a clifftop, the call to leap into night, not to fall, but to fly, a weight drawing him in, the depth of the stars and what lay beyond. The Old Great Gods, calling. He was leaning on the mattock, eyes shut, shivering as sweat and tears dried on his skin.

The god, he had said. Well. Still work here for the god's priest. His assassin, his gravedigger, his stray dog.

A spade was the tool he needed, but he had none. He made shift with the mattock again. The sun was low before he had the earth mounded over them, and then he began to pile the stones. A rough cairn to keep the scavengers off and mark the spot even once the forest took it back.

Full dark before Ahjvar sought the path to the sanctuary, and he trusted to Niaul to find the way. He noticed, though, that they crossed no brook, not even when they came to where the rapids rang below the joining of the outflow of the springs. He stripped and washed again, scrubbed mud from his clothes, washed even the shirt he had not been wearing, and hung all on a branch to dry. Covered only by his blanket, he tended the horse, who got most of the cracked barley for his day's work, and lay down fireless once more, on his back, watching the sky.

Think on what you want, what you need from him. You are a weight on him, a burden . . . all Nabban falls on him and he needs either his champion at his back . . . or to be free of ghosts. Your ghosts. You.

Find your way out of the fire, or go to find your road. Choose. For young Nabban's sake.

Three nights for a vigil. He had not thought of it so, till now. A vigil of sleep, not waking. Vigil by a grave-side that should be his own.

You don't dream of acorns. He clenched it in his hand, open-eyed. Remember Miara, living. Face that. Remember them, all he had killed as the hag's hands. Remember . . . deaths. His own. Remember he had burned with Hyllau. He was murdered, and cursed, and it was over, her very soul destroyed, his goddess put sleeping in the earth, never to wake, his chains taken from her, and if he was bound still—he trusted where those bonds were held. He had been drowned and made a necromancer's slave and he had destroyed a devil's web of devoured souls from within and that, too, was over. They were not real, any of them, when they took him in the night. They were memories. They were dreams, scars on his mind. They were done with; he would have them done with. He would remember the waves on the shore below the cliff and a hawk plunging from the sky and the cool green shade of the oaks. He must. Or let all go, and be gone. No more harm in the night.

He thought that after all he could not sleep, shivering and sick with cold and memory, but something stalked him and the body failed and let him fall. Something . . . reaching, to hold and destroy what was suddenly denied her. Hungry . . . *Hyllau, reaching for him. The Lady of Marakand, but her face was burnt black, charred and flaking away like Hyllau's and she closed her mouth over his, pressing down on him, tongue forcing—He caught her by the throat, to choke and throttle. She was burning under his hands, his hands were burning and there was some thing in the fire, in his hand, held hard enough to be a harsh near-pain amidst the burning, hard. Fingertips dug it into his fist and he could not bring both hands to grip on her because he held—he dreamed and he should dream of oaks instead. This was nightmare, this was over, this was done, and he opened the burning hand and shoved away, flung himself from her, crying out—*

"No!" He struck a hand against the ground and pulled himself to his knees, crouched gasping, fingers splayed, both hands digging into the deep litter of needles. Could hardly breathe. But he was awake. Wiped his mouth on his sleeve, shaking. He wanted to crawl to the water but did not think he would have the strength or the will to crawl out again. Crouched and shivered. His hands were empty, fingers spread to anchor him. He forced his breathing to slow, sat up, hands spread on his knees. Dream. Only nightmare.

He had let go. He had remembered and he had let go.

Bowed his head to his knees.

The acorn he had held was lost somewhere as he had jerked awake, but some distant clear thought of sense said that was no bad thing. It was his mind, not his hand, that must learn to remember.

But Old Great Gods have mercy, he did not want to sleep again. The nightmares still pressed thickly on him, smothering any will . . . that was fasting and exhaustion, fool. If he could not drag himself to his feet . . . then do not. Then fall.

It was a night of years, the stars frozen in the sky, the birds, the owls and the silver singer and the barking foxes silent. He let himself fall, he drowned in dreams as he had once tried to drown himself in the sea. Let go, sink, don't fight . . . The waves had rolled him up on the shore, the barren, sharp-toothed coast below Noble Cedar Harbour, even the sea refusing him. Nightmares drowned him, and he could . . . remember. *No.* One word.

Not pleading, not crying out against the hag or the devil of Marakand or Catairanach his goddess. One word for himself. *No.* He did not fight them, did not strike, did not seize. No, he said, and shut his eyes within the dream and found his image of the cork-oak grove. He shaped this dream; he would not allow nightmares to raven unchecked. They were not his truth in this place: this pain, this fear, this rage, these enemies . . . they were not here with him, no hungry fire, no deep black devouring water. These hands, those dead eyes, deformed and defiled face—*No.* Remember her hawks and the blue sky. Horizons, Miara had said. The horizons were always too close and narrow, when I served in the royal *dinaz.*

You would have liked him, he told her. *He's very strange. He's all horizons.*

He dreamed she kissed him, holding his hands in hers. He dreamed she opened her hands and let him go, flung wide her arms as if she launched an eagle, and looked away, into the depths of the sky, fading to light herself as the old priestess had, and the light lost in the sun.

Dawn. He had been lying awake since before the first paling of the sky gave the pines form. Birdsong had pushed into the last edges of the night and uncoiled like the ferns to fullness, echoing and re-echoing through the forest. Ahjvar pulled himself to his feet and went slowly, light-headed and unsteady, down to the pool below the rapids. He bathed yet again, for all cold water and no soap could do, washed even his hair, which was full of pine-needles, dressed in clothes still damp and mud-stained, and walked back, gathering twigs and cones, to make a fire. His hands shook so badly that he gave up on flint and firesteel and cut the signs of birch and of alder, and without considering, of rose, which was not for a cooking fire but a holy one, on a stripped green branch, and felt the fire warm and rushing life in his hands, waking easily in the kindling he had laid.

Tea. He divided the broken barley with the horse and made porridge with the little that was left, walking like an old man as he gathered more wood; there was a wealth of winter-fallen branches when he looked, and they cracked and spat with the pine-pitch and scented the air.

Warmth. Food. And more tea. It was good just to hold the cup in his hands and breathe the steam.

He found the acorn he had dropped in the night, put it with the other two in his purse. Thought of the dead tree and the black stone in the shrine that had been the Mother's and wondered if a cork-oak from the warm coast of the Gulf of Taren could grow on a Nabbani mountain of winter blizzards. There should be a tree again.

The horse wandered off down the path, not quite out of sight, grazing the new-springing green along the brook.

He fell into a state half-sleep, half-waking, dreaming not night-mares but waves and gulls. The fire died to embers, but the sun was warm and high. He ought to gather more wood, not let the fire die, if he was to wait another night. He ought to find his way to the mountain, to worry about more assassins, more servants of the empress hunting vision-led for the heir of the gods.

Niaul raised his head, pricked his ears. Not the path but the forest drew his attention, away to the north and east. Open pines running there, a long rising and dip of the land and a steep climb behind it up a ridge. Flash of distant white.

So, then.

There were words to be spoken.

CHAPTER XXVI

The sound of Snow's hooves was soft, near to silent on the thick cushion of fallen needles beneath the pines, rising to a muffled hollow thud like distant drums when Ghu set the white stallion to a canter through the pillars of the trees, impatient, dreading. Riding to have it over.

The sanctuary of the Mother, the cold springs. The birth of the Wild Sister. He had never been to this place, and knew every tree, every stone, every singing bird. Evening Cloud whinnied to his stablemate. Ahjvar was sitting by a fire, leaning against one of the great pines, unsheathed sword within reach, shoved upright into the pine mould, dull silver in the sun. Not sleeping, but open-eyed. Waiting. He thrust himself to his feet as Ghu reined Snow back to his flowing walk again. Jui and Jiot coursed up to Ahjvar, tails wagging, and he gave them a hand to sniff, absent of attention. That welcome taken care of, they coursed on by to drink noisily from the nearest of the sacred springs, Jui wading right in to wallow, joyously irreverent.

Ahjvar simply stood, waiting. He looked exhausted, gaunt, eyes hollow, dark-ringed, but there was a calm to him, a peace.

What he had feared, when Ahjvar had said he would not follow to the mountain. What he had known. Ghu dismounted and looped the stallion's reins up, left him loose to wander to the water or his fellow as

360

he would, but stood still himself, to have a moment to watch Ahjvar, to hold him whole in sight. To not cross to him, not hear the words said.

Ahjvar came to him instead and fell to his knees at his feet.

"I've been wrestling dreams." Head bowed, voice low, hoarse.

"Ahjvar . . ."

"I've found my way through them. I can wake myself. Wake myself up knowing I dream, not reaching for a weapon, not trying to choke— I've done it, three times, four, I don't know, but one, one was very bad. I'm still dreaming, but I have *broken* them. I *know* them. I do not think—I do not think I will wake trying to kill long-dead enemies any longer. I do not sleep easy, or quiet, but . . . I wake and I can sleep again. Even—even when I dream I am burning, even when the Lady takes me in the well, I can make myself wake and know I am dreaming." Almost a whisper.

"Ah, Ahj." Ghu hardly dared to touch him, to set a hand to that bowed head. But he did. The bright pale hair was finer than one would think from its unruly wildness, warmed in the bough-broken sun, golden light on gold. All his resolution—he held it firm. He could not deny and would not plead. He should take what warmth there was in knowing he had, after all, been able to give that gift of time, that Ahj did not die in flight from the haunting of his own mind, but went to his road, long though it might be with the murders he carried, with some small peace.

"If I can sleep, even brokenly, I don't think I'll dream when I'm waking. I don't think I need you sleeping by me for fear I'll wake mad and trying to kill. Or that I need you there, to stop me killing." Ahjvar dragged a deep breath. "But I think, I think there is no one I would want there by me, but you. I—would give you that."

Abrupt words, dropped heavy between them. Ahjvar would not look up. Shaken, Ghu went to his own knees in the needles and moss, hand on his shoulder, hand on his jaw, in the coarser hair of his beard, forcing Ahjvar to meet his eyes.

"Ahj—Ahjvar—"

"I want that. You."

"Not men, you said."

"No. No. A man." A rush, words desperate to be spoken. "I—I find you are become my—exception."

And however much Ghu might have wanted that—to hear it chilled him.

"Did I do this to you, wanting you? I change things. I know I do. Not intending, but—the dogs are not what they were, because they've come to follow me. Father, Mother forgive me, Ahjvar, I did not mean to—"

A gaze so raw—naked, burning as flame. Blue should be cool as the sky overhead, not hold the sun's hot heart. It took all words away. But the corner of the mouth turned in that faint, amused shadow that was not quite a smile.

"Gods, don't think that of yourself, Ghu. You wouldn't change someone against their nature. I *know* you would not."

"Not knowingly. But unknowing—" Old Great Gods above, he feared it. And was kindled none the less to fire, to have Ahj look at him so.

"No. *No.* If you could shape a person's will all unknowing to what you wanted, to what served you, you would have had Zhung Musan at your feet swearing fealty like Daro Korat, so much bloodshed spared. Hah, you would have had me at your feet long before this. True?"

He couldn't help it. That made him laugh.

"Ghu, love without desire, you know you have had that of me for years, but I have been—I have been seeing you all too unsettlingly in the body for—when I think—since before Deyandara came and we set out for Marakand. Last spring. Noticing you, since you grew up—in ways I would not have expected and could not let myself think on, could deny and bury, because—you know why. Because I couldn't feel such things without seeing, *feeling*, Miara dead under my hands." He swallowed. "And you had not begun to take on any touch of your godhead then. So don't think that you've drawn me to you against my nature, ever. Two lovers only, in what, almost a century? That's not any great history either way. Who's to say whom I might not have loved in my natural life, woman or man, if I had not been thrown all into damnation by Hyllau? You haven't forced me to this, not you. Never." Another nerve-ragged breath. "And I would not care if you had."

"You should." Ghu should. Ghu should care for both of them, if Ahj would not, and—and what could he know, but what Ahjvar said?

He gives himself to you. How do we deny that? Father Nabban would not have left Ghu to hold the stolen curse, if he saw harm in it for Ahjvar. The Father would not condone, if Ghu witting or unwitting had through that bond shifted his friend's love for him from one course to another he might not have chosen on his own. Surely not.

"I am not always sane; I am not safe, even if I have broken my nightmares, and you are my safety, and my still centre, and all my trust. I am who I am now, where I have come to now, not who Catairlau was or might have been. I am yours, soul and body. Whatever you want of me. Take that. It's all I have to give you."

"*No.* You've given me everything I needed, all these years. You gave me—a place to grow into myself. I would not be the man I am if you had driven that boy from your wall and your hearth." He added, because it was true, "Nabban would not be—what it will be. What I will be."

"Damn your gods." Ahjvar turned his mouth against Ghu's fingers, eyes shut.

"Don't. They haven't damned you."

Trust himself? He did not know. But Ghu slid his hand around to wind into the tangled fall of Ahjvar's hair, kissed him, hesitantly, hardly more than a brushing of the lips, as he had kissed him in the burning tower of Dinaz Catairna.

A moment. Ahjvar leaned in and opened his mouth to him.

Daylight, still, and he did not think the Mother, had she been there, could have minded what they did in that sacred place beneath the pines. His place, this was, now. She was gone. What she had been in her strength was growing anew in himself. If he reached for it, it was there. The river. The rivers, the three great, the countless lesser, the lakes, all the waters of the land. The Father held on a little longer, withdrawn into himself on the mountain, waiting, but this, this was already become Ghu's place, water and pines. So where better? The horses dozed, hip-shot and nose to fly-flicking tail. The dogs slept in a patch of sun. Sun found and lost and found them again, moving above the pines. Ahjvar . . . simply slept. Deep and still and beautiful. Ghu closed his eyes himself. Not to sleep. To listen, in this small place. To the wind in the pines, the springs and the streams that chimed over the rocks, through the ferns. Birds, spring birds in wild carolling. The man breathing slow beside him. That, most of all.

"Did you find your god?" Ahjvar, woken, speaking out of long, easy silence.

"I did."

"And?"

"We—spoke. I see my road. That's all. For now." He rolled to his side, pulled closer yet to Ahjvar. "I thought—I thought you had come here to find some quiet."

"I did."

"I thought you would ask me to let you die." Ghu traced the line of neck and shoulder, collarbone, the delicate hollow of his throat, awed anew. That solidly-muscled chest, that unsunned skin a palest brown no darker than his own hand, which showed a warmer sunlit tone against Ahj's Praitan earthiness. The cold blanched silver of old scars, crossed and recrossed. Ahjvar had taken no care to avoid his enemies when he sought and dealt death in the Five Cities. Knives mostly, and the crossbows of house guards. Only the newest, from Marakand, were purpled still. Spears and swords, those. Ahj did not speak of what had happened when he went to murder the Voice of the Lady, but they had not taken him easily. Fingers combed through thick and curling golden hair, followed the narrowing line of it, flattened over those most livid scars, two of them crossing the last ribs and biting below, deep and knotted. Slid over to his hip. "I thought you had come here, to—wait, and ask for death."

Ahjvar turned to face him, arm over him, and it seemed a wonder again that they could lie pressed body to body and Ahj not be merely lost in desperate need to have an anchor in the night. A greater wonder that his hands could touch, careful and wondering, and find a way over Ghu's own skin in turn, caress muscle and bone beneath, grip hard in urgency, demand and make and give a closeness that had no root in fear, that wanted Ghu for life and breath and heat of desire, not for a wall against terror in the dark.

"If I hadn't been able to fight the dreams at the last, I would have. You don't need me to take Nabban."

"Not to be my *rihswera?*" Ghu asked. A king's champion. Teasing. Neither to be my champion nor my lover, he had said after the battle at the Orsamoss.

"I will be, if you will it, but *need* me for that, no. You don't. You have Yeh-Lin for a weapon and the Kho'anzi for the shield of a lord's name. You have the place of the gods to fill. You don't need me to face the bloody lords who destroy this land and this empress who thinks she's been made a goddess, or whatever drives her to oppose the will of the gods."

"I need you to see me," Ghu said soberly. "No one else does. To know me. To remember me. No one else ever will."

"I do know that. I saw it, in the castle. I don't know how long I can give you. But what I said before: I will try. Each day. That's all I promise."

"As long as you will. No longer. It's enough."

Later, they went back down to the ruin of the shrine in the slanting afternoon sun, walking, horses and dogs following. Ghu dipped his hands in the pond above the terraces and stood a long time by the grave, but if he prayed it was without words, eyes open. Inside the enclosure, he walked a circuit of the fence, still silent. Ahjvar trailed him, not certain what he did. His path took him spiralling in to circle each of the springs, then the stone and the dead tree.

He hurt. Ahjvar could feel it. Deep, deep hurt, he and the goddess within him. No. Not two. What she had been was within him, growing to something new. Ghu was god, in this place, and not a child whose hurt could be eased by a kind touch and a word. Ahjvar put a hand on his back anyway. Thought of the acorn, found again in the pine mould, and took all three from his purse, held them out in his palm. After the dead, the dead tree was somehow the deepest wound in this place, as if it, rather than the hot springs, had been the sign of the goddess here. Zhung Musan's soldiers had not only stripped its bark away but hacked great gouges in the exposed roots. He didn't recognize its species, bark or form or stillborn buds; it might send up suckers in new life, but it might not.

"These wouldn't grow, would they? Too harsh a winter." Almost a profanation, to speak, but Ghu looked at him, blinking some—some humanity—back into eyes distant as the night sky. He took one, rolled it through his fingers.

"They might, here. The springs warm the air. They might, with a god's blessing. But do you want to plant them?"

"They're in my mind," Ahjvar said. "I shouldn't need to carry them. Better they send down roots and live."

Ghu abruptly pulled him close and kissed him, hard; clean fire of warmth and light, a hearth of life and he could have let all thought go and lost himself, drowned in that, but for the hand clenched over his and the acorns held between them.

"Yes," Ghu said, turning him loose. "Do. And the forest is called in. This place will be holy again, someday."

Ahjvar paced off distance enough for a full-grown cork-oak to be content at three points around the black stone, dug with his dagger and planted an acorn at each. Ghu had leapt to the top of the boulder and perched there cross-legged, watching, looking more like some ragged and wild forest demon playing with human form than any god.

"Or at least," Ahjvar said, sitting back on his heels, the last acorn pressed down near where the young priestess had lain, "there will be an exotic treat for the local squirrels to dig up."

"They wouldn't dare." Ghu's smile flashed. "Browsing deer, now—"

"Ghu, do the deer in this forest eat meat, or was I hallucinating?"

"Hallucinating what?"

"Deer with fangs."

"Oh, those. No. I think they fight with them."

"Ah."

"And grub up seedling trees, probably." He vaulted down, solemn again, and walked a circuit of the ground Ahjvar had claimed for his planting. He had cut three symbols into the earth, wounded with fire and blood and pain as it was, one for each tree that might be; they were oaks, but he had made the sign of cypress for healing, elder for rebirth, and elm, which was for peace, and holiness, and godhead.

"Priest of Nabban," Ghu said, coming back to where he had started. Ahjvar had not told him what the ghosts had called him. "Be that, for me, and *rihswera* too, if you will. The tree and the sword. Come. We'll take the main track down. Still a few hours till sunset."

CHAPTER XXVII

The pebbles fell and rolled in a wide scatter, red and black and yellow, over the painted calfskin. Barrast, the ox of evening, who had carried the dead heroes of the burning river to the stars. Irtennin, the seer of the white waters, whose father had been a demon of the steppes. Etic the archer. Both Irtennin and Etic had died in the battle of the burning river, among the heroes all named and honoured in the map of the sky. Etic's daughter had taken up her mother's bow, a gift of the gods, and led the band of demons and heroes to victory over the mad god of the eastern hills, in days of legend long before devils ever walked the earth. What did such a casting mean?

Death was what Ivah read. Sacrifice and upheaval. A changing of the world, as the world of the Great Grass had been changed forever when the river burned, and humankind learnt that even gods could die at their hands, and the betrayed tribe of Irtennin went to the west across the Kinsai'av. The daughter takes up the mother's bow . . . and her unknown brother, her father's son, had come riding from the north to join her, with his demon-forged spear, and together they had rallied the grief-stricken warriors who had followed the twelve heroes of the river and . . .

Hooves. Ivah looked up. Sun speared through broken cloud, dazzling off the water, making a golden haze where wind gusted pollen from a bankside tree.

It had been the coins had led her here, to this road, the coins and a restless unease that kept her from sleep, hovering on the edge of dream in the back kitchen of the inn.

Blue banners, blue as sky, whipping free, flying, turned to dragons white and muted gold, and the white horse climbed into thunderclouds and its rider turned his head, almost, to summon her, but the camel could not climb the clouds. . . . She always jerked out of her dream at that point, the rider turning to a banner-lady armoured in black, long black hair rising on the wind, staining the blue banners like ink, and red fires deep in the woman's eyes, and she woke sweating, hearing a pounding on the door that was all her imagination. If Yeh-Lin came for her, it would not be with soldiers and some pretext for arrest. There would be no knocking at the door. She did not suppose there would be a door for very long.

The coins had called her to the road that led to the mountain, but it was waiting, not journeying, that they had both foretold and counselled. She had spread the sky-map in the shadows under the bridge, squatting on heels, let the sound of the flood-swollen stream, not her father's narcotic smoke, carry her into that place where dream and sky and pebbles all danced a pattern for those with eyes that saw beyond to see.

The god was coming. The devil had promised him to the folk of Dernang, and before he came there, she would see him, and she would know. True god, or devil's lie. She could not, being prepared, be deceived. Old Great Gods, please.

Hooves, and coming swiftly. Not couriers from the outpost at the border, not on this road. She abandoned the painted skin and the pebbles and her pack lying on the cold stones beneath the arch—caught up her sabre only by a lifetime's instinct—scrambled up the bank, at the border between dark and day, blinking the water-glare blindness from her vision.

Shredding cloud, black and thunderous, and the sun pouring like water. Wind rising with a spit of rain and the blue, the blue . . . She was still caught in the seeing dream, the shaman's trance, and her pulse was a drum in her ears . . . No caution. She was falling into the sky.

She stepped out onto the bridge just as they took it, flying.

Not flight, not rout, not courier's haste but a race, a grin changed to a warning shout and they swerved one to either side, whiff of horse, flash of colour—bright as a mountain peak, dark as oiled teak.

Ivah spun around—to call, to run madly after them—but they had wheeled in the road and the bay was on her again. Touch of steel, resting on her shoulder, but she didn't even see the rider.

The black-legged white horse circled the both of them and came to a stand before her, and the light and sky fell around the man, shimmering like water.

"You've cut your hair," he said, in the Nabbani of the road, and—it was not even a jerk of the chin, just the slightest of movements, and other man turned his horse aside, the pressure of the blade leaving her shoulder, though he did not put up his sword. Some far-away last ember of common sense noted that.

"You've let yours grow—I thought you were *dead*," she said. The words seemed to come out of dream, foolish and small.

Ghu laughed—*Ghu!* He was not that hunted boy from Marakand, who had been older than she thought him even then when she looked at him properly, and was older now, lean and with a weight of weariness on him, in the haze of her vision, but he had not laughed like that in Marakand. All dark eyes and gravity and worry, there, searching for his friend.

"Me? No, but you . . . what are doing here, Ivah?" And that was the boy, who spoke with a child's simplicity.

"Waiting," she said. "Nour said—Nour survived, too. A friend found us—we were saved. Nour's gone to Bitha with his caravan but he said—I dreamed and he said . . ." She shook her head. "Was it you, all along? I was waiting for you?"

The man she had again forgotten spoke from behind her, deep voice and lilting words; she recognized the rhythm of her gang-mate Buryan's speech, the tongue of Praitan. Ghu said, "No, she's not."

Not what? Drunk? Mad? She rubbed her temples with the back of a hand, blinking, and the vision of sun and a sky flying like banners faded. Only a slight young man, lean and shadowed on a white horse.

She looked around, because something was cold and prickling warning of the uncanny on the back of her neck, but there was only the other, a yellow-haired man of her own years, maybe, but aged by illness, she thought, gaunt and grey about the burning blue of his eyes. He wore a bright headscarf pulled down about his neck and a blanket in a more muted plaid slung as a cloak and pinned with gold like a twisted flame, but his shirt was stained and scrubbed almost to rags. Beggar king of a ballad. His hands were torn and black, with scabs that seeped yet, dirt ground in, as if he had dug his way out of a grave, why such an image in her mind? He carried death like a shadow, a second skin, and he watched her utterly without expression, like a hunting cat. Ghu's lost friend, whom she had thought surely dead even while Ghu was searching. Ghu's assassin, she thought now, remembering what he was and why the pair of them had been in the city—this was the killer of the Voice of the Lady, the catalyst of all the catastrophe and rebirth of Marakand.

"No horse?" Ghu was asking.

She blinked again, broke away from the tribesman's unwavering stare. "Camel. The army took it in Dernang." Inane.

And she had learnt on the road to alter her speech, the words her mother had used, especially the first person that had made Wolan and Koulang laugh at her, saying she had learnt her Nabbani from old puppet plays of the emperors in the Five Cities . . . and she forgot again, and used the "I" that none but the imperial family might claim. Ghu didn't appear to have noticed, but he had not, in Marakand, either.

"Better come up, then." He offered a hand.

"Wait." She dodged away, leaping and sliding down the bank to retrieve her belongings, hastily scooping the pebbles into her pocket, rolled the painted skin and bundled it into her pack, bow-case, quiver— slung the belt of her sabre over her shoulder. Low voices above, both of them speaking Praitannec. The tribesman, at odds with his chill study of her, sounded amused about something. Ghu laughed softly and answered in the same tone.

"Ivah," Ghu said, introducing her to the Praitannecman as she climbed back to the road. "A scribe and wizard of Marakand?"

"Of the Great Grass, I think," said the other, in good Imperial Nabbani, the accent of a scholar of the Five Cities, bizarrely clashing with his appearance, and he gave her a nod.

"This is Ahjvar."

A name belonging to the eastern deserts, not to Praitan, but she returned the nod.

"And Snow, and Evening Cloud."

"Gorthuerniaul," Ahjvar said, but whether that was formal greeting, or what, she didn't know. It made Ghu laugh again. Ghu had seemed to be introducing the horses, which didn't surprise her somehow, that he would, and the white stallion had lowered his head to sniff her at his name.

"And Jui and Jiot have gone off hunting, I think."

"Dogs," Ahjvar explained.

Ghu offered his hand again and this time she took it, a foot on his foot, to swing up behind him. The white horse flicked his ears and strode off without further remark on the extra weight, the bay matching him stride for stride like a wagon team. They did not resume their flying race.

Ivah felt oddly shy, this close to him. Ask a man you had abandoned to die at the hands of Red Masks in the street if he was actually your god . . . ? He wore no coat and his shirt was torn, and though she was careful not to touch him, her hands resting on her thighs, she still felt the heat of his body, the barest space between them. He smelt of camels and horses and earth and smoke . . . camel was the sheepskin coat beneath her, insecure pillion. She did not know what she felt. Not attraction. It was almost fear.

"Castle or town?" Ahjvar asked.

"Castle, I think."

"Assuming she's left it standing."

She. "Ghu—" Ivah said. "Ghu, there's a devil in Dernang. She's saying she serves the—the heir of the gods. She's killed the imperial general and his lieutenant, a week ago, and taken control of the town. She claims she speaks for the lord of Choa and all his folk are as obedient as if she does, but—is it true? You do know what she is?"

"*We* killed the general," Ahjvar observed. "Or I did, when some fool took him on with a knife."

"Hah. What was I supposed to do, since you weren't handy to hide behind?"

"There's a *devil*," she repeated. "One of the seven. Yeh-Lin Dotemon."

"We know that." The assassin's tone was mild. "How do you?"

There was challenge under the soft words. Skin prickled. She looked to see him watching her, unblinking. Mad, she thought. But no. Not that. Not quite. But deeply, searingly scarred—trailing tendrils of other sight still wrapped her. Something broken and reforged and all the veiling skins that folk grew over their raw bones of the soul to deal gently with the daily world pared away. Which might be to say mad, after all.

"Dotemon is my captain, for the time being," Ghu said, as it were an everyday thing to speak so. "I do trust her."

She pulled her eyes from the assassin. "You're my god," she said, to Ghu's back. She could not have said it to his face. Wondering. Certain. "You're my god, and you were running from the street-guard in Marakand—but I dreamed of you, in the desert."

"Great Gods, another one," Ahjvar said, and followed it with something incomprehensible, which made Ghu snort with sudden laughter.

"No," he said. "I think not." He turned his head and she glimpsed a flashing grin at the assassin.

Half a guess as to what that was about. She could imagine he drew women, yes, now that he wasn't hiding himself. Her face heated, but the grin was catching, and the laughter. "No," she said, and managed almost to sound indignant. "*Not* that sort of dream." It was Ahjvar chuckled then.

Ivah made an effort to speak soberly, though she felt almost drunk, still walking the edge of vision. "Yeh-Lin Dotemon. Your captain."

"She says she's mine," Ghu observed.

"*Says.*"

"How did you know her?" Ahjvar persisted, as if the brief flurry of—of not-flirtation had not been. But he looked less burningly intense now, less like a predator about to strike.

"I—" she picked careful words, not to lie, and again forgot care in others. "I've met devils, before." Ghu cocked his head and considered that, and again did not remark on her royal form of the pronoun.

"So have you," she said in haste, to distract him. Man. God. He might know all her secrets. But he would not take them; he would wait till they were given.

"Have I?" Ghu asked. "You mean the storyteller in Marakand, the Northron skald. You knew her."

"Ulfhild. Vartu Kingsbane, they called her in the north."

"Ah."

"There was more than one of them there?" demanded Ahjvar.

"I did tell you," Ghu said. "One of the bad nights, when I talked halfway to dawn because you wouldn't sleep and kept dreaming awake, you said."

"I don't remember."

"She was telling stories. I told you the story she told. I didn't know what she was, then, in Marakand. Not for certain. Not till later." Ghu considered. "She knew me. She saw me. I didn't see myself."

The assassin said nothing to that but went suddenly alert like a hound scenting prey and put his horse a little ahead. She saw then what he had—a dark movement that was not the sway of roadside willows but distant riders. The road had descended and water lapped the verge of it here as if they followed a causeway, the flooded fields a wind-riffled lake. No way to avoid a meeting. Banners unfurled, a pale blue without device.

More movement, another and larger company away east and south, just breaking free of the dark scribble of the taller trees that marked the true bank of the river. They flowed up what might be some flooded lane, a dark blot against pewter, stretching out and still coming. Ahjvar unslung a crossbow, freed a foot to span it and slot an arrow in without dismounting. His attention was on the far, not the nearer, company.

She considered her own bow, wrapped and strapped to her bundle, but began pulling off lengths of yarn and leather cords she had slung around her neck instead, knotting them into loops, doubling and redoubling those loosely about her wrists.

"Yeh-Lin," Ghu said, with a nod at the riders on the road. "The others, I don't know." He urged the white to a canter. Ivah caught at his hips at last at the sudden change of pace and they overtook Ahjvar's bay, the pair stretching into a run together as they had raced, close enough to touch.

The small party of riders waiting on the road opened out to admit them as they slowed, the devil's piebald stallion flinging up its head to trumpet, half challenge, half greeting.

Ghu shushed it like a father might a froward child.

"Yours?" Ahjvar demanded.

"Dead king." The grey-haired woman half-bowed in the saddle. "I find I am glad to see you with us yet."

He gave her a long and—definitely challenging—look. The corners of her mouth turned up. "Guess," she said, as if she replied to some unspoken question, and Ivah wondered. The Blackdog had spoken once into her mind, and she knew he and the bear-demon Mikki did so, too, but for all the skin-prickling unease Ahjvar gave her, he was human, she would swear to that.

"That's an answer, Dreamshaper. Don't you *dare* try that again."

Ghu gave him a sharp look. "Ahj." The nearest rider, that weather-beaten lord of middle years she had stood next to as witness when the devil fought Hani Gahur, she now knew for the high lord's son and castellan Daro Yuro. He was frowning thoughtfully. Ghu said something in Praitannec, which could equally well have been a warning not to quarrel with a devil, or not to do it in a language they all could understand. Ahjvar only shrugged, but the flare of anger—Ivah felt it almost as a fire—died. He gestured with the crossbow to where the other company neared the road and repeated himself. "Are those yours?"

"Nabban's, you mean? I have no idea. They ferried themselves over in barges they dragged across the floods beyond with buffalo. Before I realized you were on the road and going to be cut off by them, I had thought to let them reach Dernang, rather than sending the army out to drown in ditches intercepting. Half of the conscripts lack even sandals— they are appalling ill-equipped. Shall we try to avoid them by going west of the town, Nabban, if you can find us a route through the floods, or do we carry on regardless?"

The castle was a distant mound of white on the horizon, Dernang a dirty smudge like its shadow. The riders from the river would be on the highway ahead of them before they could reach it.

"Go on," Ghu said.

"Holy one," the castellan protested.

Even the devil frowned. "Is that wise, Nabban?"

"I don't know." Ghu urged the white horse on, leaving the company—half a hundred riders—to turn through itself and follow. The young lady with the largest of the silken banners spurred after them, taking station to their right, a pace back. Ahjvar had put himself ahead again, vanguard of one which, if he was going to carry a loaded crossbow like that, Ivah rather preferred. No point to running; they could not get ahead of the others. She wanted a horse and probably her bow, and to be out free of the mass to circle. . . .

"And you've acquired another pretty shaman?" the devil asked.

"A friend from Marakand," Ghu said.

"Ivah," she said, best court Nabbani. She bowed.

The devil tilted her head. "You—saw me. When I fought in the circle. I saw that you saw me, and knew me, and I meant to find you, afterwards, to learn what you were." Waggled fingers. "But it's been so hectic, lately. Wizard are you? More a shaman, to see so deeply. As I said."

The enemy company—if they were that—was flowing up onto the road ahead now and spreading to either side. One horse plunged into an unseen ditch, floundered out riderless, a woman following moments later, struggling. The gaps in their ranks marked the ditches, Ivah guessed. Folly to charge through those. Ghu had neither sword nor spear and she was going to hamper him regardless, perched on a coat behind his saddle, but there were no spare horses.

"Let me down," she said.

"Safer up."

She might be, unless she could put a ditch between herself and whatever melee ensued, but he was hardly safe with a stirrupless rider clinging behind to unbalance him. He gave her no chance to dismount, and Yeh-Lin and Daro Yuro were too close; she would be under their hooves.

The devil's—Ghu's—riders wore no badge as the imperial soldiers had done in Dernang, but the banners and the ribbons of their helmets were sky-blue and the devil was all in black with blue ribbons and lacing. The company ahead wore no token of any allegiance at all, but they obviously misliked what they read, or were heartened by counting the numbers, because what had looked at first as though it might be a wary but peaceable confrontation shifted rapidly as the three conferring riders in the centre separated and one, lowering the mask of her ornate helmet, drew her sword and gestured a half of each wing up on to the road after her, to come on at a gallop.

Cut out the leader and those about him under the blue banner, riding so rashly ahead, then talk afterwards with the leaders captive. . . . One of the charging enemy swung a shouldered spear upright, unfurling a banner not of the imperial peony and gold but deep yellow above and brown below, and the characters in the roundel, white on black, reading *Dwei Dan* and *The gods of Nabban*. Her uncle renounced the imperial clan. Interesting.

"Let them come," Ghu told the devil, voice calm, and reined in, bringing the whole company to a halt. He called ahead to Ahjvar in Praitannec and the assassin set the bay into a smooth canter. He did release the bolt, but it tore through the fluttering roundel. Not an accident, that. Ivah shook yarn down her wrist and began weaving a cat's-cradle, caught a loose hair from Ghu's shoulder into it, coarse and slightly curling. Felt the devil's eyes on her.

Caught a loop in her teeth, twisted and inverted, felt the pattern take, the heat build and she shook burning yarn from her fingers, gone to ash in a moment, and the torn banner of Prince Dan followed it.

"Not," said the devil, "very original. Or—oh, nicely done."

It was not the fire, but the small knot of chaos it spread, which it need not have done.

The rider with the spear had flung it from himself with a cry as the torn and now-burning cloth fell around him, and the others in the centre had scattered away. Ahjvar, whatever he had meant to do, saw that opening and yelled something incomprehensible, weaving through them; his smoky bay turned like a good Grasslander, low on its haunches as he struck down the standard-bearer and tumbled him from his horse— open space about him and the fallen man would not be trampled, had he considered even that? Clashing swords, the bay rearing, striking out, the other horse answering, but he had disarmed the lady, disarmed and thrown down a third man, and wheeled away, flying back with the standard-bearer's dun trailing him.

And none, she thought, dead. Challenge and declaration, and would they read it?

"A horse for the Grasslander," he called, wheeling before them again to keep himself between Ghu and the enemy, and the dun came to Ghu's outstretched hand. Ivah was over on it in a matter of a heartbeat, and weaving a new pattern. The wind rose and the blue banners snapped and shimmered, the water running in patterns of dark and silver. Fingers of sunlight through the clouds, burning on the water, on sword's edge, on the white horse and the assassin's hair. Not her doing, that heart-stopping moment when the world hung in light and shadow. She made protections around them. The devil, ridden up alongside her, looked entirely innocent.

"Lady Ti-So'aro," Lord Yuro said suddenly, "the holy one has no herald."

The woman who carried the standard gave a nod and passed her banner to another rider, who came to take her place at the white stallion's heel. She pushed up her helmet's mask as she rode forward till she was a horse's length ahead of Ahjvar, who had loaded his crossbow again. He turned aside to the edge of the road to be clear of her.

"Who comes armed against the holy one, the heir of the gods of Nabban?" Ti-So'aro cried with high formality.

They came on more warily, at a walk, now. No archers among them, no crossbows, not in the party that had charged ahead. A man from behind rode up, lean, grey, his visor raised—recognizing the restraint of Ghu's company for what it was, Ivah thought—and they reformed around him.

"This is Lord Dwei Ontari," called the woman who had led the charge.

"Commander of the army of Alwu, cousin and servant of Prince Dan, the upholder of the gods and defender of the folk. By what right do you dare claim title of holy one for your—lord?" A sneer in her voice. Ghu was too obviously the centre they formed on, and too obviously no lord.

"Is Prince Dan with you?" Ghu asked, riding forward before the new-named herald could respond. Ahjvar didn't shift his position but lowered the bow he had held angled at the sky to cover the lord of the opposing company.

"The prince is with his army," the supercilious woman said. "We acknowledge no—" The commander, Dwei Ontari, cut her off with a sharp gesture of his hand.

"Enough, Baya. My niece is precipitate. Word came over the three rivers that Lord Daro Korat had retaken Dernang. We've come to meet with him, to discuss matters of importance to us both. But you ride armed on Dernang under an unknown banner."

Ghu eyed the sheet of blue silk as if he, too, found it mildly puzzling.

"It was your people who rode against us, Lord Ontari," the herald said, "and that none are dead, you have the mercy of the—the servant of the holy one to thank."

"Ride with me to Dernang," Ghu said, abruptly. "How long has it been since you lost your prince, Dwei Ontari?" He simply started forward into them, leaving Dan's folk to stop him or seize him or get out of his way. The lord of the army of Alwu was the first to rein his horse aside and, after only a moment's hesitation, turn to fall in with Ghu—Ahjvar, unsummoned, flanking him. Though he did unload his crossbow. With the herald hastening to weave herself through them and to the fore again, and the niece of Lord Ontari matching pace with her, defiantly, they were rapidly and in some disorder intermingled. Ivah found herself riding behind Ghu, between the devil and Lord Yuro, cut off from the rest of Ghu's folk by five of the enemy abreast behind her. The man whose horse she bestrode was taken up by one of his fellows. No one made any attempt to dispute her claim to it.

"The prince is over the river," Lord Ontari said stiffly. "Over all three roots of the Wild Sister, deep in Alwu."

"No," Ghu said. "And you don't know where he is. What happened?"

"By what right do you claim to speak for the gods?" the Dwei lord said, almost plaintively. "The prophets say . . ." He shrugged, looked around.

Ivah patted her horse's neck and affected not to be craning forward to listen. Yeh-Lin winked at her.

Lord Ontari lowered his voice. "The prophets say the gods are dying."

"The Father is dying. The Mother is dead. All that she was, I am." Ghu spoke so matter-of-factly. "They've left you to me." One might almost hear that as apology. "Prince Dan? I wanted to send to him. How long has he been lost?"

Lord Ontari sighed. "Since the late winter. He rode to rescue his ally, Lord Daro Sia, when General Zhung Musan forced him back on Dernang. We couldn't save Choa and its loss cut the provinces that had declared for Dan in half, severing Shihpan from Alwu. Lord Sia was no strategist, but as a leader in the field they would follow him, love him. Lords, peasants, slaves . . . I was still in the south, about my prince's business there, or I would have dissuaded him from taking such a risk on himself. He might have listened to me. Perhaps. But Lord Sia was his friend, and I think Prince Dan was a little under the spell of his charm himself."

Ahjvar said something Praitannec, a low grumble with Daro Sia's name in it. Yeh-Lin snorted. Ghu ignored them both.

"The prince isn't dead, I think," he said, but he did not sound certain. "Ivah?" A glance over his shoulder.

"I can divine for him. Holy one." That felt strange. She would rather just use his name, but no one else did, save the assassin.

"*I* could—" the devil said, and shrugged. Smiled at Ivah. "I suppose you make the more respectable wizard. I am merely his captain, he tells me."

"Our wizards have divined for him," Lord Ontari said, with a doubtful look at Ivah. "They say the prince is neither dead nor taken. But find him, no, even Lord Mulgo Miar, who was appointed Pine Lord by Buri-Nai but fled to us, cannot find him . . . We think him still in Choa."

"You're another from the west?" the castellan demanded of Ivah, interrupting her eavesdropping. "You knew Ghu there?"

Someone who did call him by his name. "We met last summer in Marakand," she said, and the man nodded, lowering his voice. "You know that one, the lady wizard?" Not, she thought, a lord's manner of speaking.

"Not . . . no."

"The answer," Yeh-Lin said, leaning over, "to what you really want to ask, Castellan Yuro, is *yes*. As I feel our Grasslander friend has already understood, though I would like to know how. Now be good and don't mention it to all the others who are so much happier with an old lady making feeble jokes about her ill-omened name." A dismissive wave of her elegant hand at Ivah. "You saw the duel. Ask Daro Yuro here to tell you about how I drove that fool young man to take my challenge, although perhaps he ought not to tell the—tell the god's champion, who may feel I have perverted the rite of his people and the role of the *rihswera*, which is his, in what use I made of the Praitannec judgement circle. Call me Lady Nang Lin. Or Captain Lin. Such a usefully vague title, at present—the holy one's captain-general, before whom even baffled high lords and their commanders give way. Everyone will be happier with Nang Lin, except the honourable castellan there, who is rather sharper than those who would like to think themselves his betters. But we all here find we serve Nabban, according to our abilities. We all here find he gathers our hearts in." She continued to watch Ivah with more interest than she ought to have deserved. "Strange, is it not, for the godless to find they have a god?"

Ivah gave her a vague smile and turned her attention to watching Ghu's back, but she could not catch their voices now, he and the prince's lord riding closer, talking more earnestly, quietly.

She did not feel forgotten, though. Gathered in, rather. Yeh-Lin's word was apt. Swept into her place. She rolled her shoulders, stretched her neck, stiff after long sitting in the damp under the bridge. Divine for the missing prince, whom the Pine Lord of wizards had failed to find? Rash offer? But Ghu had asked her, not Yeh-Lin, in seeming confidence that she could.

Ivah combed fingers through her own hair, came away with two fine threads of black. Began not a cat's-cradle but a simple four-strand braid, amber yarn and brown, black and, did she have blue? She did. Darker than the colour of Ghu's banners, but near enough. She bound the two hairs of her head into it as she worked. The braid formed only the first part of what came to her mind, a weaving and the coins, a pattern to be worked in full later. Blood might be needed, in the Northron way, but she would see what the hair gave her first. Find a prince, no. Find her uncle—a thread that the rebels' Pine Lord did not possess to follow—perhaps.

By the time they neared the camp, ditched and palisaded, that occupied the grounds of the annual horsefair to the north of Dernang's wall, Ghu had Dwei Ontari addressing him as "holy one" and planning conference with Captain Lin, someone called Lord Raku, and the Kho'anzi on the organization of the imperial army, whose command Yeh-Lin had usurped, and the reassertion of Daro rule over the province, all in the name of the heir of the gods.

"And the folk?" Ghu asked.

"The folk?" Lord Ontari was puzzled.

The castellan spoke a quiet word to Ti-So'aro and they took a dozen riders on ahead, towards the rough wooden tower that overlooked the gate to the camp. Blue banners hung there, too. Ghu watched them go, his face unreadable. Met Ahjvar's eyes a moment, very far away. Turned back to Ontari.

"Lord Sia's folk. The runaways. The slaves, the serfs, the conscripts. The folk Prince Dan promised their freedom. The folk of all the land. The land is the folk as well as the rock and the waters, and they are starving in the wilds, driven from their homes. Preying on one another. How do they live, when they are free?"

First thought said, here on the edge of war, did it matter? A problem for later. But Sia had cried freedom and left the folk who answered abandoned. Had Dan done any better? Hope took you only so far. They needed more than hope of their god.

"It's a difficult question," Ontari said. "The prince's council is still debating how best it might be done."

"I don't know these things," Ghu said, very quiet. "I'm not come to be your emperor and make your laws. But there will be justice and freedom in this land, and the folk of this land must make it, the powerful and the powerless together, or there will be—" He hesitated.

"What, my lord?"

"Fire," he said. "You can't treat the folk of the land as cattle forever. Someday they will remember they are human, and that they stand equal with their lords before the gods and the Old Great Gods. And if there is no justice in the land now, there will not be, then. Only fire, and blood, and death, and a new tyranny turning on the old. It grows already. Folk driven from the villages, folk run from their lords, folk with nothing left to lose, losing their humanity. Find them. Bring them in to us as free folk in more than name. Give them some beginning of what must be. Sia's promises were empty. You don't say Dan's have been any better. Ours must be."

"How?" Ontari asked, bewildered, as if he were being asked to solve the problems of the empire single-handed. Perhaps he was.

"*I* don't know. I only know horses." Ghu shrugged. "Some right in the land. Some recompense beyond food and shelter for their labour. The right to leave their masters. There's where you start. And with the ending of the buying and selling of people."

"Give serfs and slaves rights to the land they work and be sure there will be landlords and masters who will see it mortgaged and sold for seed, and they will be serfs again in a year," said Yeh-Lin behind, which was what Ahjvar was thinking. The land was the lords' and the villages' and the kings' under the gods at home . . .

"The shrines," he said aloud. "The land is the god's and not for selling, held of him, not owned. Can the priests deal justly, as stewards of their god?"

"They're human," Ghu said.

"Many are dead," Ontari said. "Killed in their shrines for speaking against the empress's cult. Or they've run to hide, or they've abandoned the gods to serve the empress."

"It's a place to start, though," Ghu said. "Ahjvar is right. And the

slaves must be free. There is land enough. The towns are great enough
for those with other trades. They will have their places; they must. I say
again, they must go or stay with those who've been their masters as they
will, and with fair return for their service."

"Prince Dan said so, but to do it—"

"Do it. There is wealth enough in this land."

"Have you any idea . . . ? In the imperial treasury, maybe."

"Then we will take the imperial treasury," Ghu said. "Because I will
have no slaves in my land, Ontari. And no one needs to wear six layers
of silk."

"My lord." Another fallen at Ghu's feet? Those who truly were
seeking their god knew him, but—no. This one seemed more to simply
feel himself outnumbered, since he found the heir of the gods had the
support of his hoped-for ally Daro Korat. They would all bear watching.
Ahjvar did not like to have anyone armed and riding between them.

The gates of the camp stood open, their herald riding on towards
the town. Yeh-Lin stirred herself, ordering more of her own riders ahead,
engulfing them. A word from Ontari to his niece put Prince Dan's folk
to the rear, which made Ahjvar's skin crawl, but he supposed those bee-
coloured banners ought to follow, not lead. He did not trust, was all.

"Lord Ontari, pardon me . . ." Yeh-Lin turned a bright smile on the
Dwei nobleman. "But before we come to the castle I need to report to
the holy one all I've set in place since I took the town. If you would be
so good . . .?"

Ontari made a courteous brief bow to Ghu and reined back to join
the Grasslander wizard. Ahjvar closed Niaul in before Yeh-Lin could get
between them, though perhaps she had not meant to try; she took position on Ghu's other side.

"I duelled and killed Zhung Musan's lieutenant with the town and
all Choa as the stakes," she said in Praitannec, without preamble. "It
seemed most efficient. It was a fair fight, Nabban, my word on it. Daro
Korat is on his feet and holding his lordship again, and the town in some
order after the riots—"

"What riots?" Ahjvar asked.

She shrugged. "These things will happen. It's quiet now. Officers I don't think we can trust have been imprisoned—and I still do not know what those tattoos mean, but the few who bear them are among those I will not trust, save your wizard Nang Kangju who so mutilated himself to be rid of it. Most of the officers seem willing enough to follow their lords, though, and we hold, for now, the service of enough of their lords . . . they come to Daro Korat, most of them, not to rumour of the holy one, but that will do. The soldiers and townsfolk care little so long as someone feeds them. . . ."

Ahjvar let her talk, drifting.

". . . I've formed a company of foresters and sent them to the western uplands with most of the draught-animals of the army. Zhung Musan at least saw those were fed, no matter how he neglected his men. And another company of those who know the rivers. They're working at that village—what do you call it? The one you can see from the castle. They were up to their waists in water half the time but none have drowned yet, and now that the flood is dropping all is going better, save moving the logs. I would dig a canal so far as the highway, at least, were I lord of the province. A short stretch; it could be done in a season."

"Not this season," Ghu remarked.

"No."

"And why?"

"Why?" she echoed.

"Why build rafts?"

What rafts? He had not drifted so far away that he lost half the conversation, had he? Not this time. Their thoughts chased one another on some track he did not see.

"What rafts?" Ahjvar asked aloud.

"Can we live off this land that is already so warred over? We must move, we must keep moving, not sit here waiting for our enemies to come to us. We go over the river or down it, do we not, Nabban?"

"Maybe."

"On rafts?" Ahjvar asked. "With horses?"

"No. But we can move no faster than our provisions, yet when we do move, when we know where to move, we must go with speed. We may need your style of warfare after all, dead king, or as close as we can come with our barefoot infantry. Look at these soldiers. Would you take them into the field?"

That was addressed to him.

They were come to the camp of Zhung Musan's army in the horse-fair, inside a palisade still new and yellow, pales stripped of bark. The soldiers were a poor lot, thin and bandy-legged, for the most part, as if they'd grown up half starving.

"What? No. I wouldn't set them to herd sheep."

"I have sent a party over the border into Denanbak, to see if we can trade some of the castle's store of silks for sheep and seed, in fact. Rather more valuable pound for pound than cloth to us, at present. There will be no trade with the caravans this year." She considered. "I doubt they will return in time, and those caravans that have fled have lost most of their goods to Zhung Musan's expropriations already. They will not be back this year, maybe not next. We must gather what we can and hope that we can supply camps in the south from Shihpan and Alwu. Dwei Ontari is the man to deal with for that. But the town and the villages must also eat and, just as urgently, have flocks in the pastures again. Zhung Musan seems to have wanted to leave Choa a wasteland, inca-pable of rising again once he and the greater imperial army spread out into Alwu and Shihpan. I wonder what he did with the flocks and herds of Choa? He doesn't seem to have fed his own folk on them. Driven south, I suppose, though they'll be butchered and salted and fed to the lords and the empress's officers by now; nothing you can go raiding to bring home again, dead king. The central provinces and the south are all croplands, not pasture. I imagine meat will buy a great deal of love for the empress, for a time."

"You think she'll come north?" he asked.

"Choa was clearly only the start of a greater campaign to retake the northwest. More would have come north with the summer. I think they will not, now. *I* would not. The southern tribes are causing trouble, for which we should be thankful. Regardless of what is happening around the Golden City, we must move what force we can down to the southern border with Shihpan and to the ferry above the Dragon's Gorge. We don't know if the empress may move against us out of Numiya or up from Vanai or what high lords may decide to act on their own against us, to seize what lands they can; we don't know how firm Dan's hold on Shihpan actually is, since his folk have apparently misplaced him."

Ghu was looking dark and abstracted. Yeh-Lin fell silent, watching him. Frowned. "Is it well done, Nabban? I see nothing for certain, but—"

"Yes," he said, focussing on her again. Gave her a nod. "Sheep. Good." And seed.

They needed to put some flesh on these men. They could do with cloth, too. Not silks, though. Ragged, dirty uniforms. The little armour, on those who held the gate—standing stiff and, yes, proud—was no more than lacquered leather breast and back and a helmet. Square shields were marked variously with the Zhung or Daro or Min-Jan characters, meaningless now. Such wealth pouring into Nabban, the great lake that fed and received the rivers of the caravan roads, and they could equip their soldiers no better? There was gold somewhere, and silk such as the castle's slaves spun and wove, and jewels and rare things. Most of these—boys, really—were armed with spear and knife, no more. Barefoot, some. Yeh-Lin had not been exaggerating in that. They were not only on formal display at the wooden gate in the palisade. They lined the broad road through the camp, drawn up in ranks—warned by Ti-So'aro. They were still assembling at the far side before the town wall. Officers and banner-lords and -ladies. Men and women who had served Zhung Musan. Spells drifting, like ash, settling around him, tickling on the skin, subtle and strong.

"Protections against arrows," Yeh-Lin said, looking over at him. "Let her. Leave them." The Grasslander.

"Don't trust your prize, old woman?"

"I could hardly swear each one to Nabban in person. They made their oaths generally."

"It's all right," Ghu said. "Trust Ivah, Ahjvar. She's my friend. She helped me in Marakand. It's all right."

Trust the Grasslander, maybe. Trust these conscripted men and their masters? Not likely. Even Ghu watched them warily, still and deep, though the wariness was not fear. Sizing up a burden, Ahjvar thought. They were still themselves, or went so, rank on rank. Silenced the whispering, the muttering. An officer fell to her knees. Some young conscript right before them was scrubbing at his eyes with a grubby fist, hardly the only one in tears. What did they see?

A cloudy day and a sudden gust of wind driving a curtain of drizzle over them, and streaks of sun following.

Ghu simply—watched them. Each and every one, and saw them. Each and every one. Bowed gravely from the saddle. Then he rode on. Yeh-Lin did not find words again until they were riding through the town gate, and the road was barred—or at least filled, with lords and officers come to meet them.

"Any chance of alliance with the southern tribes?" Ahjvar asked. "I suppose there's no way of negotiating with them. All Nabban between us. What would we have to offer, anyway?"

"Barbarians," Yeh-Lin said. "Buy them for a season, they'll come back wanting more the next year."

The corner of Ghu's mouth lifted. "My mother," he observed, "would have said the reverse, Dotemon. They've ceded and ceded their lowlands, and the border keeps creeping south." Eyed her. "All Nabban between, and only the winds to bridge it? Maybe we should send an ambassador to offer them what they want, Ahj. Darru and Lathi and the old border kept."

"That's—!" Definitely a yelp from Yeh-Lin. "Which old border?"

"The true one. The one the land knows. The watershed of the Little Sister."

"Asagama and half Upper and Lower Lat on top of Dar-Lathi? They have been Nabbani since before my time, and Taiji—"

"Little of Taiji was ever Lathan. But the rest, yes."

"No one will let you give away—"

"We will run our old courses again, hold our old names and new names . . ." Ghu's voice, very soft, trailed off. Ahjvar had thought he was teasing Yeh-Lin. No. "You'll go for me, Dotemon. Not yet. Not while we have Buri-Nai and her lie of the Old Great Gods yet to deal with. But when I send you to the queens, you'll go and speak as I have said." He added, as if it somehow followed, "They never told me what my mother's name was. I wonder if anyone ever knew?"

"Nabban." She bowed low. "As you will."

In the town they cheered, the people, pinch-faced, crowding what was probably a market square. Cheered as though a conqueror rode in. Ghu paled, his mouth tight.

"They need to see you, Nabban," Yeh-Lin said, and added, with a return of her usual manner, "Be glad I have cleared the gallows away and buried all the exposed dead."

Ghu turned Snow abruptly and Ahjvar moved to guard him, not certain what he'd seen. Nothing of threat. Stone wall, with a burnt ruin of scaffolding about it and burnt beams and posts beyond. Children had climbed the wall, ruined or unfinished, and stared down. Ghu smiled up at them, and startled, shy, they stared, and then smiled back. He turned again, across the square and to the south, weaving through the crowd that shifted and flowed to be out of his way, not afraid, but cautious, and all the cavalcade that had preceded and followed them waited, watching.

"They've destroyed the Father's shrine," he said, when Ahjvar came up beside him.

It was only the entry porch to another earth-walled courtyard house like all the rest of the town, but the gates were broken down, and beyond, the pillars of the gallery were scorched, its posts and railings charred, one side of the gallery consumed and a ruin of tile and blackened timbers edging a square of mud and weeds and broken stone, a pine tree hacked down and left lying.

"The priestess is dead," he said.

"Aoda," Ivah said behind them. "She—spoke a prophecy and jumped from the wall of the empress's temple. They hanged her corpse. They burnt her library, but I have a book. . . ."

"Aoda, yes. I remember her. She fed the beggars, always. Every day." Ghu took a breath, wheeled Snow. Light in his eyes again. "I have your book, Ivah. But I lost your sword." He added, when she said nothing, "Sorry."

Half-wit boy. Ahjvar didn't say it. Ghu gave him half a grin for it anyway, and called, "Captain Lin, Castellan. Who governs the town?"

It was Yuro who answered. "We've set Lord Zhung Huong, Lady Ti-So'aro's brother, over the guild-masters and the magistrates, for now. There's been much ruined. But he's with the Kho'anzi waiting for you. Holy one."

"Who's seeing people fed?"

Uncertainty.

"Houses burnt and robbed, and storehouses burnt and robbed, and landless lawless lost folk everywhere? Are there even granaries unlooted?"

"Only the castle."

"Better we feed the people here now, and the soldiers too, than hoard it longer. Call these masters of the town together, and tell them both these shrines, the true one and the false, must be made places where the folk who have nothing can come, to share out what there is. They must eat, Yuro, and the soldiers too, or how are any of us going to stand?"

The dogs came trotting after them, panting, muddy, but looking well content with something, as they rode over the bridge.

The old lord had come to meet them, afoot, with his granddaughter grave at his side, her face black with healing scabs, her cropped hair uncovered, unashamed.

They saw that, the folk who crowded at the town end of the bridge to watch through the open gates, saw the high lord of all Choa creak down to his knees and Ghu, a ragged beggar with the sun still catching him, leap down and offer a hand up, and speak, and turn to say something to the stable-hand who came to take Snow's reins, too.

Yeh-Lin knew the play of a court. All a game, a display, here, before the soldiers, and the town, and now the castle, because Ghu had not let her make a show of him in the aftermath of the castle's fall. And yet she was right: the folk must see their god and know their god had come among them, and that their lord acknowledged and honoured him. . . . With a word and a pat, Ahjvar left Gorthuerniaul to a shy-smiling woman and strode after Ghu and Daro Korat.

No surprise to find the Grasslander moving to the other side, as if she belonged there. *Gewdeyn* of the god, maybe. What would her folk call it? *Noekar?* A lord's vassal. She offered no oath; Ahjvar found he accepted her there as Ghu did. Wondered at it.

The dogs are not what they were. . . .

Neither was he.

Long meetings, after greetings, and introductions, and oaths given again unasked. Food, plain and simple fare; perhaps the Kho'anzi had after all begun to take thought for provisioning town and army through a long, hungry spring. The day spun away. Ahjvar was *rihswera* of the god and stood at his back, and kept silent, mostly, since words grew too heavy. It had been too long since he was a king's councillor, and the law he had made a study of in the Five Cities was not the law of this empire. Yeh-Lin was better fit to understand what they must deal with. Ghu said little, but listened, and patiently drew them back to his points when they strayed too far. The folk, the folk of the land, always first and foremost, and what they would do, they must begin here in Dernang and Choa now, not later, not someday—now, here.

There was no grace given to a land whose folk were chattels.

Lady Daro Willow came to order her grandfather away to his bed, with a smile at her new-declared uncle that suggested conspiracy, and Ghu and Ahjvar were harried out, in the end, from argument—debate—with Lord Ontari about the possibility of bringing barley across the Wild Sister from Alwu on rafts, since boats seemed in short supply, by unexpected small tyrants whom Yeh-Lin declared her pages. The holy one, they said, must bathe and sleep and in the morning ride again to the town, to bless and reconsecrate the shrine of the Father his father. And to be seen again by more of the folk. She did not have the children say that, but she might as well have done.

Ghu seemed very small and weary, following the children down more stairs. Bathhouse, very grand, cedar-panelled, wall-carvings of willows and dragons and naked women with streaming hair, goddesses. The Wild Sister—who was, now, Ghu? That made Ahjvar's head ache. The pools were tiled, blue and green and white, and there would be some stove beyond the wall where the water was heated before it was allowed to flow in; no doubt slaves tended it and had been told they were greatly honoured to heat the holy one's bath and probably believed so. Which also made his head ache. Slaves no longer. The Kho'anzi would declare it tomorrow, and set proclamations through the town and the baileys of the castle, even. No branding of freedom, either. Just—free, and taking on the name of the Daro Clan, which—he was not sure he would want, if he carried that brand on his shoulder. And their service to their lord would continue as folk of the lord's household, and maybe . . . all else would be worked out, later. Ahjvar did not think the family connection of tribe, that brought folk to serve in the king's hall for their keep and gifts and mutual honour, would work in a land of cities and long oppression, no matter what the Kho'anzi himself said about all being the family of the castle, but for now, for tonight . . .

Steaming water. Though he had washed, repeatedly, in the cold spring of the Wild Sister's rising.

"Not," Ghu said, "the slaves' bathhouse." A wry smile. "Have you asked Yeh-Lin about the rancid *rykersyld*?"

"I don't want to."

"No. But I think Ivah speaks a little Northron, if we ever get curious."

Ghu stripped, regardless that one of the pages laying out towels was a girl a bit too old to be stripping in front of, and slid into the water, sinking beneath it.

"Out," Ahjvar told the three of them, and the tallest, the girl, with the littlest half-hiding behind her, bowed, and said, "Yes, my lord, we're to go bathe Jui and Jiot now, but Lady Lin says we have to tell you to wash your hair. And the holy one's, too. And there is a comb. And a razor."

"You've told me," he said levelly. The smallest boy was afraid, though the elder two were old enough to sense they were being used, and they seemed to trust it was not to their harm. Yeh-Lin was cruel to use any of them to carry her jokes, regardless. "Now go tell her you've said so."

He waited for their retreat and wedged the door with a knife, since there seemed no other way to hold it against casual entry—it was mostly

Yeh-Lin he expected to stroll in, truth be told. But he laid his sword unsheathed on the pool's edge before he ever took of his boots. Ghu had resurfaced and watched him undress, eyes solemn.

"*Are* you going to wash my hair?"

There was soap, good Five Cities soap smelling strongly of lavender, left pointedly by the pages. Ahjvar threw it at him.

Better to think of Yeh-Lin as playing auntie again than as quietly appointing herself overseer and master of the god, as though he were some favoured pet being groomed to perform well and prettily for guests. The children had left clean clothing for them, and all the outer garments, trousers and smock-like shirt and quilted knee-length coat, low boots, were black. The style of north Nabban, not the light gowns of the south. Wool and cotton, not lordly silk. She risked no arguments from Ghu on that point. Ahjvar might have objected, but even he had to admit their old rags were better burnt. These were not redyed cast-offs but hasty work by some seamstresses, he suspected. Everything fit his height and length of limb. The work of slaves, again. Praitannec blanket and headscarf he kept, and found she had been into their belongings. Ghu turned from shaking out a coat to hold up the leopard-headed bracelets that had tumbled from it.

Ahjvar, strapping on knives, shook his head.

"Wear them," Ghu said, and brought the gold to him. "Yes."

So he did not argue, but let Ghu put the royal bracelets of the Duina Catairna on him, turn him and tie back his hair.

"Respectable?" he did ask.

"No." A slow curl of smile. "But something."

The last of the sunset had faded from the west and fog was crawling over the castle's curtain wall, rising from the flooded lands that had made them an island; rising, too, from the ornamental pond, flowing up the narrow alleys between the walled gardens and courtyards. No pages waited like herd-dogs to chivvy them, only Jui and Jiot, fluffy and chastened and smelling of rosemary against fleas, not that they had had any. No lurking devil. The castle appeared to sleep. The moon rode, a waxing crescent, high overhead, a narrow boat hidden and revealed in a churning sea of black cloud. The wind gusted uncertainly.

"Is she waiting to corner us again?" Ahjvar asked, and found it easy to stand with his arm around Ghu, there in the dark, taking his leaning weight.

"Probably." A yawn. "Can you sleep, if we go in? Under a roof?"

"No." The old panic edged nearer at the thought, the closeness of people, of lives, breathing. His grip tightened on Ghu, whose head turned against his shoulder in response.

"We neither of us belong within walls anymore," Ghu said, muffled against him. "Not these walls. Come."

They found a walled garden, a small place all moss and stone, dead feathery grass bleached white by winter, new shoots rising from the heart of the clumps, sculpted junipers scenting the air. Art making an echo of the wild.

"I never knew this was here," Ghu said. It was a shrine to the Father, of course. There was an altar of sorts, an unshaped slab of stone, half wrapped in junipers and tall grass.

Again, Ahjvar jammed the gate with a broad knife. Ghu pulled him in under the layered trees with the altar at their backs, out of the drizzle that was beginning again, breathless suddenly, urgent, not yawning now, stripping sword and knives and coat from him and not worried where they fell.

The soap may have been scented with lavender; Ghu's skin and hair smelt of moss and water-splashed stone and crushed ferns, like the springs above Swajui. Ahjvar breathed him in, tasted him, lips, fingertips, gave himself up to the hands and mouth that travelled the shape of him in the dark, teeth, tongue, till they were wound together skin to skin and he was lost in darkness, dissolved in the chill of rain and drowned in the deep moss under him, and the man was a river, and starlit snow, and stone. If he cried out, it wasn't in protest at his dreams. Slept, holding Ghu curled half over him, head on his shoulder, and woke only once clenching his fingers in Ghu's hair, the sparse flesh of his ribs, the bone beneath. Ghu made some faint moan, caught at his hand without waking, fingers coiling to ease the grip. Ahjvar was shivering but silent. *No.* Only dream. No fire, no burning flesh. He forced his breath to slow, turned his face in Ghu's hair.

Warm. Held. Safe.

CHAPTER XXVIII

A sea coast, somewhere. Jagged grey stone slick with bladder-wrack, conifers Yeh-Lin did not recognize tilting over and tumbling down a seamed cliff, clinging with roots like snakes. Towering things, the ones more firmly-rooted, marching inland, bigger around than the house in which she had been born. Tree like a mountain, to hold up the sky. A small shape, bird-tiny, moved among the broken stones where the low cliff crumbled, climbing, but the size was illusion cast by the trees. A human shape, a tall woman all in grey and earthen-brown, her hair a long, pale braid. Hardly to be seen when she stood still. She did move with the surety of a bird over the stones, swift and balanced, never hesitating over a foothold, hardly needing to use a hand to steady herself, even where the tumbled rocks were steepest. She reached the top and stood looking into the trees.

Yeh-Lin knew her. Surely.

Two swords. A Northron sword belted at her hip, gilded hilt, a flash of garnets. Slung on her back, another. Black scabbard. Silver hilt. There was . . . a heaviness to it. Something that drew, not the eye, but the centred heart of her, as if deep in Yeh-Lin's chest a lump of iron were pulled to a lodestone. Where? She had never seen such trees.

The woman turned, met her watching awareness. Knew her presence, as Yeh-Lin knew that pale, harsh-boned Northron face. Smiled, not in welcome. Yeh-Lin would have spoken regardless, called to her, but the waves rolled and curled, foaming white as they flung themselves up the rocks in a sudden gale that whistled through the needles, moved branches like scudding clouds, like rafts against the sky, tore leaves from the heavy green undergrowth. And she was gone. Lost in that wild movement, slipped away into the forest, or flown like a leaf ripped free.

Yeh-Lin reached into the vision after her, but there was nothing to grasp, no trail to follow. The Northron might never have been.

"Vartu!" she shouted anyway, breaking the silence of the night.

No answer. Of course not. Only the children in the outer room stirring, mumbling.

"Go back to sleep," she whispered, and felt them sink away again, into quiet dreams. She put her mirror aside and rose from the pallet that was her bed to cross to the window in this upper apartment of the old north keep. The shutter was lifted, letting the night air in. The scent of the river was strong, the fields to the north pale with moonlight. Bats, owls, foxes out there . . . all the creatures proper to the night. Nothing more.

Yeh-Lin padded back to the bed and lay down, hands folded over the mirror against her heart, not looking into it. Cold. It did not warm to her flesh.

CHAPTER XXIX

Ghu and the assassin who was his shadow drifted about the castle and the town, rarely seen, once the lords had been set to make their own way on the path the gods approved. The holy one was among them often enough that they appeared to feel him a presence in all their counsels. The castle folk took it for granted the heir of their gods might come and go like a bird, a ghost about the town and the White River Dragon, with no regard for walls. Ivah thought they actually lived in the gardens and the loft of one of the stables and simply avoided the folk because they were as shy as thieves. They had the look of wild things, the wary watchfulness, as well as the calm assurance of a wolf in its own land, and they carried the scent of the river and the forest. And horses, and hay, which was why she suspected the stables, and possibly the collusion of Castellan Yuro and his people in their avoidance of Yeh-Lin's civilizing intentions.

It didn't matter if Ghu were some physical avatar or incorporeal god who chose to take so ordinary a man's form. Those who had come to the holy one in a fervour of faith did not waver; others, who followed where the Kho'anzi led or because they did not approve a faith that slew the priests, kept perhaps their doubts, but found nothing to denounce. He was there when he was needed; the folk of the town and the countryside said that. They came to him cautious, shy, carrying troubles too great.

So many lost ones, so many slipping away into despair. He rarely said much, but the folk, and the land itself, seemed to take new heart as the floods receded and the earth greened, walls, roofs rising, the oxen put to the plough, the little fishing boats on the river again.

A week, she had been working on this binding. No divination. She thought she already knew where the lost prince might be found. She had her father's eyes. Her uncle had his sister's. And the set of her mouth in a jaw that was hers made masculine, and . . . she did not know, she only suspected from the nagging familiarity there had been in his face when first she saw it, and what the coins gave her confirmed what she thought. Which made this a matter for the god, not for Dwei Ontari.

Better to leave him lost. There were heirs enough to the Peony Throne without him.

No. She pushed the thought away. Nagging. Scratching at her.

She did not want the damned empire. Why did her thoughts keep whispering that she should? As if her father's ghost lingered and reproved her lack of ambition, her hiding, as she had used to hide her face, eyes downcast, behind the curtain of her hair.

Meet me, she had asked, this morning at the shrine of the Father in the town. She had given the message to Yeh-Lin's pages, with no idea where the god might be. If he could be found, they would find them. Meanwhile she waited, tried to meditate, finding her way, warily, into yet another of her father's practices that she had once rejected.

To clear her mind of the chatter of the world, the stir and hurry of it, was no easy thing here at the gate of the shrine, though it was habitable again, and inhabited. She had claimed the bench in the porch, new and yellow as the unpainted doors, with bark still clinging to the edges of the raw planks. There was even a priest again, a worried little man who had arrived only the day before, saying his dreams had called him to serve in Aoda's place. He had come up through Vanai and Shihpan from Taihu away down the western mountains, a free tailor's youngest who, for all his hard-won education, had never before left the town of his birth. His first act had been to borrow a mule, to go up to the forest of the holy mountain; he intended to bring back a sapling pine to replace the sacred tree. In his absence, the handful of homeless folk set by the new governor of Dernang to rebuild the shrine and to round up and care for the lost and homeless and orphaned children there carried on. Ghu seemed to approve both the priest and the gathering of orphans.

The children were playing some noisy game in the courtyard, shrieking and laughing. Cross-legged on the bench, Ivah dropped her mother's divining coins into the circle of the four-strand braid that was only one part of the larger binding, drawn in ink up and down both arms. Nabbani characters, not Northron runes, and ink, not blood, but the working had more the feel of the north than Nabban, she thought. Her father had worked much Northron wizardry into his Grasslander practices. She, too, could make a thing of her own.

For all her mother had claimed otherwise, it was not wrong to break and overturn and remake the patterns of one's traditions. Ahjvar worked so. She had watched him in the castle gardens, and perhaps others who did thought it only a sword-drill, but she saw the meditation it wove, and the way it worked, like Yeh-Lin's nightly circling of the castle walls, to brush away some attention that reached and drifted and sought to see them. She knew Praitannec magic used no such dance.

They talked in their councils of the empress as an usurper, the murderer of Emperor Otono and possibly Emperor Yao—small loss from what she heard—and many lords of the city. They did not call her Daughter of the Old Great Gods or debate why she took such a title. But that was there, she suspected, when Ghu and Ahjvar and Yeh-Lin talked alone. That was behind the devil's nightly patrols and Ahjvar's sword-patterns and restless fidgeting with broken twigs and sprigs of greenery. They did not include her yet. It didn't matter. She would bring to them what she could, when the time was right.

Would they come? And if they did not, should she go ahead? She was not sure.

"Ivah?"

Ivah looked up, startled. Ghu and Ahjvar, trailed by their dogs. No Yeh-Lin—good. Her inattention, their footsteps lost in the noise of the market and the shrieking of the children. Something about the assassin still prickled warning on her skin, and not only, she thought, the sense he always gave of being a predator only lightly leashed.

"You already know where he is," Ghu said. Not bothering to ask why she had wanted him.

"I . . . think I do. A divination I made. It spoke—it wouldn't have meant anything to anyone else. And—" Honesty, before her god. "I suspected anyway. There was a man I wondered about, before ever you came to Dernang. But Ghu, now I—I'm not sure, what I should do. I know Lord Ontari doubts me. His people have searched every cellar, every place a prisoner might be hidden and forgotten." She shrugged. "But Dan isn't hidden. He's *lost*. Wounded and lost, and if he's so hurt, if he is no longer able to be himself, should we bring him back at all?" From her satchel she pulled out the bound codex and the scroll both. "You read Nabbani, don't you, Ahjvar? And you're a wizard. What do you make of it?"

She threw rapidly the remaining five falls of the hexagram, dropping and gathering, dropping and gathering the coins, forgetting that he wouldn't likely be able to hold the unfamiliar patterns in memory.

Ahjvar shrugged, squatting down beside her, watching the coins unblinking. Disturbing, the way he would stare like a cat, too singly focussed. Shook his head.

She showed him the text in the bound book. "The gates stand closed without the key." He took it, frowning over the official interpretations and commentaries, which were not entirely helpful, she considered, not in this case. Advice on further reflection and patience. She found, by long practice, the place in the scroll, and her mother's tutor's notes. That which was locked might be unlocked, if its truth could be recognized, said that commentary, but to recognize the truth, one must unlock the gate. . . .

Ahjvar read that too, shrugged and pushed it back at her. "Means nothing to me, but my training's a completely different tradition. I'm good at locks." A narrow grin. "Find me one, and I'll teach you."

"It doesn't mean he's a prisoner."

"No." He sat back on his heels, peeling off a strip of soft, almost ropey bark from the fresh-split wood of the bench, shaving that into slivers with a narrow knife, rust-red and fragrant. A pattern, fallen half over her coins and the circlet of braid. But he lifted the braid clear with the point of this knife, delicately, disrupting his pattern, or reforming it. "There's hair in this. Yours."

"Yes."

"Why?"

"I'm his sister's daughter." At his raised eyebrows, she added hastily, "Not the empress. The younger sister. She was wizard-talented, which meant they allowed her to be only the lowest rank of diviner for all her ability to be more, because of Min-Jan's law against imperial women holding power. But she studied in secret; she fled to the Five Cities and Marakand, went to the Grass with my father." A touch of pride. "Escaped all the Wind in the Reeds they sent after her. I never believed her stories, when I was young."

She gathered her coins up, warming them in her clasped hands. A trading of answers? Worth a try.

"What are you?" she asked.

A glance up at Ghu. "His."

"I know that."

"A murderer," he said levelly.

"Ahjvar." Not exactly reproof. Just something Ghu would rather were not said.

Ahjvar ignored him. "Mad. An assassin of the Five Cities."

"Ahj, don't."

"The folk say you're a king."

"Not really. And that was a long time ago, anyhow."

She snorted. "You're hardly that much older than me, Ahjvar."

He shrugged, looked at the pattern his bark parings now made, met her eyes again. "Lost within himself," he said.

She wasn't sure why she had pressed him. Why Ghu had let her. But it . . . mattered. Ahjvar was not lost, but—she thought he might understand why she asked. "Yes. I think so. So tell me. You, not Ghu. Lost within himself. Hidden within himself? Maybe we should leave him there."

His look was . . . considering.

But, "No," he said flatly. "Ghu wants him. Dwei Ontari isn't Daro Korat, blind with faith and trust. Ontari will be gone and over the rivers again himself before long; he'll sit quiet in Alwu and let Choa fall to ruin on its own, if we don't have his prince to hold him."

She dropped the coins, holding his eyes, but his hand flashed out and caught them before they hit the wood.

"No," he said, very soft, and if she'd been a dog all her hackles would have risen and she'd have been backing and licking her lips and crouching. "Don't."

"*Ahj.*"

She wasn't a dog. She only swallowed and held out a hand. Ghu took the coins from Ahjvar, dropped them into her palm. A quick glance, to know what they showed, and she slipped them into her pocket. Later.

"Whatever I am, I'm his," Ahjvar said again. "Leave it at that. You mean to bring Dan to you."

"Yes."

"Good. Do it."

"Ghu?"

"Yes," Ghu said. "Lost, but not, I think, of his own will, Ahj. Nor for his own healing." He considered. "Why the shrine? Ah." And a smile, beginning. "Here all the time?"

"I think so."

"Let's see."

Ivah forced the assassin, the nearness of the god, from her mind. Pushed herself away from the calls of market vendors with greens and eggs and oil to sell, and the children, who were still running and shrieking and squealing, and took up the braid, weaving it through her fingers, then a long loop of leather thong twisting, doubling, passing and crossing, a cat's-cradle the folded over and under and through it, a path, a labyrinth, a calling through the endless circling of a mind bemazed.

The threads of hair were warm, burning like sunlight against her fingers. She let thought trace the way, breathed a name, another, and again, and again, to the beat of a drum that was only her heart, swaying to its rhythm where she sat. When she looked up again, the shadows had moved around her and the children were quiet. Ahjvar was propped against the wall, looking bored, but she thought that boredom a shield, not truth. Ghu sat cross-legged in the street, watching her.

And Dan had come out from the shrine.

As she had expected.

One of the littlest children clung to his hand.

"Uncle," she said respectfully, to the mute and sightless man who had shared Aoda's refuge.

They had to shift out of the way then, Ivah taking Dan by the arm to steer him inside. He seemed almost to be sleepwalking. Daro Korat had sent a wagon-load of supplies. It barely scraped through the gate. Lady Willow, as his heir, had come to escort it. What was she, nine? Ten? She wore such an air of gravity, but Ivah had seen her running laughing through the garden with Yeh-Lin's pages in some game, and it was she the devil had charged—or bribed? to begin teaching them the first sets of the syllabics, the simplest of the Nabbani writing forms.

An old woman appeared to take charge of the unloading and Willow, putting aside her quilted over-robe, plunged into helping the various children and cripples and old people unload alongside the slaves of the castle. Former slaves. Twelve thin moon-crowns a year was the wage to be owed by lords to the lowest of their labourers, six if they had their board and lodging, and it must rise with skills and trades. Easier to say so than see it done, but even the promise meant much already in Dernang, which surprised Ivah somewhat. The folk trusted it would be done. She did wonder, would the lords wear less silk and drink less wine of the Five Cities, to see that made so? Daro Korat, certainly. The lame old man would do whatever the holy one asked of him. But all of Nabban?

A fire-hot faith in a god might change a land.

Cynicism said, a god with an army at his back.

Willow was struggling with one end of a chest far too big for her and the scrawny little boy who had grabbed the other rope handle. Dan gripped Ivah's arm, his hand shaking, too tightly for her to plunge away to rescue them before they crushed their toes, but Ahjvar was there, plucking it from them and saying, "Grab those jars instead." Ghu disappeared into the throng and reappeared with a dusty sack of grain on his shoulder, meekly trudging off in the direction the old woman indicated before she saw who he was. And then they were not sure, all that crowd, if they should appear to notice, or not, their god labouring among them.

Ivah tugged Dan along out of the way, into the shelter of a far corner of the gallery, where old wood met new. He trembled like a man in a fever.

"Just sit," she said. "Wait. He'll come back in a moment." She put his hands together, clasped her own over them, studying his face. He was younger than he looked. Pain there. Defeat. He had been losing his war, had led thousands to die for a freedom they had never achieved. How was Ghu to do any better?

Not with the sword, in the end.

She was no healer, but she knew enough to wonder how much of the man he had been might be left to bring back. Lost. Or destroyed. Those scars. Head wounds could have strange effects. But he still understood speech, and he had been taking care of the child all this time, which suggested a mind still intact. The little girl was grubby but looked better fed than she had been, surely an achievement in this town.

The wagon emptied, Ghu came over to them dusting hands on his clothing. Ivah moved aside and he settled cross-legged before the prince, taking his hands. Ahjvar found his usual place, leaning against a wall, watching everyone. Willow drifted after him, squatted down a respectful distance off. Others followed, and followed Willow's example, sitting, standing, silent.

Awaiting miracles.

Ghu smiled at the little girl, who had her thumb in her mouth.

"Don't be afraid," he said, though to which of them, Ivah didn't know. He leaned forward and touched the scars that ran up the side of the man's head just in front of his ear, bald ridges through his matted hair, then touched his temple, his lips. Sat back, frowning. Ivah almost held her breath. She thought the watchers did. Even she was waiting for a miracle of the gods, like lightning from a clear sky . . . but Ghu only said softly to her, "Lost, as you said, but not beyond recall. The channels of his sight are broken. He might find his voice again, though, if he can come back to himself." He sat in silence for a while longer, eyes closed. Thinking? Praying? Did those who harboured godhead need to pray? No one else dared speak; the castle servants whispered together and then turned the oxen with muted commands and tugging on horns, prodding of haunches. They trundled off, leaving behind the armed Daro woman who was Lady Willow's bodyguard. The shrine grew very quiet, children hushed, beggars and strays all sitting out of the way. Waiting wide-eyed on wonders.

Ghu still held Dan's hands with his own wrapped around them, still sat with his eyes closed, but something had changed. They all felt it. Ivah shivered. The wind was off the mountains that morning, finding its way even into this enclosed corner. The smell of snow, clean and cold, sharp-edged, like moonlight on angry waves. She remembered winters on the Great Grass, the dry wind cutting, the horses and cattle standing tail-to, heads down, and the sky grey, the ground like stone. The injured man didn't seem to react, but then he raised his head, attention, if not sight, focussed on the holy one. Something in his face that had not been there before. Listening, she might have thought, but Ghu did not even whisper.

"My lord," the prince said. The merest broken whisper. The little girl stirred and sat up.

"Dan." The holy one opened his eyes. "People have been looking for you, you know."

He released the prince's hands. Dan rubbed his eyes, blinked, and drew a deep breath, putting an arm about the child. "Have they? I didn't know." His voice was weak and cracking like an old man's. "I'm sorry. It's all been—dark." He touched his eyes again. "All shadows, like leaves against the sun. In my thoughts. Just shadows and glare. I don't—but I thought I heard my sister An-Chaq calling me. I was a child again . . . But you came into the darkness, my lord. I saw you. You were there and you led me out."

"Yes," Willow said, agreement like a prayer.

"We need you, Dan," Ghu said. "Dwei Ontari thinks we're doomed. He'll hoard his forces over in Alwu like a miser for fear of losing them, keeping them against some future need of yours that will never come, but we need more than Dernang, more than Choa Province, to stand behind us, when we go south against the empress. I need the lords of the land to stand behind me and the folk of the land to see that we can do what we say, that we can break this empire and remake it, one province at a time if we must. Or we lose Dernang and Choa and all Nabban. Forever. I need you to bring me Shihpan and Alwu, to stand with Lord Daro Korat and Choa in the eyes of the lords of the land. Buri-Nai doesn't serve her own ambition in claiming to be a goddess, whatever she herself may believe."

"Does she believe it? I thought she only spread this new faith to justify her breaking of Min-Jan's law, a way of claiming the throne."

"No."

"What is it, then?"

"I think . . ." Ghu said. Hesitated. Lowered his voice, hardly more than a whisper, not to carry to the witnessing crowd. "I think we won't speak of that yet."

"Did she," the prince also whispered, and his voice went high. "Holy one—did she kill Otono, then? We didn't, my lord, I never asked that of my wizards or prayed for such an end."

"I don't know, but it wasn't any act of the gods. Or of wizardry. Knowing that, will you come, Dan?"

"My lord, you called me and I heard. I'm yours. Command me."

His sightless eyes were leaking tears, though his face didn't change. The child climbed up, clutching him, wiping at them with her dirty sleeve. The prince sniffed, most unprincely, laughed, and pulled the child down to his lap, wiping his own eyes and then his nose on his own equally grubby sleeve.

"This is Jula, lord," he said. "I couldn't find her grandmother again. I think Musan's men killed her, and the brother. Jula, look for me. This is our god."

The child stuck her thumb back in her mouth, studied Ghu gravely, then buried her face in the prince's chest.

Willow rose then and came to crouch by them. She touched the prince's hand and said, "My prince, I'm Lady Daro Willow, the heir of Kho'anzi Daro Korat. Come to the castle, you and the child. My grandfather will be eager to welcome you back, and your cousin Dwei Ontari is there, too."

It broke the solemn air of folk gathered for a ritual. People picked themselves up, murmuring together. Blessed, witnesses to miracle. Retelling, already, what they had seen, to those who had also seen. But the story would be out into the market and the town and the camp even before they walked back to the castle. And probably by the morning the god would have arrived in light and glory and restored the mad, mute prince to health and voice and sight and strength with bells and thunder.

That he was still blind, and the lines of pain in his face put ten or fifteen years on him, and that he pushed himself from the ground carefully as an old man, taking Ivah's arm when she touched his hand to offer it, would make no difference to how the tale grew. He had heard and answered his god, and that, whatever poetry they dressed it in, was the story they needed carried through the land, as much as couriers to carry his own words to his lords and officers in Shihpan and Alwu and out to the lords of all the provinces, who might, they could hope, only be waiting for some change in the wind.

CHAPTER XXX

The vast hall was very dark, but Yeh-Lin recognized it. She had been brought there once, in chains and escorted by twenty-four wizards sworn to her son's service, her own daughter among them . . . She hadn't survived long for all her great abilities, poor betraying and betrayed An-Chi. Min-Jan had been as paranoid as some of his descendants. Yeh-Lin had warned her . . . The artists had still been working on the wall panels then, carving the delicate flowers and leaves and insects that made it a wonder of the world, picking out the colours with gold and the metallic sheen of butterfly wings.

Dark with smoke. The ranks of pillars, wood painted to resemble marble blue as the twilight, were bubbled and charred. No carved panels now. No glazed butterfly wings.

Stumps of pillars.

The peony throne had been a work of art greater than the walls, some held: more leaves and blooms, jewels sparking throughout. The carved canopy had always looked to her like a trap for dust and spiders. She did wonder if anyone ever climbed up to dust it.

A moot point. A few boards, scabbed with charcoal, might be its remains, down in the ruin of the dais of nine steps. Omen. One could make much of the destruction of the throne, for either side. Though when the word came north would be time enough.

It wasn't the throne she needed to see, but the one who claimed it, who was not here.

She drifted. Fallen beams. Posts where walls had been. Shattered roof tiles, water making deep pools where cellars had been. That was all that remained of the central palace. Many of the satellite buildings had been smashed to kindling. A few still stood. Doors open, clothing chests flung over, shelves half-cleared. In a range of kitchens, braziers abandoned, some with pots still sitting on them, most overturned. Few bodies, though. A woman struck down by falling roof tiles under the eaves of a gallery, a man in a room of scattered documents, buried under a wall of pigeonholes. A few dogs who roamed furtive, wary of her. They would probably find their way out of the gardens to the marsh and go wild.

"What happened?" she demanded of the ghost of the woman, but her presence was too tenuous, and the ghost could not hear her. She let her vision flow outwards to the wider expanse of the gardens, was awed, then, at the destruction. Whole groves lay flattened, rubbish flung everywhere: weed, stone, shells, dead fish, timbers, spars, rope, an anchor, a doorframe, boats . . . no bodies. Or a few, lost in brush and other wreckage. Overlooked. Skeletal, now. There was much upturned ground, great squares of it, green with new-sprouted weeds.

The pits into which one would dump bodies in haste.

Many dead. She tried to shift her vision, to remember what had been here. Men, women, children. Townsfolk in the gowns of merchants and shopkeepers, townsfolk in artisans' smocks, crop-haired slaves in hemp shirts or fine quilted cotton, boatmen in loincloths, pigs, buffalo, dogs, cats . . . a dolphin. Drowned, battered, swept inland. And all the marsh about was flooded, sluggish with flotsam . . . trees, house timbers, the broken wrack of ships, bodies pulled down to the mud, lost, to wash ashore a bone at a time over a century of storms and tides to come . . . Trapped in the pool of the dykes, which were broken, but not enough to flush clean with the tide. That had always been a problem with the lagoon, once she built the breakwaters.

The Golden City, her beautiful city floating on the mists of the lagoon. Gone.

Stumps, sandbars, jagged islands of ruin. Her palace, long abandoned, cursed by An-Chi at Min-Jan's order to remain forever derelict,
still stood, but roofless.

No ships in the harbour.

No harbour.

Inland . . . there was life on the Beacon Hills and in the shelter of
their western slopes. A palisaded camp above, almost a Praitan hill-
fort, and below, a village, a town, of tents and shacks built from salvaged timber and canvas and bundled reeds. A well-worn track led away
through the hills, and coming down it, trotting, were riders wearing the
badges of the lords of both Upper and Lower Lat. They were met by a
skein of men and women on rough ponies, their faces painted in swirls
and spirals. Amicably, if formally, met, and escorted towards the fort.

In the distance, a pack-train of asses and buffalo plodded towards them.

What story here? Dar-Lathans allied with two provinces; they had
conquered Taiji and the Imperial Demesne months before, that rumour
had come north. She tried to see, to find memory. Wind. Waves. Darkness
like night, and it was day. A wind impossible to stand against. The city
taking to boats, to ships, to anything, in hope of safety on shore among
the feared tribesfolk—waves towering to the rooftops, houses that had
stood since her day collapsed, folded in on themselves by the waves, col-
lapsing, sandbars and pilings washed away.

The empress. The imperial corps of wizards. The folk of the palace.
Drowned?

Ships. Gone, gone with the storm called after them, and the city
abandoned behind.

"I will see you," she said aloud. "*Now.*"

A woman, her outermost robe shot through with gold thread, glittering and glinting in the purple-black brocade, a coat of scale gilded so
that she resembled some glittering fish as she passed along an avenue of
soldiers. Her hair poured loose down her back. A carriage awaited her,
gilded, enamelled, a suffocating box on high wheels for all its doubtless
cushioned luxury. Ten oxen to pull it, snow white with gilded horns. She
strode, masterful, light-footed. It was the people surrounding her whose

feet scuffed or tramped. Four women, two with long hair dressed with jewelled combs, two with the short hair of slaves or labouring folk, but all in brocade court robes. Eight men of towering height, their armour coats, their greaves and helmets, even the shafts of their polearms gilded.

Buri-Nai, goddess and empress. Murderer of her father and brother. Murderer of the Golden City. Murderer, with her word, of the priests of the shrines who resisted her assumption of godhood. Yeh-Lin brushed against her, tasting her, as a snake tasted the air. What was she? Anger, a deep anger. A life of years sped too quickly and yet too slowly, too much the same, waiting, always waiting, waiting for nothing, while anger grew. Purpose. A purpose fixed like a rock, regret and excitement in that purpose. A fierce devotion, born out of emptiness, of searching, searching, and then discovery, like a beacon blazing in the night. A flood of love, of being loved, wanted—chosen. A choice made.

There. A fleeting touch, a scent on the wind like that which told of the passage of an animal through the forest—city folk did not think a human could know such but they were wrong. Faint, but—scent, colour, the feel of the shape of the light—

Buri-Nai stopped and looked back over her shoulder, her silk-gloved hand clapped to her heart.

There. Under her hand.

The guards and two of the women—one of the apparent ladies and one of the slaves, spread out about her, facing in all directions, alert for whatever she had heard.

Nothing. Yeh-Lin held her breath, which was ridiculous. The woman's eyes sought and passed over her, but the attention of something that was no human gaze . . . thickened.

A . . . taste. Sound to the bat's ear making shape . . . a light . . . milky, shot through with colour, cold as the dance of the north, crackling on the edge of hearing. Kindling into fire.

Sudden savage rage, like a mother's defence of her infant. She was slammed away and without thought, without consideration of consequences, struck back. Was deflected. Light flared, white, and the wounded air roared. The carved roof of the carriage, curling and ornate as a keep's eaves, cracked. Iron tyres smoked and the axles snapped. It sagged. Oxen bellowed, pulled to run from the smoke and dragged it swaying, capsizing, after them.

And she was falling, tumbling back into herself. Her eyes burned and her head thudded and she lurched up graceless, an arm groping to find support on the wall, but it was the dead king who caught her.

Nabban had caught the mirror she flung away. The Grasslander shaman stood like a statue where she had been the whole time, at the northern node of the cat's-cradle pattern she had traced out in red and yellow and black yarns about them all, the ends of all the skeins wound through her fingers. Her eyes were wide and dark, amber-ringed. In the far corner, the prince, clean and tidy and decently dressed in a plain robe like a priest's, but black rather than white or brown, his little girl prised away from him to the pages' care, sat on a cushion. His head was flung back, one hand braced to rise, the other at his sash, where there was no weapon. He would carry none now, he swore. He was priest, priest of the god of Nabban, and when this war was over and the land restored to its true god he would keep a hermit's shrine on the mountain.

Nothing had come into the room. They could not have heard the thunder, the cracking of the axles. Yeh-Lin did not have too much pride to take the support Ahjvar gave. Her knees had gone weak.

He looked as though he had caught the edge of—whatever it was, that look of headache tight around the eyes, and he let her down onto her bed with more haste than courtesy, reaching, as if he expected something to strike out of it, for the mirror, which Nabban was studying with childlike curiosity.

"It can't follow," Yeh-Lin snapped. "Give me that."

"Lady Lin?" Little Ti in the doorway from the antechamber, eyes wide. "Are you all right?"

"I'm fine. Go back to your lessons. Or go play."

"You yelled, my lady," Kufu announced over Ti's head. He had Jula on his hip. Her thumb, for once, was not in her mouth. Jang squeezed in beside them, and Lady Willow, clutching the sheet of the syllabics the pages had been studying under her supervision.

"I did not."

"You did," the god said. "It's all right now, Ti. Her divination startled her." He waved the children off as if shooing hens, with about as
much effect. "Go on."

"Out," Ahjvar said. Him, they obeyed, Ti last of all, shutting the
door, his brow still wrinkled with doubt and concern.

Yeh-Lin sighed and rubbed her temples. "I should at least have had
a very good evening, if I'm going to feel this way in the morning."
Shut her eyes a moment against the jagged wash of light through the
southern window, which was only a bright and pleasant noon. Ghu wandered over, in passing handing her the mirror he had failed to surrender
to Ahjvar, and leaned out to lower the blue-painted shutter. He had
crossed through the cat's-cradle to do so, but Ivah had begun winding
up her stands anyhow. It had all flown loose—not the physical pattern
but the powers it shaped—in the fierce brief exchange. Like a flickering
clash of blades, and now they fell back, she and her enemy, and caught
their breath, each with gaze fixed on the other . . . except they did not.
She had lost the feel of the shape of the thing, the taste, the humming
chord . . . gone.

"What was that?" Ahjvar demanded. He was fidgeting a knife
through his fingers again, flicking it end for end, and she did not think
he even realized he had it in his hand. Missed, and the blade plunged,
skewering a tangle of black and red just as Ivah jerked it towards herself
by the black strand.

Not missed, no. Not him.

"Pine, myrrh, yew," he said in Praitannec. And then, "The west."

"What?"

"The west," he repeated, Nabbani this time. "Out of fire and ice.
Don't ask me. You explain it." He scooped up the knife and made it vanish
up his sleeve. Show-off. But now too late she saw, almost, the pattern
steel had woven in the air, and what the yarn had written . . . almost. For
all the antipathy the dead king had to wizardry, he seemed lately to be
finding his way back to it. Not terribly usefully, except for the restless
guard he sometimes flung about the pair of them, a strange and unset-

tling wizardry that was half drawing on the god's own nature, rather than on the pulsing heart of the world at large. As if young Nabban's person were the earth that had given him blood and bone and soul. The mortal lovers of the gods should not lose themselves so, even were they wizards. Too closely bound.

"That," she said, "was not helpful at all, even as cryptic Praitannec divination goes."

A blank look. Not incomprehension. He simply gave what he found and didn't care what she did with it. Ghu touched his hand, as if to get his attention. Or bring him back. Ahjvar blinked at him and relaxed a little.

"What was it?" he repeated. "Fire and ice?"

Ivah had drifted closer, winding the last of her yarn up. Silent, watchful. Always. Dan said, "I smelt smoke." She noted Ahjvar's flinch. "I thought I heard thunder, far away." And the prince waited. It was Nabban's insistence that he was there. Buri-Nai was his sister. Dan had a right to know the truth of her. But no Nabbani ritual of vision carried the smell and sound into the room of the diviner.

Her mirror should not have, either.

"The devils, Ahjvar," Ivah said. "Light, fire. Out of ice. So—since she is here, who is our enemy?" Glanced at Dan, bit her lip.

The prince frowned.

"Like you and your niece, Dwei Dan, I have found my god," Yeh-Lin said. It was oddly difficult to say, though she had meant it as a joke. Half a joke. "I am Yeh-Lin Dotemon. I have given my oath to Nabban, to the heir of the gods of Nabban, to—Ghu." Name him, pin herself so there was no squirming away, no trickery of language open to her. An oath to this damnable boy, who looked right through her into the stars and the hells.

Ahjvar's eyes mocked her. But the words felt heavy with truth on her tongue.

"Ah," Dan said.

"Better the lords don't know, old woman," Ahjvar put in. "They may lack the prince's faith. We don't want this to look like a war of two deluded puppets."

Nabban snorted.

"My lord . . ." Dan hesitated. "My lord, you—how does she come to serve you? My lord, she tried to destroy the gods."

Silently, she shook her head. Put the damned things in their place, maybe, in an empire she in her folly wanted to move at her word, not theirs, but destroy, no.

Nabban seemed uncertain of that himself, if his silence meant anything.

"He pulled me from the sky to fall at his feet," she said, which was in fact the truth. Ragged young man on the road Over-Malagru. "He broke me to bone and buried me." A quiet fury that rose against her with the strength of a typhoon, confined in the stillness of stone.

"*Ghu* did?" Ivah's astonishment suggested she did not yet understand her god, if she could not believe anger in him, or strength to face a devil—admittedly a restrained and weakened devil, but she did not need to share that with either of her descendants just now. But let his cursed king be threatened; then the child would see what the quiet depths might hide. It was a weakness, a very human fracture running through his godhead.

"What could I do, when I recovered myself, but follow him? He was what the goddess south over sea—the tree who had held me in my long grave—what she had set me free to seek. I knew it. Not then, but in time I came to know it."

Dan sat considering. Finally he nodded. Just that, nothing more. It would have to do.

"Not a devil in person, but there is certainly devil's work in the land," she said. "The empress is only a servant, but a knowing one or one deceived—whether she truly believes herself a goddess, I couldn't be certain. At least we are warned. I think we must put the south from our minds for now, whatever may be happening there between the Gentle Sister and the Little. At least the Dar-Lathans are a human enemy. They can wait. The empress, I think, is travelling. I do not know where she is, I could not tell. I don't know her destination, but I can guess it. Unfortunately, I was seen. And Nabban, I'm sorry. Our enemy knows

I'm here now, where before he only suspected. I don't think he'll let me come so close to her again."

"Who is it?" Ivah demanded.

"Jochiz, Vartu, Jasberek." Yeh-Lin considered. Jochiz, who had been Sien-Shava, a man of the southern islands. He knew Nabban. Vartu, Ulfhild, King's Sword of the North, whom she had dreamed distant among unfamiliar trees. Jasberek, the wanderer Anganurth, the stranger, the wizard of no known land, no folk, no gods that he had ever named. She shrugged. "I say he. Convenience, two out of three? It was so brief a touch."

"Not Vartu," Ivah said with certainty.

"You think not?"

"I know it."

To play games with another's mind—was not Vartu. She admitted that. "He, then. But not in the city, Ivah."

"In the west," Ahjvar said hoarsely. Ghu gave him a sharp look.

"Buri-Nai." Prince Dan sat with bowed head. "Can she be saved?"

"I have no idea." And Yeh-Lin didn't much care. Neither, by his expression, did Ahjvar. Ghu, she thought, could be necessarily ruthless, if he saw the need. Did he mean to make himself emperor?

"We don't wait here for her to come against us," Ghu said.

"No." That was Ahjvar, agreeing, not arguing, and watching her as if he expected hers to be the contrary voice.

"Children, I'm all in favour of falling upon my enemies like lightning before they think I can even have a force in the field—I am known for it, if you would only read your histories—but we don't know where she is."

"Find her."

"Kozing Port? The Old Capital? How will you raise an army great enough to take either of those? How will you raise an army to hold even Choa against her, if she gathers the armies of Solan and Numiya? She—and he—will know you're coming."

Ahjvar asked, "Even Kozing—six weeks?"

She blinked. "Are you mad? Don't answer that, we both know the answer. We can hardly move like couriers. Even if we sent only you—"

"No," said Ghu flatly.

"—you could hardly call on the courier stations for remounts."

"We should still move swift as we can, old woman. Not an army."

"You'll need an army to cross those lands. Where we'll find one that's not barefoot and half-starved—"

"A small company," Ghu said. "A herald's party, to treat with her."

"Do you mean to?" Yeh-Lin asked.

"No. I mean to take the land from her. But we'll talk, not fight, if we can."

Ahjvar snorted. Ghu just shrugged. "We wouldn't win a war anyhow, even if we could march every soldier and rebel in Choa and Alwu and Shihpan east or south to wherever she is."

She wondered if he did mean to let his assassin loose in the end. She saw no other way.

"Let me be your shield, my lord," Dan said. "Who'll dare hinder me, if I ride to offer submission to—"

"Will we ride under a lie?" Yeh-Lin asked. "I have no objection, myself, to such policy, but it's hardly what one wants of one's god." She didn't bother with any honorific. Besides, even if Dan claimed to have laid down arms and to be willing to offer his submission to Buri-Nai, the odds were the first ambitious banner-lord they met would take his head in hope of the empress's favour.

"No," Ghu said. "Dan, I need you in the north."

"What for?" Yeh-Lin wanted to know.

"We need the shrines and the priests of the shrines," Ghu said.

"Hardly a force to conquer with."

"A web, a spread of streams through the land. Yes."

Yes, what? Yes, it was such a force? Yes, she was right, it was too weak? He had an absent, abstracted look and did not seem to hear when she demanded to know. He wandered to the eastern window, propped that shutter open, and vaulted up, sitting framed there like a cat, back against the stonework, one knee drawn up, one leg dangling out over far too great a height.

One could see the river from that side, but he tilted his head back, eyes shut.

After a moment, in which every one of them but blind Dan considered the drop beneath him, Ivah asked, "If we go as heralds of the gods, saying we want to meet with the Daughter of the Gods, then will they dare oppose us?"

"She kills priests," Ahjvar said.

And there was the matter of the stolen souls of the tattooed dead. They had seven prisoners in the cells of the keep marked with *the gate and the bridge* in a language and script no human had ever used. Two, Zhung Musan's chief clerk and a young banner-ranked, had declared themselves willing to make an oath to Daro Korat and the heir of the gods, but they lied. Nabban would not have approved if she had suggested she kill one, to observe first-hand that moment of death and loss. A pity, from the point of view of one seeking knowledge, but it was not an act worthy of his trust or that of the goddess in the tree and she had not seriously considered it. Not for more than a moment or two.

"Ride fast and hard," Ghu said, opening his eyes, breaking the silence that had followed Ahjvar's grim reminder. What had he seen? Something, Yeh-Lin was certain. "Fast and hard and secret as we can be." Ivah and Ahjvar exchanged identical looks.

"Cattle-thieves," Yeh-Lin said.

Almost a smile, from the dead king. "Damned right, old woman."

"But first," Ghu said, "we move in force to hold Choa and the crossing of the river from Numiya. Let them see that, let word of that go south, as it will, because if it's known we've left Choa, it might begin to seem good to her lords bordering us to take it."

"And we want them to know the north is in arms behind you, waiting." Dan nodded.

"Waiting, united," Ghu said. "Let them think we might fall on them across the river, whether we really have the strength to do so or not. Let them think Numiya and even Solan within our reach."

That, she hadn't expected from him. It was the dead king's thinking. Numiya might even be possible, depending on what provisions might come from the north or Dan's provinces, and once they held Numiya, then the rich fields of Solan and its harvests . . .

"We need to take this to the Kho'anzi and the lords," Yeh-Lin said, and sighed. "Dwei Ontari will argue."

"Dwei Ontari will remember his oaths to me," Dan said. "It's time to gamble our last coins, isn't it?"

"I think so." Ghu seemed apologetic, now he had them all—where he had meant to have them, from the moment he and the dead king came to find her with the dawn.

They dispersed, then, Dan collecting Willow and his child from the antechamber to go in search of the Kho'anzi and Lord Ontari, Yeh-Lin's pages sent in search of Lords Raku and Yuro, Governor Zhung Huong, and Lady Ti-So'aro. Ivah went to summon the other wizards, dream-drowned Nang Kangju and timid Gar Sisu, the young woman of Hani Gahur's staff who had witnessed the challenge and his death.

Ghu flowed like a cat down from the windowsill, a hand on Ahjvar's shoulder. The dead king had moved to be there. Did he feel how the god's own being began to wind through him, like the finest roots of some great tree? Did either of them?

It was wrong. Such surrender was wrong.

Time was she would have destroyed him, destroyed the both of them if she could, and thought she saved the land from the horror of a god turned necromancer.

Ambition. Power.

Dotemon, here. In this land, his land. Dotemon's hand on the wretched boy the gods think to make lord of their land. Dotemon's hand, Dotemon's games, mocking, seducing, twisting all to herself, even the dead, now. Playing the games of the Northrons, raising the dead from their bones? There is necromancy about them. It must be she who has dragged the soul from its proper road and set it to walk in life again, with the scent of the stars and the well of night still upon it. Set it in play to seduce the godling, to make him her own, bound to her, though no doubt she would rather have done that herself, that being her way. No doubt a disappointment to her, to find the heir of the gods not amenable to her usual wiles.

Clever, though. The dead and not-dead man is more than a Northron bone-horse, more than a usual necromancy, and very hard to kill.

He will learn how it is done, before he unravels that binding and takes the soul for his own uses.

The days were full and wearing. The nights were restful. In the darkness, there was—not silence, but a quiet that the daytime lacked. The many-layered noise, the weight, almost the battering, of the souls about wore at him. In the night, fewer were wakeful, and those that were, were—closer to themselves, for the most part. In the night, their burdens might seem even heavier, but they were more clearly seen, too. In the night, it was easier to come close to them without foundering in their noise. The night made a silence in the hearts of the folk, where a path, narrow, winding, not certain, not untroubled, but still, a path, might begin to be found, to some better way.

And simply, there was quiet, and not folk hunting him to fill the place of general and king and priest, none of which he meant to be, for all he might use the authority some were so desperate to give him, to coax, to lead, to drive them where he needed them to go.

He needed the river. More and more often Ghu found himself seeking her shore once darkness fell, rather than the garden of the Father. The guards at the castle gates rarely noticed or remembered that they had let him pass out or opened to his return. Waking or sleeping, he was a dream to them when he drifted by, once sunset came. Ahjvar trailed him, silent in his silence. An oak at his back, bedrock beneath his feet. Hearth in a cold night.

The river was broad here at what had become his favourite place, upstream from the castle, deep and wide, though by late summer it would run shallow and fordable over a flat bed of stone. The banks were shelving stone with elms rooted in the cracks, not the willows down where the village boats put ashore, where Yeh-Lin's company of riverers camped and worked, and where the log-built skid-road from the uplands came to its end.

Here, there were no fires, no sleepers, no smell of timber and tar and smithying and muck. Here, the dreams of the sleeping and the wakeful were so distant as to be less than the sound of the wind in the riverside weed. Only stone and water and the frogs singing, the water a music, coiling over and under itself, changing its note with the seasons, but unceasing.

He could lie in that current, on the stones, let it flow over him, through him, lose himself, find himself in it. Ahjvar's tolerance for nighttime wanderings would probably be pushed too far if he began sleeping in the river. He would take Ahj into the river one day. Not yet. For now he simply sat listening, learning, taking into himself the currents of his land. All too soon there would be no quiet nights, no escape to solitude. Not till all was won or lost. Ahjvar lay stretched out behind him, not quite sleeping and close enough to touch if he reached back, sword held with arm against his chest, like a child clutching some necessary toy.

Not quite sleeping, but near enough, and Ahjvar muttered suddenly, nails of his outflung left hand scraping the stone. Falling into the claws of nightmare, catching himself before it seized him. For a moment Ghu was fully there again, stone, night air, a few gasping breaths behind him, a sigh as Ahj forced himself into slow-breathing stillness again, resumed his watch of the circling stars. Ghu shut his eyes again, let the river reclaim him, let himself go, now, till awareness of stone and frogs and stirring leaves, even Ahjvar's careful soft breathing, was left behind and there was only the water. If he breathed himself, he did not know it.

PART THREE

CHAPTER XXXI

D amn Dotemon. *What game does she play? She stalks him, stalks the empress. If she understands what he wants, she may yet deny it to him, destroy her own tools to keep them from his hand.*

Empress of Nabban with a god leashed to her hand? An empire in the east? Would Vartu ever ally with Dotemon again? Would Nabban follow Yeh-Lin the Beautiful, twice rid of her before?

She is nothing to fear. She never has been.

He does not want her loose to interfere regardless. Difficult to destroy her.

Drown her, break her, leave her trapped in long years to pull herself back together. The best course. And it will shake their confidence in their slave-born god.

Over five thousand men, nearer six, marching, but not on the highway, which swung away from the river to hug the shadow of the escarpment. The river road was shorter, though in this season it was also muddy, puddled, and outright gone half to swamp. They had no wagons and wrapped in the river's breath, they were harder to see. So said the heir of the gods.

The important thing had been to get them out of Dernang, which could not feed them. They were joined by straying bands of rebels and fugitives, drawn to the banners of the god and Prince Dan, who would be making his base at the fort of the Dragon's Gorge. One could not have two cooks in one kitchen, in Yeh-Lin's opinion, and two lords in one castle, even serving the same master, would be ill-advised as well. Leave Dernang and the rule of Choa to the Kho'anzi, leave his lieutenant Daro Raku to command the sizeable garrison left behind to guard it against brigands and banditry, or against some counter-rebellion of hidden imperial support. Zhung Huong remained as governor of the town under the two Daros to deal with the day–to-day practicalities. Dwei Ontari was sent into Alwu with Dan's orders, which he would follow where he would not have followed the god's. Couriers were sent to Shihpan, announcing their prince's restoration, commanding the borders be held against any imperial incursion, summoning certain lords to their prince at the Gorge. Couriers were sent, less openly, out south and east, carrying messages to the shrines, or to hunt those priests and families of the shrines who had fled into hiding. The dreamer Nang Kangju had been left with Lord Daro Korat. The young wizard Gar Sisu, who had given her oaths to the heir of the gods, travelled with that part of the army sent down the river and was to remain with Prince Dan.

And all in less time, Yeh-Lin thought, than any army had ever been stirred to move in all Nabban's history. A few thousand men and, as the strays joined them, women as well, still winter-weary, many still barefoot, for all the soldiers might be somewhat better fed than they had been under Zhung Musan. As they wound their way down through Choa they could see the village fields being planted and tended again, and they did not raid them, nor trample them. But the river could not feed them all with its fish. If Dwei Ontari proved false . . . but she thought him true to his lord, willing to set aside his own doubt for Dan's faith in the heir of the gods, so long as the god's aims seemed to follow the same path Dan had committed to when he raised his banners the previous year. So long as the heir of the gods did not drag Dan to death in his confrontation with the empress. Nothing to lose. They were condemned traitors, both Dan and Ontari; if the god proved true, then well and good; if a deluded madman who journeyed to his death, at least he left the north in better order than he had found it, and under Dan's hand. And the restoration of his prince to himself would count for much with Ontari, she judged. So he would come with the cavalry of Alwu. The eastern ferry landing, where the river made a border between Alwu and Choa, was very close to the border with Numiya. It would be held for them.

Her mirror showed her nothing of the empress, though Yeh-Lin sought her almost nightly. Nothing. Divination—hers, Ivah's, Gar Sisu's—found nothing. Even the dead king was persuaded to make a drawing of the wands in the Praitannec way, but no revelation came to him. It was as if Buri-Nai, and whatever force she travelled with, had vanished from the world. Enclosed in a devil's fist.

A worry. But it was a long way from the Golden City to Choa, even if the empress went first by sea to Kozing Port or the fishing towns of the lower mouths of the Wild Sister, and the imperial armies of recent history moved broken, crawling, driven by fear at an oxcart's pace.

Yeh-Lin was impressed with what young Nabban had, by contrast, inspired—persuaded, driven—his folk to achieve. Speed, most of all. They marched light, and in hope and trust of their god. They were organized in half-companies, bands small enough to start to feel kinship, to know and maybe to trust. In the five weeks they had been encamped at Dernang after she took the town, she had seen that their officers drilled them with spear and what swords they had, and new crossbow companies had been formed.

It was her rafts freed them to move. No clumsy platform of logs but a shaped thing given form by their layers and lengths, higher in the water—a vessel, not a desperation. They rode the water as if it carried them willingly, and maybe it did. Even the one that had run aground the day before was floated clear undamaged, losing none of its load. The god blessed his own. The riverers, proud of what they had achieved and in so short a time, held themselves to have become the personal followers of Nang Lin, the god's captain-general. That she had named herself after a devil in her challenge to Hani Gahur was her biting humour, and they loved her for that, as well. It was that brought her out onto the rafts. She would rather have ridden ahead with the advance guard, who were also hers and who would have the camping ground chosen, hearths and latrines and laneways marked out with flags before even the rafts, always the last to leave and the first to arrive at any camp, ever arrived, but it mattered to the raft-captains and the folk who crewed them that she be among them sometimes, that they not lose her entirely to Prince Dan's army before they came to their end and their craft were broken up for their timbers. While they had the river and their unity as a company, they wanted to have her.

Nabban was somewhere out here on the water today, too. He, too, had come to understand the need to give himself to his folk, to share himself.

The chill of fog stroked over her skin, but there was no fog. The raft, heavy thing that it was, nevertheless danced with the water, no contrary wind catching their load like a sail and sending butting waves to make them labour at poles or oars to force their way downriver. The two sisters at the great steering oar at the stern sang with it, a song of menfolk left behind and the river's freedom. Ti sat out of the way, as enrapt as if he listened to one of the great poets. Folk had sung that same song on the river in Solan when she was a girl. Jang and Kufu were up in the bows sitting with the grizzled raft-captain, who was teaching them, so far as Yeh-Lin could overhear, the river, talking of currents and winds, floods and storms she had known, the lore of the sky as it related to winds and water. The rafts did not keep the strict order of the marching companies and half-companies. Sometimes, where it was broad enough, two might even race, raise a bit of sail on stubby double masts, if the wind was right. One swung close now. Half a company of the archers on that one, rather than tents and provisions, a great offering of souls to the river if they tore one another apart. Though every raft-captain seemed to fear the shame of carelessness, with the river's very eye upon them.

Green fields to either side. The river was safe and quiet, the god's own place.

But the fog Yeh-Lin could not see felt greasy on her skin.

She stood up, swaying atop the net-bound stack of their cargo, turned through a full circuit of the horizon. For what good that would do. The scouts were out of sight ahead, the main force behind, hidden by the river's twisting course. Nothing moved on the eastern shore. Alwu, like Choa, was a sparsely populated province, though between the rocky, forested hills its soil was deeper and its grazing fatter. Once into Numiya, the pastures and meadows that made a web around the crumpled hills would fade away into cropland and villages and manors each nearly within sight of the next. She was still not certain how best they might travel, Nabban and what she could not help thinking of as his hearthsworn, old phrase of the north. Disguise meant giving up their far-too-excellent horses for commonplace nags, and what to do about the dead king's hair and height . . .

They should have been secret on the river. She had the chill conviction they were not.

Yeh-Lin descended to the deck in a few hops.

"My lady?" The captain broke off her talk.

"Children, go to the stern with Ti. Get your backs to the cargo and stay away from the water."

"Why?" Jang asked.

"Now!"

Too indulged. She was not their grandmother. But they ran without further word. The captain had bounded to her feet at Yeh-Lin's tone, taken up the long-hafted boathook of her authority. Blunt, maybe, but the bronze head was no weapon to be discounted.

"Danger, my lady?"

"I don't know."

The gentle sway of the raft was changing. The river was narrow here, swifter, deeper than it had been. Dark. Tangled stands of willows lined the shore. Ambush? No, nothing living there but what one expected: birds, snakes, frogs, voles.

Silence. No song. The water was loud, slapping against them, under them. The captain breathed too loudly and Yeh-Lin almost snapped at her to hold her breath, as if that would help.

Small clouds above made patches of shadow.

Cold, cold, cold. Claws of ice, not fog, striking, freezing, ice in her veins, ice to hold her, stilling thought, paralysing—

Waves gathered. The motion of the raft changed, diving and bucking, a gathering of current like a bunching muscle, a snake coiling to strike. The captain shouted, turning, so slowly, too slowly, to stare at the darkening water, shadow coalescing into . . . life.

The shadow gathered itself, creature of old bone and mud and water, reared up high as a tree, struck. Fangs long as a hand splintered logs; the prow ducked low, flinging a wave over them all, but it surged up again as the fangs tore free. A child screamed and a woman cursed. The captain had fallen to her knees, but struggled up again, water sheeting from her hair, her boat-hook gripped like a spear.

"*Dragon!*" the woman shouted—warning, terror, disbelief in equal measure.

The great head, the size of a man's torso, had disappeared beneath the water again. River water, cold river water, soaked her.

Move! Dotemon raged, burning in her veins. *Move!* But ice held her.

At the steering oar they were shrieking of dragons, repeating their captain's cry though they hadn't seen what hit them. Trying to summon the crossbows of the following raft. No good. The river carried them all.

Stench of old rot long buried, ancient death, forgotten, gone to slime and stone. The water heaved and churned, brown and frothing. Something dark beneath the surface, arrowing towards them. *No. No, no,* and *no.*

For a moment Yeh-Lin felt herself what she was not—*was not*, bone, gaunt skin, old wounds, and the fire beneath, the fire within her marrow, cold and hungry, the stuff of stars, of ice—

The raft-captain glanced her way, stared, mouth opening on some cry of horror.

Unravelling—

No. We are not.

Yeh-Lin tore herself away, pulled herself together.

"Behind!"

And as the captain spun back to the river it thrust from the water again and Yeh-Lin leapt to meet it, snarling, her sword a song in the air. Skylark, she had named it long before, that voice that only she-Dotemon heard clear as water, edged as glass, keen and piercing as the sun in the sky. But the ice still clutched at her to slow her, ice or memory of ice, and the creature struck the captain, seized and shook and tore shoulder and arm away, flung back its head to gulp and swallow even as what was left of the women fell away and the Skylark sang, carving the snake-neck to the spine. They were screaming at the stern, the raft tossed and flung, new shadows coiling under the water, darkness in the air. This head was the length of a tall man, maw snarling wide enough to engulf and bite a woman in two. It snatched and tossed the bulky green-brown body of the first aside, lashed away as Yeh-Lin swung for it, whipped around and struck. She stepped aside and brought her blade sweeping up, but the thing was fast as a striking snake, fast as her own thought. So was she, rolling away. Wood splintered from its missed strike.

Yelling. Another raft angling close, the crossbows shooting at the shadows, the dark thickening of air that was striving to become—something. Fools would hit the children. She screamed at them to hold, *hold* as another massive head reared itself over her, Skylark's edge opening a gouge in one great throat and at the same time she reached into the water, the air, reached for what shaped this forgotten monstrous life . . .

Something went into the waves from the other raft, smooth and silent as a diving bird. She knew him before her eyes had understood, felt him, the river suddenly a live thing, and it sucked down the smoke-shadows and the cold fire burned free through her veins, waking from its ice. Her second kill slid away, dissolving into river-muck and weed. The last head lashed back the neck's own length and plunged down after Nabban. The raft rolled over god and monster both, carried by the current, as Yeh-Lin leapt the mangled body of the raft-captain and raced to the stern and her children.

The water roiled. The creature thrashed half out of the water alongside them, a thing that should not have been, streaked now red and white, rolling, its belly opened like a gutted fish.

They had pushed little Ti up tight against the net-bound storage jars, Kufu and Jang shielding him, all clinging together. The steerswomen knelt, one with a knife, one with another boathook. The head began to rise again, wounded as the creature was, snaking across the surface of the water for them. Yeh-Lin stood with a foot braced on the frame of the steering oar, waiting, but steel flashed up its neck and ripped a gash a yard long before it reached her. It sank. Red curling and coiling in the water, darkening, water foaming pink along their sides, fading, shadow, dissolved into nothing, the river quiet, gone bright and dark and sparking in the sunlight. The god hooked his knife into a crack between logs and heaved himself onto the deck, black coat and trousers clinging, hair slicked flat. No expression, none, as he came to his feet. Cold eyes, black and deep as night's own ocean. But it had not been she who summoned the creatures from bone long gone and the memories of the ancient seas held in the stone, and his anger faded as the shadows had. He went around her with merely a nod of acknowledgement— going to the dead captain. She turned and the pages were staring, but Ti broke from the other two and rushed to her. She dropped her sword in time to catch him, hold him against her, and Jang and Kufu followed. Ti was sobbing. He was so very young. She tried to remember being so young, and went down to her knees to hold them all, three shaking young bodies pressing close.

"Captain Lin?" She looked up into the face of one of the women, grey, sweating, river-soaked. "That—was that a dragon?"

She had no name for it. "I don't know. But it was sent by the enemy of the heir of the gods. Look to your steering!" They were drifting out of the current, twisting sideways, and other crews were recovering from alarm to hail them, crying out for news.

Ghu came walking back down the deck, sombre, as if shadows still clung to him.

"Your sister died fighting the monster," he told the two leaning on the steering oar again. "I gave her to the river."

A fit funeral for a riverer, and better that they did not see her dismembered body, Yeh-Lin thought. Better that the children did not see.

Did she mean to take them beyond the fort of the Dragon's Gorge? Had she given it any thought at all? Better they stayed with Prince Dan, who had left his little Jula in the care of Lady Willow's governess at the White River Dragon. Better she had left them behind to attend on Lady Willow and chase after Jula.

The sisters of the raft wept, but they did not leave their steering.

"Take us in to shore," Yeh-Lin said. "The danger is past . . ." Switched to Praitannec. "Is it, Nabban?"

He considered her. "I wasn't their quarry."

She had not given that thought. "Ah. Take us to shore, if you would, sisters. The danger on the river is past and Prince Dan and the lords must be shown the heir of the gods is safe."

"You knew," the younger of the sisters said, and Yeh-Lin was about to deny any such thing, but it was Ghu who shook his head.

"You knew," she insisted. "You knew the false goddess sent dragons against us and you came to the rafts with Lady Lin today to protect us." And she loosed her hold on the oar and went to her knees. "My lord, I know you would have saved my eldest sister if you could, but she died honourably and is surely blessed on her road, to die fighting your enemy's creatures. My lord, is the river safe now?"

"They're gone," Ghu said. "I don't think there will be any more." But he looked worried, and too young, with it, until his gaze fixed on Yeh-Lin again. "At least, not of that kind. But we need to raise some guard against any further attacks by whatever it is the empress has made her ally. Lin."

"Yes. I—will work on that. At once. Shall we find your *rihswera* and Lady Ivah?"

"Best we do, yes."

"Take us in to shore, sisters. The river is safe for now." She felt confident of that, at least. Nothing watched; no attention stroked over her skin, raising warning hairs. Not that its defeat had been any of her doing.

Humbling that.

Perhaps it was good, to remember fear.

But not at the cost of these children. What had she done, taking them to herself?

Ivah's eyes had snapped suddenly to the river, leaving some remark to Prince Dan unfinished. Ahjvar, riding aside, beyond the crowd of the commanders in a solitude no one was going to break, had felt it too, a silent thunderclap, a burst of light he could not see—something flooded the world and Ghu's attention fixed on it with the total focus of a striking falcon. *Felt* it, as if the light, the sound that was neither light nor sound coursed through some invisible channel between him and Ghu.

And then he was shut away, as if a door slammed to between them.

Ahjvar could have drawn a line straight to him nonetheless, ahead on the river, the rafts, late starting, slow in passing the march this day. He had already set Niaul to a gallop, swerving around the herald and banner-bearers who preceded the lords, startling the archers of the vanguard, even before he heard the hooves behind. Ivah's grey Denanbaki, gift of Daro Korat to the god's Grasslander. She wouldn't catch Gorthuerniaul and he didn't wait, though she caught up when he had to rein in, a cat-scramble over scrubby ground, down to the riverbank. The dogs, too, hurtled after him, barking, for what good that would do. He had his crossbow out, spanned and loaded, the moment Niaul was still. Could see the one raft beset, the water dark and churning, rising in storm-waves, something hidden there, flash of sleek greenish-brown, gone again, nothing to aim at. Shark, was his first illogical thought. Wrong colour, wrong water, but that slick hide and the twisting speed in the water—he couldn't see Ghu, only a slender figure shrouded in pale fire, and the creature fell away, was gone. Ghu heaved himself out of the river to the deck, forage-knife in hand. Ghu was the only real and solid thing, a stone, as the rest of the world went thin and blurred as ink on wet paper.

Ivah was swearing in a language he did not know and his skull was splitting with the sort of headache he used to get in the aftermath of the hag's hunting, vision gone half-blind and ragged. Then the world took slowly its proper solidity again. The burning figure of light was gone, become Yeh-Lin, down on her knees engulfed by children, and he had nearly squeezed the trigger.

Ivah knocked his aim down to the stones, snatched the bolt and shook it at him.

"Whatever that thing was, it's done for. What's wrong with you? You could have killed one of the pages. Bloody fool, can you not see?"

"No," Ahjvar said through clenched teeth. "I can't. What in the cold hells was that?"

"I don't know. I don't know what lives in Nabbani rivers. Crocodiles? Horse-whales?"

"Burning."

"What?"

"She was—" She was Dotemon, and *I do not think you would see the difference between us, naked of the body of this earth.* "Was she—did you see her all burning, turned to pale light?"

"No. Ahjvar, do you have seizures? You look—"

"No!" He tried to slow his breathing. Niaul was tossing his head, ears back, catching his—panic, was what it was. He slung the crossbow behind the cantle, quieted the horse, reassuring himself just as much as the stallion. "What in the cold hells is a horse-whale?"

"I don't know. Something in the sea. The Northrons hunt them for ivory and rope, though."

"What?"

"It's what my father said."

"Hunt them for rope?"

"Never mind." She offered him the crossbow bolt back. He rammed it into the quiver as a party of the lords arrived, confused and questioning and noisy. Ivah turned her grey to deal with them, letting him escape down to the water's edge as the raft grounded its nose in the shallows. His vision was clearing, though every step the horse took jarred up his spine as if he'd leapt and misjudged the nearness of the ground.

Ghu was giving Yeh-Lin's two elder pages a hand to leap over to the shore. Yeh-Lin swung the youngest herself.

"Lord Yuro!" she called. "Will you look to my pages? They're unharmed, but I fear rather shaken. Gar Sisu, the danger is past for now but look to your lord—the empress's reach is greater than we realized and the prince may be in danger." The devil went back to the two rafters, standing arms about one another, and spoke to them softly, heads together. A second raft had followed them in. Yeh-Lin leapt over to it, was giving its captain orders. While she waded ashore, a party of a dozen soldiers with crossbows crossed to the first, helping to push it back out to deeper water, climbing aboard as it came to life again.

Someone had died out there. Ahjvar knew that as if he had seen it. Ghu stood at his knee, apart from the flurry of questions, Yeh-Lin's firm seizure of the moment holding all their attention: an attack against herself as the chief wizard of the heir of the gods, the holy one's defence of her, the heroic death of the woman who had captained that raft.

Ghu would fade away and leave them if he could, Ahjvar rather thought, but this was not the moment for their god to drift from their view and Ghu knew it. He leaned against Niaul's shoulder, arms folded, looked up at Ahjvar. The dogs were silent at his feet.

"All right?"

"No," Ahjvar said. Should it not have been he doing the asking? "What was that?"

"Something sent by the devil behind the empress, I think. It wasn't after me."

"Wasn't it?"

Ghu nodded at Yeh-Lin.

"Huh. And she failed to stop it."

"Yes."

He could let his hand rest on the wet hair a moment, reassurance.

"Time to haul her off for a quiet talk?"

"It might be. Bring Ivah."

Ahjvar gathered his reins, turned Niaul as Ghu went to the lords and their officers, reassuring them the danger to the rafts had, for the moment, passed. He caught Ivah's eye, crooked a finger at her. She followed obediently. Some of Yuro's folk were bringing up Snow, saddled and pulling ahead, scenting his master, with Yeh-Lin's cranky piebald and the pages' ponies. Ghu escaped, moving through the folk with an assurance that parted them like blowing leaves, a straight line to Snow, a nod to the young man who turned the bridle loose, and he was up, barefoot, still dripping.

"Y—Lin. Ivah. Ahjvar. Come." And Ghu was shaken, for all his apparent calm. Her name had almost escaped him.

Yeh-Lin bowed. "Children, stay with Lord Yuro and the prince. It's safe now."

Companies of foot had passed on the river road when the lords turned aside. They folded themselves back into the line, with the blue banners and their household warriors about them. Ghu set off inland, crossing a field, furrows crumbled and rounded by the winter's frosts and tangled with weeds, but still uneven going for the horses. A ditch to jump and then a narrow cart-track angling up a low green ridge that had surely been an island in the spring floods.

Deserted now. Stitchwort, pigweed, foxtail grass. Blackened timbers hidden beneath. Village straggling along the lower ground, manor house above? Nothing, now. No sign of any folk having returned to raise a shanty, plant taro and beans, round up straying swine. Zhung Musan's handiwork on his march north.

Clean wind, no scent but bruised green and horse. There was still a stone coping to the well in a hollow of the hillside; Ghu turned there, watching the last companies pass below. He might have only been seeking privacy, and a place they could speak without watching for ambush, but the folk below would see their god watching over them, the black-clad figure and the white horse standing like a blessing, and be reassured against whatever rumour might be passing up and down the line.

"What was that?" Ghu asked.

"I don't know, Nabban. They were creatures made from the memories of the stone of the river."

"Don't play games."

"My lord, I—do you want a name? I do not have one. You know what it was. The devil who serves or is served by the empress is not in Nabban, but he reached, from wherever he is, to strike at me."

"A woman died, Dotemon, and you stood by and watched. You didn't even try to defend her."

"I could not. I could not—her death is my failure, and I am sorry for it. I was overmatched and held, for just that little. I told you, I am . . . restrained. The goddess-tree of the underground river still holds a part of me. If the captain had not attacked the monster herself, it might have taken me in that moment."

"A river monster could have killed you so easily?" Ivah voiced Ahjvar's scepticism.

"Oh, I'm sure I could have survived, and recovered, but taken me into the river, yes, left me wounded and useless to you for a time, yes. And forced me in doing so to reveal myself as something other than a hale old wizard-woman. Which may have been what was intended."

"Why?" Ghu asked, and Ahjvar demanded, "Why not attack Ghu directly? Assassins in Denanbak, on the mountain."

"I don't know. But consider, dead king—" At least she used the Praitannec words and Ivah might think it title or insult or a byname as she chose. "—that it is the empress who sends the assassins. This was *not* the empress. This was not an attack on the convoy or on the army. A single raft's worth of, what, barley and oil? What sort of a target is that? They could expect us to lose so much by mere everyday accident, the hazards of the river. It's a miracle of your young god we have not."

"Why attack you and not Ghu?"

"How should I know? Because our enemy does not believe we are anything other than what he himself is, a power holding a human mask before it."

"He thinks you're his real enemy?" Ivah asked.

"He thinks. Maybe. Am I not? Nabban, what, in the name of the Old Great Gods, do you think you can do against a devil? Against Jasberek or Jochiz or Vartu, what do you think you can possibly do, in the end, god of all Nabban though you may become? Yes," to Ivah, "you deny Vartu is our enemy and I do admit this is not her—her style, but—"

"Not my enemy," Ivah said. "Not Ghu's. She is yours. Yeh-Lin, she's killing the devils. The rest of you. She's hunting you all."

Yeh-Lin's expressive face was masklike in its stillness then.

"The black sword," she said.

What black sword? But there was the chill of deep water in Ahjvar's marrow. It stirred beneath the surface of nightmare, the Lady's mad dreams spilling from her lips. *The sword of the ice is coming is death . . .*

Ghu, unspeaking, reached across the space between them, brushed the back of a hand against his cheek. He blinked and gasped and felt the sunlight again.

"Why?" Yeh-Lin demanded. "And why does An-Chaq's Grasslander daughter know this?"

"I'm also my father's daughter."

The devil considered her a long, cold moment. Ivah just raised her chin, but her horse shifted nervously under her.

"Ahh," Yeh-Lin breathed. "I see. You have his eyes. And his way of knotting your forms into the unexpected when you weave your strings. I should have known you sooner. So Tamghiz Ghatai has had another daughter. Well. We shall see what comes of that, when it comes. Ulfhild Vartu I will face if I must, but she is not here. Her, I have seen, and I think we have an ocean between us now. And I also think that you are correct and that it will not be she we find holding the mask of the empress before her, at however great a distance. So. Nabban. I ask you again, what do you think you can do against a devil, alone and without me?"

"But it's what he thinks that matters, whoever he is," Ghu pointed out. "So that's answered. The empress may believe me her rival and her enemy, and send her assassins because of whatever her wizards see, but the devil holds me of no account and attacks Yeh-Lin. Good."

"Good?"

Ghu shrugged.

"Not good if our devil is going draw the attention of our enemy to us all the way to the Golden City, whoever's will was behind this attack," Ahjvar asked. "How do we prevent him striking again?"

"I was foolish. I thought of the empress as our enemy and whatever she served as too distant to be a threat till we came to her, unlikely to act except in her defence. He will not fix on me again."

"Are you so sure, old woman?"

Yeh-Lin only looked at him. There was fire living in her, white, now, and cold. He could see it for the space of an eye's blink.

"Fine. Ghu?"

"If she says so. But we should do more to be certain we have some

warning, if she is wrong. Ivah, work with Yeh-Lin. We want to know—
what? When we are watched. When something begins to reach for us.
We want these companies on the road and the rafts on the river protected, so much as they may be, from this sort of attack out of nothing,
this shaping of the stuff of the world against us. I can . . . maybe. On the
river, now, I might know sooner what he began."

"Yes," Yeh-Lin said. "I did feel it. Not soon enough. I was not certain
what it was I felt until too late."

"If he does strike at you again and you're warned, can you do anything?" Ahjvar wanted to know. "Or do you just stand by helpless a
second time?"

"That's unfair, dead king. And yes."

Ivah had pulled leather cords from her pockets and was weaving
cat's-cradles, frowning, shaking her tangles free. She might as well have
been muttering, thinking aloud. "Trying to shield against a devil's
attention, when he already knows where we are?"

"He may not," Yeh-Lin said. "We may be—I may be, only glimpses
in the fog." She shrugged. "Difficult to explain, if you do not see as I do."

"So show me," Ivah said. "And guard yourself better in the
meantime."

Ghu's face, watching the devil, seemed less hard now. "Go with
her, Ivah. Go now. Do what can be done, both of you, together. If she's
some bright spark among us to draw a devil's eye, she puts all the folk
in danger."

"And you, Nabban?"

"I—am only the river, Dotemon. Do you see me, when you look?"

"Not always."

"And you know where to look and what I am."

"The assassins have found you twice."

"Yes. And you weren't much help on either occasion. No, sorry. I
didn't mean that. You saved Shui from the poison. I don't expect you to
guard me, Yeh-Lin. Leave my *rihswera* to do that and look to yourself,
so that you don't draw the lightning down on the march again. Go on
ahead. We'll follow."

"My lord." No argument, and no snide remarks about the god wandering off alone with his dead king.

They watched as the women rode away, down to find themselves in the dust of the rearguard.

"You want to stay here, catch up tomorrow?" Ahjvar did. He felt as though the world had gone quiet, clean; as if he could breathe again, and it was not the absence of the noise or the smell or the dust, but of the people, that freed him.

"Yes. But better not. Better I'm seen in the camp tonight. Yeh-Lin would say so."

"Don't let her decide what you should do."

"It's common sense, Ahj. My folk, here because of me. I need to wander the fires, to be seen."

"Is that what you were doing out on the rafts?"

"I suppose."

"And that was so very safe."

"Hah. You. Come here." Ghu reached over to embrace him one-armed, cold and damp and smelling of the river, horses jostling together. Pulled his head down to kiss his forehead. "I'm all right. I am."

"Ghu?" His head still ached. Something he wanted said, because around all the fires tonight they would be saying it with awe but also with acceptance, because the holy one was their god and of course he had killed a dragon for them. It wasn't awe Ahjvar felt. What? Pride? Something that made him want to laugh. His starveling stray cat, his half-wit boy. "You killed a damned *dragon*. With a forage-knife."

"Didn't have anything else," Ghu said, with that slow smile that was like the warmth of a hearth in the night.

"I shouldn't let you out of my sight."

"Those weren't really dragons, anyway. Did you see? Something the devil made. Memory. Ancient, older than the river. Older than men." He considered. "The dragons of the river—are mine."

"What dragons?"

Ghu looked over, gathering his reins as the dogs plunged ahead down the hillside away from the river, barking at nothing more exciting than a hare. "I don't know. Maybe they're long gone. Maybe they never were. But I dreamed a dragon once, when I was small. I dreamed dragons again last night, Ahj. I think we may see dragons again, before we're done." He set a course after the dogs. "Let's see what's inland. Don't need to catch up till evening."

Did they not?

Good.

The empress had given herself to a devil. No, there was a devil in the north, who set up a slave as a false god to deceive the folk. A necromancer led an army over the provinces of the north, leaving villages burned and empty behind her, and the holy empress, clothed in the radiance of the Old Great Gods, marched to oppose her. The Mother and Father were reborn in a champion who would end the tyranny of the Min-Jan and throw down the Peony Throne, and all the slaves of the land would be free.

These were now the whispers that flowed south to meet them, here in Numiya Province. Somewhere, the empress's army prepared to move—she was in the Old Capital, she marched through Solan, she was in Kozing Port and sent her generals of the northern provinces to encircle Choa, who could say? Rumour at least was certain as rumour could be that to the north the rebels of Prince Dan and the holy one of the gods—the devil's puppet, the necromancer's toy, the false god who was only another rebelling slave—held Choa and maybe even Alwu and to the west Shihpan as well.

Nearly all the length of the empire crossed, night-travel, in haste and secrecy, hidden under wizardry Rat said was something else, a blessing of the goddess of the Little Sister, who had given herself up to become part of Mother Nabban, to fight Yeh-Lin long ago. A Nabbani goddess, yes, but the Little Sister was Lathan too, Rat claimed, and some echo of what she had been blessed them. The few men and women with whom they dared speak, being without papers, were mostly outliers of the villages—the poorest, the outcast, the least likely to hear reliable news. They had found secret dwellings of priests, more than once, but their news was no more certain. The holy one was in the north—was that not enough? As warriors travelling to the service of the heir of the gods in the battle to come, Kaeo and Rat went on their way from such folk with a blessing, if no other aid, poor as such priestly fugitives were.

Rat might be touched by holiness, but Kaeo no longer dreamed visions, not since the night of the typhoon. It was as if all the prophecy had drained out him as he lent his voice to Rat's—to Anlau's prayers and her magic that had built some little protection against the storm. Had the dreams of the gods left him, or had he walked away from them? He no longer wanted to find Prince Dan, to lay his sword at his feet. The sword of a free man. The freedom of all the folk might have been Prince Dan's desire, but it was the Wild Girl of Darru and Lathi who had freed Kaeo and given him that sword. He no longer even wanted to lay it at the feet of the god, who should be his god, the holy one, the heir of Nabban. Not that he doubted the god's holiness or his cause. Not that he regretted his service to Prince Dan, either. It was only that he gave himself elsewhere.

But he did not know if that was something a god of the land would understand. Nabbani birth and blood and bone, the land was in him; Kaeo was of the land. How could he face the god whose prophet he had been, to say, *I've given myself to a priestess of Darru and Lathi and through her to her gods of the jungles and mountains and the river she says is hers as much as yours—I cannot serve you?*

Rat stirred, warm against his side in their hollow nest. Sunlight had finally found them beneath the canopy of young leaves, coppery sunset striking low through a gap in the greenery. Another night's journey.

"Soon," she said.

"Soon, what?"

"Soon we eat."

They had only a handful left of the roasted sedge tubers, grubbed out of a forest pond and softened in the ashes of their cautious little fire as the sun rose. It was going to be a long and hungry march this night, and that Rat could nuzzle at his ear, a cold hand warming itself inside his shirt, and ignore a gnawing belly made him feel . . . most thoroughly desired, and rather less weary than he knew he was.

"Not that we have much to eat," she said, voicing at least the more practical of his thoughts. "I'll hunt when dawn comes, find us a lizard, at least. No, I meant, soon, we'll find him."

"The god."

"Yes."

"Oh." He folded arms around her, held her close and gave up what he had begun, which was undoing the ties of her shirt.

She lay over him, cupped his face in her hands, kissed him. They made a long moment of it, but the time for lovemaking was past, or had slipped away with the growing dark. Miles before them, and the nights grew shorter, the roads, even these byways between villages, more dangerous. They had spotted scouts in imperial colours only the previous evening, heading to a manor house they were circling at a wary distance. There had come a heavy smell of smoke in the night, after that. They had not gone back to look.

"And then?" he asked.

"Then," she said. Her smile was lost in the gathering dark. If it was a smile, and not a grimace. "Kaeo, I don't know. I only follow, now, where I am led. Or go where I am moved to go, and what our two swords may do . . . but if we do not win the god of Nabban to be a friend to Darru and Lathi, and not another conqueror, then we will have war, still, and no peace in the south, and how many more generations can live so, before all our very souls are born crippled in our hate?"

To that he had no answer.

It did not take long to eat their sparse meal and gather up their small bundles. They passed from the forest eaves to the rutted cart-track beneath a clear sky and a full moon rising bright and silver. If he were a poet and not a mere singer of the songs of others, he might make it a portent of hope, of new light in the world.

But it could as well be said it was a very cold and distant light. A poet was not a prophet and could make of a sign what he would. There was a chill in the air that night, a wind from the north.

CHAPTER XXXII

The pace of the river quickened with the passing days as it narrowed and deepened and the land about became more rocky. It demanded all the skill of the rafters, but also carried them more swiftly, so that they often reached the next flag-marked camping site with much of the day to spare, and twice overshot it altogether, causing acrimony and weary marches into the evening for the footsoldiers.

The moon had been new when they left Dernang; now it rose in the deep night and stood high in the morning sky, diminishing dawn by dawn. It had been three days since anyone had sighted the occasional scouts that shadowed them on the eastern shore, sent out from Dwei Ontari's cavalry, moving south through Alwu. Gar Sisu, travelling with the rafts, had been set to divine for the Dwei lord. They had, however, made contact with couriers from another of Prince Dan's lieutenants, a Lady Dwei Liu, who had moved to secure the crossings of the Shihpan River against possible imperial movements north, as bidden, and sent her imperial cousin promises of her continued support—and proclamation throughout Shihpan of the falsity of the empress's claim to godhead and the coming of the heir of the gods.

Ghu still went to the rafts every few days. Ahjvar followed, now, though it was hard to endure. Too small a space, no way to escape the nearness of other people, and on another level of irritation entirely, the chopping of the raft through the water made him feel vaguely sick, though it was nowhere near as bad as being on the open sea, crossing the Gulf of Taren on a ship, which he had done once, and once only.

By night, there were fogs over the camp, and the breath of them lingered through the day, even under blue skies. That, at least, was Ghu, and not wizardry, and Ahjvar did not think it was the fog itself that shrouded them. The fog was only what he might shape as walnut, yew, rowan—secrets and shadowy illusion and protection interwoven, drawn softly over them and nightly renewed.

He and Ghu were both ashore and among the rearmost company the evening that a pair of exhausted scouts returned from a cast far ahead, horses hard-ridden and failing. They were two day's march from the ferry at their current pace. To the south, steep hills rose harsh against the sky. Somewhere there the Wild Sister earned her name, plunging through a gorge that, so legend told, had been torn through the hills by the birth-throes of a dragon, draining the great lake that had drowned the land. The same dragon who had been tamed and broken to obedience by the goddess of the river long before she ever was lost into the Mother. The same whose bones had been the first foundation laid for the castle of the White River Dragon after death in some battle against . . . no one remembered what. An ancient darkness of the dawn of the world. Usually conflated with the seven devils, but the tales had been ancient when Yeh-Lin was a girl, she said. And another story said it was the Wild Sister herself who was the dragon.

It was Ivah came back down the line to find Ghu.

"Captain Lin needs you," she said briefly. "Will you come, holy one?"

"What?" Ahjvar demanded, as they swung away to bypass the road. Not immediate threat; she carried her own bow cased. Half the march was already spread into the camp. A good time for an attack, but there was no alarm ahead.

"Imperial forces have both ferry landings."

"Dwei Ontari?"

"They found a wounded man who'd gotten over the river, stole a fowler's skin boat after he escaped an imperial patrol. He was one of Ontari's scouts. He said Lord Ontari must have had enough warning the road was held there, because he never came to the ferry. Yeh-Lin's trying to see."

"A raid, an army?" Ahjvar demanded. "Or treachery? How secure is Alwu?"

Some old woman of the Dwei Clan was the Kho'anzi, if he remembered correctly, but she had ceded authority, in most practical matters, to Lord Ontari in Prince Dan's name. She had sons and adult grandchildren, though, and their commitment to the past winter's failed revolt . . . He wouldn't rely on it, whatever faith Dan might have. The young had more to lose in a lost cause, and Dan and Daro Korat must certainly look like that, outside the reach of those who saw and recognized their god. He didn't understand faith anyway, mistrusted it in Dan, in Ivah, in Daro Korat. It baffled him. His trust in Ghu was something entirely other. Had to be. Grown over years. Part of himself.

"Dan says this will be some raid up from Numiya, either Lai Clan loyal to the Kho'anzi of Numiya or imperial conscripts under the high lord's officers. The border's very close."

"I want to know where Dwei Ontari is."

"Yeh-Lin said you would." Ivah's voice didn't give away her own opinion. "She's searching. We don't know anything. I don't, anyway. She sent me for Ghu before she had asked many questions. She told Lord Ontari's scout the holy one would hear his report."

Numbers, Ahjvar wanted to know. And what they were, horse or foot, archers. What they had on the water, what kind of defences they had taken or raised, how long they had had to prepare . . .

"Scouts," he said. "Patrols down the river."

"She's doing that, yes." Ivah didn't quite roll her eyes, but her careful mouth tucked up a smile. "I thought you claimed to be an assassin, not a captain."

He shrugged. Realized how very little he liked having Ghu—and himself, but his impulse for himself would be to simply ride away—engulfed in this herd. Not comfortable and not safe, not a safety he could take on himself to ensure, no matter what scouts and patrols were out about them to watch the land.

What simple tents they had were going up, the first companies in already at their cookfires, as Ahjvar and Ghu followed Ivah's grey up the central laneway of the camp. The weeds were already trampled into earth. Yeh-Lin, Prince Dan, Yuro, a handful of lords and officers, waited at one fire, folk of Yuro's following—mostly former stable-hands with no official title—and Lady Ti-So'aro's were scattered out, marking out a private space more effectively than any tent could.

The alleged scout of Dwei Ontari's forces was hunched by the fire, an arm swathed in clean bandages, a cup in his other hand. A boy, not a man, and his cheek torn and black with bruising, too, as if he had rolled down rocks.

They rode right to the fire. Yuro rose to take Snow's bridle, give Ghu a nod that was a lord's hasty and respectful greeting, not in any way self-conscious. A couple of his girls darted in to lead the horses off.

The scout was looking up at them doubtfully, but when Yeh-Lin flowed to her feet to make a graceful bow, he staggered up and did his best. Ghu caught him, hand under his arm, as he stumbled. The boy was shivering and his face, where it was not bruised, was the colour of greasy clay. Whatever those bandages hid was ugly.

"Sit, Gar Oro." Ghu helped him down, settled on his heels before him. "You're safe here. Lady Lin's had someone tend you?"

"I saw to him myself," Yeh-Lin said. "He won't lose the arm after all, but we should tuck him up by a nice warm fire so soon as he's told all he knows."

"Is he truly Ontari's man?" was what Ahjvar wanted to know.

"Oh yes, and if there is any betrayal in Ontari's vanishing, he knows nothing of it. He risked much to come so far up the river and cross in search of the prince and the holy one, believing it was what his lord would have wished and having no way of knowing if any other message might have been sent. The village just below us, where he stole the boat, is Dwei and its banner-lady had joined Dwei Ontari as he passed, but the boy didn't want to risk discovering its overseer had decided otherwise. We'll put a half-company of Dan's men over by raft in the morning, to make sure it remembers where its loyalties lie. They may even know where Ontari will have gone. Don't loom over him like that, dead king. Even if he is Wind in the Reeds, he would fall over before his knife could touch your horseboy. Gar Oro," she addressed the scout in Nabbani again, "now that the holy one is come, tell us all."

Gar Oro drained the last of whatever they had given him, set the cup carefully aside. His report was delivered with equal care. He had witnessed the imperial forces crossing the Wild Sister to the western ferry landing, seen the dozen Dwei retainers who manned the ferry and the courier post on the eastern shore beheaded, their bodies, and those of two imperial couriers as well, thrown into the river. The couriers were by tradition held to be neutral and untouchable, because even in civil war, lords must speak with lords. Had this been murder or had they defended the post against the forces from Numiya rather than standing aside? Gar Oro did not know.

There was only the one ferry, held against the push of the current by chains cast in bronze and wizardry, and in the time that he observed only a single company of footsoldiers and crossbowmen were assembled on the western shore, where they began to erect a palisade across the road, as if they would enclose and fortify all the landing. There was the ruin of an old watchtower on the steep and barren outcroppings of rock that began to rise as the river dropped. A jagged, broken land began there, much of it unclimbable except perhaps for goats, but they seemed to be trying to make the tower secure. An outpost for archers over the road. But on the east there were the banners of the empress and the high lord of the Lai, and he had counted two hundred banner-lords and perhaps two thousand men, imperial soldiers and Lai retainers of the banner-lords. Their camp was set with its back against the broken hills, with the river where its white waters began to guard their left. There was a ditch and palisade going up, enclosing road and the little village of a dozen huts that served the ferry post. The fortified house had been taken for the commander, who was, the scout thought, a lord of the Lai.

They had horse, yes, he said, in answer to Ivah, but only one company, the lord general's escort. Numiya was not a province of pastures, Yeh-Lin observed, but of ploughlands. It did not breed riders.

Yeh-Lin asked what little more needed asking—what the scout could guess of the manner of their patrols, if there were wizards of the imperial corps among the Lai lord's officers, what other vessels they might have access to besides the ferry. Patrols were mostly on foot, with a few mounted, he thought, and there was at least one blue robe that he had seen in attendance on the Lai lord, before he himself was seen and hunted and lost them in the night and the riverside scrub. There were canoes and a few fishing boats in the ferry village, a few skin boats, nothing of any size. They could still have carried more men over to the west, yes. Many more, but the area they had been enclosing there was small.

"They won't abandon the east," Yuro said. "They'd risk cutting themselves off from Numiya. They only want to secure the western landing. Probably the idea is take southern Alwu for the empress, annex it for the Kho'anzi of Numiya, force any movement out of Choa to go down the highway and over the Shihpan, through Vanai and Jina."

He might be illiterate, but Ahjvar had seen him with Daro Korat and Daro Raku, and a table spread with the sort of maps Yeh-Lin claimed were forbidden to leave the imperial library but in the possession of a wizard assigned to an imperial general—not an artist's story but the land as a bird or visionary with a mirror might see and measure it.

"We have the numbers," Dan said.

"On the wrong shore," said Lord Zhung Ario.

Ghu, who had been silent, only nodding now and then and making some encouraging noise to the weary Gar Oro, looked down to the river.

"My river," he said. "There is no wrong shore. Someone find Gar Oro a place to eat and sleep, if Lady Lin has done all that's needed for his wounds. Lin—ask your pages to round up the raft-captains. Yuro, Ti-So'aro, Ario, Dan—we'll want the captains of the companies. The cavalry and the archers. Ivah—horse-archers?"

"We have some. Most were with Dwei Ontari, though. Men and women of Alwu."

"Two days' march yet to the ferry, Yuro thinks."

"If we go on as we have, holy one," Yuro said. "But we could move faster."

And show up with weary soldiers who would still, once they had dealt with whatever enemy forces were on the western shore, need to be ferried over the river, and could they use rafts for that, there where the current strengthened above the reportedly unnavigable gorge? The enemy could pick them off as they landed.

"Wait," Ghu said. "Wait for the captains."

And when the captains came to sit around the fire with those who thought themselves the great folk, he laid out what they would do. Ahjvar stood behind, watching them all, the faces attentive, solemn—delighted, a few. Doubting, some.

"You can't," Yeh-Lin said, and switched to Praitannec. "You're not thinking of the weight of the water, the push of it, Nabban. You don't understand the strength of the river. Even iron bends under the force of water . . ."

Her voice trailed to silence.

"My river," Ghu said quietly. "Don't tell me its strength. Ivah will look to the ropes."

Ivah's eyebrows went up, but she only nodded.

"Tomorrow," Ghu said. "Eat, rest. Tell the people. Tomorrow's will be a long march, and then we'll begin."

The stone steps are high, and she climbs them alone to the summit. Red pillars support a soaring roof high above, and the eaves are gilded, bright in the sun. She turns, slow in her heavy robes, brocade of crimson and gold over layers of silk that trail a train. Her golden headdress is rayed like the moon, like the crown of Mother Nabban, and set with pearls rose and white and gold. She rests her hands on the hilt of the sabre in her sash and watches them all so far below, the lords and the ladies, the nobles of the land assembled in the great plaza. The priests, too, in their robes white and brown, the priests of the empress, the warlord and wizard who has brought peace to the wounded land.

They go to their knees, the folk, and bow their faces to the stone.

A cold wind stings tears from her eyes. She shuts them. Cold wind, chill heart.

Don't leave yourself hollow, a devil says in memory.

Wind rises. She opens her eyes, raises her chin, grips the sabre's hilt. The wind strengthens, blowing like a storm off the mountains. Robes become banners, rags, streams of snow snaking over the paving stones below, around, over the hunched bodies, which are no more than the undulations of the land, and the waves of the grass, lying near-flat in the wind, and she stands on a hill, one of the old mounds, grave of a forgotten hero. The roof is gone to churning grey cloud, the pillars are leaning stone, minimally shaped; faint lines still trace broad-antlered deer, aurochsen, bear. She staggers against the wind, bare-headed, flings her arms wide, flourishing her sabre, her sheepskin coat flaring like wings, as if she would turn to a hawk and fly.

No! she shouts, and she stumbles to the grey rock, the low one, not old hero-stone but a heart and warm and she crouches, sets her back to it, watching, seeking her enemy.

Show yourself! she calls. Let me see you, and I'll deny you to your face. Stay out of my dreams.

Empress, he says. Your own dreams, not mine. You know what you are. Daughter. Chosen. Worthy to be mine.

Ivah muttered in her sleep, in the tent she shared with the banner-lady Ti-So'aro and four warriors of her retinue, and rolled over, half-waking. It was the uncertainty of what might come disturbed her unremembered dreams. She did not sleep well, these nights on the river road. Who could?

Ahjvar had grown used to sleeping while Ghu sat wakeful by the water, used to hard ground under him, dew and the river's fogs dampening his clothes and curling his hair, a chill that once would have set old broken bones to aching but never seemed to bother him anymore. He wished Ghu wouldn't sit up, because it left him vague and distant, less human, for too long the next day, but maybe it was something he needed, as a snake needed to bask in the sun. He never seemed tired as a man should be after such a vigil. He sat, and Ahjvar slept, and he might wake with Ghu lying open-eyed alongside him, or sitting where he had been like some outcropping of the stone, misted pale like a spider's web. It wasn't yet dawn when a touch on his face woke him that night. The moon was past its height, hazed with fog that rose and wavered, filling all the broad valley like a tide.

"We need a boat," Ghu said, crouching over him.

Ahjvar groaned, tried to bury his head in his arm. He hadn't been dreaming. Sweet dark depths of dreamless sleep, and he wanted to crawl back there.

"Hey."

He lipped the hand that burrowed in between face and elbow, then bit it, not terribly hard.

"Idiot." Ghu rolled him over. "Boat?"

"Don't have one. Go steal a raft. A change from horses."

"Wake up, you."

He considered trying to pull Ghu down on top of him, decided against it and pulled himself up instead, hands on his shoulders. Sat wrapped around him. That proved distracting to Ghu, at least for a few moments. Mouth on his neck, his ear, mouth lingering on mouth. But this was hardly any private place.

"Why a boat?" he asked, and disentangled himself to walk the two steps to the shore, wake himself properly with cold water.

"I want to look at the river."

He didn't have to speak his sarcasm, crouched and splashing river water on his face.

"The other shore. Have you ever handled a skin boat?"

"No."

"Like a canoe, but crankier."

"Nor a canoe. I can row, you know."

"Not a boat for rowing. Probably you should just sit still."

"That, I can do. But are we leaving the dogs behind?" The dogs were there, ears alert, the roots of their curled tails wagging in that gentle, questioning way that meant, *us too?*

"The dogs will wait over here." Ghu rubbed both wolfish heads, light and dark. "I don't quite trust you two not to go off looking for excitement."

Two tails slowly uncoiled to the straight and then drooped.

"Go find Ivah," he said, which seemed to cheer them. "I'll want her, and the horses." Tails rose and they trotted off. Ivah, wherever she slept, was about to get a cold nose in the ear. Or two.

Ahjvar swept up sword and crossbow, trailed after Ghu upriver, to where the fogs smelt of smoke and horse and humanity and the rafts were grounded in the shallows or moored to those that were. A few of them carried lighter vessels, property of the rafters, double-ended bark-skinned things that rode the water like gulls, but it was the boat the scout had brought over that Ghu sought, and found as if he had, like the dogs, nosed it out, hauled up on one of the rafts. A watchman came walking down across the decks, swaying gently with the river's motion.

"Holy one." He acknowledged them without question and gave Ghu a hand unlashing the boat and sliding it into the water, but seemed to consider Ahjvar doubtfully, as an awkward piece of baggage better left ashore.

Not so doubtfully as Ahjvar studied the boat, though. It sat far too lightly on the water for his liking, a framework of woven bamboo covered in hide, wider than the bark canoes, but not so long.

"Up towards the bow," Ghu said helpfully. "Stay low."

No thwarts, only a couple of bracing crosspieces, and short paddles shoved in beneath those. He didn't plummet through the bottom, which he half expected. It was lined with split bamboo and doubtless tanned bullhide fit to cover a shield in. The boat shifted and bobbled as Ghu stepped in behind him, kneeling up on one knee, not sitting to row like the coastal boats of Gold Harbour. The thing spun and shot away, caught in the current in a few quick strokes. Ghu chuckled with what sounded like delight. Ahjvar just kept still. Balance, no different from a horse. Very different from a horse, and like no boat he'd ever used before. Not that he did so except in desperation.

"Want me to take a hand?"

"Just keep an eye out ahead."

There was a greyness to the east, and the half-moon towards the west making the fog pearly. On the water, they moved in a muffling cloud of night. By the time he saw anything, they'd be on top of it. They seemed to scud like bubbles kicked along by the wind. As if the river breathed and they rode the flutter of its pulse.

Ghu was taking them downriver, not across, and keeping in the strongest flow of the current, too, he judged. They passed the village on the east; smell of pigs and cattle and lingering smokiness. Ahjvar settled back, warily, and the boat did not tip or dive. Relaxed, a little. Oddly, he wasn't feeling the motion as much as he did on the rafts. The night faded and the fog turned to white banners around them, glowing with captive dawn.

Daylight. He found it hard to judge their speed, but they passed a point where Ghu said, "That's where we would have camped, but they'll have to march on." Their marches so far had been short, though. No great hardship.

He began to wonder if Ghu planned to take them all the way to the ferry. If they got into the current sweeping to the gorge, there would be no turning back. And it was broad daylight; eluding the sight of a distant and possibly dreaming devil would not be to elude keen-eyed watchers on the shore, or their arrows.

An island divided the river ahead, low and marshy, overgrown with tall willow, thick beneath with tangled scrub and some pink-flowering weed clambering through everything. The scent carried on the wind, sweet and harsh in one. The broad, twiggy nests of herons filled some half-dead trees at the gravelly point that faced them like the prow of a ship.

The skin boat swirled sideways and held place, suddenly out of the current. Turned to face the western shore. Tangled, marshy woodland there, too. Ghu turned the boat again. The east, though, was flat water-meadow and more of the steep, forested little hills beyond. No herds grazed, no village smoke rose, but still, at some point in the year it must see use, or it would be gone to scrub as well. Perhaps the interval-land was pasture of the ferry village.

"Here," he said.

"The swamp will be a problem."

"Might not be so wet as it looks."

"Is that the river knowing, or just hope?"

"Where are we without hope?"

"In a swamp with our feet wet."

"Yeh-Lin is right about the strength of the river. The island will help."

"Did you know it was here?"

"I'm not sure."

"Ghu . . ."

"Well, I'm not. Sometimes I know, sometimes I don't. Sometimes . . . I don't know if I know, Ahj. I see things . . . Let's look."

The woodland continued the length of the island, and half a mile back upriver. Impossible to see from the surface of the water how far inland it ran. Ahjvar caught an overhanging bough as Ghu brought the boat nosing in under the trees. No stony ledges here, but mud and roots and winter-broken boles of some tall bush rising from the water like spears, but they managed not to hole the boat as they snugged it in deep under the branches, probably impossible to see even from the island, and tied it there. Getting out involved crawling like a squirrel through a random jumble of branches and boles and discovering the ground to be fern-hummocks with water between. Ahjvar hoisted himself up onto a branch of the big willow that brooded over all the snarl like a hen on her chickens. Ghu came up after him, more gracefully, less encumbered with weapons. Also shorter and thinner, which made a difference when it came to weaving oneself through branches.

"We can't march them through this, unless you want to take the time to lay a log-road."

"Wouldn't take long if this wetland's narrow."

Whatever kind of willow this was, it flung up multiple leaning trunks, reached out branches near-horizontally, seeking light. They made it across two trees before they had to take to the ground again and there it was drier, less tangled. Ghu took the lead, keeping his back to the river. Ahjvar followed, watching the wider field of view while Ghu dealt with finding the immediate path, slipping around bushes, under the snagging pink-flowered whatever-it-was. When Ahjvar seized his shoulder, he froze. Ahjvar moved in close, pointed, but Ghu was already looking where he wanted him to, sliding aside, reaching behind for the hilt of his forage-knife.

Ahjvar kept his hands free. Certainly no place for a sword or the crossbow. For all their care, they were leaving a clear trail behind them, and something else had as well, angling up their way from further downstream, heading, like them, for the higher ground, but with less certainty. Too broad a path for any smaller woodland animals and this was no country for bear or boar. Not broken enough for cattle or buffalo, no sharp-pointed hoofprints in the mud, either. Not the old track of some hunter; the crushed plants were still green. Someone else had come from the river and was trying to strike through. Come up the river? Nobody had passed them in the night, that was certain. If whoever it was had gone down the western channel, odds were they'd have found a canoe or some such vessel hidden like their own.

Ghu gave way to him and they made a slow and near-soundless progress. A muddy puddle in the deep shade of a tree gave them the footprints of two people wearing soft shoes, not horseman's boots, but they'd come by water, of course.

He doubted any fisher or hunter of the village would wear anything better than sandals, if that, for this season.

The light brightened, trees thinning; the ground, though not rising enough to be noticeable to the foot, was drier. The undergrowth thickened with the strengthening of the light. Coming to the edge of the woods. Narrow enough that they could slash a way through and lay the trunks and brush to make a roadbed in hardly the time it would take to bring up a company or two. Better if the empress's forces weren't warned they were coming, of course.

Knife in his hand now, moving very slowly, watching all ways. And up. Up was where a man lay along the broad, sloping branch of one of those willows. Watching up the river road with the patience of the hunter. No weapon ready, though, no bow or crossbow. The other, another man . . . sitting at ease beneath the tree, leaning on it. Ahjvar couldn't see his face, only one shoulder, the outstretched legs, crossed at the ankle. Rough sandals. The shoes . . . had been replaced. The feet were clean, too clean for anyone who had walked that path in sandals. Their clothes were hempen trousers and smocks, shabby. They could have been any of Prince Dan's rebels.

Waiting for the army. They might have been scouts sent to count Ghu's army, judge its pace, if the Lai commander had some warning of their coming, which he might very well have. Gar Oro might not be the only one of Ontari's scouts to have had too close an encounter with the enemy, and another might not have been lucky enough to escape them. But scouts would not come prepared to join the march and pass as followers of the holy one, and how the Wind in the Reeds knew where to lie in wait . . . with all their careful shielding of their march and the river from wizardrous watching. But perhaps what Ghu could summon, the shadowing essence of the river, was not enough against the empress's devil. Or perhaps it was simpler than that, rumour travelling down the eastern shore.

He wanted one alive. Not even a whisper, though. Slid his knife away again, touched Ghu's hand, pointed to the man on the ground. Ghu nodded. Deep breath, running the tree in his mind, branch, handholds, feet, knees. Surged up it, a foot against the angled trunk, sideways to a branch, another, seizing the man's far arm, flipping him, flinging him— the man twisted, falling, so that he landed crouched on his feet, but Ahjvar kicked him as he rose, knocked his head back, not hard enough to kill—he hoped—followed in as he fell. The man rolled and staggered up, unsteady as a drunk, fumbled a knife. It slipped from his fingers and Ahjvar kicked him down again. He struggled weakly, tangled in the whippy branches of a bush. Ahjvar dragged him out, dropped him facedown in the trampled mud and green, cut his rope belt and used it to lash his arms behind his back. Took the time to tie his ankles, too, since all was quiet beyond the tree. He rolled the man to his back. The eyes wandered a bit and he panted, but he didn't seem likely to die in the next little while. Went around the tree to find Ghu crouched by a body. Bloody mess, literally. The forage-knife was not a weapon for neatness and Ghu must have been face-to-face with the man when he slashed his neck half through. Ahjvar prodded the narrow-bladed knife dropped in the old leaf-mould. That, and a short sword. Neither showing any staining or oiliness to the blade. Well, you wouldn't poison a weapon you might have to carry around with you a day or more yet. The sword's point was bloody, and not with spatters.

"All right?"

Ghu shrugged. "He came up at me like a shark. So fast. I didn't mean to kill him."

Ahjvar hooked a finger through a tear in the breast of Ghu's coat, four fingers broad, and hot and wet beneath. He didn't think that was the assassin's blood, though Ghu wore a mask of it. The man must have heard something, probably Ahjvar's rush up the tree, and been rising into his own attacker. Hadn't meant to kill him but hadn't had time to think through any other choice, Ahjvar judged. His fingers were busy with the knotwork buttons of the coat, ears strained for any sound, but there were only the birds of the morning singing, now that the scuffle was over. What had he taught the boy? To defend himself without hesitation for thought. Ghu batted him away.

"He didn't touch me."

"Yes, he did."

The proof was in his slashed shirt beneath the coat, but yes, the main force of the blow had been struck aside. There was a cut running along the ribs, ugly and bleeding more than he wanted to see, welling up and streaming down, but not the deep thrust that would have, and Great Gods Ahjvar felt sick, likely killed him.

They should have backed off. He could have shot the one in the tree and gone after the other himself.

"Doesn't hurt."

"It will. Now who needs sewing up?"

But a pad of torn shirt and the rest of the shirt as bandage around the chest to hold it was going to have to do.

"Tattoo," Ghu said. He hooked his left hand through the sash of the coat to keep his arm steady, with his right, cleaned his knife methodically. "And his soul—I lost it. He was terrified. I don't know what he saw, but as he died he was suddenly terrified. Of me, of dying, of something else, I don't know, but I tried to hold him, Ahj; I'd killed him and for a moment he clung on to me, to the road through me, but he was torn away. I—didn't dare follow. There was—light. White, but murky. Darkness. Like water. A weight. I don't know."

Ahjvar would take Ghu's word for the tattoo. Wind in the Reeds, though. Ghu's knife had snagged and ripped the fine chain of the man's badge.

"Sit," he ordered, but Ghu was already sitting. The blood on his face was drying and cracking. Never an obedient servant, he grabbed Ahjvar's arm and pulled himself up, stood, head low, finding his balance. He was too pale around the eyes, but he let Ahjvar move his supporting hand to the tree instead, turned loose from that after a few breaths to follow to their prisoner, who had gathered his wits enough to be trying to scrape the ropes loose. Ahjvar put a foot on his chest.

"Wind in the Reeds," he said. "Any more of you?"

The man just glowered, but his eyes kept sliding to Ghu, bare-chested and bathed in blood. Ahjvar sat down, picking up a broken willow switch. Eyes back to him, following the knife that began peeling off strips of bark. "Be good and answer, or I'll let him have you."

Ghu's lips tightened. He didn't find that funny.

"Maybe," the man said. Ahjvar stood the knife in the earth at his side and twisted bark strips, knotted them. Cornel cherry. *Truth.* Dropped the sign on the man's chest. He flinched, expecting who knew what. Maybe the knife. Ghu had turned to watch the other way. Nothing moved.

"Others. Anyone at all."

"No," the man spat. "Not on this side of the river. Damned devil-deluded barbarian—"

He didn't hit him, just poked him with his toe.

Ghu turned back, leaning over Ahjvar's shoulder.

"Your empress," he said, "is the one devil-led."

"The Exalted is the chosen daughter of the Old Great Gods."

"They were alone," Ahjvar said. "Leave him to me. Go wash your face. Don't fall in."

He thought Ghu might warn him off, but he only nodded, faded away, shadow into shadow. Ahjvar could hear nothing of his passage.

"You were sent to join the holy one's followers, that much is obvious. Where did you come from?"

"Kozing Port." The man sneered.

"Did I ask where you were born?" He would really want to hurt him if he kept that up. Started weaving another character, a triad, cornel interwoven with blackthorn for *strength*, walnut for *secrets*. Laid it, more carefully, over the man's heart.

"Did you come from the Lai, from Numiya?"

The man licked his lips. "Over the river."

He did hit him. "Who sent you?"

"Lai Sula. Mulgo Miar."

"Who? The Pine Lord?"

"Him. Yes."

"He takes Buri-Nai's orders?"

Treachery, double treachery. Mulgo Miar had fled to Dan's service the previous autumn. Mulgo Miar was supposed to be in Alwu, awaiting Lord Ontari's return. Should be with Dwei Ontari now.

"He obeys the will of the Old Great Gods. The Daughter of the Gods speaks to him in his dreams."

"So what's their will? You were sent to do what your captain—tall woman, scars of the pox on her face—failed to do?"

"No."

"What, then? The holy one," Ahjvar said, when there was no answer, "won't have me hurt you, but you'd rather speak the truth anyway, wouldn't you?"

"*Him?*"

"Yes."

Silence. Cold consideration of his options. Unlike the woman Meli, the assassin rejected the temptation to offer himself to them, in any capacity. He abruptly bunched himself and tried to kick. Ahjvar hit him again for that. His face was swelling from the first blow that had sent him down.

"Your empress lies. She lies when she says the Old Great Gods speak to her. She lies when she claims godhead. She's the tool of a devil, or the master of one. Tell me, are you tattooed for her? Foreign script like thorns, over your heart. Something stole your comrade's soul as he died, you know. Something takes you all, every one marked with the empress's tattoo."

"You lie. And the Old Great Gods are the guardians of our souls. If the Daughter of the Gods needs mine, it's hers."

"So you weren't sent to kill the holy one. What, then?"

The spell still pushed against the man, urging confession.

"To capture him. He's only a man, not even a wizard. Nothing but a runaway slave to beat to obedience, once we get him away from the wizard. And his Northron guardian, the wizard's slave. You. You won't die, she said. A necromancer's slave. Cut off his hands but don't think him harmless even then. Bring him bound in chains."

"I'm not—Northron." Don't get sidetracked. "What does she want with us?" No point telling the man he and his partner would have been doomed even if they had succeeded in their abduction, or that their empress—or her master—had likely already written them off for dead. Something knew Yeh-Lin now, even if it hadn't when these men were sent out.

"The Exalted doesn't need to explain herself to me. Her wisdom sees what I can't understand. She does as the Old Great Gods desire."

"Or the devil ruling her changed his mind. Why?"

A man hearing blasphemy. The rage as he flung himself at Ahjvar despite his bonds was that of a maddened animal. And that was what blind faith gave birth to.

Love, too, Ahjvar supposed. He knocked the man back into the bushes.

"She is no goddess but the puppet of a devil. That's truth for you. How many more of you? Where?"

Ghu had come back, so soft-footed Ahjvar had not heard him. His hair was wet; his coat, rinsed and inadequately wrung out, was draped over his shoulders, dripping. Had he gone right into the river, with that wound? He was clean, but the bandage was wet. A sure way to fever and festering.

His river, he would say.

And how long had he been standing there? The coat was dripping a puddle.

"Enough," the man said. "You'll find out. There's enough of us. You won't get past Lai Sula, and they'll come to find you."

"Where?" He pushed. "Where are they hiding?" Truth and secrets pressed. The man snarled, screwed his eyes shut. "Don't need to hide. They're with Lai Sula and the Pine Lord."

"How far away is the empress? How great an army?"

"Don't know."

"What does Buri-Nai want with me that dead isn't enough anymore?" Ghu asked.

"How should I know? To send you to a traitor's death and lay out your guts for the birds to fight over while you still breathe. To burn your Northron abomination, I hope, if it can't be killed. She'll know what to do against necromancy. The Exalted is guided by the Old Great Gods. I'm Wind in the Reeds. I serve. To the death, I serve."

Ahjvar sat back on his heels, spoke Praitannec. "They were sent to take us alive to the empress, you and I. Change of plan from the winter."

"I heard."

But he thought Ghu had stopped listening. . . . *necromancer's slave* . . . *cut off his hands* . . . He couldn't have been to the river and back when that was said, could he? *To burn your abomination.* That, Ghu had most certainly heard. Ahjvar wished he hadn't.

Would rather he had not heard it himself.

"He has allies over the river. He's not Meli, a mind easy to turn aside, thoughts only for himself. And I don't trust he doesn't already have allies, or can't find them, in the camp, despite the compulsion of truth on him."

Ghu said nothing.

"Ghu?"

"I know. You're not wrong."

"Go. Out to the road. I'll follow."

"No." Ghu rested a hand on the man's chest, over where the tattoo must be, the heart. "Ahj, I said: you don't kill for me. Not like this."

"No. Don't—"

The man's eyes widened. Breath stuttered. Ceased. Gone. Like a candle pinched out.

No blessing for the road. That it would have been empty, with his soul reft away, was not the point. Ghu never left the dead unblessed.

Ghu flung himself away even as Ahjvar reached after him. He caught him on the wood's edge and they sat there in the sun, wrapped in a heavy silence.

"I shouldn't have done that," Ghu said at last. "Killed him. Not that way."

"It was fast. What's the difference, if you'd cut his throat?" But the difference was there and he knew it.

Ghu shook his head.

"You should have left him to me," Ahjvar said. "I don't mind."

"Yes, Ahj. That's why." But Ghu didn't turn to him, just watched the road. Hadn't looked at him, since then.

Ahjvar put a tentative arm around him. He was relieved when at last Ghu sighed and pressed a cheek to his shoulder. Wet and shivering, now. Ahjvar draped the plaid blanket over him, paced about a bit, loaded the crossbow against—whatever, and settled in to wait for Ivah and the dogs and the camp-marking party to find them.

After a while it occurred to him what Ghu had forgotten. Ghu had his eyes shut, leaning back against a tree. Probably not asleep; he looked round when Ahjvar stood up.

"Rafts."

"Oh. Good." Ghu shut his eyes again.

Ahjvar went back to the river, to hang Ghu's black coat like a scarecrow in the shallows as a flag for the raft-folk. Perhaps it would dry in the sun.

CHAPTER XXXIII

By mid-morning the next day, there was a roadway cut through the boggy woodland, a bed of brush and logs laid, and the camp almost in holiday mood. Excited more than apprehensive. They had taken a patrol from the western landing, but held the four men prisoner now, and from the east they were hidden by the woodland. Their own patrols were already over the river; luck with them—it was not something Ahjvar thought his god could influence—they would be able to stop any scouts or villagers taking news of the crossing back to Lai Sula. But they weren't counting on it.

"Mulgo Miar," Dan had said in distress, hearing their news the previous evening. "I thought him a true servant of the gods."

Small wonder Dan had been losing his war, was Ahjvar's opinion. A man who ought to be kept quietly to his prayers, and his declaration that he would be no emperor but a hermit and priest of the god of Nabban when all this was settled was perhaps the greatest wisdom he had shown in his life. They needed Ti-So'aro's brother Zhung Huong, the practical governor of Dernang, down here; Daro Raku could look to the town. A word with Yeh-Lin last night, and a courier had headed north with that order. They could not count on Dwei Ontari being either alive or true.

Ahjvar found Yeh-Lin down at the water's edge, watching her riverers impassive, arms folded.

"You still think it won't work?"

"I think we're fortunate the island's here." But she smiled, raised a hand. "Do you feel that, dead king?"

"Feel what?"

"The wind."

"So . . . there's wind?" It was blowing up the valley, warm with a promise of summer.

"I will leave the charming of the ropes to the Grasslander. She does have a way with bits of string. We, however, will set our sails, to carry some weight of our own. You, captain!" Switching languages. "There must be more slack in the ropes. Think of what happens when you cast a line across the water, how the current shapes its curve. Let our bridge make a great bow, let the river play with it, and it will be gentler." She ran light-footed as a girl out across the decks, started some sort of explanation with much hand-waving, gathering a crowd of her workers. Ahjvar shrugged and settled down to watch.

After a while, as shape began to emerge, and order, he continued across, deck to deck, so far as the bridge now went. Ghu was where they were shifting and lashing a last raft into position, the bow angled into the current. It was like the keystone of the arch, but the weak point, he thought, not the strength. They made a great arc sagging downriver, stronger, Ghu said, than if they had been lashed to make a straight line flung from shore to shore. Or even shore to island to shore. Two arcs bellied like nets, noses upriver and now, under Yeh-Lin's direction, some raising sails on their stubby double masts. Wind to push against the water, not enough to move them. Enough to hold.

"If the ropes fail . . ."

"They're still rafts. They have sails and poles and steering oars. It won't be a disaster."

It would be if Lai Sula's scouts had marked them, and they were flung off their bridgehead, rafts scattered downriver, the army trapped on the west, the leading party cut off.

Ghu was the first to cross, over and back, leading Snow. Where the white stallion went, the other horses would follow without acting up—or so Ghu's folk all seemed to believe. Ahjvar and Ivah walked with him. No straight line, as he had said, but two curving bridges riding the water, each deck bobbing and swaying with a life of its own, and gaps enough for human or horse to drop a leg in if unwary. The water, in such gaps, rose and foamed. The endmost rafts were grounded in the shallows, anchors as much as the trees to which they were lashed. They had had to dismantle several rafts to salvage enough heavy cordage. The island shore was algae-slicked, gravel and broken riverstone; their pioneers had hacked a trail beneath the heronry, though they left the birds their nesting trees. The stronger current took the eastern channel. Here the rafts bucked and jerked more, and Ahjvar had the uneasy feeling the river chewed at them, trying to gnaw one loose. Ghu didn't seem troubled by it. No fog. The water was all dark and dazzle, broken points of sun. Yeh-Lin had followed them halfway and stood at the island's northern point, ankle-deep in water. Moving, her steps slow and careful on the stones, her sword drawn. A dance, almost.

Protection.

So he made nothing new after all in what the Denanbaki shaman had called his prayers with the sword, but only found something that already belonged to Nabban. Well.

Across and back and it held. Knotted braids trailed like some sort of festival tassel from the ropes, Ivah's work. Setting strength on the ropes, wishing them to hold.

Crossbow companies first, with spearmen among them. Small parties, but crossing quickly. Some had been landed from the rafts at the start, to guard the bridgehead and dig in the posts—timbers of a dismantled raft—that must anchor them on the treeless east. They fanned out as more joined them, began an advance. No road on this shore, only a winding cattle-track.

The cavalry next, horses led. The rafts moved differently under them, rocking more, but of course they had carried far, far heavier cargoes, and the danger lay in some beast taking fright at a bellying sail and shying, or slipping.

It seemed a long afternoon. The foot and what baggage they needed for the night's camp crossed intermingled. Not all the great host. Prince Dan, guarded by the wizard Gar Sisu and with most of the conscript imperial footsoldiers Yeh-Lin had won them, would travel on downriver. Nearly all the horse but the banner-ranked of the prince's household guard had been diverted to the east.

A sombre mood descended as they broke up their bridge, coiling ropes, rafts drifting, bumping, as their crews turned them. A short night and fireless. Uneasy, with patrols and pickets flung far out about them, and the weight of Yeh-Lin's wizardry over them. Nothing, not even fog, obscured Dan's companies on the rafts, even the horses of the banner-lords of his guard, the only cavalry left to that party. Let the watchers look to the river and the west. Ghu stayed among the sleeping soldiers that night, but the river shore was churned and muddy, owned and human. He slept as if exhausted, dropped down like the dogs in the open, but Ahjvar couldn't, sliding towards nightmare every time he began to drift. He gave it up and sat by Ghu, watching the moon rise. Yeh-Lin drifted out of the darkness to sit by him, close enough he could feel her warmth at his shoulder.

"Keep him out of it, tomorrow," she said after a while. "They need to see the god they fight for, not have him lost among them."

"Yes." Agreeing with what she said, that was all. Ghu would be where he felt he needed to be.

"What?" she asked, of his silence before, not his answer.

"He shouldn't have killed that damned assassin. Not a prisoner."

"Simplest. You would have. I would have. Once."

"Now?"

"I would have—considered it. I don't know what I would have chosen."

"Simplest isn't right. I was wrong. He's god of this folk. He's—he should have found someone else to follow, back in Gold Harbour, not stayed to grow up in my madness. He should have gone on west as he meant to and left me behind."

"Choice, not chance. He followed you. And if that captive had been brought before us all and been still swearing death to the holy one, we would have decided to take his head, rather than keep prisoner an assassin with a devil's hand on him."

"For that. Not because it was easier than dealing with him living."

"You think that was his reason?"

No. Ahjvar thought it was deep anger that killed the assassin, not reason of any sort. He shook his head.

"Go to sleep, Ahjvar. You don't want to be half dreaming through the day tomorrow."

He did not want to be dreaming this night, either. But he tossed his sword at her feet, and stripped himself of knives—pointedly. Dropped them in her lap and rolled to lie along Ghu's back, arm over him. No intention of sleeping. People all around. Breathing. Alive. Dreaming. Afraid. He could almost taste their dreams. Water. Blood. Ghu rolled over himself and clung on to him. Ghu's dreams, his, he wasn't certain any more. They blurred like blood in water.

"Shh," he said, and walked them through the oak grove in his mind.

Rising by the light of the waning half-moon. Cold food. Quiet reports, patrols in, patrols out. Armour like a skirted coat, more shaped than a Northron byrnie, enamelled scales of plate and lacquer-hardened leather. Black, and sky blue ribbons. Greaves, gauntlets, helmets in the current Nabbani style, ornately crested to give somewhat of a beast-skull shape, horns or fins. Yeh-Lin had had armourers busy as well as the tailors, or she had changed the colour of what she scrounged from Daro Korat's armoury. They looked good banner-lords, not great lords: no gilding. Ghu laughed at it, not happily, but did not protest the need. The slash over his ribs of the previous day had healed to a purpled scar overnight. Horse-armour as well, burdens of the rafts. Niaul looked well in that and seemed to know something more serious than yet another jaunt down the river was in store, nuzzling at Ahjvar's cheek, prancing with the same sort of restless tension as the men and women were showing, watching the horizon, where the sun was rising red. They were trained for battle, had seen fighting, or Snow had, in the rebellion. He didn't know about Gorthuerniaul. But Ahjvar was still surprised when Ghu, circling Snow close about, took a spear from one of Ti-So'aro's followers. He handled it with old ease, smiled for the first time that morning and raised eyebrows at Yuro, standing by his big black.

"Don't you dare, boy," the castellan said. Shrugged at Ahjvar's questioning look. "Someone has to train the horses for the lords, eh? I wouldn't ride against him. Or bet against him, in the harvest games." A slow smile. "Of course, I usually made sure I drew him for my team. Baril always claimed I cheated."

"You did. But so did I. I didn't want to ride for Baril." Ghu tapped him with the spear, flipped it to his other hand, spun it end for end and back again, Snow moving, muscles gathering, leaping like a bird into flight. Pursuit of Ivah, who was away beyond the assembling companies, taking her dappled grey through some rapid turns and changes, a course set only in her mind, dropping arrows into tufts of grass.

An edgy restlessness all round.

Ghu rode her line, brushed each arrow where it stood, Ahjvar thought, but didn't strike even to damage the fletching. Except the last, which he split and skewered to the earth, wheeling back to reclaim the spear. He did not relinquish it when they rode out.

They made a swift and winding passage around the hills, leaving riverside grasslands for fields where green spears were already beginning to thrust from the furrows. They were seen; men and women out with hoes, children with slings and bullroarers against the plundering birds. Such watchers might come to the ferry before they did; a single runner who knew the paths of the hills . . . maybe. Maybe not. The horses set the pace; the crossbow company and the foot jogged where they could, and the curving path was not always the slower, not when the hills were a steep scramble tree to clinging tree. They ignored the village folk— serfs, slaves, or free tenants of some Dwei manor, they did not ask— and the folk fled them where they could. Where they could not, Lady Ti-So'aro proclaimed the heir of the gods and Prince Dan, riding against those who had invaded Alwu to enforce the tyranny of the empress and put the priests of the shrines to the sword.

"Tell it in the villages," she said. "Tell it in the markets; the heir of the gods, the holy one, rides to free the folk of Nabban. The empress is no goddess but a murderer of priests and the children of priests."

They had prisoners already, bound and roped in strings of five or six in the rear—patrols from the ferry landing, soldiers in imperial colours. Some had been shot by Ivah's small company of horse-archers, fleeing to carry their news; more than Ahjvar would have expected discarded weapons and went to their knees in surrender. The holy one of the gods, they asked? There was a priest among them, somewhere among Lai Sula's folk, secret. There were whispers. The empress was the enemy of the gods . . .

"There," Ghu said, about noon. They had lost sight of the river; on their right hand was rough terrain of rocky woodland, and left and ahead as well. A gap, though, where he pointed, and already a pair of scouts were riding back.

"Swamp, captain, as the holy one said." The girl—a former slave of the stables and hardly older than Yeh-Lin's page Jang—grinned, as if the holy one's knowledge of the river's terrain reflected well on Daro Korat's grooms. "And a hard path hugging the toes of the hills ahead, between them and the wetland." Her partner—father, maybe, they looked near kin—nodded. "Bound to be watchers along it somewhere, but none here at the gap." Not an archer, but he had a sling tucked through his belt.

"Do we divide?" Yeh-Lin asked.

"Have you seen Dan?"

"The mirror, you mean? I am trying not to attract notice, dead king. Nabban?"

"He's off the river," Ghu said.

No delaying, then, or they left the blind prince to be slaughtered like a calf among wolves, the imperial forces on the east able to cross freely over the river. Dan's force would have put ashore at a bend between another borderland of stony woodland to their north and swamp to the south, and marched a quick quarter mile between the two unopposed— they hoped—to gain the road again.

"So, yes?" Yeh-Lin persisted. Captain-general, but important they know they had their god's blessing—or that he was no adjunct to his wizard.

"Yes," he said. "Go well. March swiftly." He swung Snow away.

"Nabban! Stay out of the fighting. Be the banner of your folk. Let your champion stand between you and the enemy, yes?"

Ghu waved a vague hand.

"Hrm. Dead king—"

"I know. Yes."

Yeh-Lin issued a few quiet orders. Scouts—archers, this time—started out.

Ghu looked back then. "Leave the children here."

"I intended to."

Folly to have brought them even this far.

Some two companies of horse and all the foot were Yeh-Lin's, now. They would leave, concealed on the forested hillside, what they must abandon: the handful of horses and humans who had succumbed to illness or injury or exhaustion since the river crossing, the prisoners, the pages, the followers that every force on the march gathered but the holy one's more than most: the unarmed youths, the fugitives, the honestly devout who felt the pull of their newborn god's gathering strength, or those who only wanted something, anything, to take them away from wherever and whoever they had been.

"Hold this point," was the last he heard Yeh-Lin saying, to a banner-lord left to keep order. No, to all the gathered irregulars. "Hold yourselves under Lord Daro Ruhi's command. Rearguard is no dishonour but a great service to the holy one's cause. Jang, Kufu, Ti, you have charge of the holy one's dogs. Do not let them follow."

Ghu's companies—his, Ivah's—it was Ivah and Yuro who set the order of march and Ivah's helmet that fluttered with the red ribbons of command along with the blue and black of the holy one—took the crossbows up, once all the remounts, of which they had far too few, were also carrying two. They would not be coming fresh to the fight by any means, but their strength lay in speed now, and stealth, and the weight of a first rush. Lose that by miserly hoarding and they probably lost all.

Ti-So'aro shook out the sky-blue banner under which the god rode. Each company swung into line under their own, blue and black, no clan-emblems, only a coloured strip or two for their captain, and they sought their own road, east of another uprising of precipitous hills, a land made like a forested version of the badlands in grey, but on a greater scale. And Ahjvar wondered, surprised, what waters had shaped these stones, and if they whispered into Ghu's dreams. Sometimes he thought he heard waves.

He carried no second rider, and those who did traded them about, to spare the horses as much as they could. Speed, though. Ivah's fleeting archers, scattered ahead, brought down an imperial patrol and took no prisoners.

Mid-afternoon. Ghu and Ahjvar went forward once the advance patrol sent a message back that had the lookout post; Ivah and Ti-So'aro went with them. They left the horses while they were still concealed, went afoot the last piece, to where the land dropped before them. No great height, but enough, and village fields below, village houses, and the burned ruins of houses—small, rectangular, wooden-walled, with thatched roofs. Their patrol of twenty lay concealed, corpses and bound prisoners of the sentries who had held this height dragged together in the shadow of the trees. A brief flurry under the eaves of the wood and the shadow of the hill, that was all it had been. No alarm given.

It was not a great height, but a long, slow descent, to the gap of the road to Numiya. Below, new bamboo posts blocked a gap in the older defence of the wood-built courier outpost—it looked like an inn to Ahjvar, three wings around a well, a stable detached and behind—and the square stone tower that overlooked the ferry landing. The imperial camp spread through the village and out along the road. A line of slanted poles sliced to give a deadly point arced from the rocky hill-foot around to the road, partially shielding both village and camp, meant to force an attack, at least by horses, around to a narrower gap, but no ditch fronted it. They were not spaced closely enough they could not be avoided by a skilled rider, either.

They could not quite see the ferry landing itself from here, only the higher hills that marched along the gorge, but there seemed too few soldiers about for the size of the camp. Knowing that there was a rebel force somewhere to the east, as they must guess if they had been hunting Ontari's scouts, would they leave their rear so weak, even expecting the threat to come from the west over the river? Sula should be worried by the vanishing of scouts and patrols over this past night and day; some should surely have been expected back before now. Some should, god's luck and devil's magic or no, have been missed, and given him warning of some kind of threat moving. Ahjvar could not quite believe a wizard skilled as the Pine Lord must be would not notice at least some prickling unease.

Altogether too weak. A party of five to watch from this critical vantage-point that gave sight along the edge of the woodland running north?

Ivah was frowning.

"There's something else there." She rose up on her elbows, eyes half shut, fished coins out of her gauntlet. "I think this ridge is watched, too."

Ghu had a hand bare, splayed on the earth.

"It was," he said. "It wasn't when our patrol came up."

"Why not?"

"I took it back from him," he said. "The wizard."

"Does he know?" Ivah asked in alarm.

"I didn't mean him to. I'm not sure. Probably not. Nothing's changed down there."

A windless day. Black smoke rose, a high plume of it, thinning to grey, over the river. It wavered, strengthened. Gar Sisu.

"The prince," Ti-So'aro said. "Holy one, my lady—orders?"

"Fire," Ghu said. Eyes shut and fingers digging through meshed roots into the damp earth. "That's what it is, Ivah. Fire in the earth."

"The ground's disturbed behind the line of stakes," Ahjvar said. "Not just from planting them."

"Graves?" said Ti-So'aro.

"Maybe those too," Ivah said grimly. "Can fire-powder be lit, under the earth? If you bury a fire, you starve it."

"Lai Sula's face is to us, not the river," Ghu said. "Mulgo Miar is hiding the tents. Dwei Ontari is traitor to Dan. He was always—of two

minds about us. I think I am not his idea of a god, Ahj. And he stood by
Dan honestly all through his rebellion, faithful then, and true. Poor Dan."

The tents were in plain view. But what was in them, to wizardly
searching—maybe not. Ahjvar didn't bother to try.

"Show me the fire," he said, pulling off his gauntlets. He laced his
fingers through Ghu's, against the earth.

Darkness, a drowning, airless darkness. Strange and vertiginous, the
restless earth, the stone that was shell, the hidden waters loud. Roots
breathing. He could taste the fire, sleeping, smell the ash, the terror of
the horses, the men that would die, devoured, hair burning and flesh, skin
bubbling, charring, flaking away . . . Ghu knocked him over and stifled
his cry, but he'd struck out at something in the attack. Ghu, of course.

"I thought you were going to stop doing that," Ghu said, but his
voice shook, not for his bleeding mouth, but for what he'd done himself.
"I'm sorry, Ahjvar, I'm sorry. I don't see what you see; I didn't think
what you'd make of it. I'm sorry."

Ti-So'aro had her hand on a knife. Ivah was half up on her knees, all
the patrol about them confused and uncertain.

He lay where he was, sky over him, and shut his eyes. Forget the
damned and damning nightmare and the past, what he'd seen was words
interwoven, and symbols cast into ornate firesteels, painted in ink on
flints. Simple symbolism, and a web of word and syllable that wound
into itself, waiting to be uncoiled, to call out sleeping potential in the
buried jars. Far from simple. Opened his eyes again. "I'm so tired of
nightmares," was what he whispered. "Sorry." Caught the beading blood
on his thumb. "I knew a Northron caravan wizard once, in Two Hills.
They say they have to mark their runes with blood."

"Their own blood," Ivah said distantly, watching them.

Ahjvar shrugged, rolled over to press his bloody thumb to the earth.
Cut a triangle around it, then another, touching those points, and the
third encasing those. Set the twigs—none of them the true thing but
whatever it was that grew at arm's reach, some scrubby little shrub he
didn't know and didn't like the smell of, either—upright at each point,
three and three and three, alder, yew, elm, and reached for the old, deep

naming of the names, the truth of fire, the truth of death . . . the name of his god, whose earth this was. Didn't need to speak the secret verses; he could taste them in his mouth, like blood and earth and ash. He laid his left hand over his right at the centre, covering the smear of blood the earth had taken.

"I can—halfway see what you're doing," Ivah said. "I'm not sure I understand it all, but halfway. Want some help?" A loop of yarn dangled from her hand.

He shook his head. "Go bring them up. Let me do this. I can do this. I don't think you can."

"Why not?"

He whispered it. Secrets of the night. "Because I am fire and I know what fire is."

"Ahj." That flat warning.

What had he said? "I'm all right. I am. Go back to Yuro. Don't let them ride over me."

"Leave the patrol with him, Ivah."

"Are we going?" she asked.

"Oh yes," Ahjvar said, "Straight down. If Yeh-Lin's not in position yet—we can't wait."

Because he did not think he could hold this in place for long. It flared around the corners of his vision, edged his bones in pain. Fire remembered him, wanted him. How the man Mulgo Miar held such a thing sealed in steel and ink he could not imagine. A different magic, a different set of forms, of temper—a greater wizard. They would have to kill the Pine Lord, the empress's spy, Dan's traitor, before he could kill the god of Nabban half born.

He could feel the fire in the earth, but the earth, and Ghu's blood on his right thumb, under his left palm, were safe. They tamed it, held it. Made it his, to burn at his word, no other. To burn, and if it turned on those who laid it . . . Old Great Gods take them quickly.

They came quietly, as if the very horses wanted to pace lightly, secretly, over the earth. The crossbows slipped away into the woods eastward, to angle down towards the Numiya road. They carried spears as well, shields at their backs, for when attack came against them and they could not reload. Or they might have no more to do than pick off any lords who chose to flee rather than surrender. Being optimistic. They had their orders: let the conscripts run as they would.

Whether Dan, over the river, could draw the imperial forces out of their enclave there by his presence, or whether his companies would have to attack their ditch and palisade, made little difference. Hold their attention, prevent whatever forces had been sent over the river from returning. He might already be engaged. The smoke was only to say he was there, and within sight.

Dark hoof, black pastern and fetlock in the corner of his vision. Fire trailed sight as he blinked, could hardly move to push himself to his knees, as if he had become rooted into the earth. He was glad Yeh-Lin was on the other side of the hill; he did not think he wanted to see what his eyes would have found in her, just now. Knife in his hand, wiped clean of earth. He looked up. Ghu, good shield-bearer, leading Niaul, who blew at him, rolled an eye askance. Smelling the unborn fire.

Ghu nodded, and was already dismounting, spear planted in the earth, as Ahjvar cut the back of his wrist, just below the twisted heavy gold of the bracelet, one hand still pressed over the heart of the inter-locked seal of the triad, fire and death and the god who held him. The blood welled, burning, he thought, sheeted down the joint of his thumb, not so very much blood but fire had taken him and was in him still and he understood its hunger, its rage to be free, and so he let it go with a word and shut his eyes against the savage screaming pain of it, the searing air that paralysed the lungs.

"Up," Ghu said. "Look up, look at me."

At Ghu kneeling in front of him, gripping his shoulders. Beyond Ghu, over his black-armoured shoulder. Not himself burning. The earth, a long arc of it, half the perimeter of the stake-guarded camp, erupted in flame, soil, gravel, flung skyward, bamboo burning, whatever else had been laid in the buried trench to feed the fire-powder blazing up like a bonfire, sparks carried skyward, drifting, embers snapping and spit-ting. A tent caught, another. Thatch that should still have been winter-

sodden and reluctant glowed and took as a wild wind flung the wall of
flame back over the camp that had set it. Mulgo Miar had meant his fire
to cling and burn and so it did, and soldiers hidden in the tents and the
houses fled them in disorder. No village folk, which Ahjvar had feared.
Fled or driven out to hide in the hills of the gorge, he could spare a
thought to hope.

"All right?"

Ahjvar nodded. Throat too raw and rough with remembered smoke,
ghosts of smoke, to speak. Found gauntlets, knife . . . feet. Ghu held his
stirrup.

"Mulgo Miar," he said. "Lai Sula we take or not as we can. We
want Mulgo Miar, Ahjvar. Alive. A man who was close to the empress,
who maybe still is. He'll know where the empress is. She speaks in his
dreams, the assassin said, though more likely it's the devil."

Certainly the Pine Lord would be more use alive. But he wanted
the man who planned this fire dead. He nodded, and Ghu sprang back
to Snow's saddle, swept up his spear, lowered the mask-like visor of his
helmet, a creature suddenly strange and terrible, not human, shadows
of dragons . . .

Ahjvar lowered his own visor as they started down, trotting, gathering to speed only as the companies spread out from the narrow defile
they had come up, swinging to left and right as was their place. The line
of fire was dying, quickly starved, though roofs still burned, and officers
were shouting, screaming, driving men to form up, archers taking aim,
but crossbows in disarray, and the main companies of spearmen looking
more like badly driven cattle in their milling panic to spill off the sides
and scatter away.

His place was Ghu's right. Yuro with his mace and Ti-So'aro had
the left. Ti-So'aro rode with the blue banner braced in her stirrup, her
retainers about her to guard her and it and their god. Zhung Ario had
the company of the right flank; Ivah and the archers of Alwu swept away
to the left—riders under an imperial banner broke from the opened gate
of the courier post. A few tore away down the road, which would give the
crossbows something to do, but the rest swung towards them. Into range

of a Grasslander's bow. One shot. A rider next to the banner fell. They
scattered apart, closed up, but the archers of Alwu had their range now.
More fell. No horses killed, save one. They needed horses. The imperials
found themselves riding parallel to their enemies as Ivah's wide-spaced
company wheeled and turned, driving them as a falcon drives its prey
in the air, and then the charge upon the churned and broken ground of
the fires and his attention needed to be before him. They jumped the
sunken, sulphur-reeking ruin of the trench and were within the camp. A
company to the right had charged the archers and if they had shot more
than a single flight before they scattered in their fear, he did not see it,
but there were imperial soldiers ranged against them now, order and
discipline reasserted. A long front on the road, spears braced for the first
clash, rocks against the mounted wave that would break over them, or
break. A long front was not what these defenders needed—

Uproar towards the river, but . . . Yeh-Lin they must trust to be
there, having had a shorter march by virtue of it being flatter.

And then there could be nothing but what was before him.

They were flung against the line, and the soldiers were scattering
from the man on the white horse, crying, "The holy one!"

Priest secret among them, that prisoner had said.

Ghu ignored them, searching. The imperial line sagged around
him, fraying. Lai Sula's army had the numbers to engulf the banner-
lords and their household troops, to open like a mouth and swallow
them, but fear of their own officers would only hold them so long. The
imperials should have had archers throughout, not bunched away in a
corner, but then they had been planning to be the ones emerging to fall
upon panicked and disordered survivors in some grim rush from the fire
and smoke. Ahjvar killed an officer who came screaming curses against
them. The man had cut down one of his own who was trying to shove
his way to the rear. Snow struck down another and they were engulfed,
a churning mass, those willing to die for their empress or for fear of
the lords who drove them, or of shame, or trapped and having no way
out. He kept them from Ghu, did not number those he fought, who
came battering against him and Niaul to be broken, and torn, and flung

underfoot. Break the line, split it, find the lord who commanded here. A few mounted imperials charged up and down beyond, but no stand of banners, no clustering, observing command—if all this trap was only the rearguard and Lai Sula himself down by the river, Yeh-Lin would deal with him and his traitor wizard, too.

Ghu found what he sought, maybe, swung horse and spear to point like a hunting dog. Movement amid movement. Ahjvar swore and swept around him, another officer, cut down and under Niaul's hammering forefeet. "Run!" he roared at the boys who had dropped spears and shields and clutched at one another, two shielding a third as if he would kill the bloody child on the ground, and they grabbed up their comrade and dragged him away. It was another three running at the rear, struggling to break into, not out of, the crush of panic, that held Ghu's attention. Ill-equipped conscripts, bare-legged, but among the few to have lamellar armour for breast and back, and one a woman's face. They did not conscript peasant women. And too well armed. The woman and one man had swords, the other—a hunter's blowpipe.

CHAPTER XXXIV

Man with long hair in caravaneer's braids, not a nobleman's knot, and he saw Ivah, knew her, as she knew him. Grinned, swung his horse her way, reined in and bowed in the saddle.

Ride with him.

The words crashed like a wave through her mind. *Daughter of emperors, daughter of devils. An empress to fear . . . your god is nothing, a slave, a dreamer, all hope and no strength to fulfil those dreams. He drags you to your defeat and death and you have never belonged to him, you are your own, my own chosen daughter, and I will show you what your father never did . . . Buri-Nai was only ever a place-holder. I am Jochiz, the Stonebreaker, they called me in the north, and I have been waiting for you. Ivah, come. The Pine Lord waits to show you the way.*

"Exalted!" the man cried. "Come! Hurry!"

Mulgo Miar, the Pine Lord appointed by the empress and supposed traitor to her, ally to Dan and traitor to him, and in Dernang, hunting him, witness to Yeh-Lin's challenge of Hani Gahur. Mulgo Miar, crying, "Exalted, come quickly! Ride! Your army, your folk . . . ride with me!"

Ride with him. Go now, go quickly, before they notice, before they see you, before they understand what you truly are, daughter of Ghatai. Come! Now! To me!

What he truly was, was a dead man, and he spoke Grasslander, which had never passed the tongue of that wizard before her.

Red Mask, dead thing, soul torn away—

Arrow on the string, free like a falcon, and it burned in the air, a fire on it that she had not even shaped a word to set. Wrath. The sun's heat on the dry earth, the golden grass and the searing blue of the sky—

It pierced his armour, his heart, but his heart did not beat. It pierced the black knot of thorny script over his heart, which she could not read, but which she had struggled to decipher, the script on the prison-tombs of the gods in Marakand. The writing of the devils.

It sliced the threads that bound him, the puppet's strings, and he fell, and his horse ran, shaking the corpse loose.

He was all burnt away within, taken by the devil. A husk.

She remembered, Old Great Gods, she remembered the voice, caressing and vaunting, words in her dreams, one night, two? More? Many, many more. She gagged. Remembered suffocating, cobweb in her mouth, her throat, spreading.

Clawed her helmet free, raked unbraided hair, yanked at it, bit her lip hard enough to bleed, wiped fingers in the blood and smeared it on the hairs she had torn free. Knotted loops so fine they might be lost in a careless breath and wove. Careful now. Cold, deliberate, though her heart raced. A wrath that might have been her father's, as his sabre took her betraying mother's head.

Held the pattern to the sky. Parted her hands, tore.

The threads pulled from her, ripping, as if a thousand tiny hooks had been set in her flesh, her mind. Leeches. Worms in the gut, a cramping pain that faded and was gone, and there was a strange, calm coolness behind her eyes, an ease of something so subtle she had not felt it, till it was gone.

Ivah leaned over, vomiting, and Steelgrey pranced and sidled, ears back, snorting. Her hands shook so she could hardly manage even to wipe her mouth.

"Lady Ivah!" A man wheeled around to her. "Riders from the east! Prince Dan's banners—Dwei Ontari's proved true!"

She looked where he pointed, eyes narrowed against the distance.

She remembered the helmets, the masks—

"Not Lord Ontari," she said. "That's Lady Dwei Baya, riding ahead."

The archers of Alwu were spreading out, a great skein of them, riding to intercept the fleeing imperials, the lords and officers who abandoned—cowardice or orders?—this army of the ferry landing. She stood in the stirrups, gathering her people to her, a shout. "With me!"

They rode to meet Baya, with Lai Sula's escort caught between.

Jochiz Stonebreaker. Understand what I truly am. Daughter of An-Chaq, daughter of Ghatai—what is that? I am only Ivah, and I claimed myself for my own on the battlefield where I fought what you had left of your mad sister.

My god sees me.

She would make her heart a shrine for her god, and the stone core of her—oh yes, she had that image now; she saw where Jochiz had gone before, the stone and the grass beneath the wind. For all he thought he had hidden his tracks the grass showed them—she would make that shrine within herself, and be the stone at the heart of it.

Stonebreaker. Hah. A Northron byname, nothing more, as they called Vartu "Kingsbane" for her brother's murder, and that was a lie.

I am the stone, the altar of my god, that you will not break.

Serve Nabban.

He is my soul's home, she had said to Nour.

Most people never feel that for their god at all, Nour had replied. *The ones who do, we generally call priests.*

The old Nabbani word for emperor, empress had also meant the priest of all the land, once upon a time.

And Dan would be a hermit.

Understanding settled on her with the inevitability of winter's snow, soft and heavy.

CHAPTER XXXV

Lady Ti-So'aro saw it too, the dark, straight bamboo tube. She spurred ahead, swerving in front of Snow, sweeping her banner down like a lance, but too late for the silk to be the shield she intended. Her horse dropped as if struck down by lightning, still, not a twitch, a last spasm, unwounded. The stinging of a wasp, a dart, on the soft lips below the chamfron's protection. Ti-So'aro dragged herself from under it only to struggle in a flurry of battering blows, swarmed by soldiers. Motionless even as Snow wheeled about them, savage teeth and hooves and the spear taking the one with the heavy horseman's mace. Those that fled were ridden down by Ti-So'aro's retainers. One circled back, dropping down the side of his horse to snatch up the banner. They needed Ivah and her bow, now, now. Ahjvar swept around them all, kicked Niaul to surge ahead. If they had that poison on a blade as well this was the end of Evening Cloud, this was why he didn't name horses, damn the boy, and he did wonder how long it would take him and his curse to fight off the frozen death of the islanders' arrow-poison.

The assassins killed two of their own who pressed between, stabbed in the back and thrown aside and Ahjvar cleared their way for them, cutting down conscripts who had a will to stand and fight. Something slammed into Niaul's shoulder and the horse stumbled, didn't fall, seized and shook and flung a man. Snow flashed by in that and an assassin's blowpipe could hardly miss the naked flaring nostril, to put Ghu down at their feet—or to be run over by the racing knot of Zhung retainers and stable-folk turned cavalry that trailed him like a ship's wake. The horse spun and turned, turned back and the assassin went down, Ghu's spear pinning him to earth through the throat, arms flung wide. Ahjvar let Niaul's momentum make his sword a spear, dropped low at his knee, ripped his blade up and free and leaned to the side to take the head off the third even as Snow wheeled left, Ghu coming back for his lance, but one of Ti-So'aro's riders had crashed sideways into it, snapping the shaft, narrowly avoiding bringing himself and another down, and Ghu spun Snow away again, to clear ground. They were on the road, and behind the mass that surged and heaved.

A spearhead thrusting through, they were, beneath the stained and torn sky-blue silk, and there was a roar, a surge like the sea, or that was how it felt, as if they were gone to one will—but the imperial soldiers were each a frail body alone, and each to save himself. Just as well. Ghu didn't have the bodies to spend, to throw wave after wave at the imperials, or to force a slow way through with every step paid in blood.

"Lai Sula?" Ahjvar shouted.

Ghu shrugged. One of the riders offered him her spear, bloodied and unbroken. He shouldered it with a nod of thanks and she unhooked the axe from her belt. Ahjvar leaned over to pluck the feather-fletched dart from the breast of Ghu's coat. He dismounted long enough to bury the point in the ground, take the hardened leather pouch from the assassin's belt for later burning, and split the pipe, long as a man's arm. Into the saddle again, and the imperial soldiers were falling back around them, parting as if they were some headland. They didn't flee, though, but remained, washed up on the shore of them. As if the blue banner were their rallying point and not the death that had come upon them. Yuro, out of nowhere, striking a mounted imperial officer with the Lai badge on his helmet to the earth, roaring, "Kneel! Lay your sword at the feet of your god! Where's Lai Sula?"

"Find me Mulgo Miar," Ahjvar muttered. "Ghu?"

Ghu shook his head. Ahjvar set Niaul between him and a sudden new rush of imperial soldiery, but the men went to their knees, their faces, crying on the holy one of the gods to spare them. There was still fighting, but it had broken into chaos, knots and swirls, a pattern Ivah could weave, hazed white, pearl-streaked, edged in ghosts. Ahjvar was blinded by them. And all this folk was Ghu's, all these deaths . . .

Spears were cast down as if wind swept through a field of ripening oats. Ripples, spreading. Lords and officers, too.

The sun was dropping towards the hills over the river. A rider—she raised her visor to be recognized, a woman of the stables in the armour of a Daro banner-lord—pallid and her left arm resting awkward over her lap, reins in her right hand. "My lord!" she called shrilly. "Master Yuro! Holy one! Lady Lin says, she holds the landing and the ferry, and the commander of the western tower's surrendered to the prince. They didn't put up much fight across the water at all—thought Dan had all the army of Choa with him."

"Lai Sula?" Yuro demanded.

"No, my lord." Remembering Yuro's rank now. "There's a Lai Acen commanding; only a banner-ranked."

"Tell Y—the captain-general to take charge here," Ghu said. "Thank you. Yuro, round up the lords and officers who've surrendered. Isn't there any command here? Can't they signal a retreat, a surrender? They're lost and they don't all know it, and they're still dying. It's a damned tavern fight."

Yuro snorted. But it was like that, the disorder. No one to cry out, enough. "Drums," he said. "Have we taken their drums, any of their runners?"

Some of his people scattered, presuming the question a command. It was over here, about them, but up and down the village and beyond, no. Like a fire, breaking out renewed. Fewer and fewer though.

"Have all the houses and the station searched," Ghu said. "There's a priest somewhere, remember, who gave these people hope of our coming. Find him, Yuro, please. Ahj—Ivah."

They gathered a large enough party around them to move with impunity now, and where they went, the fighting faltered.

"The banner of the god," he heard.

Drums broke out behind them, signalling something. A call to throw down arms, Ahjvar guessed. Niaul had lost his easy flowing stride, moved halting, stiff. Bruised, but no worse than that beneath his battered armour, Ahjvar could hope.

Ivah, coming towards them, her lightly-armoured grey blood-spattered but moving unimpaired. Archers of Alwu in their hundreds swept up around her, and others, mounted banner-ranked with the god's ribbons and the badges of Alwu. Dwei Ontari's folk. Ahjvar had not sheathed his sword. He urged Niaul ahead, barring their way to Ghu. Riders spread themselves out to either side of him, a pitiful handful to throw against Ontari's companies.

"These are true," Ivah called, and one rode forward, lifting her snarling mask. She bowed. Dwei Ontari's niece, Dwei Baya.

"Holy one," she said. "My uncle is dead, for his treachery. I don't say you're the god of this land. I don't say you aren't. I say my family will keep faith where they have given it, and Prince Dan is still our lord, and he has given his oath to—at the least—a man there is no dishonour in following, whatever his birth."

She looked ten years older than when she had challenged them on the road from Swajui.

"Why?" Ghu asked. "Dwei Ontari served Dan so long, so faithfully. Why now?"

"You, my lord. Daro Korat's stableboy. He despaired of the prince at the end, when he gave up all command to you and was willing to follow you down the river, thought him witless and broken in the mind, to find his god in a Dar-Lathan bastard, forgive me, his words. He said we could never return to imperial favour but we might yet hold Alwu as princes. He offered you to Lai Sula, you and the southern manors of Alwu, in return for the north."

Ghu bowed gravely. There didn't seem much that could be said.

"I give you my sword," she said, and held it out across her hands. "And my life, if you will, for my uncle's betrayal."

"Prince Dan needs both," Ghu said. "He'll need this river crossing held against anything else that comes from Numiya. He'll need Alwu held for us, for the old Kho'anzi—Dan's mother's aunt, isn't she? He's over the river. Leave your companies to Lady Ivah just for now; take your household folk and go over the river to Dan, with my blessing. Let him know that you, at least, have kept faith."

She bowed, signalled her people, and rode on. Ivah spoke a few words and some of her archers went with Lady Baya, to see she wasn't challenged on her way, Ahjvar supposed.

"Lai Sula's dead," Ivah said. She sounded exhausted. "We shot him unknowing. They told me just now—the prisoners. They're telling the truth. There'd been rumour going around—Lai Sula killed two soldiers just this morning for repeating it—that the heir of the gods was bringing his death. He thought it was prophecy. It might only have been a whisper the priest started to break his nerve, I think. So when their own trap was sprung against them, he panicked and fled with his tent-guard." That was her weariness showing, certainly, the Grasslander term translated. As if for a moment she lost her Nabbani. "A coward," she added dispassionately. "He was very young."

So many of them had been. But maybe that was his age.

Ghu was watching Ivah gravely. "Mulgo Miar?" he asked.

"I—destroyed his link with the devil. He was dead already. He was—sent to take me back to them. To Buri-Nai, I suppose. To Jochiz. The devil is Jochiz."

Ghu said only, "Ah." Gave her a long, long look, and a grave nod. "I'm glad you're still here, then." Turned Snow away. "We have the field, I think. Don't we? Ti-So'aro is dead. I think—I have lost too many folk here. Ahj?"

"We need to stay," Ahjvar said, though Great Gods, he did want to ride away.

"I know. Come down to the river. I need to hear it." He glanced back. "Go to Captain Lin, Ivah. She may have wizard's work for you, and she'll know where she wants the archers of Alwu. We need scouts sent out, far out. The empress is somewhere, and if wizardry can't find her, human eyes may."

Changing tongues: "Ahj, you wish we were home?"

"Where's home?"

Ghu shrugged. "Stone and water," he said. "Sand Cove. I miss the sea, you know. I think—I'll always miss the sea. Come with me to the river, now." He pulled his helmet off, shook flattened hair free. He looked exhausted, drained of life. Godhead burned him up like he was only fuel for a fire, the oil, not the lamp. Find the river, yes. Ghu seemed to need it as much as food or sleep.

They didn't make it, of course. The blue banner betrayed them. Yuro needed the holy one. Yeh-Lin needed the holy one. The surrendered and captive banner-lords of the Lai needed the holy one, and most of all the dying, their own and the empress's, needed their god, to see him and hear him and touch him, to take his blessing to their road. It was past the middle night, well past and there was a greying in the east, their far-too-mortal god stumbling, his voice faint, gone to single words like a child, before Ahjvar was able to persuade him away, pull him down just anywhere, lee of some unburnt hut, to sleep still armoured as he was, with his head pillowed in Ahjvar's lap.

He didn't mean to sleep himself. Woke to sudden assault and seized—only the page Kufu, shaking frantically at his ankle, afraid to touch the holy one even in his urgency. Strong sunlight in his face, back against a clay-plastered wall, Ghu rolling sleep-dazzled to his feet and the dogs racing up, bristling.

Ahjvar rocked upright, snatching up his sword and dropping the boy, who had yelped in terror and was still trying to stammer out words regardless.

"*What?*"

Kufu repeated himself, "Captain Lin says, the empress. An army. Here, already."

CHAPTER XXXVI

Yeh-Lin had taken over the courier station as her headquarters. They found her in the dining hall with the commanders. Surviving commanders. Ti-So'aro's was not the only face missing. He did not see Gar Sisu, the prince's wizard. Yuro was there, though, and Prince Dan, armoured but still keeping to his oath to carry no weapons, with Lady Dwei Baya at his side; Ivah, a number of imperial commanders and Daro retainers . . . one tall, bald old man dressed for rough labour in hemp trousers and smock, but Ghu, for all the gravity of the summons, broke into a sudden smile.

"Awan!"

The man squinted and thrust his head forward shortsightedly, but Ghu was crossing to him, a hand raised to silence Yeh-Lin a moment. He took the old man's hands.

"Shouja Awan! You fed me, when I was travelling south. Years ago."

The old man tilted his head, frowned. "Holy one . . . ?" And laughed. "You! I do remember. Fed you? I caught you thieving from the offering-box of the shrine."

Ghu shrugged. "You were the only one who ever did. And you cuffed my ear and fed me."

"That boy." The priest shook his head. "Like a lost fawn, my poor blessed wife said. All eyes and bones and silences. She wanted to keep you and fatten you up a bit before we let you go, but you were gone the next night. I wouldn't have known you, but . . . your eyes haven't changed. My lord."

"I think I was far from the only runaway you sheltered."

Awan shrugged. "I did what seemed necessary."

"Nabban!"

"Yes." And Ghu wheeled on Yeh-Lin. "Buri-Nai." Among those grim men and women, in dirt-dulled black armour, he did not look anything that had ever been fugitive and thief. He was wolf, not fawn, and even Yeh-Lin gave him space. Only the old priest, Awan, seemed not to feel the tension. He picked up a bowl he had set aside at their entry and, squatting with his back against the wall, returned to eating soup.

"I was blinded to her. Nabban, I swear I—"

"*Don't* swear. I believe you. I didn't—call it see, I didn't see her either. I didn't feel them moving over the land." Very softly: "I should have. We knew they were coming. I was . . . listening, for her."

"I searched for her. I sent scouts so soon as we had Lai Sula out of the way and they are taken and dead, all of them, Nabban, every man and woman. And this morning at last I saw. I couldn't count. Twenty thousand, thirty, three rivers of men. Numbers hardly matter—ten, twenty, thirty." Praitannec, then. "It is Jochiz Stonebreaker, as Ivah says. Sien-Shava. He holds his hand over them like a god, greater than a god. Greater than I, at any rate. Nabban, what will you do?" Nabbani once more. "If we move now, abandon the dead unburied, we might with the rafts take some—maybe all, this folk over the river. Though the current is stronger, here. Cross, and then raise the river against her? Hold till what strength is in Shihpan can come to us? She must have gathered all the imperial soldiery of the central provinces, and how she moved them so—"

"Does it matter? We did not see."

He stood head bowed. No one spoke, till at last Yuro stirred. "Two-thirds of Lai Sula's people are wanting to swear their oaths to the holy one. Do we take them, or leave them to reinforce her, or—" He shrugged.

"My folk," Ghu said. Looked up, looked around them all. "You are all my folk. All the folk of Nabban. We never did come here to fight her. We came to hold the north safe against Buri-Nai while I went on to meet her and what governs her. I go on, as I meant to."

"She's not going to forswear her delusions for your sake," Yeh-Lin said.

"You'll get yourself killed," Yuro said flatly. "You'll never persuade her to acknowledge you, or to change how she rules."

Ghu shrugged. "We'll see. Get over the river. All who will, all you trust. Hold there. I leave them in your hands, Captain Lin."

"Great Gods, Nabban, you are mad, I did say so. Ahjvar, tell him."

Ahjvar just shook his head.

"You are not going without—"

"I need you here, Lin. I leave all in your hands. Do you hear me? All."

"I'll ride with you, my lord," Prince Dan said. "I'm not much use here—"

"No," Ghu said. "Thank you, Dan. But no. I don't think there is—is anything anyone else can do."

Ghu bowed to them all, turned and walked out from the rising voices. Ahjvar strode after him, spun to glower at Yeh-Lin when she would have followed.

"No."

She grabbed at his arm, but he caught her wrist before she could and they stood so, blocking the door. She didn't try to twist away.

"Break whatever link Jochiz has with the empress." She spoke Praitannec, low and intense. "He can't reach into the land without her, he surely can't. Kill Buri-Nai and whatever of her command you must to stop that army and put Dan on the throne."

"If Ghu asks it."

"Cold hells, Ahjvar, what use is a damned assassin if you leave him to walk into her hands?"

"Nabban's champion," he said. "Nabban's sword. Nabban's damned priest, a dead woman called me. I am not anyone's assassin. Do as he bids you." He turned her loose and she swung round on the watching commanders.

"As our young god says, then, and Old Great Gods be with him and us all. We cross the river and hold Choa. Get the wounded over first and mix what we can of Lai Sula's supplies in with them. Zhung Ario, if you would look to that . . ."

He left her driving them, her words riding over argument, and they were anyway too overridden to rally much of one. No one else had any action to offer. Flight or surrender . . . no one voiced it.

He overtook Ghu halfway to the horse lines, caught him and turned him face to face. He knew that look, fey and dark and vision-drowned.

"Why?" he demanded. "Yeh-Lin's right. The empress isn't going to listen. She's not Daro Korat or Ti-So'aro, looking for her god. She thinks she is that. You're not even a rival for the empire, in her mind. You're someone who's stolen what should be hers alone—the worship of her folk. She'll simply kill you."

"If I don't try, she kills all these who've followed me. That, I see. Inevitable."

"They could scatter and run . . ."

Ghu shook his head. "All these dead here, still unburied. Do you hear them?"

"No. See them, yes. If I try. I'd rather not."

"Mine, all of them. I should have just gone from Dernang, but—I thought to come from some strength, to meet with her with the northwest provinces behind me—it's not only Buri-Nai. It's her court, her lords, her generals I need to hear me." The night-drowned look was fading from his eyes; he was . . . wolf again. But a weary one, and his face was bruised. "To remember their gods. They wouldn't hear Daro Korat's horseboy. I thought we could give her pause, make them doubt her, if we had the northwest, if there were time so the folk could see—change was possible, a free land was possible. I don't know. I didn't think she could move so many, so quickly." Half a smile. "Under a month from the Golden City to the Old Capital is quickly, even if she's been at a cart's pace since then. But for being so well hidden . . . I shouldn't have trusted I could see all the river's length. Maybe knowing Yeh-Lin has made me view the devils as too—human. A devil took Nabban from the gods before, after all."

"Ghu . . ."

"I can't see, Ahj. I only . . . Beyond the empress, there's only darkness. The darkness at the end of all dreams, all my life. I'm sorry. If I could—"

"Don't. My soul's in your hands. I'd have it nowhere else."

"Then trust. And stay with me. Just—stay with me. Remember my name, Ahj. Don't let me drown with them and be lost. Find me, hold on to me, no matter what."

"Sh," Ahjvar said, catching him close a moment. "Don't. What are you seeing? It's all right, I have you."

A handful of Yuro's people came up. Ruckus down the line. Snow, scenting his rider and impatient. They were riding to meet the empress, Ghu said, as he might have said they would take a little exercise, all that fey moment shrugged away.

"Will you take another horse, lord *rihswera*?" a girl asked at Ahjvar's elbow. "Evening Cloud's shoulder . . ."

"Is he lame?"

"No, lord. Tender. A little stiff."

"We're not going to be fighting," Ahjvar said. "Or going—how far are we going?"

"We'll come to them by late afternoon, going gently," Ghu said. "Sooner if we want to. He's no longer hiding them. They would be here by tomorrow's dusk. So." He shrugged. "Maybe we delay them, a little, and Yeh-Lin can hold the river. Yes, bring him his Gorthuerniaul. But you two—" He dropped to a knee and the dogs crowded in to him, tails wagging. "Jui, Jiot. Go with Yeh-Lin."

Tails drooped. Ears went back, as when he had refused to take them in the skin boat. Jiot whined, pawed at him. Ghu kissed each between the eyes, which chilled Ahjvar when nothing else had. "Go on, dogs. Remind the devil she's watched. I'll call if I need you."

The horses, in their full barding, as if for battle again. Niaul seemed to move easily enough.

Word of their riding had spread like fire. There was a silence that ran before and trailed behind, a widening wake. Ghu was a weight that drew all eyes after him.

The heir of the gods rode to confront the empress, who called herself Daughter of the Old Great Gods. To challenge her, delay her . . . fold her into his following and bring on this new age of Nabban that the prophets had foretold. Did they think so? Could they?

They couldn't know what whispered in her mind.

Ghu's gods had been nothing, ever, but what they were now. Ghosts drowning or drowned in their own desperation. A last flicker of light lost in darkness, failing.

A godless land—Nabban had been falling to that before Ghu was ever born, and the Mother and Father had taken their child and cast him into the world too late, left him to make himself a man in the shadow of murder and horrors, where it should have been priests and captains had the making of him, holiness and true kingship. And their dying land had drawn a devil's eye.

We will never be his again . . . A fortress against what gathers in the west . . . my champion. An empire Over-Malagru, because he will come . . . The whisper of Ahjvar's nightmares.

He held himself still, made himself remember, and not react. It was not her voice in his ears, not the Lady, not her hands on him, her breath. Memory. Only memory. Something that had so terrified the devil Tu'usha in her madness.

Her enemy, her brother, the devil Jochiz. He leapt over what she would have made, the fortress-empire she would have held against him astride the caravan road. Planted seeds, a fence of thorns to surround her. *What gathers in the west.* While something flung down roots in the east, in a deceived and usurping princess. How long had that false faith in her destiny been germinating in the darkness of the princess's mind? How long had the gods of Nabban known? Both ends of the caravan road to be held for a devil that even the devils feared. And a despairing captive drowned the child of rape, drowned herself—gave herself and the infant to the river—and the gods took him to be their own, gave him their land, gave him to their land, and turned him loose to wander.

Was it Ahjvar who knew these things? It was there. A knowing in his memory.

West. Ghu had always been going west, even when he went east and south to the sea, when he ran from the high lord of Choa. West, following the sun, he said, till following the sun brought him to the Leopard, and the Leopard's garden wall in the rain.

Ghu looked around, found him watching. Said nothing.

CHAPTER XXXVII

Ghu remembered his first journey south more as vivid bright flashes of fear and wonder amid the long weariness of being hunted than as any clear story. Then, there had been an urgency almost animal, unthinking, unreasoning, driving him to seek the sea and a way to the west, and there had been no particular foe but sometimes, it seemed, all the folk of the land who prowled ready to raise a hand against him. Branded, paperless, far from his proper place in Dernang.

There had been kindnesses, too. Servants of the gods like Shouja Awan, a young couple of serfs on a manor in eastern Numiya, a pilgrim here, a merchant's guard there, a slave message-runner in the Old Capital, a gap-toothed woman of the river and her brood of loud and cheerful fatherless children, who did not ask questions of a furtive flitting thief and beggar, too obviously a runaway. They had all shared food or offered some shelter; even a kind word had been precious in those days. With the boatwoman and her children, he had had a few days and many miles of the river, and taken away words of the ships and the sea that unfolded a greater world to him.

This was the same. The urgency, unreasoning. The fear.

If he had had to go alone . . . but he could feel Ahjvar, keeping Evening Cloud a little behind and to the side, as if he had some other sense to know him by, like the eyeless fish that hunted in the lightless caves under the eastern mountains where the Gentle Sister had her source. Not sight, sound, smell, not the warmth of him, but as he knew where his own hand was, certainty without thought.

They were still in Alwu Province, and all was peaceful, green and growing, except that there were herds untended, and they came to a village that was emptied, all folk, he judged, fled, rather than driven out by Lai Sula. They did not follow quite that army's route. It seemed a forlorn place to halt, but yesterday had been hard and it was time to rest the horses. And some blessed person of the horselines had slung kettle and tea on them as well as a little grain.

Not entirely deserted. An old woman stumped up, leaning on a stick, as they brewed tea beneath the village meeting-tree.

"The gods be with you," Ahjvar said, sitting up. He had been lying on his back by the well, staring at the sky. But he didn't take up his sword.

"The gods are gone," she said. "Who are you, then?" She measured them with a keen, if watery, eye. "Mercenaries out of the north? I'm through with fear of masters and steel. Kill me now, kill me later when the empress comes, it makes no difference. I buried my last grandchild three days since. They said, come, come to the hills, the lord's gone to the wars on the river and they'll kill us if we stay, and I said, I'm not running, I'm done."

"Sit down and have some tea, grandmother." Ahjvar waved a hand at Ghu. "This is the heir of the gods, the holy one, riding against the empress."

The old woman studied him, and sniffed as though he left something to be desired. Ghu poured tea and offered it. It was strong and smoky, caravan-tea shaved from a brick, and there were plain dumplings wrapped in leaves, as well.

He should want to speak to her, to ask her about the folk of this village, but he knew the answers anyway. They were Dwei-Clan, serfs of a minor banner-lord of the Dwei who had ridden to join with Lai Sula in the empress's service, and who was dead and still unburied at the ferry. His wife had taken her children and the folk of the manor that lay just beyond the coppiced woodland north of them and gone with the serfs into the hills, for fear of the empress's coming.

He could not find words. Ahj would have to speak for him. The old woman had fallen silent, watching him over the rim of her cup.

"Why has the village run away?" Ahjvar asked. "What have you heard?"

"Everybody knows. Don't you? There was a boy come from Uro away down in Numiya, and that's a day's journey. I've never been. My husband went once, when he was young. The lord sent him. But this boy, he was half-crazed with terror. He said he'd been in Uro-Over-Hill on an errand for his master the wainwright—that's I don't know where, far and far away—and soldiers came, and wizards, and called all the folk of Uro-Over-Hill to the village well, out of the fields and all, and the steward from the hall and her family—and they lined them up kneeling, said they were to make their prayers to the Daughter of the Old Great Gods, but it wasn't for prayer at all they called them out. They made a great ring around them, and they went with swords and axes and forage-knives and killed them all, all up and down the rows, and they ran and screamed and the children cried, and the wizards tangled and held any who broke away out of the ring until the soldiers could kill them. And they left them lying, unburied, he says, and a captain on a horse said, the empress will give them their blessing, and he laughed. And the boy was lying up under the eaves of the great barn with a girl, up in the beams, which sounds a good way to break your neck, getting up to that sort of thing on the beams, and he saw through a chink in the wall, and the wizards searched, and the girl, poor child but it was her own folk dying, she went screaming down to kill them with nothing but her bare hands, and they killed her too. But the wizards thought she was the living thing they'd sought, I suppose, and they didn't look any further. So the boy lay there till nightfall and crept away, and he found his donkey straying and rode for Uro and his master beat him for being truant and lying and blaspheming, and so he stole the donkey and ran again. And our lady believed him, and the headman did, and they've all gone."

"Cold hells," Ahjvar said. "Souls. Left for her."

No words.

There might be visions painted in the fire. Ghu could not see them. He looked up when Ahjvar pressed the cup into his hands. "You're shaking," Ahj said quietly. "Drink." He wrapped his hands around the cup obediently, Ahj's for a moment over his. Rough warmth.

"Ghu, let me go on ahead of you. Yeh-Lin's right. Make an end of her and he has no foothold here."

Ghu shook his head, found words at last. "Not by murder."

"Challenge her, then."

"I . . . don't know. Perhaps. We'll see. Just—stay with me. Besides, last time you went to kill someone touched by a devil, it didn't go so well. I don't want to lose you that way again."

"Heir of the gods, you say?" The old woman gave Ghu another long look. "Huh. I'm through with the gods, too. Through with everything and waiting for my call to the road. But are you sure? Because he's a pleasure to an old woman's eyes, no doubt, but if he only speaks some heathen tongue, how does he know what the gods say?"

That broke something. Ghu laughed and leaned to the old woman and kissed her on the lips. "What makes you think the gods are through with you? You're not ready for the road yet. Go find your folk and this lost boy of Uro, Dwei Dolan. He needs a grandmother."

They set the old woman a mile on her way, a foresters' track into crumpled hills so steep it seemed only a squirrel or monkey might climb them. They were come into where the land changed, dropping down out of the spaciousness of Choa and Alwu. Soon there would be no wide fields or deserted lands, no wilderness but the occasional outcroppings of these steep, worn hills, water-gnawed stone to which bamboo and forest clung like a woodpecker against the side of a tree. If the empress had cleared her path with the deaths of villages all the way from the Old Capital . . . how could he not have heard the stone and the waters cry out against her?

He was overmatched. Dotemon was. They always had been.

Lai Sula had been a net to gather any fleeing to the northwest with rumours of Buri-Nai's great army.

At some point they crossed into Numiya. The provincial borders meant nothing, though he could feel, sometimes, where what had once been the land of one small god or goddess faded into another. He brought them cross-country, not following the muddy tracks. They missed the villages of Uro and Uro-Over-Hill, riding southeasterly, though there was smoke away to their right.

All the folk were fled. Some rumour had come.

Ahjvar gave him silence and watched all ways, the crossbow loaded.

The green narrowed, hills humping up above the fields. A village in the lee of one, empty of life but not of the dead, and the ghosts, and the miserable and terrified dogs who had survived their masters. Already he felt the weight of those souls, drawn to him but trapped, bound to their bodies, lives and seething life ripped away from the land. And beyond, within the narrowing land, the empress.

There was no time.

"Be blessed," he told the ghosts, but he needed to be among them, to know them, to touch. There was no time, and they pulled at him, as if they begged, clawed. He might begin to unravel.

Ahjvar was anchor. Stone. They must have the hunter's focus on what they stalked, the leopard's unblinking gaze. The dead would have to be abandoned, and hope the empress might be so delayed in whatever she intended for them that someone might send them free to their road, if he could not.

"We're seen," he said. A lone rider. Ahjvar moved up to his side.

Two more. Mounted scouts, by the village. They turned away, receded.

"Are you sure about this?" Ahjvar asked.

"Yes." No.

"Wait or follow?"

It made no difference. He let Snow walk on.

It was a troop of twenty banner-lords rode against them, and ten more who were armed like horse-archers of Alwu but were probably Wind in the Reeds, six of them women.

He drew rein as the imperial riders swept up, spears lowered, and made a half-circle about them, with their archers swung out and behind.

"The empress," he said. Request or command, they could take it how they would.

Their officer, or at least the man who now urged his horse a few steps ahead, raised his visor. Ahjvar had gone too still, but they were all living folk behind the masked helmets. He held the crossbow ready to bring up to the level.

"You are to come before the Daughter of the Gods," the banner-lord said. A Gar-Clan man of Nan-Ya province and he had little fear of them, only contempt for the traitors and the enemies who would learn to fear his goddess. A tattooed man, Ghu was certain.

"Yes," he agreed, but the word was heavy.

"Your weapons." The man spurred forward, another at his side, a hand out imperiously to Ahjvar. There would be a dead banner-lord, in very short order, and it would take a breath, just one word, to let Ahjvar do as he would and try to ride through, for he himself to think the Father's hand over them in some impossible miracle . . .

"Let it go, Ahjvar."

"Ghu, no."

"Yes, Ahj."

Ahjvar, with slow deliberation, disarmed the bow, though he dropped it rather than handing it to the man.

"And your sword and dagger, Northron."

"Not a Northron."

"Sword!"

"Ahj . . ."

"No."

"Great Gods, Ahjvar, do you think I want to see you cut to pieces here? Just do it, it would make no difference in the end if you killed the half of them before they cut you down—" His voice cracked. "Just let them have what they want," he said. "If it gets us before the empress, let them."

Ahjvar's sword and the obvious dagger, Ghu's forage-knife. But they did not search Ahjvar, and they did not see the small knife in his own boot. A pointless comfort. He did not see destroying the empress's devil with a little knife. Nor with Ahjvar's long Northron sword, if it came to that.

The path was only ever at his feet, a few steps. Falling into darkness now, drowned and lost, and pulling Ahj after him.

They rode amid their escort, hemmed close. Archers at their backs. The press of the ghosts faded.

The track they had followed climbed a bank and came onto the paved highway. In poor repair. Stones were missing, the land to either side trampled, rutted, puddled. Lai Sula had passed this way. They came to outliers, the suburbs of the camp, cavalry lines. Pickets afoot came to meet them. Banners. A fresh-dug ditch, a palisade of sharpened bamboo flung half across the valley. Tents going up along the avenues, and soldiers about the business of settling in, though it was not yet evening. But down the valley they still trudged, and wagons, endless wagons, laboured. They would be half the night coming in, and in the morning it would all be harried into motion again, and the men staggering weary, half-starved, not even a little dried fish or mutton to their rice and barley, though she had come from the sea and the flocks of Choa had been stolen away.

The pretender of the gods is defeated, is taken, is brought prisoner before the Daughter of the Gods . . .

But there was another thought running too . . .

The holy one, the heir of the gods, is come . . .

Ghu shivered. There were clouds piling on the horizon, spilling down from the north and west, from Choa, from the mountains. The wind was out of that quarter, and cold. Less than a month till the solstice and the midsummer festivals, but suddenly the air remembered snow. The horses snuffed and tossed their heads.

Another bamboo fence, this one a complete circle. Banners, imperial purply-red and cloth of gold, flew at its gates. They were ordered to dismount, and the horses taken. Snow snapped, and they dragged merciless at his bit. Evening Cloud followed mule-sullen, ears back. The guards of the inner compound had gilded armour, and checked them again for weapons. Took another knife off Ahjvar. Only the one.

Inside there were wagons and carriages, a tent of red roof and golden-brown walls central, others about it. Guards stood at each corner of that one. Two at the looped-back doors were the tallest men he had ever seen, overtopping Ahj by more than a foot, and broad to match their height. Two carried halberds, the others broad-headed spears.

Long shadows reached from the west and the roof of the tent suddenly glowed. He looked back. The sun was edged in fire. That meant fair weather, in Praitan. He did not think so tonight.

The giants took them in charge, dismissed the riders who had brought them, though two of the archers followed when they were gestured, not shoved, within. That much dignity, at least.

The tent was divided by screens, and this first room was carpeted, thick and soft as moss underfoot. The empress had prepared to receive them. It ought, he supposed, to be a compliment of sorts. At least they were no minor irritation. She sat in a carved and gilded folding chair, a travelling throne. Her court robes were a dozen layers, black through all the richest shades of red to palest pink, and a coat of gilded scale overtop. Her hair cascaded down about her and was held back from her face by a sun-rayed headdress set with pearls, white and pink and golden-hued. Her face was painted, red lips very small, blue about her eyes, drawing them up, cheekbones dusted with gold. The tent was lit with lamps burning scented oils. She flicked a slatted fan in her gloved hand, open, closed, open, the only sound. Restless. She touched her other hand to her chest, between her collarbones.

Someone might wear an amulet there. A caravaneer might, a token of their god. Ahjvar noted it. Of course he did. Ahjvar had marked every man and woman visible in that tent, even the attendant slaves in their court robes who meekly knelt aside and back of the throne, and who watched from beneath their downcast eyelids, marking targets as Ahjvar did.

Two more giants, one in each furthest corner, standing like guardian statues. Four about the empress.

"Your messenger from the Old Great Gods is a devil, Buri-Nai," Ghu said. Speak now, or he would lose all words forever, he felt, and sheer terror drive him back into the child who cringed from the cook's iron ladle. "Nothing has chosen you but to be the destruction of this land. His name is Jochiz Stonebreaker. He will make Nabban a wasteland, empty of life. How many deaths have you given him? You've killed your father and your brother and your brother's children and his wives and the crew of the ship that carried them. You've killed the priests of the land. You've killed folk in their hundreds, ever since you crossed into Numiya." He saw it now, felt it in the land. She had not flung slaughter out before her in her march through Solan. A small thing. She would say that proved she did not murder; she killed only by necessity as she drew nearer to Choa.

The Old Great Gods would weigh the lives.

The fan flicked, and flicked, catching the light.

"Don't you see what you do? Don't you fear him? What kind of god asks for the deaths of the folk? The Old Great Gods receive the dead, they don't seek death."

Flick. The fan closed, pointed to Ahjvar. "That," Buri-Nai said, "is a dead man. The mark of the Old Great Gods is on him. You have stolen his soul from the road."

"So?" Ahjvar growled.

What did she need to feel against her skin, under her hand? There must be some doubt in her, that nervous fidgeting fan, that search for reassurance.

"He lies to you, Buri-Nai," Ghu said. "I think you begin to know it. You're only a tool, convenient to his hand, and he'll throw you aside once he has what he wants from this land." Whatever that might be. "No god, no goddess, would do as you have. If you'd be holy, if you'd be even the empress this land needs, look, now. See what you do and change it."

"Your lies are empty. I have seen you in my dreams and I know you for what you are. A slave from Dernang, a runaway to the caravan road. A simpleton, when the devil is not putting words in your mouth. There is a devil in this land, yes, and she stands behind you. Yeh-Lin's puppet, that is all you are, you and the necromancer's swordsman, the Red Mask you stole from the Lady of Marakand."

A thick rage was building up in Ahjvar beside him, a storm gathering and no release for it, no way out . . .

Ghu had hoped she would hear, that she would be able to hear. He had thought she must doubt, somewhere, in some last corner of her soul, her own certainties. Simple, yes. Because he kept hoping. Because sometimes, out of all despair and all horror, hope did find something to save. Ahj.

He had killed where he ought not to have, taken away chances that he ought to have given. She was less worthy than some he had given no chance at all, he knew it, but—all those who followed him would pay the price if this came to battle.

He wanted the fighting ended, yet he would not have Ahjvar do murder for him. Challenge her, then? Throw Ahjvar against her or her champion, with the devil capable of reaching through her into the land, to do as he did on the river?

Let the folk at least know what led them.

"How can you not see what you do?" Ghu asked. "Where's this messenger you say the Old Great Gods have sent you? Let me see him, let him show himself and say why any true servant of the Gods would want this land in such terror of its goddess, if that's what you are."

"Souls," Ahjvar said. His voice was hoarse, a dog's snarl. "The souls of your servants, the souls of your slaves. The tattooed ones. Do you feed him on them? Do all these here know how your servants die?"

The empress pushed herself to her feet.

"Kill them," she said.

"Hells!" The knife left Ahjvar's hand as he flung himself on Ghu, both of them crashing to the carpeted earth, which was hard as stone and he felt Ahj's body buck as the spear took him, the empress a creature shrouded in pale and milky flame, her hand glowing against her breast and the half of her face washed dark, a knife's hilt standing out of her eye. Warmth. They fell into the springs of Swajui, but no, it was blood flooding over him, Ahjvar's blood, his own. Voices shouted distantly. A man towering against the red sky, the roof, another spear's broad and spell-edged blade and all a giant's weight behind the thrust, punching through, tearing metal, leather, tearing flesh and shattering bone, to be sure of them.

Cold, for all Ahj was so very heavy over him.

It hurt, being torn apart.

The empress was on her knees, drowned in light.

He drowned, in the pain, in the darkness, in the cold. In Ahjvar's blood.

CHAPTER XXXVIII

Ivah made braids as she rode, following the track, not the highway, and then village paths. Two horses, long-striding Denanbakis. Not so difficult to track, and the archers of Alwu were mostly hunters off the grassy hills, half Denanbaki themselves, like their horses. She left them to it, knotting the braids up into shapes like some unopened bud. In a deserted village they found signs the men had made a fire and rested. Reassuring to know she and hers had not gone astray. She used her teeth as well as fingers to work the final knot, as the sun set.

Difficult to find their way in the dark. No wizard's light. A scout in the lead carried a lantern on a pole, held low. Just the one. It would be taken for fox-light, maybe. They kept their ears open for any sound of an alerted watcher. Tendrils of fog began to creep out of ditches, pool in hollows. It had the smell of wizardry. Yeh-Lin's, not hers. Clouds rolled over them, shutting out the stars and the rising of the moon. After midnight, for certain. She smelt the smoke before she saw the fires, and the man in the lead put out his lantern.

"Fire," she said. "Like fireworks, it will be. You'll see it even in fog. Ride then."

They carried smouldering pitch in jars swinging from yokes. Even the clay grew hot. Yeh-Lin's wizardry, not hers. It was not only tar meant for ropes and rafts. Other things had gone into it. A foul weapon, the devil had said. Ask Kozing Port why they forbade building in wood and thatch. Her smile had been—unpleasant.

They left the archers under the eaves of a forested hill. Ivah did not really expect ever to see them again. She traced, in spit, with apologies, characters on each forehead, each wrist, of the three of them. Grasslander and Nabbani, woven together.

"We're invisible?" Awan asked, curiously.

"Not yet. And no, we won't be invisible. Difficult to notice. Don't walk into anyone. Don't go near wizards."

A final character.

"Now," she said. "Keep quiet, as well. They'll notice sound."

Yuro and the old priest followed her, walking softly, unhurried. Awan stubbed a sandalled foot on something and grunted, stumbling, but Yuro caught him before he fell. Past sentries keeping watch, huddled close together. They seemed to peer inwards as much as out.

Stench of smoke and dirt, after the green lands. She had no idea what they sought. Prisoners? Some late council, some debate? Ghu should not have gone alone. She had completed that hexagram she had begun to throw weeks ago. It had been, *The open arms of the Old Great Gods*. Some commentaries had it *empty arms*. It was generally read as an unequivocal foretelling of death, regardless. It had not been a foretelling she had meant to throw, only a question she sought to answer for herself, regarding the god's champion and the unease he gave her. *What is he?* she had asked.

His, Ahjvar said of himself.

What is he?

The empty arms of the Old Great Gods.

But she had been wrong. It was not a puzzle but a foretelling after all. She did not think they would find the god in council with the empress, arguing, persuading. She did not know how they could have let him go, except that it was his will to go alone and somehow . . . he had edged them into allowing it. Yeh-Lin said he went to distract the empress, to delay Buri-Nai while his captain-general moved, because surprise was all they had to give weight to their numbers, and to sit and wait at the ferry would be to offer themselves to inevitable defeat and he had not meant her to do that at all, whatever words he had spoken. Perhaps he meant to set Ahjvar loose among her command. Ivah was not so certain.

Ahjvar might be an assassin, might once have been king's sword among his own people, but the only person Ivah knew who had ever truly slain a devil was far away, trying to hide herself from the Old Great Gods, to escape the doom they had set her, which was to slay Dotemon, and Jasberek, and Jochiz. If she could summon Moth to plunge from the night sky, bird of prey shaped from the Northron wizardry of the feather-cloak, she would. Whatever the cost, even to Yeh-Lin.

Find Ghu. Get him out, if they could. Hope he had learned what Yeh-Lin thought he intended to learn, the truth of the empress and her devil and some way to sever them, or that Ahjvar had slain the empress.

Hope he was alive to find.

They drifted, like the fog that wrapped their ankles, to the inner compound. The gates were closed, but they circled to where there was less torchlight. A spell was laced through the bamboo, a thing of warning. Ivah caught and wove the characters into a ring of yarn, white like the fog, and they went over using Yuro's coat to cushion the sharpened stakes. Wagons, covered ones like huts on wheels, several more ornate carriages, and wagons with open beds. One grand tent, several lesser ones. People, in clusters, muttering, anxious. Banners hanging still. Fog pouring tendrils over the fence. Torches burning, mostly before the grand tent, and it glowed, lit bright within. She moved that way. The other two followed.

To cross that threshold . . . no. That would push the spell too far, under the eyes of the watching giants. Another of her mother's stories proven true, that the imperial bodyguard were giants. A blue-gowned wizard strode out, paused, looked around, eyes lingering on them. Frowned. Continued on her way to one of the other tents. Sudden voices. Ivah caught at Awan's arm, drew him down. Yuro followed into the shadow of a wagon, crouched in blackness, fog caressing like a friendly cat.

"Exalted, the surgeon—you must let him attend you now."

"The Old Great Gods hold me in their hands. There is no need."

"Exalted, please. For the sake of your people—"

"One more word and I will have the tongue out of you! I am going to rest, yes, and that will suffice. Any fool who disturbs me—"

The speaker bowed and fell away from the hurrying knot. Two women carrying paper-shaded lanterns, four giants, a handful of more ordinary men and women in armour coats, all armed, though some wore long gowns beneath. In their midst, a long-haired woman whose robes gave her the shape of a young spruce tree, Ivah's first thought. She strode out unhampered by them, but stopped suddenly and stood, peering around.

Her head was wrapped in bandages, covering one eye. Blood seeped through, and her chest and one gloved hand were stained. She put that hand to her breast, closed her visible eye as if she prayed.

A groping hand, reaching for them . . . Ivah set her own hands to the earth, to Nabban's earth, and slowly, because she was only drifting fog, a stirring stem of grass, wrote. *Beneath the sky, the sea of grass, the breathing hills.* The empress breathed out audibly and passed on, into the largest tent.

Ivah breathed again herself. She touched Yuro's hand, Awan's. The priest had his own eyes shut, praying. He looked up, pointed. She nodded. The empress had come from the further side of the compound. They went that way, crouching in deepest blackness, crawling, even. No oxen or mules, but there were people sleeping under many of the wagons. The more menial slaves of the imperial household, she supposed. Some lying wakeful, too, pressed close for comfort, whispering, afraid. Guards patrolled.

One wagon had been pushed away from the others. Guarded, where no others had been, and a lantern hanging from a halberd driven into the earth at its rear. Two men. Not giants, but they looked like imperial guard, until one walked over to speak to the other, heads close together, and that was not a soldier's way of moving but a hunter's, light on the feet. Ivah waited until they separated again, touched Yuro, found his ear.

"Wind in the Reeds."

She pointed Yuro to the left. He had left his mace with the archers, but he carried a forage-knife at his back as Ghu did. She tugged at the high collar of his coat of scales, reminder of the enemies' armour. The forage-knife was no stabbing weapon. He nodded.

A sudden head-on rush would be seen. Yuro followed her lead, approached warily, circling to the side as a dog would. He stepped behind his man and jerked his head back. She was a pace behind, damn, and took hers in a lunge, arm over his mouth, dagger punching between plates into his back, down on top of him so her whole weight made the blow. He still struggled, biting her. She got a knee between his shoulders and both hands on his head. Their helmets were plain, without the visor-masks of a lord's, and she pressed his face into earth, leaning on him, as he bled to feeble twitches and suffocated together. She cleaned her hands methodically, rolled to her knees and looked around, jerking her knife free. No stirring. She had lost the spell, though, disrupted by the man's blood spattering it. Yuro was rolling the bodies under the wagon. No one sleeping here. Awan dashed over. Had she warned them not to make sudden movements—no one cried alarm. Fog rose waist high now, as if it were water, trapped and pooling.

Absence of light, where there likely was not usually light anyway, would be less noticeable than absence of guards. The wagon was a rough carriage, a wooden box with louvred windows to its sides. Yuro unlatched the door and went through like a badger into its den, on his belly. Ivah blew out the lantern and gave Awan a hand after the castellan, then followed, pulling the door closed behind her. The latch could be worked from both sides, good. She secured it before she sketched a light.

Yuro had already found them, down on his knees, and she had known; she could smell the blood. They had thrown Ahjvar in all anyhow, dumped like rubbish, but Ghu they had at least laid on his back, arms at his sides, and his eyes were decently closed. His coat and shirt were flung open and she shut her eyes a moment.

Didn't need to check for a breath, a heartbeat, not with such wounds, and Ivah was not one of those who saw the waiting dead. There was an emptiness, though, that made her think their ghosts already gone. Sent to the road. She might pray so. That rather than taken, please. She knelt and touched his lips. Cold, already. Her breath was catching in her throat, sobs stillborn, because she must not scream and wail, not here. She had believed, she had truly believed, that he could come to no harm, that he had some foreknowledge. He was *god*, he must have seen . . . Yuro had turned away. Awan was praying, a low mutter, rocking where he knelt.

"We can't leave him here. Either of them. Not like this. Can we carry them away?" Yuro asked, still not looking.

A gasp, horribly gurgling, like someone fighting lung-fever. Not the last sighing of the dead. Another, deeper. A muttered unintelligible string of what sounded foreign cursing.

"What was that?" Awan looked up, eyes wide in the dim light.

Ahjvar's corpse shifted, shadows moving.

CHAPTER XXXIX

Light. Many lights, small lights, faint. Stars. Fireflies. They swam and stirred, stars in water, but that was only his unsteady eyes. He hurt. He was cold. Could not remember how to move. Remembered trying to breathe, drowning, that bubbling in the chest, that fire.

"Can we carry them away?" someone asked, the faintest whisper.

Ahjvar took a breath, a deep one. It seared like a slow knife, gods, yes, dragged and rattled, but the next was easier. Not, after all, dying. Again.

"What was that?"

Light, growing, coalescing. Light in a wizard's hand.

Fit of coughing, choking. Hacking up clotted blood.

"Oh gods, Ahjvar's still alive." Ivah, down on her knees by him. The floor moved, was still. "Ahjvar, hush, be still. They'll hear." Her hand covered his mouth, which made him taste the blood that filled it, think he would choke again. He tried to turn his head aside. Weak as a new pup.

"Cold hells." Yuro, moving carefully around him. The floor shifted again. A small space.

Third man. The priest Awan, his face expressionless, crawling over to him.

"There is something very wrong in here," Awan whispered. "Ivah, don't you feel it?"

"Where?" Ahjvar muttered, against the hand he was too weak to push away. Managed to clench and unclench one hand. They hadn't cut his hands off, anyway. Not that one. The other—hurt, rather, but it moved. A very faint hurt, under a weight of pain that was a sea, drowning him, too great to understand.

"A wagon," Ivah said. "Hush, they—they've brought you to a carriage in the empress's compound. I don't know why."

Not what he wanted to know. He did get free of her hand, rolled to his side, or tried to.

"Ghu."

"Great Gods, don't move. You'll bleed again." She had found the buckles under his arm, was undoing the coat now. He clenched his teeth and still a sound escaped him, hardly human in his own ears, when she folded it back, flesh and leather pulling apart.

"Gods, gods, gods." Her hands did something, which also hurt, did him up again, with shaking care. Bloody hands took his head. "Ahjvar, gods. How—There's nothing I can—it's beyond anything I can do. I'm sorry. Just—lie quiet. It—won't be long. We'll stay." Tears ran faster.

He struggled over again and she put arms around him, trying to hold him down, and he did not like people touching him, clinging, pulling him into the fire, into the well, holding him down.

Ivah. She was trying to be comfort, to be kindness. To help. Don't hurt her.

Too weak to be a danger anyway.

"Not dead," he said. "Not dying."

The next breath was easier yet.

"Ghu," he insisted.

"They killed him, Ahjvar. They killed you both together. He's here. He's beside you. There. Don't move. Just turn you head a little. Can you see?"

Her light moved, a little higher.

"Too bright," Yuro whispered. "Cracks. The shutters. Someone will see."

It dimmed.

Beside, on the carriage's floorboards. A shape, only. Not close enough to touch. He made it onto his side. Good. Arm.

"Ahjvar . . ."

Up onto his elbow. Knee, next.

"Don't!" But now her hands hovered, afraid to touch. The priest knelt beyond.

"He's not dead," Ahjvar said, and fell beside Ghu, arm over him, leg. Hauled close.

Ghu's armour and shirt had been half stripped from him, baring his chest as if someone frantically sought to staunch the blood. Pointless. A grey taint to his skin, no warm colour of life. Cold, to a hand on his face, his neck, spread palm to his chest above the jagged, black crusted slits. One to his chest, one his lower ribs. No rise and fall. No breath against a hand. Cold and still.

"He's not dead," he repeated.

"Ahjvar, he is. He'd bled his life away before they ever brought him here."

He hurt and he was tired, and he'd had a spear run through his back and out and into Ghu, twice, and still he breathed, and hurt, and woke to crawl onwards.

"I'm alive. So he is."

"You're dying," Yuro said bluntly. "Man, they've ripped you through the lungs and how you breathe—"

"I died almost a hundred years ago. I was cursed. I don't die." Cursed, and now trailing into the borderlands of godhead at Ghu's heels. "My stepmother burnt me to death and a goddess cursed me to live, to always live, trapped me in life no matter what's done to me. Why doesn't matter. That's done with, the use she had for me. But I heal. I survive. Fate and bloody chance will twist the world to keep me living, the blow is never quite fatal. Gods, they tried to behead me in Sea Town once sixty years ago, and the executioner slipped and fell beside me when there was no other way he could miss his stroke. Broke his neck. Or I did, can't remember. I *survive*; I'm trapped in life. I can't be killed for all so many have tried, myself included, and the bloody Lady of Marakand

But the goddess who cursed me is put from the world and I am taken from her. I belong to Ghu, my curse does. He holds me in the world as she once did. 'S'why they keep hunting a necromancer."

His laughter was a horrible sound even to himself, thick through clotted blood. They thought him mad, raving.

"He's alive, or I wouldn't be. Dust an' ashes. How you'll know. I go to ash and bone, you know then, he's dead. Saw my own hand. Bone and ashes. I know what I am. I saw, I knew, when the curse took me and I crawled from the ruin of the hag's bower . . ."

But Ghu seemed cold and still and dead; he knew death well enough when he saw it.

No. Ghu would not die and leave him behind, leave him trapped, immortal, enduring and unending, in this life he persisted in only for Ghu's own sake. He would not, he would not. Ahj had faith in that one thing, beyond all else.

"How long?"

"What do you mean?"

"How long since we came here?"

"You were only half a day ahead of us, maybe."

"When?"

"Well, today," Ivah said.

That confused him. He shouldn't be moving. Not yet. He could lie like the dead for days, while the curse pulled him back into life and wounds that should never heal knit themselves to yet more scars of bloody history.

Or Ghu was dead and he himself dying in the ordinary way, too stupid to know it. Why should he think he would burn again?

No.

"We need to get them away," said Yuro. "The empress might come back."

"She's dead," Ahjvar said. "Killed her."

"She isn't."

"Knife in her eye. Deep. Blade's full length. She's dead."

"She was walking back to her tent from this wagon. That's how we found it."

"Her eye was bandaged," Awan offered. "Perhaps you missed, only wounded her."

"Don't miss," Ahjvar muttered. "Lots of practice. Been killing people a long time. *Tired* of it." Long sigh. "Devil." It came out like an obscenity, not an explanation.

He shut his eyes, still wrapped around the dead man as if he could warm him. Cold, cold, cold and heavy flesh, unmoving. All the world, centred on Ghu. They were bound; it was not a fool's thought. Ghu held all the web of the goddess's curse that kept him in the world. He'd never felt it as a *thing* before, as if for a moment they were one creature, shared nerves and blood and soul, or he some lesser part of Ghu's greater being.

Some other thing. Some other web, some clinging, burrowing, sucking thing—

Opened his eyes and pushed himself up on one arm.

"Where?" he said.

"What?"

"Priest said, something's here. Wrong. Where?"

"I don't—I'll throw the coins." Rustling behind him. Looking for her damned coins. The priest came to kneel by them, his hands on Ghu's temples, brushing back the hair that lay over his face, blood-sticky.

"The holy one should not be so cold," he said.

"He's *dead*."

"Don't shout." Yuro put a hand on Ivah's shoulder, warily, as if she might bite. It hadn't been a shout so much as a strangled whisper.

"At my age," the priest said, "I've sat with many dead. Laid them out, blessed them, buried them. I've never yet known one be colder than the air, unless they were taken from the river and even then, they have only the river's chill."

Too weak, too heavy, and the pain grew deafening. Ahjvar was lying down again, and the priest was right. Winter-cold, seeping into him. Flesh. Bone. Heart. Creeping down the chains that bound him, spreading, frost on spider's web, ice. Spreading to him from Ghu, through what bound them. Blood, thick in his mouth. Ice. Stone beneath his tongue. Not his. Ghu.

He fumbled a hand that could hardly move, pulled Ghu's head to the side so that they were face to face, too close to focus eyes on, but his eyes were blurred and hazed anyway. He shut them, the better to feel what he did. Cold lips. Fingers clumsy, pushing clenched teeth apart. Tongue, that had shaped such careful, wary words, tongue that could be so sweet and gentle, urgent and teasing, to give him back what he had forgotten and teach him what he had never known. Tongue that could whisper comfort even against the worst of the darkness in him. Stiff and dead, sheathed in a web of ice. Under the tongue. Sharp. He fumbled it up against the lower teeth, hard needle of not-ice, hooked it out, lost it on the floorboards, groped and pinched it as if it might turn to some many-legged horror and skitter away.

"Light," he demanded, and when Ivah's dim light settled over him he struggled to sit up and pressed the sliver of stone into her hand. Pale, like milky quartz; a splinter, nothing more. Cold, biting in the fingertips.

"What in the cold hells . . . ?" she asked.

"Don't know." But the icy horror that had been sinking roots into him was melting. He let himself down again. No change in Ghu, except that a hand laid on him warmed, slowly, the skin beneath. Only as any dead thing warmed to what touched it. No life, no breath.

Remember my name, Ahj. Don't let me drown with them and be lost. Find me, hold on to me, no matter what.

Call him. But he was not here. Lost.

Find me.

He was no damned shaman. He did not know the way of wandering in souls and dreams. Did not want to. Hold onto Ghu, though, he could, and did.

Mouth on Ghu's mouth, one last breath between them. *I have you.*

"Ahjvar—Gods be merciful, he's stopped breathing." Hands on him. Very far away.

"Leave him," the priest whispered. "Let him go."

He fell, as if into dark water.

CHAPTER XL

Cross the river and hold Choa.

Was she his dog?

The damned dogs trailed her, wolf-shadows, looking accusing, as if Yeh-Lin were the cause of their banishment. The clouds that had threatened in the evening had rolled in overnight as they marched, and fog had followed and overtaken them out of the river valley. Not the god's fog, but her own, drawn about them, cold and chilly. The air was heavy, though. Past the dawn, but hardly lighter than the twilight. Storm coming. The clouds were black and churning, somewhere above the fog, and she could only hope that Sien-Shava could not pierce it, to know for certain more than that she moved. It was not only fog she shrouded them in.

They were near, she thought. Near, very near. Her folk—Nabban's— sat or lay and rested, even slept, in their ranks, and had water and what food there was so, as well. Waiting. Few lanterns, kept low and shrouded, just enough to help them keep their place.

Her children were tight-lipped and shadow-eyed with their fear. They had not gone when she ordered them, with the wounded and the exhausted over the river under Prince Dan's command. Could she argue? Jang had said, "You're going after him. We'll come after you."

This was not the proper behaviour of a page. She would have to point that out, if they all survived.

A frenzied night. A weary march. She had not been able to pull together the force she wanted in an hour, which fear screamed at her to do. The Grasslander had gone ahead. The priest Awan had gone with her, and Yuro, and a company of mixed rebels and archers of Alwu. Yeh-Lin supposed she was fortunate Dan had remained in command of the companies left to hold the crossing, though she would rather have had Yuro's good sense than Dan's utterly irrational faith in his fool god's wisdom. There was an apprehension among the soldiery, conscripts and converts and rebels alike. The holy one of the gods had ridden alone against the empress and her army. They followed, awaiting some sign . . . They might already be doomed and damned and godless.

Not godless. The empress had wanted him alive. The assassin the dead king questioned had said so. Alive and captive, and he counted on that, her mad, beautiful, innocent god.

Half-witted fool. He didn't even wait to ask what she might do, what they could do, she, he, a devil's daughter, and his half-mad champion. Just went and left her bound in the weight of an army and his word, his trust, his thrice-damned eyes.

Yesterday's rumour had run like fire through the companies, the numbers coming against them, ten thousand, twenty, fifty, a hundred, all the armies of all the provinces of the south. Tell them the south is fully engaged fighting the Wild Girls, she told the officers. Tell them there is not enough grain in all the provinces north of the Gentle Sister to feed the numbers they fear.

But there had not been panic, and she had not after all withdrawn from the east, only sent what she must, to secure the west, which confidence must, she hoped, spread downward. She did not like retreat. If she had done as Ghu had seemed to order, they might march and countermarch up and down the Wild Sister for weeks and gain nothing. No. He said one thing and willed that she listen. *All in your hands, do you hear me?* And so she left Dan to pull together what he could from the wreckage of her own ruin, if it came that.

If it came to that, they were all lost, godless together.

"My lady?"

Zhung Ario, leading his horse into the lantern-light she made. A lantern carried by Kufu, but wizardry lit it.

"What?" she snapped—too angry, tired, hopeless, she did not know. All courtesies fled.

"My lady, the scouts have brought in two you should see."

"Imperial spies? Wind in the Reeds? All scouts from the empress's army are to be killed." She was not feeling forgiving, and she did not want assassins getting loose at her back.

All too clear Ghu did not trust even to the Praitannec tongue to keep secrets within the camp, or they would have been able to make some more co-ordinated plan.

Or perhaps he really had that much faith in her.

"I don't know, my lady. They say not."

"And you believed them, of course."

Zhung Ario rubbed mud from his cheek. "I wasn't sure, my lady. One says, well, she says she's an ambassador of the Wild Girls, come to speak with the heir of the gods of Nabban. She says the other is a servant of Prince Dan. Wiser to let you see them than to obey mindless and kill an ambassador, I thought."

Give the man greater command than he had, for that. When she had time and leisure to think of such things. "Yes. Take me to them, then."

The captives sat under a tree, guarded. She could not see them till she was almost on top of them. That they had been taken at all in this fog argued that they had wanted to be found. A man with a crooked nose and a face cross-hatched with fine scars, a sharp-boned woman, both young, both road-ragged and dirty. Their quilted gowns might have been decent ones, once.

They had been disarmed of swords. Not the beggars they looked. There was an air to the woman, something to her, a presence. Not wizardry.

And her eyes, the clear brown of hazelnuts, went wide, seeing Yeh-Lin. She rose to her feet, her hand pressing her comrade down when he too would have risen. Their guards stirred warily.

They faced one another in silence.

"The heir of the gods of Nabban," the woman said at last. "What have you done with him?"

Truth in her. Yeh-Lin gave truth back. "My lord rode yesterday to meet the empress."

"*Your* lord."

"Yes. He is."

"Alone?"

"He ordered—"

"You let him go alone? Do you know what whispers in the empress's ear?"

"Sien-Bloody-Shava," Yeh-Lin snapped. "Yes, I do, and I see you do too. And what are you?"

"Anlau, a queen of Darru and Lathi. Call me Rat."

"Queen is hardly all, is it? But I'll let it pass for now. And who is he?"

"Dwei Kaeo? My friend. A singer and actor. A prophet of the gods of Nabban, maybe. A spy of Prince Dan's in the Golden City, till they took him. He came to keep me company on the way."

"I've heard that before," she muttered.

"Queen?" Ario was asking. "One of the Wild Girls, she means? Here? Her?"

"You left him to go alone?" the rat-girl persisted.

"He—Why in the cold hells do you think we are here?" Almost on top of the enemy, not even a mile between, and the fog smothering all.

"The empress is nothing. Why the god of Nabban there and you here?"

Because he arranged it so. To give Buri-Nai what she wanted, her rival, the heir of the gods in her hands. To distract her, let her think she'd won, while Yeh-Lin . . . did what she could. Or just as likely, for all they denied it, to put Buri-Nai within his assassin's reach.

The fool who had taken a castle with two swords and a forage-knife.

Had he even believed the empress to be the enemy he must face?

Did he see—

To the east, and high, the fog glowed, showing itself smoky and restless, pearly. Ivah's signal loosing the archers. Time to go, and now she saw, now—

"Cold hells damn him for a half-witted fool!"

And herself, blind, blind—blinded, known and blinded from the moment Jochiz smelt her hovering to spy on the empress in her mirror.

She spun on her heel, hair flying, loosing all hold on her form. To the cold hells with all of it. She was through with playing games.

Now.

All in her hands. He put *Nabban* again in her hands.

She did not want it. She would not be his heir. It was not the empress he had gone to distract and draw out but the devil and he did not know, he did not understand, he could not, what that might mean.

"Jang, Kufu, Ti! Go tell the commanders to follow the plan. I go to our lord, and they must follow on." And die, and all Nabban was lost. "You understand? Go now. Run!"

Kufu nodded, backing away before he ran. Ti and Jang both stared a moment. Then they, too, ran, Jang calling some instruction to the boys, sending them different ways.

And so she broke her pages' hearts.

Zhung Ario backed a step or two. "My lady—"

"Go, go, if you love our blasted young god," she said. "*Our* god. *Mine*. Yes, I am Yeh-Lin Dotemon. Did you think I lied in my challenge to Hani Gahur? My *god*, he is. I have given myself to Nabban, to his Nabban and what he will make of it, and he is gone to face not the empress but a devil, a tyrant to make Bloody Yao look a kindly grandfather. Trust me, there are powers we never yet unleashed on the world, even in the end, but our enemy is one who would break the very heavens if the power to do so came into his hands and I see, I did not understand and now I see. *And* there's another damned goddess half-formed wandering out into the land. Turn these two loose. They are what they say and the Wild Girls and the Little Sister may yet be your best hope, if all else fails."

"My lady," Zhung Ario said. He bowed to her and mounted, a curt gesture sending the prisoners' guard running ahead. One delayed only to offer them back their swords.

Yeh-Lin drew her own sword and turned through the circle, the steps, weaving a pattern to call the wind. And the wind, pulling storm in its wake, shredding fog, came to take her.

CHAPTER XLI

Two corpses and they could not just leave them, not knowing. Ahjvar sounded mad, but a man so torn through could not live and move and speak, and keep speaking. The splinter of crystal in Ivah's hand was chilling her palm, not warming to it. She wiped frozen blood from it and wrapped it in a length of red yarn, knotting it as if might escape the cocoon, and the knots were ones of sealing and holding. She added a hair from her own head, winding it, making the same knots, and put it in the purse with her oracle-coins.

"Is Ahjvar mad, are they dead, or do we have any hope?" she demanded of Awan.

"Hope," he said. "I don't know. I have faith."

She had thought she did. Tried to remember the warmth that had filled her, the safety, the sense of being home. The rider of the white horse, the sky breaking into blue banners. She had known, then. She remembered. It was very far from the stench of congealing blood and the fear that made her hands shake. Old Great Gods, she had ridden a demon into battle against the Lady of Marakand; she was the daughter of Tamghiz Ghatai, of An-Chaq who had escaped the palace and all the Wind in the Reeds sent after her; she could not be so weak now.

"He came back to the castle," Yuro said. "Everything changed. And Yeh-Lin calls him her lord. Yes, I know what she is. I do notice things.

If Ghu's man says he is a hundred years old and immortal, I believe him. A man doesn't move and speak, doesn't breathe, with wounds like that. Not this long. And if he says Ghu is not dead, I believe that too."

They had to, because otherwise what was the point in anything? They were defeated and lost and could only go on twitching, like a hooked fish tossed up on the riverbank, until the empress made an end of them.

"We still have work to do," Ivah said. "The three of us can't carry them away through all this camp to any place safer, even if we took them one at a time, and I don't think I would want to separate them."

The empress had said she was going to rest; she had threatened any who disturbed her. That might mean a certain reluctance on the part of Buri-Nai's people to report any minor strangeness. Ivah found colours, red, white, black, began a cat's-cradle that grew long, a net that caught the stars of winter morning in its pattern, the wounded hero Khumbok asleep, cradled like a child in the lap of the lake-goddess Aiakayl, while his enemies searched blind along the shore.

"Out," she whispered to Yuro. "Not you," to Awan. "You stay with them."

He nodded, settling down cross-legged on one of the cushioned benches that ran along the sides, where he could watch over the dead. Holding the pattern taut in her hands, she spread it out on the floor.

"I can't leave the light. Don't disarray this or it won't hold. If someone comes in—it won't matter anyway. Do you have a weapon?"

The priest shook his head. "I came to be by my god, that only. I'm an old man, a priest of the Mother. I eat no meat. I've never so much as killed a fowl."

"Pray Ahjvar wakes up then, if someone comes."

She let her light go out and followed Yuro into fog that wrapped and clung, so that almost at once she felt as damp as if it drizzled. Thick fog should help. The air had the heavy feel of coming storm, pressing down.

She was holding too many threads in mind. To recast the spell that made her difficult to see would be too much. Trust to the night and the fog.

A little moonlight would have been nice.

She and Yuro caught hands, not to lose one another, and walked with the careful, soft steps needed when one had no idea if the ground might rise or fall in a sudden rut. Her shoulder hit something. Another wagon. That dark. Too close, a woman's voice whispered, "I can't pray. I wish I could," which was so much her own thought . . .

They had counted on a glimpse of moonlight, a faint lightening beyond the cloud in the east, to let them know it rose, days into its last quarter, and that the dawn was coming. Already she had lost all sense of direction. Yuro tripped and in his falling something caught her across the thighs and they both went down, a heavy thump.

"Who's that?" a man called.

Guy-rope. In their silence, picking themselves up, they heard someone move near. Sudden murky lantern-light, almost on top of them. But the guy-rope found him. Grunt. Thump.

"Devils damn this fog."

"Maka?"

"Yeah. Where are you?"

A snort. "Tell me and I'll let you know. Just stay put. No point trying to walk the rounds in this. Go stumbling into the wall of the Exalted's tent and your head will be right up there with tomorrow's haul of deserters."

Yuro tugged her sleeve. On hands and knees, they moved away. They needed to be feeling their way with a stick, like Dan. No sticks to hand and she had left her bow with her horse.

They weren't crawling in circles after all. Bamboo stakes. Her knotting of the wards still worked, whispering reassuring lies into whatever mind had set this. It was a fence put up and taken down with every camp, a barrier for privacy and the setting apart of their divine empress, not true defence. The pales were not planted all that deeply, and the split canes that wove through them, helping to hold them aligned, were growing brittle. Yuro's forage-knife sliced through those with little sound, and they rocked enough stakes loose to squeeze through, setting them back in the loose earth. Not straight, but who would notice? They should mark the point somehow, but in the fog how would they find it again anyhow?

She really wished she knew what direction she faced.

Faint wind. The fog was nearly drizzle, and her left cheek was colder. Whatever direction that was. The clouds had been gathering in the north. Perhaps they crept east, now.

The archers were waiting behind them, then. Couldn't be helped.

The plan was that they would find Ghu and his champion, to extract them if they could, before signalling the raiding party. Holding off on that until as near dawn as possible, to give Yeh-Lin's rapid night march most time. Failing that . . .

Strong scent on that faint breeze. Cattle.

"Yuro?" Murmur against his ear. "Ever work with oxen?"

"I was my lord's stable-master, not a ploughman."

Damn. Daughter of the warlord she might be, but no daughter of the Grass grew up a pampered princess—her father's bellow at her mother, some argument yet again. There were tasks for bondfolk, but if she could not do them herself, how could she know well from ill done, and how could the folk she might one day lead respect her? But it was she who needed to do what they had come for; she could not be teaching Yuro to wrestle with yokes and accidentally-goring horns in the dark.

On the other hand . . . the ox-drivers would sleep near their charges.

"Yuro, you're a captain of the Wind in the Reeds. You need two yoke of oxen and their drivers."

No protest. He simply took a deep breath. "You coming with me?"

"I need to set the signals. Just be a lord. Arrogant. Certain. Walk over them. You were a slave in Dernang. They're slaves. You know the sort of captain and lord you need to be to stop them questioning."

"No slaves, he says."

"Not if she comes back and kills him while he lies—" Not dead. They were pretending they had faith. "—lies helpless in some shaman's trance."

"Yes."

"Good. Tell them—the gate-guards can't be trusted. That's why you're taking them through the fence. You'll have to widen the gap or make a new one. Gods be with you." Which god or gods or Gods? She left him.

It was easier moving on her own, and if she shut her eyes against the blindness and merely felt, in the soles of her boots, in the damp breath of the north on her face, in the air she breathed—smoke, dung, animals, human sweat, crushed greenery, mud—she found her way. A way. A straight lane, mucky and rutted, the central avenue of the camp, and there was occasional light, a fire, a lantern, suddenly emerging and quickly passed. There were others who moved likewise, most often in pairs, muttering for their own encouragement, grumbling against the dark and the night and cursing the weather.

Distant thunder.

She began to lay the knotted spells that she had made as she rode, setting each with a breathed word over it.

A section of a spiral, working inward, back to the empress's compound. She had meant to lay most of them along the main avenue, but she did not after all want to end up on the edge of the camp, where she and Yuro and Awan were meant to be with the holy one, to reclaim their horses.

Now, before whatever uproar was going to follow when Yuro began trying to steal a wagon.

She nicked her wrist. Northron wizardry, the sacrifice of her own blood, binding this. Brought the few welling droplets to her tongue, felt the words grow, strong, fierce.

In the Mother's night, the Father's fires bloom. The mountain is alight and the waters hold the fire of life.

Pillars of light, rising, breaking, and falling back like fountains. The fog glowed, showed itself not still but roiling, troubled with currents, as if unseen creatures warred within it like monsters in the depths of the sea. A stunned silence, then a shout. The usual human foolishness of one asking another just as ignorant, "What's that?" Watchmen rushing, then thinking better of it and advancing cautiously, to investigate.

The knots would burn and the light fade as they were consumed. They would find nothing, a pinch of ash, maybe. Ivah used the light to find her way back to the inner compound, began walking that fence into darkness again. One fountain died, another, another, burning down more quickly than she and Yeh-Lin had intended. Some other will quashing them. Horns blowing alarm.

Shouting, a disorder of weary, sleep-stupid men, and officers shouting with no idea what the alarm was and no enemy to see. Shouting within the compound as well, people calling out. She began to jog, one hand trailing along the fence.

Splintering. A gap not made wide enough. In the light of the last fountain, bamboo pales fell outwards, a woman scrambling through them, nearly trampled by the team she tugged along by a horn of the near ox, shouting encouragement or abuse, Ivah wasn't certain. The driver dodged away, flicked a red-roan rump with her whip. A man on the other side slapped a blue flank. Two were cattle, two looked like buffalo. Both pair leaned into their yokes and the carriage came swaying through, its high wheels making no difficulty of the ridge of broken stakes.

"Quietly, fools!" Yuro snarled, but there was such a noise everywhere . . .

Her last light-pillar died but a new light was born, red, hungry. Little flowers, devouring grass, canvas, leather. Every arrow planting a bloom of flame. Fires spread, difficult to smother. They clung and grew, creeping together. The riders were making a circuit of the camp.

"Go," Ivah said. "Go, go!" She wrote a light and flung it ahead. The oxen, sensibly, had decided to stand still until they could see.

The nearest ox-driver looked at her, at Yuro, and turned and bolted into the night. The other had already disappeared. Ivah picked up the discarded whip, snapped it by an ear, shouted a command, but of course the oxen didn't understand Grasslander. A shove on a broad shoulder got her point across, and they swung to the right and lumbered off.

Couldn't tell if the rushing clusters of soldiers, half-dressed, were obeying some drilled procedure, rallying to some point, or just stampeding in panic. Whooping cries, horses whinnying, oxen bellowing. Her archers were into the camp now. Fire-arrows landing within the imperial compound, but there Yeh-Lin's clinging fire failed to take.

Riderless horses bolting. An ox, trailed by its yokemate, came swinging after them, seeing, she could only suppose, calm purpose and fellow bovines. Or perhaps they were part of the same team.

Pale light in the fog, a horse copper-lit and its dark shadow, two horses, and damned if it was not Ghu's white stallion and Ahjvar's dark bay following. Yuro made encouraging noises, held out a hand that was disdainfully ignored, but the pair seemed set on following anyway, like dogs that had caught their master's scent.

Perhaps they had.

And that, that was what started hope, like a tiny spark of Yeh-Lin's fire, blooming in her heart again.

"Go on, get on, get on!" she shouted, and set the oxen to a jolting trot.

Snow. Jochiz brushes the image from his mind. Sien-Shava has always hated the snow, the dark dead season of the north, and snow is no better, no kinder, lying deep and ancient on the mountain's peak, compressing slowly under its own weight, year after year, birthing ice.

Jochiz hates the ice.

The god, the Father, the god the heir, they are one, or very nearly. There is a shadow, a light, over and through the man, but now he is a boy, curled into a tight and huddled knot like a baby in the womb, and the snow wraps around him. It tries to be a shield, a wall, a fortress, but it cannot keep a devil's great will out; he is already here in this place and he can feel between his hands the threads, the roots, sinking deep, and then he feels them as the cords of a net and he begins, slowly, carefully, to draw them.

The wind rises against him, flings ice, needles, blades, and he reaches. The Mother is gone, and the Father—he sweeps a hand clawed with fire, to rip him from what he guards, but the ice melts into the boy, and the snow, and the Father is gone as if he had never been there—dead. His victory over the old mountain does not yet feel like one—and the boy is a man, lying still and cold on the river's shore. A god. Pinned and powerless against him, senseless.

Dying.

Roots spread through the god, roots bind them, and Jochiz begins again to draw the strange, multi-stranded soul, to drink it into the cold fire that lies like a splinter of starlight between the empress's breasts, over his heart. She stands with him, within him, eyes unseeing, ghostly, like a reflection in water. She is nothing but a vessel to carry him now, a great canoe, on this Nabbani sea.

Slowly. Carefully.

Light. Fierce and golden. It drives the cold of the snow from what presence he has here. It is a man, or like a man, all bright and burning and phoenix-heat, and it tears the threads from his grasp, from the stone's white-burning heart, and for a moment its flames wrap the dying and unborn god. They merge to one creature, the god and the thing of necromancy, a shape not seen by eyes, golden light and dark, deep shadows, slow and flowing, and a wind sharp and silver-bright with the breath of snow and it is not a net he draws but the roots he has planted, and the fire rips them free and they burn, red, hot, angry.

The golden flames roar up towards him, brighter, white, tinged with red rage and the shadows behind stir, the scent of river and pines and stone strong.

The empress cries out, a voice to give breath to pain and rage. She falls to her knees in her tent, struggles to catch her breath, his breath. Composes herself, he does, as she would, sitting back on her heels. Her women fuss about her, guards with no enemy to fight, and the giants come to her.

Dotemon's heavens-damned necromancy?

Flame, is he, the guardian of the god, in the secret language of the god's heart? Jochiz will see that dead man burn.

A rider came at them, drawn by Ivah's light, whooped and raised his aim to shoot over her head. Someone cried out behind. He passed her and wheeled, returned, yodelling some call that didn't sound Nabbani. They intermarried with Denanbak a lot in Alwu. More riders, forming an escort. Some carried torches of the devil's fire, smoky and swirling wild. One tossed Yuro his mace. Ivah put her light out. Now they were only hurrying shadows, firelit, like all the rest. And a carriage, even a plain one like this, was clearly an imperial thing. Rumours of the empress's wounding . . . perhaps they hurried her away. Soldiers parted for them and showed no inclination to argue their passage.

Into the night, what was left of it. Find the forested hills, get them into some hidden place there . . . wait, trust, pray, and hope Yeh-Lin had made her night march. Terror, confusion—set the imperials to flight before they realized they had twenty men to the rebels' one, or whatever it might be. Let the fog and the dark and the fire fight for them. Dawn was nearly come. There was a lightening to the fog on her right hand.

A wind, wild and roaring. Fog rising, churning. It was as though the sea of her mother's stories rushed over them. Tents tore and flew, flapping overhead. A tree snapped.

The oxen bellowed, bolted, the carriage rocking wildly. Horses scattered. Inside, Awan yelped.

Yeh-Lin plunged from the sky to the roof of the carriage and her upraised sword met the sheet of lightning that broke from the imperial compound upon them. It burned about her, painting in white and black and threads of scarlet—sword's edge, tassel, a fiery snake coiled in her chest. White sparks flew from her hair.

Darkness blinded Ivah in the lightning's passing; noise deafened, as if the sea truly had broken over her. Vision returned as streaks of green and red, then fog, and light enough to see there was fog. The first edges of the dawn. She had dropped to the ground, cowering with her hands over her head, a good way to get herself run over. Get up and moving. Legs gone shaky. One of the scattered bodies about her was Yuro. She seized him by the shoulder—alive, not trampled, and he climbed upright using her as a prop, more unsteady than she was. Others were stirring. Imperial soldiers and serving-folk, a couple of her own archers unhorsed. Some did not move. Struck by lightning, broken by the wheels or the oxen. Some tried and could not, and their cries were terrible. Had to leave them to what help or mercy their comrades could give. An unmoving darkness in the fog not so far ahead was probably the carriage. She let Yuro go and they ran for it.

Stuck. Awan and Yeh-Lin—conqueror, empress, devil of legend—had set shoulders to it, heaving at a rear corner, wheel deep in a puddled rut. They were not doing much good; the oxen were standing, switching their tails; the immediate emergency, so far as they were concerned, was over and done. Ivah went ahead to shout and tug them into movement again, and the carriage broke free. Devil and priest went down in the mud together.

They kept going. The fog seemed to be thinning, the wind gathering strength as the light grew. Yeh-Lin came to walk with Ivah. The leading ox rolled an eye at her. "Get on," Ivah growled.

"That was exciting," Yeh-Lin remarked. She handed Ivah her sword, began braiding her hair, then begged yarn to tie it with before reclaiming her blade. She was mud from head to foot, her face streaked and spattered. Not an old woman. Not young, either. "Why are we stealing a carriage?"

"The empress laid them there. They're dead. But Ahjvar says he's not. Ghu—he can't be alive, but Ahjvar says—Ahjvar's not breathing either and he can't be, but he was." Sudden incoherence. She felt about five, on the edge of tears, stammering out some tale of childish woe. Scowled at the ox.

The devil walked in silence, her gaze inward.

"The dead king is—complicated. Whatever love there is between them, it does not demand—Nabban does not want—that Ahjvar surrender himself so utterly. And yet he does, and did long before he ever could recognize what else was growing in his heart. Perhaps after so long possessed, he knows nothing else, or gives himself away so entirely in order to leave no space for something else to take him. Or because he is too exhausted of life to claim it for himself any longer, I don't know. However it is, he has been growing so entangled with his god, ever since that young fool took his goddess's curse—as I might lift a cat's-cradle from your hands, Grasslander—that they might as well share one heart and blood between them. They are so bound now, if he says Nabban is not dead, I will believe him till I prove otherwise myself."

More silence. Still no one appeared to take an interest in the carriage. Ivah could not believe her spell held after being so flung about. There were drums, horns, distant sounds human and animal and metal, away to the west.

"I think," Yeh-Lin said at last, "that Ahjvar has gone to look for his god. We may make a shaman of him yet. Or a priest. Or a lesser avatar of Nabban; who can say what is possible? The gods of the earth are not my study. But wherever he has gone, he will need time for the journey.

Pray it is not days. I'm not certain how long I can hold the attention of Jochiz away, though perhaps slaughtering our poor folk may distract him a little while. Under the trees, there, where the hill rises. Let's take them out to the clean earth, at least. Leave them to finish dying, or not, as they must. And perhaps the carriage may make a useful false front to defend, when what pursuit will certainly come after us, does."

CHAPTER XLII

Ahjvar had hoped he would find the boy gone when he returned, wandered off to some better shelter in the village or absent entirely, back to the city or gone to sea or down the coast, anywhere but the ruin he called his house. To have a breathing, fragile life sleeping so close, curled in the blanket he had flung him that first night, even with the hearth and the breadth of the old broch between them, was keeping him from sleep altogether, and that only made the hag more restless, the curse more hungry. She pressed on him, a fretting around the edges of mind. Headache. Someone had died in the city, and it had not been in the service of the clan-fathers. She was fed. He was safe for a few weeks, maybe.

But when he had tended to the old chestnut mare and left her grazing by the shed, climbed over the stile in the thorn-hedge, the boy was sitting there on the garden wall, which was not right, because he always knew when Ahjvar was coming back and was always there to take the horses. Horse. Ahjvar had only the one horse. Horses, and they rode together. Always there, sleeping across the door of his room at the Seahorse in Gold Harbour come morning, no matter what he got up to with that red-haired boy of the stables in the evenings.

No. Why would he think he had taken the boy to the city? He was there, waiting on the wall, and he needed to be gone, before Ahjvar woke to himself some night to find him dead under his hand.

Ahjvar walked along the narrow neck of stone that connected the eroded headland to the cliffs, steep fall down either side to weed-slick rocks far below. The tide was out. Gulls cried, circling. Also far below. The wind pushed at him.

The garden was gone to weeds, brown and seedy with autumn. Why think of it green, planted, tended? He never did bother. Why expect hens scratching for bugs and the plum tree pruned and blooming with spring?

"My Father is gone," the boy said, his eyes still on the sea, which was odd, because this starveling stray had never mentioned having a father to mourn.

Ahjvar dropped down to sit, back against the sun-warmed stone wall, legs stretched out in the dry grass. Cliff's edge not a pace from his boots and a long fall below, if you missed the clinging path down. He leaned back, face to the sun, eyes shut. The boy rested a hand on his head.

He hated to be touched, couldn't stand to have anyone within arm's reach. It set him cold and angry, fighting a sweating panic that threatened violence. But there was safety, here, and the hand a comfort.

There was no safety. He needed to send the boy away before he killed him.

"Hush," the boy said. "You won't."

Not a boy. A man's voice, and a man. Why had he lost his name?

He tilted his head back, eyes open, looked up at Ghu, who still watched the sea.

"We could stay here," Ghu said.

"No. We couldn't."

"I was happy here."

"I wasn't."

"No? Where were you happy?"

A strange question to consider.

"Swajui. The pines."

A strange answer. Corner of the mouth lifted, half a smile.

"Who are you?" Ghu asked.

So many names. Catairlau was dead and the rest had only ever been masks, discarded when outworn. Only the one mattered, because it belonged to this life and this place and was what this man called him. "Ahjvar," he said. "Not even the Leopard. Always Ahjvar."

"Who am I, then?"

"Ghu," he said. "Always."

"Are you sure?"

"You gave me your name to hold. You said, remember you. Hold you. Don't let you drown."

"Did I? I thought I had drowned, already. But it might have been the snow."

Drowned in the goddess's river, lost on the god's mountain in spring storm. Sacrificed to godhead, to the land. Twice over. Three times. A Northron magic, and a Praitannec one. He felt again the first spear biting, even as they hit the ground. Blood soaking the empress's carpets, blood soaking the earth beneath, Ghu's, his own, flowing together. Ghu's earth. He was standing, hands on Ghu's shoulders, blocking his fixed gaze out to sea.

"Ghu, yes. Look at me."

Nothing human had eyes so black. Sky between the stars.

"*Ghu.* See me."

Eyes found his, blinked, focussed.

"Ahj." That was pain, seeping back into the face. The hands that rose to his were shaking. "I didn't think that anything could hurt so very much."

"Dying does."

"Yes. Ahjvar, the Father is dead. The devil killed him, in the end. He kept me from the devil, a little space, and died into me when he could do no more." The gaze sharpened. "You kept the devil's thorns from me. You came and—" he shook his head. "Ah, Ahj, what have I made of you? A thing of fire."

"I am not."

"You are. I've always seen you so. Hearth and sun and candle's flame I circle."

"I am yours. You know that. Whatever you make of me. Even fire."

"Ahj, you shouldn't say such things. You shouldn't surrender yourself. Even to gods."

"But I have. I'm safer that way. So."

Ghu just shook his head, brought Ahjvar's hands to his lips.

"What am I without you? I don't know that boy; I only remember him in pieces. He only ever lived in pieces. We make each other whole, I think."

Ahjvar wrapped his arms around him. Ghu leaned into him. They held so, a long moment, till Ghu sighed and pushed him back.

"There's a devil trying to root himself in my land, Ahj. Time to find out what we can do." Ghu vaulted off the wall, but then pulled Ahjvar close again. Kissed him hard and fierce and there was blood in his mouth—

They were falling, he thought, and the cliff was high, the rocks savage below, but the tide was rushing in, a storm off the deep ocean, waves climbing—

Rain, and he lay half over Ghu, holding to him, and held by him, as if they might drag one another from drowning, but it was only rain and thunder, not waves and deep water, and a tree lashing back and forth overhead, churning grey clouds, a day so dark. Headache flaring white around the edges of his vision.

Sounds of battle, far too close.

He rolled away, retching. Dull ache within his chest, but a horse could have been kicking the back of his skull.

No coffee. It always eased the headache.

Cool hand found the back of his neck.

"Sorry," Ghu said, which was just so . . . He choked on laughter, fell into a coughing fit that left him gasping for air.

"Hey. It's all right. Breathe."

Rolled to his back. Ghu kneeling by him, coat and shirt still all undone, filthy, torn, broken scales. New scars, ridged and purple. Entirely beautiful. "Kill the empress for you?" Ahjvar offered. Rain cooling on his face, clean, washing headache away, or probably that was Ghu.

"You already did. I want the devil out of her, out of Nabban. She's not him. There's no true bond between them, only chains. He's only—wearing her, does that make sense? He has his own body still, wherever he is. I want the souls he's taken freed to their road. The assassins, the officers, the villagers of Numiya. Even hers."

"Yes. Good." Breath, still rasping. Another, easier. A third, and he could sit.

"I don't know how we do this, Ahj. I don't know what I can do."

"You never do."

"True."

"It may be as much wizardry as anything."

"Necromancy." Easy to say the word. It didn't touch him.

"Enslavement of a soul? He's taken her, but I think she is not—in any way bound to her body, any longer. Possession of a corpse."

"Red Masks. Something similar. Dealt with that."

"You were part of that wizardry; inside it. And it was a great wizardry, not a devil's powers. You said so."

"Did I? Maybe not easy, then." It was hard to care. They were alive, Ghu was alive, and Ahjvar felt drunk with it.

Which was a good way for them both to end up dead for good and all. The devils had destroyed gods. Remember there had been a true Lady of Marakand, once.

"Something you need to see. Some devilry. I don't know what it was doing to you, but I took it from you. Ivah has it now."

"I—remember. I told you. I saw you do it. The devil's thorns. Growing into me."

"A splinter of stone."

Ghu shrugged. "Poetry. Words make a shape in the mind. Things make a shape in the world, for what has none. I saw thorns."

"It was stone, and Ivah has it."

"If you say so."

Easier for him to deal with Ghu's buckles than for Ghu to reach them himself, under the arm. Even torn and broken scales were some protection. It was that or go shirtless.

No sword. No forage-knife. Scavengers, the pair of them. There was bound to be a blade or two to be picked up between here and wherever the corpse of the empress walked.

They were in a hillside woods, the ground rising steep and rocky, and how they had come there he had no idea. Fallen from the cliff at Sand Cove—not likely. Ahjvar took the longest of the knives left to him and set off in the direction of the closest fighting. Trampling behind. He spun about to put himself between the threat and Ghu but had to jump back as Snow barrelled forward like an eager dog, dropping his head to push his long face against Ghu's chest. Niaul, behind him, flicked a casual ear at Ahjvar like a nod.

They trailed the cut ends of rope halters. He wasn't going to fight from horseback with neither stirrups nor bridle, but he gave Ghu a leg up and with Niaul at heel went beside the white horse.

An ox blocked their path, snuffed the air, and lowed. Another answered it off among the trees and it lumbered away.

Down a sudden steep plunge of stone, and the forest thinned, so that the brush and ferns grew thicker. A carriage, canted to one side and wedged between trees, an axle broken, its team—free and roaming up the hillside, which meant someone had taken the time to unyoke them. Just beyond, soldiers beset. They wore blue ribbons for the holy one, light leather armour. Archers of Alwu fighting now with sabre or axe, and Ivah, on foot. The old priest, his back to a tree, swinging a stick. Yuro's mace descended on the imperial soldier pressing him.

Snow plunged ahead.

"Ivah!" Ahjvar shouted. "Sword!"

She didn't look around, but when the man she fought went down she kicked him into Ahjvar's path and he switched his knife over to his left and scooped up the short stabbing sword. Not his weapon of choice for such a melee but it would do. Ghu had taken Awan's branch and was blocking the imperials from coming at the priest. A still and threatening island they did not want to approach. Had that word gone through the camp, *the false heir of the gods is dead*? And now they saw he was not. Ahjvar and Ivah pushed to collect Yuro. The Alwu folk gathered to them. Gave up his knife, short sword to his left to take up a dead man's sabre. It was like dusk in under the trees, and rain spit suddenly down, but the white horse held what light there was as Ghu rode forward into them. The imperials fell back. Yuro beside him was panting, leaning on his mace.

The imperial officer rushed at Ghu, sword raised, blind or uncaring, and met Ahjvar's left-hand blade. His men didn't choose to follow.

"Go," Ghu said gently. "You don't want to be here. Your empress is dead. She was never the Daughter of the Gods. The devil Jochiz is in her. Lay down your weapons and go."

And they did.

Not even the officer had carried the antique court sword, damn him. Damned the man was. No ghost.

"Where's Yeh-Lin?" Ahjvar demanded.

"Gone to take over command," Ivah said.

"Can you lot not count? What in the cold hells was she thinking? Ghu said to hold at the ferry."

"What were you thinking, to let him just—make us all stand aside and let him go? You're both mad. And you weren't—Old Great Gods, Ahjvar, how can you be standing? How can he? Even demons don't recover from something like that, nor heal so quickly. You weren't breathing, either of you."

"He's not a demon."

"Empress," Ghu said. "Ahj?"

"Yes. If we see a heavier sword, I want it." He offered Ghu the short sword, but he shook his head. He'd discarded even Awan's branch.

The Alwu-folk who had made their stand under the forest eaves afoot were retrieving horses. More horses than riders now, even though some must have, like the oxen, decided discretion was the better part of valour and headed up and deeper into the woods. He didn't bother taking one of the saddled spares, got up bareback on Niaul anyway. He didn't think they were going very far.

A smothering heat in the air. Sheet-lightning flared in the west, and the thunder rolled above them. Smoke hung over the imperial camp and many of its tents were gone, overrun, trampled down or burnt from a grassfire that had blackened half the valley. The blue banners were within the camp, bunched into a narrowing front, the imperials folded around them. Fighting towards . . . nothing they could hope to oppose. Drawing the devil's attention away from the woods . . . all those lives no more than another wrecked carriage, artfully crammed between trees.

They had no banner to ride under, but as they drew nearer the camp two of the huddled figures—the dead, the wounded, the overcome— rose up in their way. Girl, young man, slight figures unarmoured. The girl wore a collar of heavy jade beads, many strands, leaned on a spear-headed standard now, not threatening, but like a bored guard. And the youth had two hilts slung at his shoulder, one most familiar, and a forage-knife in his sash.

"Nabban." The girl straightened up, nodded. The other bowed.

Ghu sat back, bringing Snow to a halt. Seemed to consider the girl a long, long time.

"Little Sister," he said at last, and there was something ironic to his tone.

"Well, that's yet to be seen. Maybe. Someday. Or maybe the devil takes us all. Call me Rat, for the time being. Do you want this? Darru and Lathi will ride with you, but I think we'll not carry your banner."

"I—" the young man began, doubtfully.

"No, you won't, Kaeo, my boy. You're mine." A wicked grin. The man Kaeo didn't look displeased.

Rat swung the spear down, offered it over both hands. Sky blue silk, stained and torn, furled around it. Ti-So'aro's, their own and first banner. It was Ivah who brought her horse up to take it.

Kaeo shrugged the long Northron sword off his shoulder, held out it and Ghu's forage-knife too. "Yeh-Lin took them up, back there. She said you would want them."

They did, and Ahjvar took both weapons, but when he would hand the forage-knife over to Ghu, it was refused.

"Carry it for me."

Ivah shook the banner loose and someone brought up horses for the strangers. The Dar-Lathan girl took her companion up behind her, though; he seemed as ill-at-ease on a horse as the priest. She had claimed another spear before she mounted. Weapons to spare littered the field.

Lightning tore the sky once more, and thunder, closer.

"Where have the dogs got to?" Ghu asked, of no one in particular.

"Haven't seen them," Yuro answered. "Anyhow, it's no place for them, my lord."

"You think?"

They were a handful, and something waited behind the imperial centre; the peony-red and golden banners clustered there, while those about the blue were pushed back into themselves. Yeh-Lin, on her piebald, held her place like a statue, or the boss of a shield, sword raised as if she caught some descending blow on it, and around her the air was edged in a shimmer of heat.

Ghu cast a look around. Whistled.

The lightning cracked over them. Thunder answered.

They came like storm, and rain in their wake, a rolling grey wall. Shadows in the clouds, racing the rain, descending, pale and pewter-streaked, tawny and black. Wolfish heads, wild-maned, bodies iridescent, scaled like fish. They ran with the clouds, on the wind, and the wind struck in a rush. Ghu laughed aloud.

"Go!" he shouted. "Ride for Yeh-Lin!" and in Praitannec, "I told you, Ahj."

They rode in the wake of the dragons, and the rain rolled over the field. In a broad path before them, men flung themselves flat or turned to flee for the forest and the hill. A few shot wild in the downpour before they scattered. There was a rippling like currents stirring with the change of the tide through all the companies, scattered thin or clustered in savage packs, and it was the many of the imperials held in reserve that began to break first into disorder, after those beneath the dragon's flight had fled.

The storm-wind flung the blue banner streaming ahead, as if it cut their way.

The imperial right wing that had turned in about the wedge of Yeh-Lin's companies was fraying and unravelling, and broke entirely as the dragons dropped over it. Lightning tore the clouds, deafening in its roar, blinding white. Ahjvar felt it, as if the heavens had fallen on him, through him, burning. "Yeh-Lin!" he shouted. She was gone, where the lightning had fallen.

All about them, horses reared or ran wild. Niaul's ears were back but he held to his course. People dropped to cower, covering their heads. They lost some of their escort, carried away by panicked mounts, and more imperials were in flight, men as mad with fear as horses. They were in among their own folk and officers. Drums and shouting forbade any flight or impulsive pursuit of the fleeing foe, but it was the sight of the white horse brought them back. Order was lost regardless, horse and foot all sweeping wild about them, the sides of the wedge that had turned to face outward as it was engulfed and pinned down turning to a rush, a charge that quickly spent itself, horse outrunning the foot, losing themselves ahead. But all faltered, even as the rain crossed them and passed. Ghu's small party swept in around where Yeh-Lin had stood. The piebald stallion was down and she knelt by it, holding herself up only by her sword planted in the earth, leaning head on hands on hilt. Dead horse. Dead standard-bearer beside her, half under his dead horse, and others were fallen, horses struggling up sweating and unsteady, banner-ranked and messengers on the ground or struggling like their horses to stand again.

The dogs pushed in beside her, wolfish, barking a deep and deafening defiance, fell silent and circled away, bodies lengthening again, and snouts, fur silvery and burnished pale gold merging over their shoulders with scales, tall, horse-high as they crossed and returned, to crouch like sentinels. Jiot snarled, an echo of the thunder.

The empress strode to meet them, her giants about her, and her commanders. She still wore the court robes and armour of the previous day, and the bloodstained bandages still covered her eye. She carried a long court sword lightly in one hand. Not Buri-Nai, only the shell of her. Ghu leaned over and brushed the back of a knuckle over Ahjvar's face, as he had before, to gently nudge him back when he fell into darkness, but Ahjvar hadn't lost himself here, he did not think.

The touch lingered like a ghost on his skin.

Yeh-Lin found her feet. He was seeing her strangely now, all edged in light and a fire behind her eyes. The empress was an empty thing with light like a star cold between her breasts, and thread-fine roots flying out and away from it, or into it, too attenuated to follow.

Not his vision.

"You should have come against me in your own right, and not as a godling's lapdog, Dotemon," Buri-Nai said. "Why so willingly hobbled? Did you let them break your mind and chain your souls as well as your body? What use are you to him now, do you think?"

Yeh-Lin didn't answer, but though breathing heavily she stood straight again, between the empress and Ghu.

"No," Ahjvar said. Not her place. This battle—could not be fought between devils. Must not be.

"He has no foothold in this land but her, Ahj," Ghu said, softly speaking Praitannec. "He is not here. You see it?"

"Yes."

Ahjvar dismounted, warily, with an eye to the giants. They were afraid. It was in the set of mouth and eye, the tension of hands on weapons. The dead returned, and there was a weight to Ghu, as though the broken light and the shadow both were on him more strongly—as though he were real, and the rest of them only dim ghosts.

Watch the waiting-women. Ladies, slaves—some were Wind in the Reeds. Maybe all.

"Neither I nor Dotemon is the necromancer here," Ghu said. "Your empress is a dead woman. Buri-Nai was deceived and seduced by the lies of a devil. She was never any chosen or champion of the Old Great Gods. You are a devil and you lie. What goddess of the land kills the children of the land—"

"Kill them," Buri-Nai said. "Cut the Northron slave of the devil in pieces, once he stops moving, and bring me the body of the pretender." She clutched at the light against her chest, and it glowed through her hand, made shadows of her bones. Stone, with a sliver sheared away, or a knot of thorns, fed by many roots?

And what could the god's champion do that Yeh-Lin Dotemon could not, against the devil Jochiz?

He was already moving inside the reach of the spear and halberd, and now they had missed their chance to keep him at the distance they would prefer.

Nothing against a devil, but rather a dead woman unburied, who was an open door into Nabban.

The sword of the god.

The giant in his path shouldered his spear and leapt back. "We killed them yesterday, Exalted. We saw you killed, yesterday. I don't know what any of you are, but none of you are the Peony Throne I was sworn to serve."

One of the ladies-in-waiting flicked a knife that took the giant in the cheek. He dropped, too swiftly for that wound.

"Poison!" Ahjvar shouted, and dodged the other giant, who was swinging his halberd around like a scythe. Yeh-Lin could deal with him. An arrow took the woman who had thrown the knife. One, at least, had kept a bowstring dry. The bodyguard closed up around the empress, who swore at them in some language he didn't know and swept a hand that trailed fine white threads of light. They dropped, the closest three. Souls ripped away. The remaining three gave her space.

The women had scattered. Not in flight. Bring her the god, she had said. Or his corpse.

And the mother of that splinter under his tongue to be bedded in his heart, Ahjvar saw it, vision, nightmare, her desire—the devil's—so strong.

The air was growing heavy again. Thunder gathering. Not, he thought, hers. The dragons were out over the field, driving flocks of men before them, bunching them like sheep.

She laughed at him, brought her blade up with much of Yeh-Lin's grace. One eye to spoil her judging of distance, and what strength in a body confined to the quiet life of a palace daughter? But she had had months of travel to make something other of herself, and the skill that handled that sword was old.

She grinned, teeth bared, as they closed together.

"What does Dotemon call you? The dead king? But you bleed, and dream, and weep. What your necromancer god should make of you, if he wants you obedient in his bed for long, is what my dead empress is."

"A corpse and a puppet? Not his taste."

She did not bleed. His point had scratched her face. She flinched, though. The devil felt it, and didn't like it.

"The sword of the ice is coming for you." The Lady's words, almost, and he was sick to find them in his mouth.

"I expect it to." She had him pushed away, turned. Deliberate, to make him face his embattled comrades. Couldn't afford distraction. Yeh-Lin by Ghu, defending him. Ghu with his head bowed, hands braced on Snow's shoulders, not wounded but fallen into some other place. Don't look. Buri-Nai pressed Ahjvar hard, and there could be nothing but her unwavering eye and the blade's edge. Not the light that reached for him, like cobweb on the skin, and reached—leave Ghu to do what he did. Ahjvar could feel him, as if he stood almost within the same space, the same skin, breath within his breath. It was not his own vision saw those tendrils. A blow that should have sent her reeling. Should have ripped through and laid half her arm bare to shattered bone. Had. She lost her left-hand knife and the hand hung strangely, but no blood and no weakening followed, only fury. Sword's point punched through already-torn armour into his ribs. She leapt back and a whirling blow came at his head. He went down avoiding it and she recovered, reversed her grip and stabbed. He was already rolling aside and came up to his knees, sword thrusting up over his shoulder.

That bit more than her cheek. He pulled away and found his feet again, and she still, with face ruined and eyeless, struck another blow that caught the edge of the damaged armour and opened scars. Strength beyond what that body could claim. He fell to his knees.

She had him then. Threads of light clung. He drew Ghu's knife, tucked into his belt at the back. He could feel her, crawling on him. Into him. *Not again not again not—*

I have you, Ahj. And we have him. There.

"A mistake to discard you last night, dead man. This time I will hold onto you, I think, and bring him to me through you. Humanly weak, your little god, but his land is great."

Ahjvar pushed her head back, hooked the knife and ripped, not flesh but steel scales fixed to leather, the silk beneath, and the golden chain and the amulet, a crystal of milky quartz the length of a man's thumb, bound in golden wire—

—caught it on both shaking and bloodied hands, and she shrieked—

And silence. She crumpled up half over his knees, cold, dead meat.

Stone cold in his hands, and the tendrils of white light writhed. They clung, and pulled, web spreading over him.

You are a fool, dead man. Your soul is not even your own.

"You think? I know all that I am. What I've been made, good and ill, by my road. What he made me."

Every man's dream, a lover who surrenders self, who is nothing but a part of himself. It won't last. You'll run from him in the end, and he'll have to kill you. I know.

The threads burrowed deeper. Ice in his veins.

"His champion. His sword. His priest. His friend."

His betrayer. You're an open road into his heart. Your soul winds through his, and through you, I reach into him and take you both. See? It's already too late. You, him, Nabban. A great land.

"He is deep water, you know. Darkness. Stillness. Peace. But he says I am a hearth. A fire. And maybe I am. I know fire. I have burned."

It was in him, always. All his nightmares.

Fire might break even stone. Fire purified. Fire freed the dead.

A fire not of wood or oil or sea-coal. A fire fed on bone and soul, and what froze his hands was soul and stone. His fire had slept in his bones over ninety years. He held it in his mind, wove them together. For fire, alder. And alder, and alder threefold untempered by any other sign. He could feel Ghu's hands over his, though the white horse and the black-armoured rider were beset, and Ghu had Yuro's mace.

Distraction. There must be nothing but what he held in his hands.

His name was Ahjvar, not Catairlau. He burned regardless, as that self-damned prince had burned.

In his hands, stone hissed, and seared, and cracked. Gold wire softened, ran, seared him. Stone gone brittle crumbled to sharp-edged grit between his hands and he heard the devil shriek all the way from the western sea, some fragment of his soul broken and destroyed. He felt the souls fly free—Buri-Nai, Zhung Musan, assassins he had killed, wizards and banner-lords chosen her own, her faithful dead, her murdered lowly folk—felt the road opening out before them, drawing them, enticing, fearful, innocently short or penitentially long. And still they flew to it. He could not. He had known this would be and he could not, and neither could he after all endure—

The fire would not let him go till it was through with him. Skin bubbled, blackened, flaked, and flesh, and there was white bone beneath. The pain screamed through him but he had no breath to scream—*Not again, not like this, let me go, let me go, let me go*—

CHAPTER XLIII

All that way, to have found—whatever it was he had found. If Kaeo were only a passing pleasure for the youngest of the queens of Darru and Lathi, even that was enough, though he would rather it were more. Kaeo thought it might be more. But all that way, to die at the hands of imperial soldiers at last, when he had found his god . . .

That was the shape of a poem, but it was not truth. He had found *the* god, the heir of Nabban, and the god had not, in the end, been his. He had come to understand that on the road north. His heart, his soul, had known it, even on the night he sang with Rat against the typhoon.

"Thank you," the god had said. For what? For acting as the devil's messenger and carrying the yellow-haired man's weapons back to him.

Thank you. Like a dismissal. Releasing him. Not for fetching that sword along, but for all that went before. Not for what the dying gods had done to him, witting or unwitting. For what he had tried to do, for the Traditionalists, for Prince Dan. For trying, even if he had failed. Kaeo felt that. He understood it. Thank you, for being willing to die. Not for godhead, but for what mattered. For what was right.

He was not Nabban's. He was given to himself, to give himself where he would.

You're mine, Rat had said, more than once, and whispered it with something like surprise the first time they lay together. He hoped there was not some man back in Darru and Lathi who thought he had an understanding with the youngest queen, and that her sisters did not decide his skull would look better on a royal doorpost.

Except . . .

Little Sister, Nabban named her.

He was not a fool. She had said she was not a wizard.

He leaned against her back, and she looked over her shoulder.

"Mine," he said. "Even if you grow up to be a tigress."

She snorted laughter. No denial.

"Someday," she said. "Maybe. When I am old, I will go to the river. Until then, I am only your queen and a priestess of a goddess who was and may yet be." Her Anlau voice, he called it in his mind. An accent of the south, a formality. Rat's grin. "And whatever else you think I might happen to be. The queens live celibate, you know, but I am—not counted quite in the traditional pattern."

A kiss, awkward, she twisting far to meet him.

Not a fool, and wise enough to know he was a danger to her, clinging to her belt, spy, queen, goddess that might be . . . wife? He was liable to fall off this tall horse and take Rat with him.

"Let me down," he said. "I'll only be a danger to you and fall off and get trampled. I'll stand by the priest."

And what that old unarmed man was doing here, rather than left with the reserve at the river commanded by Prince Dan, he did not understand. Rat hesitated. Then she nodded, seized his arm to steady him as he slithered down. The old priest clapped him on the shoulder.

He looked up at her and found Rat still looking down, her eyes gone . . . remote, and wide, and glistening. Seeing . . . What he saw, reflected in her eyes. He swallowed, and blinked, their hands still caught together.

Thank you, the god had said.

He let her go.

CHAPTER XLIV

"Kill them!" the empress shouted. "Bring me the body of the pretender!" And Ahjvar went for her through her giants as the court-dressed women of her bodyguard rushed for the blue banner.

Ahjvar shouted warning—"Poison!"—and someone shot one of them, but Yuro's horse crumpled down as if clubbed on the head, and the woman who had raked its nose with a blade like a fruit-knife fell herself, skull smashed by his mace.

Two were swarming Ivah, aiming for the banner she held set in her left stirrup. She cut down one and the good horse took the other, but two had gotten past and gone for Ghu, who sat motionless, lost in some trance, and weaponless besides, though Snow shifted his weight, preparing to strike. Naked of any armour. The Dar-Lathan man Kaeo flung himself on top of an assassin who dodged Yeh-Lin to come at Ghu. Kaeo knocked the imperial to the ground and was kneeling up to stab her with his sword when she pricked him in the thigh.

He brought his blow down anyway, even as the Wild Girl screamed his name and wheeled her horse about to come to her comrade. Kaeo pinned the assassin to the earth, fell over her, losing his grip on his sword, and did not move. He had only a scratch and hardly bled at all.

The rarest of poisons, Ivah's mother had said. The Wind in the Reeds had them, kept them secret even from the wizards, lest their workings become known. Venoms from jungles south-over-seas, from fish of the islands where the pearls were found. To be used only at the emperor's will.

One had cut her above her boot, but she felt nothing other than the pain she might expect. Clean blade, and as no other wounded dropped dead, the blades of the others were clean, and the Wind in the Reeds died in short order, in the wrath of the Wild Girl of Dar-Lathi and Yeh-Lin's guarding of the god, and Yuro's fury, and her own.

Yuro fell at the god's side, struck down by some imperial banner-lord who did not live long after, and Ghu, wherever he had been, seemed to wake then, and rolled down his horse's side and back, an arm wrapped in his long mane, with Yuro's mace. One of the archers dragged Yuro up across his own horse, weak but moving. The dragon-dogs were gone out over the field. Fear of them broke the companies there, made them bunch and cower or scatter to the woodlands, though Ivah didn't see them make any actual attack. Sheets of rain chased them, the wind gusting wild from every quarter.

Cold as winter, and they were being forced away from where Ahjvar fought the empress. He should make short work of her but Buri-Nai—or whatever used her body—seemed a swordswoman of skill to hold her own against him. Ivah unhorsed the banner-lord she fought and killed him as he struggled up, and Ahjvar was down—the empress falling, and he knelt over her.

Not lightning, but flame red and angry, cupped in his hands—born of them, flame springing up along his arms, flame a bonfire and he lost within it—

Roaring red, yellow-hot, bright and savage and nothing she could do, no time to weave a spell and it was already too late to save him, no matter what held him bound in the world. The empress was nothing but a dark lump, not even a human shape, and Ahjvar knelt still unmoving, not falling but—a black and hideous thing—hands, teeth, a cheek pale bone, burning into her memory. Ivah could not shut her eyes against it, never would in all her dreams, she thought, and slashed at the man whose halberd tried to tear her down from her horse. The white stallion plunged past her, trampling the last giant standing, and Ghu flung himself down and into the pyre that was his man or took it in his arms, body, fire, and all, and—was gone. Both of them. A clear space, a moment's calm, breathless.

The wind died to nothing.

"The empress is dead!" someone shouted, or wailed, and the dragons circled them. Some of the empress's people turned to run and thought better of it, as the paler dragon settled behind them, baring teeth, or grinning. A woman with long hair falling from her ornate combs fell to her knees, reversed her knife and drove it into her own belly.

Not a swift death, that. Ivah rode over and leaned to slash her throat, though it was a mercy she gave because she thought it was right, not one she was inclined of her own heart to give. That one was the last of those women of the Wind in the Reeds.

A man slid from his horse and went to his knees, his surcoat proclaiming him of the Shouja Clan, the badges of his helmet, his ribbons, marking him a lord, a captain-general of this army, or a part of it. Others, seeing this, dropped as well. Banner-ranked men and women, greater lords of the court in arms, the empress's own folk.

"Stop this," Yeh-Lin said. Their god was gone. Someone had to stand at their head now; they could not wait for his return. "Signal your companies to lay down their arms, and stop this. You make war on your god in the name of a lie, and a fratricide, and an usurper who would have given this land into the hands of the worst of devils. Do not damn yourselves further."

Ivah rode to her side. She meant only to say that Dan—anyone but Yeh-Lin Dotemon—should formally take the surrender of the empress's lords, but Yeh-Lin gave her suddenly a most wicked grin, a dragon's grin, and bowed, standing at her stirrup.

"The captain of the archers of the god of Nabban, Lady Ivah, banner-bearer of the god of Nabban, heir of Prince Dan, princess of the Tamghati of the Great Grass, and daughter of Princess Min-Jan An-Chaq, will take your surrender."

CHAPTER XLV

——drowning in deep water. Not the Lady's well, not the sea.

River. Current, pushing him. Dimmest of light, golden, faint above. Ghu, holding him against the push of the water that would carry him away, lying with him, and water filling his mouth, breathed in. The pain was in hands and chest and eyes and he had burned.

Not even a voice in his mind. Only a touch. There was quiet. Safety. Water neither cool nor warm, wrapping close, and he could lie back against Ghu and be still. Not burning. Not drowning.

Better. That, Ahjvar did hear, and feel as a touch at the same time.

Water, current wrapping his hands, calming the fires. Water like lips brushing over closed eyes, lips against his ear, but the words were still in his mind. *You're not burnt, Ahj. You're safe. He's gone from our land. Lie still.*

You're not burnt was a lie, but Ghu never lied and Ghu had him, so he was safe.

"Cold." His voice was a croak. He was soaking wet, shivering.

"It's raining."

So it was. Rain, and breaking clouds, and shafts of sun. No people. No voices. Only the sound of the river, loud over stones. How had they come there? Not the important question.

"Have we won your war?"

"I don't know." Ghu had an abstracted look, hand wound in Ahjvar's wet hair. Listening. Or searching. "Yeh-Lin's looking after things, and Ivah is. Buri-Nai's commanders have offered their swords, though."

"I hope the devil broke them."

"She has let them keep their heads. I was—not so inclined. For a little. It's as well as I was not there. You say you're not safe. I don't know; I'm not sure that I am, either. They obeyed Yao, they obeyed Otono, they obeyed Buri-Nai—not for any great fear, even, but because they were lords and emperors and that was how things were meant to be."

"The ones who chose not to didn't manage to achieve much."

"Dan, you mean. At least they chose to try."

"Daro Korat. Daro Sia. Slaves and the poor run off to the edge of the wild and only setting up armed masters over the weaker again."

"Yes. They don't know anything else. They can't see anything else. Their stories hold nothing else, any longer. Ahj, this land makes me so—angry."

"Change it. Give them new stories." New heroes. The slave who overthrew a tyrant and set free the folk and drove a devil from the land.

"To shift all the weight of the land?"

"My granddaughter would say so. Your little bard. But someone's going to have to set new laws and take thought for new order. That can't wait. Harvest coming. Winter. Start somewhere. Choa."

"Village by village, manor by manor, city ward by ward. Province by province. Yes. Did I say law-speaker?"

"You said clerk. Be your clerk. It wasn't imperial law I studied. Five Cities is very different."

"Different may be what we need. Law of the Five Cities, law of the *duinas*, law of Marakand. There was a code of laws before Yeh-Lin. I don't know what it said. Different, though. Different after Min-Jan, too. Do you think we could make a senate of some sort work?"

Ahjvar didn't want to think about it. A land the size of Nabban, a village council, which was what the senate of Marakand was, grown grand and full of itself, with all its factions and family compacts. Or the Five Cities, where the clan-fathers lived in their fortified houses and warred by assassins.

"God of this land. Will you be emperor too?"

"No."

"Then you can't do more than push them to face the right direction. They need to find their own paths, if anything they make is going to endure."

He hurt all over, and felt his age, which was considerable. Good just to lie where he was, with the sky over him and his head on Ghu's lap, Ghu's hand over aching scars. Unmerciful Great Gods—Yeh-Lin's blasphemy—his head throbbed, and there was no coffee in all this land. His chest ached, too, and his hands felt raw.

"Ghu, did I—" He held up a hand, studied it. It shook, and hardly seemed to belong to him, for all its familiar old lines and scars. "Was it nightmare, again, or shaman's dreaming, the place where I burnt the stone?"

"Does it matter?"

That was not an answer. He struggled to sit up.

"Did I burn again?"

"Hush. Lie down. I held you. I said I would. I couldn't let you go like that."

Curled away, into darkness. Far away, far as he could get. Tasted tears on his face, not his own, cheek pressed to his cheek.

"Ghu."

"I'm here." In the night. The water sang over its rocks. They were by the rapids. The gorge. Leaves whispered, and a bird was singing. Time lost, as it had used to be, on the road, in hills of the eastern Over-Malagru, in the desert.

"Don't leave me alone." *I thought I was better. I thought I'd broken this.*

"I don't. I won't." *You are. You have. This, you'll pass through too. Old scars opened. They'll heal again. Give yourself time.*

And oak trees. Almost a joke. A shaky one.

Time and the cork oaks. Mouth moved against him. A smile, a slow kiss. "You put the devil out of Nabban, Ahj. Yeh-Lin didn't do that.

Ahjvar, you know you don't—" Breath against his ear. "Don't—bind yourself here, for my sake. Go, if will. If you need to. I didn't think, when—when you cried out of the fire, that you—I do not think I should be trusted with what you give me. I took you into the river instead. I didn't think you knew what you said."

"And you ask now?"

"Yes."

"You still want company on your road?"

"Yes, Ahj."

"Good. Don't let go of me."

"No. I have you still."

CHAPTER XLVI

Nabban came and went about the camp at the ferry landing and those set up and down the road, a few miles from the battle-field and the hill of his death and rebirth, which they were calling the holy hill, now. There was an old shrine high up there, forgotten and overgrown. The folk of the nearest village had come back, proudly protective of it, and were clearing the old path that snaked up along the ledges, between strange pillars carved in the rough shape of a human figure, head and shoulders, featureless. A holy place before there was Father or Mother, made holy again. Would the god send them a priest, they asked? Their lord and his sons and daughter were all dead in the fighting and his household fled. It was the smith, a serf of the dead lord, who came to them, and Awan who went up the steep path, leaning on his stick, to see the old holy place.

"There's a spring," he said, when he came down again. "A spring, and the altar-stone, and a pine-sapling growing by it, and they will build me a cabin once they've cleared the yard within the old stone fencing. I think I'll keep a cat for company."

They buried Kaeo in the Nabbani fashion, in the earth, and set a stone over him. Rat had tied her river-stone amulet about his neck. A promise, as it had been to her, when she took the smooth, holed pebble from the Little Sister's bed, that dreaming night when she was fourteen. She would come back someday, Rat thought, while she was still Anlau, before she went to the river. She would gather his bones and take them to her father on the mountain. Dwei Kaeo had died for Nabban, but it was the Little Sister who would remember his name.

Something remembered. Ahjvar found Ivah, claimed that splinter of the devil's amulet from her. She had cocooned it in thread and hair, a binding he did not trust to last, but did not want either to disturb. He took it to Ghu.

"Empty of souls, I think," Ghu said. "I think . . . seal it, as your goddess sealed your wizardry, till we know better what to do with it. I don't suppose an ordinary fire would do much to it at all."

And he did not want to burn again, no. Ahjvar cased it in river clay and wrote his own bindings on it: elm, rowan, hazel. Ghu set his thumbprint in it, like a seal, before they fired it.

"Bury it at Swajui, under the roots of the oaks," he said. "They'll hold it till we need it."

"What are we likely to need it for?"

"I don't know. We may, though. Someday."

"I am not your emperor," Prince Dan said. Lords, officers, rebels and imperial conscripts, village folk—and priests, because there were priests coming into them from hiding in the hills, day and night—they were gathered to witness. Folk in their thousands. Most could neither see— except that there were small figures stood on the bed of a wagon beneath the blue banners—nor hear. "It is not my place. It never was. I am a servant of the god of Nabban, a servant of Nabban—as the emperor must be, first and foremost of all his servants—but that is not the service I am best able to give. I will retire to the mountains of Choa and keep a shrine to Nabban there, and watch a child I have adopted as my daughter grow. You have heard the prophecies that were spoken. The Peony Throne is cast down. The rule of the sons of Min-Jan is ended."

"The holy one will be emperor!" some soldier called, and *Nabban, Nabban*, they echoed it.

Ivah saw Ghu, all in black and half lost in shadows behind Dan, shake his head in denial. They saw that refusal, the front ranks, at least.

"Nabban says, the Princess Ivah will serve him in this. A daughter of Nabban, a daughter of the Great Grass, his wizard and his captain of archers. If she is Min-Jan, the daughter of my lost sister An-Chaq, she is also Tamghati, come out of the west, and her house is the house of the Grass. It is a new era. We start again."

They cheered, whether they had heard or understood or not. They would have cheered anything.

No gold, no jewels. Archer's leather and her hair in a warrior's knot, not a caravaneer's braids. She wore sky-blue and black for the god, a robe sent from Dernang by Lady Willow, something that had been the girl's mother's, the colours a fortunate chance. She left it sashless, open, showing her leather and sabre beneath.

Empress might mean something more like a high priestess. She would make it so, and make certain her heirs, however she came by them, remembered it.

She might wish for Nour's good sense here, but Kharduin was not a man to bring harmony and reconciliation to a land, unless it could be brought by knocking heads together. It was her father's example she needed, strange thought. His leadership, but not his ambition and his evil. No mound of heads. His warband had followed him with loyalty and affection and respect, and not for fear. Her father's example, in some things. And she had known good men and good women, and had seen how they lived, and how they dealt. She might try to be so. She must.

A morning of clear skies and warm winds, and the birds singing up the steep sides of the gorge. Yeh-Lin came to them there, where they were clambering among the lilacs that covered the slope, with the river growling white below. Not there for any great and divine purpose, only that it was a quiet place, open and wild, and there were no people there.

"Nabban. You wanted me?"

"Yes. Something for you to do. Go south." Ghu nodded to Ti, who followed in Yeh-Lin's path. "Take your pages, since they'll only follow you anyway—"

Ti nodded, edging up beside her. "Even Kufu," he said. "You scared him, my lady, but not anymore."

She took the boy's hand.

"Your pages, and good horses, and a few of Yuro's folk to look after them. Yuro, if he's fit to ride and wishes to go with you. Go as my ambassadors, and as Ivah's, you and Lord Daro Yuro. Go with the priestess of the Little Sister and speak with the queens."

"Me? Are you out of your mind, Nabban?"

"You began this. You end it."

"All the lands drained by the Little Sister?"

"Yes."

"Why?"

"Because they were Lathan long ago, and no one asked my mother's name."

"Jochiz tried to take you, you know. You understand that. You could have turned on him. Fought him for his soul. Taken him into yourself, as he meant to take you. Did you not even think it, you and the dead king between you?"

"No," Ahjvar said.

"What would we have become, if we had?" Ghu asked.

"Something—the world has not seen. God and Great God."

"Devil," Ahjvar said.

"Yes, that."

"Something," said Ghu, "to break and burn the land, to let all anger loose and leave Nabban barren and lifeless as they say the deadlands are along the Kinsai'av?"

"Yes," she said steadily.

"No."

"Why not?"

"Because it would be too easy to become so. Go to the Wild Girls for me, Yeh-Lin."

"Yes, my lord."

"And come back."

"For a while?"

"Ivah might need your advice. For a while."

"We will," said Ahjvar, "be watching."

"Dead king, I do expect so."

Couriers riding, it seemed day and night. Shihpan embattled along its border with Vanai, a lord declaring himself a free king. Daro Korat and Zhung Huong the governor of Dernang sending accounts of village councils established and lands given to the shrines to keep for the god, and serfs of the manors to hold each their own, under, ultimately, the god. The governor of the Old Capital sent his submission. The widow of the admiral of the fleet, who had killed himself at news of the empress's death, sent hers, with thanks and her oath as her husband's successor, which might or might not be let stand. High lords were raising their banners or sending their submission, but the folk were rising, too, for their god, and it was not good to be a lord who denied the god of Nabban, and the empress, and the changes they would make in the land.

A great senate. A council, and not only of the lords or the merchants or the heads of the clans. Voices which might speak for all the folk. Let them throw the stones to be chosen, and come to the capital, the Old Capital, which was new again, for a term of three years. Fools and the wise, appointed by chance. The voices of the land. The empress would hear them, and would remember that the god most certainly did.

Always.

EPILOGUE

They have been coming for six months, the lords of the land, and the common folk too. Pilgrims. Priests and priestesses of the shrines. The tomb had been intended to stand alone, visited perhaps on certain anniversaries, formally, but that is not what the folk want of it, and she belongs to the folk.

The tomb is built into a green hillside in Solan, south of the Wild Sister, looking north over the river. It is stone quarried of the hills in Numiya, where the empress won her first battle, its pillars and the swooping eaves of its porch reflecting the entrance of a keep. The path down the hill descends in shallow steps, the way marked by stones carved with verses by the poet Yeon Silla, who was the empress's lover for half her life. The poet herself is buried nearby; it was seeking a place for her that led the empress to choose this hill for her own tomb.

There are horses and hawks in flight carved on the sealed doors, and the sun ascendant over them. Groves of flowering trees are planted, making the hill a garden. She began this with her own hands, setting lilacs about Yeon Silla's simple tomb.

She would have had her own the same, and set by Silla's, but the senate of the land and the Emperor Sanguhar, her son, wanted to do her greater honour. It was grand, but not overdone. They did not aspire to the opulence of the Min-Jan. She had sent the emperor and his younger sister, as he had later sent his three daughters, to be fostered for two years each in turn in Choa, on the mountain, and they learnt simplicity there. Humility. Service. Among other things.

"The emperors must learn the ways of the god," the empress had said. "We will not become the Min-Jan again. We will remember that we serve the land, and why."

That they came back horsemasters to satisfy even a Grasslander, and rather better with knife and sword and the arts of unarmed fighting than had been the Nabbani custom of imperial youths previously, was not considered, by the House of the Grass, any ill reflection on their god or his man.

For six months, the folk have come to the tomb. It had not been considered how the folk of the land have taken the empress to be their own. She fought for them, they say. She is theirs, and a saint of the holy one, of Nabban. They come, and they leave scraps of prayer, gifts of verse. Through her, they address their god.

The tomb must be meant to be a shrine, the emperor says. There will have to be a priest to tend it. Not a large establishment, not a temple, as some shrines near the towns have become. A shrine like a shrine of the wilderness, with its sacred tree and boulder and spring or well. A hermit, perhaps, or a couple. Someone will come. It is the way of things.

But meanwhile the pilgrims come, and leave their prayers.

It is evening, and the sun is setting, dusk spreading through the young trees. The pilgrims are gone. The wind stirs the prayers and the poems, which the folk leave pinned to the bark of one of the few older trees, a camphor that stood before the hill became a grave.

A hawk circles in the fading light. A white owl. It lands, wings spread, ruffles its feathers and is a woman, tall, lean, harsh-boned. Not Nabbani. Skin very pale, hair the colour of old flax-stalks in a long braid. Northron, and her eyes are grey. She wears a cloak of silk sewn with feathers and a mail hauberk, a long sword at her hip, its hilt gold and garnet, and another, the grip wrapped in leather, at her shoulder. She reads Yeon Silla's verse on the nearest stone, and does not hesitate over the Nabbani characters. Walks to the door of the tomb.

"She is gone, you know." A soft voice. "I'm sorry. You've come late."
She turns.

A man, and another at his shoulder. Horses, maybe, wait, dim and
ghostly. The light is fading. Dogs watch her. One marks the tree of the
prayers. The men themselves are dim, there and not there.

"Seeing," she says. "It's not knowing. I thought I might have time."
Her Nabbani is accented, harsh, overtones of both the caravan road
and archaicisms long forgotten. She sets a hand to the sealed door. The
empress's daughter the Princess An-Chaq, whose wizardry takes its form
in carving, has made the roundel of running horses interlaced.

The men are more present in the darkness. Sound of footsteps,
brushing cloth. Scent, too. Man, horse, pine trees, snow, wood smoke.

The tall man is not the sort she likes moving to stand behind
her, and he knows it. He has a Northron sword, older maybe than he
knows. One of the demon-forged from the isles, though a lesser and
later smith claimed the work than the Wolf who made hers. Its name
is lost. He keeps his hands from it, at least, but he does not like his
lord standing so close to her. She keeps her hands from her sword.
From either sword. Sets her back against the door instead, to watch
them both.

"This is the storyteller, Ahj," the god says. "I don't think she means
any threat, here."

"No," she says.

"Ulfhild Vartu."

"Moth," she says.

"Yeh-Lin said you might come, someday."

"Where is she?"

The god smiles. She does remember him, that odd, half-understood
creature in Marakand, human and not, god half-formed, watching her,
listening to the tale she performed in the market square.

"I sent her away."

"Where?"

"Do you really want to know?"

"No," she says, low, intense.

"Ivah," he says, "said you were set to destroy the devils. All of them. She says you killed her father."

"Yes."

"And the Lady of Marakand."

"Ya."

"And have you come for Yeh-Lin Dotemon?"

"Should I tell you? What does it matter, if she's not here?"

"It matters."

"No. I came for Ivah. To—say farewell. Only that. I should have come sooner."

"She wasn't your daughter."

"No."

"She remembered you with—" The god shrugs. "Respect, honour, affection."

"Ah."

"She left a message for you," the tall man says. He is a strange thing, not exactly a bone-horse like Storm, whom she has lost somewhere in Marakand, and his skull has probably been ground up to fertilize the fields long since, poor faithful, cranky ghost of a horse that he was. This man is a thing that is a part of his god, as a demon is a thing of the world, and yet like a demon is his own self, whole and certain. A beautiful thing. This world is always a miracle, in what it finds it can be.

She envies the pair of them.

She misses the bear with a pain that she cannot let out, even so much as the glimmer of a candle in the night, or she will not endure it.

The god's man is waiting.

"A message?" she asks, as he wants her to ask.

"Ivah said, 'Ulfhild will come. She must. If she comes too late, tell her. I left the skull and Mikki's axe and chisels with the god Gurhan, when I set out from Marakand. Tell her, she has to go find Mikki. She can't do this to him. Tell her, the Old Great Gods do wrong. Tell her, for Yeh-Lin, for the Blackdog, for herself, she must find a way to refuse the Gods. Tell her, she can't do this to Mikki. She must find him. He needs her, as she needs him.' She never did say who Mikki was."

"Who's Mikki?" the god asks, with childlike curiosity.

"A bear. Sometimes. A man. A half-demon. I . . . left him. He was safer so."

"Ah," the god says, and the word is heavy.

"He was."

A gesture, an open hand.

"I need him," she says. "I forget who I am, without him."

"Yes," the god says. "Why chisels?"

"He's a carpenter."

"Ah. A maker of things. Not a breaker."

"Mikki? Yes. He is that."

"Good."

"Something for you," the man says. He holds out an open hand. In it is a small thing, a lump of fired clay that looks as though it was formed to a rough disc by pressing between two hands. Symbols inscribed on both sides, which she can't read, and a thumb-print. The characters are Praitannec, she guesses. She's seen such writing before, on stones in the Malagru mountains. That fits with his looks, not Nabbani, not Northron for all his pale hair, and the plaid cloth around his shoulders.

She takes the clay disc. It is . . . cold.

"What is it?"

"A sliver," the god says, "of the soul of a devil. We think." He shrugs. "I don't understand such wizardry. Ahjvar doesn't."

"Jochiz," the blond man says.

Her turn to say only, "Ah," closing her hand over the disc.

"Take it out of Nabban."

She nods. They all stand in silence, as the full moon rises.

"She is gone," the god says again. "I'm sorry. But she thought well of you, always."

She nods.

"Go find the one who helps you remember who you are," he says. "That matters."

"Does it?"

"Always. Ahj?"

"Yes."

They leave her, quiet on the hillside. Some few words together, not meant for her, in a language which she does not know, but who does speak Praitannec anyway? They mount the horses and move off into the mist seeping up from the summer grass. They are gone before they should be, dissolved into the night.

Someone whistles, and the dogs abandon their sniffing to follow.

Moth stands for a time at the door of the tomb.

Better not to have seen her become an old woman anyway?

No.

"You did well," she says, her hand on the carved horses. "You did better than I ever did. Safe journey on your road, Ivah."

She draws the Northron sword. Kepra, it is named, Keeper of the hall. *The Wolf made me for Ravnsfjell*, the blade says, and, *Strength, courage, wisdom.*

Until the last road and the last dawn, is the inscription on the guard.

It is not a blade for carving, but it cuts the wood of the door like an engraving chisel, fine lines, deep, above the horses. Old runes of the north. A blessing.

Journey. Joy. The harvest. Which is completion, and success, and a victory.

The fragment of the soul of Jochiz is heavy in her satchel.

She turns away, the cloak of feathers swirling, rising in the wind. The owl flies west.

The last road and the last dawn foreseen by the Wolf may not be so very far away.

Finis

ACKNOWLEDGMENTS

I leaned on my friends for advice and assistance on various aspects of this one, and many, many thanks are owed them for taking the time to answer my questions and guide me to the right resources for further research. Psychotherapist Brian Walsh advised me on PTSD and nightmare disorders and also found me some very useful articles to read. Jason Johansen-Morris, P.Eng., gave me two pages of equations, diagrams, and notes on the construction of a bridge of rafts. (I have, of course, woven my secondary world's cosmology and wizardry into their primary world psychiatry and engineering. Do not try this stuff at home.) Connie Choi helped out with some more names. Tristanne, Marina, April, and Chris were, as always, there to be talked at during plot emergencies, as were a few others from time to time—particularly Jenna, Paul, Laurie, and yes, the Twitter gang. Ivan, the Wicked White Dog, kept Jui and Jiot honest—and Jonathan Harpur supplied the alphabet pretzels.

ABOUT THE AUTHOR

Photo © Chris Paul

K. V. Johansen was born in Kingston, Ontario, Canada, where she developed her lifelong fascination with fantasy literature after reading *The Lord of the Rings* at the age of eight. Her interest in the history and languages of the Middle Ages led her to take a Master's Degree in Medieval Studies at the Centre for Medieval Studies at the University of Toronto, and a second M.A. in English Literature at McMaster University, where she wrote her thesis on Layamon's *Brut*, an Early Middle English epic poem. While spending most of her time writing, she retains her interest in medieval history and languages and is a member of the Tolkien Society and the Early English Text Society, as well as the SFWA and the Writers' Union of Canada. In 2014, she was an instructor at the Science Fiction Foundation's Masterclass in Literary Criticism held in London. She is also the author of two works on the history of children's fantasy literature, two short story collections, and a number of books for children and teens. Various of her books have been translated into French, Macedonian, and Danish. Visit her online at www.kvj.ca or find her on Twitter—@kvjohansen.

18x